The
Jongleur

A Fantasy Novel
by
Isabella League

HELENENTHAL
BOOKS

FIRST EDITION
10 9 8 7 6 5 4 3 2 1
ISBN-10 1-888071-16-8
ISBN-13 978-1888071-16-0

Cover Art by E. E. Coad
Layout & Design by Gregory S. Coad

For Gail Altman, my 'real' sister –
for all your encouragement and love.

Go raibe mile maith agat!

Prologue
Paris In the Spring, April, 1811

The cold spring rain had stopped only an hour earlier and everything in the street dripped with wet. The ancient cobblestones gleamed in the pale moonlight, like a Faerie road beckoning to the unwary traveler. Rainbow outlines shone about the street lanterns, lending a magic aura to the quiet streets of the city. Remnants of the rain and cold, soft wisps of mist drifted across the face of the moon, like ghosts reluctant to return to their graves.

Although the month was April and spring was advancing in the trees and plants in the gardens, the air was cold, with a hint of frost. It was a quiet night, a week night, and the many amusements, the theater, the opera, salons, concerts and the masked balls, had ceased some two hours ago. No one was abroad on any business save the creatures of the night, both the hunters and the vermin, both human and animal.

A tall man, cloaked, with a bicorne hat covering his dark head, strode along the *Rue de Rivoli*. He was perfectly at home in the dark, not apprehensive as most would be, alone in the city of Paris at three o'clock in the morning. He seemed to belong to the night. The moonlight, peering through the mist quickly and then disappearing as suddenly, caught at the gold tassels that swung from each corner of his hat. Of his face, little could be seen. He wore the hat low on his forehead, and the cloak's high standing collar was pulled up to his ears. It seemed more a shield from intrusive eyes than a protection against the cold, for the cloak flew free from his shoulders, revealing a coat of glittering brilliance. He did not seem to regard the frosty air, for he made no attempt to pull the cloak close. Nor did he pay attention to the scuttling hunters and vermin. His attention lay on his goal – the gardens of the Tuileries.

Although he had been born in Paris he had spent but little of his time there. His life had taken him to strange places, in search of equally singular knowledge. The last few years had been spent in St Petersburg, at the court of the Czar. They had been profitable years, but he had hungered to return to his native soil. He had followed the events in France – the Revolution, the ascendancy of Napoleon – from afar. He had come home to offer his services to his country, the type of services he and he alone might offer her.

His instructions had been to go into the gardens of the Tuileries and wait there. But he first had a pilgrimage of sorts to make.

The gates of the Tuileries – that was where *Madame la guillotine* had stood. He had much regretted being from his home when he read of the deaths from her sharp blade. Thousands had died here, in terror and despair, some in anger and some resigned or senseless. Thousands had been filled with blood lust and triumph, sorrow and even pity. For nearly three years the headsmen had done their bloody work. And the resonance of it was still present in the very air and the stones of the street. It echoed in his bones. A grim smile crossed his face and he licked his lips. Blood! It called to him. He stood in that place of lingering horror and seemed to glow, as if he somehow took strength from it.

A few moments later he shook himself from his reverie. Time was passing and the man he was to meet in secrecy had no tolerance for those who were not prompt for appointments.

Paul Janvier, a mere private in the Imperial Guard, shivered and stamped his feet as he waited in the gardens of the Tuileries. His sergeant had hand-picked him for the task. Paul, only seventeen years of age, did not know that Sergeant Le Grande had chosen him for his youth, his almost fanatical devotion to the Emperor and his country-bred belief in superstition. Le Grande had emphasized what an honor this detail would be, and hinted at a promotion. If Paul had known he would have to stand, alone, waiting in a mist-shrouded garden at three in the morning for a mysterious gentleman

5

known only as *Le Jongleur*, he might very well have refused the assignment, promotion or not. All he knew of the man he was to meet was that jongleurs had been entertainers in his great great great or even further back, grandfather's time. Sometime to do with juggling, Paul thought. He liked juggling very much, but not in what he strongly suspected was a haunted garden at three in the morning. Had there not been rumors that the former Empress, Josephine, had seen the ghost of Marie Antoinette here at the Tuileries? Paul shivered again and drew his cloak still tighter over his uniform. He had a rifle, with bayonet affixed, but of what use was a gun or a bayonet against the spirits of the dead?

A sound of gravel crunching beneath the feet of someone or something – brought Paul to full attention and he swung his rifle down from his shoulder and leveled it at the sound. That was at least a *human* sound, he hoped. "*Arrêtez!* Halt! *Qui êtes-vous?* Who goes there?" he challenged, his voice shrill in his own ears.

A low chuckle sounded. "I am the man you wait for, fool! Do you think me a ghost?"

Paul flushed, grateful for the darkness that hid his shameful blush. "*M'sieur le Jongleur?*" Paul queried as the tall figure emerged from the mist and shadows of the garden.

"*Clabaudeur!*" swore the jongleur. "Is it that you have assignations with many people in this dark garden at this hour of the morning?"

"*Mais non...*" Paul was thrown off balance and stammered a little. He did not like this mysterious figure. "I am to take you to..."

"Then be quick about it! " the other snapped.

Paul saluted – it seemed the correct thing to do – and led the way to a small door, concealed by shrubbery.

"Not even the tradesmen's entrance, *hein?*" the jongleur muttered to himself as he followed the nervous private.

The door opened with a small key and the Jongleur was led past what were obviously box-rooms, until he came to one that, unlike the others, had a closed door.

"I will leave you here, *M'sieur,*" said Paul, with a short bow. "What you seek is within." He did not expect this strange man to thank him and he was not disappointed.

6

The Jongleur knocked on the door and was admitted at once, by another soldier, this one in the uniform of a Field Marshal. He wore a look of distaste on his face and disapproval came from every pore of his being.

"The person has come, Sire," he announced in the tones of one who preferred to say "The night soil collector has come."

The Jongleur chose to be amused.

The box-room had hurriedly been arranged as an office. A small desk, crowded with papers, a map hung on the wall and several chairs made up the furnishings. Several branches of fine wax candles spread light.

A man rose from behind the desk. He was short – about five foot six to the the Jongleur's height of two inches over six feet. His head well shaped but large for his size, his complexion was rather sallow, his eyes brilliant and mesmerizing. "We meet at last," he said.

The Jongleur made an elegant leg, hat swept from his head and held against his breast. It was a bow of the *ancien régime*, not seen within these walls for a long time. "Majesty," said the Jongleur. "I am yours to command."

"We shall see," The dark eyes studied him curiously. He saw a man of late middle years, perhaps fifty or slightly less. Without his hat his face was revealed as thin, long and lugubrious. The Emperor was irresistibly reminded of *le entre-preneur de pompes funèbres*, a mortician – he had seldom seen one more suited to the profession. The Jongleur's eyes were black, with a curious flat sheen – it took the Emperor of all the French but a moment to decide where he had seen eyes like that before – on a snake. The Jongleur's still dark hair curled madly over a well-shaped head. As he threw his cloak aside, uninvited, his body was revealed as tall and thin, clad in the most extraordinary suit of clothing. It clung to his lean form like a second skin, making the Emperor think again of reptiles. It was all of black, save for the jacket or tunic, which was encrusted with *diamenté*, sewn in diamond shapes of black and silver.

"My working costume," he said, noting the Emperor's expression.

"I surmised as much," said the Emperor. He turned abruptly to the Field Marshal. "Leave us."

7

"Leave you?" the Marshal cried. "*Mon Dieu*, Sire! By his own admission he is a sorcerer! You have read his letters!"

"Are you frightened that I may turn your master into a mouse?" queried the Jongleur. "I assure you, it cannot be done, even should he desire it. *Allez-vous en maintenant*."

Against his wishes and over his voluble protests the Marshal left the room.

Bonaparte and the Jongleur studied one another for a long moment. The Emperor made up his mind and said, "Sit, *M'sieur le Jongleur*. You have another name, I presume, rather than this theatrical trapping?"

The Jongleur took a seat. *He even moves as does a snake*, Bonaparte thought.

"I call myself Jean-Claude Malcoeur, Sire," He was completely relaxed in the hard chair, and made a steeple of his fingers. He stared over this at the Emperor, an odd little smile on his face, a smile that did not reach his eyes. "Jean-Claude is the only part of my baptismal name that I have retained. Your Majesty sees before yourself a reinvented man. My father and brother dishonored our name – I repudiated it and them."

"Surely baptismal is an odd word for a self-confessed sorcerer to use?" the Emperor queried as he poured two glasses of brandy and pushed one across the table to Malcoeur. "The Catholic Church denounces magic in all of its forms and forbids even white magic. The Inquisition burns magicians at the stake. Why would you risk the Inquisition to return to France, Malcoeur? Why should *I* risk the Inquisition in order to avail myself of your services? Why should I even believe that you are what you say? In your present guise you seem more of a mountebank than a dangerous sorcerer."

Malcoeur did not care for the way the conversation was going. This little man was not in awe of him; he did not even seem afraid! "I find this disguise helpful," he said retaining a hold on his temper. "An entertainer is welcome everywhere and hears many things. I have heard, *par hasard*, that the war in Spain does not go well, and that that invasion of England has proved impossible."

"The weather has not allowed –" began the Emperor, his face lighting in quick anger at the audacity of this charlatan.

Malcoeur gave a huge crack of laughter. "The *weather* does not allow – the *English* did not allow! The Wizards and the Witches, they raised a cone of power to keep your *Grand Armée* from their shores. When you attempted to invade the British Isles from the Channel Islands eight years ago they sent what they call in England the Wild Hunt after your forces and drove them from the Channel!"

Bonaparte flushed. That defeat still rankled.

"They are still employing these magicians, Sire. There were Wizards with Nelson at Trafalgar. There are Wizards with the upstart Wellesley in Spain," Malcoeur now leaned forward in his chair, his languid pose forgotten. "Do you wish to see all that you have gained disappear? I offer you the certainty of *la gloire*! With my sorceries you will be invincible! And when you invade Russia..."

"Where had you that?" Bonaparte demanded. At the strange, almost unearthly, look that came over Malcoeur's face he left the question unanswered. There was something not of this world about the Jongleur.

"I make it my business to know these things, Sire," That odd little smile flickered on Malcoeur's lips again. "One never knows, *n'est-ce pas*, when that knowledge might become useful."

"Or dangerous," Bonaparte interrupted. "I find myself wondering, *M'sieur*, what might be your gain from this so generous offer? I do not think that you are a patriotic citizen, disinterested in any self-gain. It is self-interest that governs every action of man or woman. Is it money or perhaps power? I warn you, *M'sieur*, that power is *my* mistress. I have worked too hard at her conquest to allow anyone to take her away from me, or even to covet her."

"It amuses me to manipulate events and persons," Malcoeur said. "And like you, Sire, I do not like the English. Years ago, I had the misfortune to cross swords with an arrogant fool of an Englishman. I was but an apprentice to my craft then, and now I am a Master. I live for the day I might meet him again, yes, and best him! It is my destiny."

Bonaparte understood destiny and her demands. "All of my life" he said slowly, "I have sacrificed everything – comfort, self-interest, happiness – to my destiny." *Ah, Josephine!* he thought with a sudden, sharp pang of loss, and then thought too, of the infant King of Rome, scarce a month old, asleep in his nursery. Destiny must be served.

"I may rid you, Sire, of this Wizard menace. They are very powerful, but not as powerful as I. And they are complacent. Since 1066 their little island has not been invaded – it is time they were taught a sharp lesson, *non?*"

"And you will have need of how much gold to accomplish your goal?" Bonaparte asked.

"None." Malcoeur grinned. "I am a man of great wealth. I might even offer you gold and jewels, Sire, for as well as *le sorcier*. I am an alchemist of rare talent." Malcoeur had no false modesty about him.

This did him no disservice in Bonaparte's eyes. "I see, *M'sieur*, that we have much of which to speak to one another. What is your plan of attack on these Wizards *Anglaise?*"

"I shall begin with the assassination of the Arch Druid of all Britain," said Malcoeur. "And he will not die easily, *vous voila enfin!*"

Bonaparte looked again at him. "I still require proof, Jongleur. Are you what you say you are? Conjure me something – and something more impressive than colored silk scarves or a trick with the cards."

"I should like to introduce your Majesty to a small demon," Malcoeur said silkily.

1

New Beginnings

"Diana, I shall not allow you to go to your uncle Lyonshall dressed as a starveling crow! It is time and past you put off your blacks!"

Lady Diana Stillfield looked up from the black morning gown she had been about to lay in her corded trunk and met her mother's eyes. Lady Augusta Bryant, Countess of Eastcote, had set her jaw and looked remarkably pugnacious for a lady of middle years, more known for her amiability and charm than any great determination. She now leveled her gaze at her daughter. "It has been two years since you were widowed and it is time to begin your life again. It is not forgetting Jonathan to leave off your blacks! You are but three and twenty..."

"And shall no doubt marry again," Diana finished bitterly. "How can you say so, Mama? Jonathan was my life!" Tears sparkled in her large, expressive violet eyes. "I shall never marry again – the thought is utterly abhorrent to me!"

Oh, my dear child, her mother thought sadly. *You are acting as if you died in Spain with Jonathan.*

The Earl and Countess of Eastcote had not demurred when their eldest daughter had wished to marry a serving soldier. Captain Jonathan Stillfield held a commission in the Light Bobs, and was well spoken of by his fellow officers and his commander. It was felt that he would go far in his profession. Although his fortune was genteel rather than munificent and his but a good county family-gentry, not nobility – the Earl and Countess, indulgent parents, had allowed Diana, at seventeen, to make a match many thought decidedly shabby. But the two young people were so in love – no one who saw them together could doubt that. He was older than she, a widower with a small son, who resided with his late mother's elderly parents. The Earl and Countess had not been pleased when Jonathan had been posted to the Iberian Peninsula, in '08, and had taken Diana with him to follow the drum. The Earl had been hoping to obtain a transfer for Jonathan, to a safe post in London, but his son-in-law wanted to see action. And Diana would not be separated from him. Then, just before the disastrous retreat from Corunna, in January of '09, whilst on sortie, Jonathan was captured by a French patrol, tortured and killed.

What else Diana had suffered in that terrible time was never known to her parents. The retreat from Corruna, in which so many had died from the elements as much as from the depredations of the enemy, had been well-documented in the news-sheets, but Diana had maintained a silence that could not be broken. She had returned to her home, a pale wraith, with only two emotions besides grief – a bitter hatred of the French and a complete loss of faith in her magic.

For all the charms and spells she had placed upon her beloved husband had been to no avail, and everything that she had always believed in and trusted had failed her miserably.

Lady Eastcote now chose another tactic. "It is an insult to your uncle to hold to your mourning, He expects you to be his hostess for the magical convenes he must needs host as well as his other hospitalities and duties." She thought briefly of her brother's letter "...*not only do I need a lady's touch about this great barracks of a place – in actuality it is more like an undiscovered tomb - but I shall need a hostess for Druidical gatherings & worse luck! - it seems that I shall be made Lord Lieutenant of the county, curse it,...*" Lady Eastcote's brother had recently and unexpectedly, succeeded to the room of the late Marquis of Lyonshall, and as his interests were purely magical — he had been a fellow of the Merlin college of Magic at Oxford – he found the governance of a large estate and its attendant wealth and responsibilities, more than a little annoying. It had been his suggestion that Diana come to him as his hostess and help him turn the moldering mansion of Lyonshall Abbey, long neglected by its reclusive master, into something approaching a home. The former Lord Lyonshall had been many years a widower and his children, two daughters and a son who had predeceased his father by only a few months – long grown and out on their own. His magical colleagues and the gentry of the neighborhood would expect a lady in charge of his household, not a paid housekeeper. Diana had agreed to his proposition, but she seemed determined to take her misery with her. Her loving Mama was equally determined that she make a new beginning.

"And," she now added, "you must think of dear little Simon, as well, Diana. You are his mama now and it would not do for you to be forever reminding him of his loss by being clad in black for the rest of your days."

Diana sighed and put the gown she held aside. She was so tired of everything, of well-meaning advice, of plans, and even, guiltily, of grief. Her bereavement gnawed at her, day and night, a heavy, painful burden. She had no more tears to cry and had accepted this offer of her uncle Lyonshall because she felt as if she could only get away and undertake a task that would keep her very busy she could fall into her bed at night and sleep dreamlessly. From the description in his letters, the rejuvenation of Lyonshall Abbey would be such a task.

"I will concede, Mama," she said now, sinking down on the edge of the bed as if too tired to stand any longer. "I shall leave off my mourning and go into colours."

Lady Eastcote clapped her hands in delight. "Betty!" she called "Has John brought those pack-ages from my bedchamber?"

"Oh, yes, my lady!" came a voice from Diana's dressing room. "They're all here."

"Pray bring the largest of themin, Betty, if you would be so good," Lady Eastcote requested.

Betty, an apple-cheeked country girl, was never-the-less on the diminutive side and she staggered beneath the weight and bulk of a huge bandbox, emblazoned with the name of a fashionable London *modiste*.

"Your papa and I have determined to outfit you for your new position," Lady Eastcote said happily as Betty, as carefully as she might, dropped the bandbox on the chest at the foot of the bed. "And before you protest that you are a woman grown and well able to shop for and chose your own gowns, I put it to you that you did not do so and showed no sign of ever doing so! *Madame* had your measurements and we chose the colours together as your colouring is so like mine." Lady Eastcote, like her daughter had violet eyes with exceedingly long lashes, dark, curling hair and a fair complexion. She was no longer as slim as was Diana, for the presentation to her lord of five pledges of her affection, a taste for bon-bons and time had wreaked havoc with her figure. She was still a remarkably attractive female, and as her husband often teased, a cozy armful.

Betty, showing more interest than her young mistress, tore enthusiastically into the box and gasped with pleasure as she pulled each gown from the depths of the bandbox. Each was neatly folded and wrapped in silver paper.

It was a wardrobe to gladden the heart of any young lady. There were walking dresses, carriage dresses, morning gowns, round gowns, evening gowns and pelisses, spencers, riding habits, and zephyr, paisley and Norwich shawls. Betty returned to the dressing room again and again, bringing back more bandboxes which she unpacked just as eagerly as the first. There were shoes, bonnets, parasols and reticules, *robes de nuit*, and other intimate articles of apparel. And not a one was black. They were all in the strong clear colours that looked best on Diana – true red, Chinese blue, lemon yellow, true green, emerald and pine green, royal blue, deep pink and Parma violet as well as cooler, paler versions of each colour. All were in the very latest *mode*, exquisitely trimmed and finished.

To Lady Eastcote's dismay, Diana was indifferent to this bounty. "Thank you, Mama," she said rather woodenly. "I shall be sure and thank Papa, also."

The Countess and the maid exchanged worried glances. Betty said, too loudly, "This'll never all fit in th' corded trunk, my lady. I'd best get John and Thomas to' go t' th' box room and fetch in th' big trunk."

"Do, Betty," agreed Lady Eastcote. "We shall definitely need the Imperial trunk, as well as portmanteaux for both Simon and Diana to use at the various inns on the way to Gloucestershire."

"Simon hasn't much to pack," said Diana. "His grand-parents seem to neglect him." She spoke rather absently.

Lady Eastcote sniffed audibly. "I have known Maria Stillfield for thirty years. If she were in her full health, things would have never come to such a pass. But that daughter–in–law of hers–! A ramshackle, indolent female who can not hold household! I shall never know what Frederick Stillfield saw in her – a chitty-faced ninnyhammer without two thoughts to rub together in her head! It is little wonder to me that she allowed those great sapskulls of hers to ride roughshod over poor little Simon."

"You are very severe, Mama," said Diana.

Lady Eastcote snorted – a most unladylike noise. "Simon was miserably unhappy once those young ruffians came to stay. They seemed to think that he was some sort of punching bag!"

Due to the circumstances of his widowed father's profession being one that took him away from his family for long periods of time, Simon had made his home with his grandparents. This had served very well until Jonathan's elder brother, Frederick, had been forced to look for a new home for his ever-expanding family. His father, Mr. Charles Stillfield, had suggested that Frederick and his family come and live at the family estate, Field Grange, in Norfolk. It would be Frederick's one day and it seemed time and past that he began to learn the business of the estate. The younger Stillfields eagerly accepted. And all Simon's peace was cut up forever.

Frederick Stillfield had five sons – Tom, Dick, Robert, John and James, all as ordinary as their names. Their only interest was in sport and bullying. They were large, rough boys, poor at lessons, but with a true talent for making mischief. Within a sevenight of their arrival at Field Grange they were the terrors of the neighborhood. They ranged in age downwards from sixteen to nine. Robert and John were twins. It might have been thought that such well-grown boys would be at school at their advanced ages, but they had been expelled from so many schools that their frustrated papa had lost count of the headmasters who had written to him, in uncompromising terms that the Masters Stillfield were NOT welcome at any school of theirs. The boys were completely

15

spoiled by their doting mama, who would allow no fault in them. To keep them somewhat in line Mr. Stillfield had hired a tutor who was more qualified as a games master than a pedagogue.

Simon was a natural victim to such as his cousins. He was a slight, shy boy, who had no talent or liking for sport, particularly the rougher forms preferred by his cousins. He disappeared into books, air-dreamed continuously and was rather clumsy when frightened or nervous. He had a great thirst for knowledge which was not being quenched by the addlepated young tutor.

Then the elder Mrs. Stillfield, who had been of an invalidish habit for years, became severely ill, and her physician prescribed a move to Bath, where she could take the waters daily. A wise and knowing man, he realized that her grandsons were doing their level best to hurry her into her grave. But the elder Stillfields thought that Bath was no place for Simon, and, at eight and small for his age, they did not feel that he was ready to be sent to school. They knew what had been his lot, but were as powerless as their son to prevent it. Feeling that Jonathan would have wanted it, they wrote to Diana and suggested that she take charge of Simon. Lord and Lady Eastcote felt this to be an excellent notion – it might take Diana out of herself and give her thoughts a new direction. Simon had arrived a week earlier, ready to go to Gloucestershire or any place else where he need never see his hated cousins again. He was a very shy boy, with little to say for himself. So far he and Diana had not seen much of one another. All of his time had been spent in the nursery, with old Nurse, who had come up from her retirement cottage to oblige. She reported that Master Simon spent all of his time reading big, thick books. A nice, quiet, obedient child, she said approvingly.

Lord Lyonshall had no objection to another addition to his household, and indeed, had offered to find a tutor for Simon, one who "knew his stuff" and could start Simon on his very first magical lessons. Simon was somewhat fearful of learning magic – none of his cousins had any talent for it (a circumstance that gave all who knew the Stillfield boys a profound feeling of thankfulness), and he had little experience of magic at all. It was not practiced to any degree in his household. But his step-great uncle Lyonshall had been recently elected Arch Druid of Britain, and it only seemed natural that everyone in his household should be able to do magic.

"I hope, Diana," said Lady Eastcote "that you will come to be a true mama to Simon. He seems to be a sweet child and you will be able to comfort one another."

"I like him very well, Mama," Diana replied. She had risen and began to take the black gowns from her trunk. But in truth, her numbed emotions allowed her very little feeling for anyone or anything.

Betty arrived at this moment with the two footmen, who carried a huge trunk between them. Betty directed them where to place it. She was carrying a portmanteau, which would be packed with toilet necessities and several changes for the trip.

"Nurse is packing up Master Simon's new things as well, my lady," Betty informed the Countess.

"New things?" queried Diana, looking up from her task.

"Your Papa took him into Dover and fitted him out. They had a fine time, looking at the ships and visiting the shops. Simon bought quite a few books and Papa made certain to buy him some toys as well," said her mama.

Diana felt vaguely ashamed. She should have thought of Simon's needs. After all, she was his stepmama.

Lady Eastcote was pleased by the look, however fleeting, on her daughter's face. Diana felt something, a little something, at long last. Her mother felt a surge of hope. The responsibility of Simon, the task before her, and a change of scene would awaken Diana to life again. And if the Countess knew her brother Lyonshall at all, he would not let Diana slip into a deeper melancholy from which she might never recover. No one could remain melancholy near Eliot Lyons for any length of time.

Most young gentlemen had dreams. Some dreamed of becoming a Pink of the Ton, a leader of fashion, or a wit or wag, invited to all the best routs and revels, their epigrams repeated by every one in Society. Others dreamed more of the realm of sport, perhaps of popping one over Gentleman

Jackson's guard in the select boxing salon in Bond Street. There were those who dreamed of the day they would be asked to join the Four-In-Hand Club, and drive out with the Club, four times a year, from George Street in Hanover Square, out to Salt Hill at a flat trot, tooling shining barouches, pulled by high bred, superbly matched cattle. Some young gentlemen dreamed of culping sixteen wafers in a row at Manton's Shooting Gallery, to the envy of their bosom-bows, or bringing down a record number of grouse on the Glorious Fourth of August. Many young gentlemen dreamed of the charms of an opera dancer or a bird of paradise, or perhaps a young lady they hoped to make their bride. Some dreamed, no doubt, of scholarly accomplishments or military glory. But René Roussillon dreamed of food.

It was always the same dream, with little variation. He was seated at the inn, the *Beetle and Wedge*, or perhaps in the kitchen of the tiny cottage he shared with his grandmother, mother and their elderly servants, Jacques and Marthe Bonnard.

There was a huge baron of beef on the table, along with all of the accompaniments – hot bread, roasted potatoes, several vegetables (usually asparagus and carrots, two of his favorites), steaming gravy – all of which was piled high on his plate. Mouth watering, he lifted a forkful of the lovely beef to his mouth – and woke up.

And tonight was no exception. He woke abruptly, finding that he had fallen asleep at his desk – or rather the rickety table that served at his desk. His neck was stiff and he was cold, for the April nights were chilly and they could not spare the fuel for a fire in the miniscule fireplace. Above his head hung a mage light, which he had conjured several hours ago when he sat down to work. It now lit up the disapproving face of his grandmother, Ninon de Varien who was standing over him.

"*Bonjour*, René," she said rather sarcastically. "It is two of the clock! Have you been to bed at all? Me, I think you have not!"

She was a tiny woman with bones like a bird, but she managed to look very fierce. Her eyes were black and snapping, her once dark hair completely silver. She wore a badly knit, voluminous shawl of a nasty shade of green over a worn, high waisted gown that had not been fashionable since the early years of the century. She had knit the shawl herself and was quite proud of it, even though a child of six could probably done a much better job of it.

"I had to finish this," said René, indicating the mass of papers on the table before him. He stretched again and winced as his right hand twinged. Writer's cramp, again. "*M'sieur* Timpson wants it in London by the end of the week." He rubbed his eyes wearily.

His grandmother took the opportunity to snatch up one of the papers and began to read it. She pursed her lips and looked disdainful. "What is this supposed to be?" she demanded. "*Ceci ne marche pas!*"

Horrified, René leaped to his feet and grabbed the paper away from her. "*Grandmère*! You should not be reading that – !"

"Ah, bah!" she declared. " It is not as if I do not know what it is about! But, *mon cher* René, if you write *pornographie* it should be at the least *good pornographie, non?*"

"*M'sieur* Timpson wishes an exact translation, *Grandmère*. He cares not if it is well written." His lips twitched with a smile as he regarded his grandmother.

"Ah, bah!" she said again. "Only *les anglaise* could make the act of *l'amour* dull. Me, I do not think this was penned by a Frenchman, even if it was written in French."

He stacked the papers neatly. "This is finished and I may send it off tomorrow. And we shall have six shillings by return post."

Ninon made a noise rather like a growling cat. "Six shillings! No doubt *M'sieur* Timpson would be in the house of the poor if he were to pay at least ten shillings for bad *pornographie, c'est vrai*! He is of a most assured cheapness!"

She expected her grandson to laugh. When he did not, but continued to study the papers and jog them into neatness, she looked at him intently.

She saw a tall young man of nearly – what was it now? – she asked herself, five and twenty. Like everyone in the family, he was far too thin, and dressed in clothes that had seen better days. He did not look French as she did – his hair was the colour of mahogany, and in the bright mage light it gleamed with chestnut highlights. He had the sensitive face of a scholar and what one of her teachers called 'Elf features' – brows that arched towards each temple and eyes of silver that reflected every mood, as the ocean reflected the sky. Those features must have come from a remote ancestor, for the Duplessis, Ninon's family, were of the Old Blood of Celtic Brittany. Long ago, there had been more than one marriage with the Shining Ones. She could sense his distress at something, and with a sinking heart she realized that it must be, as it ever was, money.

They had come here, to Silverbridge in Gloucestershire in 1790, fleeing both the Revolution in France. Ninon's husband, Louis, had been alive then, René a small child, and Lucie, Ninon's daughter, newly widowed. They had escaped from France with very little – a trunk between them, and that false bottomed, full of handwritten grimoires, used in secret for generations. For the family was magical and to be magical and fall under the eyes of the Church was to court the Inquisition.

Sir Jason Mildmay of Silverbridge was a distant relation of Louis de Varien, and the baronet had offered them the tiny May Cottage, and arranged for Louis to teach fencing to young gentlemen and for Ninon to obtain her license as a practical Witch and herbal healer. All went well for a while – Louis was popular with his pupils, and although in these modern times, many people turned to a university educated Wizard rather than a Witch or Herbalist, Ninon managed to make a little money, every ha'penny of which she put aside. Her goal was to send René to University – to either Merlin at Oxford, or the College of Dee at Cambridge.

For René was a brilliant (even though she admitted to a certain amount of prejudice) magician. Even his tutor, the Reverend Mr. Arabin, agreed. Had not René passed his *Magus Novitiate* at the early age of eleven, and his *Magus Minorus* at fifteen? At University he would earn a Baccalaureate in Wizardry, Even did he not attend University he could take the independent ex-aminations allowed by law – but these were expensive The fee for the *Magus Majorus,* the next step after Minor Magus, was two hundred and fifty guineas.

Ninon and Louis dreamed of seeing their grandson the first in the family to be able to practice magic openly for many, many generations. Ninon even harbored dreams of René's becoming a *Magus Magistra*, of which there were fewer than one hundred in Britain. There were more Masters in Ireland, Wales and the Isle of Man for some reason. It was said the Old Blood ran stronger there than in Britain, Scotland, Cornwall or Brittany, the other Celtic countries.

As for Lucie, René's mother, little of what went on mattered to her, for she lived in a world of her own. An horrific event had turned her brain, and at times she was sweet and child-like and at others quite violent. No one was quite sure what had caused this change and no one had been able to affect a cure.

Their plans might have come to fruition had not Louis de Varien died when René was fifteen and preparing for Merlin. Louis had failed to come home after an evening overseeing a fencing match in a nearby town. The next morning the horse he had been granted use of by Sir Jason turned up dead lame at his stable. A search had discovered Louis's body with a broken neck, in a ditch. No one had ever ascertained whet had happened – the Coroner and the investigating Forensic Wizard had ruled it 'death by misadventure'.

Louis' death changed everything. Their income became virtually non-existent. It also became apparent to René that he must give up any idea of furthering his education. His grandmother could not be left to tend to Lucie by herself – Marthe and Jacques were elderly and Jacques' health was poor. They could not afford to hire an attendant. They all recoiled from the thought of abandoning Lucie to the rigors of a mad-house. And to make matters even worse, their kind patron, Sir Jason, suffered an apoplectic fit at this same time and was thereafter confined to his bed, leaving the day to day tasks of running the estate to his son Piers, of whom the kindest thing said of him in Silverbridge was that he was not the gentleman his father was. Piers was no friend to the *émigrés* – he hated them. He could not openly rid himself of them, for his father still retained enough wit to govern through his bailiff and attorney-at-law. Both of these men dreaded the day the reins were handed over to Piers.

Sir Jason, after ten years of increasing suffering, had at last quit the earth at Christmastide of 1810, throwing the small community of Silverbridge into prolonged grief. He had been a true gentleman, a fine Squire and fair-minded magistrate. His death, it was presumed, had been hastened by the news of his only grandson, Geoffrey, falling at the battle of Bussaco, in the Peninsula, on September 27th.

And Piers, now Sir Piers, was left in charge of most of Silverbridge. Nearly all of the farmers were his tenants. He owned many of the buildings in the village as well. And it seemed to René that barely had Sir Jason been decently interred before Sir Piers began to harass and persecute the de Varien family.

For, in spite of passing his *Magus Minorus*, there were little employment opportunities open to a non-University trained Mage. As the law would have it, René was qualified to do very little with his standing as a licensed Minor Mage. The neighborhood of Silverbridge was a limited one. He ended in doing agricultural labor, helping with the vast herds of sheep that gave the county its wealth, sowing, ploughing, harvesting, even picking stones. Some people had refused to employ him – the war with France had been going on for a long time and there was more than a little prejudice against the French.

Sir Piers had been livid to discover, upon the reading of his father's will, that Sir Jason had left Ninon a life interest in May Cottage. Legally, the new baronet could not evict his despised French tenants. But he could and did make their lives difficult indeed.

Ninon said, "What has that pig person now done?" Her hands tightened on her ugly shawl until her knuckles shone white. Her eyes glittered angrily.

"I am not to work on the farms any more. I went to *M'sieur* Handy today, to see if he needs me for the sheep wash. He told me, *Grandmēre,* that the Squire says he wants only good Gloucestershiremen to handle the sheep, not foreigners. *M'sieur* Handy apologized to me – he did not think that this was right, but the Squire is his landlord and he cannot risk his displeasure."

"*Chien de voleur! Crétin! Ane bâte!*" Ninon swore. "Pig person!" She looked like a fierce eaglet, quivering with rage.

"*M'sieur* Handy has also warned me that it will be much the same at any of the farms, save those that are freehold," René added.

"And that is ONE farm in Silverbridge! *Ce n'est pas de veine!*" Ninon threw up her hands in despair. "Oh, René, I wish that alchemy were not prohibited in this country! Me, I would buy lead and turn it to gold of the utmost purity. And then we would buy the whole of Silverbridge and sweep out the pig person! I do not know where this Piers obtains his ugliness – his *maman* most assuredly was a pig person also, for *le bon* Sir Jason , he was a *preux chevalier!*"

René sat down on the edge of the table. It was very late and he was suddenly very tired. "*Je ne sais pas.* Why does he hate us so much?"

A stricken look came over Ninon's face. "This*, je crois que oui*, is my fault. You are old enough now to know – when your *grandpère* left us, the pig person came to me and offered me *carte blanche*, acted, if you may believe this, as if he were doing me a great honor! He told me that I was a little – what is the English term – oh, *oui*, 'long in the tooth'...."

Fatigue forgotten, René came to his feet again. "Sir Piers dared insult you!" he cried. "He wanted you to become his mistress? I will kill him!"

"You shall do no such thing!" Ninon declared. "And how do you propose to kill him, *hein*? You had to swear an oath to do no harm with your Wizardry and you cannot make the duel arcane with a pig person who has no magic! We have not the pistol and we have sold your *grandpère's* swords. This is why I did not speak of this ten years ago!"

René realized that she was right. He had no recourse. As a resident alien he would hang if he were to challenge Sir Piers. But it rankled deeply that a woman of his family could be insulted by such a man.

"I turned him down, *naturellement*. Me, I told him that a de Variens did not sleep with pig persons!" she continued.

René would have given much to see Sir Piers face when he was called a pig person.

"And, too, René, you must know that he hates you. For you are everything that Geoffrey was not – his son had no magic, which the pig person wanted desperately. So desperately did he want it that he married that girl of Wales, who ran away from him. You were a scholar, Geoffrey could scarcely write his name. You had friends, Geoffrey had only toadies and bullies. We are ever a reminder of his failures, *non*? It is little wonder that he hates the very sight of us and wants us gone. He cannot make us leave this cottage, so he thinks to starve us out."

"He will not succeed at his tricks. Tomorrow I shall go and consult with Reverend Arabin and hear what he suggests," René vowed.

Reverend Arabin had always been a good friend, even offering René employment whenever possible. But Reverend Arabin had very little private means and his living was not a rich one. Fortunately, his living was in the gift of the Marquis of Lyonshall, not that of Sir Piers Mildmay.

Ninon brightened "The good *M'sieur* Arabin will have a suggestion – *penser a quelque cose*! And now, I have a nice surprise for you, *mon cher*. Today the little Emma from the village comes to thank me for the love charm I have made for her. And she brought a gift, René, of cream from her cow, four eggs and *la bouteille* of dried cherries! Marthe and I, we made a *clafouti*! I have a piece for you in the kitchen."

René brightened visibly. He had expected to go to bed hungry. "Your are a wonderful woman!" He picked up his tiny grandmother and whirled her around the room.

"*Oh, la la!*" she cried breathlessly, laughing. "Come." she said, tugging at his hand when he set her upon her feet. " *Viens avec moi*! Before the good Jacques walks in his sleep and eats it all!"

2

The Cotswolds

It was a beautiful morning for a journey. Not a cloud marred the pale blue sky. Birds sang rapturously from every hedgerow and tree. Up above the Kentish Downs, a lark was ascending, liquid gladness pouring from his throat. From her second story window in the Palladian mansion of Eastcote Hall, Diana could see a herd of sheep up on the gradual rise that sheltered the house. The lambs were gamboling about the elder sheep, intent on play. The shepherd and his dog were silhouetted against the horizon. It was a lovely, peaceful and familiar scene.

Diana sighed and turned away from the window. Her hat lay upon the bed and she picked it up, with a last glance about the room. When she had married Jonathan, she had thought to never see this room again, for when visiting her parents with her husband, they would have been put into one of the State rooms, such as the Queen's Chamber. But she had come back here, to become a daughter again, no longer a wife, nor the mistress of her own household. The Chippendale furniture, the light floral hangings, the blue of the walls and Wedgwood overmantle – all had been her choice, but she had left its familiar safety eagerly on her wedding day. Would she return here yet again?

She stepped to the long pier glass in the corner, and fit the hat over her high piled hair. She saw a stranger staring back at her – a solemn woman who wore a Chinese Blue pelisse, trimmed with Van Dyked lace on hem and shoulders, over a butter yellow morning gown. The bonnet had a huge, upstanding poke and was adorned with two curling ostrich feathers. Her eyes looked enormous beneath the lined and pleated brim. She knew she was too thin now — her cheekbones stuck out too much and her straight little nose looked sharp. There was little colour in her cheeks or lips. But she had no appetite. Food tasted as if it were made of dust and, like dust, stuck in her throat.

The ormolu clock on the mantel chimed nine and just as it finished striking the hour, an impatient voice called "Diana! I don't want to keep my horses standing any longer!"

That was Peter, Diana's second oldest brother. At one and twenty he was next to her in age. He had recently come down from Merlin as a fully qualified Weather Prognosticator, or Augur, and was to escort Diana and Simon to Gloucestershire. Then it was Portsmouth for him and the HMS Nimue, to bear him to the Peninsula and service in the Wizard Augury corps. Diana dreaded this — she had tried to convince Peter that the Peninsula was not glory and adventure as he seemed to think, but mud, blood and death.

She picked up her reticule from the now empty dressing table and put on the white kid gloves that lay beside it. Closing the door quietly behind her, she went down the hall and on down the curved staircase. Most of the servants seemed to be in the hall. All bobbed curtsies or bowed, and many wished her a safe journey. She thanked them all, rather absently, and was let out into the spring sunshine by the butler, Jorrocks

It seemed as if her entire family was there to see her off. Her eldest brother, the heir to the Earldom, Viscount Weylin, was there with his new wife — they were presently occupying the Dower House — and her younger sisters, Harriet and Selena, as well as the Earl and Countess. Now they crowded around her, offering last minute gifts, advice and good-byes.

Simon was already in the traveling carriage. This was an elegant equipage, with the new elliptical springs, the Earl's crest on the door and drawn by a team of perfectly matched greys. Another coach stood behind it, laden with baggage, but not Betty. Diana's maid was walking out with the young son of the blacksmith and much disliked the thought of an indefinite stay in Gloucestershire. A new maid would be hired for Diana at the Abbey. And behind the coach was Jed, one of the grooms, who had on a lead line Diana's dappled riding mare, Luna. And, there also, to Diana's consternation, was Peter's curricle, with his bays harnessed to it, and his tiger at their heads.

"You are not traveling with Simon and me?" Diana asked her brother.

The Honorable Peter Bryant looked nothing like his sister – he took after the Earl, in being tall, sandy-haired, blue-eyed, and at the age of one and twenty, still rather lanky for his height. He considered himself a prime goer – a real Corinthian and sportsman. He said carelessly, "It will be a dead bore, shut up in a carriage on such a day! Simon tell me he gets carriage sick, too. I daresay that's why Papa did not hire a dragon transport for this trip." The Eastcotes had never kept a dragon of their own as so many great families did, for Lady Eastcote became distressingly dragon-sick whenever she flew.

"And you're to leave me to cope with that by myself?" Diana said through her teeth.

"You're his mama, ain't you? And besides, females are much better equipped to handle that sort of thing." Peter's attention was on his team as he drew on his driving gloves of York tan and settled his glossy beaver hat on his head.

Diana exchanged a look with her mother, who stood nearby. It clearly said "Men! What else might one expect from them?"

Peter mounted his curricle and took the reins from his tiger, who then scrambled up behind his master and they set off at once at a spanking pace.

"You shan't see him again until you stop for a nuncheon," said the Earl dryly. "My only hope is that he remembers the stopping points we decided upon. Ah, well, you have Thomas up behind and John Coachman is a sensible chap and can be trusted to do just as he ought." He gave Diana a quick hug and then handed her up into the carriage. "Good-bye, my dear, and scry us when you have safely arrived at Lyonshall."

"I had Betty place a vinaigrette in your reticule in case Simon should become travel-sick," added the Countess. "But I am quite certain that he shall be as right as a trivet!" She smiled up at the anxious little face peering down from the carriage window. "Good bye, Simon dear. You must be certain to write to us and tell us all about Lyonshall."

"I will," he promised in a small, solemn voice. He said goodbye to the Earl, whom he liked, and the others, with whom he was not very well acquainted, for Harriet at seventeen, and Selina fifteen, were rather too old to be playmates of his, and the Viscount and his wife were infrequent visitors.

Thomas the footman closed up the steps and the door of the carriage was secured. He leaped up to his perch on the rear of the carriage. John Coachman gave the office to the team to be off and they were on their way.

Diana looked out he window as they left, waving at the frantically fluttering handkerchiefs behind them.

"I shall try very hard not to be sick," came a little voice.

Diana drew her head back into the carriage and looked at Simon. He seemed lost and alone on the blue velvet squabs. He also seemed absurdly small.

There was nothing of Jonathan in Simon. Jonathan had been a big man, not heavy, but strong and clean-limbed. His hair had been gold brown, bleached to blonde by the harsh sun of the Peninsula and his complexion tanned. Simon was pale, with dark brows, but with fine, very light flyaway hair that reminded Diana of thistledown. She supposed that he took after his late mama, for he looked unlike the other Stillfields with whom Diana was acquainted. But now, with a sudden shock, she realized that Simon had his father's eyes — a peculiar shade of hazel that never seemed to be the same colour twice, with a dark ring around the iris.

For some reason this served to endear Simon to her and she resolved to love him for his father's sake, if not for his own. Now she smiled at him, and said, "Come, sit beside me, Simon. I think you are less likely to be sick should you sit facing the horses."

"But Uncle Frederick said that to sit facing the horse is for ladies, invalids and persons of rank. Gentlemen and boys and servants must sit with their backs to the horses," Simon said, his eyes growing very wide.

"Nonsense!" said Diana. "There are but the two of us in this carriage and we may sit wherever we like. Come along and we shall have a comfortable cose. I am your Mama now and we should learn to know one another."

Simon obeyed, but the look on his face said that he was not sure that he should. He sat a distance away from Diana, as if he were not certain that she would want to have him near to her. "Am I to call you Mama?" he burst out.

"Only if you wish to do so," said Diana.

"Well, I should like to do so," Simon said in a rush of frankness, "for I have never had a mama, and it seems to me as if it would be a nice thing to have. Your papa said that I was to call him Grand-papa. I liked your family."

"They are your family now, Simon." Diana's heart went out to him. She thought that he was much too solemn and reserved for a child of his age. Perhaps there would be some children in the area of Lyonshall with which he could play.

"And I shall try NOT to be sick," he promised again. "I do not want to spoil my new clothes." He looked down, rather proudly at his new nankeen suit and frilled shirt.

"If you feel sick you are to tell me at once. I was carriage-sick when I was a girl – it is something you will grow out of."

Simon looked dubious, and said "But we are expected in Gloucestershire ..."

Diana said firmly, "We have no real schedule. Should any one of us become ill, we will scry a message to Uncle Lyonshall at an inn since my scry bowl is buried in the luggage. He will not be looking for us if we send a message explaining the circumstances. So there is no need to worry about anything, Simon." Impulsively, she reached out and patted his knee.

He smiled at her, rather timidly.

"And now, suppose I teach you a word game that we played when I was a girl, whilst on long carriage trips," Diana suggested.

Simon nodded eagerly.

It was a splendid April morning when René set out to walk to the Vicarage on the other side of the village of Silverbridge. Everything was springing to life again – the buckthorn had burst overnight into bloom and a thrush sang madly in the fresh warm air. May Cottage lay within the bounds of Sir Piers Mildmay's lands, to the east of the village of Silverbridge. The Vicarage of Saint Swithin's, close to the church and graveyard, lay to the west of the small village. Further to the west, nearer the Cotswolds themselves, lay the large estate of Lyonshall Abbey. It was a rather long wall, but René, like most countrymen, was well used to long walks. It also led through some of the prettiest country imaginable, particularly at this time of year.

There were innumerable little lanes through the thick forest of beech oak, ash, elm, hazel and sycamore, all of which were in flower or verdant with new leaves, as were the blackthorn, and crabapple and many other shrubs. Under the trees and on the verge of the lane bloomed a variety of wildflowers – primroses, wood spurge and anemones amongst them. In more open spaces there would surely be daffodils and if he returned by the southern road, there would be an immense wood, where bluebells made a carpet beneath ancient beeches. In the space of five minutes René saw and heard robins, chiff-chaffs, wrens and several great tits, all singing as if it were the only spring day that would ever exist.

He bypassed the village where joined buildings of the mellow oolite stone so common in the area shimmered golden in the sun beneath tile roofs. It was a very small village – it contained a receiving office, a tiny apothecary shop that also sold dry goods, a sweet shop/bakery, a blacksmith, and an extremely small circulating library. Silverbridge also had a miniature inn, barely deserving of the name, for it boasted but one guest chamber and no private parlour. It was not a posting house, nor even a livery – those seeking a change of horses or a vehicle to hire were doomed to disappointment. But it was where the locals ad-journed for their pints after a hard day's labor, tending sheep or working on the farms.

Two rows of houses surrounded a duck pond and a green, where willow trees lined the stream that flowed into the duck pond. Over this stream was an imposing arched bridge of imported stone whose colour gave the hamlet its name. Scholars such as the Reverend Mr. Arabin thought the bridge to be Roman. They were probably right in this, but the mystery remained as to why a bridge of such workmanship and beauty had been built over such an insignificant stream in an equally insignificant little town.

René took a longer route around the village – he had no wish to perhaps be accosted by Sir Piers, who seemed to spend as much time in the village as he did riding about his estate.

His long legs made short work of the miles and he was soon at the site of a pretty Norman church. St Swithin's was a large church for such a small area. At one time Silverbridge had been more populated and more prosperous. The sheep had brought great fortunes to the Cotswolds in times past, but the wool trade was not what it had been, due to the popularity of lighter fabrics, such as muslins and the great new machines that spun faster than any man or woman, even a Witch or Wizard, could spin.

René had passed fields of sheep on his way – most with lambs at their sides. Earlier in the year, in the frigid air of January and February, he had been in the fields with the shepherds, playing the traditional calming songs for the sheep on the flute. There was magic in his flute and the birthing went far easier when the sheep heard the strains of "Sleep, sleep, stupid sheep." And he performed th same services at the sheep wash in June, for the sheep did not view the business of having their fleeces cleaned with any degree of equanimity. Rene sighed as he thought about the sheep wash. There was another source of income closed to him.

Reverend Arabin was in his garden, checking the progress of spring. He greeted René with delight and invited him in for a cup of tea.

The Reverend Matthew Arabin was some sixty years of age and of a hale and hearty constitution. He was of medium height and spare of body. He was well-suited to be a country vicar, both in disposition and looks. Indeed, he was almost a caricature of what a parson should look like. He had a nimbus of silver hair, a high forehead, and mild blue eyes that peered nearsightedly from behind thick spectacles. His expression was lively and interested and he truly cared for all of his tiny flock.

Ho lead René into the parlour, where, as everywhere else in the Vicarage, there were books where ever one happened to look. These volumes covered virtually every subject under the sun, from theology and magic, to botany and natural history.

Now he moved a stack of books from an overstuffed chair and said "Here, my dear boy, sit down and I will ring for Mrs. Parker to bring us a tray! Is it not a glorious morning?"

René agreed and they talked for a few moments about the beauty of the spring and Mr. Arabin rang for Mrs. Parker and ordered a tray of tea and baked goods.

"And what has brought you out on such a fine day – other than to enjoy the splendor of nature?" Mr. Arabin beamed at his young friend and sat down on a curved back chair, carefully lifting his black coat tails.

"It is Sir Piers..." René began.

"Oh, dear," said Mr. Arabin, distress filling his face. "I was afraid that he would do something. I spoke to him at Candlemas – no, wait, it was the second Sunday after Septuagesima – and I told him that this unChristian persecution must cease! But of course he paid me no heed," he added sadly. "I cannot reconcile Sir Piers with his father – a noble old gentleman. If I were not fully aware that Faeries do *not* steal babies, I would think that Piers were a Changeling and a Changeling from the Unselighe Court at that. But I fear that he is just like his mama."

"She was such a one – mean and holding grudges?" René inquired.

"Oh, yes. It was an arranged marriage, you must know – quite the thing in those days and many people were made pitifully unhappy by the custom. She – her name was Maude – resented the life that Sir Jason desired her to live here in the country – she wanted to live in Town and cut a dash. For some reason she thought herself a great beauty, which she was anything but. And she took offense at the slightest things! It seemed to me as if she were looking to be offended. An unhappily married, discontented woman of great passion – and Sir Jason did not love her, nor in the end, even like her. A bad atmosphere for children to grow up in, I always thought."

"And her son is much like her," René said.

"I am afraid so," Reverend Arabin sighed. "And he has decided to persecute you and your family, particularly since Geoffrey was killed by the French."

René quickly informed the Reverend of Sir Piers' latest campaign against them as Mrs. Parker, a stout, cheerful woman, bustled in with a laden tea-tray and waited patiently as Mr. Arabin moved several stacks of books from a Pembroke tea table. "Thank you, Mrs. Parker," said Mr. Arabin, and began pouring tea, adding one lump of sugar to a paper thin Minton cup before he passed it to René, as a special treat.

"Had you not come to me this morning, my boy," Mr. Arabin said "I should have come to you this afternoon. I have come upon a situation for you that is most particularly suited to your talents."

René took a long sip of tea – it was good China tea, full-bodied and strong and he relished the flavor. Equally alluring were the rock cakes and Banbury buns on the tray.

Reverend Arabin continued, "I called upon the new Marquis of Lyonshall yesterday. He is my patron and I did not wish to be backwards in any attention. I was most agreeably surprised in him. He is nothing like his cousin, who, you will remember, was an old squeeze-penny, cross as crabs, and completely reclusive in his habits. A complete care-for-naught, really, for neither I nor any one else, could never interest him in his duties to his tenants and to the county. No one could!" Absently, he pushed the plate of rock cakes towards René.

"But this man is completely different!" he went on. "He has already set about an inspection of the estate and has a long list of improvements he will be making. He tells me that he will soon be confirmed as the new Lord Lieutenant. And, my dear boy, he is not only one of the few *Magus Magistra* in Britain, but he has also been newly elected Arch Druid of Britain!"

René's brow shot up and he swallowed a mouthful of rock cake hastily before he said, "A Druid – here? A Druid *de meilleur rang?*"

"Of the highest rank, yes!" Mr. Arabin became even more enthusiastic. "And he feels just as he ought about the subject so dear to our hearts! In point of fact, he is the very Eliot Lyons who has writ all of those wonderful letters to the *Gentlemen Wizard's Magazine!*"

Both René and his mentor were passionate about the reform of the laws governing magic in England. So many laws had been passed (almost as many as had Game laws) that magic had become a gentleman's profession and was more and more becoming the plaything of rich dilettantes. Just as the Game laws prevented a man who did not own property from taking a pheasant or a deer to feed his family, the Mage laws prevented a man like René, who possessed only a *Magus Minori*, from profiting by it. Reverend Arabin often pointed out that nowadays one needed a *Magus Majori* to sprinkle the dust from the roads as a "Dust Wizard", as the position was popularly called. A sinecure! the Reverend said bitterly. An hour's work a day – and none at all when it was raining! And for this the Wizard was paid £150 *per annum*! One could not practice any of the professions in which magic could be used, such as doctoring, teaching magic at a school or at university level, or many others, unless one had, at the very least, a baccalaureate from an accredited college of Wizardry, which meant Oxford, Cambridge, Edinburgh, Dublin, St Daffyd in Wales, Kernow in Cornwall or Manx on the Isle of Man, or the equivalent pass in the approved independent (and expensive) examinations. It had not been so in the "Golden Age" of Wizardry, in the days of Queen Elizabeth, Sir Francis Drake and John Dee, the Queen's personal Wizard, when talent was every-thing and many a great Wizard had served as an apprentice under a system now abandoned. The last century had seen more and more legislation pushed through Parliament, all seemingly bent on making magic an exclusive right for the aristocracy and the wealthy.

The new Marquis of Lyonshall had been writing letters to all and sundry for years, protesting the rigid laws and the hardships they created and pointing out the sheer stupidity of wasting a good deal of talent because one did not have the money or the status to pursue a natural knack for magic. Eliot Lyons had even stood for Parliament, but had been ignominiously defeated. The fact that he was a blunt-spoken man without an ounce of tact might have had a great deal to do with his defeat.

"His Lordship also informed me, René, that he seeks a tutor for a small boy that is to join his household. His Lordship's widowed niece is to come and play hostess for him, and she brings her stepson with her. The Marquis had heard that I tutor boys and asked me if I felt able to take on one more, for I told him that I have four young gentlemen at the moment."

"But will he require the training in magic?" René queried, putting down his tea cup. "I am not qualified –"

"But you *are* qualified!" said Mr. Arabin, beaming at him. "Young Master Simon is only eight years of age! A *Magus Minori* can teach elementary magic, up until the pupil is twelve. Then, of course, he must go to a *Magus Majori* or *Magistra* to prepare for university. Had I any pupils of the young enough since you yourself came of age, I would have suggested this sooner! My dear boy, you could teach even my older students with one hand tied behind your back, did the law allow it! And as for the other subjects he must learn, mathematics, Latin and Greek, the use of the globes, and logic, the natural sciences – you've had a better education than most young men, and I know would be glad to impart it."

René could scarcely believe it. To teach was what he wished for, since his first choice of profession had been closed to him. He had hoped to become a teaching fellow at Oxford, to further the knowledge of magic, to conduct arcane experiments and discourse with other learned magicians...And this dream, in a minor way was to be his! "*Je vous suis trés reconnaissant,*" he said rather huskily.

Fortunately Mr. Arabin was fluent in French and realized that René was expressing his profoundest gratitude. "Not at all!" he said "Why, you will be doing me a favor, my boy! My young gentlemen keep me busy enough, what with my parish duties as well. I did not like to refuse Lord Lyonshall. And my young gentlemen are so much older than Master Simon. He will do far better, particularly in his first magic lessons, with a younger man who remembers how intimidating those first lessons in magic can be."

René expressed his thanks again and then said thoughtfully, "My *Grandmère* will be much interested to learn of a Druid come to Silverbridge."

The Reverend Arabin looked surprised for a moment and said, "I had quite forgotten – yes, she will be, won't she?"

He then put down his cup. "I have a meeting with the sexton in fifteen minutes, but perhaps we might meet later this week and discuss a syllabus for Master Simon. They are not to arrive until next week, I believe his Lordship said."

René rose to leave and thanked his host for the tea. The rock cakes had been particularly welcome.

"Pray give my regards to your grandmother," Reverend Arabin said as he walked René to the door. "I shall be most intrigued to find out what her opinion of a Druid in the neighborhood might be. Oh, do go by the bluebell wood on your way home – it is truly astonishing this year! I have never seen so many bluebells – it looks as if a piece of heaven has fallen to earth."

"I will be certain to do that. I will sit with *Maman* this afternoon so that *Grandmère* may go and see the wood," answered René. Both of them knew better than to pick bluebells, for the flower began to rapidly wilt as soon as it was picked. And the flower Faeries of the bluebells were particularly fierce in their defense of their own flowers, even if the tiny creatures were not often seen.

As René bade the Reverend farewell and started on his return journey he felt more hopeful than he had in quite some time. The tutoring would probably be but a half a day, for Mr. Arabin did not care to keep young boys too long at their books. Perhaps he could find something else in the afternoon, or if it paid well enough, sit with *Maman* to let his grandmother and Marthe rest. And spring was coming – there would soon be new vegetables in the garden. *Grandmère* sold a good many of her herbal beauty treatments in the spring, when the young people of the village were courting. Matters were definitely improving.

3

The Horse Fair at Greater Biddlesham

Much to Peter's disgust, Simon did indeed prove a poor traveler. By two o'clock of the afternoon of each day they had to seek an inn, and let Simon sip a *tisane* that Diana brewed for him and lay down until his stomach settled. By the time he was somewhat recovered it was far too late in the afternoon to proceed. A trip from Kent to Gloucestershire, which in Peter's estimation ought to have taken but two days ("Yes" Diana had retorted "if one does not care for having one teeth's rattled form one's head and sick as a cushion by noon!") was going to take a week. Dragon-back would have taken but a few hours.

Every day Simon grew paler and ate less. Diana soon learned that anything else than a milk posset or some minced chicken failed to agree with his constitution. It broke her heart to have to ask him to climb back into the carriage each morning, but he bore it all with remarkable fortitude, neither crying or whining.

Peter actually complained the most, so much so that she was glad to see the back of him each morning when he mounted his curricle and whirled away – not with so much panache as usual, for he had been reduced to job horses, his precious bays having been left at the first stage, and some of these hired cattle were "regular bonesetters". Diana was very glad when Sunday came and they were able to rest for the day in a charming village and go to church. Sunday travel was much frowned upon and even Peter could see the sense in allowing Simon a day to rest and recuperate, and as Diana pointed out to her brother, a family who had more than a few men of the cloth and even a bishop within their kindred, it behooved the small party to make their proper religious observations.

Simon did not attend morning services with them. Diana thought it much better that he stay in bed under the watchful eye of the landlady of the *Clock and Bells*. It was a small house, but very clean and the fare was surprisingly good, as was their cellar, to Peter's delight.

On Monday morning John Coachman suggested that they forgo the secondary roads that they had traveled thus far and turn to the main posting roads. The press of traffic would be heavier, true, and their would be tolls to pay, but the post roads were as smooth as glass, and it would be much easier for Simon. Even though the secondary roads were kept in excellent repair by a cadre of Wizards who did nothing else, the Post roads, that carried the main traffic of travel and commerce, were undoubtedly the finest roads in England.

Simon felt that he might improve on the Post road, and he entered the carriage feeling more cheerful than he had in the earlier stage of the journey. The day of bed rest and carefully chosen food had revived him. He was more alert this morning, Diana noticed with satisfaction.

The village of Houltin, where they had spent Sunday, proved to be not far from the major east to west Post road and they were soon bowling along a broad, dust-free highway on another bright spring morning. It so far had proved an exceptionally sunny spring, with refreshing showers at night.

By casual questioning Diana had begun to learn of Simon's life. She was surprised and horrified to learn of the circumstances of his existence. In spite of her mama's opinion of Maria Stillfield, Diana judged that Simon had led a half-life, ignored by his grandparents, who seemed far more occupied with Mrs. Stillfield's health than might have been thought possible. Simon had been instructed from an early age to keep quiet and not bother his grandmamma, and no one had seen to his education (the tutor hired by Frederick Stillfield sounded a fool) or his emotional needs. Diana was astonished that Simon had somehow learned to read. She had been appalled to learn that he had never been given such childhood essentials as *My First Book of Dragons* or *What*

38

Magic Is. Nor had he been exposed to any sort of magical learning. And she was equally horrified to find out that he had never celebrated any Celtic/Druidical festivals such as Samhain, Alban Arthuan or Beltaine. He could not even conjecture a guess as to what they were or discern the meaning.

He turned an anxious glance to her when this information came out. "Did I do something wrong?" he said in a small voice, for he could sense her displeasure.

"Not at all, Simon!" she patted his small hand assumingly. "I am very surprised at what you tell me, that is all. Your family is of the Old Blood – all of this is part of your heritage and you ought to be learning about it from your earliest days."

"My grandfather Stillfield said that the blood is run very thin in us and no one has the talent for magic any more. I never saw him do any magic, nor my uncles nor my cousins," Simon offered. "Every-one was very thankful that my cousins had no magic."

"Your cousins sound as if they are a set of horrid rudebys," said Diana firmly. "We shall attend your first Beltaine together, Simon, for Uncle will no doubt have one planned. It is May Eve, you must know, and it is perfectly splendid. There is food – wonderful food, dancing, singing, and there are Bards, who chant the story poems of our heritage and play upon the harp. And then there is the ritual at midnight, during which we light the sacred fires and is so moving. My Papa always invited the whole village to our Beltaine fest – the non-magical persons leave before the ritual, of course."

"But I am not magical!" Simon protested. "Will I have to leave?"

Diana looked at him, surprised. "But, Simon, you *are* magical! In fact you have the potential to be *quite* magical! Has no one ever told you so?"

He shook his head, eyes large in his pointed face. "How do you know, Mama, that I am magical?" There was a note of doubt in his voice.

"Why, my Othersight tells me so," she said, with a smile. "Your aura is a deep blue, much like my Papa's – it is darker than Peter's."

She saw by his face that he did not understand what she meant and once more she mentally cursed his relatives. None of this should be new to Simon. At the very least he should have been given the "First" books that were readily available everywhere.

Simply and gently she explained to Simon that Othersight was a magical talent that most, but not all Wizards or Witches possessed. One was born with it or not. In her family, she and her eldest brother Edmund had the knack. One could see things that others could not, such as elemental creatures and the aura that each person carried, an outline of colour that shone around them, much like a halo, although not just about the head. Non- magical people shone with various colours of yellow, while those who had the potential to work as Healers – such as doctors and surgeons — shone green. Magical persons ranged in colour from pale blue all the way to violet and dark purple. "And the most accomplished Mages gleam purple, tinged with gold or silver about their edges. Uncle Lyonshall has such an aura, but then, he is not only a *Magus Magistra*, but Arch Druid of Britain."

"Will I be able to see people's auras?" Simon wanted to know.

"Perhaps," said Diana thoughtfully. "You tutor will awaken your magic and sometimes it will happen that a dormant Othersight will awaken at the same time. That is what happened with my brother Edmund. I had it from early on and had to be trained how to stop it – for it is rather disconcerting to see on two levels at once, for the Othersight allows you to see many other things as well. We shall just have to see if you have the knack or not."

Simon had been paying excellent attention. "You did not mention orange, black or red."

"All of those colours are a bad sign, Simon. Orange indicates a person who is very ill, usually unto death – either physically or mentally. Black is evil incarnate and red indicates blood magic – the worst sort of magic that there is. It is illegal in England and in most civilized countries where magic is practiced, as well it should be, for blood magic draws on pain, terror and death, and only a necromancer – an evil sorcerer – would use blood magic. I have never seen a black or red aura and hope that I never shall," said Diana seriously.

Simon was silent for a moment, ingesting this information, and secretly pleased that he seemed to have the potential for magic. Wouldn't he like to go and turn his cousins into toads or something truly disgusting?

He was lost in the thought of wondering what type of creature was horrible enough to be his cousins' new home, when a large shadow blotted out the sun over head, making the carriage interior as dark as night for a moment. And then it was gone.

"What was that?" Simon cried, rather frightened. He clutched at Diana's arm.

"Why, 'twas only the Post Dragon," Diana was surprised at his fear. "Since we are now on a post road, we shall no doubt see many dragons carrying the Royal Mail, for they follow the post road as a travel guide."

"They won't eat us, will they?" Simon's eyes, ever an indication of his feelings, were dark and wide. He still held onto her arm.

"*Eat* us?" Diana exclaimed. "Dragons do not eat people, Simon! They only eat sheep and cattle and then only those in the Royal Pens that are built for their use or what their employers provide for them. Why do you think that dragons eat people?"

"My cousin Tom told me that if I tattled on him, my uncle Frederick would take me out on a hillside and stake me out as dragon bait," Simon said.

"Your cousin is stupid as well as a horrid rudesby!" Diana realized that Simon might never seen dragons in the air over his grandparent's estate in Norfolk, for all the Royal Mail was kept to the same route as the post routes, and the estate lay far from the main roads. Unless someone in the neighborhood kept a dragon, Simon would not have seen one. "Did no one ever take you to Dragon Day so that you could meet a dragon and pet it?" Diana was feeling more and more as if she wanted to write a very nasty letter to the elder Stillfields.

"I could PET a dragon!" Simon stared at her in disbelief.

41

"Once a year – it takes place at different times in each county – all of the children in the area are invited to the Posting grounds to met the dragons. You can feed them dragon treats, talk to them and pet them, and many times, the officials of the Royal Mail have a small Welsh Red available so that the children may ride upon it. The Reds are the smallest of the dragons and they are able to fly quite low to the ground. Dragon Day started over six hundred years ago when the decision was made to start delivering the Royal Mail by dragonback. Many people were very superstitious then and still believed in the old myths about dragons – that they ate maidens, burned villages and destroyed crops. It was thought that if people, as children, could meet dragons and see how kind and friendly they are, and how useful, that there would be no more fear. It was so popular that the idea has been kept up each year ever since. I shall look in the guide book, Simon, and find out when the next Dragon Day in Gloucestershire might be."

She pulled a volume bound in red vellum from her reticule and turned to *"Important and Diverting Events for the Education and Ente-tainment of the Traveler of Taste and Refinement"*. She perused the page eagerly. "Simon, we are in luck! Gloucestershire Dragon Day is to take place upon the tenth of June! It takes place in Cheltenham, which is not above twenty miles from Silverbridge. I own, I shall be glad to go to a Dragon Day again." She then told Simon about her first Dragon Day. A child, by law, had to be six years of age to attend. Diana had been so envious of Edmund, two years older, who had already been twice. He was rather smug about that. Diana had not slept at all the night before the event, and it had more than lived up to her expectations. She would never forget the first dragon she was presented to – he had such a friendly look in his eye and spoke to her so kindly. He had been a Highland Dhu – a black dragon and his name was Angus. She could still feel, in imagination, the amazing softness of his forked tongue as he took the preferred treats from her palm.

She wanted all of this for Simon. It was his right. And she suddenly wondered why Jonathan had not insisted on these rights for his son. Did she ever remember Jonathan writing a letter to his son? A careful question to Simon revealed that he had never written to his papa nor received a letter from him.

Diana realized with profound shame that she had only met Simon once before, when she and Jonathan were first wed. In the four years they had been married she had never once thought of writing to Simon, so that they might begin to know one another, or insisted that Jonathan write to his son. *How could I have been so selfish?* she thought, thoroughly ashamed of herself. Things would change, she resolved. Simon should have all of the advantages that should be his. And she would start by finding a large bookshop and buying him all of the books he should have had so long ago.

The Post Road took them through Oxford – no better place to find a well-stocked bookshop. They were over two thirds of the way to Gloucestershire, now.

A bookshop was located and Diana, finding that her father had still an account there for Peter's recent use, ruthlessly pledged her parent's credit to an astonishing degree. She purchased every title in the *My First Book of –* series, explaining to Simon that they might be written too simply for him, but the pictures, in full colour, and particularly those that folded out into a three dimensional representation, were an explanation in themselves. There were additional volumes on the Celtic Rituals, and Magical Creatures as well as the sacred sites of the British Isles and a volume on the Druids. She bought him a book of Bardic poetry, a copy of the Mabinogion. in translation from the Welsh, and a very fine copy of the Book of Kells. Thomas the footman stared when he saw the size of the parcel he was to carry back to the inn where they were stopping for a nuncheon.

The inn, *The Jolly Student*, was located in a small side street away from the bustle of the colleges, which were, as it was still Easter Term, choked with students. John Coachman was quite familiar with Oxford, having driven both Edmund and Peter, with paraphernalia, back and forth from Kent several times, and had no trouble finding a quiet, clean place for his charges.

Simon made quite a good meal. Wisely, Diana ordered a breast of chicken, poached, and a haricot of vegetables with sweet rolls and milk pudding for both of them

43

They were in the midst of this plain but good meal when Peter burst into the room. "There you are! I had the devil of a time finding you! What do you think, Di? There is going to be a mill quite near here – there is a horse fair at Greater Biddlesham, which is on the Gloucestershire road so that it is right on our way. There is a Learned Pig and fairing booths and a fortune teller as well, but I don't regard those!"

"No, you want to see a horrid bout of pugilism," said Diana dryly. She had never understood why gentlemen so enjoyed watching two men beating each other to unconsciousness.

Peter paid her no heed. "I daresay Simon would like to see a mill," he said hopefully.

Simon had no desire to see a fist fight. It would remind him of his cousins. "I would rather see the Learned Pig," he said in a small voice, looking from one of them to the other. He had become quite comfortable by now with Diana – she was pretty and talked so nicely to him, as well as being sympathetic and patient when he was ill, but Peter, or rather Uncle Peter, as he had been urged to call young Mr. Bryant, was a different matter altogether. He was quick of temper, impatient and most often seen swirling away in his curricle.

"And so you shall, my dear," promised Diana. Here was a treat she could give Simon! They would visit the Learned Pig, have gilded gingerbread (ginger was excellent for the digestion), ride the roundabout, try their luck at the games of chance, and have their fortunes told. She smiled at Simon and for the first time, he smiled back with confidence and trust. Lady Eastcote would have been glad to see the very maternal expression on her daughter's face.

The horse fair was quite crowded with humanity. John patiently edged their coach through a press of vehicles of every kind, partcularly those of the sporting varieties – curricles, tilburys, gigs and a number of high perch phaetons, full of gentlemen who wished to see the mill. John out-maneuvered a basket phaeton full of schoolgirls to a place beneath a shade tree. Diana and Simon, accompanied by Thomas, went to see the delights of the fair. Peter, of course, had tooled his curricle as near as to the prize fight ring as he could manage, so that he might watch the fight in comfort.

It was rather a close mass of humanity and Diana kept Simon's hand firmly in hers. His eyes shone with excitement as he looked about him, trying to take everything in all at once. They stopped at every booth that offered a game or a chance to win a prize. Simon was not very good at ring toss or at the coconut shy, but Thomas was surprisingly adept, not averse to showing off his skills, and enjoyed it even more when a trio of bucolic beauties rolled their eyes and flirted with him.

They took in the Learned Pig, who, not surprisingly, was rather unlearned, saw a Fireproof Man, rode the roundabout and had their fortunes told – Simon was to become a world famous Wizard and write many books and Diana was to marry again – a tall, Elfin gentleman from far across the sea. Privately, Diana thought that Simon's fortune had more chance of coming true than did hers. Far across the sea could only mean America, and insofar as anyone knew, there were no Elves in America. And the days in which the Shining Ones had intermarried with the Celts were long gone. One seldom ever saw an Elf nowadays – indeed, some scholars held that the Elves were long gone and the Hollow Hills were empty. And at any rate, she would never remarry – not even to an Elfin gentleman.

Midway through the afternoon they adjourned to the refreshment tent for gingerbread and lemonade. Thomas fetched a tray for them and at Diana's invitation, sat down with them and enjoyed the treat.

Simon was in alt. He had never had so much fun in his entire life. It was marvelous to share this experience with someone like his new mama. And the treats ahead for him he could scarce believe – a Beltaine fest, Dragon Day, and all of those lovely books! He looked about happily as he munched his gingerbread and his eyes fell on a poster hanging on the inside of the tent.

Underneath this hyperbole was a silhouette of a man tossing eight balls in the air. Since the poster had been produced in a Wizard print shop, the balls actually spun through the air in breathtaking fashion.

'Look, Mama!' Simon drew Diana's attention to the poster. "May we go and see the juggler?"

"Rather too many exclamation points, but think we might," she said with a smile. "Thomas, do you return our fairings to the coach and join us there. If I know John he will already be at the horse ring. And, if the fight is done, we shall in all probability find Peter there as well." She checked the ball watch that hung on the lapel of her green spencer. "It wants but ten minutes to the hour. We had best go and find a place if we want to be able to see everything."

It seemed as if everyone else at the horse fair had decided to see the juggler as well, for they were soon caught up in a stream of people heading towards the horse ring. Their progress slowed and Simon began to get impatient, trying to stand on his tiptoes so that he might see better.

Up ahead, the show had begun with a fiddle and a horn making a poor sort of overture. Something was thrown up onto the air and the crowd oohed and ahhed in delight. Simon pushed against the wall of legs before him and it actually opened, and he was out in front, pulling Diana after him.

Simon was at once mesmerized by the flying golden balls. How fast they flew, in a circle, back and forth from one hand to the other! He paid little attention to the man in the bicorne hat and spangled suit. He attention was all for the skill of the long, thin hands.

Diana had but one quick sight of the man. Ever afterwards she could never describe what he looked like, only what his presence did to her.

For her Othersight surged up, blinding her to all but the appalling sight of the soul before her.

It was black – ebony black, and full of nameless Things that writhed and screamed soundlessly. That black soul blotted out his face and form – he seemed an outline, a holding place for this horror. Around the edges it flared scarlet, like fire running along the boundaries of the outline. Within the red flames were faces of people, shrieking for help, for release.

Diana felt her senses slipping away. She felt as if she were choking and could only manage a faint croak before she fainted from the horror of that black and red aura. Simon felt her hand slip from his and turned quickly, just in time to see Diana collapse to the ground, eyes rolled back in her head and as pale as death.

"Mama!" he screamed and ran forward, as people began to turn about and notice that a lady had fainted.

"Step back; give her air!" a heavy-set, self-important looking man directed. An older woman with a kind face knelt down beside Simon, who was clutching Diana's limp hand to his breast and crying, great silver drops streaking down his cheeks. "Is this your mama?" she asked Simon, as she fished in her reticule for a vinaigrette bottle.

Simon nodded, unable to speak.

"She probably fainted from the heat and the crowds, poor pretty dear! But my smelling bottle should bring her right around." She unstopped it and began to wave it under Diana's nose.

But it didn't work. Diana remained unresponsive, limp and white.

"Is your Papa here, little boy?" the woman asked, a frown creasing her brow. "We had best find him."

Before Simon could find his voice, which seemed to have deserted him entirely, Peter pushed his way through he crowd, closely followed by John Coachman and Thomas. "Diana!" Peter exclaimed, appalled. "What has happened? I'm her brother," he explained to the many interested faces

47

clustered about, and who all tried to tell him what had happened at the same time.

"You'd best get a doctor to her" the self-important man declared. "We have a Wizard Healer in the next town but one – I shall send someone for him at once!"

"Thank you – you are very good," Peter murmured distractedly. He was remembering in all too much clarity, a conversation overheard between his mother and father about Diana slipping away from life. Had she finally slipped away – for good? Her pallor and stillness frightened him.

"Mister Peter, we'd do well to get her ladyship out of the hot sun," suggested John Coachman, his tone adding *and away from all of these Paul Prys.*

Peter began to gather her up, but John said, "Let me, Mister Peter. Master Simon needs some comforting, I reckon. Me and Thomas'll take care of her ladyship."

So saying, he picked up Diana as easily as if she were a child, leaving Simon looking lost and bewildered. "Mama..." he barely managed to whisper.

Peter, on whom Simon had made little or no impression, was suddenly sorry for the boy. After all, the poor little chap and just lost his papa and was probably afraid that he was to lose his new mama after so short a time. "Come on, Simon," he said coaxingly. He knelt and opened his arms to the boy.

Simon flew to him, clinging like a cockleburr and sobbing. "It will be all right," Peter said soothingly, "you will see. Why, they have a Wizard Healer here who will see her shortly. You cannot ask for any better than that!"

But Simon could not be comforted. He sobbed bitterly as Peter walked towards the refreshment tent, where Diana was to be made comfortable in the cool, dark shade. He quite ruined Peter's neck-cloth, turning it from a well-tied Oriental to a sodden mass of muslin. It was much to Peter's credit that he did not even mind.

And behind them, the gold balls, now joined by those of scarlet, still spun in the air.

4

A Sleep and a Forgetting

Jean-Claude Malcoeur glanced sourly about the little closet that served him as a dressing room. And it was in a wagon! That he had come to this, performing for a lot of rustics at a horse fair! He, who had supped with the Czar of all the Russias, as an equal! But at least, he told himself, he *was* in England. It had been more difficult to get here than he had supposed.

His plan had been, he thought, foolproof. He would enter England through Holland, where many French émigrés had fled, some from the terror of the Revolution and others from the Inquisition. Holland, solidly Protestant and steeped in magic, offered a refuge to the Wizards and Witches who otherwise might have been burned at the stake in France, Italy, Spain, Portugal, Italy, Germany and other European countries where the armies of the Inquisition held sway. Those stolid Dutchmen, who seemed more to use magic to line their pockets than for anything else (their magics made Holland one of the most economically prosperous countries in the world) had proved a surprise to Bonaparte. His *Grand Armee* had failed to penetrate the etheric barriers of Holland, and Louis Bonaparte. who was promised the throne of the Dutch people, had little to do other than twiddle his thumbs at the Tuileries.

Holland was the best choice for entering England – the mages of Holland avoided the French blockade with ease and avoided too, the ships of the Inquisition which prowled the waters of the North Sea, trying to catch a shipload of Protestant, magical heretics.

It had been an exhausting experience to shield himself from those who might have read his aura and found out that he was not what he professed to be – a Hedge Wizard, quite the lowest class of Wizard and performer, on his way to join exiled relatives in the Six Nations. He had had to time it perfectly – when the stars and the moon's influence were at their weakest.

It had required several blood sacrifices to gather the amount of power that was needed. Those he remembered with pleasure. His favorite sacrifices were the little *poules* who walked the streets of Paris, the younger the better. The sex act before the killing added greatly to the power he accumulated from their terror and death.

His second problem had been one he had not anticipated – money. His wealth came from alchemy and most of the gold that he made was ephemeral, as Faerie gold was reputed to be. It mattered little to him that what he paid out to tradesmen or other debtors soon faded away. Only when he was to reside in a place for a length of time did he take the added trouble to make his wealth 'real'. He had learned from a spy that the English law stated that all persons entering England had to exchange whatever amount they had to English coin immediately. Persons coming from Holland had to exchange their currency in Holland, and rigorous magical tests were applied in both countries to any coin, to avoid all specie that might have been created by an alchemist. To Malcoeur's chagrin, alchemy was strictly illegal in both countries and alchemical supplies were rigidly controlled. When he had asked Bonaparte for gold, in exchange for his alchemized specie, the Emperor had refused. That little Corsican was far more shrewd than Malcoeur had counted on. "Do you think me a fool, Malcoeur?" the Emperor had asked dryly. "I give you good French gold and you give me a bag of what will fade to nothingness. You told me that you needed no gold. I expect you to honor that promise."

He had sold a number of jewels that he had created in Germany, but not enough in price and quantity to yield what he felt that he needed in England. There would be travel expenses and perhaps bribes, for he wished to use as little magic as possible until he determined if the English Wizards could detect his presence. Money was tight on the Continent

50

– the endless war had made jewels a difficult commodity to sell. He had exchanged this gold in Holland for English coin. For in spite of the blockade, England and Holland still had a profitable trading relationship and there was actually a branch of the Bank of England in the Hague where such transactions were generally conducted.

So he was reduced to performing at horse fairs, in order to save as much of his money as was possible. He could not perform at larger venues – he wanted not to be noticed.

Another great problem was his lack of knowledge about English magic. Books on England and English magic were banned on the Continent... The Inquisition forbade such books and any found were burned. There were severe penalties for selling or reading any books on magic. There was no way to scry over the sea to spy upon them

He had found few enough books in Holland – everything they read seemed to relate to commerce. Bonaparte should have referred to the Dutch as *a nation of shopkeepers*, not the English! In Russia he had found books on English magic (for the Orthodox Church did not forbid magic). But he found them sadly out of date, most of them having been written in the reign of Queen Elizabeth of England. He had found the Russians a most insular people. They seemed to have little or no curiosity about the rest of the world, except in how it might affect them. There were few mages in that vast land.

Some of the things he had seen in his but two days in England had amazed him. The sheer volume of dragons in the sky – he had been told that they carried the Royal Mail. He had never seen a dragon before – since the massive dragon hunts of the sixteenth century by Papal armies, and the St Bartholomew's Day Massacre, which had killed thousands of dragons, Witches and Wizards in France, few were left on the Continent. There were said to be dragons in Russia, notably Ice dragons in Siberia, but Malcoeur had never seen one. The British accepted the dragons in their complacent way. No one looked up when one flew over, nor were the English horses in the least bit frightened. When he had landed at Hartlepool, on a sloop that ran regularly from Holland, avoiding Bonaparte's blockade with magical ease, he had seen a small dragon land right beside a gentleman's phaeton, in a field. The horses had not turned a hair.

He was impressed in spite of himself , by the broad, dust-free roads and the sense of order everywhere. The fields were rich and green with fat cattle and sheep. There was no trash or litter as there was on the Continent. There still seemed to be the ubiquitous poor, but even their homes and condition seemed far better than their counterparts in France. His lip curled as he thought about this. How stupid the Church's ban on magic was! Only look what it had done for the people of England, and Holland too. And how stupid was the English and Dutch ban on black magic!

Malcoeur was heading south to the Vale of Avon. One of the books he had read in Russia had stated that the Arch Druid was to be found at the Isle of Avalon, the most sacred place in all of Britain to those of the Druid order. There was where he would begin. He had no doubts but that the death of the Arch Druid would throw the English magicians into fear and disorganization. But that was not the only killing he could do. He could kill the King and the Prince Regent as well. The death of two consecrated Royals would provide him with almost invincible power. And it would bring down the government. He had no doubts that he could accomplish this. He only had to remain undetected, and so far the spells and glamourie he had cast about himself had baffled everyone, even that young Wizard at the Immigration office in Hartlepool. Malcoeur had not sensed much power in that bored and rather lazy young man. The young Wizard had seen what Malcoeur wanted him to see – an tall, older man, rather stooped and tired looking, who had come at long last to join his *émigré* relatives in England. He had had a long sojourn in Holland, where he eked out a living as a street performer, so his false papers claimed. His luggage had not even been searched.

But today, during his performance, he had definitely felt something odd. He frowned at his reflection in the tiny spotted mirror. It was as if someone had touched his soul for a fleeting moment. It had not been enough even to disturb his concentration on the golden balls that flew through the air so easily.

He shrugged, dismissing it. Perhaps it had been a bit of wild magic, the sort often found in rustics. He had felt it amongst the serfs in Russia. They were entirely untrained, of course, and usually could not do anything with their small talent. He assumed it was the same here. It probably amounted to nothing – nothing *he* need worry about, at any rate.

Peter was very glad to learn that the Wizard Healer who was to see Diana was Scots. Everyone knew that Edinburgh had the most exacting standards for its physicians and turned out the most competent doctors and surgeons in all of the Six Nations of the British Isles. And for some reason, the Scots Celts made the very best of doctors. He hoped that this Dugald Buchanan could find out why Diana was still in a swooning state. She had roused briefly when John laid her upon a table in the refreshment tent, hastily converted to a bed. She had not really seemed in her right mind and had babbled of necromancers. But she had returned quickly to unconsciousness, with a rapid, shallow breath that Peter could not like.

Simon was inconsolable. When they had reached the tent he had wriggled from Peter's arms and had gone at once to sit by Diana, stroking one limp hand that lay by her side. Tears still trickled down his face.

The kindly woman had followed them. She introduced her self as Mrs. Burnett and proved invaluable in the next few moments, performing duties that Peter had not thought of and would have been embarrassed to do. Mrs. Burnett removed Diana's bonnet and kid slippers, opened her spencer and the ivy sprigged muslin gown beneath and loosened her stays as well, all without disturbing Diana's modesty.

She also sang the praises of Doctor Buchanan, She knew exactly how high in his class he stood (first!) and told of several miraculous cures he had made in the district since he had come into the area. When she was done, Diana looked a bit more natural and less like an effigy on a stone.

Dr. Buchanan arrived shortly after that. An express rider on a hippogriffe had been sent for him, and since, like most doctors, he rode a hippogriffe in preference to a horse (as flying was faster than riding across country), his arrival was quick indeed. He proved to be a tall man, not much above thirty years of age, with a shock of red hair and beetling eye brows. He looked both shrewd and competent and carried saddle bags full of the most modern medicines and instruments.

He was well acquainted with Mrs. Burnett. "Ye were most fortunate that this guid lady was here," he informed Peter in a slight brogue as introductions were made. "She is a most excellent nurse and has oft assisted me on a case."

He went over to Diana and began to examine her As the green light began to flow off his hands he questioned them as to exactly what had happened.

For this they had to depend largely on Simon. No one else had been near to Diana when she collapsed, and even he had not seen what caused it. Mrs. Burnett had been back to Diana at the time, and Peter, John Coachman and Thomas had not arrived until later. And Simon had only seen her fall.

"Don't ye worry, laddie," the doctor said in a kindly voice to Simon. "We'll soon have your mama sorted out." His strong hands lingered in the air over Diana's head, the green light pulsating as it penetrated her head. The doctor could read the light that pulsated back into his hands; it told him what was not normal and healthy.

"Humph," he said, frowning. "She's had a psychic shock of some sort. She has strong Othersight – she's most competent Witch, I should judge."

Peter agreed. "She was first in her class at school – she is a graduate of Miss Minchin's Select Female Academy for the Daughters of Gentleman Wizards in Bath."

"That's a fine school," the doctor said absently. "And I would say she's a rare sensitive." He added with a slight frown.

"She came to consciousness briefly, Doctor, and talked rather wildly of necromancers," said Mrs. Burnett.

The doctor exchanged a quick look with Peter and then looked beyond him, to where Thomas and John stood anxiously in the background. "There has nae been a necromancer in England since the last one was drawn and quartered at Temair na Rig in Ériu in, I think, 1430. Did ye feel aught, Mrs. Burnett? I know well ye have the sight."

"I am not that sensitive, Doctor," she said apologetically. "I felt nothing."

"Then I am going to assume that what she saw was a boggart. One will slip out every now and then, in spite of the best efforts of the Repressors in the Containment Corps. Boggarts are tricksters. To one as sensitive as this lassie, a boggart 'twould be a frightening thing and she would be able to see through its invisibility," said Doctor Buchanan.

"Can you help her?" Peter asked anxiously, conscious of Simon's big eyes fixed on his face with a painful intensity.

"Och, yes," said the Doctor easily. He drew the green light back into his hands and reached for his bag. "'Tis a simple incantation and a wee herbal drink, but I'll need your permission, Mr. Bryant, to administer it, as it is a spell of forgetting. Ye are of age, I presume, and can take the responsibility?"

Peter nodded. He had turned one and twenty six months earlier.

The Doctor drew a scroll from his bag and gave it to Peter, telling him to fill it out and sign and date it. Mrs. Burnett would sign as witness. He then asked Thomas to find a kettle of boiling water for the herbal drink. "The wee drink comes first," he said. "She will nae forget completely – sometime in the future she will remember, but without pain and fear. The law does not allow us to completely remove the memory, no matter how bad that memory is. Taking the memory of her fear away will allow the lassie to heal."

Thomas hurried up with a kettle. One of the workers at the refreshment tent had assumed that the doctor would need boiling water – doctors nearly always did, as many treatments were a combination of herbal decoctions and incantations.

Dr. Buchanan had taken a mortar and pestle from his bag and flipped open a pocket in the side of the bag that revealed row upon row of cork stoppered bottles, all neatly labeled with inscriptions in Wizard's Latin.

He chose among them, swiftly, then measured out exact portions in silver spoons, graduated in size. He then ground them together in a brisk fashion. Peter was impressed. He had always found herbs and potions the hardest part of his basic Wizardry studies and had been glad that Augury had few herbal requirements.

In a moment's time the doctor was done and he poured a measure of the boiling water over the herbs in the mortar, mixing them thoroughly. These were then poured into a crystal flagon, through a silver strainer. A sweet, spicy fragrance rose into the air. The 'wee drink' was a pale rose in colour. He tapped it with his wand, a slender rowan rod with an emerald, the Healer's stone, on its tip.

When it had cooled to comfortable drinking temperature, Doctor Buchanan, with Mrs. Burnett's help, raised Diana's head and bade her drink. With the power from his fingers compelling her, she had to obey. Almost immediately colour came into her face and she gave a sigh.

He then lay his fingers on Diana's temples. The incantation was silent – most accomplished Wizard Healers did speak minor incantations aloud — but they could all see the green light of power surge into Diana. She gave a little shudder and then completely relaxed.

"She will sleep naturally now," Dr. Buchanan said, withdrawing his hands. "In all probability, until tomorrow morning. Convey her carefully to an inn where she may be made comfortable. I recommend the *Cat Nap*. 'Tis a small place, but clean and the landlady is a superb cook. Mrs. Burnett may direct ye."

"And I shall come along," said that good lady "and help get the young lady into her nightclothes."

"Mr. Peter, why don't Thomas an' me go an' bring the carriage up as close to the tent as we may?" John now suggested.

"An' the seat facing the horses folds out into a bed," Thomas suggested. "There's carriage rugs an' pillows beneath th' seats."

"Thank you, please do so," said Peter greatfully.

Simon, who had been holding his breath during the doctor's examination and treatment, now let it out on a long sigh. He rubbed his face with his sleeve, for his eyes were wet and his nose dripped. She looked better – she looked as if she was sleeping. As he watched, she turned over onto her side in a more natural posture.

He had been awed by the magic he had seen. He had never been allowed in the room when his Grandmama Stillfield had been treated by her doctor. Learning magic would be a good thing, he decided, suddenly eager to begin his studies.

The doctor and Uncle Peter were talking in low voices, but Simon felt better now and he paid little attention to them. He would remain on watch.

"I think it important that your sister go to a place that is properly grounded and shielded," Dr Buchanan was saying to Peter. "I assume a boggart, but I cannot be sure. Her psychic senses will be fragile for a se'ennight or so."

Peter grinned. "We are journeying to Gloucestershire, to my uncle, the Marquis of Lyonshall. Not only is he a *Magus Magistra*, but the Arch Druid of Britain. I cannot conceive of a more grounded or shielded place."

"Indeed!" the doctor returned. "Ye yourself are an Augur, I see." As required by law Peter wore a tie pin of a crystal ball, mounted on a bolt of lightning. This informed all and sundry that he was a qualified Weather Augur. Lapel pins were also allowed, as were fobs and rings. By law, this identification had to worn daily. The good doctor wore a silver caduceus, on a green ground, on his lapel.

"What is your fee?" Peter asked diffidently. He always felt awkward, asking what he owed for a service.

Dr. Buchanan was not shy. "Call it a Yellow Boy," he said, and accepted the proffered guinea with thanks. "Ye may wish to have her seen by a local physician. Should he have any questions about my treatment, ye may send a 'griffe express to this direction." He gave Peter a calling card from a silver case.

"Thank you," said Peter. They had been fortunate that such a fine physician lived in the vicinity. So many villages had only a semi-trained apothecary, who relied on a mumbo-jumbo of large words and little real knowledge. "I shall see you to the door."

Simon asked, and was allowed, to sleep on a trundle bed by Diana's side. He knew that he would not sleep at all unless he could be near her. He had said all of the prayers of thanksgiving that he knew, once he was in bed. The relief was over-whelming.

Simon was literally starved for love and attention. In his short life he had received little of either. And in this journey, Diana had been so kind to him, so sweet and good. He had given her his heart and never again would think of her as anything else other than his mother. Today he had come perilously close to losing that which he had possessed for such a small while. It didn't bear thinking of.

He could not sleep. Peter had gone to bed, and had hired the landlady's daughter to watch over his sister. But the daughter had fallen asleep by the fire. Simon felt that he had to keep checking his mama in case she were to become worse again. The trundle bed had been pulled from beneath her large bed and he knelt upon this, clutching the edge of the bed, looking anxiously and lovingly at her.

And so it was, when near midnight Diana awoke, the only familiar thing she saw was a little pointed face with wide eyes, staring at her.

"Simon?" she said in a low, husky voice. Her head felt muzzy and she was but half-awake. Wherever was she? Only Simon and the scent of lavender on the sheets seemed familiar. But it seemed too great an effort to try and figure out what was going on.

"Mama!" Simon whispered joyfully. He had been told time and again that one had to be very quiet when one was near sick persons. He stretched out a hand to hers.

Diana found it a nearly impossible task to move her hand and it cost her not a little effort to lightly meet his fingers. Why was she so tired? "Simon! You're freezing!" she felt how cold he was. "Get under the covers with me and warm yourself up." It was such an undertaking to speak.

Simon did not need to be asked twice. He lifted the blankets and got into bed.

"Come, cuddle against me," Diana whispered. "We must get you warm."

Simon, bursting with happiness, scooted beneath her arm and lay his head on her breast. "Mama," he sighed in happiness and was asleep almost instantly.

Diana sighed. It felt so right to have him cuddled against her. She closed her eyes and fell down a long dark corridor into a refreshing and dreamless sleep.

When Peter came in the next morning, he found them like that.

Practical Magic

"Good morning, Mrs. De Varien," came a hesitant voice.

Ninon, kneeling in her herb garden, looked up at once and smiled when she saw who it was. *"Bonjour, Mam'selle* Mildmay!" She straightened and put a hand to her back as she stood up. These days it seemed more difficult to keep up with the garden.

Hester Mildmay returned the smile in her shy fashion. She was a thin, very plain woman, with dark, lusterless hair worn in a bun at the back of her head. Her skin was sallow, and her near-sighted eyes were a muddy colour between brown and green.

And to add to all of these disadvantages, she had to suffer Sir Piers as her brother. Ninon felt sorry for *Mam'selle* Mildmay, for the woman was timid to the point of self-effacement. She seemed to strive to be as drab and unnoticeable as was possible. The gowns she wore were of dull colours and her bonnets were of plain unglazed straw in the beehive shape. No one had ever offered for her, indeed, Ninon doubted that any man had ever looked at her, in spite of a tidy portion of both land and money. "For who," Ninon often said to Marthe, "would wish to have a pig person as an in-law?"

And several weeks ago, when she and René had actually been able to attend church together, Ninon had discovered a secret about *Mam'selle* Mildmay. The woman was in love with René. There was no mistaking the looks she gave him when she thought that no one was looking. René was totally unconscious of the fact, Ninon was certain. Why,

Hester was old enough to be his *maman* – she was of Lucie's generation and looked even older than the mentally ill Lucie. Wisely, Ninon decided to keep this secret to herself. She did not think that Hester would ever act upon her feelings – she was a sensible woman, not given to fits and starts. But she more than likely dreamed and on occasion cried when she face the facts that those dreams would never come true. And in spite of the fact that she was the pig person's sister, Ninon liked her.

"You wish for some more herbs *pour le chat?*" Ninon inquired. Hester loved her little white cat, Minou, inordinately. She was the only thing the poor woman had to love. Minou, longhaired and fastidious, groomed herself constantly and as a result suffered from furballs. Ninon made an herbal mix that worked very well on keeping furballs from forming.

"And I have some good news for Mr. Roussillon," Hester offered. "Is he here?" she queried, looking about eagerly.

"*Je suis désolé* – he is with the good *M'sieur* Arabin today," said Ninon, secretly glad that René was not at home. "But me, I will take a message for him, *oui?*"

Hester blushed. "Minou is to have kittens," she explained, as if mentioning such a thing was socially unacceptable. "Reverend Arabin told me that Mr. Roussillon was looking for a familiar, as his cat had died. And their father," she confided in a whisper, "Is the Reverend's familiar."

Gil Blas, who had been familiar and friend, had died during the winter, of sickness, leaving a hole in their home and hearts. A Wizard needed a familiar, as did a Witch.

"We would be glad to have kittens of such parentage," said Ninon. With one familiar parent, the Reverend Arabin's familiar, Plato, the kittens would undoubtedly be familiars as well.

"When they are old enough to be weaned I shall bring them by so that you may chose. I know how important it is that you chose just the right kitten," Hester said eagerly. She knew it futile to even suggest that they come by her home to look at the kittens.

"*Merci,*" Ninon said, not correcting Hester's assumption. It was the kitten who chose the Magus. "You will wait while I fetch the herbs, *non*? Come into the garden and sit upon this so ugly little seat." The seat was of wood and leaned rather drunkenly to one side. Ninon was convinced it was cursed – no spell ever succeeded in making it sit straight for more than a day or two.

It took Ninon but a few moments to slip into the cottage and fetch a mix of herbs in a green glass bottle from her tiny still room. '*Pour les chats*' read the label.

She looked in on Marthe, who sat with Lucie in a corner of the room on the ground floor. Marthe was knitting a pair of stockings for René and Lucie was sleeping. Against her better judgment Ninon had dosed Lucie with valerian tincture that morning. Lucie had had one of her nearly uncontrollable days, with screaming and striking at anyone who came near her. They never knew why some days she was so violent and on some days so gentle. Unfortunately René had to meet with Mr. Arabin this morning – they were to write a syllabus for the new pupil, and René had not the time to play the violin, which he played as well as he did the flute, for his mother – it always soothed her. Thus the valerian. When Lucie grew violent, René was the only one who had the strength to handle her. Jacques could barely walk – he suffered from rheumatism – and Ninon and Marthe were too old and lacked strength. Sometimes Ninon prayed to *le bon Dieu* that Lucie would die and cease to suffer. She always felt horrible pangs of guilt after such a prayer, for she loved her daughter dearly. But remembering the bright flame that had been Lucie and the wreck that she had become brought tears and wild grief.

With a nod of her head Marthe indicated that everything was fine and Ninon, bottle in hand, went back outside.

Before she reached the garden she heard the loud, angry voice. She knew at once to whom it belonged.

Sir Piers Mildmay was a man most inaptly named, for there was naught mild about him. He burned with anger and it showed in every look and line of his body. He was of rather less than medium height and almost as wide as he was tall. His face was pugnacious in expression – Ninon had never seen him smile. He had thick lips, small porcine eyes and a bald dome of a head, with a thick fringe of grey hair. Bristling grey brows met in a perpetual frown. His hands were heavy – to Ninon his fingers had always looked like overstuffed sausage casings.

His hands were heavy on the mouth of the cob he rode as well. His horses had to have cold blood – draught horse blood – for no thoroughbred could carry his bulk. This unhappy animal jibbed at the bit, rolled his eyes and wrung his tail as he was held in an iron grip and had to endure the great booming voice of his master in full spate.

"What are you doing here, woman? Have I not told you often enough that you are not to come near this place? You must be deaf as well as stupid!" he yelled at his sister, a vein throbbing in his temple.

Ninon often thought that if she could only make Sir Piers angry enough, he might go off in an apoplexy, to everyone's immense relief.

"I needed medicine for Minou," Hester offered timidly, stammering a little and shrinking back from the torrent of her brother's abuse.

"Minou!" he growled. "I ought to ring that animal's neck! Useless flea-bag!"

A look of horror spread over Hester's face and Ninon lost her temper.

"*En voilē assez!*" she snapped. "That is enough!" she marched forward and gave the little bottle to Hester. "A shilling, *s'il vous plaît!*"

Hester, hands trembling, fumbled in her reticule, and finally drew out a coin, which she gave to Ninon. Sir Piers sputtered, calling down threats against Hester's little cat.

Ninon made a very rude noise. "Pig person, have you nothing better to do than berate your sister and threaten little animals? *Sortez! Et allez appendre la politesse!* Go to learn the manners, you!"

"You shall not speak to me in that way, woman!" Sir Piers thundered, leveling his heavy wooden riding crop at her. "I am your landlord, pray remember that!"

"Ah, bah!" Ninon said, tossing her head." I have the life interest in this cottage – this means I am as good as owning it! So *le bon avoué*, M'sieur Barrow tells me. And there is nothing that you can do, pig person! Now go! *Je ne veux pas vous parler. Allez-vous en maintenant!*"

Sir Piers nearly choked on his rage. How he hated this little French termagant! There must be someway that he could rid himself of this thorn in his flesh. He was even willing to destroy the cottage...destroy the cottage! An idea came into his brain and he involuntarily tightened his hands further on the reins.

The cob had borne enough. With a squeal of rage, he put down his head, kicked out and bucked, twisting his back.

And Sir Piers went sailing through the air, to land in the lane in a mud puddle left by the night's rain. He screamed, and sputtered, landing face down. When he rose on all fours, dripping with mud, Ninon burst into laughter. "Oh, la, la! A pig person indeed!" she gasped, holding her sides.

Angry beyond reason he hauled himself to his feet and started towards her, intent on wringing her neck, oblivious to Hester's cries of distress.

But at this moment Jacques came slowly around the corner of the cottage. Although old, he was armed with a formidable weapon – a newly sharpened pitchfork. "*Qu'est-ce qu'il y a?* What goes on here?" he demanded, looking from Sir Piers and his sister to Ninon. "Does this person bother you, *Madame?*" He leveled the pitchfork at the enraged baronet.

"He dares not," said Ninon scornfully. "I bid you a good day, *Man'selle* Mildmay." With great dignity she walked into the house.

Sir Piers and Jacques glared at one another for a moment until Sir Piers looked away and said in a loud voice, "Hell and the Devil confound it!" and stamped away down the lane to look for his horse. A few moments later, Hester, who had walked over from the Hall, scurried after him like a frightened rabbit.

Hester, her precious jar clutched close to her chest, ran as fast as she could through the woods. Her heart was thumping and she could scarcely breath. She had to get back to the Hall before Piers! Minou had to be protected! Hester knew her brother all too well – his temper was ungovernable and when he was angry or thwarted he looked for something to blame and punish. He was perfectly capable of wringing Minou's neck. At just the thought of her little cat dead with a broken neck, Hester began to cry, tears blinding her as she ran and sobs making her breathing more difficult. Please, please let her get to the Hall before Piers! She would bundle Minou into her basket and beg Reverend Arabin to give Minou sanctuary. Hester didn't know if she could bear living at the Hall without Minou, but it was far and away better to have Minou safe than dead, even if it meant doing without her company.

Not for the first time Hester wished that she did not have to live with her brother. The Hall was an unhappy place, with even the servants trembling at Piers' frown. She knew that he had struck some of the servants, more than once. He had even hit her, his own sister, when he thought she was interfering with his affairs or thought she was being stupid. She could not seem to please him. Only Geoffrey had ever been able to accomplish that. Hester felt guilty for being glad that Geoffrey was dead and would never torment her again – he was rude and mean and called her names, amongst them, 'Old Horse Face". She supposed it was a sin to be glad that someone was dead, but she had never been able to bring herself to talk about it to Reverend Arabin. He was always so kind to her, and she did not wish to see his expression change to that of disdain when he realized what a very bad person she was, to hate her own brother and be glad that her nephew lay dead in a foreign land.

She could hear Piers thrashing about and cursing at the top of his lungs to her left. Her heart lifted in spite of the stitch that was forming in her side. He had not caught the horse as yet! And she knew well that her brother would never go back to the stable block and order the groom to fetch in the loose horse – to admit that he had been thrown and lay himself open to the humiliation of appearing the fool before the servants! If the horse went back to the stables on his own, Piers would probably tell the servants that the horse had been tied and pulled the reins loose. Hester could not imagine how Piers would explain being covered with mud. But she didn't care. She was now certain to make the Hall and be gone before Piers arrived! With her free hand, she picked up her skirts and put on a burst of speed. Minou would be safe! She could count on Reverend Arabin.

Simon woke very early on the his first day of school. He supposed that he couldn't really call it school, for Uncle Lyonshall had explained that he was to have a tutor and be the only pupil. This tutor was to teach him magic and all of the other subjects a gentleman needed to be accounted as well-educated. It sounded a formidable amount of learning and Simon was more than a little anxious. His stomach hurt, rather. Would the tutor like him and not think that he was stupid because he didn't know much about magic – or anything for that matter? Would he like his tutor? What if he were like that horrid Mr. Appersett that only wanted to play cricket and rugger with Tom and his other cousins? Every time Simon had a question Mr. Appersett made a rude noise and told him to go look it up. Sometimes Simon didn't know where to look. But Mama said that Uncle Lyonshall would not pick a fool for his tutor – Simon could count on his great uncle.

Remembering that, Simon relaxed a little. He felt that he *could* count on Uncle Lyonshall, or Uncle Lyon, as he preferred to be called. Uncle Lyon hated his Christian name, Eliot – he said it sounded too much like *idiot* – so for all of his life he had been called Lyon. It was a singularly appro-priate name, for Uncle Lyon was a great deal like the picture of an African lion Simon had seen in one of his new books. To begin with, he was tawny – his hair was the colour of a lion, and it was wild and curly, and, unfashionably, he wore a beard. His eyes were a curious amber colour, full of humor and intelligence, and he moved like a cat, in spite of his size. He was a big man with a deep chest and a well muscled body. He was extremely fit – Simon was to find that Uncle Lyon thrived on exercise and when not riding or rowing was tramping through the woods. In spite of his size he exuded a feeling that made Simon feel safe and secure. And he was easy to talk to – he was really interested in what even a little boy had to say and never talked down to Simon. Even his frequent bellows of "By the Horned Moon! "or "Morons!" didn't frighten Simon, for he sensed that Uncle Lyon was not mad at him.

Lyonshall Abbey was a strange and rather exciting place. It was very old in places – it had originally been a Benedictine Abbey, and had become a home after King Arthur had driven the Catholic Church from England and established the English Church, when the Pope had ordered Merlin burned at the stake.

The Abbey was also in a remarkable state of decay. Portions of the roof had fallen in, mice had run havoc in most of the rooms and no one seemed to have thrown out the trash in many a year. There were only about ten or so rooms that could be used. Uncle Lyon had been in residence not above four months and since the first day he had had workmen busy on the structure. There was still a great deal of work to do. There were men busy on the grounds and the stable block and on tenants' cottages and barns as well. The gardens bore a remarkable resemblance to a West Indian jungle and ancient trees were quite close to the house, as well as lining the drive. Simon had never seen anything like it. When the carriage had come to the huge gates of the Abbey, two great stone lions, perched atop two pillars of Cotswold stone, had turned their heads and looked at them, with bright blue magical eyes – on of them had even roared!

Simon's Mama had been abed and cosseted for nearly a week. They had brought her to Silverbridge by easy stages. Uncle Peter actually let his groom drive the curricle and had journeyed in the closed carriage with them. Simon had been very proud of himself – he had not gotten sick once — even Uncle Peter said he was a regular right'un. Once Mama was placed tenderly into bed and Uncle Lyon had her looked at by another doctor – the famous Sir William Knighton, the Regent's own doctor – flown dragonback to Cheltenham at great expense – she seemed to get better rapidly.

Simon spent every moment he was allowed with her. When she was stronger, they looked at the new books together and Simon even read to her. He was not used to reading aloud, but she praised him and said she enjoyed hearing him read.

Uncle Lyon sometimes joined them of an evening, just before Simon went to bed, and sat sprawled in an armchair, puffing on his pipe, making comments on the lack of intelligence of the authors of the books. He did not seem to know or care that a gentleman did not smoke in the presence of a lady, or sit so casually in her bedchamber, nor make rude remarks prefaced by "Oh, Gad!" or "Curse it!" Diana, well-used to her uncle, never remonstrated with him. Uncle Lyon made Simon laugh.

Another change, a happy change, had come for Simon. He was not to be sequestered in the nursery. For one thing, the roof had fallen in up there and Uncle Lyon said Simon was too old for petticoat government. Simon now had his own valet – a young man from the village, Bob Sanders by name. Sanders was seventeen, freckle faced and friendly, and this was his first position in service. He was very proud to be earning good money to help his widowed mother and siblings, eat with the upper servants and wait on such a nice little gentleman as Master Simon. Simon liked him very much and it made him feel very grown-up indeed to have a valet rather than a nurse or a nursery maid. And his room was on the same floor as was his Mama's – indeed, he had only to go to the end of the hall and there was her door. The Abbey was well lit by blue-white mage lights, not flickering candles, so it was not scary, as it had been in Norfolk, to walk the halls of an evening.

Simon sat up against the mound of pillows and looked out of the window. The sun had risen and was sending a shaft of light, fluttering with leaf shadows into his room. He rather liked the trees so close to the house. In low lying Norfolk Simon was far more used to a great deal of open land and sky – even the Eastcote mansion had in Kent a view of the open downs. This hilly country was far more heavily wooded and almost secretive, but Simon was coming to enjoy it. There were a profusion of flowers everywhere and right outside his window the long branches of an elm swayed. On a branch sat a great tit, seeming to watch Simon with a bright black eye. It was going to be another beautiful day.

He still couldn't help being nervous, though. Beginning anything was difficult. And he wanted Mama to be proud of him.

He gave a start as the door opened. It was Sanders, with a can of hot washing water. "Good morning, Master Simon!" he said cheerfully, a wide grin splitting his face. "You're up wi' th' birds! Thought you'd be up early, seeing as how today is your first day."

"Good morning, Sanders," Simon returned. His stomach gave a jump.

Sanders gave him a shrewd glance. He well understood how Simon felt, for had he not felt the very same when he began this position less than a week ago? And now look how well he was suited! "Don't you worry none, Master Simon. I knows th' young gentleman who as goin' to be your tutor, and 'e's a prime 'un. He was a friend of me brother Will, the one as I told you about, that went to Canada. Used to let me tag along when 'im an' Will was off on one o' their starts. Allus kind to us littles. You'll like 'im."

Simon's rather wistful face brightened. "Really, Sanders? I do hope so!"

"Would I tell you somethin' that ain't so? I'm true blue an' will never stain!" Sanders solemnly crossed his heart. "Now, lets gets you washed up an' dressed."

Simon's stomach relaxed, and he climbed out of bed feeling better.

When Simon entered the breakfast parlor he found only not Uncle Lyon eating an enormous plate of ham and eggs and grilled tomatoes, but his Mama, up and dressed and looking fit and pretty.

"Mama!! You're better!" He ran to her and hugged her joyfully. Laughing, she hugged him back. "Simon! Good morning!" she kissed him fondly. "I am going to take you to your first lesson in the pony cart…"

"But herein after, you will rely on your legs to get you there," said Uncle Lyon. "It is a short walk and the exercise will do you good."

"Unless the weather is inclement," Diana said firmly. "Now, Simon, sit down and make a good breakfast."

"I am not very hungry, Mama," he said, sliding into a chair besides hers. Uncle Lyon had decided that unless there was an adult dinner party Simon was to eat with them. "How is the boy to learn company manners if he is never in company?" he had said.

"Nonsense, my boy," said Uncle Lyon. "You're going to begin your magical career today and you need a good meal to work magic," he said, taking a giant forkful of eggs.

"You must be planning to work a great deal of magic today, Uncle Lyon!" said Simon, eyeing the mound of food on his uncle's plate.

Uncle Lyon gave a great shout of laughter. His laugh even sounded like a lion roaring, Simon thought. But it was a friendly lion.

The butler came forward with a plate for Simon. On it was a baked egg and fingers of buttery toast. He smiled at Simon encouragingly as he set the plate before Simon. "I fancy this will not upset your constitution, Master Simon," The butler was called Seppings, and like the rest of the servants here at the Abbey, he was very kind.

Suddenly, the food smelled good. Diana prepared a cup of Cambric tea for Simon, with plenty of cream and sugar. Simon began to feel a little pleasurable excitement about the day to come.

Diana drove the pony trap to the Vicarage. It was a little wicker vehicle drawn by a fat, wise little pony, caramel in colour, who was named Butterball. Diana was a notable whip – her father said she was a better driver than Peter – but she would not set up her carriage until the stables were in better order. What horses there were crowded the very few stalls that were in decent condition. Lyon's carriage pair, his riding horse, her mare Luna and this pony were the only inhabitants at the moment. There would have to be a pony for Simon as well, for Diana had been surprised to learn that Simon could not ride. She had been tossed into a saddle before she was four and always hunted , since she was ten, with her father's pack of hounds every season. She could not imagine not knowing how to ride and determined that Simon should learn as soon as was possible...

They passed the short drive to the Vicarage discussing what kind of pony Simon wanted – his only desire was that it be small and kind, not given to making a fuss. Diana decided to look for a nice Welsh – it might be a little large for him at the moment, but he would grow into it. She was confident of her ability to pick a good mount for him.

The Vicarage was reached, perhaps too soon for Simon. He remembered the church from Sunday services the previous day, and the Reverend Mr. Arabin as well. Uncle Lyon approved of Mr. Arabin. His scholarship was sound, he said, and the pastor preached an admirably brief, to the point sermon. His rating in the *Magus Registratun Britannae* was more than satisfactory – he was a *Magus Majori* and held an Honors Baccalaureate from Merlin.

Simon liked the Vicarage at once. He had never seen so many books in his life. There was a little white cat, too, that met them at the door and purred when he petted it.

"My dear Lady Diana!" cried Mr. Arabin when they were shown into the drawing room. "I did not expect you!"

"I would like to meet Simon's tutor," she explained, offering her his hand.

"Oh, dear, I'm afraid that is not possible for a while. You see, I sent him on an errand this morning. One of my young gentlemen thought it would postpone his examination if he were to make all of the pencils and blank paper vanish. Well, he muddled the spell and he could not get them back again. So I sent Mr. Roussillon to the village for more equipment," the Vicar said apologetically. "And in his absence – although he should be back shortly – I am going to ask Simon a few questions, so that we can find out where he is in reading, mathematics, geography and the other sciences."

Roussillon. It sounded French. But there were many people in England with Norman French names, since the Invasion in 1066, Diana thought, although the way she presently felt about the French, she rather thought that they should all return to France, as soon as was possible. Why could the tutor not have been named Smith or Carter, or some other truly *English* name?

Diana looked at her ball watch. She was due at the drapers in Knightswold, which was some five miles away; within the hour where she was to choose papers and fabrics for the rooms on the ground floor of the Abbey. She had made the appointment on Saturday, by scry. And she very much doubted if Butterball could manage more than a slow trot. "I am afraid I must be on my way. If you recommend this young man so highly, Reverend, he must be all that is suitable."

"Yes, indeed. I am certain that he and Simon will take to one another and work well together," Mr. Arabin said eagerly.

"I will take my leave, then," Diana said and bade a fond farewell to Simon, who was not as upset as he might have been, being enthralled with the cat and the piles of books.

Simon did not find the Reverend Arabin's questions too difficult, He sat in a chair, cat in his lap, purring away, as the Vicar gently questioned him as to what work he had done, what books he had read and what he liked to study. At the end of fifteen minutes the Vicar, who had been making notes with a stubby pencil – it had been in his pocket and therefore had not been magiced away – said "There, Simon. I think that I have established that you are an excellent and wide-ranging reader, but you mathematics are shaky, you know little of geography and the natural sciences and have had no experience with even the most elementary magic. We shall know how to go on, I think."

"Please, sir," said Simon, suddenly remembering the few times Mr. Appersett had set them to their lessons (usually when Uncle Frederick began to demand just what he was getting for the outrageous wages – £30 a year – he was paying the sports-mad tutor) They sat in the stuffy classroom at the top of the house, repeating things by rote and writing endlessly, copying from very dull books. "Will I have to drone on and on and write things over and over?"

Mr. Arabin blinked in surprise. "Good Heavens, no! What a horrid way to learn! I have never believed that rote learning accomplishes any thing!. I teach – and so will your tutor, my dear Simon – by letting the pupil do and explore. Much more interesting for the pupil *and* the teacher."

A door opened in the hall and a murmur of voices was heard. Simon gulped suddenly and his stomach fluttered. This had to be his tutor. He put the cat on the ground and stood up.

His first impression was favorable. His tutor was tall and nice looking. Mr. Appersett had no chin, and a supercilious expression. This gentleman reminded Simon of Uncle Lyon in some strange fashion, even though they looked nothing alike. In fact, Mr. Roussillon looked rather like a picture of an Elf Simon had seen in one of his new books except that his ears didn't seem to be pointed. He had a friendly smile on his face and came at once to Simon and shook hands, which made Simon feel quite grown-up.

"It is such a beautiful day," he said, adding to Simon's surprise, "Why do we not do our lessons in the garden?"

Simon had never heard of such a thing. But since he hated being in a gloomy school-room when the sun was shining, he eagerly assented.

There was a large circle of gravel in the midst of the garden, ringed by masses of spring flowers, and in the midst of this stood a carved square block of Cotswold stone. It seemed to be covered in sculpted vines and flowers. There were two cushions placed in the middle of the circle of gravel and Mr. Roussillon indicated that they sit down on the cushions.

Had Simon but known it, René was nearly as anxious as he was. So much depended on the success of this position! When Reverend Arabin told him that he would receive a pound a week for teaching Simon he had felt the room spin around him. Never had he earned that much – for doing something he wanted to do, for only a half day at a time! It was unbelievable, munificent! Ninon had shrieked and jumped up and down like a schoolgirl when he told her.

"You have no experience with magic, I think," René said when they had settled themselves comfortably.

Simon shook his head, "No, sir."

"We shall start simply and go slowly . If you do not understand, you must ask as many questions as you like," René said.

"Even if they are stupid questions, sir?" Simon was desperately afraid of being thought stupid.

René smiled at him. "Do not worry about that – only those who pretend to understand are stupid. The intelligent person seeks to know. There are no stupid questions. I want you to truly understand what you are learning, whether it is science, magic, mathematics – so that you feel confident every step we take, yes?"

Simon nodded. "That's what my Mama said."

"Your mama is correct," René approved. "The very first lesson that any magician learns is about the Circle in which you perform your magic."

"Oh, sir, I read about that!" Simon said eagerly "Mama and I read *What Magic Is* together. and she explained a little about it."

"Why don't you tell me what you know, Simon and we shall proceed from there?" René suggested.

Simon had a retentive memory and the capacity to put facts together in a logical fashion rather than just memorizing. In a precise pain-staking fashion, he recounted that the altar always faced east and was covered by a cloth that was the proper colour for the ritual one was about to evoke. "And Mama said when the magic is worked indoors that the walls ought to be covered with drapery of the right colour too."

"That is correct,"

"But how do I know what colour is correct?" Simon asked.

"You will learn as we go along. And I have made for you a little book, which I will give you today before you go home, that has the Tables of Correspondence in it." René had spent a good deal of time on this – simplifying and making it easy for a young magician.

"Did you read about the Circle and what it means?" René asked.

When Simon said he had René stood up and reached inside his jacket to withdraw a wand. It was not like Uncle Lyon's wand, that Simon had seen in the Wizard's tower at the Abbey. It was wooden, like Uncle's, but lacked the gold tip and jeweled handle, and the large moonstone set into the end of the handle. Mr. Roussillon's wand was plain, with a carved handle and a tip of some dull metal. Simon stood up too and watched in wonder as his tutor drew a circle of violet light around them and the altar. He did not, however, finish the circle entirely.

"If you must leave the circle," he explained to Simon, "you must go through this gap and leave the same way. This is not a very powerful Circle – it is what we call a Teaching Circle – but we should begin as we mean to go on and treat every Circle as if it is indeed a thing of power. It will be a time of perhaps some length before we work in a closed Circle."

Simon nodded.

Then René told Simon that the carved stone was their altar and that the Circle would be oriented to it, He then drew a circle about them, encompassing the altar and then drew a symbol in the gravel – ∇ – and then drew a line across it, bisecting it. "This is the North, the symbol of the elemental king who governs –"

74

"Earth! "Simon supplied eagerly. "He is Uriel."

"Very good!" said René. Pleased. The boy was very quick and attentive.

René moved on to the next station.

"South." said Simon without prompting as René drew the next symbol, Michael's. △ "Fire."

The next station was West, Gabriel's water. The symbol was a plain ▽. The last station, the East was of air and Raphael. This was ☉, which was also the sun symbol.

"Would you like to try?" René asked Simon. "I will give you a little boost so that you may see what you have drawn."

Simon was confident that he could do it and nodded.

With a wave of his wand René restored the gravel to its undisturbed state.

A stick lay on the altar. René handed this to Simon. "For now," he said, "this will represent your wand. You may never use another magician's wand – that can be very dangerous, *non*? Tomorrow we will go to the trees and ask for a wand for you. Now, Simon, how are you orienting yourself so that the symbols are in the right direction?"

"By the altar. If it lays to the east, this – " he pointed "is North.'"

"Ah, you have a very good sense of where you are, which is most excellent. To carry always with you a compass is difficult," René approved.

With little hesitation Simon drew the correct symbols in the proper places.

René drew a deep breath. To teach this boy was going to be sheer joy. And he was so appreciative of praise, as well.

"When it is half after ten," he informed Simon, after telling him what excellent work he was doing. "Mr. Arabin will come out to us while his young gentlemen take a rest from their studies. We shall have a small ceremony to awaken your magic. And then we shall study the solid symbols of each station, and I think that before you go home you will know how to make a mage light and ground and shield yourself."

A mage light! Simon could hardly wait.

6

Afternoon In Knyghtwood

Diana was quite pleased with her morning's work. Knightswold had proved a larger place than she had guessed it to be and the shops were very good. She had spent an agreeable couple of hours choosing fabric for curtains and paper for most of the ground floor rooms. The draper's shop, Aldershot's, had a connection with a London warehouse and their own delivery dragon, so that she could have any choice not in stock within two days. They had furniture as well, under the same arangement.

She had sat in a sunlight room, at a wide table, with the pattern books spread out before her. Mr. Aldesshot himself brought her a cup of tea and Faerie cakes. Together they made the critical decorating decisions, based on Diana's copious notes and rough sketches of the rooms. Mr. Aldeshot was at first distressed that Diana had not let him come to her, but she had wanted to see everything available and there was but a limited amount he could send out for her appraisal, even with a delivery dragon. And she had other errands in the town.

Since Uncle Lyon had given her *carte blanche* – he was an extremely wealthy gentleman – Mr. Aldershot was more than pleased by the size of her order and Diana had the gratification of seeing what was not immediately available of her order scryed before she left the shop.

She found a sizable circulating library in the town and took out a subscription for herself and Simon. She found several novels that looked interesting, and, for Simon, chose a book on King Arthur and Merlin – his knowledge of history was not wide, and this particular book looked as it would be as interesting as a novel, not dry as dust as many histories were.

To Diana's pleasure there was a large shop that sold Wizarding needs, called *The Cauldron – Fine Needs for the Discriminating Witch and Wizard,* and boasted the Royal Warrant. It had a little of everything, from grimoires, bottles of such necessities as eye of newt, mermaid tears and bat wool, cauldrons and scrying bowls, crystal vessels, silver implements and measurers, wand tips and handles, and a notice board, indicating familiars available in the neighborhood, suitable for young Wizards and Witches to visit so that the young familiar animals could make their choice.

Diana's familiar, a sweet little hedgehog named Harley, had perished on the retreat from Corunna, dying in the snow like so many others, in spite of all she could do to protect him. At the time she had thought she would not need or want another, for she felt that she would never practice magic again. But now she was not so certain.

Another time, perhaps, she might think of a new familiar. And Simon was of an age to be chosen as well. She would bring Simon to this shop for he would need his own magical supplies, and would need to chose a tip and a handle for his wand. This made her think of his first lessons and hoped he was doing well this morning.

The Cauldron also sold robes, so she ordered Beltaine garments for herself and Simon. Now she *would* have to bring him here, for he had to be fitted. Perhaps tomorrow afternoon, for Beltaine was but a week away now and Uncle Lyon indeed had plans for it – there had not been a proper Beltaine celebration in the neighborhood for years. That was a duty of the Marquisate and the old Marquis had completely neglected his duty in this regard as he had in many others.

At the recommendation of the clerk at *the Cauldron,* Diana went next to *The Ladies' Emporium,* which was not, as the name might have indicted, a *modiste* or a milliner, but a shop full of amusements, needlework and art supplies for ladies. Here were parchment and pens for calligraphy, watercolours, brushes and papers, wool and silks and linens for embroidery, needles and tambour frames, books of instruction to make all sorts of pretty and useful things, and the supplies to make them, beads and loose jewels and trims and ribbons. There were musical instruments and the very latest sheet music from London publishers. It was quite as good as anything Diana had seen in Town, a veritable treasure trove, and she enjoyed poking amongst the wide selection of goods. She left the shop with a sizable bundle of embroidery silks, pattern books, needles and hoops. If she got right to work she could at least embroider the collars of their Beltaine robes. Robes were never sold embroidered – the design was a personal, meaningful choice, and the embroidery was usually done by the Witch herself, or by her, for a male family member.

After that, she stopped for a nuncheon in a pleasant tea shop, and then went to the local inn, the *Green Man*, where she had left Butterball. She was anxious to be home and to hear all about Simon's first lesson and how he had liked his tutor and it was nearly noon. Simon's lesson ended at one.

The ostler at the inn advised her to take a route home through Knyghtwood, since it was such a pleasant day and the primroses and bluebells were a fair treat. Diana was had no objections – the directions were easy to follow and he assured her that it would add but a few moments to her journey back to Silverbridge.

Butterball, having eaten a measure of oats at the inn and stuffed himself with timothy hay, had little desire to be poled up between the shafts and trot into the forest. He grumbled audibly, stamping his tiny hooves. He protested until they were into the forest of Knyghtwood,

Diana paid him little attention, for she was entranced by the beauty of the greenwood. She had never seen such old trees of such huge size – and England was full of very old trees. Even not yet fully leafed out, they cast deep shadows between them, making mysterious tunnels of darkness. It was a quiet wood, an enchanted wood. In the few beams that managed to break through the canopy of the forest were flowers – bluebells and primroses as the ostler had promised, but also wood spurge, pasque flowers and anemones. It was so lovely that Diana felt her spirits, which had been so low for so long, start to rise. She heard a cuckoo deep in the woods and suddenly found herself singing the ancient song celebrating spring:

"Sumer is icumne in
Lhudë sing cuccu!
Groweth sed and bloweth med
And springeth the wodë nu!
Sing, cucu!
Awe bleateth after lomb –"

"Help! Oh, help!" A shrill cry interrupted her song. That was a child's voice! Diana pulled up Butterball and looked around hurriedly. She could see nothing. "Where are you?" she shouted.

"Oh, thank God! We're at the bottom of the coombe!" There was a distinct sob in the young voice.

Diana saw no coombe, but she was unfamiliar with this wood. "Pray keep talking," she directed. "I don't quite know where you are.
Tell me who you are." She could hear an edge of hysteria.

"I am William Clifford and I am visiting my grandparents, Mr. and Mrs. Barton of Coombe Grange. My grandmother and I came out in the trap this morning and when we reached the edge of the coombe a hare ran across our path. Grandmama's horse is particularly afraid of hares and he shied and the wheel went over the edge and we fell out. He ran away! And Grandmama has fallen in a deep pool and I can't hold her up much longer! It's cold and she is heavy.! Oh, ma'am, do hurry!"

"Be calm, William, and I will help you." Diana located the coombe at last. The lane lay right along its edge. She could see where the trees started going down hill.

She grabbed the horse weight at her feet and clipped the lead to Butterball's headstall so that he would not wander off and went to the edge of the coombe and looked down.

What she saw dismayed her. It was a deep narrow coombe, with steep and wooded sides. At the bottom ran a rapid, clear stream over numerous rocks. William and his grandmother had fallen into a deep pool – fortunate for them, or they might have been killed. The elderly lady seemed to be unconscious and the boy, about twelve, was crouched underneath her, holding her head above water. From the top of the coombe Diana could hear his teeth chattering. Mrs.

Barton was stout; Diana could see that to pull her out of the water would be beyond William's strength.

"Her leg is caught between two rocks!" William shouted. "I can't get it out!" He looked terrified and desperate.

Diana knew that even if she managed to get to the bottom of the coombe they would never be able to get up again. She had no idea where the coombe might end up, if they followed it. Somewhere ahead she heard falling water — that would be impossible to negotiate. And there was no time to fetch help. She would have to use her magic — but would it be enough?

"William, do you have any magic?" she called down.

"No, ma'am," he returned. "I wish I did!"

It would have been helpful if he had even minimal magic, for she could have drawn upon it. "William," she called "I am going to conjure a rope. When it reaches you I want you to tie it about your Grandmama's waist." She only hoped that his hands were not too cold to tie a good knot.

As if he could read her thoughts he shouted, "I can tie a good knot! My brother Denny is a sailor and he showed me how!"

For the first time in over two years Diana called her magic to her, and felt it flowing through her veins. A blue light appeared in her hands and she began to pull at it, almost just as she had the other evening when she had Simon had invaded the kitchen to make and pull candy. Steadily a rope of blue fire grew in a pile at her feet until she judged that there was as much and more than she would need. At a Word, one end flew down to William and she tried to secure the other end to the pony cart.

Tried, for it dissolved beneath her fingers. At William's despairing shout, she realized that the same thing was happening to him. It really needed two mages to make a good stout rope. She sagged against the wheel. What was she to do?

"Let me help," said a voice at her shoulder.

Startled, she turned to find a gentleman at her elbow. Before she could say anything, violet light began to flow off his hands and split into two, winding itself around her blue rope, making it braided and heavy. It flowed down into the coombe, following her line.

"That's done it!" William cried. "I can tie it!"

The gentleman strode to the edge of the coombe. "I am coming down," he said, and slid done the rope hand over hand.

Diana watched anxiously as he helped William get his grandmother's booted foot from the cleft in which it had lodged itself. At his signal she ran back to the cart and tied the rope firmly to the axle of the pony cart.

"Pull!" the gentleman shouted and she picked up the horse weight and led Butterball forward.

The conjured rope did its work properly and pulled the lady safely through the tangle of trees – it knew just where to go.

Ruthlessly, Diana dragged the cushions and two carriage rugs from out of the pony cart. She untied the rope from the unconscious Mrs. Barton and made her as comfortable as was possible very quickly and, backed Butterball up, directing the rope to return to the bottom of the coombe. When the two in the coombe indicated that they were ready, she then led the pony forward again, and pulled the unknown gentleman and William up.

William ran at once to his grandmother's side. Like her, the boy was dripping wet. Diana hurried forward with a carriage robe to wrap about him.

Then with her heart full of gratitude, Diana turned to the gentleman who had so fortuitously appeared. "Oh, sir," she began.

But he was gone.

Diana took William and his grandmother home to Coombe Grange and stayed until a doctor came. Mrs. Barton had bumped her head but was not concussed. The greatest danger was a chill from the immersion in the cold water, but she was given an herbal drench, as was William, and both put to bed to steam beneath a pile of fleecy blankets.

Mr. Barton and William's parents were effusive in their praise and would not hear of Diana leaving before they offered her sufficient thanks and hospitality. Diana thought they owed more to the strange gentleman that had so mysteriously appeared and disappeared. When she described him to the Mr. Barton and the Cliffords, they did not recognize him. But Mr. Barton said apologetically that he and his wife knew little of the young people hereabouts – on this side of Knyghtwood they attended church at St Anselm's – perhaps the gentleman was form her own parish, or perhaps St Sebastian's? And the Cliffords, of course, were visiting here from the Lake District, and knew no one in the neighborhood. Mrs. Clifford had not grown up here – Coombe Grange was her parent's retirement home – he had been a mer-chant in Bristol.

All the way home Diana thought about the unknown gentleman. For something very strange had taken place when his magic had begun to interwork with hers. There had been the most profound feeling of unity, of oneness, as if he could read her mind and soul, and she his. They Worked together in perfect harmony. She had never Worked with anyone else where she had achieved that sense of accord, as if the were not two magicians, but one.

Such was the ideal. At school, the girls had dreamed of it, hoping that the man they eventually married would be able to work that sort of magic with them. There was much giggling over the whispered stories that it was said to be a union of ultimate bliss in the bedchamber, also, if one was fortunate enough to find such a Wizard for husband.

Jonathan had had very little magic, almost none in fact. Had he ever even passed his *Magus Novititae*? And she realized, he had really not much liked her using her magic. She suddenly remembered that when they were first wed, she had thought him jealous of her skill. Because she loved him, she had stopped openly using magic, only employing it to spell his safety.

She had to find out who this gentleman was.

After a most satisfactory morning with Simon, René decided to scope out various parts of the woods, in search of trees that might offer Simon a wand. His own wand came from Knyghtwood, very deep in the heart of the trees, where there was a sacred place, long deserted. A wand from there, for Simon, should the trees agree, would be a special one for the boy's use.

It was a very long walk, but a lovely warm day. He hoped it might not be too long for Simon to walk. The boy looked rather frail, and Reverend Arabin thought the lessons, especially with summer coming, ought to be conducted out of doors as much as possible.

He was very pleased with Simon's progress, as had been the Vicar. Simon had gone home able to make a mage light – a small, but warmly glowing mage light and had learned how to ground and shield. The ceremony to awaken his magic had gone very well, and the Vicar had blessed Simon's magic and his learning. The awakening, which was allowed to a *Magus Minori*, would create a special bond between pupil and teacher for the sum of their days. They had discovered Simon had Othersight, which by the end of the day he had learned to shield.

Yes, it had been a good beginning. René hoped that the Marquis and Simon's mother were pleased and wished to retain him as the boy's tutor.

The way to the sacred place had grown tangled – it had been a long time since he had been here – too long, as the trees informed him. Would he tell the Druid of this place? The trees would be very happy to see the ancient ceremonies performed here once more.

René gave his word and received the promise of a wand for Simon. He then left the grove, to go home. His grandmother needed help in the vegetable garden this afternoon. Jacques had not been able to rise from bed today, for the pain of his rheumatism. And Lucie could not be left alone.

He heard the cuckoo sing out in the woods for the first time this spring. Cuckoos were not charming birds – they had very nasty habits, among them, laying their eggs in other's nests so that they could cadge someone else into raising their young, but their song always meant that summer was coming and living would be easier – there was more work and food was abundant.

René wished that he had not thought of food – it had been a long time since breakfast and that breakfast had been woefully inadequate – three eggs to make an omelet for five people, and to accompany it, but a cup of very weak tea. If he had been thinking, he could have begged a hunk of bread and cheese from Mrs. Parker – she was very good about that. It was a long walk back to May Cottage and no guarantee once there that there would be much to eat. René shrugged. *Ça ne fait rien*. It was not important.

He went towards the cuckoo, admiring the carpet of flowers between the huge old trees. Truly, England was a beautiful place, and this area perhaps the prettiest of all, although he had not been elsewhere to compare. But all of this beauty lifted the soul and made hard times a little easier to bear.

The cuckoo sang out again and then René heard the screaming. He began to run.

By the time he reached the place where the screams came from, someone had already arrived. He had run quite a distance – he had thought he heard a horse clatter away earlier but he was not certain.

He took in what was happening at a glance. The woman had made a nice rope, but it always took two magicians, in concert, to make a rope. He stepped forward and said, "Let me help you."

He was surprised at the ease with which his magic blended with hers. It was as if they had Worked together all of their lives. It was even better than Working with Ninon or the Vicar, the only two people he had really ever Worked with. And there was an added element to it, a feeling of union and completion. They worked without words and in no time at all he was able to slide down the rope and help free the woman's foot. With the boy, he rode the rope to the edge of the coombe. Without a backwards glance the boy flew to his grandmother's side and the woman with the pony cart threw a carriage robe about the soaked child.

And René staggered into the forest. A little ways in, where they could not see him, he collapsed beneath a huge beech tree, in a patch of bluebells.

He lay back against the pale trunk, closing his eyes. He had never felt so ill in his entire life, not even when, as a child he had had an extremely severe case of influenza. "*Balourd! Crétin!*" he admonished himself. One of the cardinal rules of magic was to never do a working on an empty stomach. Magic required fuel.

He really had no idea how he was to get home. Even with his eyes closed he was so dizzy that sitting up was almost beyond him. His legs and hands were trembling with weakness and he was very much afraid that he was going to be violently sick.

"Man!" a voice like silver bells heard far away said near his face. He heard a sound like a humming bird's wings. "Man!" the voice repeated "Open your eyes and look at me!"

"I do not think that is a very good idea. *J'ai le vertige*," René said weakly, feeling himself slip further down the tree and powerless to stop himself. "*Je me suis très malade.*"

"Speak English!" said the little voice crossly. "Oh, this is impossible! Here you are! Don't bite me!"

Something flew against his lips and surprised, René inadvertently opened his mouth. Something small popped in.

And immediately a warm glow spread through out him, starting near his heart and flowing outwards. He felt wonderful – as if he had had a perfect night's rest and had feasted at a bountiful banquet.

His eyes flew open. Right in front of his face hung a tiny blue Faerie. She was no bigger than half of his clenched fist and her gauzy wings moved exactly like a humming bird's. She had a cloud of blue hair, skin of blue and was a perfect little naked female with translucent blue wings like those of a dragonfly.

But she wore a very cross expression. "Are you better now?" she asked in exasperation. "Do you know that you have quite crushed a particularly fine clump of my bluebells? If I were not under a strict order to aid and succor you I should be biting your nose for that!"

René got up at once – so easily! – when just minutes earlier he had imagined dying beneath this tree. "*Je vous demande pardon,*" he said, feeling it might be a good idea to bow to her.

"I told you to speak English! I am a good English Faerie, not a bloody foreigner!" She scowled even deeper.

"I am very sorry to have destroyed your flowers, but I could not seem to help it," he amended.

"That's better," she said. "Do you feel well now?"

"I feel wonderful," said René, careful not to speak any French. "I thank you very much, my lady Faerie. What was that you gave me?"

"A little remedy," she said carelessly. "Useful for stupid Wizards who overextend themselves."

"Do Wizards often overextend themselves?"

She rolled her eyes, as blue as the rest of her. "Oh, yes! After all, Wizards are mortals and everyone knows mortals are not very intelligent!"

"Why did you help me?" René asked curiously, ignoring the insult.

She folded her hands together and, like a child reciting a piece, said in sing-song tones, "My name is Medb. I am sent to tell you that you are counted a Faerie friend – "

"But I have never had anything to do with Faeries!" René protested.

"Don't interrupt me!" Medb scolded. "Where was I? Oh, yes – you are counted a Faerie friend, for it has been noted that no matter how little you have for yourselves, you always leave a bowl of something for us at the back door, as is proper – we particularly liked that cherry thing – " she interrupted herself "and you and yours are respectful of the flowers – except for now – and as a Faerie friend, we have aided and succored you in your hour of need. Expect a summons."

"A summons? From whom?" René asked.

"That is all I was told to say. Don't sit on any more bluebells!" she added severely. "Goodbye!" And she was gone, winking out of existence.

7

A Cry In the Night

The golden late afternoon sun streamed through the tiny windows of May Cottage. It spread across the floor and onto the table where Ninon sat and lit up the object in front of her.

It was a silver cauldron of great antiquity, undoubtedly worth a great deal of money. But it could not be sold, for she was tuned to it and it to her. To allow it to pass into other hands would be dangerous, for one did not rid oneself of a cauldron lightly. If it was stolen the thief would die.

It was a beautiful thing, one of the finest examples of old Celtic silversmithing that existed, Ninon often thought. On the outside were raised relief panels, each representing a Celtic God amidst branches of mistletoe. On the inside a stream of dragons chased one another endlessly.

It was filled with water that caught the sun and sparkled like diamonds. Normally, this bowl, wrapped in silk, lived in a wall cupboard by the chimney, pushed quite far to the back. It was used once a month now. At one time the contents of the bowl had served as a sort of school-room for René, and then for simple communication, about once a month.

But all that had now changed. Ever since her grandson had told her of the Druid *de meilleur rang* who had come to their little neighborhood, she had known that change was in the wind and she must do what she had sworn to do. What she had seen and done with the bowl today disturbed her profoundly. She had used the cauldron for so long that its messages were usually clear to her and the messages she received from the Others were to the point as well. But the images she got today were murky and obscure – there was danger, but to whom and what form it would take she could not be certain. It did not even tell her where. And the message from the Others was a simple "It is time." At least she knew what *that* meant – she had been waiting for it for years, but she had never really thought that the time would come. She felt suddenly inadequate to bear the burden.

She sighed and rose from the table. Lifting the cauldron with a little difficulty, she took it to the back door and threw the water out on to her herb garden. That water was as sanctified as if Mr. Arabin had blessed it and would do the herbs good.

She then went into the curtained corner of the room where Marthe sat with Lucie. Lucie had had a very good day today – they had been able to go out into the garden. Now she was sleepy after all of the fresh air. She looked up from her pillow and smiled at Ninon, blinking. That smile twisted Ninon's heart. She could see the young Lucie in it. She went forward and dropped a kiss on her daughter's forehead. "*Pauvre petite*," she murmured, smoothing back a lock of dark hair – how grey it was getting – from Lucie's face.

Lucie smiled at her again and then turned away, burrowing into her pillow.

Marthe was asleep in her chair, snoring lightly. Her knitting had fallen to the floor and Ninon picked it up and put it on the tiny table that stood by Marthe's side which contained her rush knitting basket. Dear Marthe, she never complained; she just did what had to be done. Ninon could not imagine what she would have done all of these years without Marthe and Jacques. But now they were growing very old. Jacques had been unable to rise from his bed for the last two days. She gave him herbal remedies for the pain, but she suspected more and more that he was just wearing out. What would they do without the good Jacques?

And Ninon did not know what René would do for stockings should anything happen to Marthe. The one pair she herself had knit – with a large amount of help from Marthe – were so lumpy that they made him limp. Nor did

Ninon know how she would take care of Lucie without Marthe's help – or what she would do without Marthe, period.

Pulling the curtain closed behind her, she went back into the little kitchen. There was no closed stove, only a fireplace with a spit and a row of pothooks, one of which held a battered kettle. After she carefully dried the cauldron and re-wrapped it in silk, and stored it in its cupboard, Ninon stirred up the hearth fire, which was never allowed to go out. She felt in need of a cup of tea – weak though it would be. With René making such a good wage now, perhaps they could afford to buy some pure tea, not the adulterated, poor stuff that they had from the peddler, which, Ninon suspected, was more dyed sawdust sweepings than tea.

The door opened and Ninon turned from the fireplace. "Here you are at last!" she said as her grandson entered, trying not to let the emotions of the afternoon sound in her voice." Did it go well? And then, frowning, "René, *qu'est-ce qu'il y a*? You look strange."

"I feel strange," he returned, sinking into a chair at the table. The Faerie remedy was wearing off and he was beginning to feel both tired and hungry. "*Grandmère*, I have this afternoon met a Faerie."

"Surely you are joking – *les feés*, they do not show themselves to us! Tell me what happened. I shall make tea for us. And there is bread and butter!"

René was too tired to inquire from where had come the bread and butter – he was too grateful to have it. As his grandmother bustled about, slicing bread and making the tea, he told her what had happened. She scolded him roundly for working magic in such a condition.

He shrugged. "What could I do, *Grandmère*? The lady would have drowned had I not helped."

She shook her head at him. "Do not do such a foolish thing again! Now eat more of *le bon pain* – there is plenty! I have sold some charms today and spent the shillings at *la boulangerie*. And *les saucisses* form le *charcuterie*. We will eat well tonight, us!"

"Now tell me how it has gone with the little Simon?" she continued and said to herself "*Later. I will tell him later.*"

Diana was very late arriving back at the Abbey – the afternoon sun was declining and she hoped that no one had been worried. Butterball had actually almost cantered, so eager was he to reach his stable. Diana expected Simon to be laying in wait for her.

There was no sign of Simon, but there was an undue bustle about the house. As Diana drove up to the front door, it opened and Seppings came quickly down the shallow steps, followed by a footman. "Oh, my lady! Such a to-do! We've unexpected guests!" He came forward and handed Diana down from the pony cart. "Don't just stand there, Edward!" he said impatiently to the footman. "See that the pony cart gets to the stable block and take her ladyship's packages up to her chamber."

"Who has come, Seppings?" Diana queried as Seppings escorted her up the steps and into the hall, Behind them, Edward was ringing the horse bell for a groom to come and fetch the pony cart. It was beneath his dignity to take a pony and cart to the stables.

"It's the Arch Druid of Ériu, my lady, Con-chobar Ó Clérigh, and his secretary, a very nice young gentleman called Diarmait Mag Uidhir."

"Were they expected?" Diana frowned. The Irish Arch Druid, here? Surely Uncle would have told her? If they were staying the guest chambers would have to be hurriedly readied.

"Oh, no, my lady. And I gather," he lowered his voice confidentially, "that the news they brought is not good. His lordship began yelling almost as soon as they went up to the tower."

Diana took off her bonnet and gloves and handed them and her reticule to the butler. "Where is Master Simon?"

"He is out in the stableyard, my lady. His Grace the Arch Druid came dragon-back and Master Simon could not wait to meet his dragon. A most pleasant creature, called Pádraig. I took the liberty of arranging a little meal for him. Mr. Mag Uidhir is with them, my lady."

"I shall go and see my uncle first, Seppings. I must find out if my uncle's guests will be staying," Diana said, mounting the bottom step.

"Very good, my lady. I fancy they will be at least staying for dinner, as his lordship bade me lay two extra covers," Seppings bowed.

Diana could hear her uncle's raised voice even before she reached the tower. Traditionally, Wizards Worked in a tower when not out of doors. Modern thought held that it was not really necessary, but most Wizards still preferred a tower for a Workplace and every great house in England that was owned by a Wizarding family had at least one tower.

Diana tapped lightly on the door but no doubt due to the loud cries of "Curse it! How could they do such a thing?", no one heard her and she pushed the door open and went in.

Her uncle was pacing up and down the floor, swearing. With him was a man of late middle years, with a crown of silver hair and the look of a poet about him. Before he had been elected Arch Druid, Conchobar Ó Clérigh had been one of Ireland's most famous and best-loved Bards. He was attempting to soothe Lord Lyonshall.

"Now, Lyon," he was saying in his soft Irish voice." It may not be as bad as you think. We'd do best to wait and see."

"Wait and see!" Lyon exploded. "I tell you to your head, Con, this is one of the worst things that could happen!"

"What has happened, Uncle?" Diana came forward worriedly She was used to her uncle's rages, but she had never seen him so upset.

"Diana! You're back!" he said, and very briefly introduced his niece to the Irish Arch Druid. "Con has brought the worst news!" he growled. "Oh, you tell her, Con! I cannot bring myself to do so."

Although his expression was grave, there was still a twinkle in the Arch Druid's green eyes that told Diana he had a keen sense of humor. "You must be understanding, Lady Diana, that my wife's nephew, Fergal Fearghail, is after being a runner between the parliaments of Britain and Érui."

All the Six Nations of the British Isles – Érui, known as Ireland in English, Scotland, Cymry (Wales) , the Isle of Man and Kernow (Cornwall), had chosen allegiance to Britain and recognized the British sovereign as the High King, but each country had its own Parliament and runners were employed daily either dragon-back or on hippogriffes, to keep the six parliaments in touch with one another.

"Fergal brought some distressing news from London – it has not yet been made public, nor have we even received the official dispatches –"

"That coward Perceval is afraid to tell me!" Lyon cut in.

"As it may be," Conchobar continued mildly.

"As you are probably being aware, the Chancellor of Magic and Enchantments has but recently passed away."

"Yes." said Diana. "Lord Bluestone died in office, did he not?"

"Yes, the poor man was very overworked and not in the best of health..." Conchobar said.

"Who cares what his health was!" Lyon almost shrieked. "Diana, that fat idiot of a Regent and the Prime Minister, Spencer Perceval – another idiot! – have appointed Chenevix to the post of Chancellor of Magic and Enchantment! Chenevix!" Deep loathing was in Lyon's voice.

"Oh, no!" Diana was shocked, for she could not imagine a worse choice.

To begin with, the Duke of Chenevix was a lapsed Wizard. He had given up magic some years before and in the last few years had begun to speak out against the over use of magic in daily life. He was a cold, austere man who seemed to have no family or friends. He had a biting wit and had such a freezing stare that he had become known as "the Icicle". He was no friend to magic and Wizards.

"And what, pray, is the justification for this appointment?" Diana inquired.

Lyon ground his teeth. "To promote a more balanced approach to magic, if you have ever heard such damnable nonsense! The government is becoming top heavy with Wizards! The non-magical peoples deserve their own voice! BAH!" he spat. "Why Chancellor of Magic – why not Chancellor of the Exchequer? Or Minister of Fisheries! Or Keeper of the Privy Stair? There's a position for him – Wiper of the Royal Bum!"

"Lyon!" Conchobar was shocked. "Not in front of your lady niece!"

Lyon had the grace to look abashed. "Sorry, Diana," he mumbled.

Diana let his transgression pass. "Will you be staying the night with us, sir?" she asked the Irish Arch Druid.

"'Twould be a pleasure, Lady Diana, for haven't we been in the air since early morning, having stopped in at the Isle of Man on the way here." He smiled at her. She decided that he was a very nice gentleman.

"What did Douglas Ramey have to say about this?" Lyon demanded. Ramey was the Arch Druid of Man.

"He was – err – not being happy," Conchobar said carefully.

"I am going to scry Myfanwy, Iain and Pengelly," said Lyon. These three were the Arch Druids of Wales, Scotland and Cornwall – Myfanwy Gryffydd, Iain McAslan and Pengelly Tregaron.

Diana left them, then. She wanted to get the preparations in train and find Simon. They were still arguing over whom to first notify when she started down the stairs.

Most large houses in England had, near the stableyard, what was known as a dragon pen. It had no railings or fence, but was a large sandy area for a dragon to rest in, as dragons liked nothing better than a sandy wallow in the sun. A canvas top, quite high, protected the dragon in inclement weather and could be rolled back on a fine day as well.

Here Diana found her small son, sitting on the bank of the dragon pen, talking animatedly to a medium-sized bright green dragon. Beside him sat a darkly handsome young man, throwing in a laughing word once in awhile. Simon and the dragon appeared to be making great strides toward a lasting friendship.

Simon heard her footsteps on the gravel and scrambled up, running towards her joyfully. "Mama!" he cried and threw himself at her. "Mama, it's a dragon! His name is Pádraig! And he says if it is all right with you, he will give me a ride!" His eyes were shining with excitement.

The young man rose from the bank and strolled towards Diana. "And I'll be going up with them, do it please your ladyship. Diarmait Mag Uidhir at your service, my lady," He bowed extravagantly. "And this is Pádraig." he waved his hand towards the dragon, who inclined his head graciously.

"May I, Mama, may I?" begged Simon. "I should like to do so above all things!"

Diana looked at the dragon. "I understand you've had a long flight today, Padrág. Are you certain that you want to go up again tonight?"

"Sure, and why not?" the dragon said pleasantly. Like most dragons he had a rich, mellow speaking voice. "We'll go but a bit about the village – not too high or long – just so the little lad may have a taste of flying."

"Very well, then," said Diana and Simon jumped up and down in glee. "After your supper, Simon. Uncle and I will be dining later tonight with our guests. Seppings is arranging a little meal for Pádraig, too."

The dragon looked interested. "'Tis starved that I am," he said with a mock plaintive note.

"'Tis a great overfed gowk that you are," said Mr. Mag Uidhir teasingly.

The dragon stuck out his long forked tongue at the secretary and they both laughed.

Mr. Mag Uidhir offered his arm to Diana and they strolled back to the house, Simon running in front of them as if by doing so he could make the time for his dragon ride come faster.

Simon lay in bed waiting for Mama to come and kiss him good night. While she had been abed he had gone into her and perhaps read a story with her. But now that she was better she would come to him each evening.

Sanders was still in the room. picking up and putting away. He had been there to see Simon, firmly strapped in, with Mr. Mag Uidhir's arm about him, take off from the dragon pen. It had been so exciting — the cool rush of breeze as Pádraig spiraled up into the evening air. It was dusk, but still light enough to see and Simon watched in fascination as the ground fell away beneath them. He was not afraid – he could feel Pádraig's muscles moving beneath him and hear the mighty flap of wings.

The miniature world beneath them was beautiful at this time of evening, a time that many people called Elf-light. The village lay lost in the dense woodland and Simon saw the Cotswolds rising up from the valley floor. He saw the church and the Vicarage as well as the village and he wondered where Mr. Roussillon lived and if he was out of doors where he might see Simon flying overhead on a dragon. As Pádraig circled back towards the Abbey, Simon saw his new home from above and was certain that he could pick out his own room where a light shone from the window. Uncle Lyon's tower blazed with a blue-white light.

It was over all too soon. Pádraig landed neatly in front of the dragon pen and Simon waited until Mr. Mag Uidhir slid off and then unstrapped Simon and helped him down.

Simon thanked Pádraig and the young secretary profusely. "Ye can go up with me any time, lad," said the dragon. "'Tis happy to have you I'll be."

Sanders then came forward to collect Simon and ready him for bed. Mama and Uncle Lyon and the Arch Druid, as well as most of the servants had come out to see Simon take his very first dragon flight. Mama kissed him and promised to come in and say good night when he was ready for bed.

When she came, Simon's mouth made an 'o' of surprise. She looked so beautiful! She was wearing a gown of some purply-blue gauzy stuff and jewels in her ears and at her throat. "Mama!" he said, lost in admiration. "You look like a Faerie Queen!"

She laughed, the low pleasant laugh that he loved to hear. "I am dressed for dinner, since we have guests," she said, sitting on the edge of his bed. "Now, Simon, pray tell me all about your lessons!"

"Oh, yes, Mama!" He sat up in bed and held out his hand, concentrating and visualizing just as he had been taught. And in a very few minutes, a blue white mage light, albeit a small one, appeared.

"That's wonderful, Simon!" Diana was surprised. Simon must be very clever – it had taken Peter two weeks to make a proper mage light. "What else did you learn?"

Simon put out his little light and told her all about the Circle and the ceremony to awaken his magic. "And do you know what else, Mama? Mr. Arabin has a little white cat that is named Minou. She's going to have kittens! Mr. Arabin said that I should ask you if I might be presented to the kittens as I shall need a familiar."

"I thought you wanted an owl, like Uncle Lyon's Leander," Diana said.

"Oh, I like Leander, but a kitten could sleep with me and a kitten would like to play. Minou likes to chase string," Simon explained.

He *would* need a familiar – it was probably a good plan. "You may have a kitten Simon. It's a good idea to grow up with your familiar." Diana was almost squashed by his enthusiastic hug.

"Did you like your tutor, Simon?" she wanted to know.

"Oh, yes, Mama!" Simon was very enthusiastic. "He's very nice and kind – not like that Mr. Appersett! Tomorrow we are going out to chose a wand for me."

"You'll enjoy that." She smiled at him and bent to kiss him. "I'm very glad that everything is going so well for you, Simon. I must join our guests. Sleep well."

But no one in the whole of the British Isles was to sleep well that night.

Midnight. Earlier in the evening between dusk and the end of the hours of the day it had rained lightly – a true April shower – but now the skies had cleared and the moon, a gibbous waxing moon, glowed amid a million stars in a blue velvet sky. It was very quiet – not even a night bird sang and very little breeze stirred the new leaves of the trees. All had retired for the night – all the occupants of the Abbey, the horses in the stables and even Pádraig, snuggled down into the sand to reap the benefits of as much of the captured sunlight as was possible, slept deeply.

At May Cottage everyone slept peacefully as did people throughout he Village. At the Hall Sir Piers snored thunderously in a chair in his library – he had drunk two bottles of port and whipped a too-slow servant. In her bed, Hester had cried herself to sleep. She missed Minou so much – there was no sweet little face to look up at her with love, no one to cuddle in the night. It was even more difficult than she had thought it would be to be without love.

All over England clocks were chiming out midnight when the first scream sounded. It was a scream of pure terror and it echoed from John O'Groats to the cliffs of Dover, from Tyneside all the way across the sea of Érui. It was followed by another – this a scream of death agony, of the horrible end of a life in the extremity of pain.

And all over the British Isles, people tumbled from their beds, sickened and horrified. Dogs began to howl everywhere, dragons roared and the earth itself shuddered.

Simon awoke at once, terrified. "Mama! Mama!" he screamed. Sanders came stumbling from the dressing room where he slept on a cot. Every hair on his head stood on end. "God help us!" he exclaimed "What was that?"

He gathered Simon against him. "Your mother's coming," he said, his teeth chattering. Suddenly he felt as young as Simon and wished he might have the comfort of his mother's arms as well.

Diana had been catapulted from bed by the sound. What was that? She had never heard anything like that and she was sickened by the pain that resonated in it.

Her first thought was of Simon. She managed to find her dressing gown but not her slippers and pulled the gown on as she opened her door and ran down the hall to his room, barefoot.

The scream seemed to have awakened everyone else, for she saw her uncle's door open violently and heard the servants, some sobbing and at least one of the maids screaming, coming down the stairs. Mr. Mag Uidhir and the Irish Arch Druid, both looking profoundly shaken, had burst into the Hall too.

Diana ignored them all and ran into Simon's room.

"Mama! Mama!" he was sobbing.

"I'm here, sweetheart, Mama's here," she said and took Sander's place, holding the little body against hers, stroking his hair and rocking him back and forth.

"My lady," Sanders moaned. "What was that?"

Diana shook her head, Simon still tight in her arms. She had no more idea than he did.

"Is he all right?" came Lyon's voice.

Diana raised her head. "He's terrified."

"We all are," said her uncle. "By the Horned Moon, I never heard anything like that!"

Outside, Pádraig bellowed again. Further off towards the village, they could hear dogs howling.

And then a horrible keening arose from outside, like a soul in torment in the deepest grief imaginable.

"Is that a –" sputtered Lyon, glaring at Conchobar, who had followed him into Simon's room.

"Yes, it is my *bean-sidhe*. She will follow me everywhere you know, and I imagine Diarmiat's is not far behind." The Irish Druid sighed. The *bean-sidhe*, or banshee as they were known in England, were Irish death spirits, who keened for the death of a member of the family to which it was attached. When two or more keened together it meant the death of someone very great or Holy. Even as Conchobar finished speaking a second wail joined the first and the Irish Druid's expression grew grim. "I'm not liking this at all, Lyon. 'Tis something dreadful that has happened! And draw the window shade!" he ordered Sanders. "The lad must not see the *bean-sidhes* – it will turn his brain – they are a fearsome sight."

Sanders leaped to obey – he didn't want to see them either.

"I'm going to the tower," Lyon announced. "Either I can find out what has happened in my scry bowl, or there will be a hippogriffe landing on the roof with a message. I'm also going to brew a calmative in a vast quantity. It sounds as if it is sorely needed around here."

"I'll go with you," said Conchobar. "Diarmait, go out and speak to the *bean-sidhes* – see if you might quiet them. And be telling Pádraig that we'll let him know what is wrong as soon as we are finding it out ourselves." He followed Lyon out the door.

Simon continued to sob quietly. He had had such a wonderful day! And now this fright in the middle of the night. But Mama was holding him and soothing him and it felt good to be in her arms. He felt safe.

Diana felt him relaxing. She wished that she had someone to hold her as well. Her heart still thudded erratically and she still felt terror beating in her veins. She hoped that the two Druids could find out what it was – and prevent it from happening again.

At the Vicarage, Reverend Arabin was awakened not only by the screams, but by two extremely distressed cats. Minou and his familiar Plato were on his chest and shivering and mewing with fear. Plato seemed to be shocked speechless – he usually had quite a bit to say.

Poor creatures! He comforted them as best he could and then making a quick decision, got out of bed and into his dressing gown and slippers. "Come," he said to the frightened little animals. "There is only one place for us at a time such as this." He led them out of the house across the yard and into the church. "Others will be afraid and will come here for succor. We must be ready for them," So saying, he went about the church, lighting every candle and conjuring a large soft white mage light on the angel roof. Then he knelt down at the altar, the cats crowding close to him.

At May Cottage, they all had been shocked from their beds. René, and Marthe, slowly followed by Jacques, came down the stairs in a rush, Ninon, who slept on a folding cot by Lucie's side, sat bolt upright. And Lucie began to scream. It took the combined efforts of all of then to calm her. Ninon finally resorted to the valerian yet again.

"*Mon Dieu!*" said Jacques "What was that horror?" He was a little, thin, stooped man, bald, with a face so wrinkled his features were not easily discerned. His hands and joints were swollen. It had taken an effort to get out of bed, even with such a propellant. Marthe, except for her thin grey hair, looked much like him.

"I do not know," said Ninon. "But it is something terrible and evil, of this I am certain!"

They were sitting at the table, exhausted after the fight with Lucie, for she had struggled violently with the strength of the mad. René held a wet cloth to his cheek, for she had hit him in the eye when he was attempting to hold her arms while Ninon administered the draught to her.

Ninon persuaded Marthe and Jacques to go to bed, but signaled to René that she wanted to speak to him.

René sighed. It had been a long day – he wanted nothing more than to return to his bed and get a little more sleep before it was time to get up in the morning. But he could tell that she had something important to say.

She came right to the point. She could put it off no longer. Something awful had happened and she very much feared that it was just the beginning of the things she had glimpsed in her cauldron.

"It is time, René," she said abruptly. "Are you able to help me?"

Startled, he looked at her. " You have heard?"

"This very afternoon. And I, think, me, that this night is part of it. Are you still willing to help?"

"I gave you my word, did I not?" he said. "I shall not cry quits on it now."

She smiled at his use of English slang. *"Trés bon*. Here is what I want you to do."

8

Familiar and Unfamiliar

True to Reverend Arabin's prediction, St. Swithin's was, within an hour, crowded with people in all stages of dress and distress. Many thought that the end of the world had come and Judgment Day was upon them. Others did not or could not even begin to guess what the events of the night might mean, but were frightened out of their wits and needed reassurance as much as they needed news. Many more people went to the Abbey and stood in a restless, anxious crowd beneath the brightly lit windows of the tower, thinking that surely the Marquis, being Arch Druid, would know, if any one did, what had happened and what it meant. Still others stayed in their homes, huddled together, windows and doors bolted and shut, too fearful to try and find out what had happened.

Lyonshall made an appearance on the balcony of the tower, trying to reassure people, telling them that as soon as he had news, they would have it too. He was frustrated, for he had not been able to scry anyone as yet – it felt as if everyone in the British Isles who had a scry bowl was trying to use it at the same time.

But by one in the morning they had news at last. And it was terrible news indeed.

It arrived with an exhausted young messenger on a hippogriffe. The 'griffe had obviously flown fast and hard for its feathers were sweat soaked and it gasped for breath through its open beak, unable to speak a word. Lyon and Conchobar, in the laboratory, heard it land on the roof and raced up the circular stairs before the rider could put his silver horn to his lips.

The rider was equally exhausted. Wordlessly, he held out a folded parchment to Lyon.

Lyon recognized the livery in the mage light he quickly threw up – it was blue and silver, that of those in the service of the Arch Druid of Wales.

The parchment had been folded over and sealed with the seal of Cymru – the leek. It read:

Llyn Cerrig Bach, Ynys Môn, Gwynedd, Cynru
To his Grace, the Arch Druid of Britain:

Our beloved Myfanwy has this very night been foully murdered by a power or powers unknown. As was her custom she walked and meditated late, before retiring. She was some distance from the House of the Derwyddon and was unaccompanied, even by her familia, the white cat Pangur Bán.

There is no sign of how this atrocity was accomplished, for all that she left her death cry behind her. Forensic Wizards from Bow Street in London have been summoned. We know naught else.

Yours in sorrow and
haste,
Cynndelew Brydyad Mawr,
second to Myfanwy Gruffydd, Arch Druid, Cynru

Lyon read this aloud and Conchobar looked at him blankly. "Murdered? Myfanwy?" the Irish Druid said in disbelief. "Who would do such a thing – and right on the Isle of Anglesey, too, in the Holiest place of the Druids of Wales! Why would anyone do such a thing?"

Lyon had gone pale. "And how was it accomplished.?" he demanded. "She was a very great magician!" He turned to the young rider. "Did you see the body? How was she found? You're Owain Cyfeilcawg, if I remember correctly, from the last time I was on Ynys Môn."

"Aye, my lord," answered the young rider. "She was found by Pangur Bán, who fetched the second. He then fetched the Healer, but she was full dead. They did let none of us see her." Tears stood in his eyes. "They do say, there is no sign of anyone else being with her and she had a look of horror on her face that would fright you to your own death. There is horrible, it is! Who would want to hurt Myfanwy bach? Loved by all, she was!"

Conchobar patted him on the shoulder in silent sympathy as the young man impatiently dashed away his tears with the sleeve of his jacket. His 'griffe, Gwion, nudged him sympathetically.

"I'll tell the rest of them," said Lyon in a low voice, gesturing towards the crowd below, many of whom had seen the hippogriffe and its liveried rider arrive and knew that it must bear an express. They were calling up anxiously.

Conchobar nodded wearily. It was going to be a long night, full of anxiety. "Come, lad," he told Owain, "I imagine you're under orders to be taking a message back with you, but take time to bait yourself and your 'griffe. I'll be finding Diarmait," he told Lyon. "He can make himself useful writing letters and such. At least he's stopped those beansidhes from screeching their blessed throats out. And we know now why they wailed so – someone great and Holy has died."

"Damn!" Lyon swore, perusing the very bottom of the letter. "Look at this, Con!" It was easy to see in the steady glow of the mage light.

Copies to His Grace the Arch Druid of Britain, His Grace the Arch Druid of Cornwall, His Grace the Arch Druid of Ireland, His Grace the Arch Druid of Man, His Grace the Arch Druid of Scotland, HRH the Prince Regent, His Excellency the Prime Minister Mr. Spencer Perceval, His Grace the Duke of Chenevix.

"Oh dear, oh dear!" said Conchobar.
Lyon snorted. "Oh dear, oh dear indeed!"

All night long 'griffes arrived and left. Dragons did not see as well in the dark as did 'griffes', but Diana had no doubt that the stableyard would be full of them at first light.

She sat in the window seat in Simon's room. He had finally fallen into sleep at about two-thirty, but slept very restlessly indeed. She wanted to be near in case he should awaken and be frightened again. He was the only one in the Abbey who appeared to be getting any sleep at all.

There were still people below, waiting for more news. Diana has sent the servants out with chairs and blankets to sit on, and trays of hot coffee and sandwiches. Mr. Mag Uidhir had gone both to the church and the village and read aloud a copy of the letter and posted a public notice. Messages had come from the other Arch Druids and from London, including from the Prime Minister and the Prince Regent, and a directive from the Ministry of Protocol. Public mourning of black gloves, wreaths and bands would be observed. Flags of all the countries of the British Isles would be flown at half staff.

The Arch Druid of Wales would not be interred at the Welsh Druid burial tombs of Bron y Foel Isaf near Dyffryn Ardudwy in Gwynedd until the Bow Street Runners had had time to examine the body and the scene of the crime. Her body was put in a spell of keeping.

A fiat from the Prince Regent begged that everyone, while observing respectful mourning, would go about their proper business. The government had all in hand. A regiment of the crack Dragon-back Riflemen of his own Life Guard had been sent to protect the other Druids at Llyn Cerrig Bach and the Runners had the investigation under control. The peoples of the British Isles would serve the investigation and the memory of the late Arch Druid best by going on with their ordinary lives.

Diana had first thought to keep Simon at home today. But upon reflection she decided that it would be best to keep him – especially his mind – active and busy. That meant going on with his lessons. She foresaw that she was going to be very busy indeed, making certain that people were fed and rested, and the messenger beasts as well. Unless she received a message that his tutor wished to cancel the lessons today, she would send him to the Vicarage, but under some sort of protection. But right now, she thought as she yawned and stretched, she had to get a least a few hours' sleep. That would be more than Uncle Lyon would get. Her worry over this shocking event must be put aside for a while.

Mr. Arabin yawned loudly and muttered "Oh excuse me!" to no one in particular. Here he was, still in his dressing gown at nine in the morning in a now nearly empty church. Many of the people who had come for comfort had slowly drifted home, once the news had come out. That very nice young Irish gentleman had brought notices down from the Abbey every time that any message of general interest had arrived. He could have just magically transported the notices of course, but people had questions and he had patiently answered them. Non-magical persons were apt to get flustered by magically changing notices when they were already in a state of anxiety.

He stretched and yawned again, and snuffed all of the candles in the church and the mage light with a gesture of one hand. He then left the church, closely followed by Plato and Minou. They had not left his side all the balance of the night.

He saw René arriving at that moment, coming from the direction of the village. He waved, and called out, "Have you had the news, my boy?"

René walked towards him. "I saw the notices at the *Beetle and Wedge,* early this morning and then went to tell them at home. *C'est incroyable!* Why would someone harm a Druid? And, one wonders how there may be such a power that kills a Druid."

Reverend Arabin sighed as he joined his young friend at the gate. "I have been worrying about that all of the night," he confessed. "Whatever could it – my dear René, whatever did you do to your eye?" he said in some concern. "If I did not know better than to even suppose such a thing, I should think you had been in a mill!"

René grimaced and touched his cheek carefully. "My *Maman,* she has the good right hook."

"Oh, dear," said Mr. Arabin solicitously. "She was much upset by the screams, I daresay."

"Vous avez raison. I have never seen her so bad – it took all of us to dose her," René answered.

"Oh, dear!" said Mr. Arabin as they began to walk into the Vicarage." I am very much afraid that many people will be terribly frightened, just like your dear mama. That is why I am planning to go all about the parish today, calling in on every one and offering what aid and news that I might. I shall be certain and stop at May cottage and offer a service of comfort for her."

"Thank you," said René gratefully, for such a service often served to soothe and calm Lucie.

"You've a few minutes before Simon arrives, my boy. Do you go in and ask Mrs. Parker for some sausage rolls and coffee. We fed twenty people at seven o'clock – I am certain that there is a good amount of food left. I must make ready for the day," Mr. Arabin said. At the mention of sausage rolls, Plato gave a loud meow. "And our little friends will be wanting some breakfast as well. I did make mention to Simon that he might like a kitten ."

"I should like to have one as well, if it pleases Plato and Minou, and there is a kitten who will have me," René looked down at the little white cat, who looked up at him with enormous green eyes. Minou was not a familiar and she could not speak to anyone, including Wizards, but Plato, who had been uncharacteristically quiet since the events of the night before said suddenly, "We should be happy to have the kittens go to such a good home. Does Madame De Variens not need a familiar as well?"

"Yes, she does –"

"Two kittens, then and one to Master Simon," said the cat complacently. Plato was that exceedingly rare thing – a male calico. He was inordinately proud of this fact, and, as the Reverend Arabin said on occasion, rather vain about it.

"They will be born before the end of the week and there will be four of them," said Plato." I feel certain that someone else in this neighborhood will need a familiar as well. I shall sit out here," he jumped to the top of the fence post "and tell Master Simon that we approve of one of our kittens going in to his service. Pray save me some sausage." He put one paw up to his face and adjusted his spectacles.

"I am glad to see that Plato is back to his old self," said Reverend Arabin dryly, as the two men, with Minou dashing in front of them, went into the Vicarage.

Simon had slept through the rest of the night, although not very well. His first thought on waking had been of the scream he had heard. Had anyone found out what it was? He had never been so frightened in his life!

But Mama had come right away and held him and protected him. The last thing he remembered, she had still been holding him. He must have fallen asleep in her arms. Thinking about that gave Simon a warm feeling.

There seemed to be a lot of noise out side his window. Simon slid from bed and padded across the floor to look out.

There were hippogriffes and dragons everywhere! As he watched, a large black dragon took off, spiraling up into the sky. Its harness and rider was red and gold. Those were Royal colours, Simon knew. A hippogriffe landed in the space the dragon vacated, its rider slipping off before it had really landed, taking off at a run towards Lyon's tower.

Simon heard a noise behind him and turned to see Sanders coming in from the dressing room. He was yawning, looking as if he had not slept at all the night before. "Good morning, Master Simon," he said, his jaws cracking on another yawn. "Dunno as when I've ever seen so many dragons and 'griffes in one place at one time!"

"Why are they all here, Sanders?" Simon queried eagerly.

"Messages for his lordship. Comin' in from all over the place, they are, 'bout last night," Sanders answered, He took Simon's dressing gown from the top of the chest at the foot of the bed and helped him into it. "Where's your slippers then – oh, here , under the bed."

"What was that last night, Sanders? " Simon asked. He was both fearful and curious about that scary noise.

"Her ladyship's goin' t' tell you all about it," said Sanders. "You're to have breakfast with her in her bed-chamber an' then a nice hot bath here."

A bath would be nice – unlike most little boys Simon adored splashing about in hot water.

"Come on, then, her ladyship's waitin'," said Sanders, and lead Simon out of the room.

Diana had not been certain what to tell Simon. She felt an almost overwhelming urge to protect him from the horror of the news, but a brief conversation with Lyon that morning had changed her mind. "Tell the boy the truth," Lyon had said bluntly. "I remember when I was a child – my father lied to me about my mother's illness. He said it was to protect me. What I made up from bits and pieces I overheard were far worse than the truth could ever have been. Imagination can be the very devil! And when she died, in spite of all his lies that she would be just fine, I was not able to forgive him for years. Simon is far from stupid. Don't tell him the horrid details, just the facts, and answer his questions the best that you can."

So when Simon joined her at a cozy table for two overlooking the park, she let him sit down and have some fruit, and then said, "Simon, you are probably wondering about what happened last night."

"Oh, yes, Mama," he put down his spoon and looked at her wide-eyed. "It was something very bad, wasn't it?"

"Very, very bad, I'm afraid," she said soberly and then told him briefly that the Arch Druid of Wales had been killed and that it was her screams that they had heard. She explained that someone very bad had killed her and that the screams were left behind to perhaps help the Runners find out who or what had killed her.

"But why would someone kill her, Mama?" Simon wrinkled his forehead in thought.

"We don't know yet," Diana said.

"Will some one try to kill Uncle Lyon?" Simon was fearful of losing any one in his new family.

"We don't know. But we are going to take all the precautions we can. The Prince Regent wanted to send guards, but Uncle Lyon said no. He is going to release the stone lions at night so that they may prowl the grounds and has asked some griffin friends of his to come and guard us. Leander is organizing all of the owls in the forest to be on the watch, as well. So you do not have to worry. We shall be well guarded. But there is a part that concerns you, Simon. Mr. Ó Clérigh has returned to Tara briefly. He will return within a day, for there is to be a Druid conclave here in two days time to discus this matter. Mr. Mag Uidhir and Pádraig, however, are still here. We have arranged for Pádraig to take you back and forth to your lessons –"

"Do you mean that I am to ride a dragon every day to go to my lessons?" Simon cried joyfully.

"Indeed I do, for a while at least," Diana smiled at him, relieved. The joy of a daily dragon ride seemed to have calmed his fears remarkably. "And Pádraig is going to watch over you and your tutor as well. I know that you are to go into the forest and chose your wand today and that is too important to put off. Pádraig will be flying overhead to keep an eye on you at least twice an hour. Now, eat your eggs, Simon Sanders will have your bath ready soon and then it will be time to leave for your lessons."

To Simon's intense delight, he was to go up on Pádraig all by himself. Mr. Mag Uidhir showed him how to mount, get in and out of the harness and how to slide down Pádraig's leg to reach the ground safely. Simon was also given a dragon whistle – no one but dragons and dogs could hear it. If Simon was to see anything or hear anything that made him feel afraid, he was to blow this and Pádraig would be there in an instant. Pádraig would come to the Vicarage and fly him back to the Abbey – Simon was to wait until Pádraig came for him and not attempt to walk home alone. Simon agreed to all of these conditions eagerly. He was so proud and excited to be flying by himself.

Diana went outside to see him off and watched his enraptured face as the green dragon took to the air. She waved until they were just a speck in the sky.

"I am going to have to have to hire a dragon," said a gloomy voice at her elbow.

Diana turned and saw her uncle standing behind her, seemingly lost in contemplation of the last glimpse of Pádraig's tail.

"It's a great expense, I know –" Diana started sympathetically.

"Oh, hang the expense!" Lyon growled. "It's the change I hate – I shall have to travel more now that I'm Arch Druid, and have a secretary around my neck like a millstone. That means a dragon to haul the two of us. I have tried several times to have a secretary cum assistant ands it seems to me that all I have to do is put an advertisement in the Wizard's Times and every idiot in the country decides that being my secretary is precisely the post he has been waiting for all of his miserable life! I get replies from people who barely squeaked by their exams, and think that I should employ them because dear Papa is the Earl of Nincompoop, even though one in their right mind would employ such a chowder-headed want-wit. Anyone who has their wits about them and is a competent magician doesn't WANT to be a secretary or an assistant!"

"Mr. Mag Uidhir seems competent and intelligent," Diana pointed out, following her uncle back into the house.

"Con was just lucky to get him. The luck of the Irish, you know! Iain McAslan has gone through nine secretaries in as many years, and I haven't time to enumerate the problems Pengelly Tregaron has had. After this night, it's obvious I need to hire one of the creatures."

Diana wasn't certain whether her uncle was referring to dragons or secretaries as 'creatures', but could only imagine an average young Wizard, like her brother Peter, fresh from school and trying to get along with her uncle. She felt sorry for anyone who tried to do so.

"Oh Gad!" he uncle bellowed as they heard the flap of dragon wings behind them. "What idiot is sending a message now!" He turned and rushed back off towards the courtyard.

Diana continued into the house. She had best order new trays of tea and coffee made up, and consult with the cook about sandwiches and biscuits.

To Simon's disappointment, there was no one but a cat to see him arrive dragon-back. Pádraig landed quietly, with neatness and precision, in the lane outside the Vicarage, crouched low for Simon to get down and reminded him to remove the basket that Cook had fastened to his harness. This basket contained a nuncheon – Cook being afraid that if Simon had to walk in the woods all morning looking for a wand he might die of starvation before returning to the Abbey. She had packed enough, she assured Simon, that he and his tutor could share and keep up their energy. Pádraig took right off, again promising that he would be available if needed. "Just whistle!" he said, giving a nod at the silver whistle that hung about Simon's neck, and launched himself into the air.

"Good morning," said a voice as Simon turned from watching Padraig fly away.

Simon looked around carefully, but saw no one. He picked up the heavy basket and started to open the gate.

"I said good morning!" came the voice, sounding a little peeved.

"Good morning," said Simon carefully, still not seeing anyone. There was just the cat, sitting on the fencepost, a cat wearing spectacles...a cat wearing spectacles! Simon, shocked, took a closer look at the cat as it yawned and politely put a white paw to its mouth.

"I have decided," it said clearly "that you may have one of the kittens, if one chooses you."

"You can talk!" said Simon, in a disbelieving whisper.

"So can you, but not very intelligently," returned the cat. "I should think that 'thank you for your condescension and generosity' might be a more suitable reply. All that is needed now is an equally unintelligent comment on my spectacles and the boredom level of this so-called conversation increases beyond my capacity for endurance. Sometimes I don't know why I tolerate human beings." With this he stood up, stretched and leaped from the fence post, and sauntered away, his plume-like tail in the air.

Bemused, Simon headed into the Vicarage and found Mr. Arabin and Mr. Roussillon sitting at a table drinking coffee and eating sausage rolls. The little white Minou was in Mr. Roussillon's lap, being fed bits of sausage and purring loudly. Simon wondered why his tutor had a black eye, briefly, but he wondered more about the cat.

"A cat just talked to me!" said Simon, putting down the basket rather abruptly. "He was wearing spectacles!"

"That would be Plato, my familiar," said Mr. Arabin. "I hope he wasn't rude to you, my dear Simon. He is rather vain, and can be very uncivil at times."

"How can a cat talk?" said Simon in confusion.

"Because he is a familiar," explained René. "Here. Simon, sit and have the sausage roll and we shall explain."

Simon, a growing boy, had no objection to more food. He pulled out a chair and slid into it. "I am not really certain that I know all about familiars," he confessed as Mr. Arabin handed him a thin porcelain plate on which reposed a flaky roll stuffed with sausage, and offered him a glass of milk.

"A familiar is a Wizard's or Witch's helper," his tutor explained. "They may run errands, carry messages, keep track of your supplies and appointments, or prompt you when you are doing the intricate spell. They intercede with elementals, also. They can see spirits as well."

"And they can be very good company," put in Mr. Arabin. "Four hundred years ago, Wizards Worked and lived largely alone. It has only been recently that Wizards and Witches married and started families. And a familiar was a good com-panion – someone to talk to in one's lonely tower."

"But how do they learn to talk?" Simon asked.

"Ah, that is from association with a Witch or Wizard, au fond," said Mr. Roussillon.

"It seems to rub off on them – the magic, I mean," the Vicar offered. "Most familiar not only talk, but read. Unfortunately paws and claws do not allow them much success at writing."

With a few more questions Simon learned that cats, owls, hedgehogs and ferrets made the best familiars. Dogs made poor familiars as they were too easily distracted. Bats were too nocturnal and rabbits too nervous, as were mice and most rodents. Horses, most large-hoofed mammals and dragons were too large to fit into a Tower or a laboratory, and snakes and reptiles and frogs hibernated in the winter. Their life was also lengthened by magic – most familiars, baring accident or illness, lived the same life span as did their magical human companion.

The tradition of familiars dated far back to ancient Egypt, to the mystery schools there, where cats were worshipped and revered for their psychic powers.

"He told me I might have a kitten," Simon said when his curiosity about familiars had been satisfied. "I asked my Mama and she said I might."

"That is excellent, Simon," said René, smiling at him. "I am hoping to be chosen by a kitten as well for my cat died in the winter."

"Oh, I'm sorry," said Simon quickly. "But how do you choose a familiar? What do you look for?"

"You will actually do very little," the Vicar told him. "When the kittens are old enough, I shall have you both come, and your grandmother, as well, my dear René, and you shall seat yourself on the floor. With urging from their parents, the kittens will choose which of you they want to Work with. It is a partnership, you see. A familiar is not a pet, but a Working partner and if you are fortunate, a friend as well. Like most Wizards and Witches, a familiar has to have an independent spirit and free will. One's familiar is an equal, not a pet indeed, it will have powers you cannot, little matter how talented a Wizard you may be. For one thing, familiars, particularly cats, are not afraid of spirits – indeed, they like ghosts and will flock to a haunted house or to a séance. If there is any doubt about the validity of a medium one can always tell by ascertaining whether or not he or she has a cat. A cat will stay with a medium to be near the ghosts."

"But do not expect the kitten to talk right away – it will have to learn, as you did when you were little also," René cautioned the boy. "When your familiar does begin to speak you can depend on it to tell you the information about the weather, the danger and the approach of storms. And there is the bond of love as well – and love, *n'est –ce pas* — increases psychic power between you and your familiar."

Simon's head was all awhirl. Magic! Dragon rides! Talking kittens! A cat wearing spectacles! Familiars! It was a world far removed from any he had ever known. But he liked it – he liked it very much.

9

The Painted Floor

Pádraig reported that Simon had been safely delivered to the Vicarage and that there had been no sense of evil about. Dragon senses were excellent and, thus reassured, Diana was able to concentrate on the pressing problem at hand – what to do about housing and feeding all of the Druidical parties that would be arriving within two days.

It was a source of constant surprise how the mundane intruded upon events of awe and terror. No matter what happened, people had to be housed and fed. And how she was to manage that in this tumble-down wreck of a house, Diana was at a loss to know. The Irish Arch Druid and his secretary had had to share a room. Lyon had told her that Iain McAslan never went anywhere without a pair of pipers, and a secretary and an Augur. Heaven only knew what or whom the other Druids would bring. And there would be their dragons or whatever else mode of transport they might chose to come in. The Arch Druid of Man was said to drive a chariot of sea-horses who, once they left the sea, could fly through the air. Where did one stable sea-horses and what did they eat?

These and other problems kept her run off her feet all morning.

But at the back of her mind was always that encounter in Knyghtwood. Who was that gentleman? She had not had a chance to talk to anyone about her adventure, what with the unexpected arrival of the Irish Arch Druid and then the terrible events of the night. And supposition about it was fruitless, until she had the time to relax and meditate and perhaps recall more details about the matter. Perhaps there would be time before bed this night, she promised herself as she headed belowstairs to consult with Seppings on how many of the newly renovated bedchambers were habitable and if there were any bed-frames in the attic they might use and where mattresses might be obtained.

It had been misty and a bit chill when Pádraig had left Simon at the Vicarage and Simon had been afraid that perhaps they might not be able to go into the forest after all if it started to rain. But by the time the last of the sausage rolls had been consumed and Simon had drunk a big glass of milk, which he shared with Minou, the fog had burned off and clear blue sky arched overhead.

"Another lovely day!" said Reverend Arabin happily as he accompanied René and Simon to the gate. "It will be a positive pleasure to walk about the parish today! I do not recall seeing such a verdant, fair spring in many a year."

René carried the lunch hamper. It was quite full of good things to eat. He could scarcely believe it – two good meals in one day. It was going to be a wonderful day!

At the gate of the Vicarage stood Reverend Arabin's pony cart, with his little mare Chocolate hitched to it. She was the exact colour of breakfast chocolate, with a mane and tail of whipped cream. She was held by the Vicar's man of all work, Tim.

"Now, my boy," the Vicar said firmly to René, "I must insist on you and Simon using the pony cart. You plan to go to Knyghtwood and that is far and away too far for Simon to walk in one morning and be in fit case to do something as important as choosing his wand. You are well provided for the inner man," he smiled with a nod towards the basket, "and now let me provide for the outer man as well."

He was adamant and refused to listen to René's protests. "I shall enjoy the walk about the parish and no doubt need the exercise, for everyone will offer me sustenance and I dare not offend by too many refusals! I shall need to walk off all of that food! " he insisted. "And, no, it is not too far for me to go!"

To Simon's delight, they set out in the pony cart, basket stowed beneath the seat. The sun shone benignly on Chocolate's glossy rump as they set off to the woods.

Simon had almost forgotten the horrible event of the night before because so many interesting and wonderful had happened this morning. But when he rather diffidently asked his tutor what had happened to his eye and the answer was that he had had an accident on the night before, it all came rushing back. He had been chattering away eagerly about Pádraig and the visit of Conchobar Ò Clérigh and his secretary, but now he became quiet and a little apprehensive.

"Are you worried about what happened last night, Simon?" René glanced down at the boy, for he had grown so still. "You have told me that the good Pádraig will watch over us, and we go to a sacred, safe place today."

Simon sighed, and said in a troubled voice, "I don't understand how or why anyone can kill a Druid. I thought a Druid was all powerful."

"No one is all powerful," said René. "But it would take a very great, a very evil power to do so."

"That's what Mama said," Simon sighed again. "Sir, what is the difference between a Druid and a Wizard.? Uncle Lyon is a Druid, but he is also a Wizard. But Uncle Peter is not a Druid, nor is Mama."

"All Druids are Wizards, but not all Wizards are Druids," René said. "To begin with, it is difficult to become a Druid. One must study for a much longer time – ten years at the least – to become a Druid. One must learn the Secret languages, and to read Ogham, the Beth-Luis-Nion, the Tree Alphabet, and use the hidden forces of nature for his magic. A Wizard uses the power of the ley lines in the main, *n'est ce pas*? And the sign and sigils – Wizard marks, as we drew in the circle – are of the elements and the angels while the Druids use the sun. Druid magic is far more ancient – it was Merlin who devised the magic Wizards use today."

"Mama gave me a book about King Arthur and Merlin. It said Merlin was a Druid, too," said Simon.

"Yes, he was, for his teacher was Blaise of *Bregtagne* – Brittany, who was a very great Druid indeed. But Merlin, being a *sorcier sans pareil* made a magic that was easier for those of the Old Blood to learn, to help make everyone's life the better. Merlin also tamed the dragons and gave them their smell."

"Their smell?" Simon said in disbelief. "What smell?"

"Think about Pádraig – how does he smell?"

Simon wrinkled his nose. "Nice," he said at last. "Like cinnamon."

"Dragons fly by burning acid in their hollow flight cavities. And acid smells very bad, *non*? You would not wish to ride a dragon who smelled of acid. Merlin bespelled dragons for all time, so they would be helpful and acceptable to us."

"I thought dragons flew with their wings!" Simon said "Like a bird!"

"Dragons are very large – it would take much, much bigger wings than they have to lift their weight," René explained. "They eat the fire-stone, it combines with the acid in their stomach it makes a gas which fills the flight cavities and they are lighter than air and *voila* – the excess gas comes out as flame. *Demain matin*, tomorrow, we shall do an experiment in the laboratory and we shall see exactly how this works."

"Am I ever going to study regular subjects?" Simon asked "You know, sir, like mathematics and geography or I am just to learn magic?"

"This morning we have covered already history and chemistry and we shall do more history and magic when we are in Knyghtwood," said René.

"But we were just talking," Simon said, who still had somewhat of an idea that to study one must be in a classroom, listening to someone like Mr. Appersett.

"Do you remember what we have talked about?" asked his tutor.

"Oh, yes, sir! It was so interesting. Was that a lesson?"

"You have learned from it, no? Then it is a lesson."

Simon was surprised and happy. Mr. Arabin had said he would not be taught in the usual fashion, but Simon had not been quite certain that he believed this. The lesson yesterday had not been what he had expected, but at the back of his mind was the fear that he would be obliged to return to the classroom. He liked this, talking and asking questions about things that he was interested in. He liked Mr. Roussillon more and more, too, even the funny way he talked.

Malcoeur was more than satisfied with his night's work. In retrospect, though, it had been a little too easy. Wearing a cloak cast of darkness (a useful trick he had acquired in Persia) he had been able to get within a foot of that silly woman before she even sensed him.

In Malcoeur's view, these British Wizards were naïve children. They were so confident that their laws and protocols would protect them. There were no security measures at their places of magic – anyone could walk in or out. He had been shocked, but also amused that the Isle of Avalon had posted visiting and consultation hours.

But Malcoeur had been annoyed to find that the Arch Druid of Britain was not in residence at the Isle of Avalon. He had also been vastly annoyed to find that this gentleman he wanted so much to kill was NOT the Arch Druid of all the British Isles, but only one of six Arch Druids. This he learned from one of several volumes that he purchased at a bookshop. This again, he thought monumentally stupid. The British sold books on everything related to magic! There were books of, learning for children, *101 Useful Spells for the Beginner*, silly things like *Charms Anyone Can Use*, even something called *Registratum Magi Britannae*, which not only listed all the mages – Witches and Wizards and Druids – in the British Isles, but their magical ratings and achievements, and their addresses! It was printed by a magical press –*The Arcane Press, London, Edinburgh and Dublin* – and the entries changed as did the status or the direction of the persons it enumerated. To Malcoeur, the book out to have been entitled 'Come And Kill Me", for it laid out their powers – what he saw as their limitations – and where they might be found.

Once he had read the book, his plans had changed. The Vale of Avon was near the Welsh border – how convenient to cross the mountains of Snowdonia and go to the Isle of Anglesey, where the Welsh Druids' high holy place was to be found.

He had not liked Wales. Its wild mountainous beauty left his withers unwrung, for he was an urban creature – he preferred the civilized amenities to be found in a place such as St Petersburg or Paris. And what was he to make of a sign post that read "Lled-Croen-Y-Yrch" or "Barclodiad y

Gawries"? What did this mean ? And when he tried to pronounce it – ! He had seen a sign in front of a river that read "Llamhigyn Y Dwr". When Malcoeur tried to read this sign aloud, a passing rustic laughed at him and pronounced it *thamheegin er doorr*, and said it meant 'Water Leaper", and the river was the former home to the gigantic toad-like creature that devoured anything that passed by. Gone, now, since Merlin *bach* banished all such Unselighe creatures to the Otherworld.

The rustic was soon no longer among the living , but not devoured by a Water Leaper, much to Malcoeur's satisfaction.

Upon consulting the *Guide To the British Isles* he had purchased, he decided to cross the sea to Ireland and attack the Irish Arch Druid. He almost glowed with the power he had stolen from the Welshwoman. It was a heady experience, to kill someone with that much magic and he wanted to repeat it. He saw no reason why he could not dispatch all six of them. They were so guileless about the black arts!

He was still quite near to the coast – he had left Anglesey immediately, of course, in the same small boat he had stolen to get there– the book indicated that there was a ferry every day.

He closed the book and replaced it in the pocket of his cloak and then looked up into the face of the ugliest being he had ever seen. He had not heard it coming, It was just suddenly there.

"My master wants to see you," it grated in a voice like a rusted hinge. With a slight sense of shock, Malcoeur realized that it was female. Its hair was matted and filthy and it wore what resembled a pile of old rags. It had a loose pendulous lip, a hooked nose, rheumy eyes and huge, knobby hands that dragged on the ground.

"And who is your master, *Madame?*" he said haughtily. He was not certain that it was properly addressed as *Madame*, for who could marry or even lay with such a thing?

"He is Sluagh, second only to the Dark Lord of the Unselighe Court, and he wishes to thank you, mortal, for you have rendered us a great service," the ugly thing informed him.

119

"Why should I bother myself with your master? What is he to me?" Malcoeur demanded.

An evil smile spread over her horrible features. "If you do not come, he gives me leave to eat you!" The smile showed enormous sharp, yellow teeth.

He could feel the magic of her, and discretion was the better part of valor. "Very well," he said, as if he had nothing better to do. His curiosity was piqued. "I shall go and see your master."

She laughed – it was a screech, really and Malcoeur winced. He hoped that her master was not as repulsive as she was.

As they drove towards Knyghtwood, René told Simon about it. The wood was very very old – some of the trees were more than one thousand years old, and in very ancient times it had been a unicorn wood.

"Are there still unicorns there today, sir?" Simon asked eagerly. He would love to see a unicorn – the pictures he had seen were so beautiful it almost hurt to look at them.

"No one has seen a unicorn here for many years, not since the time of Queen Elizabeth, since over three hundred years ago it is now."

"What happened to them?" Simon was sad to learn this.

"There were never many of them – they are solitary creatures and do not mingle with one another. It is thought that they went somewhere else, somewhere where they can be more alone." As he spoke, René drew up to a little copse. "Here is where we must go on foot, Simon."

They tethered Chocolate with a horse weight and slipped the bit from her mouth so that she might graze. Taking the basket, they set off into the wood.

It was a place of dark and shadows and of sudden bright shafts of sunlight slanting down through the huge trees. Simon's tutor pointed out the different trees to Simon and told him their names and what to look for to identify them. They talked about the flowers, too, and why they were best left unpicked. Simon was intrigued by the subject of th flower Faeries and asked a great many questions.

He was bright and eager and René found it no burden to answer his frequent questions. Looking at Simon, René wondered if this is what it would be like to have a son of his own – something he would probably never know, for it seemed unlikely that he would ever be able to marry. For not only was he poor, but what young woman would wish to live with a mad mama-in-law? Most young women would probably be afraid that Lucie's madness was hereditary and would not wish to take the chance that one's children would be lunatics, or even that one's husband would turn into a madman sometime in the future.

"Where are we going, sir?" Simon's enthusiastic voice interrupted his reverie.

"To a grove that is doubly sacred, for it is bound by oaks and inside the trees are a circle of standing stones," René answered. "And there is something special there as well, but we will save that for a surprise, no?"

"Standing stones – like Stonehenge? I saw that in a book," said Simon, wondering what the surprise could be.

"Yes, much like Stonehenge, but smaller." René shifted the basket to his other hand. It was growing quite heavy – it must be *full* of food. After they received Simon's wand, they would have a picnic.

The woods began to grow denser and tangled; Simon could not see how they could go any further and voiced his concern.

"We shall have to ask for help," René returned. "We will stop here for a moment, Simon." He put he basket down and knelt, facing the tangle of vines and trees. "Join me, Simon, *s'il vous plait.*"

Simon obeyed, although he could not imagine what they were doing. Perhaps they were going to pray for help?

To Simon's amazement, Mr. Roussillon began to speak in a very strange way, looking up at trees and spreading his arms wide. It did not sound like words, but more like the rustling of leaves or the wind blowing. Simon hoped he did not need to learn to talk like that. Mr. Roussillon talked oddly, any way, but this was very strange.

To Simon's amazement, the vines in front of them began to sway and Mr. Roussillon was *answered* by a voice speaking in the same language. And then an opening appeared in the tangled vegetation, an opening like a tunnel. Clearly, a voice said, to Simon's relief , in English, "It is most courteous in you, child of ours, to speak to us in our own tongue. It pleases us. We honor your request and shall chose a fitting instrument for your pupil. And remember what you have promised – that which we have guarded so long will be used again. Now, come, both of you, if you please."

"Come, Simon, we have been invited," Mr. Roussillon gave Simon a hand up and then turned to the tunnel and bowed deeply. *"Oui, s'il vous plait."*

A chuckle that sounded like dry leaves blowing over the road answered him.

Simon was round-eyed with wonder as they entered the tunnel, which was a deep well of green shade. On the other side of the shaft of vines and shrubs was a row of trees, mighty of trunk, with huge branches that curved downwards until they almost touched the ground. They had barely begun to leaf out and some still had curled brown, dead leaves clinging to the branches. All were crowned with mistletoe.

"These are oaks," said René quietly. "They are the last to leaf and the last to have the leaves die in the autumn. The oak is a sacred tree, particularly to the Druids, as is the mistletoe that crowns it."

Beyond the trees was a circle of stones. They were quite high, way over Simon's head, even over Mr. Roussillon's head and Simon thought his tutor very tall. The moment they stepped into the circle, Simon felt very odd. His hands and feet tingled and he felt as if every vein in his body was sparkling. "Oh, sir," he whispered, for it seemed somehow wrong to talk loudly in this place, "I do feel strange!"

"You feel the magic, Simon," said his tutor in an equally low voice. "There has been much magic made here over the years – centuries! And it has left its mark here for us. It is a good thing – in a few moments you will feel well, *ne vous en faites pas.*"

Simon felt very well indeed in a few more moments. His senses seemed somehow heightened – colours were brighter, the sun was warmer, the air delicious – full of an earthy, woodsy scent that he wanted to draw of in deep breaths.

"And now for the surprise," René reached inside his jacket and withdrew his wand from his breast pocket.

They were standing in a clearing that was ankle-deep in leaf debris. It looked as if there were a rock in the middle of the clearing, it too, disappeared in herbaceous matter.

René raised his wand and the dead leaves spun around in a circle, which shrank into a funnel, like a cyclone, and fled upwards into the air. Simon gasped. For revealed, in bright shades, was a floor made of bits of coloured stone.

"The locals call such a 'painted floor', " said his tutor, "but it is properly called a mosaic. It was left here by the Romans."

"We did not wish them to have it here at first," came the rustling voice again. "Ah, many times did we thrust our roots through it! But when we came to realize that they wanted but to worship, we let them be. Now their power is added to ours."

"Who is that talking?" Simon whispered.

"That is Father Oak. He is the oldest and wisest of the trees and is a good friend to magical people. He is the one who will give you your wand," René told him.

"Thank you, Father Oak!" Simon bowed as he had seen his tutor do.

The tree chuckled again. "I am still ruminating on which branch to give, and must ask if it is willing. Do you look at the floor while I decide."

"We shall do that, Father Oak." René looked at Simon as the boy stared at the floor.

The designs were of reds, browns and greens on a field of cream tesserae. There were so many little pieces of stone that Simon could not imagine counting how many there were. All around the edge lay interlaced Celtic weave. Mr. Roussillon explained that the area nearest the standing stones and been built by the Celts, once the Romans left Britain. The whole floor, or pavement as Wizard archaeologists termed it, was some five hundred years in the making. There were animals and birds depicted. Simon identified them all with his tutor's help, deer and wolves, a hedgehog, an owl and a bird Mr. Roussillon told him was the winter wren, which was sacred to the Druids. In the center lay the Roman part of the floor – squared by a geometric border of black and red. Inside this was a circle fill of creatures of the sea – dolphins, fish, and sea-monsters. Around this ran a band of scallop shells . Inside this band was a portrait of a man, with a lyre on his knee, singing. He was dressed in Roman style, with a crown of laurel about his brow. Directly over his head, what Simon had thought to be an outcropping of rocks proved to be a small heavily carved altar.

"It is time for your wand," interrupted Father Oak as René was explaining to Simon that the figure in the center was Orpheus and what he signified.

"Come, Simon." His tutor led Simon behind the altar and they both knelt. "Now say 'Father Oak, I pray you give me a wand of your choosing, so that I might do magic according to the natural laws.'"

Simon repeated this solemnly and then watched as the huge oak directly opposite the altar began to sway. It then bent towards them – the branches seemed to elongate and reach towards the altar.

A short sharp *crack*! sounded and a slim straight branch fell onto the altar.

Simon started to reach out for it, but René stopped him. "Wait."

"How shall we mark it?" said the tree voice. "I know!"

The wand began to blaze with a pulsating green light and it changed from a plain piece of wood to one intricately carved with a pattern of dragons spiraling about it. In amongst the dragons were runes that glowed. The light died back. "It is done. The branch gave its life willingly. It will serve you well, boy. Make certain that you do as well by it," said Father Oak.

"Thank you," said Simon reverently. At a nod from his tutor he took up the wand. It was not warm in his hand as he had expected, but it was pliant and supple and a smooth golden colour, as if it had been rubbed and polished for years. It felt just right.

The leaves, still so near to their faces, quivered. "What is this, child of ours?" the tree said. "You are hurt! I did not see this before." A slim twig reached out and touched René 's face. As Simon watched the tiny leaf bud on the end of the twig quickly unfurled and covered the bruised eye. It then withdrew and the bruise was gone. As Simon gasped, the tree drew back. Would the wonders never stop?

"Thank you, Father Oak," said René fervently. *"Je vous en prie."*

The tree chuckled again. "Not at all. Or *il n'y a pas de quoi,* as you would say, child of ours. Now, I think that your young pupil grows hungry and it is time for my sleep. We bid you good day."

Simon was full of questions as they ate a satisfying meal. From questions about the trees to the Romans and Celts who had built the floor, he was avidly curious. René told him a condensed history of the Romans in Britain, making it as interesting as an adventure tale and Simon hung on every word.

They had just finished eating the delicious chicken and cress sandwiches, ham and cheese rolls, jam tarts and bottles of shrub when a blue ball shot into the clearing, screaming "Redcap! Redcap! Flee! Hide! Run!"

René wasted no time. He took out his wand and with extreme speed, cast a glowing violet circle around the edges of the painted floor.

"Are you certain?" he asked the little blue Faerie, who hung panting in the air in front of them.

"I know a Redcap when I see one!" Mebd said indignantly. "I remember them from before Merlin banished them to the Other world! I daresay you've never even seen one!"

"I know what they can do," said René quietly "and how to defend ourselves against it. Simon, stay behind me and believe nothing that it says to you. It wants to kill you and will do anything it can to accomplish that end."

Wide-eyed, Simon looked up at his tutor. "It wants to kill *me*? But why?"

"Because little boys are delicious and it can't kill me or this Wizard so it wants you!" snapped the Faerie. "Haven't you taught this child anything?" she demanded of René.

"I had never thought to met a Redcap – ever. They have been banished for almost one thousand years. How did it get out ?"

"I don't know," she said crossly. "Here it comes!" she announced, as a crashing noise came thought the trees. René wondered briefly why Father Oak was allowing it to even approach this sacred place, but the trees always had their reasons.

"Simon! Simon!" the voice was sweet and coaxing. "Come and play with me. I've a tray of sweeties to share with you. Me mum made them this morning and oh, my – they're so good! Just for us, Simon!"

Simon gave a start. The voice was so nice and kind, and sounded lonely. What would be the harm in sharing a few sweets with him? In spite of the fact that he had just made a very good lunch, Simon's mouth watered at the thought of those sweets. He took a step forward. But Mr. Roussillon's hand was on his shoulder and with an angry hiss the Faerie darted forward and grabbed his ear painfully, pulling back on it. "Don't be stupid!" she shrilled in his ear.

"Simon, don't you want to play? We could have such a fine time!" came the coaxing voice once more.

And a little figure came into view just behind the violet light. He was Simon's size, and the most pleasant cheerful little person imaginable, with a huge, friendly smile. "Simon," he said plaintively, "don't listen to them – they don't want us to have fun! We could be such jolly friends. I'm very lonely, you know and would really love to have a friend to play with!" He held up a tray of the most appetizing pastries Simon had ever seen.

Simon felt an overwhelming compulsion to go to this friendly little person and tried to squirm away from the two who were restraining him. Why were they being so mean?

"Point your wand at him, Simon!" said Mr. Roussillon urgently. "Use your Othersight! Do it now!"

The habit of obedience was strong in Simon and reluctantly, very reluctantly, he pointed the new wand at the friendly little being. And then he gasped and recoiled in horror.

Gone was the friendly face. Simon saw a old, short man, thickset, with prominent, yellow teeth which were sharp and pointed. He had nasty claws, with gray hair streaming down his back and eyes of red fire. The tray in his hand no longer held tempting pastries – it held rotting meat and Simon could see maggots crawling in it. On his head the creature wore a red cap.

"See that cap?" the Faerie said. "It's red because he dips it in human blood!"

Simon shrank back against Mr. Roussillon, and felt that reassuring grasp on his shoulder. "Do not worry, Simon, he cannot take you if you do not wish to go to him. I will keep you safe from harm. There is nothing that he can do to me."

When he realized that Simon had seen his true nature the Redcap gave a great shriek. "I'll get you ! I'll get you!" the voice was no longer sweet and coaxing, but evil and vicious. "You, Wizard, you can't keep your circle up forever. And then I'll have him. I can wait forty years – can you?"

"I will wait as long as I have to, you may believe that," said René calmly. "and you cannot tread on this sacred floor unless you wish to die."

Father Oak suddenly spoke. "Child of ours, call the dragon. He circles above."

"Blow the whistle for Pádraig, Simon, if you please," said René hurriedly.

"Dragon!" shouted the Redcap a sneering note in his voice. "I'm not afraid of a dragon! Why, I've eaten dragons for breakfast! Even dragon fire can't hurt me!"

Several things happened simultaneously. The tops of the trees bent back as Simon blew the dragon whistle, making a clearing through which the dragon could come. Pádraig plunged down through the opening and landed on the painted floor. And like a thunderbolt, a stream of mistletoe came from the very top of Father Oak's branches and grabbed the Redcap by the neck.

He screamed and struggled, but the mistletoe continued to wind itself around his body until he could neither move nor speak, only his red eyes glared in fury. The mistletoe held the Redcap up into the air, lifting it over the violet light, which caused it to shriek in pain until it hung over the painted floor, which caused it to writhe painfully.

"Now, dragon, if you please, flame carefully. This mistletoe is a willing sacrifice. We cannot allow our grove to be profaned," said Father Oak. "or our children to be injured."

Pádraig obeyed and the Redcap burst into flames. Simon turned away and wound his arms about his tutor's waist, pressing his face into René's waistcoat, and bursting into tears. It was suddenly all too much for him.

"So much for being fireproof!" said the Faerie in satisfaction.

Páadraig drew in his flame – a long thin stream of it , with which he had carefully avoided touching any trees. "And where was the likes of that coming from?" he demanded.

Simon was getting himself under control as René patted him on the back and said "Simon, I am sending you home with Pádraig, *maintenant*. You will be perfectly safe with him. But you must tell your uncle immediately what has happened here today. And you are to tell him of the grove and Father Oak, most urgently, also. Do you understand?"

Simon nodded, rubbing at his cheeks.

"And I'll be having a word with his Grace, as well," said Pádraig.

"I must go and consult with someone – it cannot wait," René said worriedly. "But I must also know that you will be all right, Simon, before I can go."

Simon nodded. "I will be all right and I will tell Uncle Lyon everything."

"*Trés bon!*" René swept the little boy up in a hug. "I have already sent the good Chocolate home to her stable," he said as he put Simon down.

And then, in a clap of violet light, he disappeared.

"By all the Saints!" Padraig exclaimed. "I've never seen the like of that! And me being around Wizards all of me life! Sure, and where was he learning that?"

The light of hero worship was in Simon's eyes. "He wouldn't let that creature have me. And the trees like him."

"Oh, pooh!" said Medb. "He's just another Wizard! It's not as if they aren't thick on the ground everywhere you look."

But the look on Simon's face said that he no longer considered his tutor 'just another Wizard.'

Christian Charity

Scarcely had Mr. Roussillon disappeared so dramatically than Pádraig ordered Simon up on his back. Simon had wanted to talk to the Faerie but Pádraig was adamant – they had to leave now and talk to Uncle Lyon as soon as was possible. Simon was actually a little frightened, for Pádraig flew faster than he had before and they were back at the dragon pen in no time at all.

At Pádraig's direction, Simon unbuckled and slid down. The dragon wore a look of thoughtfulness on his face. "It's fetching out Diarmait I'll be," he said decidedly, "And he can be grabbing the ear of his Grace for your uncle may not be after having the time or the inclination to listen to what he might term but Banbury stories."

Simon nodded in agreement. To him it always seemed that adults were too busy to listen unless they were in a certain mood.

Accordingly, Padráig headed off in the direction of the tower and fetched Mr. Mag Uidhir by the simple expedient of bellowing "Diarmait, boyo, I have urgent need of ye!"

A dark head poked out of one of the arched windows of the great Tower. "Pádraig, ye great gowk! We've serious business going on here! What is it that can't be after waiting?" He sounded exasperated, Simon thought.

Then Padráig said a single sentence in what Simon assumed was the Gaelic (for his uncle had told him that was what they spoke in Ireland) and Mr. Mag Uidhir said, "Be lifting me down, Pádraig, and we'll talk." He called back something that Simon could not make out over his shoulder as he climbed out the window.

Pádraig stood on his hind legs lifted a foreleg to the window and Diarmait rode it down to the ground. He then walked with the dragon to where Simon waited.

"Now then, Simon," Mr. Mag Uidhir said gravely, his usual smiling face still and solemn "what's all this about a Redcap? It's certain you are – someone's not been filling your head with nonsense?"

"No, sir, I saw it – it wanted to *eat* me, but Mr. Roussillon and Pádraig wouldn't let it. And oh, sir, there was a blue Faerie as well! She warned us that it was coming!"

Looking down at Simon's earnest little face Diarmait could not doubt his sincerity. And Pádraig, whom he had never known to lie or even exaggerate, swore on the blessed Saint Pádraig after whom he was named that he had seen and dispatched a Redcap.

"Then this is very ill news indeed!" Diarmait exclaimed. "We must inform his Grace, the Arch Druid."

"He did WHAT?!" Lyon stared at Simon in disbelief.

"Disappeared," Simon reiterated, shrinking back a little because Uncle Lyon had yelled so loudly.

They were out of doors, in the dragon pen, so that Pádraig might be included in the conversation.

Uncle Lyon exchanged a look with Mr. Mag Uidhir. Uncle Lyon moderated his tone. "Simon, you must be mistaken. No one can disappear. The best Wizards at Cambridge and Oxford have been working on the matter for years and have never managed to do it. The secret of dematerialization was lost when Merlin died. Perhaps your tutor just ran into the forest..."

"Sure, and didn't I see it with me own eyes?" Pádraig interrupted. "Beggin' your honor's pardon, but it was not the boy's imagination! It all happened, just as he told ye!"

"It's all too fantastic!" Lyon muttered to Diarmait. "But if there was a Redcap, you know what that means, don't you, Mag Uidhir?"

"It's meaning a hole has been torn in the fabric binding the Otherworld," answered Diarmait. "And we're like to be overrun with Phoukas, the Foidin Seachrain –".

"And not just Irish creatures, Mag Uidhir," Lyon interrupted."The whole pantheon of the Unselighe Court – creatures not seen here for a thousand years! Evil creatures most modern Wizards wouldn't know it they presented their calling cards! What I want to know is how your Mr. Roussillon knew what to do about a Redcap, and most of all, how the hell he dematerialized – something that no one is supposed to be able to do! And the last Wizard I heard of that could talk to the trees was Merlin himself – which art he learned from Blaise of Brittany, the very last of the Druids of Brittany. And the grove and the stone circle you tell me of, Simon! I *knew* there was someplace sacred here – I could fell it tugging at me ever since I came here! I have to talk to this Roussillon! Do you know where he lives, Simon?"

"No, sir," Simon said, but a sudden thought struck him. "Mr. Arabin would know, uncle!"

"I'm off then to the Vicarage," Lyon announced.

"I'll take you, yer honor," Pádraig offered.

"Thank you, Pádraig, but I'd like you to keep an eye on Simon. I'll take a horse. And, Mag Uidhir, I leave you to cope with the messages and letters – you've kissed the Blarney Stone, and can turn them up sweet far better than I." Deaf to Diarmiat's protests he strode off to the stables.

"Pádraig, is Mr. Roussillon in trouble?" Simon's voice sounded very small.

"Nay then, lad," said Diarmait for the dragon. "But we need an explanation, ye must see. These are important matters."

Simon looked up at the secretary and then at the dragon. Both were frowning and Simon's heart sank. What was going on?

Ninon was hanging out wet sheets on the lavender bushes. This insured that the sheets would smell delightfully, and as lavender was a relaxant, people sleeping on lavender-scented sheets would drift into a refreshing slumber.

The wet sheets seemed heavier than usual this morning, and Ninon wondered in some exasperation, (not for the first time) why magic had so few really practical uses. One could make fire and make a mage light – that was useful, and one needn't spend money one didn't have on candles that reeked of tallow or have a flint always to hand. But it took real fuel, such as wood, to make a fire burn. One could only warm the house by magic in the winter if one was able to spend a week in bed for each day of warmth created. But one could not conjure up food – that would have been more than useful! One could preserve root vegetables so that they would still be fresh in March, but that was of limited use if one did not have an adequate amount of vegetables in the first place. Nor could one magic up new clothes – even making truly old clothes look new was beyond the power of magic. If one had a pile of fabric and thread and tapes and what ever else one needed to make it, a gown could be made magically, with difficulty. But it was always the same rule – "nothing comes from nothing" and there were the magical Laws that governed what could and could not be done. There was no magical way to wring out wet, heavy laundry, or to pull up a sizable wooden bucket from the well. Ninon had heard that there were Wizards at the Universities who did nothing but develop new spells. Why did they not work on simple spells that would make one's life easier, such as a wringing spell, or one that fetched water? She supposed that it was because none of them had ever had to wring out wet laundry or fetch water from an icy well when a bitter, sleet-laden wind was blowing.

She was trying to toss a sheet up onto a tall Chinese quince bush (having used up all of the lavender bushes) when behind her she heard a *crack!* and she whirled around, to find René behind her in a swirl of violet light.

She gasped, inadvertently pressing the wet sheet against her chest. "René, what have you done! To teleport in daylight – should any one see –!"

"*Grandmère*, there was a Redcap at the grove!" he interrupted her.

"On, *mon Dieu!*" she moaned, dropping the sheet onto the grass at her feet. It left a large wet mark on her rough linen apron and gown. "Perhaps this is the meaning of what I saw in my cauldron – René, we must speak to *Madame Mère* immediately! She must know of this! Fetch some water and purify it while I get my cauldron from where it resides!" she said hurriedly in French.

"The Arch Druid will come, *Grandmère*, for I have told Simon to tell him of all he saw," René warned her as she

132

began to head towards the house and he headed towards the well. "*Je suis navré*. I know that we were to move slowly…"

"*Ce n'est pas de veine* – it terrible luck, but she will understand – a Redcap! Ninon shuddered. and hurried into the house. Behind her, she heard the creak of the pulley as René began to draw the water.

At last all the arrangements were made. Diana's morning had been busy indeed. Lists festooned the Sheraton desk in the sunlit parlor she was using as an office. A footman had been dispatched to Knightswold with an order for mattresses from Aldershot's. If she had calculated correctly, they would be here from London, just in time, along with much needed bed linens. An order had gone to Gunter's in London, for made-up pastries and ices, to spare Cook too much work. Under a preservation spell, these would be flown dragon-back to the Abbey. The attic (the part where the roof had not collapsed) was ransacked and they found chairs, bureaus and bed frames, which even now the estate carpenter and his helpers were refurbishing – old fashioned, but usable The new plate – some of Mr. Josiah Wedgwood's most attractive – she had ordered in Knightswold had arrived, as well as the new silver service and table linens, in addition to a new Minton tea set, with enough cups to serve a regiment. An order had gone to Cheltenham for foodstuffs. Seppings was in the village, hiring additional staff. Arrangements had been made for a large tent to serve as extra stabling, and Pádraig had chosen a big, well-drained meadow as a site for dragons to rest and eat. Permission to use the Royal Feeding Pens for the visiting dragons had been granted.

Diana felt that she had spent the entire morning in front of her scrying bowl, talking to various merchants, all of whom had well-paid *Magus Majorii* on their staff so that customers could place orders from any spot in Britain via scry bowls. It was also possible to actually see what one ordered in the scry bowl – a vast improvement over a paragraph or so of over-exuberant prose in a catlogue. Because no one had yet discovered a way to scry across the water, orders from Ireland and Man and any outlying islands, such as the Hebrides, had to be placed by hippogriffe, which was the way one without access to a scry bowl ordinarily ordered, or by the Royal Mail, unless one was in an extraordinary amount of hurry.

Now she was free to rest or relax. She felt as if she wanted to get away from the Abbey for a while, before anyone could ask her any more questions. She decided to combine pleasure with a task she agreed to do for the Church.

The first Sunday she had been able to attend church, Mr. Arabin had asked her if she would mind taking on some parish work. There was a crying need for a lady's attentions amongst both her uncle's tenants and those of Sir Piers Mildmay. Miss Mildmay tried, but she was a timid, nervous woman without many resources and her brother made certain that she had a woefully inadequate allowance. Much like the late Marquis who had hoarded his wealth and neglected his tenants, Sir Piers had plenty of the ready, but preferred to spend it upon himself – mostly on his cellar. "It is my belief, Lady Diana, "the Vicar had confided, "that Sir Piers has traffic with *smugglers*! From what I have heard many of the bottles on his table can never have seen Customs seals!"

Diana had little trouble in believing this, for she had meet Sir Piers at church and disliked him heartily. She had not liked the way he ordered his poor little shadow of a sister about, the way he pushed his way through the crowd outside the church door, and the way he looked at her when they were introduced. He held her hand in his far too long and gazed upon her in such an insolent, appraising sort of way that her hackles had instantly risen.

But Uncle Lyon, bless him, had been there and had said, "Mildmay, if I ever see you look at my niece, or any other female, in that way, I shall break all of the laws of England, turn you into a rat and give you to the Vicar's cat to play with. And if I were you, Diana," he continued as Sir Piers turned a bright red, "I'd go home and scrub my hand before I caught something nasty." Uncle Lyon had smiled wolfishly at the baronet. Both men knew he meant every word of the threat. Being non-magical, Sir Piers could not know that human to animal transformation spells were virtually impossible.

Diana hoped that she would not meet Sir Piers this morning. Uncle would scold her perhaps, for she knew she should take a footman with her, as she had not as yet hired a new maid to take Betty's place, but she relished her freedom as she took off in the pony cart, in spite of the danger that hung over all of them just now. She had no fear as long as it was light out and Pádraig was in the sky keeping a watch out as well.

The boot of the cart was laden with baskets, each one chosen by the Vicar for a particular family. Each had large foolscap labels indicating to whom each one would go, and contained items ranging from a large ham to tea and tobacco and even toys. The money for these had been provide by Lyon, who was much distressed to find that his new tenants had been so neglected – and robbed. The former steward, Joseph Wilkins by name, had been milking the estate for years, and was even now in Cheltenham goal, awaiting the Assizes, and no doubt transportation to the Antipodes.

And Lyon had no objection to providing baskets for Sir Piers' tenants as well. They were a part of the parish of St Swithin's, and Lyon would quite enjoy making Sir Piers look as neglectful as possible.

Diana had been brought up in the tradition of Christian charity. Lady Eastcote spent a good part of every week out upon the estate, visiting, providing soup and comforts for the sick, listening to problems and grievances. It was part of a great lady's duty and Diana fully expected to do the same once she was established in her own home. But Lord Eastcote, in sharp comparison to the old Marquis and the baronet, was an excellent landlord. His tenants lived in superior surroundings, which were kept up to the mark. He used all the newest, most modern farming methods, and availed himself of every one of the magical advantages offered to the agriculturist. The fields and the animals were blessed every spring and autumn and a local Coven, to which his wife and daughters belonged, danced to bring the goodness of the moon to the fields. He also provided a school for the children, a doctor for the tenant's ills and gave liberally to the Parish Relief Fund. No beggar or vagabond ever left Eastcote hungry – many were hired on th estate and became valuable members of the little community.

Mr. Arabin had warned her, but Diana was nonetheless shocked by the poverty and neglect she found that afternoon. She called in at five cottages – the Vicar had given her a list and directions – and was appalled at the condition of the cottages – her papa would not have kept *boggarts* in such places – and brought almost to tears by the pathetic gratitude of some of the people. Others were sullen, for which she could not blame them. They had been ill-done by and had every right to be angry and resentful. Uncle Lyon, she knew, was doing all that he could to better their lot – he had declared a moratorium on collecting rents for at least a year, and repairs were being made as quickly as possible. The fields had been properly blessed, and, in many cases, Uncle Lyon had provided new livestock and seed for planting. Diana hoped to join or start a local Coven as well, so that the goodness of the moon could be imparted to the fields through the Witches' dances.

But what could be done to better the lot of Sir Piers' tenants? They needed the comforts she carried, and she took note of who needed the services of a doctor. Perhaps Uncle Lyon, as Lord Lieutenant, could bring some pressure to bear on Sir Piers.

She decided to visit in at one more cottage and consulted her list and map. She was closest to the de Varien cottage. De Varien – were they French, perhaps *émigrés*? Diana really wanted no part of anyone even *remotely* French – she still blamed the French – *all* of them – for Jonathan's death. She still did not like the fact that Simon's tutor had a French name, although probably Norman French, so old as to have become English. Her mother had felt this prejudice unreasonable, but Diana could not help how she felt.

But Mama would also expect her to do her duty and that meant visiting *all* of the people Mr. Arabin thought worthy. Perhaps these de Variens were aristocrats of the *ancien regime*, elderly now, and pathetically poverty-stricken, as so many of them seemed to be. A relief effort *"To Alleviate the Distressing Economic Condition of the Many French Émigrés Who Have Taken Refuge Upon Our Fair Shores"* had been started by the *Wizards' Times*, but not many people had subscribed to it, for many persons felt almost as Diana did. The war had been going on for a long while and there were few families who had not lost someone in military service. The French were the enemy.

May Cottage proved to be a small place, neat as a pin, and surrounded by trees, set on the corner where two roads met. To one side, near the road, stood an herb garden, properly laid out and aligned to the cardinal points with an armillary made of twisted sticks in the center. The herb garden was bordered with lavender bushes, covered in much darned sheets. There seemed to be another garden out in back of the cottage as well – a raised vegetable bed – Diana could see a corner of it. At this time of year it was largely empty.

Diana stepped from the carriage and clipped Butterball to the horse weight. She would be glad to have her own carriage – Butterball was letting her know in no uncertain terms that he was more than ready to return to his stable.

As she stood up, a carriage swept around the corner. It was a barouche, open to the fine day. and in it sat an exquisitely attired gentleman of mature years. When he saw her, recognizing by her rose-pink carriage dress and matching bonnet that she was a Lady of Quality, he raised his glossy beaver and inclined his head graciously. She curtsied to him, wondering and hoping that he was *not* on the way to the Abbey. There were quite enough people arriving as it was. He was heading in the right direction, but the fact that he traveled in a barouche, drawn by a team of Cleveland bays with a liveried driver and footmen up behind, would indicate a non-magical personage. Elsewise he would have arrived on a dragon. She had not been able to make out the crest on the panel of the carriage.

There was no answer to her knock on the closed front door, so she went into the herb garden. She did not care to leave the basket on the step.

There she found a man, in shirt-sleeves, hanging laundry – it appeared to be a sheet – on a bush. His back was towards her and he seemed not to have heard her light step on the garden path.

"Excuse me," she said politely and was astonished when he whirled about suddenly, as startled as she.

And then – "You!" she exclaimed, recognizing the gentleman of Knyghtwood, for had he not been on her mind ever since their encounter?

He was equally surprised. "The lady of the wood!" he exclaimed.

The tug of attraction Diana had noticed was even stronger. She began to smile but was interrupted by a little, elderly woman who ran around the corner of the house, panting. "René, René, your *maman* has gone missing! One minute I take my eyes from her and she is out of the chair and gone!"

He took off at once at a run to the back of the house.

The little woman turned imploring eyes on Diana. "*Mam'selle*, whoever you are, please help us! My daughter is very ill! She must be found!"

Diana could not disregard so direct a plea for help. She put the basket on the ground and hurried after the little woman. They found the gentleman coming back from the edge of the road with a struggling woman in his arms. "Lucien!" she was panting. "I saw him! I saw him! I will go to him! You cannot stop me!" she spoke in rapid French, which Diana, who had had seven years of French at Miss Minchin's, had no trouble in understanding.

The woman was a haggard beauty, bone thin, with short-cropped, graying dark hair. Her eyes were the colour of a particularly fine sherry, but wild in expression. With a sense of shock, Diana realized that she was more than likely completely mad. Now she beat at the man carrying her with her fists. "Let me go, you! I do not know you! Let me go to my husband!"

"Valerian!" he gasped out to the old woman.

She nodded and turned, running into the house.

He could barely hold her. Without thinking, Diana stepped forward and grabbed a flailing arm. "Shh, shh," she said soothingly, as if the woman were Simon.

"Will you help me get her to her bed?" he asked desperately, as he narrowly avoided being hit in the eye with an angry fist.

Diana nodded as the woman once more shrieked "*Let me go!*"

They wrestled her inside. In the process, Diana's bonnet was knocked from her head. With one part of her mind Diana noticed a little old woman, extremely elderly, who had found the basket out of doors and had brought it in and placed it on a rickety table. She had opened it and seen the large ham, a pound bag each of coffee and tea, and other nice

138

things. "The good *café*," she was murmuring. "Oh, Jacques will enjoy this!"

The other woman, who Diana assumed must be Mrs. De Varien, came forward with a bottle in her hand. "Hold her!" she ordered and ruthlessly drugged the struggling woman by holding her nose and making her swallow. Much of it ran out of her lips onto the shabby gown she wore.

Together, Diana and the man (Mr. de Varien?) lowered her to the bed, which Diana noted, was a palette on top of a simple wooden frame.

"Get your violin," Mrs. de Varien urged, grabbing at the younger woman to restrain her.

He let go and obeyed, taking a violin from a rickety dresser. Standing close by the bed where the sick woman still struggled, he raised it to his chin.

Diana still held onto the woman, whose strength was phenomenal.

When the first notes of the violin sounded the sick woman gave a long shudder and stared intently at the faint violet light that fell from the bow.

Diana recognized the melody at once and without stopping to think about what she was doing, began to sing. She had a true, low contralto, warm and soothing. She had been told that her voice had a certain amount of healing magic.

Startled, the violinist looked up and met her eyes briefly. He immediately began to play an accompaniment and let her voice carry the melody.

He shall feed His flock like a shepherd
And He shall gather the lambs in His arms, within His arms
Within his arms.
He shall feed His flock, like as a shepherd,
And carry them in His bosom
And shall gently lead those that are with young.
And gently lead those, and gently lead
those that are with young.

This aria from *The Messiah* segued into one for soprano, but he kept the key correct for her voice and she continued:

Come unto Him all ye that labor and are heavy laden
and He will give you rest.
Take His yoke upon you and learn of Him
 For He is meek and lowly of heart
 And ye shall find rest unto your souls.

As soon as Diana had begun to sing the eyes of the sick woman had fixed themselves on her face with a peculiar intensity. She had grown still and silent and visibly relaxed. As the music ended she gave a great sigh and closed her eyes and fell back on the pillow in a natural sleep. Breathing softly, she curled up like a child and turned over on one side.

"Oh, merciful God!" said Mrs. de Varien, hands to her face and tears in her eyes. The violinist lowered his bow and instrument. "Thank you," he said to Diana, fervently.

She was thunderstruck to say the least. Again she had felt that incredible unity of spirit the moment her voice combined with the violin. It was like an embrace of the most intimate sort.

And she had felt this with a *Frenchman* she thought in sudden revulsion. One of the race that had murdered Jonathan! How *could* she do such a thing? What was *wrong* with her?

René could not understand the look on her face — while they had made music together, soothing Lucie, she had looked at him as if she liked him, and that sharing the feeling of making magic together was as special to her as it was to him. But now she looked as if she found his presence the worst thing she had ever experienced. Her looks were dagger—like, her expression contemptuous.

"*Madame...*" he began, but was not allowed to finish what he had been going to ask, for with a scream and a sob, Marthe came almost falling down the stairs. "*M'sieur* René, *M'sieur* René! I cannot awaken Jacques! I went up to tell him of the so good *café* and he would not awaken!"

René thrust his violin and bow at Ninon and went up the stairs two at a time.

Marthe, her apron held up to her face, stared anxiously after him. Ninon put the violin on the table and went to put an arm around Marthe.

140

In a few moments René was back downstairs. "I am sorry, Marthe," he said, his voice full of compassion. "He is gone. I think, *du vrai*, that he has slipped away in his sleep."

Marthe gave a great wail and cast herself at René. His arms closed about her as she sobbed. Almost incoherent, she seemed to be begging something and it took Diana a moment to make it out. "Please, *M'sieur* René, do not let Jacques be buried in the pauper's cemetery! I could not bear it!"

"Marthe, I promise you, Jacques will be properly buried if I must dig ditches to pay for it," he swore, exchanging a look with Ninon.

Diana suddenly felt as if she were an intruder. No one seemed to notice that she was still there. She was touched by the tragedy she saw here today but her prejudice against the French stood in the way of true empathy.

It was at this inauspicious moment that Lyon arrived, hatless, obviously in extreme haste. He came in through he door that had been left open to bring Lucie inside, took in the people in the room at a glance and said to René, "Are you Roussillon? I what to know about the Redcap and most of all, how the *hell* did you dematerialize?"

"Roussillon?" Diana cried, just as Ninon shouted at Lyon "Go away, you!"

"Are you Simon's tutor?" Diana demanded angrily.

He nodded, still holding and stroking Marthe, who was now wailing softly, repeating over and over, "Jacques! Oh, my Jacques!"

"Can't you make that woman be quiet?" Lyon demanded. "We have important things to discuss!"

Ninon turned on him in a fury. "Her husband has just this minute died, *grosse brute*!"

"Did you know this, Uncle?" Diana challenged her relative,

"Know what?" Lyon asked. "What are you doing here, Diana?"

"Did you know that Simon's tutor was a Frenchman?" she nearly screamed, feeling as if the whole day had turned into some obscene farce.

"What does it matter?" Lyon shot back. "There are important things that must be discussed, not among them the question of national origin!"

"I will not have a Frenchman teaching Simon! Every feeling revolts! His father was murdered by the French! And for all we know, *he* –" she pointed at René, "is corrupting Simon and intending him to become a Papist!"

"You've run mad!" said Lyon. "Now will you be a good girl and be quiet and go away! There are important things I must learn –"

"You, sirrah," Diana ordered, glaring balefully at René, "are not to come near my son ever again! I shall find a new tutor for him, an English tutor!"

"That's it!" A frustrated Lyon grabbed his niece and thrust her out the door. locking it magically after her. "We'll discuss this when I get home!" he yelled through the door. "Go home and put a cold cloth on your head!"

"Now perhaps we'll get somewhere!" and turned to find Ninon with a broom raised in a menacing gesture. "*Vieux baveux*! Leave my house!" she demanded.

"None of that!" With a gesture, Lyon whipped the broom from her hand, It crashed against the wall.

"René, do not let your *Grandmère* be assaulted by this *vieille cloche*!" Ninon cried.

"The only thing René is going to do is to tell me what I want to know. Otherwise he'll be spending the night in Cheltenham goal," said Lyon. Pleased, he looked around at the silence he had created. "I thought that would do it!" he said in no little satisfaction.

11

The Face In the Water

Malcoeur was not certain what to expect from the very ugly creature. He was not frightened of her threat, but he was curious as to what her 'Master' wanted of him. It was not as if he had not dealt with supernatural beings before – in Russia, one could not take a step without falling over vast hordes of creatures, including bath house *Banniks*, and *Rusalki* in the water and woodlands. And he had dealt with Servian *Vilas* and Dalmatian *Marlachi*, vampires in Roumania, and *Djinns* and *Afrits* in Persia, Egypt, and Baluchistan, and even the fearsome dust devils of the steppes of Central Asia. But these denizens of the British Isles were new to him and he decided to precede cautiously at first until he found out what they wanted of him.

He followed the hag up a steep path to the side of a mountain. There she gave a wave of her hand and the mountain split and parted. She gave him a sidelong glance as if she expected him to be impressed by this commonplace happening. He was not impressed in the least. He had seen too many other truly strange things in his travels and had grown all too accustomed to such.

They proceeded into a tunnel where Malcoeur, because of his prowess in the Black Arts, could see on two levels. Overlaying the rooks and the roots of trees and shrubs hanging down was a glamourie, what Malcoeur would call *le charme de grâce,* which made it appear as if they entered a world of gold and crystal walls and vaulted roof, with dazzling tapestries, and beautiful rugs underfoot, rather than the hole in the ground it truly was.

They went from the tunnel into a large chamber, where was assembled a crew of some of the most repulsive creatures the Jongleur had ever seen. There was a very ugly thing with one leg, one hand out of the middle of its chest and one eye in the middle of its face. It had not lost a leg – it was obvious that it only ever had one and it moved in a curious hopping fashion with the aid of a flailed club, bound round with twenty chains. It was hideous and dark-visaged and clad in filthy deer hides. He learned later that it was called a Fachan.

There was another old woman, a blue-faced, lean hag who seemed to be existing in a swirl of snow and icy wind. She wore garments of slushy white, had hair that appeared always to be blowing in a snowstorm and eyes of frost. She was the *Cailleach Bheur*, known to some as the Mother of Winter.

There were more of the same type of being who had brought him to this place – each uglier than its sisters. They were the *Gwillyon* – evil, and hungry. There were horrible little men with long grey hair and sharp teeth and claws, all red-capped. There were fiery-eyed, shaggy horses – Shag-Foals – and several enormous toads, with wings, and no back legs, but a tail. These were the Water Leapers. Corpse candles – will o' the wisps – hung in the air, flickering lights in which Malcoeur could see nasty little faces, with looks full of wicked mischief, licking crimson lips as they stared at him. There were many others, all horrifying and all seeming to have several things in common – long pointed teeth, claws and blood-lust in their eyes.

At the very end of the room was a dais where a large chair of twisted roots held a far different type of individual. He looked human – except for his pointed ears. Among this unlovely company he shone as if he were a star. His face was one of unnatural beauty and his hair was a cascade of gold. His eyes were like green jewels in his narrow face. But his expression was one of cruelty mingled with an almost desperate boredom. His long fingers clutched and unclutched at the arms of his chair. Unlike the others who seemed to favor rags and dirt as fashion choices, he wore silk and velvet, the finery of a age long past, Medieval past, Malcoeur decided.

The hag that had fetched Malcoeur sidled up to the throne. "I brought him, Lord Sluagh , just as you told me," she said in the tone of one trying to please.

"So I see, Jenny," he returned, bored and frowning. He lifted a long finger and beckoned to Malcoeur. "Come here so that I may see you better."

Malcoeur did not care for his tone – the Jongleur was not accustomed to being addressed as if he were some sort of lapdog – but he went nearer to the throne and bowed, but not very deeply.

"You have done us a singular service, sorcerer," drawled the non-human on the throne. "By slaying an Arch Druid you managed to tear a hole in the binding set by that accursed Merlin –for almost one thousand years we have been forced to exist here, below ground, without daylight –"

"Or human blood!" put in the Fachan.

Sluagh glared at it. "Do not interrupt me again or you will have no need for blood." His voice was cold and imperious.

"I am naturally *aux anges* to have rendered you a service, *M'sieur*, although such was not my intention," said Malcoeur coolly.

"And what *was* your intention?" Matholwch Sluagh queried.

"To cast the English sorcerers into fright and confusion so that my country can win the war we are now engaged in," was Malcoeur's answer.

A ripple of interest ran over the room. "War!" more than one of the creatures muttered. Most licked their lips. War meant fighting and blood, pain and death – the things on which they fed.

"We did not know that the humans were at war!" A very tall, red-headed , striking woman in breast plate and shield over a short kilted gown strode forward. She carried a dark spear, its tip glistening with blood. A carrion crow sat on her shoulder. She was the Morrigan, the greatest, fiercest aspect of the ancient war Goddess, Badb. War was all to her; in her other aspects she caused indiscriminate slaughter, and confusion to allies, so that they fought among themselves. Nothing pleased her as much as the horrors of human conflict. "We must be above ground!"

"You shall be – the tear grows larger every hour. Once split it does not stop," said Sluagh dismissively.

"Only the Redcaps have got out!" growled a Water Leaper.

"Aye, Llamhigyn Y Dwr, ye're too fat to get from that wee hole!" sniggered a Redcap.

Sluagh's eyes flashed and the Redcap shrank back.

Malcoeur watched with interest. All of these oh-so-wicked creatures were afraid of Sluagh. He must be very powerful indeed. Malcoeur wondered just how much.

"We want to know, sorcerer, what you intend to do now," said Sluagh.

"Kill the other five," said Malcoeur simply. A hiss of appreciation ran around the room.

"That is agreeable to us," Sluagh leaned forward in his chair, his eyes intent on Malcoeur. "We want you to look out for our interests as well, sorcerer."

"I work by myself," Malcoeur stated. "I care little if you come out of your hole or rot here for all eternity." He was growing tired of this whole proceeding. He saw no advantage in it for himself.

"You will do as I tell you," said Sluagh in a silky voice. "Elsewise, Jenny – persuade him."

The *Gwillyon* started forward, her eyes gleaming. Malcoeur spun, lifted his hands and red fire ran from the tips of his fingers so fast that it blurred in the air. The red fire grabbed her by the throat, twisted and broke her neck with an audible snap. Then she burst into flame, was consumed in a matter of seconds and left but a pile of greasy ashes on the floor of the cavern.

At the sight of the red Mage fire the creatures shrank back. "Balefire!" they whispered. "Blood magic!"

Sluagh began to laugh. It was wild and mocking laughter with more than a tinge of madness. "Oh, very good!" he said. "There is more to you than we thought! We like you, sorcerer!"

"I cannot return the compliment, *M'sieur*, for this conversation grows tedious in the extreme, *n'est ce pas*? I have better things to do," Malcoeur stated.

"So we may not command you," Sluagh said thoughtfully. "But what if we were to offer you something that would help your cause? Just as you have helped ours, however inadvertently?"

"It must depend, *M'sieur*, on what is in your mind," the Jongleur said carefully. One could never tell with creatures such as these. Mostly, alliances with them were more trouble than they were worth.

"What if," Sluagh said, his slightly slanted green eyes glittering, "we were to march at the side of your army? To throw our lot in with yours? And in exchange for our services, you were to keep doing just what you are doing – killing Druids – and Wizards. We cannot kill them, but you can. We will take care of the non-magical folk of these Isles, which is, if they hold true to form, the scaff and raff of the army. Why, between the two of us there might not be enough humans – or Wizards – left here to oppose your armies! Our folk are very hungry – it has been a long time since they fed on their natural diet."

Malcoeur thought furiously. If these creatures fought on the side of the *Grand Armée* – if they could be used against the British troops in the Peninsula, or against the Czar's forces – would such an army not be invincible? He was not concerned that they could not be trusted. Of course they could not be trusted! But he had no doubt that he, himself, could control them, and rid France of them once Russia and Britain were subjugated. He could have killed all the creatures in this room, easily, if he had desired. He had no doubts that he had magics they had never dreamed of, as old and as powerful as they were. It had been his experience that in any given locale magic worked one way and that was all that anyone ever learned and that people – or creatures – were ill prepared to face a different kind of magic. He had traveled the world and learned from every source that he could exploit. They were all combined into a power that he fancied unique – and unconquerable.

Now he said, as if it were a matter of complete indifference to him. "Perhaps we should talk of this further, *M'sieur*, in private."

The green eyes gleamed. "Bring food and drink!" he rapped out to the *Gwillyon*. "Leave us!" he then commanded to the host of creatures, waving an imperious hand. They faded away into the deep shadows of the cavern.

One of the *Gwillyon* brought a chair for Malcoeur, while others brought food and drink and a table which she set between the throne and Malcoeur's chair.

Malcoeur had no intention of eating Faerie food – he knew better than that – and at any rate, what was on the platter before him appeared to be a baked rat – and he refused the wine as well, which was not wine at all , but the mingled blood of several animals, such as moles and shrews. His Othersight told him that the rat was supposed to appear to him in the guise of a roasted chicken and the blood as the finest of burgundies.

Sluagh realized that Malcoeur could see through the glamourie and was secretly impressed. Humans usually needed Faerie help to see that clearly. He took up the rat and took a huge bite of it, wishing to gauge the sorcerer's reaction.

There was no reaction at all. Malcoeur's face was impassive. He leaned back in his chair and steepled his fingers. "So, *M'sieur*," he said "tell me more of why my Emperor should wish to align himself with you."

René very carefully helped Marthe to a seat at the table. "I have done nothing," he said carefully to Lyon, "for which you might put me in gaol."

"Of course not," Lyon flipped his hand impatiently. "But I had to do something to stop the hysterics. We'll not get anywhere with all of this brouhaha going on. What's wrong with her?" he said, leveling his glance on Marthe, who had begun to cry again.

Ninon glared at him. Men! Even the best of them could be so insensitive and not notice the nose on their face! And this one did not qualify as the best, of that she was certain! "Her husband has this moment died," she said with immense dignity, her tone saying *even you, a complete barbarian, can understand that she might be upset by this!*

Lyon had the grace to look slightly abashed. "I'm sorry to hear it, but I am the Arch Druid and it is very important – "

"We do wish to talk to you, *M'sieur le Dryadas*," said Ninon, "but Marthe must come first."

Lyon stared at her. "*What* did you call me?"

"*Dryadas* – it is a Breton term for Druid," she replied.

148

Lyon made an exasperated noise. "I know that! But how did *you* know that?"

Ninon could not help it – she was beginning to enjoy herself. He was so impatient – so easily manipulated. Ignoring him, she turned to René. "You had best go for *M'sieur* Arabin, as *quickly* as possible."

"I would like to see the good priest," said Marthe through her tears. "He can bless Jacques' journey and call upon the *anges purs et radieux* to carry him to *le ceil.*"

"I am certain that Jacques, a good man – the best! – will be already in Heaven," said René, squeezing Marthe's hand.

She looked up at him gratefully. He dropped a quick kiss on her brow, and then backed away from her. "I shall return quickly," he said. looking at Lyon and Ninon, and then disappeared in a crack of sound and a blaze of violet light.

Lyon's jaw dropped. "It is true!" he strode over to where René had just been standing. A faint trace of violet light stood in the air, but was rapidly dissipating. *"Madame,* I want – I need – an explanation! Who and what are you?"

"We are Druids of Bretagne – Brittany," she said calmly.

Lyon snorted. "There have been no Druids in Brittany since about 64 A.D.! Every schoolboy knows that they were driven out by the Romans! Many fled here, many others were slaughtered by the Romans, who knew enough to use Cold Iron and fire against them. Blaise was the last the Druids of Brittany and he was old – *very* old – when Merlin was a boy."

"Blaise was not the last. The Druids of Brittany live still, *M'sieur*, and dwell upon the *Île de Sein* – "

The *Île de Sein* is a legend!" Lyon inter-rupted. "A lost island! It doesn't exist!"

"It does not exist like Lyonesse and Ys or Atlantis from which came the *Tuatha de Danann?*" Ninon suggested slyly, for all of those places were real, or had been real. Atlantis had been the original home of the *Tuatha*, the children of the goddess Dana, who, eons before, became the Shining Ones, the rulers of Faerie folk.

Lyon flushed angrily. "Am I just to take your word for this – this farrago of nonsense?"

149

"No," said Ninon. "I will show you," she walked to the cupboard by the fireplace and pulled out the cauldron.

Lyon made a sound of awe when he saw the cauldron unveiled. "Beautiful!" he murmured, studying the artistry of it. "I have never seen its like."

"When René returns I shall scry the *Madame Mère*, Guénolé Cornouaille, of our Order. She wishes to speak to you," Ninon announced.

Lyon looked up from the examination of a representation of Taranis, the god of Thunder. "Scry the *Île de Sein*? Are you mad?" he demanded. "That means you would scry over water!"

"And that cannot be done?" Ninon shook her head. "*Non, non, M'sieur*, it can be done, and many other things as well. You will learn that you do not know everything, *n'est ce pas*? Now I will make a cup of tea – for Marthe, she needs the comfort and me, I need the *le reconstituiant* from talking to you!"

For once in his life, Lyon could think of nothing to say. No one had ever told him before that they needed a restorative to counteract his conversation.

After what was surely the worst cup of tea he had ever had (for Ninon wasn't about to waste their new, good tea on Lyon), the Arch Druid impatiently watched Ninon purify the water for the scrying cauldron, Unlike his magic, which used salt or a Latin incantation, she set the water afire with blue flames from off her hands. They burned fiercely for a moment and then died back, leaving a water so pure he could actually detect a scent to it.

Ninon had made Marthe a cup of tea and made her lay down on the cot in the curtained alcove beside Lucie. Lucie still slept, rather too deeply for Ninon's liking, but the dose of valerian had been extremely strong.

Just as Ninon finished setting the cauldron René reappeared, "He is on his way," he reported to Ninon "and has notified the mortician."

"Why did you not bring him back with you?" Lyon demanded. He *had* to know the spell for dematerialization!

"One cannot transport other people," René told him.

"Not as yet," Ninon put in. "Come, all of your questions will be answered, my lord, but now *Madame Mère* awaits."

She stood over the deep cauldron and stretched out her hands, seeming to pull air towards her with a fierce look of concentration on her face. This again was different – Lyon, like all of the Witches and Wizards in the British Isles, used a wand to activate a scry bowl.

"*Bonjour, Madame Mere*," Ninon bowed to the cauldron, and Lyon, bending over her shoulder, saw a face in the water.

She was a very old woman, her face a map of wrinkles, but endowed with a great serenity and spirit. Her eyes were blue, shrunk to slits under high soaring brows, her lips faded. She wore a nun-like habit of purest white, with a wimple surrounding her face closely and covering every bit of her hair. This wimple was bound about her head with a fillet of gold, made of tiny oak leaves and acorns, and on her breast was a enameled brooch pin, made in the likeness of a sprig of mistletoe.

Lyon couldn't help staring. He had never seen such a clear picture in a scry bowl before. And they claimed that this was coming from an island off the coast of Brittany?

The elderly woman laughed and said, "My daughter, is this the Arch Druid of the English that you have told me of?"

"*Oui, Madame Mère*, but he is worse than I have thought," Ninon told her.

Affronted, Lyon glared at her. Ninon ignored him.

"I am Guénolé Cornouaille. As you would say in Éire, I am *banfhlaith*, of Ker-Ys on the isle of Sena called so in the ancient tongue. We have long wanted to meet you."

Lyon noted her use of the ancient term, no longer used, for woman-druid. He bowed and introduced himself, adding curiously, "Why have you wanted to meet me?"

"It has long been in my mind and in the minds of my brethren that we rejoin the world. This has become imperative, for there is a great evil abroad and, as Ninon has told us a rent in Merlin's binding of the Otherworld that will grow larger every day. There is also the matter of Napoleon Bonaparte and his unhallowed ambitions. Recent events – the

Redcap in your grove among them – have precipitated matters that we thought to move slowly on. That a Redcap should dare to come so near to a sacred grove and a stone menhir is outrageous. And too, we wish to contribute to your grand plan."

An icy chill ran down Lyon's spine. How did she know about that?

She read the expression on his face correctly and chuckled. "We send our children out into the world to watch and keep close to our magical brothers and sisters. We know how you repulsed the invasion of Napoleon several years ago. We also know that you plan to gather power again, to send it to the few remaining Wizards of Russia, to repel Bonaparte, and that with the sanction of the rightful King of Spain, and Viscount Wellington the Witches of the Peninsula having been using their powers against the French forces."

"We've been spied on!" Lyon was indignant.

"Not to harm you, but to help. In one thousand years," she said, "magic has changed on both sides. We have much to learn from one another."

Lyon forgot his indignation over being spied on. "You would be willing to teach someone – me, for instance – to dematerialize?" he said eagerly.

She smiled at him. "You are probably too old to learn, Arch Druid. We have found that teleporting is best learned and done by the young. Once you reach a certain age your mind cannot accept it."

"Give me the spell – I can learn it!" he said tersely. "I have never seen the spell that I cannot master. And what is *teleporting?*"

"We have named what you term dematerialization such, a much better term for what is done – mind travel. There are few spells involved in teleporting. But René may explain it to you. He is one of our best and well understands the higher mathematics involved."

Lyon blinked. Mathematics?

"My dear, Ninon, I grow tired," said Madame. "You may answer any more questions that the Arch Druid has, surely. But we will be in touch again, soon, my lord." She smiled again at Lyon and the water was empty abruptly, just a silver cauldron full of extraordinarily clear water.

"Well, by the Great Horned Moon!" Lyon swore.

When her uncle had thrust her so rudely from the cottage Diana's first impulse had been to throw herself against the door and beat against it with her fists. He had locked it magically against her – she felt that right away. But she thought better of it, for she was fast becoming aware that she wanted nothing as much as a private place to let the tears come, which were fast overwhelming her.

Butterball had never been driven as fast in his life. He really had no objection to returning to the stable but there was no need to be pushed along at quite this gait!

Diana was so angry she wanted to scream. How *could* her uncle and Mr. Arabin do this to her? They *knew* that Jonathan had been killed by the French – they *knew* her feelings about that perfidious nation – Mr. Arabin should *not* have asked her to call on *any* French people! How could they? *How could they!*

By the time the Abbey was reached and Butterball quite run off his legs, a large lump in Diana's throat threatened to choke her. Her eyes burned and her nose felt twice its size.

She pulled Butterball up in the drive and flung the reins at a startled groom who happened to be there. Diana did not notice the elegant, crested barouche on the gravel, nor the baggage being unloaded from it. Seppings was in the hall, along with several other persons. She flew by him, on her way up the stairs, ignoring his cries of "My lady –!" as she went flying by.

"Headache!" she flung over her shoulder.

The haven of her bedroom was reached none to soon. With a sound like a banshee's wail she began to cry as she cast herself on the bed, not even bothering to remove her pelisse. Great wracking sobs wrenched her body and she pounded her fists on the pillows in a paroxysm of grief and rage.

How, for even one second, had she been attracted to a Frenchman! And how could she work magic in such a fashion – an intimate fashion – with him! How could she have been so disloyal to Jonathan, the man she had promised to love forever? Twice now, she had had disloyal thoughts about her

153

dead husband – and that was the Frenchman's fault, too, irrationally forgetting that the first disloyal thought – that Jonathan had been neglectful not to have written to Simon – was before she had met the Frenchman. And twice now, she had worked magic – which she had never thought to do again – and that was *his* fault, too.

And singing to that woman – it had been a stupid thing to do, for it brought back memories that she had put way in the darker recesses of her mind. Memories of men dying in the surgical tent after a skirmish, when she had attempted to help the surgeons by soothing dreadfully wounded men with her voice – memories of men dying in the snow on the retreat, their last vision of her singing some lullaby that their mother had soothed them with, memories of poor little Harley freezing to death – and worst of all, the memory of Jonathan's body, brought back to camp by some of his men who had volunteered to find him – a twisted, broken, black thing. For the French had tortured him with Cold Iron, more than likely, had said Sir John Moore, for information. Jonathan did not have much magic, but he still had the aversion to Cold Iron that all those of the Old Blood, no matter how thin, still carried.

She sobbed bitterly into the pillows. Why did this have to happen when everything was going so well? She had found Simon and grown to love him on a few short weeks. She was enjoying the renovation of the Abbey, even with all the attendant problems, and as she hoped, she was sleeping better.

Tears flooded her eyes anew. She had not cried this hard since it happened – no, not even then, for her grief had been dry-eyed and stony in the Peninsula. The retreat had come so hard upon the heels of Jonathan's death that she had no time to recover before one horror piled upon another. Many of her friends, her maid and her riding mare and Harley, her familiar, had died in that retreat. And Sir John, who had been like a father to her and Jonathan, had been killed.

She cried for a long time, finally subsiding to weak sobs, her throat raw and eyes aching. Afterwards, she fell into an uneasy sleep.

Seppings was much distressed. Here was an important guest arrived and no one here to greet him, save staff! Lady Diana had taken off up the stairs as if pursued by demons and no one was certain where Lord Lyonshall might be.

"I am very sorry, your Grace," he said, turning to the man who stood in the hall. "There does seem to be no one about. But I will see your Grace to your rooms, myself, and see that all is made ready for you."

"A most ill-run household," murmured the Duke of Chenevix to his manservant, Mariposa. He put his quizzing glass to his eye and stared at the decoration of the hall, which consisted of a tall case clock, a table on which reposed a litter of riding whips, copies of the *Wizard's Times*, a prayer book and a bag of dragon treats. A rather ill-done land-scape hung on the wall. His Grace gave a shudder.

He was a tall man, very slender, but with the suggestion of steel about him. He was held to be one of the best swordsmen in London. His hair was entirely grey although he was not yet fifty. He had a cold, closed, secret face with thin lips that almost never smiled. His eyes were dark grey, with a silver sheen that could chill the observer with a glance. His clothes were exquisite – he had taken Mr. Brummel's maxims to heart and dressed with neatness and propriety, and quiet elegance. His well-cut coat was maroon, his breeches grey. He wore a mourning band on his arm and a black cravat. Those were the most cheerful colours he ever wore. He always wore a quizzing glass which he used to stare the toady, the ill-bred, and the slow-wit out of countenance.

He had felt it his duty to come here. After all, he had accepted the post of Chancellor of Magic and Enchantments and as soon as they had the news of the Welsh Arch Druid's death, he had bade Mariposa pack a valise or two.

But he did not like Eliot Lyons. His Grace found it hard to believe that *anyone* liked Eliot Lyons. If this reception was anything to judge by this was going to be an intolerable visit.

155

12

Burn, Witch, Burn

When Diana at last awakened, she at first could not imagine what had happened. Why was she in her bed, in her pelisse and still wearing shoes? Her eyelids felt as if they had been glued together, her throat ached and the end of her nose felt raw. She had a sick taste in her mouth and felt both irritable and depressed and sticky and dirty.

As she woke and sat up in bed, it all came rushing back at her. And she grew angry yet again. With a wave of her hand she lit several candles, for the room was nearly dark. She stood up abruptly and staggered to the wash stand, where she found some tepid water still in the pitcher. This she poured into the basin and splashed on her face, which somewhat revived her. She patted her face dry with the towel that hung on the washstand and then went to her dressing table and sat in front of the mirror.

She was horrified by what she saw. Her hair had come loose from its pins and was a tangled mess. Her face was puffy, her eyes red and swollen. Her pelisse and gown looked to be hopelessly crushed, and she realized that she did not know where her bonnet might be.

She could not go down to dinner looking like this! She would have to send her excuses.

Diana thought longingly of a bath. It would feel good to be clean, and perhaps wash her hair. She was not at all hungry, but a cup of tea might be refreshing.

At the forefront of her mind was the fact that she had to tell Simon that he was to have a new tutor. He had had only two lessons with this Frenchman and surely there could be no objection in that quarter. When it was explained to him, he would see the sense of it.

With this reflection comforting her, Diana rang the bell for a servant. She would order a bath, have a cup of tea and then sleep and talk to Simon in the morning.

It was a dull, rainy morning. Rain fell steadily from a sullen, heavily overcast sky. Diana was surprised to learn from Lyon – they were the only ones at breakfast, for Lyon always breakfasted unfashionably early – that the Duke of Chenevix had arrived yesterday.

"Why was I not told of this?" she demanded, putting down a muffin she had been buttering.

Lyon shrugged. He had been perusing first a copy of the *Wizards' Times* and then a stack of post. "I daresay Seppings told the staff not to bother you, since you had such a bad headache. By the bye, is that how a fit of temper is described nowadays – a headache?"

"I had every justification for being angry!" Diana flashed. "I cannot conceive how you and Mr. Arabin thought I might not object to Simon being taught by the very persons who murdered his father!"

"You're all about in your head," Lyon com-mented. "From what Arabin tells me, Roussillon has lived in England since he was about four years of age and has never even been heard to express admiration for Bonaparte, which is more than can be said for some of our own poets and politicians. And besides that, he can dematerialize!"

"I don't care if he is Merlin come back to life!" she retorted. "I will not have Simon anywhere near French persons and if it means taking him back to Eastcote, I shall do so!"

A noise from the door made her twist about on her chair. There was Simon, big-eyed and anxious and right behind him, Diarmait Mag Uidhir. The young Irishman had dropped a hand on Simon's shoulder.

"Mama," Simon faltered "am I not to have lessons with Mr. Roussillon any more?"

"No, Simon, you are not. I cannot have you taught by a Frenchman and a Papist," Diana said more sharply than she had intended. She wondered how much he had overheard.

157

Simon's lower lip quivered and a tear ran down his cheek. "Oh, please, Mama! I like him so much! And the lessons are so interesting!"

She did not like seeing him upset, but she was determined on this." You shall have a new tutor, an Englishman"

"I don't want another tutor!" he interrupted her.

"Simon, the French killed your Papa! How you can wish to consort with one of the very people – "

"*Mr. Roussillon* didn't kill Papa!" said Simon shrilly, showing rather more sense than his parent. "I don't care if he is French – I like him!"

Diana rose. "That is enough, Simon! Now, you go to your room until you can speak to me in a respectful fashion, and accept that I know what is best for you!"

"You're not fair!" Simon burst out. "I hate you!" Sobbing, he pulled away from Diarmait and ran into the front hall. They all heard the great front door open and slammed shut.

"Well, you handled *that* remarkably well," said Lyon, sarcastically, to his niece.

"That was not well done in you, Lady Diana," said Diarmait quietly. "If there was ever a boy in need of a father, Simon is the one, and after yesterday and the Redcap, he's near to worshipping Roussillon *and* Pádraig. 'Tis my guess he's gone to Pádraig now to be comforted."

Perhaps it was best to let Simon seek Pádraig's company. Diana had been about to tell Mr. Mag Uidhir that what happened between her son and herself was none of his affair but the mention of the Redcap halted her abruptly. "Redcap?" she queried quickly, looking from one man to the other.

Diarmait, since Lyon showed no sign of doing so, told her the events of yesterday morning. "So you see, Lady Diana, between them, Pádraig and Roussillon saved Simon's life."

"It seems to me that Pádraig deserves most of the credit!" she said crossly. "And if it were not for that Frenchman, Simon would not have been out in the woods where he might be accosted by a Redcap in the first place!"

Lyon rolled his eyes and picked up his news-sheet. Women! They had no logic!

"Nevertheless, my lady," said Diarmait, forging bravely onwards in spite of the stormy look in her eyes and the mulish set to her jaw, "Simon has been looking for someone he can look upon as a father for a long time."

"He has found such in two day's time?" she queried scornfully, "Really, Mr. Mag Uidhir, I am certain that your theories on child rearing are quite fascinating –"

"And haven't I been there when the boy was pouring out his heart to Pádraig? And didn't I go through the same thing, myself, when me dad died when I was younger than Simon? A boy needs a man to look up to, and learn from, and 'tis a hunger in ye 'til ye find it. And no female can replace that! And finding that other father can take two years, two months, two days or two hours!" Diarmait said fiercely.

"He's got you there, Diana," said Lyon dryly.

She turned to glare at her uncle. He was no help at all!

"One does not expect to see Cheltenham tragedies enacted so early in the morning," came a cold voice, rather like an arctic frost. The Duke of Chenevix, a symphony in gray, stood in the doorway, swinging his quizzing glass idly in one hand. "I might have known, Lyonshall, that your household would be fraught with histrionics, and ill-bred strangers." He directed a pointed glance and a hideously magnified, chilly eye at Diarmait, who still stood in the doorway. "Thank you," he said as Diarmait moved away, allowing the Duke's entrance to the breakfast parlour.

His Grace stood behind a seat, and stared at Lyonshall. "One hesitates to remind one's host of his manners," he murmured "but I should like to be introduced to his lady and gentleman, and perhaps persuade the lady to resume her seat so that I may take mine?"

"I didn't think that you would hesitate at anything, Chenevix!" said Lyon, stung by the Duke's comments. "After all, no one invited you here!"

"One has one's duty," said the Duke, with a slight bow.

"Hah!" said Lyon, but introduced Chenevix to Diana and Diarmait. When everyone was again seated and the Duke had requested that the butler be summoned to serve him (everyone else had helped themselves from the sideboard) Lyon said abruptly, "I don't see what you think you can do here, Chenevix. You could have stayed in London – reports would have been sent to you. The Runners are still making their examination in Wales, I believe."

"But you are having a conclave here in a day's time, are you not?" queried the Duke as Seppings served him buttered eggs and kippers. "This coffee is not to my liking," he said, after taking a sip and putting the cup down again. "Pray have your chef prepare another pot and make certain that it is hot."

Seppings bowed. The Duke was already unpopular in the servant's hall, as was that man of his. The staff had been kept hopping all evening with requests for fresh linens, complaints about the bath water and demands for a tray of sandwiches at nearly midnight.

"I shall have Mrs. MacReady prepare another pot posthaste, your Grace," the butler promised.

"Mrs. – " a look of horror (as much as his frozen features could express) descended upon the Duke's features. "My dear Lyonshall, surely you do not employ a female in the kitchen? Had I known you exist in such a state of savagery I should have brought Alphonse with me. He is a genius. His *agneau de primtemps Madeleine* must be tasted to be believed!"

"Popinjay!" growled Lyon. He folded up his news-sheet and rose from his chair. "Come along, Mag Uidhir," he directed. "I want to tell you of what I learned yesterday." Followed by the young Irishman, who took hasty leave of Diana and the Duke, Lyon left the room, muttering to himself.

"Well, Lady Diana," said the Duke in his cool voice. "I must apologize for inadvertently eavesdropping this morning. One does not like to be impolite, but I could scarcely miss your – ah – conversation. If it be any consolation to you, I thoroughly approve. One does not like to entrust the education of the young to foreigners, particularly French foreigners. It seems as though when the French *émigrés* began to invade our shores they ought to have been put somewhere – the Orkney islands suggest themselves – where

160

they might be watched and controlled, rather than this slapdash manner we now employ of letting them settle where they will. And as for using public – or even private funds to sustain them – they ought to have thought of their future monetary needs before they inflicted themselves upon us."

Diana, whose first impression of the Duke had not been favorable, began to warm to him. Here was the first sensible person she had met in days. She ignored the fact that the Duke's French chef was not cooking for him in the Orkney Islands.

"I fancy," said the Duke, "that you must busy yourself about the household this morning, for I noticed that there are no hatchments or mourning wreaths up as yet. Otherwise, I should ask you to conduct me about, for I am always interested in both art and architecture."

Diana felt her opinion of him sinking again, for his tone implied that she was extremely remiss in not having displayed suitable mourning for the death of the Welsh Arch Druid. "We found the stored mourning to be unusable, full of mold and mice droppings. I am waiting for new mourning to come – it should arrive today," Diana found herself explaining.

"Ah, no doubt that accounts for it," The Duke took a sip of the coffee Seppings had just brought in and sighed, putting the cup down. "Why is it impossible to teach a servant to make a decent cup of coffee?" he inquired almost plaintively.

Diana was beginning to understand why her Uncle disliked Chenevix so.

Jacques was buried in the rain. Since there was no reason to wait, his interment was immediate. The Silverbridge mortician had a plain deal coffin of the proper size and the sexton and his assistant dug the grave early that morning. There were no mourners other than Marthe, Ninon and René – Jacques and Marthe had never become part of the village, for their English had always been poor.

Mr. Arabin had been a great comfort to Marthe, for not only was he fluent in French and conducted the service in that language, but he had arranged for the bell to be tolled once for each year of Jacques' life. Ninon had been stunned to learn that Jacques was ninety-four years of age, having been born in 1717. He and Marthe had been servants to the De Variens when she had married Louis, which had been, she was shocked to realize, over forty years ago. Where had the time gone?

Mr. Arabin had also arranged for his change ringers to ring Jacques out with a long peal. Marthe loved the bells, even though change ringing was an English art and never heard in France.

On the morning of the funeral Mrs. Parker agreed to sit with a heavily sedated Lucie so that Marthe, Ninon and René could all attend the services.

Mr. Arabin had stripped his garden of daffodils and tulips to bedeck the altar and the coffin. The service was short and touching and five paid pallbearers and René put Jacques in his final resting place while the skies streamed down. Mr. Arabin paid the pallbearers himself and officiated over the graveside services in his best white lawn surplice and orpheyed chasuble, last worn for the obsequies of the late Marquis of Lyonshall.

As he watched the coffin lowered into the wet earth René's thoughts went round and around in a circle. He was now unemployed. They now owed money to the undertaker as well as to the sexton and to the church for the plot in the cemetery. He could not let Mr. Arabin pay for that, as the Vicar had offered. And Marthe wanted a stone for Jacques. Where was the money for that to come from? Only that morning, after learning how old Jacques really was, Ninon had weepingly confided that she did not think Marthe could last much longer, for she was as nearly as old as Jacques, and already seemed far more frail that she had been just the day before. There would be another funeral to pay for, for no more than Jacques could they let Marthe go to a pauper's grave – she must lay beside her husband. It all came back to money – or rather, their severe lack of it.

And there was that woman yesterday – Lady Diana Stillfield, Simon's mother. He could not stop thinking about her and the disdain, the *hatred* – in her face. When they had worked magic together René had felt an extraordinary sense of completion, as if he had come home to a place he had never known. It had been the most amazing feeling, and he thought she had shared it. But her actions denied that. She hated him – and did not want him to teach Simon, a boy of whom he had become very fond in the short term of their acquaintance.

And that hurt, too. It was not just the loss of money, but the loss of doing something he loved to do, with someone he liked. And she hated him for no other reason other than that he was French! He didn't even *feel* French, only in that French was his native tongue and he had grown up speaking it rather than English as their lives were so isolated. He had never known any home except England, and having been raised on stories of the Inquisition and practicing magic in secrecy and fear, he had no desire to return to France, even should an agent of Bonaparte appear with a huge sack of gold. If the war ever ended he would apply for English citizenship.

A sound caught his attention – Mr. Arabin had finished reading the burial service – Marthe stepped forward to spill a handful of earth on the coffin and drop a single yellow daffodil into the grave. Ninon followed suit, and then he did so as well. The sexton and his assistant stood by to begin filling in the grave as soon as they withdrew to the Vicarage, where hot food and drink awaited them. In spite of heavy black umbrellas they were all soaking wet from the rain.

A closed carriage went by, drawn by a team of chestnut horses, but none of them looked up to see it pass.

Inside the carriage Miss Hester Mildmay looked out the rain – streaked glass. Oh, dear, was that a funeral? She scrubbed at the foggy glass with a gloved hand and recognized Mr. Roussillon. She could recognize him anywhere. She was not certain that she could identify anyone else save Mr. Arabin. She hoped it was not Mrs. De Varien who had died – that would be too sad for Mr. Roussillon and she could not bear for him to be saddened by anything.

She could remember the exact day she had fallen in love with him. It had been a September day, two years past, and she had gone into the woods to go nutting. She had nearly a full basket when she heard someone crying – a child – up ahead and was much distressed by the sound. She would have given anything to have a child of her own and she could not bear to see any child unhappy.

By the time she had, somewhat breathlessly, arrived at the scene, Mr. Roussillon was there before her, and was taking care of the problem. The little girl's kitten was up a tree. He climbed up and got the little cat down, and comforted the child.

It was his tenderness and care of the child that undid her. Piers would have ignored the child- one of the poorer tenant's children – or perhaps shot the cat out of the tree and laughed about it. But Mr. Roussillon had behaved as a true gentleman, a chivalrous gentleman, ought, and it brought home to Hester how very horrible her brother, and her life, were. That kind of care and kindness had not come her way since she was a very little girl and Sir Jason had been alive. She was as touched as if Mr. Roussillon had rescued Minou for her out of the very same tree.

Neither Mr. Roussillon nor the child saw her, hidden as she was in the shadow of the falling leaves. But the whole episode warmed her heart, a treasure to be taken out again and again when she was low in spirits. She began to look for him everywhere, particularly in church and felt excited for days afterwards on the rare occasions on which they actually exchanged words, for he was unfailingly gentleman-like and interested in the few things she could manage to say. She knew it was all a fantasy, for he would never look at her, and she could give him ten years at least. And Piers would never countenance such a match, even if a miracle should happen. Piers had the power to forbid her marriage, even at her age. If he ever found out how she felt, he would make of her life a misery. Therefore, she had never told anyone how she felt, nor even confided her passion to the pages of her diary. She suspected that Piers read it. Only at night, by herself in bed, did she dream.

She had been out this morning, in spite of the heavy rain, to buy darning thread. Piers, always impatient, had ruined several cravats and wanted them mended yesterday, in Hester's small exquisite stitches. She must match the thread herself, not entrust such a delicate errand to those lazy servants, he had declared. So on a morning when most people were snug in their homes Hester had gone into Silverbridge and completed her errand. Piers had given her just enough money to pay for the thread, no more. She could not even treat herself to a cup of tea, for her inadequate allowance was long gone – she would get no more money until the next quarter day, June 25th. If he could, Piers would have denied her even that, but dear Papa had left provision in his will for her. In these modern times, though, with everything so expensive since the war began, the amount was too little to stretch to an entire quarter, particularly if one dipped into one's reticule a little too often to help out the poor tenants.

Hester always was left at the kitchen door, for it was closer to the stables, where the coachman and the horses could shelter under the delivery overhang while she dismounted from the carriage.

After she came down from the carriage Hester went into the house through the kitchen and around to the front stairs. She would not dream of using the back stairs – the servants might think that she was spying on them. They were bad servants – insolent, lazy and sluttish, but *bad masters made bad servants* as the saying went, and Piers was certainly a bad master. Hester was certain that the servants despised her.

Unfortunately, the route to the front stairs lay past Piers' bookroom – why he called it a bookroom Hester had never been able to discern, for there were no books in it, only old copies of the *Racing Calendar*, the *Newmarket News* and the *Sportsmans' Quarterly*.

As usual the door stood slightly ajar. Piers often amused himself by leaping out at her or a servant and laughing uproariously at their fright.

Tiptoeing, and holding her breath, Hester began to cautiously edge by the door when a sudden phrase from within stopped her in her tracks.

"We'll burn the de Varien bitch tonight, boys," she heard her brother say. She heard the sound of liquid flowing into glasses and determined that there were at least two other men in their with her brother.

Hester gasped and then quickly pressed a hand to her mouth. Pray God no one had heard her!

But they were making too much noise drinking and laughing. "In about an hour Bill here will deliver a basket to their door, with a bottle of wine especially prepared for them," Piers said.

"'ow you goin' to be sure they drinks it?" asked a voice Hester did not recognize.

"They're Froggies," Piers said scornfully. "Wine is like mother's milk to them. They'll lap it up right enough – why we wouldn't be able to stop them!"

"And once they're asleep, you boys will put iron bars 'crost all of the windows, the door and over the chimney. That'll keep them in," Piers continued.

Hester was breathing so hard that she thought she might faint. Her heart was thudding away at a great rate. It was nothing less than murder, what Piers was planning!

What could she do? What could she do? The sheriff was all of the way in Knightswold. She was afraid of Lord Lyonshall – he looked at her and she couldn't speak. Piers would pay no attention to the Vicar – Piers hated him – they might even kill him too!

The only thing that she could do would be to warn them. She would have to go through the woods – Clarence would have put away the horses by now and he would not pole then up again for her – he had been none too happy to take her out in the first place, in the driving rain.

Sliding away from the bookroom door, Hester moved as quietly as possible and went through the hall into the kitchen. "I am going for a walk in the shrubbery," she announced to the slatternly cook and her helper who were beginning to make preparations for dinner.

Cook shrugged. If Miss Hester wanted to half drown herself, she was sure that she, Cook, didn't give a rap.

Hester maintained a sedate pace until she was well out of sight of the house. Once within the periphery of the woods, she broke into a run. It was dark, wet and chill even between the trees and her kid slippers were soon soaked. Heart in mouth, she ran. She could not bear it if he were killed and she never saw him again.

They had remained at the Vicarage for an hour or so after the services. The hot food and blazing fire had been welcome. But Marthe had eaten little – she had just sat, with folded hands, staring into the fire. She and Jacques had married at sixteen, she said dreamily and had never been

166

apart since. René and Ninon had exchanged worried glances. Even as they watched she seemed to be slipping away.

Reverend Arabin had taken them back to May Cottage and had taken Mrs. Parker back with him. Lucie had been a perfect angel, the Vicar's housekeeper reported.

"Little wonder that she was *une petite ange*," said Ninon, as they watched the Vicar and the housekeeper drive away in the rain "for I have dosed her so heavily that she could not be anything else. *Maintenant,* make a pot of *thé*, René, and I shall put Marthe to bed. And then you will tell me, *n'est-ce pas*, what so worries you."

When she returned from this task René had the tea made and had scribbled a few figures on a sheet of parchment. This he handed to Ninon when she sat down, "What is this – oh, I see, me. This cannot be right! All of this for the funeral simple and quiet?" she cried.

"The Reverend has said that we may pay for the gravesite as we may," said René tiredly. "But the sexton and *M'sieur le* mortician want theirs now."

"It did not cost this much when we lost your *grandpère*," said Ninon sadly. "I think –"

But what she thought was never to be uttered, for a frenzied pounding came at the door and they heard a voice crying "Run! Run! They are coming to kill you!"

"That is *Mam'selle* Mildmay!" Ninon said, jumping up from her chair.

René beat her to the door and opened it quickly. He had to catch Hester, for she nearly fell into the room "Oh, quick, oh quick!" she panted. "My brother has two of his bully boys coming to kill you and you must be gone before they get here! They are going to burn you out, with bars of iron at the windows!" She was shaking from the cold – she was sodden, with a pulpy straw bonnet hanging down over one eye.

"Sit down, *Mam'selle*," René escorted her to the table. She was on the edge of hysteria. Ninon quickly gave her the cup of tea she had just poured for herself and insisted that Hester drink it before she spoke another word.

Hester's tea chattered on the rim of the chipped cup as she sipped the scalding brew. It seemed to steady her somewhat for she was able to collect herself and tell them what she had overheard.

167

René and Ninon exchanged horrified glances over Hester's head. They might have escaped a fire, but Cold Iron over the windows and doors and chimney meant no way out, not even with magic. Cold Iron and fire were a Wizard's greatest fears.

"We must go," said Ninon abruptly. "René, the grimoires. I shall pack as much as I can."

"*Grandmère*, I think that if these persons do not find us here, they will look for us. It must appear as if we are here and have drunk the wine," René said thoughtfully. "I have a plan..."

13

Smoke and Flames

Simon ran out of doors into the pouring rain. He could not comprehend why his Mama was being so unfair. He had awakened this morning with a feeling of pleasurable anticipation – they were to experiment in Mr. Arabin's laboratory today and find out how dragons breathed fire! And now everything was all ruined.

He could think of no one to go to for comfort save Pádraig.

The Emerald dragon had just finished his breakfast and was expecting to take Simon to his lesson at the Vicarage. He was much distressed to see his little friend coming towards him, upset.

"What is it, lad?" he said, as Simon drew closer and Pádraig could see the tears mingling with the rain drops on his face.

"It's Mama!" Simon choked. "She says that I am not to have my lessons with Mr. Roussillon any more, Pádraig!"

"Why ever not?" the dragon queried in surprise. "Here, Simon, do you get beneath my wing and keep as dry as you might. 'Twill be serving as an umbrella." Pádraig brought one of his wings forward and arranged it so that Simon could crawl beneath it and still be close enough to talk.

"Because he's French!" Simon burst out. "She says that the French killed my Papa and he's one of them."

Pádraig wrinkled his brow. "But I was after thinking that he was an *émigré*. At least, that is what the Reverend's cat was after telling me. And I thought your father was a soldier on the Peninsula."

Simon nodded. "Papa was a soldier, but I don't know what an *emmy-gray* is."

"An *émigré* is being someone who escaped from the Revolution in France and was after coming to live here in England. You'll have heard of the Revolution?" Pádraig asked.

Simon had – adults talked about it constantly and worried that it could happen here in England. Most of these conversations were when they thought Simon to be out of earshot.

"I can't understand why, Pádraig, if Mr. Roussillon was here in England, why Mama thinks he had something to do with Papa's death, just because he's French!"

"Your Mama is like a lot of people, Simon – she's prejudiced because of what she thinks is true, not because of the actual truth. She thinks *all* French people are bad, because of what some of them were doing." The dragon tried to put it in terms that Simon could readily understand, and explained what he meant by 'prejudice'.

"But that's stupid!" said Simon scornfully.

"Oh, aye, it is that. Prejudice is very stupid," Pádraig agreed. "But the older you get, the more you run into it, laddie. Someone is always prejudiced against something. There are some people who are even being prejudiced against dragons."

"I think dragons are wonderful!" Simon exclaimed.

Pádraig turned his long neck and nuzzled Simon's hair. His breath was very warm and dried Simon's hair to a soft down.

"Mama says I must have another tutor," Simon continued. "Must I, Pádraig? We were to do experiments today – to find out how a dragon breathes fire."

"I'd like fine to see that myself," said the dragon rather wistfully. "But you must be after obeying your mother, Simon. And don't be giving the new tutor a hard time just because he's not Mr. Roussillon. 'Tisn't his fault. Ye'll be promising me that, Simon."

Simon sighed, but at last said, "I promise, Pádraig. But if Mama would only get to know Mr. Roussillon, I am quite sure that she would like him!"

"It's little chance of that I'm seeing," the dragon said sadly.

René's plan was very simple. They would appear to accept and drink the wine. But by the time the bully boys returned they would be gone, with as many of their goods as they could carry. And when the bully boys looked in the window, they would see René and Ninon, slumped at the table as if passed out from the drugged wine.

"But how can you do that?" Hester asked, puzzled. "How will you be able to get out in time if they are going to put iron bars across all avenues of escape?"

"We will not be here," said René. "But our images will be."

"You are to make a fetch of us!" cried Ninon.

"A fetch?" Hester asked, looking from one to the other.

"A fetch is a double," René explained. "To see one's own fetch – this means that one's death is near. But to *make* one, this is a different matter."

"What shall you use, René? Straw?" Ninon asked.

"We haven't enough. I shall use our sha-dows." With this he turned to the fireplace and, stretching out his hands, made it blaze up higher than normal.

Hester watched in fascination as René and Ninon stood directly in front of the fire. On the opposite wall their shadows showed, long and wavering. At a gesture from René the shadows shrank and were still, waiting until they were needed.

"Now we will pack everything we are able to do and we shall remove *Maman* and Marthe from the house and into the woods," he said. "We would be grateful for any assistance, *Mam'selle* Hester, though you have already done so much for us today."

"I'm very good at packing," she offered. "I help the Reverend pack up the poor boxes quite often."

Indeed, she proved remarkably adept and thought to pack things that Ninon would have forgotten. Everything was tied up in blankets and sheets. Hester insisted on Ninon taking her jars of herbs – it was Hester who put them in a large basket. As the women packed quickly, René carried the bundles and the trunk of grimoires (to which was added the silver cauldron) into the woods behind the cottage, hidden by the thick growth of trees. Then he carried both Lucie and

Marthe out of doors. Even bundled in blankets they would get wet, but there was no helping it.

Then they waited for the basket of wine to be delivered.

It was not long in coming. There was a quick rap at the door and Ninon answered it. No one was there, but a basket with a well-wrapped bottle sat on the threshold.

"Oh, what is this?" Ninon cried in a loud voice for the benefit of anyone who might be watching. She unwrapped the bottle and gave a glad exclamation.

"Some kind person has given us a fine *bouteille du vin!* René, get the glasses! We shall have some *maintenant!*" She felt like sticking out her tongue at the unseen watcher. Hester had told her about the 'mother's milk' remark from Piers.

She brought the wine in and put it on the table. "It is a fine *Côtes du Rhône,*" she said wistfully. It had probably been brought in by smugglers. "Could I not purify it with my unicorn horn and we could have at least a small glass?"

"There is no time, *Grandmère,*" said René. He uncorked the bottle and sniffed. "Laudanum. They will expect it to be quick to put us to sleep, *non*? We must ready the fetches."

He went to his shadow image and stretched out his fingers towards its dark hands. Their fingertips met and violet light flowed. Within moments there was a tenebrous image of himself. Close up, no one, unless drunk, would mistake the image for the real thing, but through a window, in a dimly lit room, it would pass. Ninon did the same thing to her shadow, then they pushed the fetches by judiciously applied magic, to the table and arranged then to look as if they had been drinking and fallen into unconsciousness. Two glasses were filled and one tipped over and the bottle left in the middle of the table.

Ninon surveyed these preparations in satisfaction. "There is someone watching, I think, since the basket has come."

"But won't they have seen us through the window?" protested Hester. The windows were not covered, only edged by skimpy curtains.

172

"They have only seen want we wished them to see *à travers la fenêtre* – through the window," said Ninon. "We will go out the little back door and *voilà*, we make the *reculer pour mieux sauter.*"

"Tactical retreat," René translated for Hester, as Miss Mildmay looked bewildered.

He took a quick look around the room to see if they had left anything essential. There had been remarkably little to pack, for they owned little. A change of clothing, the grimoires, a few magical supplies, a handful of books, some linens and cook pots and Ninon's herbs – that was the sum of it. Quickly, he ushered the two ladies out the door. The curtain was pulled around Lucie's corner – no one could see into it. The last things he did were to dim the fire and the candles and to lift the concealment spell from the windows, long in place for privacy's sake.

They retreated into the forest where Marthe and Lucie, both sleeping, were with the pile of their belongings.

The rain still fell heavily. Under a cedar tree, where René had left the two women and their household goods, it was relatively dry, but he worried about the health of his charges. And *Mam'selle* Mildmay –.

"You must return to your home at once!" he said urgently to Hester. "If your brother should find you here, or know that you have helped us, it will be the worse for you! And after your kindness today, we could not bear that you should suffer."

Even as Hester paled at the thought of what Piers would do to her if he ever learned she had spoiled his plans, she warmed to the concern in his voice. "I wish that I could stay," she said regretfully.

"*Non*," said René "you have done more than we may ever be able to thank you for, *Mam'selle* Hester." He took her hands in his and raised it to his lips. "*Merci bien. Vous êtes très getil. Je vous suis très reconnaissant.* I will never forget you."

Hester was in alt. Star-eyed, she looked at him as if he were her knight in shining armor.

"Go!" cried Ninon impatiently. The woman would stand there all afternoon mooning at René if someone did not do something!

Startled, Hester broke from her trance and scuttled off deeper into the woods so that no one would see her.

A quarter of an hour passed in which they shivered in the rain and waited. Lucie and Marthe were oblivious to all that was happening.

At last, when the tension was nearly unbearable, they heard the men come.

Loud rough voices – the smell of something pungent – axel grease perhaps – the clank of iron, the thud on the wet wood of the window and doorsills as the Cold Iron was put into place – a great whoosh of sound as fire caught hold – laughter, loud and cruel.

Ninon shivered, not only from the rain that seemed to be dripping down her back. Those men were committing murder! Did it not give then pause? Were they so dead to all claim on common humanity? And to be so hated by Sir Piers that he wanted them permanently removed! All because she had refused to become Sir Piers' mistress all those years ago?

René could hear the crackle of the flames as they caught. They had used something to make the fire catch quickly in this rain – probably grease on the door and windowsills. Even through the rain drenched wood he could see a glow where the cottage stood.

It suddenly struck him. Where were they going to go? The only home he had ever known was even now burning beyond the hope of rescue. It would be some little while before any of the villagers arrived to fight the fire, for sighting it would be the only warning they would get.

Sighting it! Struck by a sudden notion, René reached out with his magic and caused the fire to flare up higher. There was a great explosion and the sounds of screaming as someone who was too close was singed. Now he could see a lurid incandescence against which the trees in front of them appeared as black silhouettes. Acrid, dark grey smoke poured up into the rain, a solid column marking the site of destruction. The blaze roared and the sound of timbers and stones falling inwards was heard.

There was something satisfying in the destruction, something that pacified the anger that had been growing in him since yesterday. If they wanted a fire he would give them one that they would remember all of their days!

Several miles away, Sir Piers saw the smoke and smiled in satisfaction. As much as he would have liked to set the torch to the cottage himself, he could not risk it. But the sight of that smoke was so gratifying – that damned bitch was burning! Never again would he have to see her insolent face or see the contempt in her eyes. She would never call him 'pig person' again, or act as if she was so superior to him. He could pull down the remains of May Cottage, rebuild and put in a paying tenant.

He poured himself another drink of brandy that, true to the Vicar's suspicions, had never been scrutinized by a Customs officer. It bothered him not at all that he had killed three others as well. What did it matter? They were Froggies – the world was far better off without those French parasites. It had been a good day's work. And as for those bully boys from London – he had already arranged that they be taken up by his gamekeeper as poachers. They had no future except as remands to Botany Bay, where they would be unable to peach on him. Anything they said could be taken as attempted revenge, or the ravings of disaffected criminals.

From the window of her bedchamber Hester could see the column of smoke. Oh, thank God that they had been able to get out! She had hurried home and out of her wet things, enduring a scolding from her maid, who was upset that she would have to clean what had become little more than limp rags. Now, wrapped in her dressing gown and a blanket, Hester sat in the window seat and thought again how he had kissed her hand. She lay this member against her cheek, remembering the warmth in his silver eyes and his voice as he thanked her – she recalled enough of her schoolgirl French to know that she had been thanked and told she was very kind. And that he would never forget her.

From the top of his tower Lyon first smelled the smoke and then saw it, with the help of a spyglass he kept in his laboratory. Through the steadily increasing rain it was not obvious from where it came – somewhere on the other side of the village. He thought he had heard a rumble of thunder – the first of the year – perhaps some poor fellow's barn had been struck by lightning. Those were Sir Piers' tenants in that direction. None-the-less, he thought, putting away the spyglass, if the Vicar came to him with a sad story of want and misery, he would put his hand in his pocket again. Sir Piers was as sorry an excuse for a landlord as he was for a human being. Lyon had taken him in dislike on the occasion of their very first meeting. Too long had Mildmay had played the petty tyrant here about. It was time for the unamiable baronet to learn a few lessons. And one of the first lessons that he was going to learn was that one did not play fast and loose with the lives of people for whom one was supposed to be responsible. As a Magistrate Sir Piers had used his office to rid himself of recalcitrant tenants on trumped-up charges. As Lord Lieutenant Lyon had the power to appoint – or unappoint – magistrates within the confines of the county and the paper work was already underway to remove Sir Piers from the bench.

He glanced across the laboratory to where Mag Uidhir had set up a temporary desk. If only he could find a secretary like that one! Conchobar had all the luck! Lyon had asked for the continued loan of Diarmiat's services but Conchobar had declared that, in spite of the present crisis, he could not spare Mag Uidhir beyond the end of the week, when he himself would be returning to Érui after the conclave. Lyon had inserted an advertisement in the *Wizards' Times* without a great deal of hope. His lack of hope had been justified – he had had two replies – both from certifiable idiots. Already the work was piling up – he was kept busy answering letters and it seemed that there was always someone scrying him demanding explanations that he did not have. In the short time since Myfanwy's death no progress had been made in bringing her killer to justice. Only two chilling facts had emerged from Bow Street's investigation – she had been killed by blood magic and her soul had been stolen.

There had been no blood magic used in Britain for nearly five hundred years – and it had been rare before that. The penalties, laid down by Merlin, were severe. Blood magic was bad enough but to steal a soul on top of that – it was unheard of!

This last fact had been kept out of the news-sheets. There would be mass panic if that ever got out. To have one's soul taken – with no hope of Heaven! It did not bear thinking of – for it was not only a Wizard, a Witch or a Druid who could be purged of their souls. Anyone could be completely annihilated.

And of top of that there was the problem of the Redcaps and others like him. It seemed every hour saw a report of some Unselighe creature attacking or killing someone, somewhere in the British Isles. How had they torn a rent in the binding? The news-sheets were already saying that not enough was being done to protect citizens form this menace. And what could be done? They had no idea where the creatures were getting in. A map of the British Isles hung on the wall of the laboratory. For each report of an Unselighe creature a pin had been put at the location. They were in the process of devising security measures for the non-magical folk. And Lyon had realized something – what he had worried about was coming true – there were too few Wizards because of the policies formed by this idiotish government. And too many of these Wizards merely played at magic, and were of little real use.

On his desk lay the notes he had scribbled after talking to Guénolé Cornouaille in Brittany and Roussillon's comments on dematerialization, including some mathematics which Lyon, no arithmetician, strongly suspected to be physics on a very high level. He had not even had a chance to look these over, much less try to use them. And how he wanted to use those notes!

From out in the stable yard Pádraig smelled the smoke and then, with his long dragon sight, saw it. He lifted Simon up onto his back so that the boy might see. "Perhaps someone is having a bonfire for Beltaine," was Simon's thought.

"A little early for Beltaine, I'm thinking," said the dragon. "No, laddie, if we were in Dubh Linn it's hearing the fire engines we'd be, with the bells ringing and the clatter of the shod hooves on the paving stones. I wonder what might be is burning."

Diana, up on the second floor conferring with the men who had come with the new papers for the walls, (after overseeing the placement of the new mourning accouterments) saw the column of smoke and wondered at it. She knew by the direction that it was probably the home or barn of one of Sir Piers' unfortunate tenants. She would have to go to see Mr. Arabin this afternoon and find out if anything was needed. She intended to see the Vicar at any rate – she had a quarrel to pick out with him about that Frenchman.

The Duke of Chenevix regarded the fire as just another manifestation of the rigors of living in the proximity of Eliot Lyons. If the wind began to blow to the west, they would be able to smell it and his sleep would no doubt be disturbed, for it was of a size and smokiness that it could easily go all of the day and into the night.

Mr. Arabin, with a sick feeling in his stomach and dread in his heart, saw the smoke and prayed that everyone had gotten out safely. He directed Tim to put Chocolate in the dog cart and gathered extra blankets, foodstuffs and whatever comforts he could find in the Parish Hall. He was afraid that this was only the bad beginning of the trouble for anyone who had suffered a burn-out. Sir Piers, a very bad landlord, would do nothing for any tenant that was made homeless by a fire. In fact, he would try to find a way to place the blame squarely on the tenant's shoulders. Fire was an ongoing hazard in the country – particularly in the homes of the non-magical who had to rely upon open flames for heat and light.

And it was such a fire – in spite of the still steady rain the flames leaped high and the smoke rolled in huge clouds. Something like this could put a family on Parish Relief with little possibility of ever recovering enough to be dropped from the rolls. He would do what he could but it would not be enough. He said a prayer as he drove out into the rain that the fire would not spread to the forest and cause even more misery and destruction.

14

From Bad To Worse

Mr. Arabin was horrified when he arrived at the other side of Silverbridge. The entire village had been roused and even as he pulled up in front of a burning May Cottage, a bucket brigade was attempting to quench enormous flames and huge clouds of smoke. He sat in the dog cart, hands slack on the reins, feeling the blood drain from his brain and the world close in around him. "No, oh, no!" he whispered. "They must have got out – their magic alone would have –"
He could neither comprehend or believe the fact that his friends might have perished, but a rapid scan of the people gathered to put out and watch the fire did not reveal any of them.

In such a scene of frenzied activity no one had noticed his arrival. He shot into the air like a scalded cat when a hand touched his shoulder and someone said softly, almost in his ear, "Do not turn around."

"René!" he said joyfully, recognizing the voice at once. "My dear boy! Are you all safe?" In spite of his relief, he obeyed the command of his young friend and continued to look at the remains of the cottage as the fire began to subside.

"We are safe for the moment, but we need your help," came René's voice. "Are you able to drive this carriage into the woods?"

"Oh, yes, I've used it for nutting expeditions with the young people and unless the trees are quite close together..." answered the Vicar.

"*Très bien*. Does anyone look this way?"

179

"No, everyone's attention appears to be on the fire. My dear boy, why all of this secrecy?" the Reverend was puzzled.

"I will tell you why once we are with my family," René promised. He slid around the side of the dog cart, so that he could not be seen by the crowd. Taking Chocolate by the reins near her bit, he turned her slowly and led her into the woods. Once the concealment of the forest was about them, he swung up into the high seat of the dog cart beside Mr. Arabin. Silently, the Vicar handed over the reins.

As they threaded their way through the trees René quietly told the Vicar what had happened.

Mr. Arabin was at first speechless. His nature could not comprehend such evil. "But that is *murder!*" he whispered at last. "We must go to the sheriff, or to Lord Lyonshall at once and swear out a warrant for Sir Piers' arrest!"

"And who will believe it?" said René savagely. "He is a landowner – we are poor *émigrés* – you yourself know that we would be disregarded."

"But Miss Mildmay can attest –" the Vicar began eagerly.

"*Non.*" René shook his head. "If the judgment of the court is with her brother, he will probably kill her. She is much afraid of him."

"I am reasonably certain that he beats her," said the Vicar sadly.

René's hands tightened on the reins. "Why is such a one allowed to exist?" he burst out. "My *Grandmère* calls him a pig person –"

"And she is wrong to do so," said the Vicar. "The pig is a good, useful creature, which is more than I can say for Sir Piers!"

Chocolate's ears went straight up. She flung up her head and snorted, coming to a stop. Something was coming towards them through the forest, crashing blindly through the brush.

A few minutes later Ninon burst into sight. She looked like a wild woman with twigs and leaves in her hair, a distraught look on her face. "Oh, René!" she cried in rapid French. "It is Marthe! She has died! She sat up and looked at me and then looked beyond me and smiled. She held out her arms and said so happily, 'Jacques! I knew you would come

180

for me! You are so young and handsome, just as I remember!"
And then she fell over, dead! There was nothing I could do!"

René jumped from the trap and took her in his arms. Her frail body shook with sobs and he comforted her as best he could. Too much had happened in the last few days. He had never thought to see his indomitable grandmother in such a state. His own emotions were no less tempestuous. In the space of two days time everything had changed and not for the better. They had lost both Jacques and Marthe, who had always been a kind, helpful presence in their lives. He had lost the only lucrative employment he had ever had. And today they had lost their home. *What was next?* he wondered bleakly.

"Where are Lucie and Marthe?" Reverend Arabin asked gently. "They must be got out of the rain." It had begun to rain harder again, as if to underscore their misery and grief.

Ninon, lacking a handkerchief, scrubbed at her cheeks with her sleeve, which as it was soaking wet, did little good. "Not far from here – *viens avec moi.*"

They followed her closely. Reverend Arabin dismounted from the dog cart and led Chocolate through the trees as the trees and brush grew more dense.

It was dark in the wood and damp. Somehow the woods did not seem as friendly or as welcoming as they usually did. It was a place of cold and wet shadows with dripping trees and a cold wind. Reverend Arabin, comfortable in hat, gaiters and snug rain cloak, was concerned for his friends – they were all saturated with rain and needed to get warm and dry before they took chills.

They found Lucie sleeping quietly and deeply, for Ninon had dosed her heavily. Marthe lay as she had fallen, with a smile of peace and joy on her face. Mr. Arabin said a blessing over her as Ninon straightened her limbs. "Why do we not make a magical catafalque for Marthe," the Vicar suggested. "It will protect her until the mortician can be brought here. We will send for him once I have conveyed you to the Vicarage."

"*Je vais rester ici, avec Marthe,*" said René.

"You shall do no such thing," said the Vicar firmly. "If she is properly enshrouded there is no need for anyone to stay

— she will be quite safe until I return with Mr. Putney. *You*, my dear boy, will get yourself warm and dry at the Vicarage, as will your grandmother and mother. Now if you will be so good as to lift Marthe for me and create the scaffolding, I shall shroud her."

In a few moments it was done – Marthe lay on a pulsing violet platform, a little above the forest floor, draped in soft folds of shining, opaque blue. She looked completely at peace.

René gently placed his mother in the dog cart while Mr. Arabin, with Ninon's help, stored the pitifully small amount of their household goods in the slat ventilated compartment beneath the seat, which normally would contain dogs, carried between shooting coverts. The two-wheeled dog cart carried four, with the additional passengers facing the rear, with their feet resting on the lower end-gate. René sat there, and held Lucie, while Ninon tool her place beside the Vicar. They left the small clearing behind, the glow of Marthe's catafalque fading as the trees shut it away from their view.

Shortly after noon it stopped raining and a watery sun made a determined effort to come out and dry everything off.

Off in the distance from the Abbey the great blaze and tower of smoke had at last died down. Only the finest wisps of smoke still hung in the air.

No news had as yet come from the village, save that it had been a cottage that caught fire. No one yet knew the how or why or even who, but that information would be forth-coming before long, *via* the village grapevine that operated even more efficiently than did Lord Wellington's finest spy network on the Peninsula.

Diana was at last finished with her preparations for the coming Druidic conclave. There were more than enough rooms and stabling for any sort of creature.There were extra servants and plenty of food prepared and stored. The house shone with cleanliness – Diana had even cleaned off the table in the front hall where Uncle Lyon tossed everything when he came in – it now gleamed with polish and a brass bowl of spring flowers had replaced the bag of dragon treats. Proper mourning – a hatchment on the door, a mourning wreath and all of the mirrors covered in black crepe – had been hung. All of the household wore black armbands and she would wear black gloves to dinner.

The preparations for the Beltaine festival were well on track as well – it would be a much more subdued festival than Lyon had envisioned. Knowing that there would not be time to prepare it this year, Lady Eastcote had sent her daughter five cases of woodruff wine by dragon courier. Next year, Diana vowed, she would prepare her own. She had already brewed the honey mead for Lammas in August; it would not age as long as she would like – six months was best – but it would be tolerable. The ritual wines were a very important part of Celtic celebrations and the mistress of the house, or the highest ranking Witch of the household, was expected to brew these her own self. Tomorrow, she and Cook were going to gather violets and candy them – they were a traditional part of the Beltaine feast – a taste of spring. Perhaps that would be something Simon might be interested in. There was a coolness between them at the moment. He had been very quiet at luncheon. As she had suspected, he had spent the morning with the dragon.

As soon as was possible she would hire a new tutor – an *English* tutor – for Simon. She had spent part of the morning scrying several agencies in London, outlining what she was looking for. She had been promised replies by return post, as she wished to examine references and *curriculum vitae* before scheduling any interviews.

Since it was drying out rapidly as the sun shone brighter, and the local Road Wizard would have dried the mud as soon as the rain ceased and a brisk breeze dispatched the last remnants of the storm clouds, Diana decided to ride her mare to the Vicarage. She had not had the chance to ride since arriving at the Abbey and Luna, although she was being exercised by the groom, was probably longing for a good gallop. The fresh air and exercise would sweep the cobwebs away.

Diana's slumbers had been disturbed the night before by nightmares. She kept dreaming about *him* – the look on his face when they made magic together, the way his expression had changed from wonder to puzzled, and then to cold and hard – this much exaggerated in the dream. She had awoken from this dream tangled in her nightgown and bed clothes, and had scarcely shaken it off when she fell back into an uneasy sleep.

The next dream was far worse – it began with a feeling of suffocating horror. Everything she saw was black and red, but formless and seemed to be reaching out for her, intent on some incredible harm. In the red she could sometimes see faces – filled with unbearable despair. She awoke from this with a shudder, drenched in a cold sweat. She had been afraid to go back to sleep, and risen from bed to wash and change her nightgown. Building up the fire, and lighting a mage light, she had sat up in a chair, with a volume of Mr. Wordsworth's poetry. Just before dawn, she had returned to bed, this time to sleep dreamlessly.

But on awaking the first thing she remembered was that elderly woman, begging, "...do not let Jacques be buried in the pauper's cemetery!" Diana did her best to purge this memory – and the others – from her memory, but found it nearly impossible. At last she resolved to give Mr. Arabin some money so that the dead man could at least be buried decently.

There was a warm breeze blowing and the sun shone benignly when at last she set out on Luna. The mare was curveting as one of the grooms threw Diana up into the sidesaddle. Diana wore her new riding habit of dark blue broadcloth. It was severely cut, worn with a veiled beaver hat and lacked the fashionable military-like braiding and shako cap that was currently so popular. She had not been able to bear the thought of a habit cut *à la hussar*.

Once clear of the Abbey, she let the impatient Luna have her head and they galloped *ventre à terre* for well over a mile. There was no one else on the road and it felt marvelous to go so fast. When she at last pulled Luna up, they were both breathing fast, but were well satisfied with themselves.

The Vicarage was soon reached after that. She slipped off unaided and tied Luna to the gate, feeling the mare carefully on neck and belly, to make certain that she was cool enough to stand.

Hearing a voice saying "Oh, dear, oh, dear!" from the direction of the Church Diana headed there, rather than knocking on the door of the Vicarage.

She found Mr. Arabin at the east end of the church, in the apse, looking over floral arrangments of daffodils, primroses and branches of flowering trees, which were at the foot of the altar and on the lattice of the chancel. He looked rather harassed and said in some relief as she came closer, "On, Lady Diana! Thank goodness it is you! For one horrible moment I thought that either Mrs. Chambers or Mrs. Maynard was come back to continue their – er – *discourse* on whose flowers ought to be nearest the altar! They are very good in keeping the church well supplied with flowers, but there is an undoubted rivalry which can become most vexing!"

"I have hopes of being able to supply the church with flowers as well, by the latter part of the summer," she said, "and once we have the succession house in proper order we shall have floral offerings all year round."

"That will be very kind in you, to be sure," said the Vicar gratefully. "And since naturally, any flowers from the Abbey must take precedence, that will solve the problem of Mrs. Chambers and Mrs. Maynard."

"And now, Lady Diana, is there something that I might do for you? You came to see me of a purpose, did you not?" he continued.

"I am more than a little upset, sir, that you were so misguided as to recommend a Frenchman to be Simon's tutor," Diana said.

'Misguided!" exclaimed the Vicar. "My dear young lady, Simon could not have a better tutor, French or no! And what does his nationality matter, pray?'

"Simon's father was murdered by the French!" Diana returned heatedly. "You cannot expect me to accept with any degree of equanimity –"

His look grew severe. "I expect a spirit of Christian charity! You have no doubt been told that René – a young man as dear to me as a son – is a refugee from the late excesses in France. He has never fought with Napoleon's forces in the Peninsula, nor expressed any desire to serve the Corsican monster in any way whatsoever! And anyone, seeing the poverty in which they live, could not be so cloth-headed as to assume he is in the pay of the French as a spy. What would he spy upon, pray, in this neighborhood – we have not even a military encampment within an easy distance!"

He stopped for a moment. His face was flushed and he was breathing rather heavily. Diana could never had imagined the mild Vicar could be so incensed. "And," he burst into speech once more, "it is my understanding that your late husband was a serving soldier and was killed whilst on duty in the Peninsula. That scarcely qualifies as murder!"

"I do not wish Simon exposed to Papist beliefs –" she began.

"Papist!" Mr. Arabin cried. "Lady Diana, you labor beneath a mountain of delusions! René and his family were Huguenots in France and are now full communicants of St Swithin's and subscribe to the Thirty-Nine articles just as you do! René can repeat the catechism as well as you can yourself, I daresay! If fact, at one time, he intended to take Holy Orders, until it became readily apparent that prejudiced persons, such as yourself, would never accept a French Anglican clergyman! And now, Lady Diana, in case you had not heard, it was René's home that burned this morning, through no fault of their own, and he and his grandmother and mother, of whom he is the sole support, are left homeless, with no income and probably no choice but to go on the Parish. And I hope you are satisfied!"

With this Parthian shot he stamped away, leaving her staring after him in consternation.

When René awoke he could not imagine where he was at first. The bed was soft and pillows deep. Somewhere a clock had just chimed three, and judging by the sunlight pouring in the window it was three in the afternoon, not three in the morning. The window was open slightly – a fresh breeze blew the filmy white curtains into the room. It was a small, neat room, containing just a tester bed, a washstand a wardrobe and a tiny desk and chair, but it was far nicer than he was used to, and for a minute he thought that he was dreaming.

But the events of the day rushed over him in a huge wave of depression and despair. He was in one of the Vicarage spare rooms. May Cottage had burned down. Marthe had died. Yesterday Jacques had died and he himself had been sacked. *Maman* seemed to be getting worse. Things had never been so bad.

At this thought he almost groaned aloud, but was saved by a gentle tapping at the door. "*Entrez*," he called.

Reverend Arabin poked his head in around the edge of the door. "Am I disturbing you, my dear boy? I looked in earlier but you were sleeping so nicely that I did not care to wake you. I daresay you could do with a cup of tea. Mrs. Parker has baked your favorite rock cakes." His head disappeared: René heard a clinking of china and the Vicar reappeared with a tea tray. "No, don't get up!" he said hastily as René lifted the covers. "If you will but sit up against the pillows – ah, that is it!" He set the tea tray on his young friend's lap. The Vicar then pulled the chair out from the desk to sit by the bedside.

There were two cups on the tray and René poured a cup for the Vicar – and added lemon and three lumps of sugar. His own cup was left plain, for milk and sugar were scarce commodities in his home and he had always thought it best no tot become used to such luxuries. The rock cakes – still warm from the oven! – proved too tempting to resist.

The Vicar accepted his cup with a sigh of thanks. "I have given a great deal of thought to your situation and believe that I may have a solution."

"We cannot stay here," said René quickly.

"You are most welcome to stay here," Mr. Arabin said equally quickly. "But I have spoken to your grandmama, my dear boy, and I am forced to agree with her – this will not do for your Mama. She is much disturbed by the noise and people coming and going. I cancelled the classes of my young gentlemen this morning, but there are countless people in and about the church and the Vicarage in a steady stream, from persons with problems to ladies delivering flowers. Your Mama must have quiet. So I took it upon myself to find you a different situation."

He drained his cup and sighed, absent-mindedly holding it out for more tea. René obliged.

"A se'enight ago, one of my parishioners came to me with a problem. You probably do not know him, for he lives on th extreme Cotswold side of the Abbey lands. It would have been too far for you to go to look for work, and at any rate, I

187

believe Wilkins warned you off the Abbey lands, did he not? This man I am talking about is a farmer, by name James Cerne, and farms a little under two hundred acres. He was treated very badly by the old lord's agent and nearly ruined. He is looking for a cow-man. Would you be willing to work as a permanent farm laborer? There would be a cottage, no doubt, and usually board is included. I hear that his wife, Sarah, is an excellent cook. I know that it is not what you would like, to be sure. Cerne is having trouble finding someone, because he can pay very little and whoever takes the job will have to do a dairy maid's duties and probably a ploughman's duties as well. And, you must know, the men here-about would never consent to do a female's tasks! So Cerne is rather desperate."

René put down his half-eaten rock cake. It was not what he would have chosen. It was not even what he liked. But it was work – and perhaps a place to live. And that was an imperative need.

"I shall talk to this *M'sieur* Cerne," he said. "But I have not had much to do with the cows."

"You are not offended?" the Vicar's face, which had grown steadily longer since he began telling René about the farmer, cleared. "You can talk to him immediately, I took the liberty of sending Plato to him with a note, telling him that I might have the solution to his problem. He is below in the kitchen with Mrs. Parker at this very moment. Do you get dressed and come belowstairs and discuss this with him."

James Cerne proved to be a young man of a little over thirty, of medium height and a sturdy frame. His face was plain, but honest beneath a shock of unruly brown hair and his handshake firm. He wore rough work clothes – smock and gaiters over coarse linen trousers and shirt, but they were clean and well cared for, and the smock beautifully embroidered.

They sat at the kitchen table where Cerne felt more comfortable. "I'll be frank wi' ye," he said to René when the Vicar had introduced the two young men. "'Tis a hard job I'm offerin'. There's no one to work th' farm 'ceptin' me, m'wife Sarah and my young brother. An' we're at it from mornin' to night. Times past, I had the brass t' have two girls in th' dairy, a girl in th' kitchen, a ploughman an' a cowman, an' a shepherd. too. That bedamned agent o' his old Lordship's – sorry, Vicar - bled me white with rents an' fines an' tithes til I was near bankrupt. An' I had bad mastics in th' milch cows an' scours in th' calves an' that Wilkins put it about that my milk was no good. He wanted my farm for his nevvy, d'ye see, and even set the fields aflame onct. I just ain't got th' brass t' hire all the folks I need, not until I gets back on m' feet. Can't find no one who's willin' t' be a cow-man, dairy maid, shepherd, ploughman an' work hisself into th' grave for what I has t' offer. But I got to have somebody! 'Tis four shillin's th' week, and there's a place we can fix up for ye, an' ye'll take your meals wi' us. My Sarah's a champion cook an' th' food is good and there's plenty of it."

It was the food that decided René. Four shillings was very little – it would take him five weeks to earn what he would have made in one week teaching Simon. And he knew how hard farm work was – he would start at cockcrow and work probably until dusk, six, or even seven days a week. But to have two or maybe even three good meals a day, every day – that was worth it.

"When would you like for me to begin, *M'sieur* Cerne?" he said.

James Cerne's solemn face lit up. "None o' that Mister Cerne – I'm Jim. And you're Reny, the parson tells me. D'you have a wife, Reny?"

René did not bother to correct his pronunciation. "I have a grandmother and a mother. My mother is an invalid – my grandmother tends her."

"That's rough – m' Sarah's mother lives wi' us, but she's a tough old bird."

"I must know, *M'sieur* Cerne – Jim – do you not mind that I am French?" René did not want a repeat of what had just happened.

"I don't care is you was a Hottentot an' a heathen to boot," said Jim Cerne. "If ye be willin' t' work hard an' treat me right , I'll treat you right. Soon as I get on m' feet, there'll be more money in it for ye, that I promise in front of Vicar here, an' here's my hand on it."

They shook hands on the bargain and arranged that René and his family should come out to the farm the day after the next, for Marthe was to be buried on the morrow.

Shortly after ten, the Duke of Chenevix had shown up in Lyon's Tower, and had politely, but quite firmly, demanded to see the reports of the latest Unselighe incidents. Just that morning there had been reports from Scotland of the shapeless Brollachan, from Man where the Cabyll-Ushtey, the exceedingly dangerous water – horse, had destroyed a fishing boat and all her crew and in the Highlands of Scotland the Boabhan Sith, the very evil succubus had appeared. The day before had seen Phoukas in Dublin, while nixies had drowned two young men in Essex. Two Wizards, *Magus Majorii*, had been murdered in Cornwall, and three *Majorii* in Devon, their souls stolen. The situation was bleak and getting bleaker. Lyon's temper was not improved by the Duke, sitting at a small desk, in formal attitude, reading reports of horrors with no expression at all on his cold face. Personally, Lyon felt that the Duke was more than an icicle – he was an enormous glacier, capable of freezing an entire room to death.

With the Duke had come his officious man-servant – Mariposa, whom Lyon found as irritating as his master.

Mariposa might have been thought by most to be a strange valet for a fastidious Englishman like the Duke, for Mariposa was a colourful, if not actually flamboyant individual. He was on the short side, with a tendency to *avoirdupois* and a round face, with darting black eyes like raisins set in golden dough. His hair, what there was left of it, curled naturally. When he smiled, a gold tooth showed and he wore a gold earring in his right ear. His always wore a lush red cravat and rather florid waistcoats. In short, he looked like a Spanish gypsy. His ancestry *was* Spanish – his ancestors had come to England in the train of Katherine of Aragon in the sixteenth century.

But his name and appearance were the only things Spanish about him. Mariposa had been born in London, within the sound of Bow Bells, and had worked hard to rid himself of his Cockney accent. It might have been thought that one as conservative as was the Duke would not have stood for a manservant so *outré*, but Mariposa was a genius, for one, with the Duke's clothing. No one else, save perhaps

190

Mr. Brummel, had linen of such a pristine whiteness, well-pressed coats, or such shiny Hessian boots. Mariposa also ran his master's nine properties with an iron hand and the Duke wanted for nothing. The finest of everything was at his command – instantly. This was helped by his great wealth (he was richer than 'Golden' Ball Hughes, it was whispered) but also Mariposa's skill at anticipating his master's every desire or whim. Mariposa was an able a *factotum* as the legendary Figaro of the Beaumarchais play.

Lyon fidgeted with the sheaf of notes in his hand, He had informed the Duke of the existence of the Breton Druids and the reaction had been a raised eyebrow. Lyon could hardly wait for the others to arrive – he would enjoy the looks of wonder and awe on the faces of Iain McAslan and Pengelly Tregaron! They wouldn't act as if they'd been informed of something mundane, such as their bath being ready. They'd be eager to discuss what this meant – and to wait with bated breath for the conference he had set up for tomorrow evening with Guénolé Cornouaille. It was like waiting for Christmas when one was a child – Lyon wanted to show off dematerialization. But *he* wanted to be the one to dematerialize – not Roussillon! When told of this – the most exciting thing to happen in magic in hundreds of years! – Chenevix had politely yawned in Lyon's face and said "Are you suffering from heat stroke so early in the year, Lyonshall? Or perhaps the pressure of being Arch Druid – after such a *little* time, too! – have become too much for you? Such a thing is impossible. I don not believe in Faerie stories. They are for children."

Scowling at the Duke from across the room, Lyon gave a great "Humph!" and fell to studying the notes he had written on the process of dematerialization. He had even copied them out neatly in his best script, in hopes that he might imprint them on his brain and thus understand them better. So far it was to no avail. Roussillon insisted that teleporting as he called it, was a bend of the mind, not a real spell, and allowed a letting go of perceived notions of reality. Although what the Devil he meant by that, Lyon did not know.

Tomorrow was the conclave. The others would be arriving first thing in the morning. The most important thing on the agenda was this threat from the Unselighe Court. They still had no idea who or what was using blood magic. The soul stealing aspect had been kept quiet, avoiding a widespread panic. But they had to do something – and soon.

The Awakening

Moonlight, bright and white, shone down upon the tangled mass of the Abbey garden. It was so brilliant that Diana could see the progress the gardeners had made in clearing away the overgrowth of years. A fountain had been found beneath the entwined vines – a mermaid in a scallop shell sat in the middle of the fount; she was designed to have water pour from a Triton shell she held in her hand. The fountain, at this moment, did not work, but the mermaid had been scrubbed clean – she proved to be made of white marble – and she now shone with a pearly glitter in the intense moonlight. As yet no flowers bloomed near her fountain, but a vast quantity of rose canes had been trimmed away, revealing living plants beneath the dead canes and one day soon the fountain garden would be full of the heady scent of roses.

Tonight the air was smelled of freshly turned earth. Diana drew in a deep breath from the open window.

It was very late. Everyone and everything else lay deep in slumber.

She had dreamed again – the same dreams as the other night. One made her feel guilty, the other terrified her. She felt guilty, for to dream about *him* was to betray Jonathan. And the formless terror in the second dream left her with a feeling that there was something important that she ought to be remembering, but the memory hung just beyond her grasp. It took some little while to get back to sleep, for she was deeply disturbed by both dreams.

She thought back to the encounter with the Vicar the other afternoon. She could never have imagined gentle Mr.

Arabin so incensed. His views corresponded with those of her uncle on the subject of the Frenchman. The only one who agreed with her opinion was the Duke of Chenevix. And her overall opinion of the Duke was not such that she rejoiced in his sharing her stance. He was maddening, demanding and fussy.

She was seated in the window seat, knees drawn up to her chin, hands clasped about her knees. Her bare toes were tucked into the folds of her velvet dressing gown. She rested her head against he cool glass of the window. It felt good, for she had awakened hot and flushed with pulses pounding.

Had she been unfair? Was she wrong? She conceded that the Vicar had been right about one thing – she was guilty of false assumptions. She had not bothered to check her facts and if she had thought about it, in a calm, rational fashion she would have realized that a Catholic, of course, would probably not be practicing magic. The Catholic Church was very set against the practice of even white magic. No one who practiced sorcery, as they called it, could make the sacraments of the Church. And the Inquisition had Witch-Sniffers who would make certain of that.

But she could not change her mind now – nor did she want to do so. She still did not trust the French – particularly *that* Frenchman. She did not like the feelings he engendered in her – feelings she thought dead and gone. It was easier to despise him. No, the best plan was to keep as far away from him as was possible and keep Simon away from him, too. There would be no danger of her meeting him again – no chance of Working magic together – no more threatening feelings.

She sighed and pulled the warm velvet closer about herself. The night air was chill. The foliage and the flowers had advanced so far that it was sometimes hard to believe that it was still only early spring.

Tomorrow the other Druids would arrive to talk over the latest horrors and what they could do about them. There would be too much to do to think about this – or anything much else. Tomorrow she might even have some applicants for the post of Simon's tutor. Tomorrow she might be able to sleep the whole night through without dreaming.

"It is a cow–byre, René," said Ninon, wrinkling her nose fastidiously. The cottage provided for their use at Hillside Farm was certainly not what she had hoped for, or expected. For one thing, it was not a cottage as such. It was a former cow-byre. True, it had been scrubbed and limed – two windows had been added and the stalls removed. The floor had been planked. A rough stone fireplace had been knocked up at one end, and the large door for the animals made smaller. Jim Cerne had explained that the good cottages had burned down when Wilkins had burned the fields and that they had never been rebuilt. The new Lord Lyonshall had promised that the cottages for the farm workers would be rebuilt, but no one was certain when this would happen. In the meantime...

"I am sorry, *Grandmère* – I have not done such a good job of providing for you and *Maman*, have I?" René said bitterly. They both spoke in French, so that Jim, unloading the cart borrowed by the Vicar, would not understand.

Mr. Arabin had ruthlessly plundered his attics ("My predecessor never threw anything away!" he had said.) and found bedsteads, a table and chairs and a large chest, and some chipped, but still usable chinaware that had, no doubt, been fashionable during the reign of Queen Anne. It was these household goods that Jim and his young brother, Luke, were now unloading, under the Vicar's supervision.

Ninon was at once contrite. She did not like the look on his face. "*Mon cher* René, I am not blaming you! I do not know what else you could have done! It is just our luck, that is all." She looked about her, searching for something good to say, to lift his spirits. "But it is good sized and quiet! We can put up the curtains and make rooms, *non*? I will make potpourri and sachets so that it smells better. Please do not look so glum, *mon cher*," she begged at last, putting a hand on his arm. "We will make do and perhaps even be happy, you shall see."

He hoped so – he certainly hoped so. He felt overwhelmed, as if too much had happened in too short a time and he could not quite deal with it all. The sight of the cow-byre had been very nearly the last straw.

Jim was a good-hearted fellow – there was no doubt about that – and he was doing his best. He was under no

obligation to help them move in, and his family had taken great pains to make this place acceptable – scrubbing and cleaning and doing alterations.

But they would have to work hard to make it a home – there were no gardens and no upstairs for privacy as there had been at May Cottage and they were a great deal further from Silverbridge. Jim had already told them that except for church (since they were on the western boundary of the parish of St Swithin's) all of their business was conducted in Knightswold. The one advantage to that would be probably never running into Sir Piers. René was torn as to what to do about Sir Piers. He wanted to do *something* to punish the baronet – the man had tried to commit murder! But what to do? Ninon had begged him not to try and challenge the pig person – she was frightened of what would happen to her and Lucie should her grandson be taken up by the law. And René was well aware that in his new status a cow-man, Sir Piers would never accept a challenge from him. To be perfectly honest, Sir Piers would have never accepted a challenge from René under any circumstances, for in Sir Piers' view, René was not a gentleman and therefore, beneath his touch. And to hide behind a tree and perhaps take a shot at the baronet was beneath contempt, even if he had a gun or knew how to use it. The oath René swore when he received his *Magus Minori* began the same as the Oath of Hippocrates – "First, do no harm." Magic was to be only used in self-defense – against another magician. Using magic to harm a non-magical person was strictly forbidden. The Duel Arcane was for magical persons of equal rank, and was governed by a strict code of behavior and regulations.

It was a seemingly insoluble problem. Both Ninon and Mr. Arabin felt it best just to stay away from Sir Piers. The baronet still thought they were dead. He would find out differently in church, on the coming Sunday. But René could not be happy with this state of affairs. He ought to be doing something!

Now Jim interrupted his thoughts, which as was usual of late, seemed to be going around and around in endless circles.

"All unloaded," said the farmer. "Just tell us where you wants 'em put.Vicar tells me you was burned out – my Sarah's comin' over wi' linens an' such."

As if she had been waiting outside for a cue, there was a knock on the door and a head poked in the door. "Are ye ready for me?" she inquired.

Mr. Arabin leaped to the door and opened it, revealing Sarah Cerne and a barrow full of linen and other goods.

Sarah was a small, rather round woman with bright eyes and a cheerful, bustling manner. She reminded Ninon of a brown wren, for her hair, eyes and skin were brown and she wore as well, an old-fashioned brown dress with a spotlessly white apron and a fichu about her shoulders.

Sarah and Ninon took to one another immediately. In no time at all, they were talking like old friends as they examined the goods on the barrow. Nothing was new, but it was scrupulously clean and well mended. She had brought feather beds for the bedsteads and fluffy pillows. She had bed linens and quilts – all made by her own self – Ninon much admired the neat stitching – and a basket with fresh-made bread, honey, butter, a jug of milk and a flitch of bacon.

She told Ninon all about her two children, Sally and Joseph, four and six respectively and her mother, Maggie MacLeod, who lived with them. Ninon told her about Lucie, finding that, to her surprise, it was easy to explain to Sarah about Lucie. Lucie was at present under the care of Mrs. Parker at the Vicarage. She would be brought out to her new home this evening.

By this time the men had gone out to look over the farm. The furniture was set where Ninon wanted it and she and Sarah had made up the beds and hung some extra sheets up as room dividers. Sarah had even brought sanitary utensils – not new, but clean and they made a corner into a washroom. Noticing Sarah's work–roughened hands, Ninon went into her basket of herbs and offered her an herbal ointment that gave instant relief to cracked and dry hands, for it had a touch of magic in it. Sarah was very grateful, for her hands were often painful. "What d'you think is wrong with your daughter?" she said, as they finished up the work and sat down at the table.

197

"We have never been certain," said Ninon sadly. "When first we came to *Angleterre* we had doctors, but none seemed to help her. No one was able to find out what happened to her. When we found her, she was much like she is now, *non*? But she seemed to get worse after René was born."

"Some women get real sad and sick after havin' a babe," said Sarah. "I might be able to help her – sometimes I can get inside a person's mind and sort of take away their pain. I don't do it a lot – if I was to take everyone's pain, I'd be sick myself. Folks hereabout don't even know I can do it – not even Parson. Jim says they'd never stop botherin' me to heal what ails 'em. But twenty-five years is a long time to be sick."

Ninon stared at her. "*Qu'est-ce que cela veut dire*? Are you – oh, what is the English word ? – ah! – empath?"

"That's what our Dominie back in Scotland– afore I married Jim – called it," said Sarah.

A sudden wild hope filled Ninon. The one doctor she had really liked all those years ago had suggested that they find a natural empath to help Lucie. Her pain was so great that it had disturbed her mind. And combined with post-partum depression... But a natural empath was a rare creature, so rare as to almost nonexistent. And the one Healer they had found listed, in London, who had claimed to be an empath, was of a dubious skills indeed and wanted a small fortune for his services.

"Could you help my Lucie?" Impulsively, Ninon reached out across the table to take Sarah's hands in her own. "I would do anything, pay anything, to help her!"

Sarah squeezed her fingers in return. "There's no question of payment. If I can help her, I will. But I'd like best if you wasn't to tell anyone 'ceptin' your family here. Why don't you tell ne everything that happened?"

Lucie's story was simply told. She had run away from school at the age of fourteen. It had taken a year to find her, even though Louis had hired investigators. "For we were not poor then," said Ninon sadly. When they had found Lucie, she was living in the city of Roussillon, in Provence, in a state of extreme poverty and she was pregnant. And she was mad. She talked more then and babbled sometimes about her "husband", who she called "Lucien", but Ninon and Louis had thought this a trifle unbelievable coincidence – "Lucie and Lucien". They very much feared that Lucie had either been raped or had been taken advantage of by a rogue who had mot married her and abandoned her when she became with child. 'Lucien' was a fantasy she had concocted out of thin air. She had no marriage lines, nor a wedding ring and the neighbors were not the sort that were helpful, unless they were heavily bribed. They had let Lucie exist in a pitiable state – in fact, if Louis' agents had not found her when they did, she might had not lived much longer. The birth of her child was difficult and she became much worse, mentally, falling into deep, long-lasting fits of depression and despair. Ninon and Louis raised René from the beginning and gave him the name of the city in which they had found Lucie, for they had no idea who his father might be. It said "Lucien Roussillon" on René's birth certificate, because of the legal necessity of having a father's name therein. "And then came the Revolution," Ninon finished "and we had to run or we would have been murdered, *sauve qui peut*, and this, I think, did not help her for everyone is so frightened all of the time, and here we are *dépaysé*, and everything goes *de mal en pis*."

Sarah managed to understand this, in spite of the fact that she spoke not a word of French. "I'll come tomorrow and see if I can sort her out," she said briskly, patting Ninon's hand. While Ninon had told Lucie's story Sarah had made them cups of strong, sweet tea, and she urged the older woman to finish her cup. In Sarah's opinion, these people needed feeding up. "An', I'll ask my ma t' come sit wi' your Lucie tonight so's you can have your meal wi' us. My ma's a grand sick nurse an' she'll be pleased t' do it."

Ninon saw her off with hope in her heart for the first time in years. She would not speak of this to René, she decided, for if nothing came of it, she, Ninon, would be the only one disappointed. René had enough on his plate at the moment.

Ninon knelt before the fireplace and prayed to *le bon Dieu* that Sarah might be able to help Lucie. What a relief it would be to lift the burden of worry and care that the constant tending of Lucie had become! And to have her daughter back! For René to know his mother as the lovely person she had been, not as a pitiable madwoman! Ninon remembered oh, so clearly what Lucie had been like – the type of person that lit up a room – with an *élan vital* that drew everyone who met her. She was the first to laugh, but never maliciously, and sang as blithely as a bird. She danced through her days. It had been a wrench to send her to school, and, as events had proved, a mistake. And to perhaps have her again! Ninon knew that she would not sleep that night fro excitement.

Jim put René right to work. By the time Sarah had rung the dinner bell he had met and helped milk the cows, including the lead cow, Buttercup, who, unlike most of the Alderney dairy cows, was not of an equable temperament. He had also been on the hill with the sheep and had learned from Jim the whistled signals that instructed Sep, the black and white Scots coally. Sep approved of René, which had made Jim feel good – it was very important that the animals liked and trusted the new farm-laborer. Animals could tell a great deal about a person and Jim had never trusted any one whom the animals did not like. They had hated old Wilkins – Sep always tried to bite him and the cows kicked at him. And look at how Wilkins had turned out.

Jim Cerne, as his father and grandfather and great grandfather before him, worked his farm by the memorized verses of the Medieval Wizard Thomas Tusser's farming calendar, a *Hundred Points of Husbandry*. These rhyming lyrics told the careful farmer what to do at each month of the year and had been used since the mid 1500s by anyone who wanted to farm successfully. April was near an end – most ploughing was done and the seed scattered – the work of the farm was chiefly with the cattle, and the busyness of the dairy beginning again. Most of the cows had calved. Jim fed his cows on new grass as soon as was possible, which meant taking them to pasture every morning after the first milking and rotating them, so no pasture became overgrazed. It was Jim's younger brother Luke's duty to take them back and forth to pasture. It would be Jim, René and Luke who milked them and thirty-five Alderneys, milked twice a day, took up a good deal of time. There was really enough work for five men and two dairy maids, but they would have to make do. Jim also had René groom and harness the team of huge, gentle

Shire horses – Bess and Bill – and they seemed to like him too. All in all, Jim was pleased with his new help.

And René and Ninon were very well pleased when they saw the table that Sarah laid for the evening meal. For there was a huge steak and kidney pie, a baron of beef, new potatoes, pickled vegetables, fresh bread, a roasted chicken, stuffed, two kinds of cheese, and a roly-poly pudding with hot, sweet syrup and dried fruit. "We shall soon be fat," Ninon said afterwards.

Mrs. MacLeod, a pleasant-faced woman with a decided Scots burr to her tongue, came again the following morning to sit with Lucie while Ninon walked up to the farmhouse for her breakfast. Lucie, after her wild period, had become astonishingly sweet and obedient once again and smiled quietly at everyone. She seemed to miss Marthe, Ninon thought. They all missed Marthe and Jacques, too.

Jim, René and Luke had been up since about half after four – milking, cleaning the byres, and the other stabling, and feeding all of the animals.

It had been difficult to get out of bed at that hour, but Ninon, as she had predicted, had not slept well and had risen and made René a bacon sandwich and a pot of tea while he washed and shaved. Jim had given him a smock and a pair of rough work boots, as well as a pair of gaiters and Ninon scarcely recognized him when he emerged from behind the curtain of the washroom. "You look like one of the peasants at Château Mont du Mer," she said without thinking.

"Where?" said René, stifling a yawn. Rising at this hour was going to take some getting used to.

"Oh, where your *grandpère* and I lived once, long before you were born," she answered, cursing herself.

"In Provence or Brittany?" he inquired.

"Provence –" she began, but was fortunately interrupted by a knock on the door and Jim's voice "Reny! Time to milk!"

He left then, and she cleaned up the pans, thinking that she had better pay more attention to what came out from her mouth, or things could become more than a little awkward. She still had secrets to keep. Pray God she would not one day.

At seven o'clock Sarah served up an enormous breakfast of eggs, both scrambled and baked, bacon, fried ham and potatoes, dried apple pie, cheese tarts and Dundee cake, served with tea and coffee and rich, thick cream. There was also oat porridge and currant scones, with plenty of sugar, brown and white, and three different kinds of jam. True to Jim's promise, it was all delicious – and there was plenty of it, with no skimping.

When the men were finished and went back out of doors Ninon stayed behind and helped Sarah clear and wash the dishes. "Right after we clear up here, we'll sort out Lucie," Sarah promised.

Ninon was so excited that she had not been able to eat much. Her emotions varied between high expectations and a certainty that nothing could be done for Lucie and she was doomed to live the rest of her life in the state she was in now.

They walked down to the byre together, leaving Sally and Joseph in the hen-yard. Mrs. MacLeod would come back to tend her grand-children as soon as Ninon and Sarah arrived at the cottage. Sarah insisted on Ninon taking a basket of leftover scones, Dundee cake and cheese tarts "for later".

They found Lucie awake but sleepy. She was in a good mood – she smiled at her mother and looked at Sarah with no curiosity, even when Sarah sat down in front of her and took Lucie's thin hands in hers.

Sarah shut her eyes and concentrated, allowing her personality to melt into hat of Lucie's. Expression came and fled on her face and at last she released Lucie's hands and said feelingly, "Poor lost little thing! But I can help her. Let's get her comfortable. I have to have my hands on her temples. 'Tis best if she is lying down an' me sittin' behind her head."

Ninon helped her to get into position and made Lucie stretch out on the bed. "Must she be awake?" she queried anxiously, for Lucie seemed to be falling asleep.

Sarah shook her head. "She needn't be. She'll fall asleep when I'm done an' probably sleep very deep-like for hours. An' if I've done my sortin' proper, she'll be a different person when she wakes."

Ninon understood, as best she could, how empathy worked. The empath actually took on the physical or mental pain of the person they treated and somehow dissipated it – what Sarah called "sorting". Since true empathy was so rare, it was not really understood. One had to be a very strong, grounded person to be an empath. Ninon's admiration for Sarah was enormous. And if she could cure Lucie, her gratitude would be enormous also.

The moment Sarah's fingers touched Lucie's temples. Ninon could see a change in her daughter. Rapidly, emotions began to run over her features and she began to twist on the bed. "Hold down her shoulders!" directed Sarah. "Sit on her if you have to! I mustn't break my touch!"

Ninon did end in sitting on Lucie to keep her still. The process seemed to take forever. Each emotion of Lucie's – and she soon became vocal as well – was reflected on Sarah's face. Ninon thought hours had passed. She was surprised to learn later that it was scarce forty–five minutes.

With a last effort to throw off Ninon's restraining weight Lucie arched up, screaming "Lucien! Lucien!" And she suddenly went limp as Sarah's hands fell from her temples.

Sarah was dripping with sweat and ashen in colour. Ninon climbed off Lucie and said, "Is she – are you – well?"

Sarah wiped her forehead and smiled. 'We're both fine. Lucie'll sleep naturally for a few hours – you should see a big difference when she wakes up. And I wouldn't say no to a cup of tea. That was quite a sortin'! An' I'm goin' to tell you what I saw, because I arranged it that she won't remember th' worst of it. Poor little thing! It's no wonder to me that her mind was fair turned!"

She rose from the chair a little unsteadily. and went to the table while Ninon fetched water from the cistern outside the door and put the kettle on to boil.

"She *was* married, Ninon," Sarah and Ninon had reached the Christian name stage very early on. "I saw a ceremony with a priest, I guess he was. Of course, I don't understand French. But I guess she was real happy. And then just after she found out she was goin' to have a baby, men in purple robes with a big black cross here on a bed of flames," – she crossed her chest – "came an' took her husband one night."

"The Inquisition!" said Ninon, horrified.

"She didn't know what to do, it seems. She was terrified. An' then she went out one day and saw a big fire —"

"The *auto de fé!*" Ninon interrupted. "and she saw her husband burned to death," Sarah finished. "She couldn't accept it. What kind of country is France, then, that they'd do such things?" she demanded of Ninon. "No wonder her brain was turned!" Ninon explained about the Inquisition and that it was death to practice magic even to help someone. Sarah could not believe that any one would want to live in such a country.

"Oh, Sarah, I was not there for her when she most needed me!" Ninon said suddenly, stopping in mid-scoop of fragrant tea into the tea pot. "*Ma pauvre petite!* Why did she not come home to us when her *mari* was taken by *l'Inquisition?* Her papa and I would have helped — Louis had the ear of many highly placed nobles, *n'est ce pas?* And he could have reasoned with the Grand Inquisitor perhaps! Did Lucie make such a *mésalliance* that she feared to tell us?" "You'll soon be able to ask her," said Sarah soothingly. "Now, about that tea...."

16

Cold Iron

To Lyon's disappointment, no one at the Druid Conclave was as excited as was he over the rediscovery of dematerialization. Their chief concern was the Unselighe creatures and the soul-stealing murders. He agreed with the importance of this, of course, but could not help being a trifle cast-down that no one shared his enthusiasm. They were more excited over the rediscovery of the Druids of Brittany, and of a method to scry over water. Elation was high when Guénolé Cornouaille promised the support of all the Druids on the Île de Sein in the great sending to the magicians of Russia.

But Lyon thought they wasted far too much time in debating what or whom the killer could be and how the Unselighe creatures had escaped the binding in the first place. To him, the answer was simple – they had to find out what Merlin's original spell had been and duplicate it This meant a search of every sacred place in the British Isles, where Merlin had ever been – and he seemed to have lived a very peripatetic life – they might find something that was not in the known writings – something pertaining to the binding spell. Lyon had already sent orders to Avalon that the archivists there were to begin searching at once.

The others derided this idea, for everything that Merlin had ever written – which wasn't all that much – had been published for eons and any magician worth his or her salt had a copy of the volume of *Merlinus Magii* in his or her library. The book was never out of print and could be readily obtained even in the smallest and poorest of book shops. And there was nothing in that volume that even hinted at the spell used in the binding of the Unselighe Court, they thought

But Lyon was convinced that somewhere, there was something that had been overlooked. Merlin had been too wise to think that the binding could never be undone. And if it had been him, Lyon, doing such a working, he would have put the spell in a safe place, away from those who might be tempted to tamper with it. Somewhere, Lyon was convinced, there would be a clue to where this spell was hidden. And the logical place to look was in the sacred places of Britain, such as Avalon, Temair na Rig and Ynys Môn – even in Bryn Myrddn, Merlin's Hill, where his crystal cave lay in Wales.

Guénolé supported him in this – via their scryed conference she offered to have her archivists immediately attack their extensive library, for they had all the papers and books of Blaise, Merlin's teacher.

And to Lyon's surprise, he had another supporter – the Duke of Chenevix.

To Chenevix, (much to his own surprise to be agreeing with Eliot Lyons!) it seemed only logical to search the libraries and find the original spell. Certainly they could do that while the best magical minds at the Universities were working on a method to restore the binding. Nor did he agree with the other Druids' consensus that it was a creature of the Unselighe Court that was murdering Wizards and Druids. Why would an Unselighe creature steal a soul? They were soulless and glad to be so. If they had a soul, they would be judged at their death and go straight to Hell. Unselighe creatures had no hope of Heaven. And these murders reeked of blood magic. Most Unselighe beings, although they loved the taste of human blood (and human flesh) were terrified of blood magic. In his cold voice, the Duke directed the Conclave to implement a plan of the most fastidious search for hidden records, hiding places and for a team of scholars to reread everything they had of Merlin's writings, carefully searching for the smallest of clues to the binding spell's whereabouts. Over their protests, he said, at his driest and chilliest, "I *am* the Chancellor of Magic and Enchantments, am I not? The ultimate source on whom this responsibility falls? Therefore, you *will* obey me." No one could gainsay that frigid eye and voice.

It was also decided that both the magical and non-magical peoples of the British Isles needed more training to cope with the Unselighe menace. Most modern Witches and Wizards did not know how to deal with the Unselighe Court. Unselighe beings had become story-book characters in these modern times.

Even non-magical folk could be taught to use talismans and these could be provided free or at very low cost to the indigent. For instance, enchanted silver bells hung at the cardinal points of every home would ring madly when a creature menaced the household. Salt could be poured around the foundation of a home to make it difficult for the vile beings to enter. A protective wreath for the door could be made with rosemary branches, tied with green yarn. Crystals, blessed by a clergyman with magical powers, could be buried at each corner of the house. Necklaces, tie pins and lapel pins of blessed crystal, although of limited use, could be worn, as could bespelled herb bags around the neck.

Timetables, teaching and such matters as increasing crystal production were all agreed upon.

But there was very little that could be done to fight blood magic. They had to do a great deal of research, and sharing of knowledge. No one had fought blood magic in nearly five hundred years. There had been no need. And no one knew how to fight a soul-stealer.

By the end of his first day at the farm René was exhausted. Had he but realized it, he would have known that his weariness was mental as well as physical. Too much had happened in the last few days – grief, terror, disappointment and even a small taste of joy. There had been no recovery time in between these emotional transports before being plunged into an entirely new life.

However, there were compensations. By the end of the work day René's liking and respect for Jim Cerne had grown. Jim was patient in explaining what he wanted done and worked just as hard – or harder – then his helpers. René also liked Luke, Jim's young brother. Luke was a rather laconic youth of seventeen, who closely resembled his brother in looks, and had a occasional dry wit that set them all in whoops several times during the day.

But there was one problem that had the potential to turn into a very grave one. Many of the farm implements were of Cold Iron. Jim used metal milking pails – each of the thirty five cows had her own pail. Jim was fussy about cleanliness – each of these pails had to be scrubbed in cold running water with a clump of horsetail weed before and after each milking. Most of the buckets used on the farm were of metal. Jim considered them easier to keep clean than the old fashioned wooden pails.

And the Shire horses were shod in Cold Iron. Their huge hooves were cleaned out with iron hoof picks twice a day and the combs for their mane and tail and the currycomb were of metal. The harness was held together by buckles of Cold Iron. Wizards' horses were shod in copper alloy and the harness clasps were of brass or silver. Wizards' cooking implements were of copper and they took care that all metals were silver, brass, copper or gold, all bespelled to be as strong as Cold Iron.

But since Jim had no magic he had no reason not to use Cold Iron.

Cold Iron caused pain, and, in a great enough application, death in a Witch or Wizard of the Old Blood. René could feel it in his hands by the end of the day. They ached as if he had severe arthritis and the skin of his hands looked dark, as if it had been lightly burned. Before, when he had ploughed or handled a scythe or sickle with the harvesters, Ninon had made him triple-layered silk gloves, double-lined with crushed pine needles, which were cleansing and repelled the negative energy of the Cold Iron. He would need a new pair. But he was under no illusion – even with silk gloves and perhaps a bath of protective and clean-sing herbs, such as elm leaf, basil or wintergreen, each evening, he was going to suffer.

But this cost to himself had to be weighed against the advantages for his family. The food was wonderful – he had thought yester evening that his dreams had come true. And they needed a place to live – there was no where else to go. It had become readily apparent that Lucie could not stay at the Vicarage. And every feeling in René rebelled against hanging on the Vicar's sleeve. René con-sidered himself responsible for his family and that meant standing on his own feet and not letting any one, even a dear friend, pay their way. This was the only position that had offered itself in a long time. Ninon would not even have the miniscule income from her charms and decoctions, for with May cottage had died her herb garden and a new one must be established.

At the end of the day, nearing dusk, with the last milking done and the stock fed and bedded for the night, René was at last free to return to the byre and perhaps wash up and rest a bit before Sarah served supper, well after seven. He was tired, dirty and hungry and unprepared for Ninon impatiently waiting for him by the cistern. She looked as if a multiplicity of candles had been lit inside her and hopped from one foot to another, impatient as a child at Christmas.

"There is someone I want you to meet, René," she said, with an air of barely suppressed excitement.

"Can it not wait until I have at least washed, *Grandmère?*" he said tiredly. "I am in no fit case..."

"Ah, bah!" she said. "It can wait no longer! I thought, me, that you would never come!" She grabbed his hand and pulled him into the byre. He winced as her fingers seemed to dig into his hands.

To his surprise Lucie was sitting up in a chair in front of a small fire. Usually at this time of day she was soundly asleep. René had expected to find her sedated, so that *Madame* MacLeod could sit with her during supper.

And then she looked at him – really *looked* at him, with the light if reason and sanity in her sherry-coloured eyes.

"René," said Ninon proudly, "here is your *Maman!* Lucie, this is your son!"

"*Bonsoir,*" said Lucie slowly, as if she was not used to speaking, which indeed she was not, for save for an occasional outburst, she had mostly not spoken for over twenty five years.

"*Maman?*" René thought perhaps that he was so tired he had fallen asleep and was dreaming even now. The woman who looked at him was not mad, but she looked at him as if she had never seen him before and wanted to memorize every feature. She smiled at him tentatively, as if she were not sure that he would be happy to receive her smiles.

It was a miracle. The prayers that every evening they gave for her recovery had at long last been answered. There could be no other explanation. With a glad cry he leaned forward and kissed her. She threw her arms around his neck and said "My son! My son!" in French, in a broken voice.

Ninon was so happy that she felt faint. Her heart swelled as she looked at them. She had spent the day telling Lucie (when her daughter was awake, for true to Sarah's prediction, Lucie had slept a good deal) of the last twenty five years and hearing, in turn, Lucie's story.

Lucie had been horrified at first that twenty five years had gone past. It had taken a great deal to soothe her. It had also been difficult to tell her that her father and Marthe and Jacques were gone. It had been nearly impossible to tell her of the Revolution and the drastic change in their circumstances, and why they were now living in a cow-byre in England. And to tell her that she had a son who was twenty five! A son she had never seen! Ninon gladly told her all about René, what a clever magician he was, how hard he worked to support them, and every tale she could remember of his childhood.

Lucie could not help feeling extremely sad, with a deep sense of loss, that she had missed her son's childhood. The last thing she remembered was being *enciente* – she had been so certain that she would bear a little girl!

And Lucie told her mother why she had not come back to her parents when her husband was taken by the Inquisition. She was simply terrified. "I thought, *Maman,*" she said in her slow fashion, "that I would bring the Inquisition down on you. When Lucien was taken, he wished me to go to his brother. But his brother did not like me – he said that I would ruin Lucien's life and we should have never been married. I was afraid that he would blame me for the Inquisition taking Lucien. And I was sick from being with child – and afraid – so afraid! – of the Inquisition! So I hid as best I could until that day when I went to the market and saw the fires of the *auto de fé* . I remember running and running and a kind woman who helped me for I was sick and frightened and then I remember little else until today."

All this had to be recounted for René. He had to sit beside Lucie, for she would not leave go of his hand, and kept looking intently at him, as if afraid to let him out of her sight.

He had questions of his own for her – what had his father been like? Did he look like his father at all? What was his father's name?

Her husband had been Lucien de la Mare. He was nineteen when they married. And no, René did not resemble him. "You have his height," said Lucie" but his hair was fair – a dark blonde – and his eyes darker. He was very serious, *non*, when first we met, but I made him laugh! We met at a fair, and spent the day together. You know, *Maman*, I never meant to stay away from school – but I was so bored there! I thought if I ran away, you and Papa would let me come home. But then I met Lucien and within two weeks we were married! And I thought that Papa might have the marriage annulled, for Lucien's family were not what you would have wished for me."

Ninon shook her head sadly. "Child, I wish that you had trusted us! You should have known that your Papa and I would never had done anything that would hurt you. Papa loved you so that he would have accepted this young man if he truly loved you and would take proper care of you." It was as Ninon had thought – Lucie had been simply too young to think clearly and make mature choices. How different things might have been! Ninon herself had been married at fifteen – an arranged marriage, but fortunately for her, she and Louis had fallen in love almost at once and were very happy together. But they had wanted more for Lucie – a good education and the chance to be out in the world and make a marital choice that would make her happy.

But what had happened could not be changed. It was enough, Ninon supposed that Lucie had been returned to them. She was very quiet, though, not like the Lucie Ninon remembered, but Sarah had warned that she might be overwhelmed by the loss of so much of her life at first, and they must be very gentle with her. Ninon felt impatient, though – she wanted the old Lucie to return.

René, however, having never known the old Lucie, was very happy just to have this quiet woman with sanity in her voice and eyes. When he was little, he had been afraid of his mother, for her violent moods were terrifying to a small child. It was not until he was considerably older that he had learned compassion for her, and then love. It seemed a true miracle to have her back and when Ninon told him of Sarah's part in Lucie's recovery, he resolved that none of the Cernes should ever have cause to complain about his work and if he could do anything special for them he would do so.

The time was growing near for supper and René quickly washed up, and then escorted his two ladies to supper, Lucie leaning heavily on his arm. They were greeted with cries of delight by Sarah.

Ninon's heart was full with thankfulness and joy as she watched Lucie interact with the Cernes. She had thought that coming to this farm was one of the worst things that had ever happened to them. It had turned out to be one of the best.

"My lady," said Seppings, "there is a young gentleman here to see his lordship, but there is a large "Do not, under pain of death, disturb" sign on the Tower door. And his Grace of Chenevix is in there with his lordship. Will your ladyship receive him?"

Diana had been reading with Simon in her sitting room, a pleasant, light-filled apartment done in yellow, which in addition, had the morning sun streaming through the filmy curtains. The French doors stood ajar, allowing the sight and smells of a newly planted garden to drift in. In the absence of a tutor Diana thought that she could at least teach Simon some history and language skills, as well as botany and the use of the globes. By law, she could not teach him magic, for Witches and Wizards had different forms of magic and learning.

Today they were studying the different types of dragons. Diana had animated the paper three-dimensional dragons from *My First Book of Dragons* so that Simon could see how they moved and flew. It was a lesson calculated to hold Simon's interest and delight him and it had managed to dissipate a measure of the coldness that had come between them.

Diana frowned. "Is this gentleman from the government or one of the Arch Druids?" The Conclave had ended yesterday evening and Dian had been glad to see them go.

212

Everyone was so tense and worried and there had been unforeseen problems – for one, Douglas Ramey's seahorses had had to be stabled in the pond and they ate not hay and oats, but fish.

"He has a letter of introduction from His Royal Highness, the Prince Regent, my lady, but has no dispatch case. He did give me his card, as is proper."

Seppings extended a silver salver to Diana. She picked up the card and read: *The Honourable Augustus Goodbody, Magus Majorus, the Albany, London.*

"Goodbody –" Diana said thoughtfully. She also noticed that contrary to custom, Mr. Goodbody did not have the name of his familiar inscribed upon his visiting card.

"The youngest son of the Viscount Ffoillot, my lady," said Seppings, who made it his business to know these things. He coughed delicately. "And he has arrived with a mountain of baggage, my lady."

Not another unbidden guest! However, one could not turn away someone sent by the Prince Regent. "Send him in, Seppings," she said resignedly.

Simon had listened to this exchange with interest. He hoped this person was not his new tutor. In the absence of Mr. Roussillon (whom he still cherished hopes of having as his tutor again) he liked these lessons with Mama. He was disappointed that this fascinating dragon study was ending, for Mama was gathering up the dragons and putting them back in the book.

Voices were heard in the hall and Seppings announced, "Mr. Goodbody, my lady," and held open the door for a tall young man clad in the most dandified fashion Diana had ever seen.

His coat was of a starting bright blue with huge padded shoulders and exaggerated lapels, his pantaloons an exquisite primrose. His waistcoat was embroidered with silken peacock tails, while his neck cloth and his shirt points were so high that it was impossible for him to turn his head without putting out an eye. He wore several rings, a huge diamond tie pin and five fobs hanging from his waistcoat. all of which were large and garish. His lapel pin was that of an Augur, like Peter's, but unlike Peter's modest pin, it was

213

enormous. He reeked of a blend of Circassian hair oil and Steek's lavender water.

In person he was thin, with elongated limbs, very little chin, and a beak of a nose. Although probably no more than two and twenty, his hair was already receding and his attempted to cover this deficiency by combing what remained forward and plastering it in place with hair oil. He had a cowlick on the back of his head, which would not lie flat, despite liberal application of oil. He had small eyes, set too close together and if his throat had been bare, Diana would have been able to see a very prominent Adam's apple. All of these physical characteristics had earned him the schoolboy nickname of "Stork" whilst at Winchester and Cambridge. It was still singularly apt.

He was also smug and self-satisfied. As he came forward to greet his hostess he wore an odious little smirk that made Diana long to smack his face. His entire demeanor seemed to say, "My! Are you in for a treat! To have the pleasure of *my* company!"

He bowed low over Diana's hand, but did not kiss it, a mercy for which she was grateful. "I had no notion that Lord Lyonshall had such a lovely chatelaine to grace his home!" He leered at her and smiled, showing large and rather yellow teeth. His voice was thin and reedy and he had a slight lisp.

Diana withdrew her hand from his grasp as soon as she could without being rude. She introduced Simon to Mr. Goodbody, but the dandy ignored the boy, merely flipping his exquisitely manicured fingers in Simon's direction.

"To what do we owe this visit, Mr. Goodbody?" Diana inquired, inviting him to take a seat as she resumed hers.

"I am sent here, by HRH, to be Lord Lyonshall's secretary. HRH was much concerned, you must know, when he saw the notice in the *Wizard's Times* and determined at once to find the very best for the Arch Druid of Britain! And the very best is me!" he said in no little satisfaction.

Diana nearly choked. She could imagine what Lyon would have to say to this apparition as a secretary!

Simon was glad that this person was not to be his tutor. He had taken an instant dislike to Mr. Goodbody. In this he was not alone – most persons felt that way when they met Augustus Goodbody, a fact that that conceited gentle-

214

man always wrote down to jealousy. His self-satisfaction was extraordinary.

"My uncle is closeted with the Chancellor of Magic and Enchantment at the moment, and I am not certain how long their meeting might last. May I offer you some refreshment, Mr.Goodbody, or would you prefer to be shown a room where you might refresh yourself? Your familiar did not accompany you?" she queried. This was quite unusual – but perhaps his familiar was a female and had recently given birth.

Goodbody flushed. "It is not a tradition in my family to have a familiar," he said somewhat shortly and then , with a quick recovery he went on "If I will not offend your lovely self, Lady Diana, by sitting here in all my travel dirt, I should like a glass of port and some ratafia biscuits." He smiled again and Diana realized that his smile made her slightly sick.

"Not at all," she lied, wishing that some household crisis would develop in the kitchen or the stillroom that required her immediate attention. But she could let Simon elude this unpleasant person. As she rang for Seppings she suggested to Simon that he take the book to his room and write a little report on the dragons they had studied that morning.

She did not like the fact that he did not have a familiar – it was considered a bad sign – a sign of black magic or ineptitude, if a Witch or a Wizard had not been chosen by a familiar animal. Of course, as in her case, one's familiar might have died. Her brother Peter was at present minus a familiar as his hedgehog had succumbed to a fever.

While Simon made good his escape, Seppings rejoined them. Mr. Goodbody made his wishes known, adding that Seppings was to make certain that the wine was not corked, for he, Goodbody, would know at once should an inferior product had been passed off on him.

Seppings' impassive face did not betray what he thought of this rudeness, but beneath it, he quivered with indignation. This from a man who would eat ratafia biscuits with port at this hour of the morning! And to place orders, as if he were in his own home and not a guest – a guest on sufferance! Seppings, before now not fond of Lord Lyonshall's fits of rage, could scarcely wait to hear how this odious dandy would be torn to pieces by the Marquis's acidic tongue.

"His Grace of Chenevix is in residence here, I am told?" said Mr. Goodbody, inching his chair closer to Diana's. Really, she was a most attractive female! He had researched the entire family when the Regent had suggested this post. True, her papa was but an Earl – Mr. Goodbody had always fancied a Duke's daughter as his life's partner, for all of the Royal Princesses were far past the first blush of youth, but Duke's daughters were thin on the ground these days. But Lady Diana had a most satisfactory fortune and connections, and due to come into a more than satisfactory amount of rhino when her father stuck his spoon in the wall. And she appealed to his aesthetic senses as well – she was beautiful and graceful and he liked her large violet eyes and curling dark hair. She dressed too plain, though. He liked a more dashing style in a female. He would change that once they were married. And having made this decision in all of five minutes, for it was time he was wed and shored up his coffers for his style of dress took a great deal of money to maintain, never mind his gambling debts and snuff box collection. In his mind, he was as good as betrothed to Diana. It never occurred to him that she might have something to say about it. In his opinion, she was a very lucky young female. Not every one could have such a superior husband. Many young ladies would be in hysterics once the news was out, knowing that Augustus Goodbody had been removed from the lists of London's most eligible bachelors.

Diana tried to move her chair away from his, as subtly as was possible. He was leering at her again. Repressing a shudder, she said that yes, indeed, the Duke of Chenevix was presently in residence.

"That is very well," said Mr. Goodbody complacently, drinking his wine. "For I have certain theories about the present crisis that I fancy the Duke will be glad to hear."

Diana doubted it.

17

May Days

Lyon was not best pleased with his 'gift' from the Regent. He took an instant dislike to Augustus Goodbody – Lyon had little use for dandies and no use for know-it-alls, which was among the kinder things he called Goodbody when he was alone with Diana that evening.

"Even Chenevix doesn't like him," he told his niece as they sat in her sitting room. "Called him a toad-eating sycophant to his face. Goodbody didn't turn a hair – he seems immune to insult. Leander hates him too – what kind of a Wizard does not have a familiar, he said."

"And what did you call him to his face, Uncle?" Diana asked. She was finishing a blue and gold interlaced Celtic design on the collar of Simon's Beltaine robe, which she had ended in fitting herself. There had been no opportunity to take him to Knightswold. She had embroidered hers with a wreath of violets.

Lyon ignored her remark. "Never thought I'd be agreeing with Chenevix – twice! – in as many days," he continued, tamping down his pipe and relighting it with a small blue flame from his fingertip. "The thing of it is, as Chenevix pointed out, damn him, I can't just send Goodbody back to London. That damned fat fool of a Regent would be insulted and we've got to keep on his good side if we want to get some of our protective measures passed. The Regent can be a bad enemy and is capable of throwing all sorts of obstacles in the way."

Diana's heart sank. "So Mr. Goodbody will stay?" she asked in no little trepidation.

"I'm afraid so – for a while at least," Lyon said. "I'll do my best to keep him out of your way. I hope you realize what a sacrifice this is – I might end in killing the jackass."

"I'll retain the very best barrister in London and plead justifiable homicide. Surely anyone that has met him can understand that!" Diana promised.

Lyon grinned. "I'm amazed he's not been murdered long ago!"

They were free of his presence for this evening – Lyon had directed him to go to the Tower and read all of the reports that had come in from everywhere, to become *au courant* with the situation. There were such a volume of these that they might not see him again for days on end Lyon said. Hopefully, he was a slow reader.

The Duke of Chenevix had retired to his room rather than bear Goodbody at dinner. Diana, faced with a hostile uncle and a leering guest as dinner companions had wished devoutly that Diarmait Mag Uidhir had not returned to Tara with Conchobar Ó Clérigh and Pádraig.

Keeping away from his lecherous looks and his roaming hands was going to prove a challenge in the coming days. It made her indignant to think that he obviously felt she would welcome advances from him. Her skin crawled at the very thought. There was always what Edmund had taught her long ago – how effective a well-placed knee could be in fending off unwanted attentions. She had to admit, it would give her a great deal of satisfaction to hear that reedy voice become *coloratura*.

The next few weeks were trying, for many reasons. Augustus Goodbody proved a disaster both as a houseguest and a secretary. He slept until at least ten in the morning, demanded all sorts of special attentions, not the least of which was a list of his favorite foods and those he simply could not touch. He complained about his room – the chimney smoked, he said, when the wind was in the east, and the view of the dragon pen was unsuitable for one of his delicate sensibilities. His bath water had to be a precise temperature and his mattress had to be changed twice. The newly hired housekeeper hated him because he had accused her of putting damp sheets on his bed. Seppings' loathing of him grew daily. All of the servants tried to avoid him as much as was possible.

His valet, a thin young man with a squint in one eye, by the name of Thompson, was as self-satisfied as was his master.

As a secretary Goodbody had no notion of efficiency, priorities or good work habits. He misunderstood orders, purposely ignored what Lyon and Chenevix wanted and did everything *his* way. He had very poor handwriting, and could barely scry, read runes or the Ogham. His Latin and Greek were beyond poor. He could not seem to perform the most basic magical task without somehow ruining it. Lyon looked Goodbody up in *Registratum Magi Britannae* and was appalled to read his scores for all three tests and his baccalaureate degree. He had barely passed the Orals and the Essays and had passed the Practical part of each exam by only one point. Lyon suspected that the examiners may have been bribed by Goodbody's father. People like Goodbody, Lyon was convinced, shouldn't be allowed to put on magic acts at a Punch and Judy show. His aura was barely blue! Lyon was forced to lock up all of the books of the higher magics, for Goodbody thought himself a genius of a magician and was constantly attempting to do things far beyond his powers.

Chenevix was openly hostile to Augustus, which that young gentleman attributed to the Duke's jealousy, as his Grace told Lyon one afternoon.

"Jealousy of what?" Lyon asked Chenevix. He had sent Augustus to Knightswold on a trumped-up errand that he hoped would relieve them of his company for the space of an afternoon.

Chenevix looked as if he might be sick. "Of his style! He thinks that I am jealous of his tailor! His tailor ought to be dragged out from whatever little hole he inhabits and shot for the public good! Goodbody deserves to hang – if it were only possible to hang persons for bad taste!"

"I blackballed him from White's," Chenevix continued, "and I shall continue to blackball him from every club of which I am a member. I have it in my mind to leave directions in my will that he shall continue to be blackballed into infinity. And to think that such as he will one day marry and breed – it doesn't bear thinking on! For of course, idiots like that always have a multitude of off-spring!"

All this contention made for a delightful atmosphere at the Abbey.

They passed a subdued Beltaine, in which the only songs sung were those of mourning for Myfanwy Gryffydd. Simon had looked eagerly for his former tutor at this event but had not seen him. Of course, it had been night-time and there had been a great press of people at the fest. It had been held at the grove. Simon had sensed that the trees were glad to have the grove again in use, but Father Oak had not spoken to anyone.

And during this time, there were more and more incursions of the Unselighe court. Two very young Druids, traveling between Avalon and Cornwall, had been murdered and their souls taken. This fact had still been kept from the news-sheets, but it was only a matter of time before it became public knowledge.

Lyon was back and forth between the Abbey, London and Avalon and the other Druidical seats constantly. He did hire a dragon – Pádraig had a young cousin, Tuathail, who was eager for a position. Lyon often took Goodbody with him on these trips and was savagely pleased to find out that Augustus became dragon-sick every time they flew. Lyon was hoping that the continued insults, flying and any other ill-treatment he could inflict on him would cause Goodbody to leave in high dudgeon. But so far, nothing seemed to faze that smug young man.

Ninon had become incensed with both herself and René when she saw his hands. Why had he not come to her at once? Why had she not thought of the danger of Cold Iron?

On that first night of Lucie's recovery, she sacrificed the silk wrapped around her cauldron and made two pair of gloves, high-wristed, for her grandson. They were triple layered, with a thick cushion of crushed pine needles between each layer. Pine was a cleanser and deflector of negative energy and she hoped that it would do its job and protect René from the effects of handling Death Metal on a daily basis. She would watch him closely, also. What they would do if he became ill – or worse – she did not know.

Lucie continued to recover. Ninon sometimes felt that if Lucie had had better food and they had been able to afford a really fine Wizard Healer Lucie might not have been in such bad case for so many years. They were both affected by the good food – Ninon had more energy and slept better than she had for many a year, and Lucie became prettier daily, her lank hair becoming soft and lustrous, and the pink returning to her complexion. But the old Lucie seemed to be gone – she was no longer a bright flame, but a quiet, rather thoughtful woman. Her emotions could be very close to the surface and Ninon frequently found her in tears over the lost twenty five years, the death of her loved ones and having missed René's childhood.

Sarah was a great comfort at this time. She understood Lucie as did no one else and the two women became good friends. Lucie was a forty year old woman with the outlook and emotions of a fourteen year old girl. She had been locked within herself for all of those years – years in which a normal person grew, changed and matured. Before her illness she had been through a great deal more than some people are ever called upon to bear. Ninon had to learn to be content with what her daughter had become.

They did not attend the Beltaine feast. Jim and his family did not go, either, for it was a long way from the farm and the children too little to attend something that lasted until nearly midnight. Everyone had to rise early. And Ninon thought that René would be too tired.

He was, for even with the gloves he felt the Cold Iron sapping his strength. After a full day's work, he wanted a bath, supper and his bed in that order. The chores on the farm were broken into a time frame only by church on Sunday. Otherwise the days had a tendency to melt into one another.

Ninon had found a huge wooden tub in one of the sheds and had obtained permission from Sarah for the use of it. This she made water tight with magic and made certain that René had an herbal bath awaiting him at the end of each work day, in which he could attempt to soak away the effects of Cold Iron. Hauling the water for this bath was no easy task, but she managed it. As Lucie grew stronger she was able to help. Ninon tried every herbal combination she knew – those of cleansing, protecting, purifying: basil, chamomile and bay leaf for Protection and willow for healing in the bath. She made him drink cinnamon tea for strength. She put sprigs of tarragon in his shoes for energy, and made a mustard seed paste for muscle pain. All of these odors earned him some very strange looks from Jim and Luke, but made him very popular with the cows. But to Ninon's anxious eye, nothing seemed to help much.

Matters came to a head when the week of Midsummers Day was nearly upon them. At Church that Sunday Mr. Arabin had expressed anxiety about his young friend – René was looking very hagged, he said and hoped that working on the farm wasn't taking too much out of him. And the good food did not seem to be making as much difference in him as it had in his mother and grandmother. The Vicar had invited them back to the Vicarage to see the kittens – four, as Plato had predicted, had been born the week before Beltaine and would be in a few short weeks old enough to make their choices.

The Vicar of course, was delighted with Lucie's recovery and had been sworn to secrecy about Sarah's part. But Mr. Arabin noticed how quiet René was and how stiffly he moved, as if he were in constant pain. This was even more apparent to him than it was to Ninon and Lucie, for they saw René on a daily basis and it was far more obvious to the Vicar, who only saw his young friend every Sunday. Mr. Arabin at once guessed the cause but could think of no other remedy than to leave the problem in the hands of God.

Others had noticed too. Monday morning Jim came to see Ninon and Lucie.

It was nearly noon and Ninon and her daughter had just returned from picking strawberries with Sarah. They would spend the afternoon hulling and cutting berries and on the morrow would make jam and preserves. Tonight there would be fresh strawberry cake and strawberries and cream for tea. Sarah had left them to take a well stuffed basket to the men for their "nooning". Lucie and Ninon were washing strawberry juice from their hands and faces. The three had eaten nearly as many as they had picked.

They were chattering happily when a knock came on the door. Ninon answered it, and was surprised to see Jim at this time of day.

"I ain't botherin' you?" he said. somewhat anxiously, coming in a little hesitantly.

"But no," said Ninon, throwing wide the door. "We have finished *les fraises* – so *delicieux*! Is something the matter?"

Jim had pulled his straw sun hat from off his head and now twisted it awkwardly in his large hands. "What's wrong with Reny?" he burst out. "He's workin' real hard, but he don't look good. Sarah an' me's afraid he's sickenin' for somethin'."

"It is the Cold Iron," Ninon explained simply. But she realized that Jim had no idea what she meant as he stared at her in consternation.

She made him take a seat at the table and explained what Cold Iron meant to those of the Old Blood, particularly one of the Old Blood who had as much magic as did René.

"Magic!" said Jim. "I ain't never had no truck wi' magic and magicians. How come Reny ain't workin' as a magician?"

Ninon, as best she could, explained the laws of England governing the practice of magic and told Jim how much each test cost.

Jim shook his head. "It's a waste," he pronounced. "And t' have t' spend £250 t' take a test! Why, that's more'n this farm makes in a year, now! D'you gets your money back if you don't pass the test?"

"You do not," said Ninon.

Jim shook his head again. "Is Reny goin' t' be able to keep workin', Missus? I don't want t' lose him – he's a good worker an' all o'us like him."

"We are doing all that we can to keep him well, *je vous assure*," Ninon said. "He wishes to stay here, as do we all."

"I'll try an' work things out so he's touchin' as little iron as he has to," said Jim. "Seems t' me we've got some old wooden pails an' pitchforks an' such around abouts."

Ninon was grateful for his understanding. Although she would prefer René not to have to touch Death Metal at all she was pragmatist enough to realize that such a wish was not going to come true. She had been half afraid that Jim meant to dismiss her grandson from his service.

Lucie had listened quietly, hulling straw-berries, while Jim and Ninon talked. When he left, she put aside the berry she was cutting and said "*Maman*, how much longer can René bear this Cold Iron?"

Ninon gave a long sigh. "I do not know, *ma cherie*. René has so much magic! Was your Lucien very magical?"

"Too magical," said Lucie sadly. "And he would not hide it. That is why the Inquisition took him. I always thought that it was because he used a mage light to help a poor farmer repair a cart in the darkness – someone saw and told the Inquisition. But the farmer had sick children in the cart and the rain was pouring down. No one could see to repair the wheel, *n'est-ce pas*? So Lucien made light and the next day came the Inquisition. For such a little thing as that," she added bitterly.

"And here in England, we may practice all of the magic that we wish, as long as we can afford it!" Ninon threw up her hands. Life was not understandable.

Simon had been delighted with the kittens. They had been born just before Beltaine, and when they were about six weeks old they would be ready to go to their new partners. Simon had fallen in love with a little calico female – her face was split right down the center – one side was orange and the other black. He hoped that she chose him.

Having a pet who was also a familiar might help Simon feel less lonely. It seemed as if Mama was always busy these days. They still had lessons every morning while that awful Mr. Goodbody slept late. The less Simon saw of that young gentleman the more he liked it. Nobody seemed to like Mr. Goodbody – especially Mama. She always looked harassed whenever Goodbody was about and she often disappeared into the woods, on foot or on horseback, or did charity work for the Vicar for hours at a time.

Simon didn't see why Uncle Lyon didn't just send Mr. Goodbody away. Uncle Lyon and the Duke of Chenevix were working together, amazingly, Mama said, to drive Mr. Goodbody away, so that he would leave on his own. That way the Regent would not be offended. Simon could not see why they worried about that – the Regent was far away in London after all. It was more important to get rid of Mr. Goodbody. Simon had come to despise Mr. Goodbody – Seppings called him a Bartholomew Baby, half flash and half foolish – what that meant Simon was not truly certain, but it obviously was not very nice.

Simon still had no tutor. Mama had interviewed three young gentlemen, but she had not liked any of them. That was why, on a beautiful late May afternoon, Simon was on an excursion with Uncle Lyon.

Just after a cold collation at noontime, Uncle Lyon said he was going to drive around the farms that afternoon – it was too fine a day to spend any more time pouring over endless documents. Goodbody was at once ready to accompany Lyon, but was brusquely told that he wasn't needed. He could stay and work with the Duke. Chenevix, looking green, had declared a sick headache and the necessity of being in a darkened room, and taking one of Mariposa's sleep-inducing tisanes. Mama had said she had to take soup and comforts to some sick people in the village. Simon had hoped for a riding lesson that afternoon. He was now the proud possessor of a pale gray Welsh Mountain pony mare that he had named Gwen. He had a lesson every day, with Mama and Daniel, one of the grooms. But it looked as if he would not have one today.

Then Uncle Lyon had suggested that Simon acompany him on his rounds of the farms and Simon had joyfully agreed. No one cared that Goodbody was at loose ends. They would have been surprised to learn that, denied following Diana about like a tantony pig, (for of course, he would go no where near sick people, particularly low-born sick people) he was quite content to wander into Silverbridge and inflict his company on the locals at the *Beetle and Wedge*. He had discovered a dice game in the back room of the Inn, with other gamblers, and had already gone down to the tune of over one hundred pounds.

Simon had a good time with his great uncle. They talked about the kittens and the coming Midsummer's Day fest and Simon met other children at the various farms, as well as dogs and cats and livestock. He had not realized now extensive the Abbey lands were. Several times they were offered refreshments – creamy milk or lemonade for him and a wide variety of fresh baked breads, scones and biscuits.

The last farm they were to visit was called Hillside Farm. Lyon explained that it was on the far western boundary of his property and had a foot in the Cotswolds.

The farm road was rutty in places, but the curricle, pulled by Lyon's carriage pair, bowled along well enough. Although Uncle Lyon muttered about writing a nasty letter to the Wizard in charge of road repairs in Cheltenham. Simon was proud of himself – in spite of all the extra treats he had not become sick even once.

He was looking at the cows in the pastures on each side of the road when he saw two figures coming towards him. One was a young cow, the other a man in a smock. As they came closer, Simon gasped in pleasure."Look, Uncle Lyon! It is Mr. Roussillon!"

"Roussillon! What's he doing out here? And why hasn't he come to show me how to dematerialize?" Lyon clucked with his tongue at the horses and they trotted out to pull up beside the man and the cow.

"Hello, Mr. Roussillon!" Simon jumped up and down excitedly.

René, who had been walking slowly with his attention on the young cow (she had been purchased the last market day by a Mrs. Dabney, who lived on this road and he was delivering her purchase) looked up and smiled "Hello, Simon. Good day, Lord Lyonshall."

Lyon saw no use in conventional courtesies. "Why haven't you been to show me how to dematerialize?" he demanded with a frown.

"My new employment has kept me busy," said René.

"Sir, why do you have a cow?" Simon wanted to know.

Lyon took a look at Roussillon and said "Are you working as a farm laborer?" Sheer incredulity was in his voice. "A magician who can dematerialize?"

René shrugged. "*Il faut de l'argent.* One must have money. If I do not work, I have no money." He wished that they would drive on.

"Well, whatever it is you are doing, it doesn't suit you," said Lyon bluntly. "You look like a death's head on a mop-stick. Why are you not practicing magic?"

"Because I have only the *Magus Minorus* and do not have £250 to take the *Magus Majorii* examinations," René

226

answered wearily. He was getting more than a little tired of this question.

"DAMN!" Lyon swore. Simon's eyes widened as his uncle continued to curse, pounding the dash rail of the curricle with a balled fist, causing the whip to rattle in its socket and the horses to snort and flip their ears back and forth. "This is exactly why I write letters and make a fuss in Parliament! It is a bloody waste!" He seemed to brood over this state of affairs for several moments, and then said abruptly, "Look here, Roussillon. I have need of a secretary *cum* assistant. How would you like the position?"

"But I have never worked as a secretary and I am promised to Jim Cerne as his cow-man," René could not believe what he was hearing.

"I have a supposedly trained secretary at the moment who is as close to an idiot as one can get without being certifiable!" Lyon returned "And as for Jim Cerne, I'll make certain that he gets a cow-man and whatever else he needs. Damn, it's a crime – a magician who can dematerialize working as a cow-man – and having to handle Cold Iron, too, if I don't miss my guess," he added shrewdly, with another look at René "I'll pay you four hundred guineas the year and you and your family can live in the Dower House on the Abbey grounds. That way you'll be close if I need you."

Four hundred guineas the year! René felt a roaring in his ears and a sudden need to lean against the cow. FOUR HUNDRED GUINEAS!

Simon was in alt. "Please say yes!" he begged his former tutor. "I would like it above all things!"

René could only nod his assent. It was suddenly very hard to speak.

And so, within the space of another month, things changed radically again for René and his family. In less than three days Lyon, true to his word, had found Jim an experienced cow-man, began to rebuild the workers' cottages and made it possible for Jim to obtain more working capital and hire more help at a good wage. The parting with Jim and his family was tearful and they agreed to stay in touch, but Jim, considering René's Cold Iron sickness, thought it the best thing that could have happened.

Diana had not been pleased when Lyon told her of what he had done. But he would not listen to any of her arguments against it. "What do you have to say to whom I have working in my Tower?" he demanded. "You'd best get used to the idea, Diana, because I have a notion that this will work out very well and then Roussillon will be here to stay. And Goodbody will be out of the door faster than a cat can lick his ear."

"But what about Simon?" Diana protested.

"*What* about Simon?" Lyon growled. He was getting tired of this entire argument. "If you are going to pick out a fight over that old wrongful rationalization that he's a Frenchman and therefore evil, I don't want to hear it. I've been asking all around about Roussillon and I haven't heard a bad thing about him yet. He seems to be hard working and honest and clever to boot. And he can –"

"Dematerialize," finished Diana scornfully.

"That isn't what I was going to say at all," said Lyon, very much on his dignity. "I was going to say that there are few young Wizards nowadays who would put themselves in jeopardy for the sake of their families. He has a strong sense of duty – I like that."

"Keep him away from Simon," said Diana.

"He'll be too busy to bother with Simon. But I think you are being silly beyond belief, my girl," her uncle retorted. "I think you'd do best to offer my new secretary an apology."

An apology! Diana could not believe what she was hearing. That would never happen! He would be fortunate if she even *spoke* to him!

18

The Green-Eyed Monster

"Another sartorial disaster, Lyonshall?" murmured the Duke of Chenevix, arching an inquiring brow.

Lyon had just brought René to the Tower and introduced him to the Duke and Goodbody. Lyon had invited René to take a look about the Tower while he talked to the Duke.

"What do his clothes matter?" said Lyon in some scorn. "Look him up in *Registratum* as I did. You'll sing a different tune then!" he picked up the volume from his desk and thrust it at Chenevix.

The Duke flipped open the book – Lyon had conveniently marked it for him.

Roussillon, René Alain, he read to himself, skipping over the part about current residence – it had already changed to the Dower House of the Abbey, Rosebank – and the fact that René was listed as a resident alien. What interested the Duke were the test scores. These, for the *Magus Novitiate* and *Magus Minorus*, were broken down into Orals, Essays and Practicals (for each qualifying exam lasted three days with one part on each succeeding day). The score listed said simply, "*No higher score*", which meant the highest score in his test group and also meant that the score was perfect or very, very close to it. The Duke was interested to note that under *Magus Majori* the citation read "*pending.*"

"Pending?" he queried, handing the book back to Lyon.

"There is to be a special sitting for the *Magus Majorus* next week in London. With the current crisis on going, the feeling is that there should be as many qualified *Majorii* as is possible," Lyon explained. "I'm going to sponsor Roussillon. I doubt he'll have any trouble passing it."

"If I were you," drawled the Duke, raising his quizzing glass and surveying René where he stood talking to Goodbody, "I'd visit a decent tailor as well. Really, you cannot expect me, Lyonshall, to sit at table or work with TWO such badly attired secretaries!"

"I don't expect you to do anything, Chenevix, except perhaps leave. You've got a perfectly good place of your own in Dorset, I believe. I cannot conceive why you are still here, in spite of all my little hints..." said Lyon.

"Little hints?" returned Chenevix with a sardonic smile. "I scarcely think the Cheltenham coaching schedule, with the departure times circled in red ink, left by my bedside, constitutes a 'little hint'! But I shall remain here. In the current crisis, as you put it so neatly, my dear Lyonshall, it is more convenient to be here, where all of the reports and messages come in. And by staying here and not in London, I am avoiding the Regent, who would make of my life an utter misery. I do plan to send for Alphonse, however. Your woman is quite adequate in her way, but one misses the presence of an *artiste* in the kitchen."

The Duke then wandered away, leaving his reluctant host without a thing to say.

Augustus Goodbody labored beneath the misapprehension that René had been hired to be *his* assistant and thought how agreeable it would be to have someone to order about. He explained to René as they waited for Lyon and the Duke to finish, how they depended upon him and his superior talents and judgment. He looked pityingly at the new secretary – what a shabby coat and linens and how badly tied was his neck-cloth! Augustus preened himself – at least this poor scarecrow had the example of his exquisite self before him! He could not fail to be impressed!

René had already been warned by Lyon that Goodbody would condescend to him and think himself the superior. But Lyon had made it clear that Goodbody was to be ignored – hopefully, he would not be inflicting himself on them for much longer. René's opinion of Augustus was that he had never met anyone with such a high conceit of himself with so little justification.

It was unbelievable how much things had changed in the last three days. When the position had first been proposed to him René had scarcely been able to believe it. Lyon was like a whirlwind – arranging for help for Jim, seeing them moved into the Dower hose of Rosebank. Ninon and Lucie had been thrilled with their new home. It was completely furnished – beautifully so – and sat in the midst of lush gardens. It was a little Palladian gem of a house, in good repair and well equipped, for the old Marquis's sister, Lady Paulina, had lived there. She had a tidy private fortune and was well able to keep the house in repair. She despised her brother and would not live with him. She had died at a great age, only a year earlier.

And to be able, at long last, to take his *Magus Majorus*! Of course, he had protested Lyon's paying for this – but the Marquis had waved aside all of his objections, saying that it could be paid off in installments, if René insisted, but he, Lyon, considered it an investment.

Lyon, through the medium of an agency, had sent down from London a pair of servants. They were French, from Provence, a mother who cooked and a daughter who would be maid of all work. Ninon had said to her grandson, through tears of happiness, "You cannot say that you are not providing for us now, *mon cher!*"

Lyon walked up to the two young men, scowling as he lay eyes on Augustus. He did wish that the penalty for murder were not hanging. In a better regulated society he would be allowed to kill Augustus for the crime of simply *being* Augustus. Abruptly he said to the young men, 'Do either of you feel a ley line?"

Augustus looked taken aback. He had little feeling for the ley lines from which a Wizard drew a great deal of his power.

Lyon looked disgusted. He could read Goodbody's face all too easily. "Have you ever touched a ley line, Goodbody? I would have thought you'd have at least read about them! Well?" he turned to René impatiently.

"I am standing on one," said René.

231

"Oh, excellent!" Lyon rubbed his hands together in satisfaction. "And where does it originate?"

"In the grove," answered René. "And it ends at the Isle of Apples," he added, giving the Old Celtic name for Avalon.

"Oh, I say! Surely we don't need ley lines! They ain't that important," Augustus bleated. No one was paying attention to him. The Duke, seated on the edge of his desk, swinging his quizzing glass back and forth, looked bored, but in reality was quite interested.

"Not need a channel for magical energies!" snorted Lyon. The ley lines were natural gathering places of magic – node as they were called – in the earth and the magic flowed along the ley lines so that magicians can tap them. There were ley lines all over the Isles and they converged at the most sacred places, where power had been used for millennia. "Where do you think your magic comes from, you nod-cock?" Lyon exploded.

"It comes from nature, don't it? Why does *he* know about that and *I* don't?" Augustus said in some indignation.

René did not wish to make an enemy of Augustus on such a short acquaintance. To forestall Lyon, who quite clearly had a sarcastic answer on his lips, René said quickly, " Perhaps It is because I have been also trained as a Druid, *M'sieur* Goodbody."

A Druid! for the first time Goodbody looked at someone with envy. He had wanted to become a Druid – the prestige of being a Druid was enormous. But he had been refused admission to the Druidical colleges again and again – every single one of them. It was one thing his father's wealth and position could not buy him as it had purchased his *Magus Majori*. He had taken this position to become invaluable to the Arch Druid and perhaps earn his gratitude, which might lead to an recommendation to a Druidical College.

"Did you take your robes?" Goodbody asked stiffly. No matter how long a Druid studied, if he had not been 'robed' in the white linen of the Order, he was not a qualified Druid.

"Yes," said René shortly, more sensitive to Goodbody's expression, than was Lyon.

"He's got his Mastery," said Lyon in malicious satisfaction "or *Maitrise*, as they call it in Brittany, in spite of the fact that he did all his studying through the medium of a scry bowl!"

With this, Goodbody's dislike and envy of René was sealed. It became apparent, even to one of Goodbody's limited intellect, that this newcomer in his shabby, unfashionable garments was to be placed above himself, the Honourable Augustus Goodbody! A bloody Frenchman who hadn't even passed his *Magus Majorii* examination yet and couldn't tie a decent neck-cloth! He ground his teeth in rage. He would see about this!

In two day's time Lyon and René were to leave for London, on dragon-back. René was not completely nervous about the upcoming test, for had he not been preparing for it all of his life? The questions with which Lyon had quizzed him he had answered easily – both Orals and Practicals and a few sample essay questions as well.

Lyon was very well satisfied with his new secretary. Every evening he recounted to Diana and Simon some new talent he had discovered in René: he could read Runes, Ogham, Latin and Greek as readily as most people could read English. He knew the Malchim Alphabet, the Celestial Script and the Writing of the Magi.

Diana grew increasingly tired of this flood of praise. The night before they were to leave for London she added to her uncle's seemingly endless litany "And he can dematerialize! Do not fail to mention that, Uncle!" She gave her embroidery an angry twitch and rammed a needle into her finger.

At her gasp of pain Simon looked up quickly from the book her was reading. At the cross look on Mama's face he bit back what he had been going to say.

In a most unladylike fashion, she put her injured digit in her mouth and sucked the blood away.

Lyon looked at her shrewdly. "Give over, Diana," he advised. "There's nothing about him to dislike. You're the only one who does, for the most nonsensical reasons! You encourage that fawning popinjay–."

Diana gave a gasp of outrage. "I do not encourage that Goodbody creature! I wish him at Jericho daily! He is a guest in this house –."

233

"You needn't be nice to him on my account," Lyon informed her. "nor need you be nice to Chenevix – I'd as like see the back of him, too, but he's more difficult to get rid of than a leech. I do not deny that his presence saves me the trouble of writing reports to London, but I am tempted daily to throw him from out the Tower window."

"And I am certain that he feels the same about you, Uncle," Diana said sweetly.

Lyon snorted. 'You'll play a different tune one day, my girl." He enjoyed these little discussions with his niece. He was confident that given enough time, she would come around. Like his sister Lady Eastcote, he felt that Diana had nursed her grief and rancor for too long.

By the time that Lyon had been gone for four days Diana was ready to slip poison into Goodbody's soup. He had made her life miserable, showing up every place that she was. Chenevix had been no help at all – he disappeared in his barouche every day, to Cheltenham or points beyond. There were very few sick people at the moment in the village and Diana had already delivered more flowers to the Church than could ever be used. In desperation, she had Simon's morning lessons in her bedchamber, only to find Goodbody lying in wait for her in the hall outside her door.

He had proposed to her twice, and she had refused twice, in as strong terms as she could manage. He persisted in believing she was just being coy and would eventually accept him.

They had received a scry from London – Roussillon had passed every test with the highest scores. There was a small amount of business to finish up in London and they would be home for supper that night, as they had gone dragon-back. Diana would be glad to see Lyon home – he MUST get rid of the Goodbody menace. The Menace was talking now of writing to Lord Eastcote and getting his permission to marry her. Diana could only imagine her father's answer to this request. He cordially loathed all of the Ffoillots, and had she truly been enamored of Augustus, they would have had to make for Gretna Green and live in hiding, for Lord Eastcote would have never accepted the match.

In the early part of the afternoon Diana went out to the rose garden blooming around the mermaid fountain. The gardeners had done their magic and the area was full of roses and a lovely sight in the hot summer sun. Armed with secauters and a basket Diana went out to cut roses for the dinner table. For once, Goodbody was not in evidence.

It was a beautiful afternoon. The bright blue sky had only puffs of white fair weather clouds drifting by serenely. Everything was in full flower, the grass and trees brilliant green. It was slightly hot, and rather drowsy. A light breeze kissed the roses and lifted crystal veils of spray from the now working mermaid fountain. The scent of roses hung heavy in the air, intoxicating the senses.

Diana hummed to herself as she chose the most perfect blooms for her basket. The roses ranged in colour from red and yellow to pink and white.

Wherever Goodbody was she hoped he would stay there and perhaps never come back. She paid little attention to what was happening around her, relaxing and carefully cutting the rose stems.

Therefore she was unprepared when that odious, reedy voice that she so dreaded said, quite near, "Ah, there you are, my dear! What a charming picture you make!"

Infuriated, Diana looked up from under the brim of her Lavinia hat. Unlike a bonnet, this was a wide hat that offered protection from the sun. Unfortunately it did not shield her from a view of Goodbody, yellow teeth grinning away, and to his mind at least, resplendent in a coat of lavender Bath coating, with a eye-catching and stomach-turning waistcoat of gold embroidered puce.

"Can you not let me alone for even such a small sum of time as an hour?" she snapped. "I came out here to be alone!"

He was genuinely puzzled. "Why would you wish to do that, my dear? Of course you would prefer to be in my company!" Anyone would, his tone said.

Could nothing pierce this odious toad's ego? She had been bending over the flowers, now she turned to face him and leveled the secauters at him. "Leave – me – alone!" she said slowly. "Before I forget I am a lady and do you harm!"

He laughed – it sounded like a jackass braying. He reached out and grabbed the secauters and twisted them out of her grasp. He was surprisingly strong. "I like a female with spirit!" he said, licking his lips.

Diana was thrown off her balance when he grasped the secauters and fell back a little, slipping on the grass. Her narrow skirts hampered her effort to regain her footing and twisted about her legs. That was it! He was going to feel her wrath. But before she could free her legs from the entanglement of her skirts he grabbed her and held her against his chest and began to rain slobbering wet kisses over her face and throat. "This is what it takes to tame a female like you!" he said between assaults. "Mastery!"

She was shrieking by now and trying to kick him, but her kid slippers had little effect on his boot-clad legs. He had her hands in his grasp and she could but pull ineffectively at them. She was not only furious, she was nauseated. She never knew that a kiss – for she had only kissed Jonathan in passion – could be so horrible. She could not get away from him! She began to pull her magic in to push him into the fountain.

Then suddenly she was free and Goodbody was yelling from where he now lay on the ground at her feet, "Get your hands off me, you cur! The lady is my *fiancée!*"

"I am no such thing!" Diana looked up and pushed her hair out of her eyes, bosom heaving angrily.

René Roussillon stood there, eyes averted, holding his coat out to her. "He has torn your gown," he said in an expressionless voice.

Diana looked down at herself and gasped. Her pretty cheery coloured round gown had always a low décolletage, but now it was open nearly to her waist. Cheeks burning, she snatched at his proffered coat and wrapped herself in it.

"How dare you, sirrah!" Augustus was blustering. "How dare you lay hands on me? Do you know who I am?"

"You are a mannerless lout! *Veillez sur vous*!! To attack a lady – " said René heatedly.

"We are betrothed – we were expressing our affection!" said Augustus, swiping at his lavender sleeves as if René's touch had somehow defiled it.

"We are NOT betrothed!" Diana shouted. "There isn't enough money in the world to pay me to marry you! Under no consideration would I ever wed you! Should the Prince Regent order me to marry you under pain of going to the executioner's block if I did not, I should prefer the headsman's axe! If some mischance cause a wedding I should kill myself! Is that clear enough for you, Mr. Goodbody?" Her eyes were flaming and her voice quivered.

"Magnificent!" he said in admiration.

Diana shrieked in exasperation.

"You had best leave now, *M'sieur*," said René in a low but nonetheless menacing voice. " I cannot bear an insult to a lady or stupidity. And you have managed to step upon all of my nerves – I may find I can no longer restrain myself –"

"Don't let me stop you!" said Diana. "Plant him a facer! I'll stand here and cheer!"

Something in both their attitudes told Augustus he was treading on very boggy ground. "No need for violence!" he said. "You cannot hurt an unarmed man!" With an exaggerated bow he left them, walking away as fast as he could with as much dignity as he could muster.

"Are you all right, *Madame*?" René said stiffly, still not looking at Diana.

She could not look at him either. She blushed down to her toes when she remembered the state of her gown. Equally stiffly, she said, "I am fine."

"I will escort you to the house," he said, and would not listen to her protests. They walked to the French doors, still avoiding one another's gaze. When the safety of the Abbey was reached he said, "Your uncle sent me to find you, to tell you that we were arrived. You will find him in the library. He should be told of what this Goodbody has done, *du vrai*."

"Yes," she agreed softly. "Yes, I will tell him."

As he turned to go she said hurriedly, "Mr. Roussillon!"

He stopped and turned slightly. "Yes?"

"Thank you," she said quietly, finally meeting his gaze.

".*Je vous en prie*," he said. "Think nothing of it. Anyone would have done as much." With this he turned again and rapidly strode away in the direction of the Dssower house.

Wrapped in his coat, Diana stared after him for a long moment.

19

The Accusation

Lyon literally roared when Diana told him of what Augustus Goodbody had done to her. She had gone straight to the library, still wrapped in Mr. Roussillon's coat. She had scarcely finished telling Lyon what had happened when he ran into the hall, shouting at the top of his voice, "Goodbody! Get your miserable self down here!"

Goodbody had gone to his room, seething. How dare that Froggie lay hands on him! And what Diana had said to him rankled. Did she not realize how fortunate she was that he wished to take her to wife? After all, she was only an Earl's daughter and a widow with a small child to boot. She was shop-worn goods! He deserved better! He failed to take into account that Diana, as an Earl's daughter, outranked him – the third son of a Viscount, which was one rank below an Earl.

And to top it all, there were grass stains on his new coat! His man clucked over these – those would probably be impossible to remove.

When Goodbody heard Lyon shouting he presumed that the Marquis wanted him for his secretarial duties, or perhaps to apologize for the insult to his person. That Froggie certainly owed him an abject apology! As did Lady Diana – the more he thought about it, the more he became convinced that the entire scene was all her fault. She actually threatened him with her secauters! What was he supposed to do – let a mere female order him about? No real man would tolerate such behavior in the weaker sex!

Therefore it was a very much on his dignity Augustus Goodbody who descended the stairs at his usual leisurely pace.

But as he reached the bottom of the stairs he suddenly became nervous, for Lyon was waiting for him and the Arch Druid wore the strangest look he had ever seen on a human face.

His features were white and cold, set like stone. His eyes blazed as if there were a fire within him. "Goodbody," he said in a voice that sent chills down the hapless secretary's spine "you dared to lay hands on my niece!"

"But –" Augustus bleated.

It was all that he was able to say. With a mighty oath Lyon grabbed him, taking hold of him by the seat of his pale primrose pantaloons and the high collar of his coat.

Seppings, who was standing in the hall, opened the massive oak door. His face was impassive, but inside he was cheering. How he would relish recounting this episode in the servant's Hall!

With little effort, Lyon threw Goodbody down the steps and onto the gravel drive. "Get out!" he stated. "If ever I see you near my niece, or my house again I will make you wish you had never been born!"

Goodbody, who had landed face down in the gravel, turned over with no little difficulty and said indignantly, "I offered her marriage! And this is how I am treated!"

"Marriage to such as you! Don't be ridiculous, Goodbody! Her family would rather see her dead than married to you!" Lyon said contemptuously. "Now, get off my property before I *really* lose my temper! I have not even done half to you what I should like to!" He had not even used magic on the hapless secretary.

"My traps, and my man..." Goodbody began, whining. "And I came post! How am I to return to London?"

"I neither know nor care," said Lyon. "And don't ask Tuathail to take you! I daresay he'd just as soon flame you where you stand!"

Goodbody pushed himself to his feet, noting with horror that the sleeve of the new coat he had donned was torn, there was a tear in the knee of his pantaloons and a long deep scratch on his not-so-shining any more Hessian boots.

His palms had gravel deeply imbedded. "I shall inform the Regent of your treatment of me!" he threatened.

Lyon snorted. "I don't care what that fat fool thinks of me! You would do far better to worry about what he should say to you should I tell him the insult you offered to a lady in her own home! I would call you out, but you're scarcely up to my weight, magically or otherwise!" he added in derision. "I'll give your man an hour to pack up your traps and then he must leave."

"But, but where am I to go?" Augustus stammered.

"I suggest Hell!" Lyon gave him a last look of abhorrence and slammed the great oak door.

After telling Lyon about the events of the afternoon (and watching her uncle's reaction from the safety of the library), Diana's first desire was for a bath. She felt besmirched and dirty and was horrified to find that she was shaking all over. She was not certain whether it was with anger or fear. Would he have raped her? Precepts pounded into her head since she was a little girl had almost prevented her from using her magic on him. One never used magic on a weaker talent.

But would it have been self-defense to have tossed him into the mermaid fountain with hopes of his drowning? He might have sued her for assault – she had read of such cases and the law was very murky on what constituted self-defense. If only her skirts had not entangled her legs – she could have kicked him. And she admitted to herself that it had all happened so fast – she had misjudged him. She had never thought he would bestir himself to attack her – she had thought him a conceited pop-injay, too lazy to endanger her.

Thank goodness Mr. Roussillon had come along when he did! She shuddered to think that if Goodbody had succeeded in his attempt she might have *had* to marry him to save her good name. It was a future she could not even contemplate without acute nausea.

When she reached the blessed quiet of her room she rang for her new maid, Susan. Susan was from the village, and a most pleasant girl, who liked to chatter. She was horrified when she came into the room and saw Diana still wrapped in the borrowed coat.

241

"Oh, my lady! Whatever's happened?" she said, round-eyed. "Here's Mr. Goodbody thrown out the front door – and good riddance to bad rubbish, Mr. Seppings tells us!"

Diana took off the coat and revealed her torn dress to Susan. "He attacked me," she said simply.

Susan shrieked. "Oh, my lady!" she gasped. "He didn't –"

"No, thank God!" said Diana. "Mr. Roussillon came along and stopped him. This is Mr. Roussillon's coat. He gave it to me as soon as he had take care of Goodbody."

"It's lucky he was there!" Susan took the coat and folded it up. "I'll see that it is cleaned and returned to him."

"I will return it myself, Susan," Diana said tiredly. "It is the least I can do."

Susan looked at her in sympathy. "You need a bath and a nice cup of tea, my lady. And perhaps a little sleep before dinner."

This sounded wonderful. Diana was suddenly so tired that she wanted to cry. She allowed Susan to help her from the ruined gown. Susan lamented the damage to it, but Diana told the maid to burn it – she never wanted to see it again. Even should it be able to be mended, it would always remind her of this horrible afternoon.

After her bath and restorative tea Susan put her mistress into a peignoir and turned down the bed. She had Diana sit at the dressing table while her hair was brushed out.

The brushing, with long, firm strokes, was soothing and Diana felt the last of her tension melting away. She glanced idly at the top of her dressing table and saw a piece of jewelry there – not a piece of hers, she was certain. It appeared to be a Wizard's lapel pin.

"What is this, Susan?" she asked, touching the pin. It was a Wizards' staff, with a crystal on top, with sprigs of enameled mistletoe wrapped around it.

"Oh, that was on Mr. Roussillon's coat, my lady. I took it off so's I could brush the coat. It's his Wizard's pin, isn't it?" answered Susan.

"Yes, it is," Diana answered slowly. It was not just *any* Wizard's pin. The only one she had ever seen like it was Lyon's. Only Wizards who had completely mastered what was called 'general knowledge' wore such a pin. This was a misnomer, for 'general knowledge' was the most difficult of the Wizardly disciplines. It meant an astonishing degree of arcane expertise in all areas of the craft. The tests for general knowledge were well known to be brutal and longer than normal. Very few Wizards even sat for such an exam, much less passed it. Diana was impressed in spite of herself. And the mistletoe meant he was a first- rank Druid as well.

She would return the coat to him with her fervent thanks. And perhaps an apology as well.

Before returning to the Dower House, René went by the dragon pen. He had brought several packages from London. Lyon had given him an advance on his wages and he had bought gifts for his mother and grandmother. It had been wonderful to have money to spend on them and Lyon had directed him to a fascinating place called the Pantheon Bazaar, where there had been bargains galore. The packages had traveled home safely in Tuathail's breast harness and were neatly stacked, waiting for him, on the edge of the dragon pen.

Tuathail, his stomach showing the outlines of a very good dinner, was sound asleep, snoring blissfully with little puffs of steam coming from his nostrils. René did not awaken him, but quietly scooped up his packages and went on his way to the Dower House.

It was very pleasant to cone home to this pretty little house. He let himself in and admired how the afternoon sun filled the rooms, gleaming on highly polished furniture and floors. Something delicious was cooking, the scent of it mingling with the clean smells of beeswax and lemon oil. He took a deep, appreciative breath. There was no underlying odor of cows.

The ground floor consisted of an entry hall – with a delicate iron staircase curving up against the wall. To the right was a drawing room, to the left a music room, complete with harp, pianoforte and music stands. In the back lay a bookroom, the dining room and a breakfast parlour that caught the morning sun. Stone steps led down to a basement kitchen and a small servants' Hall, as well as pantries, a buttery and a still room. Above stairs were five bedrooms and,

243

wonder of wonders – a modern water-closet. The second floor contained. servants' quarters and box rooms. It was a home of which to be proud

Laughter led René to the drawing room. He heard his mother and grandmother talking excitedly. He left his packages on a table in the hall. When he entered the room, René was pleased and surprised to find the Vicar with his family, having tea.

There were shrieks of joy when they saw him, much hugging and kissing and the Vicar wrung his hand with sincere congratulations on his achievement.

"But how fine you look, René!" Ninon said, surveying her grandson. "You have new clothes! And you had had *le coupe de cheveux!*"

"The Windswept, is it not?" Mr. Arabin approved his young friend's new hair-style. "Most becoming."

"*M'sieur le Marquis* insisted that I had to be dressed properly for my position. He considers it a uniform," said René, looking at his new rig-out.

"But where is your coat?" asked Lucie. "Surely you are not to go about in shirtsleeves?"

"Lady Diana wears it at the moment," he said ruefully, and quickly told them of what had happened in the rose garden.

"I do not like this Lady Diana," said Ninon, "but no woman should be subjected to *le violer*! And to have to bear such a *scélérat!*"

"He is indeed a scoundrel!" said Mr. Arabin heatedly. "He ought to be horsewhipped!"

"He will be fortunate if Lord Lyonshall only horse-whips him," said René. "He has the temper, that one." He did not mention that his chief emotion on seeing Goodbody manhandling Diana, was to wish to tear the little *foutue pédale's* head from his shoulders and beat him to death with it. René had never experienced such a surge of anger in his entire life. He still wanted to do extreme violence to Augustus Goodbody. But it was not his place. He was limited to what any gentleman might have done. For she was not a member of his family, his *fiancée*, nor even his friend.

Mr. Arabin was all agog to hear about the examination and its difficulties and to see the lapel pin that was always presented to each Wizard upon successful completion of each *Magus Majorus* examination. He was disappointed when René realized that the pin was still on the coat he had given Diana. He promised to show it to the Vicar on Sunday, after church, but said that now he had to give out presents.

"*Cadeaux!*" Ninon and Lucie exclaimed as one and barely contained themselves as René fetched the packages from the hall.

There were several bandboxes and flat packages. There was even one for the Vicar.

The two ladies tore into their gifts, exclaiming with delight and throwing aside wrappings in reckless abandon. In the bandboxes were two bonnets, plain straw, but he packages contained ribbons and feathers and artificial flowers – everything one needed to trim a bonnet.

"*C'est très chic!*" said Ninon, running to a large mirror that hung on the wall. "But René, to spend so much money! *C'est trop cher!*"

"*Non, Grandmère,*" he said. "*C'est très bon marche!* Very inexpensive!" He told them about the Pantheon Bazaar.

"Me, I should wish to see this Bazaar place," said Lucie, stroking her hat and already planning how she was going to trim it. "Just think how fine we shall look at Church, *Maman!*"

The Vicar was thrilled with his books — a recently published volume *Natural Magic and Christianity* by the Reverend Rupert Baxter and a new translation of the poems of the Welsh bard Taliesin.

"It is like *le Noël!*" sighed Ninon, when more packages revealed copies of fashion magazines, *La Belle Assemblée* and *the Ladies' Monthly Museum* and two paisley shawls.

The Vicar was asked to remain to supper – and the new servants, Madame Roche and her daughter Giselle, proved to be gems of their kind. They dined on roasted chicken in the Provençal style with tomatoes, new potatoes, aubergines, courgettes, mushrooms, and onions, with olive oil and lemons brought from London, where there was a thriving colony of Provençal *émigrés*.

The food had been so good and plentiful lately that René had not had his usual dreams of edibles. Tonight he dreamed of something else entirely. He dreamed of Lady Diana Stillfield.

At first Goodbody could not think of what to do. He had no carriage. As he had told Lyon, he had come post, and since he had become a habitué of the *Beetle and Wedge* he was well aware that that small inn was not a posting house. Should he ever sink so low as to take the common stage – and he would *never* do so – the *Beetle and Wedge* was not even a coach stop. Goodbody had not the slightest idea how one obtained a seat on a public coach. He would have to pay some rustic to convey him to the nearest posting house. In spite of his gaming losses he was still relatively plump in the pocket, and could afford a post chaise and pair back to London.

But at the moment, he thought the best course was to get to the *Beetle and Wedge* and see if one of the fellows who would be in there at this time of day wetting his whistle would be willing to earn a sovereign conveying Augustus, his man and his traps to Cheltenham, or the closest posting facility. Goodbody gave little thought as to how Thompson would manage to get himself and the mountain of Goodbody baggage to the *Beetle and Wedge*. That was Thompson's problem – that was what he was paid for.

Goodbody had not realized how far it was to the *Beetle and Wedge* if one had to walk on rather tight boots. He had always taken a horse from the stables or borrowed, without permission, Lyon's curricle. It was not above three miles, but it seemed like much more. The day was hot and becoming sultry. Goodbody was so warm that he indulged in an impropriety for a dandy of his standing – he removed his coat and loosened his neckcloth. By the time he reached the little inn his handkerchief, used to wipe his sweating brow, was a limp rag, he was lame, and he was so thirsty he would have even drunk water, or as he referred to it – Adam's ale. He was certain that he had a blister on his heel. He was irritated beyond belief and wanted his revenge on all of them – Lyonshall, Roussillon and Lady Diana.

The interior of the inn was cool and dark. It was a very old building, with blackened beams overhead and a stained ceiling from the hearth fire and the many pipes smoked there daily. The windows were mullioned and stood open on the soporific summer afternoon. The streets of the village were empty and all was quiet.

There was only one person in the tap as Goodbody limped in. A large country gentleman sat at the bar, nursing a tankard of home-brewed. He wore a black look on his face, which made Goodbody hesitate to approach him. Goodbody thought he looked familiar – probably from the dice games in the back room. The landlord did not seem to be anywhere in evidence.

Wearily, Goodbody limped to a table and sat down, wincing as he did so. Every minute he was discovering more aches and pains. His palms stung and his ribs ached, and he had discovered a bruise on his chin as well as one on his *derriere* – he could not imagine how that portion of his anatomy had become injured – but Lyon could have told him – a well-placed kick as Goodbody became airborne.

The big man at the bar suddenly crashed his tankard on the bar and shouted "Landlord! Another!"

From a door behind the bar there appeared a roly-poly individual with a balding pate and an insincere smile. He wore a much spotted apron and was carrying a jug of beer, "Ah, I figured you was ready for another, Sir Piers," he said in a rather oily fashion.

Sir Piers grunted as the landlord, Josh Hibbert by name, poured him another tankard. This the baronet downed rapidly and held out his tankard for yet another.

The landlord poured it and chancing to look up, caught sight of Augustus. "Why, whatever happened to you, sir?" he asked, shocked at Goodbody's appearance. He looked as if he had been dragged backwards through a bush.

"I had an accident," Goodbody said brusquely. He wasn't about to tell this bucolic tapster that he had been thrown out from the Abbey.

Sir Piers turned about to look at him. "Goodbody, isn't it?" he queried.

Augustus said shortly "Yes."

"What happened to you?" Mildmay demanded. scowling at Goodbody.

Augustus did not like that look. That was all he needed – another large, angry man.

"I had a disagreement with Lord Lyonshall," he answered.

"There's little doubt who won, is there?" Sir Piers roared at his own joke while Goodbody winced.

"It's all that damn Froggie's fault!" Goodbody burst out. "Lord Lyonshall believed him instead of me!" Goodbody had no idea whether or not Roussillon had gone to Lord Lyonshall – he only knew that he himself would have run to the most powerful person.

Sir Piers stared at him through narrowed eyes. "What Froggie?"

"Roussillon," said Goodbody and let out an involuntary moan as he shifted in the hard wooden chair injudiciously.

"You interest me strangely," said Mildmay. He slid off the stool and went to join Goodbody at the table. "Hibbert! Bring a tankard for my friend Goodbody."

His friend? Augustus looked up at the large man as he sat down. "I remember you now –" he said slowly. "You're Sir Piers somebody or other."

"Mildmay," supplied the baronet. "Tell me about your dealings with the Froggie."

Nothing loath to pour his troubles into the ear of a man of his own class (although Sir Piers dressed badly, he was, after all, a baronet) Goodbody made his grievances known. Sir Piers kept his mug well filled. And this, combined with the unaccustomed exertions of the afternoon soon made Goodbody loquacious and belligerent.

Sir Piers had been angry ever since he found out that the French bitch and her family had not died in the fire. He cold not figure out how they had escaped and it frustrated him beyond belief. There they had been, as bold as brass, sitting in their accustomed pew on the first Sunday after their supposed deaths! His partners in crime had assured Piers that the family had been seen at the table, drunk as lords, before the cottage was secured with Cold Iron and fired. He had been mulling over his revenge for some weeks now, but had not come up with a plan. Listening to this poor fool gave him an idea.

248

"How would you like to see that Froggie swinging at the end of a rope?" he interrupted a tirade on the ruination of two of Trenton the tailor's best coats.

Augustus looked at him blearily. "Like it fine," he muttered, taking another swig of beer and managing to put a good deal of it on his cravat.

"I have a plan – you're a patriotic English-man, ain't you?"

Goodbody bristled at the very thought that he could be any thing else. "Certainly I am!" he declared loudly. The effect was somewhat spoiled by a loud drunken hiccough.

"Well, then –" Sir Piers leaned in closely and began to whisper to Goodbody.

And a slow, nasty smile began to spread over that gentleman's face.

The Duke of Chenevix was much distressed that his absence might have contributed to Diana's unpleasant encounter with Goodbody. Lyon told him about it at breakfast the next morning, for the Duke had dined in Cheltenham and had not returned until late. Although Chenevix was glad indeed to find that Goodbody was gone for good, he apologized profusely to Diana and berated himself for his desertion of her. "I was selfish – I thought only of my dislike of the puppy. I never thought that I would lay you open to insult, my dear Lady Diana. Had I been here, he'd have felt my whip about his shoulders!"

Diana had never seen the Duke so passionate and liked him the better for it. There was no doubt but that he was genuinely distressed. She tried to make light of it, for both older gentlemen were in a tear over Goodbody's behavior. Lyon penned an angry letter to Viscount Ffoillot, while the Duke declared that once in Town, he would see to it that Goodbody was banned from Almack's and from the drawing rooms of all the tonnish hostesses. Such infamy must, and would be, punished.

For once, Chenevix and Lyonshall were in accord. When they at last adjourned to the Tower for the day's work, they were loud in their praise of René's actions. He brushed their compliments aside. After a night of very disturbing dreams about Diana he preferred to forget the whole affair. Goodbody was gone. *C'est fini.*

Therefore, all three of them were surprised when at ten o'clock Seppings tapped on the door and announced "Sir Piers Mildmay, and the Honourable Augustus Goodbody to see you, my Lords. I am sorry, your Grace, my Lord. I could not stop them," he added apologetically.

Chenevix and Lyon exchanged glances. René stiffened. What was that murderer Mildmay doing here in the company of the *chien* Goodbody?

"What are you doing back here?" Lyon bellowed as Goodbody entered, hiding a bit behind the bulk of Sir Piers.

"We are here on a matter of national security," said Sir Piers. looking selfrighteous.

"National security?" repeated Lyon incredulously. "What are you talking about, you great gas-bag?"

Chenevix lifted his quizzing glass to his eye and stared up and down at this strange delegation. Both Mildmay and Goodbody turned a dull red under his magnified, mocking stare.

"You are employing someone suspected of being a security risk," shrilled Goodbody. "In a word, HIM!" And he leveled a finger at René.

"You're a blithering jackass!" Lyon exploded.

"I'm a patriotic Englishman! And how do you think Lord Bathurst at the Horse Guards will receive the news that you're employing a Froggie as your assistant? He's probably ferrying every thing he learns here to Napoleon!" said Goodbody triumphantly.

"Do not try me too far, Goodbody," the Duke said suddenly in his most arctic voice. "Take care. You have already earned my rancor."

That his two employers did not seem to believe this farrago of nonsense was good to hear, but it did nothing to improve René's temper, which was beginning to boil. He was so tired of all this Froggie business – the distrust and the veiled hints – there had to be a way to stop it for once and for all.

And there was a way.

"*M'sieurs!*" he interrupted the argument that had broken out. They all turned to look at him. "There is a way to resolve this matter. I will do whatever I can to make everyone certain that I am loyal to my adopted country. I will pledge my life on the Swearing Stone."

"The Swearing Stone!" Lyon looked at him in consternation. "Do you know how serious that is? Do you know what the consequences can be?"

"Of course I know!" said René scathingly." Am I not a Druid? But I will have an end to this doubt and accusations! *Je n'ai rien fait.* And I think the Swearing Stone is the only way that such as these will ever believe the truth! *Tant mieux!*" He was adamant.

"What is he talking about?" demanded Goodbody.

"Your ignorance never ceases to amaze me, Good-body," said Lyon scathingly. "He is talking about the Cremave."

20

The Cremave

Something was wrong in the house – Simon could feel it. Ever since yesterday evening he had surprised groups of servants talking in excited tones, who suddenly fell into awkward silence as someone noticed his approach. Mama had not come in to kiss him goodnight. Sanders had told him that Mama was feeling unwell – she had a bad headache. The way Sanders said 'headache' – rather hesitantly – told Simon that Sanders was making up a story. And this morning, he had gone down the breakfast parlour, for Mama was very late in coming up for his lesson, and he had heard raised voices before he tapped on the door. Again, that suspicious silence had fallen over the room. The Duke of Chenevix had a peculiar look on his face, which Simon could not interpret. Simon was never certain whether or not he actually liked the Duke- the Duke was so emotionless that it was like trying to decide if one liked a statue as a friend.

And Mr. Goodbody was nowhere to be found. Of course, he never joined any of the other adults for breakfast. He lay in bed till all hours. But Simon did not see him any where around. When he asked one of the maids, Nancy, where Goodbody was, Nancy gave a short laugh and said "Gone for good!"

Mama said that there would be no lessons this morning – she still wasn't feeling well, so Simon was free to play out of doors by himself. He could always amuse himself with a book or just studying things, like the fish in the mermaid fountain, or talking to Tuathail, whom he liked almost as much as Pádraig, his first dragon friend. Simon had gone to the Cheltenham Dragon Day earlier in June, as Mama had promised, and had had a grand time. He had met all sorts of dragons and ridden on a Welsh Red.

Simon was in the front drive watching the head gardener put in some new plants in flower beds that would border the drive. The Abbey was going to be beautiful when it was completed. The head gardener, McAllister, was fussy about the floral borders, but always took time to tell Simon what he was doing and why, and told the boy many interesting things about the flowers and their Faerie guardians. Simon longed to see another Faerie like the blue Medb, but had not been fortunate so far.

Therefore Simon was in an excellent position to see the carriage with Sir Piers Mildmay and Mr. Goodbody arrive. Simon disliked Sir Piers as much as he disliked Mr. Goodbody. Sir Piers was loud and large and his horses always seemed unhappy – Daniel had told Simon that a horse who wrung its tail and jibbed at the bit was not a happy horse. If Daniel had been there to see Sir Piers' driving skills, he would have stigmatized the baronet as "ham–fisted."

Why was Mr. Goodbody with Sir Piers? Simon wondered. The two went directly to the Tower, which had a door at the bottom, used mostly for deliveries. Simon heard them arguing with the footman on duty, who sent for Seppings, but the butler was swept aside like so many dead leaves by the sheer bulk of Sir Piers. Simon also heard Uncle Lyon yelling "What are you doing back here?"

But then he heard nothing else until Goodbody and the baronet left. Almost immediately after that Mr. Roussillon came from out the Tower door and went directly to the dragon pen. From behind a shrub Simon watched him as he quickly put the message harness on Tuathail and insert what looked like a folded parchment into the secure flapped pocket.

"All the way to Temair na Rig in one day?" Simon heard the dragon inquire rather plaintively.

"It is most urgent. Go quickly, *s'il vous plait*," Mr. Roussillon replied. "And return quickly as well, with an answer."

With a grumble of "'Tis lucky you are I've just had a good feed of firestone!" Tuathail crouched down and with a thrust of his muscular back legs and a long stream of fire, shot into the air and began to spiral upwards, beating his huge wings.

Mr. Roussillon stood watching the dragon become but a rapidly disappearing spot in the sky for a moment and then quickly returned to the Tower.

Simon would have liked to go and say hello to his former tutor, but it had been impressed upon him that he was not to go near Mr. Roussillon. Mr. Roussillon was here to work for Uncle Lyon in the Tower, which was a place Simon was only to go if invited. It was not a suitable place for playing – there were too many things that might be dangerous. Once more Simon thought that the world would be a much better place if there were not so many rules and if he could only understand why adults made so many strange, incomprehensible rules in the first place.

And later during the day there was more mystery. People were still whispering and Uncle Lyon wore a grim look at the noon meal. For once he and Chenevix seemed in accord, which in itself was odd. Mama was abstracted, too, as if she were thinking of something else, and had to be reminded of the afternoon riding lesson.

Simon was rather miffed. No one would tell him anything, of course. When adults behaved like this, something important was going on, And if he asked about it, he would probably be told he was too young to know about it, or he wouldn't understand what it was. How he hated being treated like a baby! He would be nine in September – that was rather grown up – certainly not a baby!

When asked outright during the riding les-son Mama said that there was nothing going on – nothing that Simon need worry his head about at any rate.

Simon had discovered that he was a natural rider and was rapidly progressing. Today they went for the first time out of the paddock and onto a long grassy ride. Daniel still kept a lead line on Gwen's bridle from his seat on a rangy bay and Mama on her mare Luna rode along side him. Today they cantered for the first time and Simon reveled in the feel of the wind against his face and the horse beneath him. It was almost as good as riding a dragon. He had no trouble staying on and was disappointed when the grass came to an end and they had to stop.

"Good work, Master Simon!" said Daniel. "Another week an' we'll have you goin' over those big oxers in th' hunter's field!"

Simon glowed with the praise. Mama too, told him ne was doing very well indeed, and when he was an accomplished equestrian she would teach him to drive, for she now had a pair of carriage horses who pulled a smart phaeton – not a high-perch phaeton. Simon would be afraid to ride in one of those with its swaying body fully five feet above the ground. Simon saw no illogic in being frightened of a high carriage and feeling no qualms about riding a dragon hundreds of feet up in the air.

It wasn't until almost bed-time that Simon found out what a part of the mystery was. He was in his room, with the door ajar, when he heard two of the maids going by in the hall. Nancy, the upstairs maid, was talking to Susan, Mama's maid.

"Never so glad to see the backside of anyone in me life! That Goodbody was a pincher and a grabber! Always hated doing up his room – I'd think him gone and go into to clean an' he'd be lyin' in wait for me in th' dressin' room! Get me in a corner an' squeeze me titties an' try an' kiss me! Ugh! An' I swear me bum is black an' blue from where he pinched me! After all the maids, he was."

"You should have seen what he done to her ladyship! Tore her gown near down to her waist, he did! Who knows what have happened if Mr. Roussillon hadn't come along?" Susan said. "No wonder his lordship threw him out the door! Mr.Seppings said 'twas a wonderful sight!"

The two maids laughed and went on down the hall.

Simon was horrified. Goodbody had tried to hurt Mama and torn her dress? And he had hurt Nancy, who Simon liked very much. Why would Goodbody do such things? All his life Simon had been told about the behavior expected of a gentleman – and hurting females was *not* the behavior of a gentleman! No wonder Uncle Lyon looked so grim.

Simon was suddenly afraid. Was Uncle Lyon going to fight a duel with Goodbody? Would Uncle Lyon perhaps be killed? He decided he *had* to find out what was going on. He would ask Uncle Lyon right out.

It was nearly dinner time. Simon had been told by Sanders that he would be eating with the adults again. Simon had wondered at that, but now he understood – Goodbody was gone. The Duke of Chenevix had no objection to Simon joining them; he had even told Mama that Simon was "a very pretty behaved child, now that he was finished his fit of the sulks." The Duke had chosen to utter these sentiments within Simon's hearing.

At this time of day Uncle Lyon could generally be found in the library. After finishing in the Tower for the day he washed up and changed for dinner, then had a pipe in his library until Seppings rang the gong and announced the serving of the evening meal.

So Simon headed for the library, down one flight from his room. Robert, on of the footmen, was on duty at the foot of the stairs and smiled at Simon in a friendly fashion as the boy went by.

The library was in the back of the house and Simon had to go through several drawing rooms and the music room to get there. The sun was declining and sent long golden beams through the stained glass windows that lit up the hall leading to the library. The carved door to that apartment stood ajar and once again Simon heard voices.

"The best, the ablest assistant I've ever had and he wants to put his head in a noose all to appease some bacon-brained addle–pots who've got a maggoty notion in what passes for their brain-boxes!" Lyon was saying. "It's past all understanding!"

"I am not certain that the hanging simile is an apt one, Lyonshall," came the cold voice of the Duke of Chenevix. "Perhaps a better description would be putting one's hand in a kettle of molten metal. But I understand why he wishes to do it, even though it is not necessary. He wants to end all doubts, for once and all. And I cannot say as I blame him. To live beneath suspicion and doubt of one's motives is very trying indeed."

"It's incredibly dangerous," said Lyon sav-agely. "Have you ever seen anyone undergo the ritual of the Swearing Stone, Chenevix? I have – once. He died."

"Then obviously he was not telling the truth and should have refused to undergo the rite," the Duke was unconcerned. "Roussillon seems confident that the Stone will show him to be truthful."

"He has to be one hundred percent committed to England and her cause, or the Stone will know it, and will punish him – to what degree I can't imagine," Lyon said.

"By this time tomorrow it will be done and finished," the Duke said coolly. "If your dragon makes good time Ó Clérigh will be with us, perhaps even by this evening, with the Cremave. My only wish is that we needn't have to have those two rank outsiders at the ceremony."

"There's no way around that," said Lyon gloomily. "If we don't let them watch they'll cry havoc and accuse us of cheating. The very last thing we need is a full scale scandal-broth and Bathurst dragged into this mess. Conchobar is willing to keep quiet. He and I will be the two Druids needed in the ceremony. I've asked him to bring Mag Uidhir, and I sent a note to Mr. Arabin, who will be the other *Magus Majorus* required by law. And you represent the Office of Magic and Enchantments. Diana can be our independent witness – it's well known how she feels about the French, so there can be no accusations about partiality." Lyon let out a long sigh. "I'm going to blow a cloud. Join me, Chenevix?"

"You know that I find tobacco a filthy habit," said the Duke. "There is a dreadful draught in here – the door is ajar." Footsteps sounded on the library floor and a moment later the door was closed and Simon could hear no more.

His heart was beating so that he thought they must be able to hear it. Mr. Roussillon was going to do something that might kill him! Something that he didn't *have* to do! He had to be stopped! And he, Simon, had to do it.

Simon knew that Mr. Roussillon was now living in the Dower House, for Sanders had told him so. The Dower House was another forbidden place. But Simon did not care. If he could stop this – and just the sound of whatever it was frightened him badly – he would not care if Mama made him spend the rest of his life in his room.

Diana had decided to wait until the next evening to return Mr. Roussillon's coat, giving Susan a chance to clean and brush the garment. She had also been remiss, she realized, not to have gone to the Dower House to have

welcomed the ladies of his family. That she could even contemplate doing this now showed how much her feelings had
changed. She had begun to think of them not so much as evil
French people, but just people – people who had been through
a rough patch and needed help. From Lyon and Mr. Arabin
she had heard of the fire and the Cold Iron sickness. And she
owed so much to Mr. Roussillon – he had saved her virtue and
her reputation. And according to Simon, he had also saved his
life. Simon kept insisting on that and she was at last
beginning to see the truth of it.

Since the Duke's *chef de cuisine*, Alphonse, had
arrived at the Abbey, they no longer kept country hours, but
dined fashionably late at half after seven. There was at least
an hour before dinner when Diana set out for he Dower
House.

The Dower House, Rosebank, lay to one side of the
main drive, down a sloping lawn and with a short drive of its
own. It was scarcely a mile from the main house, but far
enough away so that any Dowager there ensconced might
think twice about making the trek to the main house.

The sun was sending its last long golden rays over the
emerald grass and making huge blue shadows of the immense
trees in the park. A few sleepy birds tittered in the trees and
the air was still and sweet. The grass had been scythed that
day and the satisfying summer scent rose up from beneath
Diana's feet. This had always been one of her favorite times of
day. She loved to sit and watch as the day ended, the blue sky
turning to purple and stars beginning to twinkle in the
heavens. It always seemed such a magical time, as if one
might see a Faerie, if one were still enough. Diana's
grandmother Eastcote, now dead, had always said that there
were many more Faeries about in her day than in these
degenerate modern times.

Diana carried a basket, with the borrowed coat and a
gift of wines. She had at first thought to bring flowers, but the
gardens about Rosebank were much finer than those of the
Abbey, for they had never suffered neglect. But the cellars
had been neglected at the Dower House, since Lady Paulina
did not approve of imbibing alcohol of any sort and was a
member of the Society for the Suppression of Vice, as well.

Diana was admitted at once by a trim little maid, who took her bonnet and shawl, but only announced, "A lady calls!", even though Diana offered her card.

It was an awkward time to pay a call and she was aware of being stared at, rather critically she thought, when she entered the drawing room. Her hosts had obviously finished their dinner – they were drinking a postprandial cup of coffee about a cheerful little fire, for the evenings, even in June, could be chill.

Mr. Roussillon rose at once when she entered the room, putting down his coffee cup with a clatter on the scalloped-edge table between the chairs grouped about the hearth. He looked surprised to see her. Madame de Varien regarded her with hostility and the other lady, who Diana realized was the same she had last seen as a madwoman, regarded Diana with friendly curiosity.

"Lady Diana!"said Mr.Roussillon."We had never thought to see you here."

She felt herself flushing, though his tone was not sarcastic, only surprised. "I came to return this," she said, extracting the neatly folded coat from the top of her basket. The Wizard's pin twinkled on the lapel. "And I wished to thank you again for what you did. I do not know what I would have done had you not come along when you did." She looked straight into his eyes, one part of her mind noting that he had had a haircut and looked very much the gentleman in new clothes.

He took the package and said, "There is no need. It was a pleasure to assault Goodbody."

Ninon snorted in the background.

"Allow me to introduce my grandmother and mother to you, Lady Diana," René said, giving Ninon a stern look.

Introductions were quickly made and Diana invited to sit down. An awkward silence ensued for a moment, for Ninon was frankly hostile and René was puzzled as to why Diana had come on this errand herself, rather than sending her maid or one of the footmen, as he had expected. Lucie engaged in speculative looks between her son and the young lady.

Before the silence became too lengthy Diana remembered the wine in her basket. "I also brought this," she said, drawing two bottles out of the basket. "It is both a

259

welcoming gift and a peace offering," she added, as she placed the bottles on the table.

One was a very fine Cognac and the other a superior Bordeaux. Ninon's eyes lit up. How she had missed a good wine with her meals! And the brandy was just the thing for a *digestif* in the coffee. "Ring for more coffee!" she said happily. "We shall have some Cognac in the cups and Lady Diana will join us, no?" She thanked their guest for the gift and told her that she was to have a treat – Madame Roche made coffee in the French manner – she had brought a French coffee maker, a drip pot, with her from London and *le café* made in the French way was *très delicieux*!

Diana allowed herself to be persuaded and seeing several fashion magazines on the table, asked the ladies if they were choosing new gowns.

Lucie's eyes lit up. She had always been interested in fashion and had been stunned by the changes that had taken place since she remembered last choosing a gown. She remembered the stiff panniered gowns of the *ancien regime*, with separate bodices and fichus crossing the shoulders. She felt a little as if she were out in public in but her shift in these high waisted gowns of muslin. For now, she ware one of Ninon's worn gowns, a little short in the ankle. They were hopeful of obtaining some fabric and making new gowns on the style of those drawn in the fashion magazines. But the small dry goods shop in Silverbridge were not what they wanted. "*C'est laid*," sniffed Ninon, wrinkling her nose.

"There is an excellent shop in Knightswold," Diana said, "but I would think it a favor to me should you avail yourselves of the materials stored in the attic."

"What is this?" Ninon demanded.

"When I first came to the Abbey, Lady Paulina, the former occupant of this house, had just died," Diana explained. "I was given a complete inventory of the house and its contents. One of the items – I should say *many* of the items – are trunks of uncut fabrics and Lady Paulina's clothes. I am told that she dressed very fine. You would not wish to wear her clothes, but the trims and laces could be used..."

"*C'est formidable!*" Lucie clapped her hands excitedly.

"We are Frenchwomen – we are too practical to throw the good clothes away. They can be sewn so they look new!"

Ninon said, eyes gleaming. "You truly do not wish to use these things yourself?"

"My parents gifted me with an entire wardrobe when I came out of mourning," Diana explained. "It would make me very pleased were you able to use these things."

"*Bien!*" Ninon thanked Diana for her generosity and the three ladies began talking of fashion and fabric.

René, standing propped against the mantel, drinking Cognac laced coffee, was happy to see them getting on so well. Lady Diana seemed to have rather abruptly changed her attitude, for he could detect no insincerity in her manner, and she seemed to be genuinely enjoying the conversation. As if she felt his eyes on her, she looked up, blushed, looked down at her hands and very quickly replied to Lucie's question about bonnets.

It was at this interesting moment that Simon burst into the room. He looked wildly around, spied René and launched himself at his former tutor. "Oh, sir, don't do it!" he cried.

René scarcely had time to set his cup on the mantelpiece when Simon was hanging around his waist.

"What is this, Simon?" he asked urgently, for the boy was shaking all over and crying.

"I heard them!" Simon gasped out. "Uncle Lyon and the Duke! They said there's going to be a ceremony with a stone and people have died from using it and it could punish or kill you! They said you don't have to do it! Please, sir, don't do it!"

"What is this, René?" Ninon asked sharply. "What are you going to do that you have not told us? *Qu'est-ce qu'il y a?*"

"I am to swear on the Cremave, *Grandmère*, that I am loyal to England," he answered quietly, stroking Simon's head so that the boy would settle down.

Ninon drew in her breath and demanded, "Does that man require this of you? To keep your position? We will go and sleep in the forest rather than have you do this thing!"

"*Non,*" René shook his head. "It is my idea, to show everyone, for once and all, that I am not a spy or a traitor. The Cremave will prove that."

Diana felt the blood draining from her face. "Was it I who caused this – what I said that day?" she stammered.

"Never in one hundred years did I mean – I have come to be sincerely sorry – and how wrong I was –" she floundered.

"No, it was not your fault –" René began, only to have Simon interrupt, "It was *them* – Sir Piers and Mr. Goodbody, wasn't it? I saw them this morning!"

He turned about in René's hold to face the three ladies. "They came to the Tower this morning! Sir Piers looked pleased when he left!" He turned back to René and looked beseechingly up at him. "Please, sir," he begged again. "Don't do it! I couldn't bear it if you was to be killed!"

René knelt and embraced the boy. "Thank you Simon. But I *must* do this. I am certain, *tu m'entendras,* that the Cremave will know that I tell the truth. There is no danger when one tells the truth."

"And you were planning to tell us?" Ninon demanded sharply.

"When it is over," said René. "I thought to spare you worry –"

Lucie cried out in protest and Ninon looked angry, her dark brows drawn together.

"Worry!" Ninon spat out. "And did you not think that we would 'worry' when they told us you were injured or dead! We have a right to be there! *En voilà assez!*" she said, slamming her palms on the arm of the chair. "Did you know of this, *Madame?*" she turned fiercely on Diana.

"No! I would never consent to this! I have read of the Cremave! It is a fearsome thing!" Diana was as aghast as the two Frenchwomen.

Giselle came hurriedly into the room. "*Pardon, Madame!* There have landed two dragons in the courtyard of the Abbey. One is the dragon who lives here and the other is big and green!"

"Pádraig," whispered Simon.

"Tuathail has made excellent time," said René quietly. "He brings the Arch Druid of Ireland and the Cremave."

Diana wondered bitterly when Lyon had planned to tell *her* of the coming horror.

In the end, Diana had to dose Simon with chamomile so that he would sleep that night, for he could not be comforted. She also promised Simon that once this was over he might see Mr. Roussillon whenever it was convenient. "And may he be my teacher again?" Simon wanted to know.

"I don't know if Uncle Lyon can spare him — they have a great deal of work to do in the Tower," Diana said, her heart turning over at the sight of the anxious but hopeful little face staring up at her from his pillows. "I shall talk to Uncle, I promise, and see if we can work something out."

She slept no better than Simon. She was still horrified that her rash accusations might have had something to do with this. What if something happened? She would feel that it was, at the very least, partly her fault. The Cremave was dangerous. Conchobar Ó Clérigh had said as much when he and Diarmait Mag Uidhir had arrived yesterday. No one had sworn on it for many years and the Arch Druid of Ireland was very much against it being used in the present.

The Cremave was a thing of ancient Power. It was a slab of black marble, heavily carved in the elder Runic language. It was called "Revealer of Truth" and "The Swearing Stone" by the holy monks on the Irish island of Saints. It was the ancient predecessors of these monks who had endowed the Cremave with its powers. If the accused swore falsely, the Stone left its mark upon him or her, or even killed the unfortunate but guilty party. It also sent its mark on his de-scendants for seven generations – a curse to make expiation for the lie. The Cremave was only used in cases of murder, treason and necromancy.

The beautiful weather that had held sway for so long, unusual in an English summer, failed the next morning. An early thunderstorm, fierce and bright, started the day and rain poured from a leaden sky as thunder continued to growl and lightning flickered.

The ceremony was set for eight in the morning. As he had indicated to Chenevix, Lyon asked Diana to be the independent witness required by law. Lyon was not happy with the fact that Ninon was coming to the ceremony. At the last minute Lucie, afraid to lose the son she had only just come to know and love, refused to go. She wanted to go to church and spend the time in prayer. Mr. Arabin, of course, was going to be at the ceremony, but he made Lucie welcome at the church and left her kneeling in front of the lectern.

263

Diana forbade Simon's attendance. He was too young. If something did indeed go wrong she did not want him to see it. She had Sanders stay with him and bade the young valet to lock Simon in his room if it proved necessary. Simon was not to go near the Tower.

It was a sober group that gathered in the Tower room. The room that doubled as Workroom and laboratory seemed dark and haunted this morning, the familiar accoutrements of Wizardry – armillary, cauldrons, row upon row of bottles labeled in magician's Latin, the high shelves of books and scrolls, a crocodile skeleton hanging from the ceiling and other curiosities, seemed somehow sinister.

All well-thought-out Towers had a large circular space in the middle where major Workings might be accomplished. Lyon's was no exception.

Since this was a major ceremony, everyone attending had to be properly robed. The Druids wore white robes with blue sashes, while the two *Magus Majorii* wore dark blue, embroidered with arcane symbols in silver. As a high level Witch Diana wore robes of scarlet, gold-embroidered. Even though Ninon and Diana were not to be inside the Circle, as persons with magic they had to be dressed as if they were participating.

As René had shown Simon, the Circle was drawn by the two *Magus Majorii*, with the proper names of power drawn along its length. On the altar was a yellow cloth, for yellow stood for the power of the mind and divination.

Ninon and Diana stood outside the glowing violet light of the magical Circle with the Duke of Chenevix, Sir Piers and Augustus Goodbody. Augustus and the Duke were properly robed, but Sir Piers wore riding dress, as he was non-magical. There were familiars present inside the Circle – Leander. Plato and Conchobar's owl Abbán, and Diarmait's cat Ó Dálaigh, who had not accompanied their Wizards on the first trip to the Cotswolds from Ireland.

Mildmay wore such a satisfied smile on his face that Diana longed to kick him. "Pig person!" she heard Ninon mutter. The arched windows behind them showed a morning sky as dark as night, lit only by flashed of lightning.

René stood by himself in the very center of the Circle, now being made into a pentagram by the two Arch Druids. A box, intricately carved and locked, stood on the altar. This contained the Cremave. Awakened by the Circle being drawn, light had begun to pour through the seams of the box. It was a pure, white light.

The ritual candles, yellow like the cloth, were lit and the ritual began. A ritual cup was shared and a libation offered to God and Goddess.

First, the two Arch Druids said a short incantation over the box. It glowed brighter, and of its own accord the lock slid open and the top of the box snapped back. At a gesture from Conchobar Reverend Arabin came forward and blessed the Cremave, asking it to show then the truth.

He then reached into the box and removed the Stone.

It was smaller than Diana had expected, being about the size of one volume of a three volume novel. It was slim, shining black and the runes on it glowed with a gold fire.

Solemnly the Vicar handed the stone to the Arch Druid of Ireland. Cradling it, Conchobar went to stand directly in front of René. "Ye've one more chance, me lad, to be quitting this foolishness. I warn ye, whether or not it is certain ye tell truth, this will hurt, for it searches every blessed inch of your heart and soul. I have not invoked the full power yet."

"I will do this," said René firmly.

Conchobar sighed. "And may God be forgiving me if anything happens."

"It will not!" Ninon murmured. "My grandson is good and honourable!"

Conchobar raised his voice to that of the trained bard and Druid, who could easily fill a vast hall with the softest whisper. "I do adjure you, René Alain Roussillon, to speak the truth and nothing but the truth in presence of all this people, before the face of God and to the power of this Swearing Stone. Do you so swear?"

"I do so swear," said René. To Diana he sounded confident and like Conchobar, his voice was clear and steady.

"Place your left hand upon the Stone," directed the Arch Druid. As René did so, the light of the Stone began to pulse.

"Do you swear that all of your loyalty is to England, that you have never had dealings with any agents of France, that in your heart and mind you are a son of England, even though born on foreign shores?" Conchobar asked sternly.

"I do so swear," René swore without hesitation.

The white light raced up and down his form, until he seemed engulfed in it. Only Conchobar could be seen clearly by the others.

And then, abruptly as it had begun, it was over. René stood facing the Irish Druid, his hand still resting on the now lightless Stone.

Conchobar reached forward and removed René's hand from the cold surface and held it up for all to see. "Unmarked!" he said in triumph.

Diana heard Sir Piers growl in rage.

"You see, pig person?" said Ninon coldly and Lyon chortled "Foiled, by God!"

"We have papers to sign as testament," said the Duke. "We have taken quite enough time on this unnecessary nonsense." He leveled his quizzing glass at the two outsiders. "Let us not waste any more valuable time, gentlemen."

The Circle was taken down and Ninon hurried to René's side. "*Mon cher*, are you well?" she asked in concern.

"*J'ai le vertige*," he said. "I should sit down, *non*?" He sounded extremely tired and was wobbling in his feet.

"Lean on me," said Ninon, but it took the strong arm of Diarmait to get René into a chair. He sank into it gratefully, immediately putting back his head and closing his eyes. Conchobar had been right. That had hurt. But he was content. Now they would have no doubts any more about his loyalties. He did not see Diana look worriedly at him – he seemed so pale and weak!

Goodbody had been taken aback. He had not thought that it would actually come to the Cremave – he had honestly thought that Roussillon would back out and refuse to go through with it. Mildmay had been so sure that Roussillon was guilty. Even as poor an excuse for a Wizard as Goodbody had recognized the power and Truth in the Cremave. Even if he KNEW he was telling the truth, Goodbody doubted if he would have the nerve to put his hand on that awful thing.

"It's a trick!" said Sir Piers angrily. "You Wizards are all in a conspiracy together! All hocus-pocus and mumbo-jumbo! A show for the credulous! Well, sirs, I am *not* credulous and I do not believe for one minute that a chunk of rock can read a man's truth!"

"Would you be willing to wager on that, Mildmay?" said Lyon, an odd little smile twisting his lips.

"I'll wager on any thing you like!" blustered the baronet.

"Would you be willing to wager, Sir Piers," spoke up Reverend Arabin, "on swearing that you had naught to do with the fire that destroyed May Cottage?"

21

The Faerie Rade

A silence fell over the Tower room. Mr. Arabin wore a stern look and Lyon drew in his breath sharply.

"Pig person!" said Ninon softly but it was quite audible to everyone in the room.

The baronet flushed angrily. "I will swear to anything you like, Vicar! Aye, and put my hand on that infernal Stone! I had naught to do with that fire – why would I burn my own property? 'Tis more than likely negligence on their part!" He pointed at Ninon. "Everyone knows the Froggies are great boozers, probably drunk as lords, all of them, and knocked over a candle. It had naught to do with me!" He truly believed that nothing would happen to him. He was convinced that the Swearing ceremony had been nothing but lights and acting. He turned to Lyon. "I've one hundred guineas that say naught will harm me!"

"Done!" said Lyon promptly. "Chenevix will bear witness to the wager," he added.

The Duke agreed, noting the nature of the wager in his memorandum book.

"Mildmay!" Goodbody whispered, plucking at Sir Piers' coat sleeve. "Don't do this! It's dangerous! That thing can kill you if you don't speak Truth!"

Sir Piers looked down on him in contempt. "You're as bad as the rest of them. 'Tis a chunk of Stone – what harm can it do?"

"It truly has Power – I can feel it!" Goodbody was in distress. "I beg of you – don't do this!"

Sir Piers shook Goodbody from his arm, like a ferret shaking a rat. "Stand aside!" he ordered. "What do I do?" He turned to the Vicar.

"We must reanimate the Circle," Lyon said, before Mr. Arabin could speak. "Come and stand here, Mildmay." He indicated a place in the midst of the pentagram.

"Stop this!" René said, trying to rise from his chair. Diarmait, standing beside him, pushed him back down, "It is on his head, boyo," the young Irishman said grimly.

"But he is guilty of the fire!" said René urgently. "He will be punished for the lie! The Cremave has good reason to hurt him!"

Sir Piers whirled about at this. "You damned Froggie liar!" he started towards René, huge hands clenching and unclenching as if he wanted to wrap them around the Frenchman's neck.

A violet light shot from Diarmiat's hand and pushed the enraged baronet back into the Circle.

"Shame! To attack someone in his condition!" Diana had come up to stand behind René's chair and to his surprise, he felt her hand drop onto his shoulder.

"Let the pig person die," said Ninon. "It is his own evil and stupidity that will kill him. Even if does he not believe the Cremave will judge him."

"I tell you, I had naught to do with that fire!" the baronet ranted. A vein beat in his forehead and his breathing was labored. "To think that the lot of you would take the word of a pack of damned lying Frogs rather than that of a God-fearing, loyal Englishman! It don't bear thinking on!" He glared about him furiously, as if daring them to attack him.

"You have been warned, Mildmay," observed Chenevix in his passionless fashion. "As our Irish friend has observed, what happens is on your head."

"Do not do this!" René said again, rather desperately. He hated Sir Piers and had wished him to be shown as the murderer he was, but not this way! After having undergone the power and pain of the Cremave — and he had told the truth — he could only imagine what it would to do to a liar. And Sir Piers was lying – of that René was certain. They had *Mam'selle* Mildmay's witness to the fact. "*Ça alors, c'est trop fort*," he said, looking up into Diana's eyes. This was going too far.

She was surprised. He, with the greatest reason to hate Sir Piers, wanted to put a stop to this. Only Goodbody wanted no part of it. Even the Vicar seemed eager to let the baronet take his chances with the Cremave. Lyon was contemptuous, the Duke frozen, Diarmait frankly on René's side and Conchobar trying to remain impartial. Ninon looked at Mildmay with frank hatred.

"Let's get on with it!" Mildmay growled, shooting a dagger-look at Ninon. He would rid himself of that old bitch, yet. The whole nest of French vipers would be routed out!

The Circle was redrawn by the two *Magus Majorii*, Mr. Arabin and Diarmait. Then the Arch Druids redrew the pentagram.

The steps of the ceremony were repeated until Conchobar stood in front of Sir Piers with the glowing Cremave. "Think about this!" he urged. "You do not have to do this! Only think of what might happen!"

Sir Piers looked at him contemptuously. "Get on with it!" he said again.

"Put your left hand on the Stone," Conchobar directed.

As the baronet obeyed, Conchobar said, "I do adjure you, Piers Mildmay, to speak the truth and nothing but the truth in presence of all of these people, before the face of God and to the Power of this Swearing Stone. Do you so swear?"

"I do so swear," said Sir Piers, and a grimace crossed his face.

"Do you swear to the fact that you had nothing to do with the fire that burned down –"

"May Cottage," Mr. Arabin supplied.

"May Cottage," intoned Conchobar.

"And," the Vicar put in, "will you swear that you did not attempt murder of four innocent persons, deliberately and with malice?"

"Murder!" Conchobar turned to stare at the Vicar.

"I do swear!" burst out the baronet and then scream-ed.

For instantly, with a blaze of white light, the Cremave had punished him. His left hand and arm shriveled up to a blackened, skeletal ruin. His legs failed; he fell heavily to the floor, clutching his decaying limb to his chest. He screamed and sobbed in terror and denial. As the others watched he seemed to shrink in on himself, his full face becoming cadaverous, his body losing most of its bulk He rolled on the floor, no longer screaming, but moaning piteously.

Mr. Arabin's better nature won out and he went to the desperately injured man and began to pray for God's forgiveness.

At the first scream, René had put his face in his hands. Through her touch on his shoulder, Diana felt him shaking. She had had to close her eyes when the punishment began. She had never seen anything so awful – not even in Spain.

"Sir Piers Mildmay," came Lyon's voice, very sternly. "For the attempted murder of René Roussillon and his family, I hereby, as magistrate of this shire, arrest you. Mag Uidhir, will you fetch the sheriff and a Healer from Cheltenham? Tuathail knows the way."

"I'm on my way," said Diarmait, leaving quickly to clatter down the stairs. They could hear him calling for Tuathail as he went. In a very few moments they heard the snap of dragon wings opening.

Under Mr. Arabin's direction they made the baronet as comfortable as was possible.

"Uncle, I think Mr. Roussillon ought to be put to bed," Diana said anxiously. He did not look well at all. She herself did not feel well, for that matter.

Ninon agreed with this. "Me, I shall take him home," she announced.

"I have already rung for the servants," said Chenevix. "And it seems to have ceased to precipitate, the operation can be conducted in relative dryness." He then turned to look at the shrunken figure of Sir Piers Mildmay on the floor, now covered in a quilt. "Odd," he said reflectively. "I really thought he would die."

Goodbody fainted dead away.

The rest of that day was filled with tidying up, as Lyon rather facetiously called it. René was put to bed, lovingly attended by his mother and grandmother. Diana went home and after being very ill, had a cup of tea with

271

Simon and was able to reassure him that his friend was doing well, and Uncle had promised that the Healer would visit him, also.

The Healer arrived on his hippogriffe and the sheriff, on his own dragon, accompanied Diarmait and Tuathail back to the Abbey. The sheriff's dragon, a tough looking Highland black, was outfitted with saddle chains to transport prisoners, and a litter that attached to his harness that could be swung down for an injured prisoner. It was there that Sir Piers was placed after receiving an examination and an opiate from the Wizard Healer. The outlook was not good – if he lived, he would be a cripple all of his days, and there was little doubt that he would hang or at the very least be transported for attempted murder, did he cling to life. In current English law, the action of the Cremave was tantamount to a signed confession. It could not lie, nor be tampered with.

René's outlook for recovery was much happier – a few days in bed and strengthening food such as beef tea, chicken soup and Restorative Pork Jelly should set him right. Upon hearing this news Diana promised Simon that should the ladies of his family give their permission, she would take her son to visit his former tutor on the morrow.

When Goodbody awoke from his faint he found Lyon's carriage waiting at the door to take him to London. His baggage and his man had come from the Hall and Lyon wasted no time in suggesting, rather forcibly, that Goodbody avail himself of the generosity of the Abbey and leave for London immediately.

Goodbody was glad to do so. Never would he forget that scream and the sight of a terrifyingly altered Sir Piers collapsing onto the floor. He wanted nothing more than the comfortable familiarity of his rooms in the Albany, with one of Thompson's snug little suppers and a bottle or two.

Mr. Arabin went at once to Miss Mildmay, to give her the news. She wept wildly at first – Mr. Arabin thought a great part of it was relief – but by the time he left her she was making up lists and planning to see her solicitor on the next day.

"And now, perhaps we can get something done!" Lyon said to Chenevix as the two men watched the departures from the top of the Tower – Pádraig with the two Druids and their familiars back to Ireland, the sheriff with his prisoner and the Wizard Healer on his hippogriffe.

"There is never any lessening of the high drama that clings to you like a stench, is there, Lyonshall?" Chenevix studied his fingernails. noting with irritation that Lyon grinned at him, rather than taking umbrage. "There are no less than two urgent dispatches from Douglas Ramey in the morning's post. I own, I will be glad when we are ready to scry over water. All of this letter writing is too fatiguing! And Roussillon is not to be returned to us for several days. It is too bad." Chenevix yawned exquisitely and sighed. "We'd best get to work."

Diana was very tired before she went to bed – everyone was. Dinner was a quiet affair – only Simon seemed to have any energy at all and it seemed a mutual decision that they all retire early.

Diana fell into bed and into a deep, dreamless sleep. It was a warm night and she bade Susan to leave the curtains and the windows open.

When the silvery peal of a horn sounded at midnight, she instantly awakened. It was a clarion call, echoing in the air and inside her brain. She at up at once, wide awake. What was that? Had something else happened?

In a few moments she realized that no one else had heard it. The house was still. There were no doors opening, no voices raised in alarm, no trumpeting from Tuathail. How could they have missed that call? It had gone clear through her – every nerve was vibrating.

She was conscious of a need to be out-of-doors where that call had come from. Quickly, with the aid of a small mage light, she dressed, pulling the first thing she could find in the wardrobe over her head and putting half-boots of jean on her feet, rather than kid slippers. She snatched up a shawl that hung on a chair and went downstairs.

It was very quiet, which seemed strange. The whole house was in a state of suspended animation – no clocks ticked, no noise was made. The night footman in the hall was sound asleep. As Diana had cause to know, he snored. He now slept neatly and quietly.

She unlocked the front door and went outside.

The moon shone full in a dark sky spangled with stars. The light was silver and although the shadows were deep, each out of door thing seemed outlined, as if the edges had been dipped in silver. And out here it was the same, that unnatural stillness. Not a leaf stirred, not a night bird sang. No insects hummed. The world seemed to be waiting for something.

In the distance, the sweet silver of the horn sounded again. "Oh, come!" it seemed to say. And Diana wanted nothing more than to go where it called. She began to walk briskly towards the west, where the horn called.

To the west lay the edge of the park and the beginning of the forest. To the west also lay the Dower House. To Diana's surprise, there was a figure at the end of the drive.

It was René Roussillon.

"Did you it also?" he asked. He looked as she felt – as if it were Christmas, her birthday and every other holiday she had ever celebrated all rolled up into one, with a look of excitement and longing.

"Yes!" she said. "What is it?"

"I think perhaps, it is the horn of Faerie, *n'est-ce pas*? The Elfin horn. We are summoned. I was told to expect it." He sounded exultant. Every trace of tiredness and pain had left him.

"Summoned?" Diana queried. Without conscious choice they had begun to walk again, side by side.

"Look about you – the world is enchanted," he said almost dreamily. "No one hears but us." As he said this the horn sounded again, more urgent this time.

"I feel I must go to it *à tout prix*," René said.

Diana agreed. At any cost! "We must hurry!"

He took her hand and they ran into the woods. It was easy to see in the bright moonlight. They ran until they reached the grassy ride where only yesterday (which now seemed as it had been years ago) Simon had his riding lesson.

Hearts pounding, they stopped. Once more the horn sounded, clear and close. Something told then to wait.

The silence was absolute. Ahead, from the edge of the greenwood where the ride ended, something shimmered and grew and in a few breathless moments they could see what it was.

It was a fair company of gentlemen and ladies, some twenty or more. They rode horses as white as the moon, draped in green and gold. Some were dressed as minstrels and carried instruments – small harps, mandolins, flutes. Some were dressed as knights, in golden armor, golden swords at their sides and silver tipped arrows and bows on their backs. There were beautiful ladies, in all colours with fantastic hats on long, waist-length hair, sidesaddle on their white steeds. It was as if a tapestry from Medieval times had come to life.

The horses wore jewels on their foreheads and were shod in silver. They had arched necks, broad chests and long legs. They pranced, rather than walked – it seemed as if they were dancing. The riders sat the curveting horses with great ease.

In the front of the troop rose a man and a woman – their bearing was noble and their horses were even finer than the others. They each wore crowns – a crown that bore long exaggerated points – each point crowned by a glowing moonstone. Over all of these persons a pure white light shimmered and shone. "The Shining Ones!" Diana whispered. She sank into a deep courtesy, the very one she had learned for her presentation at St James' Palace at the Queen's drawing room. Beside her, René made a deep bow.

Silently, the eerily lovely procession cane on. There was no sound – not the jingle of bit or harness, nor of the hoof beats on the grass. No horse nickered. Nor did any of that beauteous company speak.

Behind the King and Queen rode a knight with a golden spear. From this spear flew a pennon of green and gold. It snapped noiselessly in a non-existent wind.

The Rade halted in front of René and Diana.

"Rise," said the Queen in the sweetest of voices.

As she came up from her courtesy Diana dared to look at the Queen. She was clad all in white, with a green, gold-fringed mantle and sash. Her hair was fair, and streamed down her back, wound through with pearls. A crescent moon hung at her throat. Her crown of gold was slightly smaller than her lord's. Her eyes were silver pools, her brows a high arch, her face narrow and the chin rather pointed, as were

275

her ears. Her eyes were set slightly aslant. And now she smiled benignly on them.

Her lord was as dark as she was fair, clad like her in shining white. A great moonstone on a golden chain shone on his chest, and like his Queen, he had slanted silver eyes beneath soaring brows, set in a narrow face. He was stern and rather haughty, but suddenly smiled, which changed his entire aspect. "Ride with us," he said.

At his signal, two horses were brought forward, one with a sidesaddle. Diana was tossed up into the sidesaddle as light as thistledown, and found that her dress, whose narrow skirt was never meant for riding dress, accommodated itself to her wishes.

René's entire experience with the equine race had been limited to the Vicar's pony and draught horses. And he had never actually ridden a horse.

To his surprise, riding this horse was about as difficult as sitting in a comfortable chair. Although it sidled and danced underneath him, as the others in the cavalcade did, he did not seem to feel it, nor did he need to hold onto anything.

The two horses fell in behind the Royal couple and the Rade began again its progress, but with a difference. Suddenly the hoof beats could be heard and the harness jingled in song. Harps thrummed and the brittle notes of the mandolin rang out, accompanied by the mellow tones of a flute. The company began to sing.

Many years later Diana read of someone being "ravished by a song." There could have not been a more fitting description for the beauty of that chorus. Crystal bells were woven into the long manes and tails of the horses and these chimed a descant to the singing. It was sung in a language of unbearable sweetness. The meaning of it lay just beyond their comprehension. It was a song both graceful and sad.

How long they rode neither Diana or René ever knew. The company sang the entire time, sometimes certain of them taking a solo turn, or once a harper coaxed notes of lyrical enchantment from his instrument. Diana felt tears pouring down her cheeks, and glancing sideways at René, saw that he was as moved as was she.

The pace began to quicken. The horses began trotting, then cantered. They broke into a gallop so fast that the two humans could no longer see. The landscape swept by in a blur, and the harp rang out even over the thunder of hooves.

Straight to the side of a green-covered hill they went, with never a slackening of the frenzied pace. At the last moment the green hill split wide open and the entire host swept inside.

They were in a huge cavern that resembled a large Cathedral. Gothic arches held up an enormous dome, its ribs outlined in gold. There were tapestries on the walls of great antiquity, showing the Fair Folk hunting, playing at quoits, dancing, making music and making merry. What could be seen of the walls were carved with flowers and little animals, all looking so alive that they might jump off the wall at any moment.

Diana was handed down by a young courtier in blue, who placed her hand on his arm and with a bow and gesture, led her forward. René was greeted by a dark lady in a very old fashioned gown – some five hundred years out of date – of scarlet silk. She wore a tall pointed hat on her dark brown hair, complete with a gossamer veil that trailed the floor.

She laid a hand on René's arm and the two escorts led their guests into a adjoining chamber where a sumptuous table was spread, laden with delectable food and set with plate of gold and crystal glassware. It shone beneath the light of two immense chandeliers, dripping with prisms that cast rainbows everywhere one looked.

Diana was seated on the King's left, with her courtier beside her. René was at the Queen's right hand, with the dark lady on his right.

"You may eat and drink of anything here without harm," the King said. "You are honoured guests and will not be fooled or tricked. Do you hear me, Puck?" He suddenly looked up at the ceiling, where a little figure could be seen flitting amongst the prisms.

"I mean no harm," came a plaintive voice." I only want a bit of sport."

"You shall not sport with our guests, or you shall feel the full measure of my wrath," the King said, frowning severely. "This gentleman is a very great Wizard and I hereby give him leave to protect himself against you. The lady is an excellent Witch – I grant her the same privilege. So none of your foolish tricks!"

"Yes, Majesty," the little voice replied.

At the first mention of Puck Diana and René knew in whose court they sat. This was High Faerie – the Selighe Court of Oberon and Tatania. Each of then could only wonder why they had been summoned. But one did not demand anything of the Faerie Court, even information. They prized daring and audacity in humans, but they prized good manners even more. There were probably more humans that had borne Faerie punishments for rudeness or ill-breeding than for any other crime done against the Fair Folk.

"Let the feast begin!" The Queen clapped her hands imperiously.

Covered golden platters began to appear, with such delicacies as a roasted peacock, with the feathers restored, small game hens, roasted in fruit juices, beef encased in pastry, so tender that one did not need a knife to cut it – the golden fork was enough. There were all sorts of vegetables, sautéed, steamed and baked, in marvelous sauces, and bread and rolls of every description. The wine was honey-based and invigoration without being intoxicating.

Then there was the sweet course – a hedgehog spun of sugar, complete to the spines, a cake, rich and full of fruit that looked like a castle, bonbons and comfits of every type, more lusciously ripe fruits and still more wine.

Diana let her Othersight have a quick glance. Everything was exactly as it appeared to be – there was no glamourie. Oberon glanced at her, with a smile. He knew what she had done and she blushed. He shook his head and patted her hand. He was not incensed as she had feared, How had she dared?

When the feast wore down to an end, Oberon rose with a goblet in his hand. "People of the Hollow Hills, I give you our guests! Long may they live and be friends to us and we friends to them!"

"*Hwacet!* " cried the company and lifted their crystal goblets in a toast. The two humans bowed their heads in acknowledgement of the compliment.

"And to our gracious hosts," René stood and raised his glass. "to an evening and a company *par excellence!*" He quickly drained his glass to tumultuous applause. Diana rose and drained hers as well. She was not certain how it was with the Shining Ones, but among humans ladies did not make toasts.

"I beg of you to excuse us," Oberon continued, "for we must speak to our friends on matters serious and of concern to man and the Fair Folk alike."

Diana and René exchanged glances as the company began to leave the table. Their escorts bowed themselves away.

"Come," said Tatania. "We shall adjourn to our private apartments where we may speak uninterrupted."

22

Faerie Gifts

Each place they went within the Hollow Hills was more beautiful than the last. Every vista, whether a corridor leading to who-knew-what delights or an indoor garden complete with plants of all seasons and great fountains, was perfection itself. There seemed to be a light breeze blowing at all times, with a scent compounded of flowers and spice, ambrosial to the senses. Gold, jewels, silver, and stained glass sparkled everywhere. Music came from all sides, too, rich and golden to the ears. It was bewitching beyond anything either of the guests had ever experienced.

At last the private apartments of the Royal Faerie couple were reached. These lay open to the night sky, or so it appeared. The walls were hung with silks of incredible sheerness, which stirred and rippled in the cool night air. Flowers were everywhere – many of which were blooming out of season, for lilacs and tulips were mingled with Christmas hellebores and autumnal chrysanthemums. Low, silken cushioned chairs stood about a table with heavily carved legs and a top of crystal. A jewel-encrusted flagon stood on the table, surrounded by four matching chalices.

As was proper, the King and Queen seated themselves first and invited their guests to sit. Titania poured from the flagon a green drink that had a sweet smell. Each of them took a sip before Oberon said abruptly to René, "We are especially glad to meet you at long last, kinsman."

"Kinsman, Majesty?" René repeated, puzzled.

"Surely you are aware that as a direct descendant of the line of Duke Huon of Bordeaux we are related, and not too distantly?" Oberon asked. "For was not Clarimonde, Huon's Duchess, a Princess of Faerie, and in that line was many a marriage between the Fair Folk and those of the matriarchal line, which became the Duplessis of Brittany. Therefore, we are kinsman to a degree – I would need the services of our heralds to be certain of what degree. But I believe I may call you cousin."

René was surprised – no one had ever told him this, and he said as much.

"Your grandmother keeps many secrets," said Titania, smiling at him. "But you will know all in time. Look you, Lady Diana, do you not see a likeness?" She lifted her graceful slender hand to point at her consort and his guest. "The eyes and the brows and something about the face."

Thee was a likeness, however fleeting, Diana thought, trying to imagine Oberon in a fashionable Windswept and the costume of a modern English gentleman, or René clad in Faerie raiment with shoulder length hair.

"We have summoned you here," Oberon continued, "to offer our support and help in two endeavors. First, we shall lend our strength to yours when it is time to send a cone of power to the mages in Russia."

René exchanged startled glances with Diana. *"Monseigneur, je vous bénisse!"* he exclaimed. He could only imagine how excited and pleased the other Wizards would be.

This was indeed a blessing, for with the help of the Selighe Court, there could be no doubt but what the transfer of power would be accomplished.

"We do this for several reasons," the King continued, swirling the green liquid in his chalice. "Most creatures of Faerie have been obliged to flee the Continent, for the Inquisition holds sway there, and they know all too well the weapons to use against us. And the people on the Continent, in large, no longer believe in us and have abandoned the old ways. We are very much afraid that this Napoleon Bonaparte will win out in the end and where the conqueror goes, there is the Inquisition, even in the New World, where New Spain has a stranglehold on much of the land. If the Inquisition holds Europe and Russia and England and most of North and South America, where are we to go? Asia has its own Faerie, who do not welcome us. The Inquisition will not coexist with us – they hunt us down with their weapons of Cold Iron, against which we have no defense. It can only be to our advantage to cooperate with this great effort of yours. We have done so earlier in this conflict and have no hesitation in doing so again. You may tell the Arch Druid that we will help with right good will when the time comes, which, I believe is to be Samhain, is it not?"

René was not surprised at Oberon's knowledge. It was always said that the Fair Folk knew everything. Since going to work for Lyon René had learned quite a bit about the Grand Scheme. It was indeed set for Samhain – All Hallow's Eve – as this was a particularly powerful time, when the new year and the old year met, according to the Celtic and Druidical calendars, and the veil between the worlds was thin. Cones of power were to be raised at all the sacred places of the British Isles and with an immense effort, commingled and sent to conclaves of Wizards and Covens of Witches in Russia, of which there were, sadly, but few nowadays. This power was to be used to fight the invaders, for no one doubted that Napoleon's ambition was such that he would strike at Russia. Alexander, the Czar, trusted Bonaparte no more than Bonaparte trusted him. No Augur had seen the end of the present war – it lay in darkness still, invisible to crystal, bowl or any other form of prophecy.

"And the second endeavor, my lord," Titania prompted.

"You may tell the Arch Druid," Oberon informed them, "that what he seeks lies in Bryn Myrddin."

"My uncle is correct?" Diana said, surprised. "There is a spell to bind the Unselighe Court?"

"Yes, there is, and Merlin left the secret of where it was hidden with us," answered Titania. "As well as do you, we wish the Unselighe creatures bound once again. They intrude on our territories."

"And as well as hunting human flesh and blood, they will begin to steal human children again, for use as slaves. Once their appetites of a millennium are sated, they will begin the other vile practices that we – and humans – find so repugnant," added Oberon,

"But Bryn Myrddin has been searched," René objected. "I have seen the reports of the Wizards who have searched, *je vous assure!*

"They had not the use of this," the Faery King waved his hand in the air and there appeared in his palm an ornately chased key on a watch chain. It was not very large, and was made of crystal, with a golden head. "This will guide you to the door where the spell lays hidden. Be certain and take a child with you to the crystal cave, for only a child is small enough to enter the room." He gave the key to René, who clipped it securely to his waistcoat with the fob chain, with words of gratitude.

"And we have further gifts for you!" Titania clapped her hands and two heavily carved boxes of ash wood appeared on the table before them. She picked up the box nearest to her and reached in, withdrawing a silver, shimmering chain. From it hung a silver oak leaf, so realistic in appearance that Diana could see it quiver in the light breeze.

The Queen stood up swiftly and dropped the beautiful thing over Diana's head. "Never take it off," Titania said gravely. "For the time will come that you will need it badly."

Diana put a cupped hand over the gift. It was warn to the touch, like a living thing, not cold as metal would be, coming from a box. "Need it, ma'am?" she queried." How? And how am I to use it?"

"You will know when the time is upon you. And your heart will tell you how to use it. Listen to your heart," said the Queen, smiling at her.

"And for you, cousin," said Oberon, taking up the second box of ash. He opened it and pulled forth a golden neck chain, heavier than Diana's, suitable for a man, ending in a golden acorn. He dropped it over René's bent head. "The same restrictions apply – never take it off! It is your protection in what is to come. We can see but a little way into future and you will soon be called upon to do a Great Task, for which you and you alone are suited. And you will find within your box, cousin, a jar of crystal. When the time comes to do your task there are instructions in the box as to how you must use the contents of the jar. Obey these to the letter."

Both of them thanked the Fair Folk for these gifts, but asked no more questions, for they could tell that all had been said.

"And now," said the King, clapping his hands, "we shall return you to the mortal world."

And as simply as that, they were back in the forest, on the grassy ride.

Diana and René could only stare at one another for a long moment. "Was that a dream?" she at last whispered.

"*Mais non*," he said, "for here is the proof." He held up the box of ash and touched the chain around his neck.

Her hand went to her breast, where the oak leaf gleamed. "We have Faerie favor!" she said, awed.

"And the key to banish the Unselighe Court!" He smiled and patted his waistcoat pocket.

"It must be nearly dawn," she said. "I hope we have not been missed."

"*Regardez là-haut*! Look at the moon!" René pointed at the sky.

The moon was in the exact same position that it had been when they first met the Faerie Rade. "Time in Faerieland is not what it is here. I am willing to guess that the moon will be so until we have returned to our homes," René said.

Diana shivered a little, drawing her shawl closer.

At once, René shrugged off his coat and threw it around her shoulders. He carefully put his ash wood box, (which seemed to have shrunk in size) into his other waistcoat pocket. Diana's box easily fit in the small pocket of her skirt.

"Thank you," she said softly. 'This is the second time I have had need of your coat."

"*Il n'y a pas de quoi*," he said.

"I do have to mention it," she said with some difficulty "for I have been wrong and unfair to you and I want to apologize. The things I said, and the things I accused you of — I don't see how it is possible for you to ever forgive me."

"It is forgotten and forgiven," he said.

"You are too good," she said in a voice close to tears. "I don't deserve such consideration..."

"*Ne vous désolez pas comme ça*," said René, a little desperately, for he did not want to see her cry. "Do not upset yourself in such a way! It is of no consequence. Come now – *il fait chaud* – it grows chill and you had best be returned to your bed." He offered his arm, pretending not to notice that she wiped her face with the end of one of the sleeves of his coat.

"Simon wants you to be his teacher again," she said when she had regained control of her voice.

"I would very much like that, but I have the position with Lord Lyonshall –"

"Perhaps Uncle would allow you at least a little time each day, for magical lessons," she said "for I am having no luck in finding a tutor. It seems that every young Wizard in the kingdom is teaching non-magicals to protect themselves or has joined the new Home Guard and are too busy drilling with his unit. The few applicants I have interviewed just would not do at all, and Simon would not like any of them."

They discussed the possibilities of this while walking slowly through the timeless enchanted landscape. All still lay under the hush of the Faerie spell.

He escorted her to the front door of the Abbey and bowed low over her hand. She returned his coat, with a smile and a word of thanks, and watched as he disappeared in the direction of the Dower House.

Once inside, she ran lightly up the stairs and went to her room. Nothing had changed since she left – the clock still read one minute to midnight. Quickly, she resumed her nightclothes and crawled into bed. As she pulled the covers up to her chin the clocks throughout the house began to chime twelve. Time had resumed its passing.

Lyon was always in the Tower by seven in the morning, an hour the Duke of Chenevix considered uncivilized to begin a working day. But none-the-less, his Grace was present by that time, ready to go over reports or whatever needed to be done. As much as Lyon hated to admit it, the Duke was conscientious and hard-working, and showed a quick grasp of any situation.

Lyon was also more than satisfied with their new assistant, for Roussillon arrived early, stayed late, never had to be told anything twice, anticipated what needed to be done, worked on his own imitative and had no trouble deciphering runes, Gaelic or Cymraeg and wrote a neat hand as well.

After the experience with Goodbody, it was satisfying to enter the Tower and find the mage lamps lit, the scrying bowl full of purified water, the first post of the day opened and sorted, in piles rated by importance save for that marked 'confidential'. Roussillon would be hard at work with a pile of correspondence. They were getting letters and scrys from all over the kingdom asking how to fight the Unselighe creatures, queries from Home Guard Units on what kind of spells they should be learning and practicing, non-magical persons who needed reassurance, and complaints from those who felt that the Wizards and the Druids were not doing enough to protect them from the depredations of these beings and demanding to know why this problem had not been resolved as yet.

Lyon had learned that of the three of them, Roussillon was the best one to answer these queries and complaints. He had the most tact. Lyon knew he himself had no tact – only impatience when he encountered whining or stupidity and Chenevix was quite as bad. The Duke felt no need to explain or apologize to those he regarded as his inferiors. And that was nearly every body, including the Regent and the Prime Minister.

At least *some* things were going well, Lyon thought as he bounded up the stairs, save for this murderous business with the Unselighe creatures. So far no one had deciphered a single clue as to what was killing Wizards and Druids.

On the other hand, the estate was coming back to life – soon Lyon would be able to spend more time at Avalon, as was proper for the Arch Druid of Britain, than here in the Cotswolds. There had been so much to do here, so many decisions to be made about the Abbey estate. Soon he would be able to put in a good steward, and turn the day to day running over to him and the steward would be directly responsible to Diana, who was more than capable of the duty.

Thinking of Diana, he was surprised to see her waiting for him when he burst into the Tower in his usual headlong fashion. She was sitting on a stool near Roussillon's desk and chatting to the secretary in quite a friendly fashion. Lyon's eye-brows shot up. Here was a new turn-out!

Chenevix was already seated at his desk, a scowl on his face. He was reading a letter with his quizzing glass. Lyon truly hated the way the glass enlarged the Duke's eye – it reminded him of dead fish on a slab in the Billingsgate fish market.

"Well, Diana, this is a pleasant surprise!" said her uncle. "Come to brighten up our old bachelor Tower, have you? Is there any coffee?" he asked René, who pointed towards a table in front of the window. Not only was there a pot of steaming aromatic coffee, but there was a tray of luscious looking pastries as well.

"Uncle, something very important happened to us last night and you should know about it," Diana said as Lyon poured himself a cup of coffee and examined the pastry. Hopefully, there were apricot tarts.

"And by us, you mean –" said Chenevix tartly.

"Mr. Roussillon and myself," Diana said.

"Flirting, were you? " said Lyon genially. "Never flirt with your employer's female relatives, Roussillon. It can only lead to trouble."

"Faugh!" the Duke made a disgusted noise. "Lyonshall, you are a cloth-head! Anyone smelling less of April and May I have yet to see. Pray, pay no heed to your loutish uncle, my dear Lady Diana, and proceed with your story."

Diana had flushed painfully when Lyon accused her of flirting and René stepped into the breach. "We were summoned to the court of King Oberon and Queen Titania," he said.

The reaction of the two older gentlemen was all that they could have wished for.

"What!" ejaculated Lyon, and the Duke's quizzing glass came up to stare at them.

Taking it in turns, René and Diana told of the events of the preceding evening. Neither one of them mentioned the personal gifts from the Faerie couple. It was as if they could not speak of them. But both wore their talisman beneath their clothing.

Lyon let out a whoop of joy when they told him of the Selighe Court's promise to lend their strength to the great endeavor. However, that was nothing as to the shout he uttered when the key was shown and its function told. René handed over the key to Lyon, as it seemed the Arch Druid was the proper person to have charge of it.

"We have it! Merlin's secret!" Lyon exulted.

Chenevix had winced at the first shout, at the second he had covered his ears. "Really, Lyonshall! Do you never try and conduct yourself with proper decorum and restraint? I daresay I shall be deaf above a week!"

"And do you never try to show some proper human emotion?" Lyon retorted. "This is what we've been searching for, Chenevix! And to have the help of the Selighe Court! Why, it is beyond anything great!" He threw up his hands and made a little dance step.

"It is indeed gratifying," said the Duke coolly.

"I despair of you, Chenevix!" Lyon exclaimed. And then, actions suiting words, he turned his back on the Duke and said to René, "We'll leave for Bryn Myrddin on the morrow. We'll take Simon with us –"

"If Simon is to be the child needed, Uncle, I am going also," said Diana firmly.

"What do you say? There is no need of that, Diana! Simon will be well protected by Roussillon, Chenevix and myself!" Lyon explained.

"You don't imagine that I am going to crawl onto a dragon and fly all over Britain, do you?" Chenevix looked at Lyon through glass as if the Marquis had run mad. " I shall remain here."

"Suit yourself." Lyon could not imagine missing out on the excitement of this find. But Chenevix was ever an enigma to him.

"There are a great deal of preparations to be made –" he began and then a thought occurred to him. "What are you doing here this morning, Roussillon? Aren't you supposed to be resting up, on the doctor's orders?"

"It was necessary to inform you – " began René, but Lyon waved his protests away.

"Yes, yes, I see that, but you really must go home and rest, for I cannot have you collapsing at the crucial moment tomorrow! As it is, the doctor will no doubt give me a rare bear garden jaw for flying you off to Wales tomorrow. He thinks dragon flight is injurious to the health of anyone of invalidish habit. So home and bed for you in that order! Mind you be here at dawn tomorrow morning. And if you intend to accompany us, Diana," he turned to his niece, "there will be no waiting – you and Simon have to be ready at dawn as well."

"We shall be ready," Diana, stung by his implication that she would be tardy, promised him hastily.

Over René's protests that he felt wonderfully fit since dining with the Faerie Court, Lyon made him and Diana leave the Tower.

"*For he on honeydew had fed / And drunk the milk of paradise,*'" murmured Chenevix. He felt a stab of envy. To have been at the Selighe Court was a privilege not granted to many.

"What's that, Chenevix?" Lyon had begun making a list and was paying scant attention to his Grace.

"Naught that need concern you, Lyonshall," said the Duke and picked up his discarded letter.

Bryn Myrddin

The more time that Malcoeur spent with Sluagh, the more certain was the sorcerer that Sluagh was quite mad. The Elf (for Malcoeur had learned that Sluagh was indeed one of those mythical beings) was prone to fits of abject melancholia, swinging to gleeful elation, sometimes within the space of moments.

He would talk wildly of his plans, his emerald eyes glittering, his voice high and shrill. In this mood he was very dangerous, for he was apt to kill at random, at the least fancied slight or opposition. When he was depressed he sought solace in, of all odd things, coffee. Coffee acted on his body as if it were the worst of alcohols, and put him into a drugged stupor in which he was stupid and useless. Malcoeur thought sometimes that Sluagh was preferable in this state. When in his full senses he gave contradictory orders, had violent displays of temper and unjustifiable suspicions of any one else's motives. This, Malcoeur had discovered, was the real source of the Unselighe Court's fear, not Sluagh's powers, but the unpredictability of his disintegrating personality. For his powers were not great – he had the power of the levin bolt, which in itself was able to kill a creature or level a large tree or small hill, but of the subtleties of magic he had none. When in the throes of hysteria – an all too common occurrence – he shrieked about the 'stolen' forces that he had once commanded and how he would take his revenge on a much hated person only named as 'he' or 'him'.

For some strange reason this unstable person had taken a fancy to Malcoeur, which that gentleman ruthlessly used to his own advantage. When Sluagh had a 'good' day, Malcoeur inveigled him into giving the sorcerer second-in-command status over the Unselighe creatures. For days on end, while Sluagh lay in a coffee-induced daze, Malcoeur directed the creatures' war on the humans. It had been necessary at first to kill a fair amount of them in order to insure their obedience, but Malcoeur had discovered that the Unselighe Court had one thing in common with their human prey – they wanted to keep living as long as was possible. The fear of death, of ceasing to exist – for they had no hope of Heaven – was a goad to obedience.

Nor had he any fear of them organizing a rebellion against either himself or Sluagh. They were, as well as sluggish and slow-witted, greedy and selfish. It was difficult to make them cooperate with one another – the only thing that worked was the threat of punishment and an instant retribution for the least infraction. Malcoeur was wise in the ways of pain and did not hesitate to apply it to any creature who did not obey orders to the letter.

Malcoeur himself had killed no less than fifteen Wizards as the summer drew towards it midpoint. They had been, he admitted, young, untried Wizards, as had been the three Druids that had died from his magics, save for the Arch Druid of Wales. But he had drawn power from them and stolen their souls. He had left most of the killing of non-magicals to the Unselighe Court, for non-magicals had no power and he was well content to let the creatures feast on blood and flesh. His only interest in blood was that of the magical energies it imparted, and that could be drawn from the prey as the creatures killed – he had found that he did not have to do the actual killing if he were close enough to the place of death.

He was anxious to resume his pursuit of the Arch Druids. Of course, security about such places as Avalon, Tara, known in Gaelic as *Temair na Rig* – Tara of the Kings, Castle Urqhart on Loch Ness in Scotland and Tintagel in Cornwall had tightened and the Arch Druids had maintained a low profile, since the death of the Welsh Arch Druid. They knew that something had targeted them, but they had no idea what. And that pleased Malcoeur. He had read all of the news-sheets, laughed scornfully at their pathetic guesses about the crisis, and, on forays into the closest large town, he listened carefully to local gossip, which was as ill-informed as was the news-sheets.

He was resident Under-the-Hill, as Sluagh called his dwelling. It was convenient and cost Malcoeur nothing. One of the Gwyllion was his servant and he had made it clear to her that she had best provide him with the finest of foodstuffs and drink or she would suffer for it. Gul was afraid of Malcoeur – she had been present when he killed her cousin Jenny – and was servile and ubiquitous, to the point of being annoying. But she brought him good food – stolen, he suspected – and kept his things in good order. She had a tendency to want to climb into his bed, but Malcoeur found her completely repulsive and chose celibacy rather than Gul's dubious charms.

It was a hazy summer day when Malcoeur found out one source, perhaps *the* source of Sluagh's madness.

Beneath the shade of a sheltering grove of firs Malcoeur sat with a map of the British Isles on his knee. He had marked off the places of power – the Sacred Places as the British called them – and the homes of the highest rated Wizards in the realm, and the schools and universities that trained Wizards. The monies he had laid out on books had been well-spent. He had been surprised to find how few really powerful Wizards there were in these islands. There were less than one hundred *Magus Magistrii* and many of those were of advanced age. There were quite a few *Magus Majorii*, the most of whom were Augurs, clergymen or Healers, or held (in Malcoeur's view) such absurd positions as dust–sprinklers, or scryers for retail shops. His scorn for these was great. Magic was all about power – did these fools not realize that? Wizards were wasted in such professions as publishing, apothecaries, animal trainers, and even Wizards devoted to providing entertainments! He had been disgusted by the rules and regulations governing Wizardry in this benighted country and the extensive tests required at each level of magic.

All of this would change when England was beneath the *Tricoleur* banner of Napoleon. He, Malcoeur, would be the supreme magical power. These Wizards would sing to his tune, or they would not sing at all. He cared not a rap for the Inquisition – it held no fear for him. By the time the

Inquisition established itself in England once again he would be so powerful that no one could gainsay him.

He was thinking these thoughts and other of an equally pleasant nature when Gul appeared, wincing in the bright sunlight. The Unselighe creatures preferred the darkness, and Malcoeur could understand that – they were even uglier and more repulsive in the light of day.

'His lordship wants ye," she said, jerking one knobby hand back towards the hill.

"He is recovered and awake, then?" Malcoeur began to fold up his map.

"Oh, aye, and a foul temper he is in," she said, rubbing the side of her face. Malcoeur presumed that Sluagh had struck her, but it was hard to tell beneath the coat of dirt she wore.

He followed her into the hill and down the corridors to the main room where Sluagh held court.

The Elf was pacing up and down, his red silk tunic flapping about his legs. Two spots of colour burned on his otherwise pale face and his features were set in grim lines, while his eyes snapped green sparks.

"About time!" he spat as Malcoeur entered the room. "You took your time fetching him!" He leveled his mad gaze at Gul.

At a signal from Malcoeur she left the room, melting away into the dark of a nearby corridor.

Malcoeur feigning an indifference he did not feel (for it was obvious that something had happened, perhaps something of great import), waited for Sluagh to speak.

"He is interfering again!" he screamed at last, after several more violent turns up and down the room. "Again! Will he never cease his endless meddling in my plans!"

Malcoeur wondered briefly it this might not be a good point at which to press Sluagh on the identity of the mysterious 'he'. But viewing the Elf's wild eyes and distraught air he decided on discretion and tact.

"That is too bad," he said with as much sympathy in his voice as he could muster. "How dare he do such to you, *Monseigneur?*"

This turned out to be the correct tactic, for Sluagh said, "Ah! I knew that you would understand, my friend, my

293

only friend! My brother Oberon has gone too far! He thinks that he can banish me from the Bright Court and now hinder me further! He stole my powers you know, for himself!"

Oberon! A shiver ran down Malceour's spine compounded of surprise and excitement. If Sluagh wasn't completely mad and his ravings contained some kernel of truth – the Faerie King was not a legend, but quite real. And Sluagh was his brother? It would indeed be interesting to learn the whys of his banishment.

"My brother has welcomed humans to his court! He took them up with him during the Rade!" Sluagh snarled. "One of my bogles was concealed near the path of the Rade and saw everything! He means to use them against me – I know it! He knows that I am weak now..."

"But I am not weak, *Monseigneur*," Malcoeur interrupted. "Can your brother know that I, the most powerful *sorcier* in the world, am at your side?"

"No!" Sluagh brightened instantly. "For he will not spy on me – he is all that is honourable – the fool!"

Eyes glittering, he turned to face Malcoeur. "He cannot know what we plan, can he?"

Malcoeur could not be certain of this but he nevertheless agreed with Sluagh – anything to placate him.

"What do you plan next?" Sluagh queried, throwing himself down on the throne.

"I plan to visit Scotland," said Malcoeur. *"Pour encourager les autres,"* he added ironically.

"To encourage the others?" Sluagh repeated blankly. "Oh, I see! To encourage the others that their time is near!" He began to giggle in his insane fashion. Malcoeur found this most annoying, and considered, not for the first time, killing Sluagh. He was almost more trouble than he was worth.

In summer, dawn came very early. It was not quite half after four when the travelers assembled near the dragon pen at the Abbey. Tuathail was wearing his heavy travel harness, with four saddle seats attached. An small adult dragon Tuathail's size could carry four to six adults and a good deal of baggage without the least bit of strain. Lyon had suggested that they carry overnight gear, in case the search took longer than he anticipated. Diana had to bring an entire change, as flying gear for ladies was not as practical as the gear for gentleman. A gentleman pulled on a cover-all that fastened up the front with metal clasps, over his regular clothing. A lady had to wear laced-up to the knee boots and a special heavy divided skirt that ended at mid-calf, for it was impractical to ride sidesaddle on a dragon. A long lined jacket was worn over this skirt. This outfit was entirely necessary, as well as an ear-flapped hat and gloves, for it was cold on dragon-back, high in the clouds. The higher one went the colder it was. The change, too, was necessary, as she would suffer heat exhaustion on the ground without it. The men were so fortunate! A quick unfastening of the clasps and a shrug and they were rid of the flying suit.

Simon had never been so excited in his life. Yesterday Mama had taken him to see Mr. Roussillon and Simon had been happy to see that no harm had come to his former tutor. He was also thrilled to see how well Mama and Mr. Roussillon got on. He met Ninon and Lucie, who made much of him and gave him some lovely pastries to eat. And then they had told him about this trip and that he was important to the success of it. He had listened in awe when he was told about the Faerie King and Queen, and had expressed hope that he might one day met them as well. Mama said that Uncle Lyon might be amenable to Mr. Roussillon spending several hours a day with Simon, teaching him magic.

And to top this all off, a note had come from the Vicarage that the kittens were ready to make their choice. The Vicar suggested the day after tomorrow for the occasion and had invited everyone to tea. Simon's cup was full to overflowing.

His excitement continued to build as they mounted up. He sat between Mama and Mr. Roussillon, with Uncle Lyon in front. They were well strapped in with shoulder and lap harnesses, which Uncle Lyon and Mr. Roussillon had carefully checked. Only an idiot, explained Uncle Lyon, went up on a dragon without carefully checking every inch of harness and the fastenings. Tuathail wore a breast harness that bore a net bag called a carry-sack that contained their overnight things and two large baskets of food as well – one full of human food and the other dragon favorites. Simon had been surprised to learn that dragons preferred cooked food, indeed, could be quite the gourmets, and did not eat only meat, but vegetables and had a sweet tooth as well.

In no time at all they were aloft, Tuathail spiraling up into the fresh morning air. A rose-gold coloured dawn lit the edges of the few small clouds on the horizon. Above them, the sky arched in an endless blue bowl. It was going to be a fine day, but hot.

But up in the air it was chill. Simon had never flown as high as this before. He had only skimmed the treetops. And Tuathail was flying very fast – the ground went by underneath them at an astonishing rate. Tuathail's wings seemed to push them ever faster, until he suddenly began to glide, wings held out almost straight and stiff, flying, Simon thought. like the seagulls he had seen in Dover.

They flew south, to Wales, with the sun on their left. It was difficult to talk dragon-back, particularly at speed, for the rush of the wind, even when gliding, was not conductive to conversation. Simon was therefore not able to ask how fast they were going, or how long they had been in the air. It did not seem to take a long time to arrive at their destination.

Caer Myrddin was in South Wales, near to the banks of the Tywy river, in the county of Carmarthenshire. In Merlin's day, the pretty little town had been called Maridunum, and the county Gwent. It had changed little since the great magician's time, for early on, the cave had become a shrine and was tended night and day by Druids who vied for the honour. Lyon had scryed ahead to tell them of their mission and expected the Keeper of the Cave to be waiting for them.

The cave was not quite at the top of the hill. Hill was actually a misnomer, for the terrain was mountainous, and had they been on foot or horseback, it would have been a stiff trek up from the valley through stands of hazel, ash and briars growing amidst rocks covered by moss. The top of the hill was home to fir trees, more suited to surviving the harsh winds that whistled in from the Atlantic, not all that far from Caer Myrddin. The cave lay on a plateau, one of a series of giant steps that straggled up the hillside. A grassy verge lay directly in front of the cave and it was here that Tuathail landed. It was not a big area – three moderate sized dragons would have filled it – but it was larger than it had been in

Merlin's day, for Bryn Myrddin was a popular pilgrimage now.

A smaller ledge lay in front of the cave entrance – here the white-robed Keeper of the Cave stood, a smile on his face. He was a young man, but appeared older, for he was almost completely bald, and had a scholar's stoop. "Welcome!" he cried, as Tuathail landed neatly on the grass. "Welcome, your Grace and party!"

Only the Keeper had been told of their quest. He had never seen anything in the main cave, or the crystal cave that lay in back, of a lock that needed a crystal key – not any lock of any kind. He was as excited as was Lyon that the end to the Unselighe menace might lay within their grasp and ran forward as soon as Tuathail had tucked up his wings. Eagerly, the Keeper – he introduced himself as Wulfric Freestone – helped the travelers down and pointed out to Tuathail a large spot on the very top of the hill that was a popular sunning area for visiting dragons. Since Tuathail could not fit into the cave his services were not needed and he liked the idea of catching forty winks in the sun. René, with Simon's help, took off the harness so that Tuathail would be comfortable.

While Diana changed from her riding gear in a little hut built just for that purpose, the men discussed how to go about finding Merlin's secret cache. Oberon had said that the key itself knew the way and that where it lay could only be entered by a child. It was decided that Simon should be given the key and let it lead him.

Of the entire visiting party, only Lyon had been to Bryn Myrddin. It was an awe-inspiring experience, to be where Merlin, the father of British magic, had had his first lessons from old Galapas. Outside the cave lay Galapas's fountain – not a fountain at all but a mere trickle of water sprung from a cleft in the rock, a tiny pool half hidden by mossy stones and a lush growth of ferns. A horn cup rested on a tiny shelf, for the visitor to refresh himself. This pool was a shrine to the Horned God, and buried deep within the shrubbery around the pool stood the image of the God. The water was particularly pure and ice-cold, even in summer. It was considered good luck to drink from it. Lyon insisted they all have a drink. It was as delicious, as heady as the finest of wines and utterly refreshing.

The cave was not what Simon had expected. For one thing, the entrance was small, rounded and not hidden. Once inside, the cavern was enormous – it was vast and tall, its ceiling disappearing into darkness, in spite of the fact that it was brightly lit with mage lights. It was well furnished with chairs and tables, crammed bookshelves and lecterns holding huge volumes, for Bryn Myrddin was now a research library as well as a national shrine. Usually it was filled with scholars and visitors, but today it would be closed to any one other than their party, per Lyon's request.

Once they were all inside and had looked around a bit, Lyon took the key from his waistcoat pocket and gave it to Simon and directed him to walk first towards the rear of the cave.

Simon took the crystal key in his hand, holding it as Uncle Lyon instructed – just as if he were going to insert it in a lock. As they drew near to the back of the cave it began to feel warm in his grasp and quivered, as if he held a live thing in his fingers.

The four adults were following Simon closely. "It is leading him to the crystal cave!" said Wulfric excitedly. "But there is no door in the crystal cave!"

Suddenly, with a very audible ping of crystal being struck, the key snapped and began to shine with a white light, a beam of which led past a corner of jutting rock.

Around the corner was a high wall, broken by a ledge that was halfway up the steep wall. A flight of steps, with a handrail had been built up to a narrow cleft in the rock. The key seemed insistent that Simon go up the steps – he could feel it pulling at him.

The cleft was a narrow fit for a big man like Lyon and there was only just room for their party to fit inside.

The crystal cave was a natural phenomenon, although at first glance it seemed as if it must have been made by man. It was rounded in shape, and floor, ceiling and walls were covered in faceted crystal. The light was low – covered mage lights shone onto the floor, which was also crystal, and rough beneath the feet. Wulfric explained that the lights must be covered, elsewise one could be almost blinded by the explosion of light and colour from the crystals. The floor, where the small pools of light shone from beneath their covers, were rich with every colour in the spectrum and reflections from this subdued source made enough light to see clearly in the rest of the cave.

There was a discernible feeling in the cave of great power. As Simon walked the perimeter of the cave with his glowing key Wulfric explained that a very powerful node lay beneath the cave, with ley lines reaching out in many directions.

The key began to pull more and more at Simon and he called out excitedly as the key drew him towards the very back of the cave. He finally had to run to keep up with its draw.

And at the rear of the cave it came to rest in a niche between two crystals. A small oaken paneled door with hinges and lock of gold appeared beneath the key. The key slid into the lock and without Simon's help, unlocked the door, which slowly opened.

"I can see why we needed a child for this operation." Lyon remarked.

The door was narrow and little more than three and a half feet in height. Even Simon, small for his age and slim, would have to slide in, rather than walk.

"It's very dark," said Simon nervously, peering into the door, which had continued to open slowly and now stood wide open. None of the others could see anything within.

"Make a mage light, Simon," René directed.

Simon obeyed and with the aid of this, peered in once again, "It is full of books!" he said. "Big books, all bound in gold and jewels!"

Lyon rubbed his hands together. "Go on in, Simon, and see what you can find!"

"But be careful!" Diana added.

Simon was no longer afraid for the mage light showed every corner of the room. It was a small room, not of crystal, but of smooth dark stone. There were three stacks of books, mostly of atlas size, and about twenty of them altogether.

All had locks on the front, of all sizes. There was no sign of any keys. Simon wondered how they would be able to open the books, until, on an impulse, he tried the crystal key.

It worked on the book he tried, which had a very small lock. The key shrank to fit it, and unlocked it. This worked on two subsequent volumes as well, the key expanding and contracting as needed. But Simon could not open any of the books – it was as if they had been glued shut. He called out to the others, telling them this, but Uncle Lyon assured him that this was the results of the preservation spell that had no doubt been put on the volumes when they were hidden. This spell would need to be removed before they could read the books.

It was all Simon could do to lift one volume. They were heavy and awkward, and barely fit through t the little door. Mr. Roussillon took each one from him and passed it on to Lyon, who could be heard exulting in the background. Diana called encouragement to Simon over René's shoulder and Wulfric was incoherent with excitement.

At long last the last volume was handed out and René reached a hand into the room to haul Simon out.

As soon as the boy was clear of the door it disappeared, as if it had never been there.

"Are you all right, Simon?" Diana came forward and put her arms around him.

"Oh, yes, Mama," he returned. "It was not even dusty in there."

"'Tis truly amazing!" said Wulfric, stroking one of the volumes, a striking book with corners and hasps of gold and a large ruby in a gold filigree set into the front cover... "They look as if they were put in there yesterday! But it has been almost a millennia!"

"Quite a piece of magic, that," Lyon said in satisfaction. "You did very well, young Simon."

"There are twenty books here, all with perhaps three hundred or more pages," said René, frowning. "We shall have to search through them all, to find that which we need, *non*? *Regardez*," he took the key from Simon and unlocked the volume he was holding "On most grimoires, the title will appear when the key is put in the lock, *n'est-ce pas?*"

"Hmm," said Lyon, "that could be the preservation spell, but I don't think so. That old devil Merlin doesn't want it to be easy for us! We'd best take these books back to the

Abbey and search them thoroughly. Diana, you can read runes, can you not?"

"Very well indeed," she said, dryly. In common with many Wizards her uncle had a low opinion of a Witch's training. True, Witchcraft had a different basis than Wizardry, the power coming from the Moon, crystals and the lunar mysteries, but it was in no way inferior to Wizardry. It dated from the same time as did Merlin's magic, for its founder was Morgan le Fay, and was meant to compliment and enhance male magics. Miss Minchin had always held that Wizardry needed Witchcraft as much as the female needed the male.

"Perhaps *M'sieur* Arabin would help," René suggested.

"A good thought. I hope Chenevix remembers how to read runes. And your grandmother, Roussillon – as a Druidess she must be able to read runes, as well. Leander can read runes and I daresay, the parson's cat as well," said Lyon. "This is going to take a while –unless the spell is clearly labeled, which they usually are not."

Wulfric was torn – he did not want to see these books leave the cave and his keeping, but this was the Arch Druid of Britain, and he certainly had a right to take the books wherever he wished.

For once, Lyon was sympathetic to another's distress. "Do not worry, Wulfric!" he said, clapping the younger Druid on the shoulder. "As soon as we have what we need these volumes will be returned. They will need to be studied thoroughly and what better place than here at Bryn Myrddin? They're a treasure trove of arcane knowledge! But they'll be perfectly safe in my Tower."

Simon wished that he could read runes – he had only started to learn and as yet could not read the simplest inscription without the aid of the *Runic – English Dictionary* compiled by the Wizard Dr. Samuel Johnson. It would be marvelous to be the one that discovered the spell!

Wulfric insisted on wrapping the books in the velvet-lined oil cloth bags they used for transporting those books which were loaned to various magicians, for Bryn Myrddin, as well as a shrine and research facility was a lending library. Certain rare and elderly tomes did not circulate, of course. A part of Wilfric's position, in addition to guide, librarian and

Keeper, was as copyist – making neat copies of older, crumbling volumes that had to be handled with kid gloves, literally.

A large part of the morning had passed and it seemed time for some sustenance. Once the books were safely packed and stacked – they would be placed in Tuathail's carry sack when they were ready to leave – Wulfric offered to make tea and coffee for the party . How they would stare when they saw the quality and tasted the flavor of these beverages made from the waters of Galapas' fountain!

Since the day was so fine, it was agreed to eat *al fresco* beneath the trees. Tables had been erected there for the convenience of visitors and they had just decided to leave the main cave and go out of doors when the ringing trumpet of an enraged dragon filled the air.

"Stay back!" Lyon ordered at once, as the dragon cry was repeated. He headed for the entrance of the cave at once, followed by René and Wulfric. The latter snatched up a spy glass that hung by the entrance.

Stealthily, the three men crept up to the mouth of the cave and peered out. At first they could see nothing, for the grass was long and the shade deep, in spite of the fact that noon was not far away.

Wulfric carefully lifted the glass to his eye and adjusted it. Then he gave a short gasp. "The field is full of Unselighe beings!"

"Let me see that!" Lyon took the glass and leveled it, twirling it to match his vision. He gave a low whistle. "I count thirty, at least. See what you think, Roussillon," he added, handing over the glass to René.

"Thirty or more," René agreed. "There are Redcaps, hags and bogles, amongst others. I think that there are more arriving."

"But what can they hope to do here?" said Wulfric. "We are all Wizards – "

"Might you guarantee to kill ten creatures or more, Freestone?" Lyon queried, taking the glass back from René and looking at the creatures once again. "Yes, there seem to be more arriving at every moment. In a concentrated rush we might be overwhelmed."

"I have never before killed anything, your Grace," Wulfric confessed." I find myself unable to kill so much as a spider."

"I hope *you* don't have any scruples about killing these things," said Lyon to René.

"*Ne vous en faites pas*. I shall do what needs to be done," said René firmly.

Lyon grunted. "The trouble with you, Roussillon, is that you have a tendency to lapse into French at times of stress. Now, we've got to come up with a plan or we'll be overrun with these damn things. This isn't the way I planned to die."

"What can they want?" moaned Wulfric.

"They can't know about the books – and at any rate, most Unselighe creatures are illiterate and they have no real magical skills. The books would be of little use to them. They must be after Simon – they steal and enslave human children – and what they do to women, particularly Witches – I shan't elaborate on. Freestone, perhaps you had best go and protect Diana and Simon," said Lyon.

"That is unnecessary, *M'sieur*," said René, who had glanced back over his shoulder to where Diana and Simon had been standing together a moment before. "She has sealed herself and Simon into the crystal cave."

Lyon looked back as well. "Oh, good girl!" he said in approval, noting the tightly knit web of blue energy that enmeshed the front of the cave. "We could do the same here – but since those creatures can go for far longer than we can without food or drink, it really is not a good idea. Do you have any food supplies here, Freestone?"

"Only the cistern of water, and the makings for tea and coffee, and a few crackers and cheese. Meals come up from the village three times a day," Wulfric groaned.

René had borrowed the spy glass again and was intently studying the hillside above the field.

"Can the dragon not do anything?" Wulfric said worriedly.

Lyon shook his head. "He's more than likely almost out of flame after this morning's flight. He'll need to chew firestone before we leave. And the firestone bag is with the food and harness under the trees, next to the field, damn it all! Dragons are not stupid – even a dragon Tuathail's size might be overwhelmed by that many creatures. What I cannot understand is how it is that they are all working *en masse* and in broad daylight! It is simply not like them! Of course, this entire thing has been strange and nearly unexplainable from the very beginning," he added, as if to himself.

René closed the spy glass with a snap. "*Est-ce que cela ira?* If I might get behind them and we cast a great bowl of energies over them, and remove the air inside – "

"It would kill then!" said Lyon excitedly.

"But how will you get behind them?" faltered Wulfric, looking from one to the other as if they were crazed. "If you attempt to cross the field, even in the shelter of the trees, they will see you and be on you before you can cast a spell to repel them!"

"Did you not hear of the rediscovery of dematerial-ization?" Lyon demanded. "This is the young man who can do it!"

"Yes, but many of us thought it could not be so –" said Wulfric in amazement.

"Make it so!" said Lyon to René. "I will be ready to join my magic to yours as soon as you reappear. Freestone, you keep a look-out with that glass and tell me the minute Roussillon reappears."

Bemused, Wulfric took the glass and started visibly as René vanished with a tracing of violet light left behind. Immediately he reappeared on the ledge above the other side of the field, and Wulfric announced the fact.

The creatures did not notice. They were busy staring at the entrance to the cave, calling out taunts and making rude noises, even fighting among themselves, jostling for position.

Blindingly fast, not bothering with his wand, René raised his hands and a curtain of violet light flashed out from his fingertips. Lyon repeated his actions, just as quickly and the two violet waves met over the creature's heads, joined and fell to form a bowl over the Unselighe beings, trapping most of them beneath it. It had all happened too fast for them to escape.

Screaming in fear and rage, they threw themselves at the violet barrier, wielding tooth and claw to no avail. So great was their terror that they hurt one another, mortally in many cases; the pikes carried by the Redcaps doing fearful damage. Even these weapons made no impression on the sides of the translucent violet sphere.

And then they removed the air. To do this, both magicians tapped into the node. Lyon reveled in the sheer ease and power of this maneuver – he had never worked with anyone so talented and competent. "That boy," he thought to himself " is *Magistrii* material!"

Wulfric had let fall the spyglass in sheer amazement. A few stragglers began to run away and a huge shadow blocked the sun as Tuathail suddenly swooped down, and singed each one he could catch with a thin flame – all he could raise without chewing more firestone – and then, falcon-like, dived at his prey with outstretched talons. He then took it above and dashed it to its death on the rocks of a nearby cliff.

In few moments it was all over. The creatures in the violet bowl were dead, suffocated. Tuathail had caught all but a very few of those who had escaped the bowl and had speedily dispatched them by hurling them to their deaths on the mountainside. Before the bowl was dissolved, Tuathail chewed firestone and then flamed the remains of the creatures so that naught was left but a large, greasy darkened spot.

"If grass ever grows there again, it will be a miracle," said Lyon, with a grimace.

René went to the entrance of the crystal cave and called out to Simon and Diana that they might come out, for the danger was past. Once they had emerged and heard what had happened Simon was sorry to have missed all of the excitement, but when Diana heard of the gruesome death of the creatures she was very glad that he had *not* seen it. He would have had nightmares for months.

They made a hurried meal and packed up Tuathail quickly. It had become even more urgent to find the spell that banished these beings, for their intrusions were becoming worse, as this morning's incident proved. There was a great deal of work ahead of them.

305

24

His Grace of Chenevix Takes a Walk

On the same morning that Lyon and his party left for Wales, the Duke of Chenevix rose at his usual hour and followed his invariable morning routine. A first cup of tea, served by Mariposa whilst the Duke was still abed – the best China, very strong, with no sugar. Then a bath, with the water heated to a precise temperature. Mariposa then shaved his master, finishing up with a careful, subtle application of Steek's. The Duke then dressed, save for his Hessians and coat, opting for a dressing gown and slippers of red Moroccan leather. He then took care of any personal post that had come, or should there be none, it was his habit to read a work of an edifying or instructive nature. And, to Mariposa's surprise, his Grace sometimes read poetry.

This morning, as Mariposa pressed his coat – the blue superfine – the Duke sat in front of a small fire in his bedchamber, a worn volume in his grasp. Lyon would have stared to see such a shabby book in the Duke's well-manicured hands – it did not look as if it would match the uniformly bound gilt- edged volumes in the Ducal library at Chenevix Duchis in Dorsetshire.

The little volume was one of Mr. Wordsworth's. The Duke had had it for quite some time and it always fell open to the same page, for he had read it repeatedly. Something in this simple poem drew him back time and again.

She dwelt among the untrodden ways
Beside the spring of Dove,
A maid whom there were none to praise

And very few to love.

A violet by a mossy stone
Half hidden from the eye!
Fair as a star, when only one
Is shining in the sky.

She lived unknown, and few could know
When Lucy ceased to be:
But she is in her grave, and, oh,
The difference to me!

The difference to me! The Duke's mouth twisted bitterly as he read this line. What a difference to him it would have been! If only the only three people he had ever loved were not in their graves – all of the deaths untimely. First his mother – dead by her own hand when he was but ten years of age. He had not understood why she had left him behind, not until he matured and realized what a hell it must have been for her, living with his father – that icy-cold perfectionist.

But he had become just like his father – he heard the whispers and his great aunt Vespasia, before she had died, had told him to his head that he was the living image of his father, in nature. Perhaps if the others hadn't died – his elder brother Stuart, and the only woman he had ever loved, who, amazingly, had loved him in turn. But they had both died young and tragically. He had never been meant to be the Duke – he was not worthy of the title. His father had made that perfectly clear after Stuart's death. "Why wasn't it you?" his father had raged on the black day of Stuart's memorial service. Stuart had been groomed and trained all of his life to be Chenevix – he was the pale copy of his elder brother. Things might have been so different if Stuart had lived to take the burden of the Dukedom, and he himself had been free to be a simple country gentleman with her at his side. "But she is in her grave..."

With a sound of disgust the Duke slammed the book shut. Where had these maudlin thoughts come from? Things were what they were and could not be changed. Now there was only one's duty.

307

Several hours later the Duke had dealt with a pile of correspondence (most of it he put on Roussillon's desk) and had ignored several people attempting to scry Lyon's Tower.

It was quiet without Lyonshall about. The Arch Druid liked to talk and the Duke realized with a slight sense of shock that he had actually come to enjoy trading insults with Lyonshall. The quiet was not to his liking today – really, he was in a very odd mood.

At long last, after wandering aimlessly around the Tower, he decided to go for a short walk. Exercise was what he needed – perhaps a turn about the shrubbery or a walk to the little folly – a miniature Grecian temple, complete with Ionic columns and a dome – that stood near a lily-covered pond, drowsy with heat and dragonflies in this summery weather. It was rather hot and stuffy – thunderstorm weather if the Duke made his guess. He decided to walk to the temple – it would be cooler down by the water. He would walk by the Dower House – it was right on the way and the gardens were supposed to be very fine, according to Mariposa, who was flirting with one of the maids. He had taken her down to the Rosebank gardens yester-eve and had told the maid that the delphiniums were the same blue as her eyes. He accounted most of his amours to his master, although his Grace had but a tepid interest in anyone's amours at all.

It was now near eleven and the day was fair and hot. There was very little breeze and the clouds that were beginning to pile up on the horizon of the brassy blue sky were the ominous anvil shape of thunderheads.

He found himself thinking again of the day he had been told of his mother's death, for it had been a hot day, like this, with a hint of thunder in the air. It was the final term at school – the very exclusive Fairfax-by-the-Sea, for the old Duke considered Eton and Rugby full of commoners. He, Lord Carlisle as he was then, was only at the school because his brother had begged for his company.

They had been called into the headmaster's room – Stuart was always toadied to by the headmaster, for he was the heir and bore the heir's title of the Marquis of Keir. The headmaster always had an eye to the main chance. As the younger, extraneous son, Stuart's brother was merely Lord

Carlisle, a meaningless courtesy title attached to his Christian name. Therefore he was of little account.

The headmaster, a chilly gentleman who would have made a good friend for the old Duke, had not his Grace held himself on too high a form to admit to even an acquaintance with a mere schoolmaster, bade them be seated and without preamble, told them that their mother was dead.

Chenevix remembered the pain of that moment again, as if it were new. There had been no sympathy from that man, no Christian compassion, for all that he was an ordained minister. He gave them no details, either, just that their dear mama was dead, and that they would not be returning to Chenevix Duchis for her internment, for she had been buried in haste. They would not have the comfort of a service for her, for she lay in unhallowed ground, a suicide. There was a certain satisfaction in the Reverend Upjohn's voice as he told the boys this fact. He had met the late Duchess just once and she had not been impressed with him and had made the mistake of showing it too clearly.

Years later, when Carlisle had come into the Dukedom the very first thing he had done was to have his mother disinterred from the vile place she lay and bury her in a place of honor. He had come to cuffs with the incumbent of St. Barnabas, the parish at Chenevix Duchis, and ended in dismissing the man and replacing him with a newly ordained young man who was too much in awe of his Ducal patron to protest anything the Duke chose to do.

But why were these memories torturing him now? The pain was still as real as it had been all of those long years ago. He supposed it was the atmosphere at this place – it was that of a family, with that small boy at meals, a lady presiding over the household, and the constant emotional dramas that seemed to follow Lyonshall wherever he went. It was not the regulated quiet and austere life that he had become used to and desired. Perhaps it had been a mistake to come here, perhaps an error to even have accepted the position of Chancellor...but one had one's duty. In the end, that was all that there was.

He walked on towards the pond.

Since Diana had offered them the use of the clothing and fabric of the late Lady Paulina, Ninon and Lucie had been busy every day with alterations, cutting and sewing. They had been quite happily occupied and it had given them a chance to be en ensembler and rediscover one another in the easy talk that comes when women sew together. They laughed a good deal and cried a little and opened their hearts to one another. At the end of this time they not only had, each of them, a stylish wardrobe, but a better understanding of the other.

There was a deep sadness in Lucie that Ninon thought would never leave her. She had lost so much – years of her life and sanity, her husband and the childhood of her son, and she struggled to come to terms with it. At times she would sit, in front of the fire or out in the garden, staring at nothing, a sad and pensive look upon her face. The brightly flaming girl was gone forever, it seemed, to be seen only in flashes when Lucie was laughing or amused by something. Ninon hoped that the coming of the kittens into the household would help lift Lucie's spirits, for Lucie had always adored felines. Another grief had been the little cat she had lost at the time of her husband's death. Two playful kittens would help, Ninon hoped, and had impatiently waited for the visit to the Vicarage.

Today Lucie seemed to be in a happier mood. Much of the sewing was done and the two ladies were able to come down to breakfast in new morning gowns, Ninon's her favorite green and Lucie in sunshine yellow, both trimmed with knots of matching ribbon and lace at the edge of the short sleeves and *décolletage*. It was so warm already that shawls were unnecessary.

"We shall have *le tonnerre*, I think," said Ninon, as Giselle served them croissants and coffee in the sunlit breakfast parlour. She didn't mind if it did thunder – this roof didn't leak as had May Cottage's – no matter how many times she had magiced it. Ninon had become convinced that the cottage had been under a curse, or more than likely under the malign influence of Sir Piers' ill-wishes.

It was so pleasant to sit at a highly polished table in a handsomely furnished room and eat delicious food that she had not had to prepare herself. She only wished that Marthe and Jacques – and Louis – were here to enjoy it with her, and to see Lucie well and recovered.

It gave her pleasure to hear the ticking of the gilded mantel clock and to look at the Wedgewood frieze of Grecian figures on the face of the fireplace, to watch the play of sun and leaf-light on the polished wood of furniture and floor, to handle fine china again, with its translucent and egg-shell fragility, and to sip truly excellent coffee and tea, and know that she need not do the washing up! Life had become a joy again.

"If it is to thunder, Maman, do you think that René will be safe, up on a dragon in the sky?" Lucie queried. She was still nervous of dragons, in spite of seeing them almost daily. The Catholic Church taught that dragons were evil minions of Satan, and having grown up in France and never known a dragon, this attitude had tainted her judgment.

"I have been told that a dragon will not fly in the thunderstorm," Ninon assured her. Ninon's experience with dragons was not large, but after over twenty years in England she had become accustomed to the casual acceptance that most of the British had for the great creatures. She was not certain that she really cared for René spending so much time on dragon-back, but it was a part of his new position and she must accept it, for the position had brought so much good fortune to them. But it had brought anxiety as well, she must admit. She was realist enough that to know if they had been in France still, René would have no doubt been conscripted into the army and then they would never have any respite from worry and the horror of receiving the news of his meaningless death in some foreign country conquered by that madman. Riding a dragon was far safer than that. She tried not to think about the ceremony of the Cremave – it had come out all right and Sir Piers had been punished, but she could not think of the terror she had suffered without feeling sick.

"I do not think that I shall ever wish to ride a dragon," Lucie was saying now, daintily biting into a flaky croissant. *"Je vais rester ici*, on the ground."

"There is a special costume for riding the dragon," Ninon told her, "Culottes!"

Lucie exclaimed at the thought of wearing breeches, even if it did look like a skirt and the talk drifted to speculation as to whether or not René would return that evening.

Breakfast finished, Ninon went to work in her stillroom. She was still organizing her herbs and had been thrilled to find a nice little herb garden here, as part of the kitchen garden. She had needed to add more of her healing herbs, and she spent part of each day in the gardens.

Since the gardens were so fine, Lucie had taken on the duties of keeping the house filled with flowers. They had discovered a remarkable collection of vases in the flower room at the rear of the house near the kitchen. This was equipped with a soapstone sink and a pump, a work table and numerous shelves to hold vases and containers of all shapes, sizes and materials.

Lucie much enjoyed this task – she found selecting the blooms, cutting and arranging them extremely satisfying. It was creative and allowed her to be out of doors as well. When she was with the flowers, reveling in their beauty and scent, she could let her mind drift and let go of regrets and the sadness that was always with her.

She gathered up a flat basket and a pair of shears and took a large Lavinia hat from a peg by the door of the flower room. The vases in the dining room and in the entrance hall were in need of refreshing. Lucie challenged herself each time to make a unique bouquet that would nonetheless compliment the décor and colour of each room.

The entrance hall was black and white, so it needed colour. That meant the gardens in the front of the house, where delphiniums and scarlet poppies bloomed, as well as flowers of yellow and purple hues. Lucie adored an exuberance of colour and it was here in the monochromatic starkness of the hall that she could give herself imagination and taste free rein.

It was hot out of doors – she was glad of the protection of the wide-brimmed Lavinia hat. The flowers were all wide opened, soaking up the sun. She filled her basket quickly with exquisite blooms. Since she preferred to do one arrangement a time, she was back and forth to the flower room twice and then for the third and final time, she went out for flowers for the dining room table. This was more of a challenge, for the dining rooms walls were a rich crimson, and she wanted a nice contrast. Perhaps a low arrangement of white and pale flowers?

As she worked,. she began to sing softly to herself, but on the still air, her sweet soprano carried quite a distance.

Ah! Vous dirai-je, Maman,
Ce qui cause mon tourment?
Depuis que j'ai un Silvandre
Me regarder d'un oeil tendre,
Mon coeur dit a chaque instant:
Peuton vivre sans amant?

At this moment his Grace of Chenevix had nearly reached the Dower House, He heard someone singing and his mind identified the tune idly. In English nurseries it was sung as "Twinkle, twinkle little star" but the French made a love song out of it. Who can live without love? ran the last line. Who can live without love indeed! He had lived without love, for many long years, very successfully, he thought savagely.

And then it struck him – that song! She had sung it! He was suddenly blindingly angry. He assumed that the singer was the maid-servant at the Dower House. She was French. How dared she? Well, he would soon put a stop to it! He strode forward angrily, his jaw set, not pausing to consider that the poor maid knew nothing of the fact that the song caused him pain, or even that he was going to be in the neighborhood.

There was a female figure kneeling in front of the smallest flower bed, a round plot between the beds edging the drive and the bow-windowed front of the house. She was cutting flowers with a pair of shears, her hands protected by gloves and a large hat shading her face. She also wore an apron over a stylish gown, from what he could see of it. Not the maidservant then – but one of Roussillon's family. Still, she had not ought to sing that song. "You there!" he called imperiously, striding forward.

Lucie looked up at the sound of a voice. The sun was high and it dazzled her eyes. Even with the shade from the brim of the Lavinia hat she was forced to put her hand up to her forehead to shade her eyes to see the figure that was still only a silhouette moving rapidly towards her.

And then the sun went behind a cloud, just as he reached her. Sherry coloured eyes met gray. And then *"Mon mari!"* Lucy shrieked and jumped up from the ground and launched herself at him.

The Duke staggered, not entirely from her joyous assault. "Lucie!" he said in shocked disbelief, feeling arms he had thought long gone wind themselves around his neck and her sweet eager kisses that he had not forgotten, cover his face. "Lucie – it can't be! They told me you were dead!" he gasped, and pulled her arms from his neck to hold them tightly. He pushed her a way a little bit. He wanted to look at her face.

It was! It was her!

"And you were dead, also, *mon mari* – my husband! My Lucien!" She was looking up at him with those enormous sherry eyes, fringed with long silky lashes, those eyes shining with love and joy. "But your lovely hair has become *trés gris!*" She raised a hand and gently smoothed his hair, for his glossy beaver had fallen to the ground unnoticed. She had become older too – her hair was short, graying and she was thinner – but Chenevix had never seen anything more beautiful. "How –" he muttered, trying to take it in.

She broke free of his hold and threw her arms about him again. "It does not matter! Kiss me!"

Since there was nothing he wanted more, he obeyed her. There was time and enough for explanations.

Ninon had worked hard in the herb garden, but was pleasantly tired. She had a large, sturdy basket of fresh-picked herbs on her arm – Madame Roche had asked her to pick some rosemary, basil, oregano, thyme and fennel to season a vegetable terrine destined for supper that evening. It was nearing noon and she was beginning to think of a nuncheon. Even in this heat one felt hungry – the food was so good – and there was so much of it, that she found herself anticipating meals. It was so good to eat excellent French fare again, particularly the cuisine of Provence, which she had learned to appreciate after her marriage. She had been surprised that Lord Lyonshall, who was anything but sensitive, had sent French servants to them. And to have servants from Provence! It was wonderful. Perhaps it had been Lady Diana behind the hiring of Madame Roche and Giselle. Ninon had now a better opinion of Lady Diana – she had been generous to her and Lucie, and most important, had apologized to René. They now seemed on excellent terms and Simon was in and out of the Dower House every day. Ninon liked the boy – she had always a soft spot for children and would have liked to have a dozen of her own. But *le bon Dieu* had only given them Lucie.

As she came around the corner of the house Ninon saw a terrifying spectacle – Lucie, seemingly struggling in the arms of a man!

Picking up her skirts with her free hand, Ninon ran forward, raising the basket as a weapon above her head. Unheedingly, she scattered herbs all over herself and the lawn.

"*Au secours! Au secours!* "she shouted, losing her English. "*Le violeur!*" She thought the man was about to rape her daughter, right here on the lawn, in the daylight! She ran at his and hit him again and again with the basket, shouting abuse in French.

"*Maman, non!*" Lucie shrieked, putting herself in harm's way to shield Chenevix. "It is Lucien! Lucien, my husband!"

The Duke had been forced to cover his face and cringe away from this attack, for he could not offer violence to a female, no matter how much she offered him. Burt now he reached out and grabbed her wrist, forcing her to drop the basket. "Control yourself, Madame!" he grated. "I mean no harm! Can a man not kiss his own wife?"

Ninon rubbed her wrist. Mon Dieu, but he was quite strong – stronger than he looked. But she did not understand what was going on. "Your wife?" she repeated disbelievingly. "But you are dead! Lucie saw you die in the *auto de fé!*"

"Lucie saw my brother," the Duke said harshly. "My elder brother Stuart, older than me by five minutes, for we were identical twins."

"Then why did you abandon Lucie?" said Ninon fiercely. "To leave a young girl, sick and alone – *Vous n'êtes même pas bon pour décharger du fumier!*"

315

If the Duke was upset by learning that he was not good enough to shovel manure for a living, he did not let it appear on his face. "I went back, secretly after Stuart ..." He could not bring himself to say 'died'. "The people at our flat told me that she had gone away. I searched for months – finally I found someone who had seen a girl answering the description I gave out. They told me she had died – they showed me where she had been buried!"

"And why did you call yourself Lucien de la Mare, when you are Chenevix?" Ninon wanted to know.

"I was not Chenevix then – my brother was due to inherit the Dukedom, not I. I was merely Lord Carlisle Delamar. My second name is Lucian Carlisle Lucian Charles Anthony Delamar, which once long ago during the Norman invasion was de la Mare." the Duke explained.

"I liked to call him Lucien," said Lucie, hanging onto the Duke's arm as if she would never let go. "Lucie and Lucien – it was meant!"

Ninon was still suspicious of him – she had never liked him, thinking him cold "Lucie did not tell us you were an English lord!" she said accusingly.

He had the grace to flush. "I never told her. My brother and I were living with my uncle, who had a silk warehouse in Marseilles. There had been a quarrel with our father. My late mother was the daughter of a silk merchant." A very wealthy silk merchant, he might have added, for that was the only reason the old Duke had wed her. He had been a wealthy man, but the silk merchant was worth millions, and, as was so common in those of enormous wealth, the old Duke never thought he had enough money "I thought that we could live simply..."

"Ah, bah!" said Ninon. "And now I have a son-in-law who is known as *le glaçon!* One could not wish for more felicité, pas possible!" she added sarcastically.

"And only think how happy René will be to find that he has a father!" said Lucie, with a smile of pure joy.

The Duke staggered for the second time. "Father?" he repeated weakly.

In the late afternoon Malcoeur returned to Under-the-Hill. He rode a kelpie, a Scots creature of the water, which was not confined to that medium, but bestrode the land as well. The kelpie's usual mode was to appear as a handsome young horse, allow himself to be caught by a human greedy to possess him, be mounted, and then, traveling at a great rate of speed, took his victim into a deep pool or river, where he either drowned him or dashed his brains out against a rock. The pseudo-horse then feasted on the remains. The kelpie could also take on human form – usually that of a shaggy old man, who would leap up behind a solitary rider and squeeze and frighten him to death. Without his glamourie, the kelpie was a collection of bad points, with a raw-boned appearance, cow-hocked and ewe-necked with a big, ugly head, ratty tail and small eyes.

With the aid of a magic bridle the kelpie could be controlled and ridden. The rider himself had to bridle the steed, but Malcoeur had had no trouble in doing this. An icing spell learned in Russia froze the beast and the bridle slipped on easily over the ice-encrusted head.

The kelpie was far faster than any mortal horse (although not to be compared with the Elvensteeds of the Bright Court) and Malcoeur had been able to journey to Loch Ness in one day, accomplish his task and go back again to the hill in Wales. It was a great convenience, almost as convenient as the magic carpets he had ridden in Persia. That the kelpie glared at him with fury-filled, red-rimmed eyes all of the journey bothered Malcoeur not a whit. It would do him a mischief if it could, but he had no intention of letting it.

Gul met him at the entrance to the cavern. "He's in alt, he is," she said glumly. "Can't wait to see you. Had me comin' up here every few minutes. Thank the Evil One 'tis rainin'! Elsewise I'd been out here in th' sun!" For the day had turned to rain and thunder over most of the British Isles.

"He need not have worried, *je vous assure*," said Malcoeur, handing over the reins of the kelpie's bridle to another Gwyllion that came up to them. "Take care that the bridle stays on him," he ordered.

"Oh, he ain't worried," said Gul as the hill split open for them to pass through. "He's done sommat he wants yer to give him a pat on th' back for, he has. Right proud o' himself, he is."

317

Malcoeur quirked a questioning brow at her, but she only shrugged. She knew no more than he did.

"You did what?" Malcoeur said coldly when Sluagh told him what he had done that day.

"I sent my minions to kill the Arch Druid of Britain!" Sluagh repeated gleefully. He could not sit still on his throne, bouncing up and down like a small child – like a youngster shouting "Look at me!" he wanted praise.

But Malcoeur was in no mood to offer praise. Holding his temper carefully, for to show his anger would send Sluagh into a fit of the sullens and there would be no information forth-coming, Malcoeur said, "Tell me, *s'il vous plaît*, exactly what has happened."

Sluagh giggled. "How clever I was! This morning one of the bogles came to me – he has been reconnoitering near the Abbey of the Arch Druid. He saw the dragon take off with a full party this morning and he followed it with the aid of a crow he knows. The dragon flew to Bryn Myrddin. And I thought, why not kill him there? If enough of my court were to attack him, it could be done! One Wizard against fifty or so bogles and hags and Redcaps –"

Malcoeur swore viciously.

Sluagh blinked in surprise. "You aren't pleased?" His voice was petulant.

"Are you certain that there was but one Wizard? Did you not go on this petite voyage your own self, to make certain that these crétins did their task properly?" Malcoeur demanded. "Have they reported to you as yet?"

Sluagh began to look uneasy. "No, but –"

"Merde!" Malcoeur swore. *"Faire une bêtisse!"*

Sluagh stiffened. He had not done something stupid!

"You'll see!" he stated. "Any minute now they'll be back – with his head! I told then to be sure and bring his head back!"

But it was not until late that evening that a single bogie returned to Under-the-Hill. The few others that had escaped were too frightened to return and tell of their defeat.

They were right to be afraid. For with a inarticulate cry of rage, Sluagh killed the bogie bearing the bad news with a single levin bolt.

When they returned to the Abbey, barely ahead of a thunderstorm, Lyon was incensed to find Chenevix not at the Tower and a bubbling mass in the scry bowl that meant many people had tried to get in touch with him that day. The early morning post had been sorted, but the afternoon post still lay on the silver salver Seppings used to bring it to the Tower.

"Damn that Chenevix !" he muttered to René as he surveyed the empty Tower. "I can't even trust him for one day!"

René picked up the mail and started to sort it as Lyon continued to grumble. "He's probably gone into Cheltenham to get some exotic tea or some such thing!" the Arch Druid muttered.

There was a sudden thump on the roof and a silver horn blew.

"M'sieur," René began.

"Yes, I know," groaned Lyon. "A 'griffe express has arrived! What the hell can it be this time? I only hope it is not some old dowager, with more money than sense, complaining about gnomes in her garden! When will these old beldames learn that a 'griffe express is for serious business?"

He lost all desire to make light of it when he saw the livery of the rider – that of the Scots Arch Druid and the look on the face of the young rider – as if he had seen something unbearable. Lyon snatched at the paper of parchment the rider offered him and tore it open.

"Oh, my dear God!" he said in tones of horror. "Iain McAslan is dead and nine of his people with him! Even the Loch Ness monster is seriously injured! Murdered – all of them!"

25

Revelations

They had barely beaten the thunderstorm home – large drops were falling and the sky growling when Tuathail landed in the dragon pen.

Leaving the men to unharness the dragon and get him into the dragon shelter, Diana hurried Simon into the house, for he was somewhat damp in spite of his too-large flying suit and she did not want him to take a chill. The ride back from Wales had been rough and cold, with Tuathail fighting clashing air currents and trying to fly above the thunderheads whenever possible. Dragons did not like lightning at all – a creature filled with gasses was not safe amongst flashing lightning.

She assumed that Uncle Lyon and Mr. Roussillon would be taking the precious volumes to the Tower. If she knew Lyon, he would start on the work this very night. Nevertheless, she ordered tea, suitable for five persons, for the Duke no doubt would be eager (or as eager as his Grace ever became) to discuss the findings. She also assumed that Chenevix would be at the Tower – that was where he was at this time of day.

Simon was bathed and dressed in dry clothing and came back downstairs for tea. Diana, too, had shed her flying suit in favor of a gown of long-sleeved velour. The rain was pouring down by now and thunder crashed, interspersed by jagged bolts of lightning. The sky, at four o'clock in the afternoon, was as black as night, necessitating mage lights. Seppings directed a footman to make a fire in the hearth, for the temperature had fallen precipitously. Immediately the leaping flames chased away the gloom of the storm and Diana ordered the amber coloured drapes drawn against Mother Nature's fury. The room was cozy and peaceful in contrast to the events of the day and the ongoing barrage out of doors.

Simon and Diana were seated in front of the fire, talking over what had happened when the door to the hall connecting the main house to the Tower burst open and Lyon rushed in. He held a piece of paper so tightly in his hand that his knuckles were white. His hair was wilder than normal – it looked as if he had dragged his hands through it. His cravat was askew and he was obviously under a great strain. He was closely followed by Mr. Roussillon, who looked grave.

"Where is that damned Chenevix?" Lyon demanded, looking about the room as if he expected the Duke to be hiding somewhere.

"I thought him to be in the Tower," said Diana. "Whatever is the matter, uncle? You look distraught."

"Distraught!" Lyon exclaimed. "I wish that I was *only* distraught!"

"There has been very bad news, *rein ne va bien...*" René began, but Lyon made a noise of derision and said, "You have a genius for understatement, Roussillon! Very bad news! A tragedy, rather! The worst possible news! Iain McAslan and nine of his people are murdered! Even the Loch Ness monster is injured, trying to defend Iain, I dareswear! And I dareswear we shall find that their souls have been stolen, as well!" He shook the paper as if it were a rat. "They sent me no details, only the barest outline of what has happened! The 'griffe rider had been out on an errand when it happened. Ten people! That is nearly the entire Druid community at Urqhart! This was penned by a student who has not even been robed as yet! How he survived the attack we do not know!"

Diana had come to her feet, her face set in shock. "But how – who?" she gasped, hand to her throat.

"We know very little as yet," said René. "We have tried to scry Urqhart, but there is no clear image."

"Yes and if you would only dematerialize and GO there –" growled Lyon, throwing himself down in a chair.

"I have told you, *M'sieu*, that one may not go to a place unseen. I might teleport into a wall, or the loch without a true picture of the surroundings in my mind," René told him patiently. Diana admired his forbearance. It was sometimes difficult not to lose one's temper with her uncle.

"Merlin could go any place he wanted," Lyon grumbled. "Oh, curse it!" he shouted, crumbling the paper in his fist and causing Simon to start. "What is doing this? Every creature in the Unselighe Court in concert could not kill ten Druids all at once! For all our magic and learning we are as helpless as non-magicals!" He grabbed at his hair and tugged as if he could pull the solution from his brain. "And where is the twice bedamned Chancellor of Magic when I actually need him?"

It was at this instant that a knock was heard at the door and they heard Seppings answer it. There was the murmur of voices, and Seppings said clearly; "Everyone is in the Amber drawing room, your Grace."

A moment later Chenevix entered the room, Lucie on his arm. Ninon, a strange look of exasperation on her face, was behind them. All of the party was more than a little damp.

René sprang forward at once to bring his mother and grandmother to the fire, but was forestalled in Lucie's case by the Duke, who tenderly placed her in a fireside chair, leaving René to help his grandmother. Startled, he exchanged a look with Ninon, who said clearly "Ah, bah!" and sank into the chair, holding her hands out to the fire and rubbing them briskly.

The Duke went to stand behind Lucie's chair, rather protectively, with one hand near her head. She turned in the chair to smile up at him.

What was going on? René wondered, his hackles rising. He did not care much for Chenevix and this proprietary air towards Lucie he did not like at all. What was the Duke playing at? Lucie positively glowed with happiness. But he was not allowed to question them, for with a roar, Lyon came to his feet.

"Where have you been?" he demanded of Chenevix. "Visiting and swilling tea while events of national importance are taking place!" He shook the crumpled parchment in the Duke's face.

With a languid hand the Duke waved it away. "Events of importance *have* happened today, Lyonshall," he looked fondly down at Lucie. "And you shall – you all shall hear of –"

"You hear this, Chenevix!" Lyon interrupted, shoving his face, beard bristling, close to that of the Duke "Iain McAslan and nearly all of the Druids at Urqhart have been murdered! Probably by the same entity that slaughtered Myfanwy!"

"What!" the Duke exclaimed. Without conscious thought he reached down and took Lucie's hand in his. She looked up at him, sherry eyes worried. Ninon was shocked by the news but her frown matched René's as she saw the handclasp. Diana too, watched this byplay, bemused, for she had never seen the Duke act in such a fashion. He was behaving as if he and *Madame* Roussillon shared an intimate connection of some sort. And *Madame* de Varien was definitely not happy.

"When did this happen?" the Duke demanded, looking from Lyon to René and back again, a frown creasing his brow. But he did not leave go Lucie's hand. Nor did she try to withdraw it from his grasp.

"Just after noon," said Lyon heavily. His fit of anger seemed to have passed, for he sank heavily into his chair, looking suddenly exhausted. "The details are still extremely sketchy – we haven't been able to scry anyone and I daresay once this storm is ended we will be besieged with dragons and 'griffes, all bearing messages."

He looked up at René. "We need to prepare a statement – there will be journalists coming here and the people in Silverbridge and Knightswold will be alarmed," he said tiredly.

René nodded and, and with a bow to the company, turned to leave the room.

"Wait, René!" said Lucie quickly. "We have some happy news for you!" she smiled up at the Duke. " René, this is your father! He was not dead after all!"

"Mama, how could Mrs. Roussillon have lost her husband like that?" Simon asked curiously as Diana tucked him in for the night.

"She is now her Grace of Chenevix, Simon," Diana corrected gently, sitting down on the edge of Simon's bed.

"And as you heard, many things happened that pulled them apart." She wished that Simon had not been there when the revelations of the afternoon were made. She would as lief he had not heard about the Inquisition and the death of the Duke's brother. But all of the adults, herself included, had quite forgotten that he was in the room.

It had been an emotional time. Lucie had expected nothing but happiness for all involved – here was her son and here was her husband all restored to one another and she had expected them to fall on each other's necks. But the actuality was very far from her fond imaginings. They were wary of one another and happiness was probably the last of the emotions either one of them felt. It was as disconcerting for the Duke to be confronted with an adult son whom he had hithertofore thought of as only a secretary – a servant – as it was for René to suddenly be joyous over the advent of a father – and such a father as Chenevix – when he had been used to having his parent long dead. It was not as if Chenevix knew of Lucie's pregnancy, and had wondered about his child's fate, for the very evening he had been taken by the Inquisition was the time she had planned to tell him of the coming child.

Lyon had dismissed this family reunion. There was no time for this sentimental twaddle now! It was very gratifying, but there were more important things to think about and do.

Reluctantly, the Duke admitted that Lyonshall was right and leaving Lucie in Diana's hands (with instructions as to what kind of tea she was to have and how she was to be dried from her wetting) he accompanied Lyon and René back to the Tower. The storm was passing – at any moment messengers would begin arriving. There was work to be done.

Ninon was unable to read René's expression as to how he felt about this development, for his face had become closed and remote. That he was as shocked as was she, she had no doubt.

Lucie had been disappointed in his reaction. "But *Maman*," she said when the gentlemen had retreated. "he does not seem happy to see his dear Papa alive and restored to us!" Tears stood in her eyes.

"And your dear Lucien does not seem thrilled to see his son," said Ninon dryly.

"It must be a shock to both of them," Diana pointed out. "It is not as if they knew one another and have been reunited. Neither knew of the other's existence. Mr. Roussillon is an adult, also, not a little boy."

"René is now le *Marquis de* Keir, Lucien says," said Lucie. "He will like that, *Maman*, will he not, to be the wealthy *Marquis*?"

Ninon reflected that Lucie had not really known René very long, if she had thoughts that he would be happy with honours he had not earned, especially from a man he did not particularly like. Ninon, too was not particularly taken with her new son-in-law. He was cold and authoritarian. She could not see what Lucie saw in him. *L'amour* was very odd.

Now Diana thought again of the very strange day that had passed, as she tried to answer Simon's questions. So much had happened – the discovery of Merlin's books, the attack and rout of the Unselighe creatures, the murder of the Scots Druids, and now this revelation. All in one day! Diana's mind felt bruised.

"Mama, am I to call Mr. Roussillon Lord Keir and his Mama Lady Chenevix?" Simon looked up at her with enormous eyes. He was done in with fatigue as well.

"It would be the proper thing to do, but the correct address for Mrs. Roussillon is now Duchess, or your Grace." She bent over and kissed him on the forehead.

Simon sighed a long-suffering sigh. "Everything keeps changing!" he complained. "I wish that it would all stay still!"

His eyes then became dark with apprehension. "Mama, I'm afraid," he confessed. "Are those things going to come here? Will we all be killed?"

Diana had dreaded this conversation, for she had no real idea what to tell him. She could not promise that nothing would happen. "We will do everything we can to be safe," she said. "But everyone must be careful and take precautions. We have two powerful Wizards here – in Uncle and Mr. Roussillon – Lord Keir, I should say, and *Madame* de Varien is a Witch and a Druid and I am a Witch. We have Tuathail to warn us and the griffins and the lions from the gates prowl the woods at night. There is little more that we can do, Simon. Tomorrow Uncle Lyon says he is going to see about more safety measures, for us and the village, including having Mr.

Rou – Lord Keir's family move up here from the Dower House so there are less people to protect on the grounds. I wish that I could promise you that everything will be all right, but I cannot!"

"Shall we still be able to fetch our kittens?" Simon inquired anxiously.

Diana smiled at him. Children were so resilient – one moment worrying over being killed and the next bothered about a kitten. "I think we might do so, but we shall have to see what safeguards are available."

Simon had to be content with this and was persuaded to settle down and close his eyes. She sat on the edge of the bed until his quiet breathing told her he was fast asleep.

On the way to her own bed she paused in the hall and looked out from the window. From here one was able to see the lights of the Dower House. They still burned brightly – of course, it was early yet. The lights of the Tower blazed in the falling dusk as well. As Lyon had predicted, there had been messages all evening once the storm had passed. Diana had taken a tray to the three gentlemen for their supper and she would lay odds that it was largely untouched still. Even as Diana watched, a black dragon in the red and gold of the Royal colours landed in the yard.

What was going to happen to them all? Wearily, she lay her forehead against the cool glass of the window and closed her eyes. It could take months to search all of Merlin's books. And after today she had the feeling that no one, anywhere, was truly safe and that time was running out.

It was well after midnight before René was able to return home. The lock of the door was magiced and he easily reversed the spell and let himself in. All was dark and quiet – he supposed everyone long retired.

But as he passed the drawing room, as silently as he could, a voice spoke out of the darkness. "René, are you only now coming home?"

He turned and went into the room, casting a little mage light so that he would not stumble against the still unfamiliar furniture.

"*Grandmère,* why are you not in your bed? It is past midnight!" he said, heading towards her.

She sat in a wing chair covered handsomely in bargello, huddled in a voluminous shawl of cashmir. She looked as tired as René felt. "I wanted, René, to talk to you about this matter."

Hr knew to what she was referring, but he was totally disinclined for talk. "May this not wait until the morning?" he suggested. "I am very tired. I am only surprised that *Maman* is not laying in wait for me as well."

"She has gone to be with him," said Ninon. "She packed her valise and was gone, as easily as that." Earlier on she had been angry about this – although she chided herself for the jealousy she felt when Lucie danced away with the Duke. Of course, Lucie wanted to be with her husband. If Louis had reappeared, after years of her thinking him dead, she would have wanted to be alone with him as soon as was possible.

René looked taken aback and Ninon almost laughed aloud. It was always difficult for the young to realize that their parents felt love and desire and were still capable of doing something about it. And it was just as difficult for a mother to realize that her *bébé* was old enough to enjoy the intimate embrace of a man.

"Your *Maman* expected you to be much pleased with this news, *hein?*" Ninon went on. "But, me, I do not think you are pleased, René."

"I do not know what I feel," he said rather harshly, turning from her. "It is a shock I have never expected."

"Perhaps this is some of the change I have seen in my cauldron," Ninon sighed. "I am too old, I think , to change."

René wondered if he were not too old, also, to accept having parents who seemed to feel that they had some control over his life. He had barely come accustomed to have Lucie sane and sensible, now he had the Duke – who had already begun his assumption of authority. His Grace had spent the afternoon and evening correcting Lyon every time the Arch Druid called René 'Roussillon'.

His son was to be addressed as 'Keir' by his equals and 'my lord' by his inferiors. He made that perfectly clear.

And this was going to take a great deal of getting used to.

26

Searching

On the following morning the Duke of Chenevix woke up feeling extraordinarily well. Usually, only strict discipline forced him from his bed. He had a deep feeling that only the invalid, the lazy, the idler and the profligate lolled about in bed. He had too many responsibilities to indulge himself in such a fashion.

But he felt extraordinarily well – and – dare he even think it? – happy! And then it all rushed over him. He had found Lucie! She was alive and well and still loved him!

And she was in his bed, he remembered, as he heard a small sigh as she turned over in the vast bed.

He turned to look at her. She still slept and she had a satisfied little smile on her face, one hand tucked under her cheek and those long lashes of hers making shadows like veiling on her face. Her hair was mussed into wild curls. Tenderly, he pulled the bedclothes up over one bare shoulder. He would let her sleep. But he had things to do.

His nightshirt and dressing gown lay discarded on the floor with her nightgown and he picked his night-gear up and shrugged himself into them.

Last night had been beyond even his most cherished memories of how it had been with her. She was so eager and responsive! It was as if they had never been parted.

Mariposa had been displeased, for Chenevix had ordered him to find a bed in the servant's quarters, rather than sleep in the dressing room as he had done for so many years. Mariposa would have to accustom himself to that, for now that Chenevix had found Lucie, she was going to be with him day and night. There would be none of this fashionable sleeping in separate rooms, even if he had to have all of the bedrooms in all of his houses refitted to accommodate her needs. They would be together. He would not lose her again.

Where would Lucie like to live? He would show her each property and let her decide. But he wanted to take her to London and properly outfit her. He had been appalled to learn that the gown she wore yesterday had been made by herself. No homemade gowns for his Duchess! He would take her to *Madame* Rose Bertin – *Madame* had once been dressmaker to Marie Antoinette, but had emigrated to England when the Revolution broke out. She was the premier *modiste* in London.

Chenevix decided he needed a list – there was so much to do. He went to the writing table and found a tablet of writing paper. He found one of the new silver-nubbed pens – a great improvement over the quill – and dipped it in the inkwell.

Gowns he wrote, *Madame Bertin.* This was followed in rapid succession by *Hats – Fanchon, shoes and accessories – Bond Street, jewels – Rundell and Bridge, have Chenevix jewels taken from vault and cleaned, need wedding rings, jewel case.*

Each thing he wrote made him mindful of others. As his Duchess Lucie would need to be presented at Court at one of the Queen's Drawing Rooms before she could properly enter Society. That could be done in the Little Season, in the autumn. He must speak to one of the patronesses – perhaps Emily Sefton; she was very good-natured – about vouchers for Almack's. Lucie would need a maid, her own carriage and pin-money. He would need to visit his attorney, revise his will and make certain that she had a generous widow's jointure, and a handsome settlement. An announcement would have to be drafted to the journals about his change in status.

And, he realized with a small sense of shock – he now had an heir, who needed to be presented at one of the Regent's *levées* as well. That meant new clothes – the clothes Lyonshall had purchased in London were not precisely disgraceful but they were not the well-tailored garments that the fashionable world would expect to see on the heir to the Dukedom of Chenevix.

329

The Duke started another page, which he headed *Keir. Tailor – Weston, boots-Hoby, hats – Locke. Tie pins, fobs, seal – Rundell and Bridge.* He was not certain that he cared for that Windswept hair style – perhaps the shorter Stanhope Crop? He wore his own hair in the severe Brutus style. And Keir had to be taught to tie a neck-cloth properly – a top of the trees valet was in order. And his heir would need to set up his carriage, acquire a high-bred riding horse – that meant Tattersall's. Vouchers to Almack's for Keir as well. And Keir was nearly six and twenty – he ought to be meeting well-bred females, marrying and setting up his nursery. *Suitable young ladies*, Chenevix noted, as his pen sputtered busily. Keir would have to be sponsored to several gentlemen's clubs, such as White's and Watier's, as well. Chenevix would ask Brummell or Alvanley to do that – but perhaps he ought to do something about Keir's French accent. What was counted charming in a female was unacceptable in a gentleman. *Speech teacher* he wrote.

And he supposed he would have to make provision for his mama-in-law as well. He did not want her living with them but there were any number of Dower Houses at his various properties – if she preferred to live in London he had a nice little house on the river in Chelsea that she might like. She would need an allowance, as would Keir.

In none of this planning did the Duke, even for one minute, stop to think that the three people whose lives he was so eagerly rearranging might have different ideas about their future.

He had covered four sheets of paper with closely written notes when he heard a stirring from the bed and Lucie woke up, stretched and yawned daintily and said, "Lucien, why are you from bed – it is scarce light, *n'est ce pas?* Come back to bed. *Il fait très froid!*" She held out her arms invitingly and nothing loath, Chenevix discarded his garments once more and slid into bed with her, his list forgotten for the moment.

It seemed strange at the breakfast table that morning, without Lucie. Her empty chair seemed to take up an enormous amount of space. Giselle was all agog at what had happened and asked innumerable questions until Ninon lost her temper and told the girl to be quiet.

Ninon had awoken in an ill-temper. She realized that she resented want had happened. She had had Lucie back for so short a time! They had been so happy to have her returned to them – and now she was taken away yet again! And into the custody of that cold man! How Lucie could love such a one! Perhaps he had been very different as a young man? Lucie still saw him as he was when first they met. Truly, love was blind – and deaf and sometimes stupid!

René was very quiet this morning she thought. He had disappeared behind a copy of the *Wizards' Times*, which was unusual for him. They usually shared the news-sheet, reading out pieces of interest to one another. He had not answered any of Giselle's eager questions, leaving it to her. Nor had he eaten much breakfast, leaving a lovely mushroom and cheese omelet largely untouched. The little she could see of his face above the news-sheet was unreadable. She had been unable, the evening before, to get him to admit to his feelings about suddenly obtaining a father, a title and a fortune all at once. He had excused himself from her questions and gone off to bed. This morning he was still uncommunicative. Ninon sighed. Men! A female would be eager to talk about her feelings and what had happened. The best thing she could do now, in all probability, was to leave him alone.

René, behind the sheets of paper, was glad of her silence. He did not wish to talk about what had happened, for he was not certain that he really quite knew what he felt. It was so shocking – to have such a change in circumstances and to discover that a man such as the Duke was his father – René was not even certain that he could *tolerate* the Duke, much less embrace him as a parent. It had hurt to see the disappointment on Lucie's face when they had not immediately taken to one another. She had expected a Faerie-tale ending of every one living happily ever after.

René realized that many people would consider him a fool. He had gone from being a poor *émigré* to being the son of one of the wealthiest men in the kingdom. He now had a title, and as Lyon had informed him, Chenevix would no doubt make him a handsome allowance. And as Chenevix's son, he was now an English citizen. That part was gratifying at least. But he had a feeling that Chenevix was not going to be an ideal or even easy parent. His nature was cold, his manner controlling and demanding. He held himself on a very high form. René's own nature was warm and affectionate. Last night had had a taste of what the future was going to be like. Over Chenevix's protests, Lyon had sent his secretary down to the butler's pantry to fetch some ale.

And Seppings had been stiff and formal with him. Every other phrase out of the butler's mouth had been "my lord". Seppings had always been friendly – they had often shared a joke and a glass of port in the pantry. Lyonshall's secretary might crack a joke with the butler, but the Marquis of Keir could not. René felt rebuffed by Sepping's formality and he did not like the feeling. What if everyone else began to act like that – Reverend Arabin or Jim Cerne for instance? Being a lord could be a very lonely proposition. Every time someone addressed him as *my lord*, or *Keir*, he had almost looked about for someone else that bore that name.

And he wished to keep working as Lyon's secretary. He liked the work – it was important and satisfying – and he hoped to begin teaching Simon again as well. He preferred to earn his wages – not be handed an allowance like a kept woman. He turned a page in the paper that he was not actually reading. Most people would consider that to be an act of driveling idiocy also – to not want a hand-some allowance that he had not earned. Maybe he *was* a fool , but that was the way he felt. But how could he explain any of this to Lucie? Ninon might understand, but he could still clearly see the hurt in Lucie's eyes yester eve when he had not responded to her news as she had imagined he would. The Duke had not been overjoyed, either. He was happy enough to have his wife restored to him, but the existence of a grown son had been a thunderbolt to match those that had been raging out of doors.

What would this day bring? After yesterday's storm it was going to be a lovely day. Today they were to remove the spells of protection from Merlin's books and begin the search for the binding spell. Lady Diana was to come and help search through the books, for she read runes very well, as did Ninon. Lucie disclaimed any such ability. She had never had any but the most rudimentary knowledge, for she had never learned much magic, having little real interest or inborn talent for it. René had learned to love his *Maman* dearly, but had to admit that hers was no great intellect. But she was kind and loving and sweet.

He found it odd, however that a man like Chenevix had chosen a woman like her. For himself – but he shook those thoughts away. That was a futile road to go down.

Everyone was assembled in the Tower by eight o'clock, even Chenevix. Although no longer a practicing Wizard he could still read runes.

Simon was to keep Lucie company, as they would be useless in the reading. He had been promised that he could run errands and greet any 'griffe' riders or dragons that arrived, for he desperately wanted to be of use. Lyon had asked Conchobar and Diarmait to come from Ireland to help in the search. He had scryed the news of the find late the night before and each Druid hold, with the exception, of course, of Castle Urqhart, had promised to send its two best rune readers to aid in the search.

More grim news had reached them from Scotland. There was no sign of how the murderous intruder had breached the security of the Castle. Urqhart stood on a peninsula jutting out into Loch Ness, and was thoroughly shielded. There was no sign that Iain or any of his people had been able to react to the attack or put up any sort of defense, and the grimmest news of all – the Loch Ness monster's injuries were consistent with the use of blood magic. The monster had reported seeing nothing until he was assaulted by a wave of blood-red energies, whilst he was on patrol.

This latest horrific event made it imperative that the binding be restored as soon as was possible. They could only conjecture that whatever was doing the killing had come with the Unselighe Court, for the murder of the Welsh Arch Druid had nearly coincided with the appearance of the Redcaps and other Unselighe beings.

But all *was* but conjecture. There was no hard evidence for anything – where or how the creatures had broken the binding, nor what or whom the slayer might be.

Every surface in the Tower laboratory had been cleared and the precious volumes laid out. There seemed to be no order to the books – they had no titles or volume numbers as they had noted whilst at Bryn Myrddin.

Lyon unlocked each volume and then attempted the standard preservation removal spell on the largest of these, a gold-edged book with an emerald of outrageous size set on the cover.

Nothing happened.

"Oh, damn!" he swore. "It couldn't be as easy as that, could it now?"

"*Puis-je vous aider?*" queried Ninon. "I wish to try something that we know in *Bretagne*."

"Oh, go ahead," said Lyon. "You can't do any worse than I did."

Ninon went to the book and lay one hand on it. She spoke one Word, in a language no one else in the room understood, save René.

The cover flew open, the pages ruffling quickly as if blown by a tempest. It was as if they stretched themselves after being too long closed, for in the next moment the pages rippled back, opening to the very first page.

"It is Blaise's preservation spell," she said, pleased with herself. "in ancient Breton."

Ninon then lifted her hands, repeated the Word and the remaining nineteen volumes sprang open all at once, ruffled themselves back and forth and then lay open.

"Impressive!" said Lyon. "It stands to reason, I suppose, that Merlin should use one of Blaise's spells. Thank you, *Madame*, for thinking of that."

Everyone knew what to look for. They each took an open volume, and then perching on a stool or standing as their inclination dictated, they began to read.

The contents of each book were indeed in runes – tiny runes written in a rather crabbed hand. Each book seemed to be the same thing – spells interspersed with a sort of journal – notes on the how and why of the spells, and there were also comments about various personages, and records of Merlin's travels, even his expenses on the trips. It was a treasure trove of information and shed new light on Merlin's methods of work and his place in history.

It was slow going however. With the exception of Chenevix all of them could read runes as fast and as easily as

334

English. The ink was as fresh and as crisp as if it had been penned yesterday, due to the preservation spell, but Merlin would never have won a prize for penmanship. The language was archaic and sometimes obscure. And there was also the digressions, as every book-lover knows, of finding something else perfectly fascinating and being sidetracked into reading it, rather than what one was searching for. The volumes were large and every page was covered in small runes, its contents made without rhyme nor reason, seemingly as they had occurred to Merlin. It was written as if he were delivering a series of very erudite, but unconnected lectures to a student or apprentice. Recipes for honey wine were on the same page with a spell to turn a cat into a canary, and a rude poem about Sir Lancelot.

Mid-morning, when no one had found anything of import, and no one was further than a sixteenth or less through the volume he or she had chosen, Conchobar and Diarmait and their familiars arrived. Lyon ordered a short cessation of work. Everyone needed coffee and some food. Simon was called and sent to the kitchens for a tray.

Shortly after that, two Druids from Avalon arrived, closely followed by two more from Wales and then two from the Isle of Man. All with attendant familiar animals. These were set to re-checking the readings for something missed. Guénolé had promised two from the Île de Sein, but they would not arrive until late that evening, as the Île boasted no dragons, and they would have to take ship for the Channel Isles and catch a dragon there.

By two in the afternoon there were eleven people and nearly as many familiars scrutinizing the volumes, all going slowly and all becoming rather frustrated.The recent deaths were always on their minds and there was a real sense of urgency in the room.

Although many fascinating spells had been found nothing resembling a binding spell had been even noted in the mass of writings.

"It will probably be in the very last volume we check, on the very last page," said Lyon glumly as they took time out for tea and biscuits.

The Tower room was crowded with people and animals , including the six white-robed Druids.

"Two more rune readers will give us nearly enough people to each read a book." Chenevix rubbed the bridge of his nose wearily. He had been forced to consult Dr Johnson's *Runic / English Dictionary* far more than any of the others, even the familiars, for he was woefully out of practice.

"The Vicar comes tomorrow," said Lyon "and I think I shall scry Cheltenham this evening to try to find enough Wizards –"

"– or Witches!" said Diana firmly.

"Or Witches," Lyon amended. "to make twenty of us, so that all volumes will be studied at the same time. The familiars can go behind us, checking for what we may have missed. Even with that, I think that this is going to take some time – time we really cannot afford to expend."

27

Reminiscence of Things Past

It was very quiet in the Tower where Lyon sat by the window staring out at nothing in particular. There was no moonlight, for the sky was obscured by clouds hanging low and thick. Thunder rumbled in the distance. Brief flashes of heat lightning lit the clouds from within. There was little wind and the air was still and heavy with the promise of another storm. The clouds were as black as Lyon's thoughts.

For the first time in his life he felt daunted by a task before him. They had worked until midnight, each book lit by a mage light of high intensity. Although many fascinating and useful things had been found, there had been no binding spell. Progress was heartbreakingly slow. Looking at the bookmarks in the scattered volumes Lyon estimated that they had not advanced as far as he reckoned – the amount read was more a sixteenth part, not one quarter as he had thought earlier on. Diana had provided wide scarlet ribbons to mark their places and the ribbons were readily discernable, even in the dim mage light that now illumined the Tower. It was not easy reading, even for highly trained rune readers. Even did they find the spell, would they be able to implement it? And did the restoration of the binding mean the ending of the blood magic?

He could not stop thinking about Iain's death. All of the Scots Druid's training, all of his expertise and skills had not saved him from a horrible death. Nor had he even been able to defend himself. Where would this slayer strike next?

Here at the Abbey? Avalon? Tara? The Isle of Man or Kernow? Or even the Welsh enclave again? There was no knowing. Every Augur in the British Isles, using every method of prognostication, had attempted to see where the next strike might be. They had all failed.

Lyon was not a fool. He was more than a little afraid for himself and his household. How did one protect oneself from such as this? They had taken what safeguards they could – every protective spell that he could devise had been used on the house and grounds. Tonight the servants had moved Roussillon and his family to the main house so that the guard griffins and the stone lions would have only to protect one dwelling. At any rate, Lyon felt better having two powerful Wizards under the same roof, although he realized that it hadn't helped Iain. And there were additional Druids as well, now in residence.

Conchobar had been reluctant to come and Lyon could understand that – the Irish Arch Druid was worried about the safety of the hold at Tara. But the finding of Merlin's spell was too important. Conchobar was one of the best rune readers in the country.

Lyon had remained in the Tower to under-take a necessary but unpleasant chore. He had to write a letter of condolence to Kirstie, Iain's wife. She had been spared, for she had been in Edinburgh, at daughter Jean's first lying–in. Iain's son, Donal, had been spared as well, for he was recently gone out to Canada to head a Druid enclave there. Lyon thought that he should really write to all of them, for they had been friends for over thirty years. He was Jean's godfather, and been groomsman at Iain and Kirstie's wedding. But what did one write in these circumstances? *I am so sorry Iain was murdered?* He could not even promise revenge, for he had no idea what he was fighting or if it was even possible to stop it.

His self-doubt led to questioning his recent decisions. Perhaps he had taken on too much – accepting the Arch Druidship might have been a mistake. He had never expected to inherit the Marquisate but the old marquis's son had died at about the same time as his father – he had thought, when he was elected, to spend most of the year at Avalon, with occasional lectures at University. Now he was Arch Druid, fellow at Oxford and Marquis of Lyonshall, which meant the Lord Lieutenancy, the duties of a magistrate and overseeing a vast and neglected property. For the first time it seemed an onerous burden. Not for the first time he wished that his wife, Amelia, had not died. A talented Witch, she had also been able to firmly ground him and make him see where he was going wrong. He missed her wise counsel and loving presence more than he could say.

With a sigh, he drew a piece of parchment towards him, and dipped a quill in the ornate ink bottle that stood at his elbow.

My dear Kirstie, he began.

Diana felt as if she had never been so tired in her life. She knew that thinking such a thing was ridiculous – she had been much more tired on the Peninsula, when she had to keep going, at a time when all that she wanted to do was lie down and die in the snow. The sense of urgency had been great at Corunna, but the atmosphere in the Tower had been worse. Every one on the retreat had been afraid of being caught by the French before they could reach the safe haven of the ships. All of them in the Tower so frantically reading were afraid of much worse. It was an unspoken fear – that whatever was doing this would succeed in destroying all of the magical persons in the realm. They had no way to fight back at present, not even a way of protecting themselves. This made for tension, short tempers and exhaustion.

Diana had left he Tower earlier than the others, in order to put Simon to bed and to make arrangements for their guests.

She had been so grateful to find that the Duchess of Chenevix had stepped into the breach and made certain that Simon had his dinner and been bathed and readied for bed. She had even read him a story and played at spillikins with him. Lucie had also suggested to Seppings that the servants ready the rooms for the visiting Druids.

Diana therefore found everything all in readiness. She had only to kiss Simon good night and tuck him in. She had every intention of returning to the task in the Tower, but made the mistake of sitting down in front of the fire in her bedchamber – for only a moment. She leaned her head back and closed her eyes – for just a brief rest, she promised herself.

She slid at once into a dream.

It was a bright spring day. She and Simon were at a fair. They were having a marvelous time. Everything was so bright and clear. They decided to go and watch a juggler perform.

And then the dream changed. She became transfixed with horror, for the juggler was not just a juggler, he was a necromancer! She saw the aura of blood magic, saw the souls trapped in his black outline, endlessly screaming, begging for their release to the afterlife. She felt again the terror, the sliding into unconsciousness – but this time she woke with a start and a cry, and found herself in her chair, heart pounding and gasping for air. Her hand was wound about the Faierie gift she always wore, obedient to Titania's orders.

There was something important to remember!

At last she had it – "The Jongleur." she whispered. "He was called the Jongleur."

It had not taken long for Malcoeur to return to Sluagh's good graces. Once the Elf had comprehended that the Scots Arch Druid and many of his people had met their fate he was all smiles and compliments. He seemed to have an especial hatred for the Loch Ness monster and gleefully hoped that it would die of its injuries. That was the only thing that he chided Malcoeur with – Sluagh felt that the sorcerer should have made certain that the monster was dead.

He was like a child – a large, dangerous child, Malcoeur thought as he watched the Elf. He was not afraid of Sluagh, for he knew his magics far outranked those of the Elf. A simple shielding spell erased the danger of frequently thrown levin-bolts. But Sluagh was becoming tedious to deal with and Malcoeur was convinced that the Elf was further descending into madness.

By dint of encouragement and endless patience, Malcoeur had found out more about his host. Sluagh was not full brother to Oberon, but half-brother, his mother being a mortal woman. It was rare for the union of an Elf and a human to result in a child, (children were rare even amongst the pairing of two full-blooded Elves) and his birth had been greeted with much joy. Sluagh had been much indulged. His magic had been not innate, but had to be endowed.

And from the beginning he had resented this. He took umbrage at the fact that his half-brother Oberon would reign over the Hollow Hills, while he was to remain a mere courtier – not even an Elfin knight, for he did not have the magic required to join that fair company. Disgruntlement grew and festered, turning at last to madness, a madness whose pressures could only be eased by killing.

Oberon had caught him killing flower Faeries. All of the Bright Court had been horror struck and many had demanded his death. But Oberon had chosen banishment and stripping of powers, save those of defense. Perhaps the Elfin King still retained memories of happier times in childhood and could not bring himself to order the death of his brother. If this was so Sluagh hated him for it. *He* would not be so merciful! Oberon was weak and stupid!

Sluagh had gone to the Dark Court of the Unselighe and offered his services. The Dark Lord, he whose name was never spoken, had welcomed him and given him dominion over many of the Unselighe creatures. Sluagh had been happy with this until he realized that it meant ruling a kingdom bound from ever visiting the Outside world. And to his chagrin this meant he was bound as well, once ne became one of them.

Then had come the rending of the spell that bound them. Sluagh's desire for a complete revenge against his brother was born and who better to help him than Malcoeur, a sorcerer who had killed a Druid – a supposedly invulnerable Druid? The Wizards and Druids were a danger to the members of his Court and Malcoeur could rid him of this menace.

When all of the Druids and Wizards were dead and Malcoeur had stolen all of their power they would annihilate Oberon and the entire Bright Court.

Malcoeur had no intention of helping Sluagh overthrow the Bright Court. He himself had no quarrel with the Elfin King and did not see that it would be an advantage to expend so much magical energy on a useless endeavor. From what he had read, the Fair Folk interfered little in the affairs of man and preferred to remain hidden and secret. They were welcome to their Hollow Hills.

But it would not do to dissuade Sluagh at this point. He might need Sluagh to help deliver the Unselighe creatures to the Peninsula and to the Russian front. If he, Malcoeur, was to kill the Dark Lord's second, the Dark Lord might not honour the agreement. There would be time enough for an 'accident' to happen whilst on campaign. One could blame Sluagh's death on the British or the Russians.

So he resigned himself to the utter boredom of agreeing with Sluagh's crazed plans and the Elf's endless complaining and whining about the injustices of Oberon.

On one of the more *ennui*-inducing occasions Malcoeur found his thoughts drifting into the past, a place he tried never to visit. But all this talk about brothers and revenge – and then too, the mountains of Wales, in spite of them being softer and greener, reminded him of his early home. To Sluagh, raving again, it appeared as if Malcoeur hung on his lips. But the sorcerer's mind was ranging back into the past.

Snowdonia was wild and rugged, but it was tame when one compared it to the French Alps where Malcoeur had passed his early childhood. He had been born in Paris, but shortly after his birth, which had killed his mother, his father had inherited a title and a small property in the area of the Alps near Grenoble. Near was a relative term. A trip to Grenoble was an expedition such as one would mount to travel the arctic wastes or the deserts of Africa. The mountainous terrain was harsh, as was the life they lived.

Malcoeur's father, Émile Vidocque, Comte de Belle-donné, was a bitter man. The tiny holding he inherited was heavily in debt. The Chateau did not deserve the name, for it was scarcely more than a series of loosely joined mountain huts – cold and dark all of the year. There were no fine paintings, silver plate or tapestries to be sold. All of the money came from the herding of goats, and selling their milk and cheese.

To Belledonné, this was the final insult. He wanted to live in Paris, where there were courtesans, bright lights and most important of all, gaming tables. He was now a Comte – but would society accept a Comte of goats? He could just imagine their laughter! He had wasted the last of his small hoard to make the journey to the mountains, intending, once there, to leave the new-born babe behind with a wet nurse, for he little cared if it lived or died. He would take the elder boy, Marc-Antoine, back to Paris with him, for the ten-year-old was very useful and had learned to pick pockets and fuzz the cards.

But that had proved impossible. There was nothing to steal or sell. The house was scarcely furnished – and that furniture was rough, peasant-made trash. There was no jewelry, or cash – only debts. Increasingly bitter with every passing year, with no money to return to the flesh-pots of Paris, Belledonné had turned to the Black Arts.

He had always possessed a little magic – enough to sometimes turn the cards his way or give a horse a little more speed whilst at the races, but he had never dared use too much, for he was terrified of the Inquisition. Attendance at the *auto-de-fés* was expected of all good Catholics. One needn't go every time, of course, but to stay away entirely was apt to bring the Holy Inquisitors down on one's head.

Belledonné began to sweat, to only think of those figures writhing, twisting and screaming as they burned. And the smell–! He could all too well imagine the agony of those flames devouring his feet and legs and screaming until his throat was filled with his own blood.

The French Alps were a closed, secretive place of nearly impossible to access valleys and shelves. The mountains were high, bare and jagged. From his small holding, on a clear day, Belledonné could see the massive bulk of Mont Blanc to the North, snow-covered nearly all of the year. Very often he looked out from his steep mountainside on a sea of mist or clouds. Many of the mountain huts were set in Alpine meadows, alive with flowers and the white cotton grass of the region. Not so Chateau Belledonné – it sat on a steep, stark escarpment, exposed to the cold wind, driving snows and sudden rain and wind storms of the mountains, the only trees coniferous and dark. They offered little protection, for they clung to more hospitable areas than that of the Chateau.

But Belledonné found to his surprise that the region was full of Witches. He found this out by degrees, seeing a hex doll here and hearing a whisper there. He wondered at it, for were these people not afraid of the Inquisition?

They were not, he soon found. The local Bishop was lax and cared more for the pleasures of the table than sending troops into the trackless mountains to put peasants to the question. Very often, the troops he had sent, when first he took up the Bishop's mantle, had never returned, disappeared into the mists. As the years passed, he cared less and less about the heresies of magic that might be practiced in those secret mountain villages. By the time Belledonné arrived, it had been thirty years since any of the Army of the Inquisition had ventured into the region. To practice the Black Arts was safe – the Bishop was a man in good health, of only late middle age. He would be in the See a long time – indeed the local Witches made spells to insure his long life and his remaining as their Bishop.

When he had been some few years in the mountains Belledonné found a collection of grimoires at the Chateau, written by a remote ancestor. He found them whilst searching for something to sell. They were written in a strange style of Old French, but long study enabled him to puzzle then out – he had always been good at puzzles and cryptograms.

What he found excited him. Here was power! Power to be wealthy and admired! Subtle manipulations that would never be discerned, even should the Inquisition come to the area!

And so it was that Malcoeur, known at that time as Jean-Claude Vidocque, began to study magic at an early age. His father had decided that if all three of them studied and learned the Black Arts, they would three times as powerful.

From the very first Malcoeur showed a precocious talent and an inborn understanding of dark magics. Things his brother and father struggled with came easily to him, with instinctive understanding. By the time he was twelve he had completely outstripped them and was actively seeking training from other sources – the old Witch women and men who hid in the secret places. From them he learned many things not in the books.

Things had begun to turn Belledonné's way. Subtle manipulations had given him good luck — he had increased the goat herd and had a wide market for his cheese, for he put a spell into the making of it that made it virtually irresistible. He took an occasional foray into Geneva, or to Italy, where the cards and the dice ran the way he wished. Money was beginning to pile up in a bank in Rome, a local bank and a Swiss bank and the investments he began to make proved wildly successful, with a little help from the dark magics. Soon he would have enough to leave this benighted place behind and live year round in Paris.

Then suddenly the negligent Bishop died, choking on the small bones of an ortolan. And he was replaced by a new, young, and ambitious Bishop, Faustin de Caivillon, who burned with Holy zeal and an intense hatred of heretics.

The Church had become concerned that there had been too few *auto-de- fés* in the region. It stood to reason that there had to be heresies – such a long stretch of time without heretics was impossible.

Bishop de Caivillon had been sent to the area with a troop of crack Inquisitors, armed with all the tools of the Question (the rack, the Iron Maiden, the *bastinado* and the more portable thumb screw, and a handsome selection of whips) and a highly trained Witch-Sniffer as well. This gentleman, Guillame de Constellet, a deceptively mild little man with cow-like eyes, rejoiced in his profession and particularly enjoyed the questioning of comely young persons of both sexes, who, of course, had to be questioned in the nude, so that the could examine their bodies for Witch-Marks, and take a good long look for evidence of carnal knowledge of the Devil. He did not pay as much attention to the old or the ugly, unless they screamed well.

Within two days of de Caivillon's arrival, the troops were in the mountains, dragging shrieking, suspected Witches from their homes and putting them to torture.

The old, the solitary, the ugly, those with a cast in the eye, the crippled, those who kept cats – all of these were suspect. And de Constellet made certain that a fair amount of the most attractive youths in the region came under his eye. He enjoyed their maltreatment as much as, or perhaps more than, he enjoyed them in his bed. For he was generous enough to offer them that option. Since the other option was being burnt at the stake, very few refused his offer.

345

De Caivillon ignored this aspect of his Witch-Sniffer's life. De Constellet had results – that was what was important. Most of those he questioned were guilty. De Caivillon wrote an enthusiastic report back to the Papal Office of the Inquisition in Rome.

And then he began to look into the nobility and the *bourgeoisie* in the area.

There were not many nobles hereabouts. Any one who could leave the region usually did so. Most of the nobility lived at Court, at Versailles, while a steward ran their estates. De Caivillon had always felt that the nobility was a hotbed of vice and depravity. Had not Louis the XIV's mistress, Athenäise, Marquise de Montespan, participated in a Black Mass and offered her own naked body as the foul altar? She had cheated the Inquisition by taking her own life. She had not cheated Hell, however.

De Cavillon had made a thorough study of the many ways that evil persons used the black arts. They used it for power over weak minds, for sex and riches. In de Caivillon's experience, one of the easiest ways to find a practicing black sorcerer was to look into his bank accounts. Those who had a sudden influx of cash, without a logical reason such as a rich inheritance, were more than likely practicing Black Magic. Hard work didn't enter into it. The *petite noblesse* did not know how to work hard, indeed, would shrink from the very notion in horror. That was how he found the Comte de Belledonné.

On a cold day in October when clouds hung low over the rocky tops of the mountains, the Comte de Belledonné was returning from a more than ordinarily successful trip to Italy. It was always a hard journey, but it had been well worth the ardor of the trip. Next week he mused to himself, he would go to Geneva and make a sizable deposit.

He heard the screaming before he rounded the hill that kept his property from the view of the main road – if one could call such a goat track a road.

He recognized the voice at once. It was his oldest son, Marc-Antoine. Marc was a coward about pain – he had sprained his ankle once and one would have thought he had been being flayed alive.

Belledonné heard the crack of a whip, heard Marc-Antoine's screams and whimpers. He knew at once what it meant. The Inquisition had come. With no thought for his sons, he wrenched his horse's head around and put spurs to its sides.

But he did not get very far before two grim looking troopers in the livery of the Inquisition appeared from nowhere and grabbed his reins, forcing the horse to a jolting halt.

"No," he whimpered, "I have done nothing!"

In the courtyard of the little Chateau sat Bishop de Caivillon on a handsome bay stallion that had once belonged to *M'sieur* Massot, a jeweler in the nearby small village of Didier. *M'sieur* Massot had no longer a need for this fine animal, since he was dead, having been convicted of sorcery. *M'sieur* Massot's shop had also yielded the fine sapphire ring on de Caivillon's finger.

Soundlessly, the troopers dragged Belledonné from his horse. And the Comte knew all was up with them when he saw, at the Bishop's feet, the pile of old grimoires. They had never hidden them – there had seemed no need.

Quickly he took in the scene about him. Their few servants were huddled against he building, guarded by troopers. On the ground lay Jeanette, a very pretty maidservant, who had been warming his and Marc-Antoine's bed for some time. She was naked and bleeding, bruised and curled into a ball, beyond crying.

Marc-Antoine, was in like case, but he was still able to whimper and cry. He had been tied to a post inserted into the ground by the troops, who never went anywhere without one of these useful items. His back ran with blood and a plump little man with the light of fanaticism in his huge eyes was examining each crevice of his body. There was no sign of Jean-Claude.

"Is thus obscene filth your property, *M'sieur le Comte?*" the Bishop said severely. He pointed at the grimoires with his riding whip. Blood dripping from it on landed on the top of the pile of books.

"I have never seen them in my life, I swear on the grave of my mother," lied the Comte. "One of my enemies must have planted them here."

"Do not lie to *me*, Belledonné!" said the Bishop in a silky smooth voice. He was a intense young man with a close clipped pointed black beard that reminded the Comte of a picture of the Devil in one of the grimoires. "Your son has confessed – he was only too eager to do so. Your entire family is a den of vipers – black sorcerers all. And like vipers we shall burn you out."

He turned his look on the troopers. "Put him to the question!"

Belledonné begged, wept and pleaded as they stripped him and bound him to the post. Marc-Antoine had been taken down, but de Constellet was still examining him. Marc-Antoine was a very handsome young man with a fine build and de Constellet practically drooled over his body.

As they laid the whip on him, Belledonné spared no thought for either of his sons, not even to be glad that Jean-Claude had escaped.

From a ledge high above the Chateau twelve year old Jean-Claude watched the torture of his family. He had to stick his hand in his mouth, for he was afraid that he would scream aloud.

He watched all afternoon as de Constellet made a proposition to Marc-Antoine and was accepted. He watched as his father screamed beneath the lash and recanted, promised immunity if he would betray others and listened as his father gave up name after name. He watched as the Bishop did not keep his word and, then and there, with the furniture from their own home as fuel, burned his father at the handy post. He listened to the screams of agony and fear from his father's throat. He watched as the troops were given Jeanette and the other maidservant, Babette, as their reward for a good day's work.

His hand was bitten deep and bleeding when at last dusk drew a curtain over the events below. The fire still blazed and the troops, having had their fill of the two maidservants, ransacked his home, throwing most of what they found on the fire. Several sacks of what Jean-Claude knew was money went into the Bishop's saddle bags. He saw Marc-Antoine go off with the Witch-Sniffer on horseback, the Witch-Sniffer licking his lips in anticipation. His brother looked dazed and sick. Blood stained the shirt and breeches he had been allowed to resume.

A deep hatred welled up in Jean-Claude, not only for the Inquisition but for his father and brother. Why had they submitted to the authority of the Inquisition? They had power – why had they not used it? And his father had recanted – to save his miserable life! Marc-Antoine had submitted to becoming the plaything of a pervert, rather than die. To die would have been more honourable.

There had never been much love or affection between Jean-Claude and his brother or between him and his father. Once he had thought that his father did not love him because his birth had killed his mother. He had found out early on that Belledonné had never loved his mother – he scarcely remembered her name. He had married her for her dowry.

Marc-Antoine was always jealous of the ease with which a brother ten years his junior learned magic.

So he did not cry. But his eyes burned hard and bright and he resolved that he would get away from this place and never return. He would seek out magic in all of its blackest forms and study until he need have no fear of anyone.

And he would no longer be Vidocque. It was a shamed name. One of the old crones who had taught him had informed him that he, who had never loved anyone, had a bad heart. That was as good a name as any – Malcoeur.

That night he made his way to the Swiss border and never looked back but once. Twenty years ago he had been in Rome and seen Bishop de Caivillon, grown rich and fat and sleek.

Malcoeur had not hesitated – he had struck and killed, magically burning the Bishop to death in his own bed.

But he had never found out what happened to Marc-Antoine.

28

Merlin's Secrets

When Reverend Arabin arrived at the Abbey early the next morning he carried a large basket covered with a cloth. From the shrill mewing that came from inside this basket, it contained the kittens.

As the Vicar alighted from the dog cart both Minou and Plato jumped down to the graveled drive, Minou looking up anxiously at the basket.

Simon, who had been laying in wait in the entrance hall, gave a whoop of joy. Mama had said that they probably could not take the time from their oh-so-important task to go to the Vicarage and get their familiars. Simon had hoped to talk the Vicar into bringing the kittens to the Abbey, and here they were – it was as if the Vicar had heard his prayers. Surely there would be enough time this morning, before everyone became so involved in searching the books, for the kittens to make their choice!

"Good morning, Simon!" said the Reverend cheerfully as Simon threw open the door. "We thought it best to bring the kittens here as we cannot take the time away from our search to have tea and a leisurely visit."

"And it is time they made their choice," said Plato at Simon's feet. Minou stood very close to her mate, looking rather intimidated and a little sad. "If they stay with us any longer, she will not wish to let them go," Plato continued.

"Is everyone gone to the Tower already, Simon?" the Vicar asked, Several little paws had poked out from beneath the cloth that covered the basket.

"No, sir, just the Druids that came to help. Everyone else is still at breakfast, for the breakfast parlour is too small for everyone to eat at once. Mama said since the Druids are our guests, they ought to eat first The large dining room is being repapered and painted," Simon answered. Was that a little black paw of the kitten he liked at the edge of the basket? Oh, he prayed that she chose him!

"Excellent!" enthused the Vicar. "Let us go then and have out familiars choose their Wizards or Witches as the case may be!"

Simon led the way to the small breakfast parlour, where they found the Duke and his Duchess, Ninon and Lyon, René and Diana and Conchobar and Diarmait discussing the day's work over a final cup of coffee.

"Mama!" Simon exclaimed, bounding forward. "Mr. Arabin has brought the kittens!"

Everyone looked up at this with varying degrees of interest – particularly the other familiars in the room – two owls and a cat and those who were to get familiars – René and Ninon – the most interested.

"Have we time for this nonsense?" said the Duke sharply.

Lyon, who had been about to say much the same thing, abruptly changed his mind and said, "Nonsense, Chenevix? If you had not been so ill-advised as to give up magic you would remember the importance of a familiar! I daresay these kittens have a good idea of whom they will choose, as everyone here that needs a familiar has been drooling over them for weeks."

"Naturally," said Plato, adjusting his spectacles. "I am proud to say that these particular kittens are quite mature and clever and ready to take up their positions. Now if the candidates will sit upon the floor – there in front of the fireplace will do nicely. Matthew," he directed Mr. Arabin, "you may uncover the basket."

Only Lucie was surprised by Plato's taking charge. The others were used to talking animals. The Duke found Plato's presumption of authority annoying. His own familiar had died in France, at the hands of the Inquisition, and since he had given up magic he had never replaced her. Ninon had never had her own familiar as there were no familiar animals on the continent. She had shared Gil Blas, who had chosen René when her grandson had begun learning magic here in England.

Simon was the first in place. René took a cushion from the window seat and helped Ninon sink down upon it before joining her and Simon.

Mr. Arabin put the basket on the floor and removed the cloth.

There were four kittens in the basket, all tumbled together from their journey. They were well-grown and active, all mewing a little anxiously. They knew what they were to do, for their father had explained it to them – that a familiar was an ancient, honourable profession for a cat, and that when they saw the person who was to be their particular Wizard or Witch they would know at once that it was that person and no other with which they could work. They could not help but be a little worried, so their cries reflected this emotion.

One kitten was a small, completely white female with blue eyes and longer than normal fur. Stepping on her siblings, she left the basket and headed determinedly for Ninon. The worried mews changed to purrs as she crawled into Ninon's lap and was picked up and held to her new partner's cheek and cooed over.

The next kitten, a black and white male who looked as if he were wearing formal evening dress with a white waistcoat, gloves and shoes, toddled towards René. This kitten had a white chin and a white streak, perfectly symmetrical, ran down from above his eyes, and around his pink nose. Directly under his lower jaw was an asymmetrical black spot. He climbed on René and settled down on his new friend's shoulder, purring loudly and began to knead happily.

The third kitten, the little patchwork of black, orange and white, nearly galloped to Simon, flinging herself into this arms and snuggling under his chin.

The fourth kitten, whom everyone thought would stay in the basket, was a tabby male, with his predominant colours grey and buff. He had very long fur and an immense plume of a tail. No white, except a little 'locket' at his throat, coloured him, but the bottom of his paws and the backs of his legs were black. He jumped lightly from the basket, and then, in an

352

astonishing leap, jumped into Diana's lap where she sat at the table, meowing demandingly until she took him in her arms. He then settled down quite happily.

"There, Diana!" laughed Lyon. "You have a familiar whether you wanted one or not! From the looks of him he won't take no for an answer!"

Diana had not thought to get another familiar so soon. It had been a 'some day' plan. But as she stroked the little kitten – who had quite the loudest purr she had ever heard – it seemed as if some day had come today.

"Names, please!" Plato ordered.

"*Neige*," said Ninon, "Snow, for she is whiter than snow."

"Beau," said René "for he is a fine little gentleman in his evening dress."

"Janus," Simon said. "after the Roman God, even though she is a female. She has two faces," he explained. looking at the perfect black and orange division of the little female's face.

"And this one can only be Rascal," Diana said, for the kitten was playing with her earrings and the lace at her throat and patting her face with his black paws. She could see that he was the sort of cat who would get into everything and had an endless curiosity.

"Celtic legend has it," said Reverend Arabin, "that the Faeries can look at us through a cat's eyes and therefore always know what we are doing. But I have never been able to discern the truth of this."

"You must allow us to have some mysteries, " said Diarmait's familiar, Ó Dáliagh, an orange tabby. The two owls nodded in agreement.

"We shall take our leave of out offspring now," Plato announced. "Although a dish of cream all around would not be taken amiss. Or some minced chicken," he added.

"We leave you, Simon, and you, ma'am," Lyon nodded at Lucie, "to take care of that. The rest of us must needs return to work."

The next fortnight was the same pattern – they began work early in the morning, eating all meals save breakfast in the Tower. The common ending time each day was ten o'clock

353

at night, for working until midnight as Lyon wanted left them heavy-eyed and sleepy, unable to comprehend what one was reading the next day. It still made for a long day.

Lyon had been unable to secure other helpers in Cheltenham. The few young Wizards that had applied had miserably failed his test of rune-reading ability. This circumstance had caused a long harangue about the low standards allowed today's youth as well as their lax study habits and their satisfaction with doing as little real work as was possible. A scry to the Universities was no better, for it was the Long Vacation and most students and professors had long since made plans and fled both Oxford and Cambridge. The few that responded were not worth the trouble and Lyon ended up in turning more than a few out of the Tower. "People have a very inflated idea of their abilities!" he growled.

Just about the time that they were beginning to feel that theirs was a hopeless task, Reverend Arabin found what they were looking for, quite accidentally.

The Vicar had come faithfully each day, save Sunday of course, and had bent over the heavy tomes with the rest of them. He was a scholar of ancient language forms and was much in demand to translate archaic phrases that defied rendering into modern English.

Late in the afternoon of the second week, on a Friday afternoon of heat and heaviness, Mr. Arabin finished up reading a slimmer than normal volume and went to the table where the rest of the books lay stacked. He was the only one to have actually completed a volume, for with the exception of the one he had just perused, all had proved to contain near to five hundred pages of close writ script. It was Mr. Arabin's theory that these volumes were Merlin's notes – the great Wizard had probably meant to write them down in orderly fashion, but of course he had been fallen afoul of that young Witch Nimue. He must have locked then away, no doubt meaning to come back one day. He had never had the chance, for now he lay in suspended animation, waiting for England's call. Mr. Arabin gave this as a good sign that they would be able to triumph in this present crisis, for if they would not be able to do so, surely Merlin and Arthur and the knights of the Round Table would awaken and come to their aid.

He picked up a large volume, gasping a little, for it was heavy, bound in gold with a large ruby and several diamonds on the front cover. He hugged the volume to his chest and as he did so, something struck him a sharp blow on the ankle and he almost dropped the book, but managed to put it back on the table before any damage was done.

Whatever was that? Mr. Arabin bent to rub at his ankle. No one else had even looked up, save for one of the kittens who always now accompanied their people wherever they went as the adult familiars did. It was Rascal, Diana's kitten, who looked up inquiringly. The four kittens were asleep in a tangle of bodies in the hazy sunlight coming in the Tower window. Rascal lay on the bottom of the pile and was forced to look at Mr. Arabin upside down.

On the floor lay a small, shabby volume. It lacked the gold and jewels of the other books, and its spine was in precarious condition. It lay open to a page, much stained and worn.

The Vicar bent to pick it up, idly reading the right hand page, which had a heading in flowing script: *Hic jacet Obligatorius*, it said in Wizard's Latin. Mr. Arabin read in wonder, *Here be Bindings*. He gave a gasp. He had to be certain, reading the spell through at breakneck speed. At the very end, he translated, it said, '*To bind and banish the Dark Court.*'

"Eureka!" he shouted unoriginally. "I have found it!"
Everyone looked up at once as Mr. Arabin nearly jumped up and down in excitement, waving the little book in the air. "The binding spell!" he shouted, for their concentration had been abruptly broken and they seemed slow to realize what he was saying.

When the sense of his telling struck, all was confusion – queries, exclamations and the tired laughter of relief.

"Is it difficult?" Lyon demanded."Shall we be able to find everything we need and do what we have to do?"

"I think so," said the Vicar cautiously, "but I have only skimmed it." He opened th book again, carefully, as the others crowded around him, even the visiting Druids very eager. "Hmmm... it seems to involve an incantation – a rather long one, a special incense, the ley lines and a locus. There are several ancient terms that I shall have to consult upon. I shall

355

make a fair copy of this and take it to the Vicarage where I may reference several dictionaries I have."

Rather reverently, Lyon took the small volume from him. "To think that this little book holds the key to our problem!" he said. "The very last place that we looked!"

"Not the very last place, your Grace." pointed out one of the Druids from the Isle of Man, who was very literal-minded. Lyon ignored him.

"Pray, Mr. Arabin," translate as fast as is possible. We heed to implement this spell almost immediately. We need to know what equipment will be necessary, when is the best time to perform it – perhaps Lammas night, which will shortly be upon us," said Chenevix in his best Chancellor's voice.

"Why did we not notice this book?" Lyon wondered, turning it over in his hands. "I will go bail it was not there before!"

"Perhaps it was not," Ninon said thoughtfully. "Perhaps we have only found it when Merlin wanted us to do so, *hein*? For this makes one and twenty books and so many times we have counted only twenty."

"I think that it was somehow stuck to the bottom of the bigger book," offered the Vicar. "But we shall probably never know if that was deliberate or an accident. It really matters little. What matters is that now we have it and we shall be able to at last start fighting back."

"René, my dear boy," he continued, "pray fetch some foolscap and pens for us. I think it best if you will be so good as to copy my transcript. We cannot have enough repro-ductions of this spell. Once I have made sense of some of the terms we shall make as many fair copies as are needed. In fact, if you would come back to the Vicarage with me – René is quite knowledgeable in anachronistic terminology," he ex-plained for the benefit of the others.

"I had an excellent teacher," said René, with a small bow in the Vicar's direction.

"Not many people are studying archaic terminology nowadays," said Lyon gloomily.

"Yes, Lyonshall, we know your views on the iniquities of modern education all too well," said Chenevix dryly. "But they are scarce to the point at the present. This task should be accomplished as soon as it may be."

They all knew and understood the urgency, for in the time that they had spent in finding this spell, there had been many more deaths of both magical and non-magicals persons. The news-sheets had found out about the soul-stealing and there had been a furor of horror from the public and in both houses of Parliament. The Regent had been booed at Drury Lane at the play for his perceived lack of action and people were demanding that something be done to insure their safety and curb the danger. Every day there had been stacks of desperate messages pleading, ordering and requesting help: scryed, written, 'griffe express and through the medium of the post. People were terrified and felt that their Wizards and their government had failed miserably. This crisis would probably bring down the current incumbents in Parliament. There were rumors of a 'no confidence' vote for Spencer Perceval's administration.

The Vicar had scarcely started copying when Simon burst into the Tower. "Uncle!" he cried. "There is a messenger in the Royal Livery! He says it's urgent!"

He was closely followed by a young man in red and gold, with the red dispatch case of the Royal household under one arm. He came straight to Lyon.

"Your Grace," he said, with a bow and held out the dispatch case. "In the Regent's own hand." He was tense and nervous, and he had actually left his 'griffe, which most riders tried not to do.

Lyon's brows shot up. The Regent almost never wrote anything in his own hand, preferring to dictate to his secretary, Colonel McMahon.

He took the case from the messenger and broke the seal, which he noticed, was not the Regent's personal seal, but the Great Seal of England. It had been magiced to yield only to Lyon.

The message was brief and as Lyon read it he felt the blood receding from his face.

"What is it?" Chenevix demanded sharply.

"The Prime Minister, Spencer Perceval, has been assassinated in the lobby of the House of Commons," said Lyon hoarsely. "He was killed by blood magic."

29

Necessities For a Spell

The entire nation was in an uproar. The news-sheets screamed for action as did huge crowds of frightened people in the cities. The day of the Prime Minister's funeral there was a enormous demonstration in Hyde Park, demanding that the government do something to protect the citizenry and halt the killings.

Both Chenevix and Lyon had gone to London to confer with the new Prime Minister, the hastily appointed Lord Liverpool. It had been agreed upon that the news of the finding of Merlin's spell was not to be released to the public. It was considered a matter of national security – they did not wish to let the enemy – the Unselighe Court – know that they now had a weapon which could be used against them.

The Vicar was hard at work on the translation of the spell (the pages had gotten wet at one time and someone had spilled something on them), assisted by René when he could spare the time. In order to free up his time, Diana offered to help out in the Tower. She was very grateful when Ninon also came every day to help her, for the volume of messages alone was staggering, and she had to decide what needed to be forwarded to London, and what could be answered by René, or left until later.

When not helping Mr. Arabin René spent most of his time writing letters and messages and scrying. The Druids had returned to their respective holds and Conchobar and Diarmait to Tara. All had thought only of getting back to their own place when the terrible news had come.

Everyone was afraid. That the Prime Minister had been struck down, in the heart of London, by an attacker unseen by anyone caused terrible fear – for that had been the reports. No one had really seen anything – only Mr. Perceval, crying out and falling to the floor, dead. The Forensic Wizards from Bow Street had determined that he had been killed by blood magic, for its stench was all over him, but they did not know how until an autopsy was performed and it was determined that his heart had exploded. There were the usual conflicting reports from eye-witnesses but no one had seen anything of import, nothing that gave a clue as to who or what had done the deed.

Diana had told Lyon of her strange dream, and although he had doubted its validity he had set an investigation in train, which so far had yielded nothing. The Jongleur had been a temporary performer with the small traveling show. They had traced him backwards to his arrival from Holland and had interviewed the Customs Wizard who had questioned the performer on his entrance to the country. He had noted nothing odd about the man, much less the taint of black magic. In fact, the Customs Wizard had been much insulted that even the faintest doubt was cast upon his abilities and wrote rather nasty notes to both Chenevix and Lyon, protesting the implied disparagement of his skills, and threatening them with his solicitor.

The Jongleur had left the show somewhere near London and it was presumed that he had gone there to join the family he spoke of. But he had named no names and his trail was cold. Diana knew that most people thought she had seen a boggart, indeed, Lyon thought so.

But she was certain of what she had seen. And that it had some bearing on what was happening now, she also was certain. She just had to find out how.

The spell of binding was lengthy and complicated. Many items had to be gathered for it and the incantations were longer than most modern ones. As Mr. Arabin read it, (the spell covered more than five closely written pages) he became more and more concerned that it could actually be accomplished.

"This spell" he said to René one morning as they worked in the Tower, "requires a *human* locus." A locus was usually a large gemstone, in particular, a crystal.

Diana, Simon and Ninon were also present, as well as the kittens and Plato. Leander, of course, had gone to London with Lyon. An entire bag of mail had been delivered and Simon had been employed running back and forth between hippogriffes on the roof and dragons in the courtyard.

"What is a locus?" Simon asked curiously.

"In mathematics, a locus is any system of points or lines that satisfies a given condition and contains no point that does not satisfy that condition," said the Vicar. " Since we use ley *lines* in magic we have borrowed the term and a magical locus is the point at which magical energies are gathered. For example, one can gather up all of the energies of the various ley lines and then focus them as one great energy."

Simon wrinkled his brow. "So that you would have one large magic instead of many little ones?"

"Exactly!" said the Vicar. "Most Wizards have a stone on their wands or staffs to serve as a locus for magical energies. When a cone of power is raises, as when the Wizards and Witches of England gathered to repel the Spanish Armada in Queen Elizabeth's time, each Coven used a locus stone to send their energies to Stonehenge, where a very large locus – a great crystal – was located."

"The magical energy from that gathering of power was used to raise a great gale, which destroyed the Armada," said Diana.

"But this spell uses a human locus," said the Vicar. "I have never seen such a requirement before. But then, they did things much differently in the old days. Merlin does say, however, that the use of a human locus is completely necessary – although he does not say *why*."

René put down the stack of mail he was sorting – he, Diana and Ninon all had a huge stack in front of them – a great deal of it hysterical in tone, much of it from government officials, some forwarded from Avalon. There was mail from anxious citizens, mail from worried Wizards and Druids. All wanted some action to be taken or reassurance that they would be safe and something was being done about the situation. Conchobar had told then that it was much the same at Tara, even though there had as yet been no attacks (save by the Unselighe creatures) in Ireland. People were frightened.

"It would be painful, *n'est-ce pas*, for the locus," René said.

"I should think so," murmured the Vicar, "especially since this spell must be repeated for three nights, with the same locus. I have not yet got to the end of the spell where it gives the requirements for the locus. Our main concern now is to gather the materials needed and that must be done quickly, for it specifically states that this spell *must* be performed on one of the four great ritual feasts, but *not* at Samhain, when the Unselighe world is too close to ours. It is beginning to look as if it will have to be Lammas."

"But Lammas is only three weeks from now!" Diana said, for the ritual, the point of mid-summer, the very beginning of harvest, was on the first of August. "Can we possibly be ready?"

"We *must* be ready," said René, "for if we cannot do this on Lammas, we will have to wait until Imbolc in February, *non*? And what will happen by then?"

"There could be no Wizards left alive in the British Isles," said the Vicar "or Druids, for that matter."

"What is needed for the spell?" asked Ninon.

"A specific cauldron, robes – white, of purest silk, anointing oil of lilac, incense of heather, frankincense and oak, candles of white of the purest beeswax and honey mead for the ritual wine," read the Vicar.

"I made honey mead," said Diana eagerly "And since we have bee skips in the garden, we might gather the beeswax and make the candles here."

"And me, I have the lilac oil – I have made this myself," Ninon offered. "And I have the incense of oak, but not of heather or frankincense."

"Frankincense is quite expensive, I believe," the Vicar mused. "Perhaps they might obtain it for us at the *Cauldron*, in Knightswold. And the robes might be purchased there as well. The spell is quite specific as to how they are to be made and what the colour of the sash should be."

"Could we get the cauldron there?" Simon had been listening closely to the adults.

"Dear me," sighed Mr. Arabin. "I do not think so. That is going to be the most difficult part. We must use something called 'Huon's Cauldron' and I have no idea what it is or where to get it."

Ninon laughed and everyone looked at her as if she had run mad.

"But this is simple! Huon's Cauldron is mine!" said Ninon happily. "It has been in my family many, many years, passed from mother to daughter. It should rightfully be called Clarimonde's Cauldron, for it has belonged to the wife of Huon of Bordeaux. I wonder, me, who gave its use to Merlin so long ago? Blaise perhaps?" But there was probably no way to know this.

That reminded René that he had never asked her why she had not told him of their descent from the legendary Huon of Bordeaux. And what were the other secrets Titania had mentioned?

"This is wonderful!" said the Vicar. "Lady Diana, when does your uncle return?"

"This evening, he hoped," she answered. "And his Grace with him."

"That one, he did not like going dragon-back!" Ninon said of her son-in-law a little contemptuously.

"My dear boy, whenever you are finished with that correspondence, why do we not see if we may finish the reading of this spell and find out everything that we need before they return? We really have very little time," Mr. Arabin suggested to René,

Diana offered to take over the reading of the mail so that this would be possible.

Lyon was not in the best of humors when they arrived back at the Abbey late that evening. The situation in London was more than tense, and talking to Lord Liverpool had confirmed his belief that politicians were among the stupidest creatures on earth. The new Prime Minister, a non-magical, did not seem to grasp the necessity for any magical intervention. He thought that the matter of Perceval's death could be handled by Bow Street and that the public, especially the magical public, was whipping itself into a frenzy over nothing. He made light of the forensic tests that proved the use of blood magic and suggested that Mr. Perceval had a heart condition that had caused a violent apoplexy of that organ. There had actually been no assassination, in his view. And he had swayed the Prince Regent to this nonsense. Even Chenevix, Lyon thought sourly, wasn't as pig-headed and foolish as were those two. It made Lyon glad that he was a Whig and not one of these blind Tories like Liverpool. The Whigs, also known as the Wizards' party, of whom the Regent, although without magical skills, had been one of the most ardent in his youth, had expected a Whig appointee as Prime Minister. Tories, by and large, were not magicians and deplored the intrusion of magic into politics an the governance of the country.

But even Chenevix, lapsed Wizard that he was, could feel the blood magic used in the House of Commons. He was almost as disgusted as was Lyon with the reaction of the government.

They left London immediately after their visit to No. 10 Downing Street – Tuathail had waited in the street for them, blocking traffic. A dragon was an infrequent sight in the crowded narrow streets of London. English horses were trained from birth not to be dragon-shy, but even a small dragon, mostly on the kerb, took up a great deal of room and caused a snarl in the flow of traffic. Usually one left one's dragon in one of the Dragon Parks and took a hack or walked from there to one's destination.

There had been no time to exchange impressions or to make plans. Lyon, for one, was determined to go on with the spell. He cared little for the opinions of two such stupid clodpoles – he knew what had to be done and he was going to do it. Even had the Prime Minister forbidden the use of Merlin's spell he would have gone ahead. Someone had to save these idiots from themselves!

Chenevix had never been so exasperated in his life. He had lately found himself agreeing with Lyonshall and it astonished him. Today had been no exception. He had wanted to thump the heads of the Prime Minister and of the Regent together and demand that they look at the facts. This problem was not going to go away by itself as those two fools seem to think. They even thought that all the killings were being done by French spies dressed as bogey men in a plot to frighten the British public! They did not seem to find it illogical that a non-magician could murder a Druid or a Wizard –without Cold Iron – and there were no signs that it had been used in any of the deaths. Even the Archbishop of Canterbury had assured the Regent that souls had been stolen and he had not been believed. Chenevix thought fleetingly of forgoing his lifelong allegiance to the Tory party and becoming a Whig.

It was nearing eight o'clock in the evening when Tuathail landed in the courtyard of the Abbey. It was still twilight, for the long summer evening had yet to end.

There were no lights in the Tower – they must have finished for the day. By this hour dinner would be over, but Alphonse could no doubt supply something on a tray. Everyone should be in the drawing room. Wordlessly, Lyon and Chenevix headed for this room, leaving Tuathail to be unharnessed by one of the grooms, and shedding their flying suits in the hall. Chenevix was somewhat stiff, for it was many years since he had ridden a dragon and would have not done so now if necessity had not compelled. His Grace did not enjoy heights.

They found everyone, including the Reverend Arabin, seated about the fire. Simon was still up, playing with the kittens, who treated him as if he were another, very large kitten.

When the Duke entered the room Lucie sprang to her feet and ran to him. He had been gone for two days – to her it was as if he had been gone two centuries and she enthusiastically welcomed him back. Although Chenevix was a trifle put out by her lack of decorum – for it did not do for a husband and wife to live in each others' pockets, nor show such a lack of proper restraint – it was still rather gratifying to see her so happy at his return. Still, he would chide her gently when they were alone together. He sat down beside her on the sofa, near the fireplace.

Preceded by Leander, who flew in and perched on the back of his chair, Lyon fell into a wing chair and ran his hands through his hair with a loud "Phew!" He was glad to be home. He had always hated London – there were far and away too many people there and most of them, in his book, were idiots.

He let Chenevix tell the others about their trip and its frustrations. He was more interested in the progress made on the spell and scarcely had Chenevix completed his narrative when Lyon eagerly asked the Vicar, "How goes the work on the spell?"

"Most excellent!" the Reverend assured him. "In fact, we have finished the translation and made a fair copy just before dinner. I am of the opinion," he said, taking off his spectacles and cleaning them with a handkerchief, "that the little book is Merlin's own personal everyday spell book, for it has seen hard use, as if it were carried about in a pocket. The rendering of the spell was made more difficult by the fact that the book has suffered spills and a wetting or two, exactly as it would do if it accompanied Merlin on all his travels."

Lyon gave a low whistle. "What a find!" he exclaimed. "When this is all over we must study all of these books carefully. Who knows what we be able to learn and add to our magical knowledge?"

"We have a list of all that is needed for the spell, Uncle, and will be able to supply most of it," Diana put in.

"Including my cauldron," said Ninon.

A stack of papers lay on the Pembroke table. René took one of these and handed it to Lyon. He read it with pursed lips and noted that most had been checked off as obtainable or already available.

But one item made him frown. "A *human* locus?" he queried. "Is that necessary?"

"Unfortunately, yes," Mr. Arabin sighed. "Merlin is quite adamant about it. And that is where we are going to run into difficulties. The requirements for the locus are quite exacting. He needs to be a *Magus Magistra*, between eighteen and thirty years of age, and experienced in the use of ley lines."

"How many *Magus Magistrii* in Britain are under one hundred years old? I'm one of the few and I am no lamb in years!" Lyon said in exasperation as Seppings brought in a heavily laden tea-tray. Diana had ordered meat pies and savories, knowing that her uncle, in particular, would be ravenous after a dragon ride.

Lyon gratefully accepted a cup of steaming tea and bit down into a flaky meat pie. He swallowed and said "Has anyone checked *Registratum* to find young *Magistrii?*"

"There are fourteen," said René, handing over another list to Lyon.

"Did not Conchobar say that young Mag Uidhir is sitting for his *Magistra* exam in Dublin very soon?" Lyon recalled. "That makes fifteen!"

The Vicar sighed again. "It would seem so, but there are other considerations." He gave a significant look at Simon, who was on the floor, teasing the kittens with a length of knotted yarn.

Diana took his hint and said firmly, "Come, Simon, it is time and past you were in your bed. Do go along now and get ready and I shall be up very shortly."

Simon did not wish to go – he knew that they were to talk about grown–up things – *interesting* things – and would not do so until he was gone. But he also knew that no one would give into his wishes. He took Janus in his arms and bade everyone goodnight and left the room. The remaining kittens ran at once to their respective people and climbed into laps.

"We have had to eliminate virtually all of the young gentlemen listed there," said Reverend Arabin, "for there is another requirement that most of them cannot meet. Merlin says that the locus must be –" he picked up his fair copy from the table, "how does he phrase it? – ah, yes – 'unknown of woman'."

Lyon, who had been swallowing a large mouthful of tea gave a great choking gasp and spattered milky tea all over the company. "*What!*" he exclaimed between coughs.

"What does this mean, Lucien?" Lucie queried, looking from one frowning face to the other.

"It means that the locus must be a virgin, my dear," said the Duke dryly. "Might one inquire why?"

"As you no doubt know," Mr. Arabin answered, "in Merlin's day, most Wizards were celibate. It was felt that the union of bodies stole from the magical potency of the Wizard. There are some who believe this, even to this day, pointing out that no one seems capable of working the magics that the Wizards a millennia ago could work, when a Wizard was always a celibate. Wizards now marry and have families, the same as any other men, since the days of Good Queen Bess. Most of the young gentlemen on this list are married or keep a mistress. There are two we are not certain of, but one is a great invalid, having had a spell backfire upon him just after attaining his Mastery."

"It's not a thing you can just *ask*," mused Lyon.

"You surprise me, Lyonshall," Chenevix said sarcastically. "I did not think that you had any delicacy of mind whatsoever."

Ignoring this byplay the Vicar said earnestly, "We must needs follow every particular of this spell! It is too important not to do so! And we all have heard what happens when one attempts to change the particulars of a spell by as much as an iota. We heard of the tragedy near Tiverton last year when a young Wizard tried to substitute one herb for another. They never found the body – only his notes indicating what he had done."

"Is there anything else I should know about this damned spell?" Lyon growled.

"The candidate must pass the Unicorn test," said the Vicar apologetically.

"Oh, marvelous!" said Lyon sarcastically. "Now we need TWO mythological creatures – a young male virgin and a unicorn – both of which probably no longer exist anywhere!"

30

Revenge On His Mind

When Augustus Goodbody reached London again he was glad for a while just to be out of that horrible situation. It took the best part of a bottle of the finest port each evening for many nights to blot out the memory of Sir Piers Mildmay's terrible transformation.

It was pleasant to fall back into the usual round of his life in Town – the day at his club, a look – in at Tattersall's or a visit to his tailor, and in the evening, a stop in at one or the other of the gambling hells he frequented. Town was very thin of company, for the *Ton* had largely fled to their country estates, where it was cooler than in London.

Still, there were some few gilt-edged invitation amongst the litter of unpaid bills on his hall table and Goodbody took every chance offered to secure a free meal and an evening's entertainment.

For things had not worked out as he hoped when he first returned to Town. Money was at low tide with him – his creditors were dunning him increasingly and he would not receive his next quarterly allowance until September twenty-fifth. His father had made it clear that if he outran the constable once again there would be no rescue from the burden of his debts. And the cards and the dice were not running his way. Not for the first time he wished that the gaming clubs did not employ Wizards whose sole job it was to find any taint of magical cheating. The dibs were not in tune –he could not show his face at any of the more popular gaming establishments, for he owed virtually everyone money. How much the final sum could be he had no idea.

With the thought that they perhaps might just go away Goodbody stuffed all of his I. O. U. s in a drawer. He did not know that the sum he owed was more than triple the amount that he received as an allowance. That sum did not include the bills he owed various tradesmen. Of course, a gentleman in Goodbody's set did not concern himself with debts owed merchants. But a debt of honour was another matter all together.

Goodbody learned of the story of the Duke of Chenevix's long lost family one morning at his club. It was not one of the premier clubs such as White's – he had been rejected by White's – and it was not on St James Street or even in Pall Mall. The membership was composed of, for the most part, by younger sons, and those were dandies, like himself. The club was called Dando's and was a haven for Goodbody, because most of the gentlemen he owed money to belonged to White's or Watier's.

When he entered the main room of the club – oak-paneled and furnished with comfortable wing chairs, sophas and low tables – the room was abuzz with the story of Chenevix. Goodbody had not read the news-sheets that morning, save for the Army lists. Several of the soldiers to whom he owed debts had gone back out to the Peninsula and with the siege at Badajoz ongoing Goodbody hoped to see the names of those men in the death lists, thus wiping out his debt.

He was as agog as anyone in society at the nine day's wonder of the dramatic change in Chenevix's circumstances. And then he realized what it truly meant – his rival, that upstart Frenchman, was now the heir to a Dukedom – no longer a lowly *émigré*, but the acknowledged *heir* – to the wealthiest peerage in the realm!

The more he thought of it, the more he resented it. And from resentment grew the desire for revenge. No one had the right to treat Augustus Goodbody as he had been treated ! When he thought of how he had been assaulted by that Froggie and then thrown from the house by Lyonshall, he writhed in fury. In no time at all he had convinced himself that he was the one with the grievance, for self-delusion had always been one of his strong suits.

But how to accomplish his revenge? He was sadly short of funds – that precluded hiring bully boys to attack his intended victims. Bully boys would be of little use against Wizards, unless one could way-lay said Wizards and threaten them with Cold Iron. But that took even more of the ready. Any plan involving expenditure was out. He retained enough sense to realize that he was no match, magically, for either Roussillon or Lyonshall.

He brooded over it, making and discarding plans at a great rate as objections, even to one of his limited intellect, occurred almost immediately. But he could not think of anything at the moment.

Two days after he heard the news he happened to attend a dinner party given by Lady Barbara Belmont. Lady Belmont was a would-be hostess on the fringes of acceptable society. She was the widow of a wealthy City merchant many years her senior. He had been knighted for covering some of the Regent's all too numerous debts. Lady Belmont desired nothing more than a place in Society, which had so far been denied her. She was undoubtedly vulgar and fast, and was infamous for sending invitations to anyone of good breeding who might ease her way into the *Haut Ton*. Very few ever bothered to answer her invitations, feeling her presumptuous and beneath their notice. Goodbody, too, usually used her invitations to light his cigarillos. But that night he was at loose ends. He did not dare go to one of the hells – he owed far too much money. Thompson had pointed out that he had not been paid in four months and he could easily find a position with one of Goodbody's friends – lord knew that they had cast enough lures out to him, for a good valet was always in demand amongst the dandy set. Goodbody had given Thompson the evening out – no other master would be so generous, he told the valet. Thompson left at once for the tavern that was so popular with valets – *the Gentleman's Gentleman*. Of course, he left without preparing anything for Goodbody's supper, as a minor form of revenge.

Goodbody had gone without a nuncheon that day, for the steward at the club had hinted, far from delicately, that Goodbody could no longer punt on tick in the dining room. Some payment was expected – immediately. Goodbody could not find anyone gullible enough to stand him a meal. Everyone, it seemed, knew his circumstances.

There was little to eat in the tiny kitchen of his flat. And he had not the faintest idea what to do with the foodstuffs that he found. He had no notion as to how to make even a cup of tea.

Fortunately, he remembered the discarded invitations on the hall table. One of them was no doubt for a dinner party.

And so it proved. Lady Belmont was hosting an intimate dinner for twenty or so people and if Goodbody hurried he could be there before the first remove was served.

A quick change to evening dress (which cost him a pang, for his usual habit was to take an hour or more to dress) was all that was required and he found enough change amongst the sopha cushions to pay for a hackney cab. He would have to walk home, but at least he would have a full stomach.

Lady Belmont lived in Russell Square in a dazzlingly new mansion. Goodbody was welcomed effusively as the son of a Viscount and given a seat at the head of the table, and allowed to take in the beautiful and voluptuous Mrs. Wanda Wycherley to dinner.

Wanda Wycherley, like their hostess, was the widow of an elderly merchant. However she had been widowed five times – each husband more elderly than the last and none of the marriages lasting longer than a six-month. Her husbands all had one thing in common, though – they were very wealthy. Mrs. Wycherley was known as "the Much Married Maiden", for there was much speculation in the clubs as to whether or not she had actually been bedded by any of her five husbands. Most doubted it, for her husbands had been mostly of an incredible infirmity, with several dying within a week of the nuptials, and one on the wedding night itself.

In person she was of middle height with a rounded, shapely figure, generous of bosom, which was always shown to advantage in clinging fabrics and a very low *décolletage*. Her green eyes were heavy-lidded and her lips full and pouting. Heavy masses of blonde hair, always a trifle untidy, gave her a look of having just risen from bed after a long night of lust fulfilled. Most gentlemen could think of little besides lechery when confronted with Wanda, and most believed her unawakened to the delights of the bedroom, despite her appearance. Such old men as her late husbands could not have pleasured her.

In spite of all cajoling and many offers of *carte blanche* from well-heeled gentlemen she had become no gentleman's mistress, or so it was thought. She always held out for marriage.

What Wanda wanted more than anything else – even more than money – was a title. She yearned to be addressed as 'my lady", to be able to take precedence over friends like Lady Belmont, whose title was *purchased!* Wanda longed for a husband with an old title, an estate or two or three in the country, a gentleman who would take her to the Pavilion on Brighton in the summer, there to mingle with the Prince Regent and his set, and to Town in the spring where she would attend Almack's and private balls at houses such as the Seftons and the Melbournes in the very highest ranks of Society. She wanted a box at the Opera (even though she was tone-deaf) and to be tooled about Hyde Park at the magic hour of five in the afternoon in a barouche and have everyone who was any one bow and acknowledge her. She wanted to wear family jewels and to have her picture painted by Sir Thomas Lawrence, thereafter to hang in the gallery of her husband's stately home. She wanted to be a SOMEONE, not a nobody. And money was not enough to do this. She needed a title, an OLD title, and the only place she could get it was to marry it.

She had been singularly unsuccessful in obtaining a title so far. She had thought that with all her beauty and money, some impecunious nobleman would come calling. But it had not happened. Her origins were too low and the money she had married tainted by trade. Her exact origins were unknown in society, but it was enough that she was the widow of tradesmen. She also suffered from another disadvantage – other women did not like her. She preferred the company of gentlemen and showed it openly. Therefore, Society hostesses never even considered sending invitations to 'that vulgar *parvenu*'.

She had been born Wanda Bosomsworthy and by the age of twelve lived well up to this unfortunate name. She was the daughter of a minor and untalented actress who had toured the Provinces with an undistinguished theatrical troupe. Wanda's mother had an unfortunate taste for low men and was left with child by an ostler in Birmingham. Wanda shared her mother's taste in men – her own personal groom could have put the lie to the "Much Married Maiden" sobriquet, as could an abortionist in Seven Dials.

She was growing desperate though – the first bloom of youth was fading, for she would be eight and twenty on her next birthday. She looked a great deal like her mother, who by thirty five had no longer looked voluptuous and sensual but fat and tawdry. She was even desperate enough, she had thought that evening whilst dressing, to take a Baronet to husband. She thought she saw a shadow of thickening about her jaw and the tiny beginning of crow's feet at the corners of her eyes.

There were no titles, save that of the lady herself, at Barbara Belmont's dinner party, but it was the only invitation Wanda had received for that evening. She was bored and at loose ends – she had just returned from Brighton where she had wasted a fortnight trying to cadge an invitation to the Pavilion, or even one to the society balls at the *Old Ship* tavern, but had been singularly unsuccessful. She had spent a delightfully erotic time with a *ménage à trois* of herself, her groom, Culver Grindle, and a lusty young sailor they had happened upon. She supposed they would never see the sailor again, for she had neglected to learn his name – but he had been *very* talented!

Wanda was singularly unimpressed with Augustus Goodbody – he was only an Honourable, which, if one was foolish enough to marry one, would not entitled one to be called 'my lady'. Even if one were announced at a ball it would be "the Honourable Augustus Goodbody *and* Mrs. Goodbody", not 'the Honourable Mrs. Goodbody'!

Wanda might have been employed by the College of Arms, had they hired females. For she knew every escutcheon in England – one would not wish to waste one's time fainting in front of a crested carriage if that crest were not of an unmarried nobleman. She knew as well the members of each noble family in the British Isles, in particular the unmarried males of marriageable age, up to, and including unwed octogenarians. She had memorized huge portions of *DeBrett* and *Burke's Peerage* was her bedtime reading.

Physically, too, Goodbody was not to her taste. Culver Grindle was heavily muscular, with swarthy good looks. That was her preference. But nonetheless, she flirted with Goodbody. It was always good to practice.

Goodbody was no different than any other man when it came to her charms. Ignoring his right-hand partner, a piece of rudeness he would have never committed in his own *milieu*, he concentrated on Wanda and her magnificent bosom, of which he could see a good deal. Wanda had her gowns made by a *modiste* famous for dressing the Fashionable Impure and the gowns were just this side of indecent leaving very little to the imagination. Goodbody was quite certain that she had not only dampened her petticoat but had rouged her nipples, which he could see plainly through the sheer spotted muslin she wore, as close as he was. He flattered himself that she found him attractive. Goodbody's delusions were many.

Wanda was relieved of the tedium of his conversation when the ladies withdrew, but female society proved so dull that she welcomed his return, making a place for him on the sopha on which she sat. She was well aware that Barbara had invited her only to make up the numbers and to show that she at least, had obtained a title. Barbara was the closest thing Wanda had to a friend of her own sex and that friendship was based largely on an ongoing rivalry.

Goodbody had been struck by a wonderful idea whilst drinking with the gentlemen after a filling dinner. Several of them had made game of his obvious interest in Wanda, warning him that she was out for a ring on her finger with a title attached. All of the other gentlemen at the dinner, save Lady Belmont's particular friend, Mr. Cunningham-Smythe, were married and in the company of their wives, all of whom, to a woman, disapproved of Wanda and showed it.

And that had given him a devilish cunning idea!

He therefore made a beeline for Wanda when the gentlemen joined the ladies, and was gratified when she smiled archly at him and patted the sopha cushions invitingly, leaning forward so that he might have an unobstructed view of that magnificent bosom.

With difficulty, Goodbody put a curb on his lust and pasted an ingratiating smile on his face. He sat beside her and stared into her face, not without an effort. His natural inclination was to look down.

"A female as beautiful as you should wear a coronet," he said in a low voice.

"But you do not have a coronet to offer me, sir, do you? And there are your two elder brothers and their sons between you and your father's coronet of pearls. Unless you plan to murder your family to oblige me?" she said bluntly, but with a brilliant smile.

"Not at all – fond of 'em," he said hastily. "But what say you to strawberry leaves?"

"Strawberry leaves? Strawberry leaves and pearls?" she frowned. "A Marquis? There are no unmarried Marquises that I know of other than Lyonshall and he is never in society."

"There is the new Marquis of Keir," said Goodbody softly,

"He is not a peer – not entitled to a coronet." Wanda knew better than that.

"Ah, but when his father Chenevix quits his room, Keir will be a Duke and entitled to those strawberry leaves on his coronet – *sans* pearls — as will be his Duchess," said Goodbody.

Wanda looked at him with narrowed eyes. She had tried to capture the Duke of Chenevix twice – to no avail. When she fainted in front of his house in Park Lane he had sent a servant out to throw cold water in her face. Accosting him at Vauxhall Gardens had earned her the coldest of cuts – in direct view of most of the *Ton*. Those eyes of ice had gone straight through her. He seemed completely immune to her charms, which she could not understand in the least. She listened intently to what Goodbody was saying.

"Keir is a young man of five and twenty who has never been in society. Until recently he was a poor French *émigré* and now is suddenly rich and titled. Only think how a beautiful lady such as yourself would appeal to an inexperienced rustic as he is at this moment! He would be swept away by your air of fashion and loveliness! And should he not prove amenable, I will be there to help you – er – bring him

375

up to scratch, for I am a qualified Wizard, well versed in love spells."

"Are not love spells illegal?" she pointed out.

Goodbody pooh-poohed this objection. "Have you ever heard of anyone prosecuted for using a love spell? You can lay odds that Chenevix is too proud to bring suit over such and would accept the marriage, even should he find out about it. Which he will not."

Wanda thought furiously. She was non-magical and had often wished that she had magical skills to entice a noble husband.

"I can brew you a perfume that makes you completely irresistible to him," Goodbody whispered to her, picking up her hand and kissing it so that anyone watching would think that they were continuing their flirtation.

"And what do you gain from my marriage to Keir, Mr. Goodbody?" Wanda asked pointedly.

"Lady Diana Stillfield," said Goodbody. The revelation had come to him over dinner. Lady Diana and her more than ample fortune was the answer to all of his problems. And after his rebuff, he wanted her more than ever, by fair means or foul. And it looked very much as if it would have to be foul.

"Oh, I see," said Wanda. "Keir is your rival and she favors him." She thought a moment, chewing on her lip.

At last she said, "I've no objections to a husband who wanted some one else – I'll be the one with the strawberry leaves, after all. We need to talk of this further, away from prying eyes and ears. You may escort me home, Mr. Goodbody."

She was suddenly visited by inspiration. She needed to bind him further to her. She leaned forward and twisted so that one breast nearly fell from her gown. "Plan on spending the night, Augustus, for I find you prodigiously attractive and can scarce keep my hands from you," she said in a husky voice, looking up at him from under lowered lashes, darkened with lamp black.

Augustus gulped visibly and began to sweat. He had never really hoped she would offer herself, for most of the females he lay with had a distressing tendency to demand payment before anything actually happened. And ones who looked like Wanda Wycherley were high-flyers, above his touch.

He could not leave quickly enough.

Wanda knew that Goodbody was likely to be a dead loss as a bed partner. He was too self-involved to have learned how to please a woman like her properly. He would probably even be shocked at some of the activities she delighted in.

No matter. Even should she snare this incipient Duke she had no intention of remaining faithful to him either. She enjoyed having many partners and exploring the new and strange with different men, none of whom could keep up with her desires. Only Culver came close, but they had been sleeping together since she was twelve and he knew her inside out.

Sleeping with Goodbody was a small price to pay, for with a sexual reward in the offing he would be all the more eager to help her to obtain her goals. And she knew enough harlot's tricks to keep him panting after her into infinity.

31

The Confession

When René awoke the next morning it was to bright sunlight in his face and a buzzing sound in his ear.

How late had he slept? He surged upright in the tangle of bedclothes, dislodging Beau, who had been curled up on his shoulder, purring.

A glance at the bedside clock showed him that it was nearly ten. Ten! He had never slept that late before! He was amazed that Lyon had not been thumping on the door, demanding his presence in the Tower.

Beau gave a squawk of protest as René's abrupt movement sent him tumbling to the counterpane. He looked up at his friend in censure. "They said to tell you that they would keep break-fast for you," he said clearly. "Everybody slept late. But I had my breakfast already. The sausages are very good!"

"You are talking already, *sans peine!*" said René in wonder.

"I am a superior cat," said Beau smugly. His voice was rather thin and piping, like a child's, but unlike a child's, within a year it would mature to something between a baritone and a tenor.

"You didn't sleep very well last night," the kitten observed. "The blankets are all tossed about and your fur is ruffled."

"My fur? My hair you must mean, *non?*" René put a hand up to smooth it down.

"It works better if you lick your paw like this." Beau put a pink tongue to his white paw and then used it to smooth the top of his head.

Absentmindedly, René smiled at him. It was true – he had not slept at all well last night. There was something on his mind and it had been there since the reading of the binding spell.

There was a brisk knock on the door and René called *"Entrez."* He assumed his caller would be Simon. Over the Duke's glowering disapproval he had arranged to begin Simon's lessons again and today was to be the first day. Simon was all eagerness.

But the caller was not Simon but the Duke's man, Mariposa. "His Grace has sent me," he said in the clipped Oxonian accents that contrasted so oddly with his gypsy-like appearance. "to help your lordship bathe and dress." He spoke better English than did Augustus Goodbody.

René stared at him. *"Merci beaucoup,"* he said at last "but it is many years since I could not bathe and dress myself."

Mariposa lifted a hand to his mouth and coughed in a deprecating fashion. "His Grace feels that your lordship needs some guidance in the matter of becoming bang-up to the fashion."

"That man will send me to the *maison de santé,"* René murmured to Beau. Raising his voice he said, "Since I do not care about being *le dernier cri,* I may dispense with your services. *Vous êtes très gentil.* But I thank you, no," his voice was very firm.

"His Grace will be most displeased," Mariposa warned.

René shrugged in the very Gallic fashion that said, "I don't care, so what? I can't help it."

Mariposa bowed himself from the room as Beau said "You are no longer a kitten! Why does your father treat you like one? Even a cat can see that you do not need to be told how to groom yourself – except in the matter of your fur," he added, and sprang to René's shoulder, where he set about pawing his friend's hair into place.

Without Mariposa's – or Beau's – help, René finished dressing, magically warming the shaving water. Just as he was shrugging himself into his coat there was another knock on the door.

This time it was Simon, bright and shining. He was the only one, he explained, who had risen from bed at the usual time. Everyone else had slept quite late. Mama had said this was a natural reaction to the relief of having at last discovered the binding spell.

"Are we to study how a dragon makes fire today, sir?" Simon asked, perched on the end of René's bed. He was stroking Beau, who had climbed into his lap. Outside in the hall there was a sudden noise and Janus mewed imperatively until René let her in. She promptly jumped on Simon, pushing Beau aside, with a look at her brother that said "You have your own human! This one is mine!"

"We shall do a bit of everything today," René promised.

"Tuathail would like to see how dragons make their flying gasses as well," Simon said.

"I want to see too," said Beau loudly.

"He's talking!" Simon exclaimed. "Janus hasn't said anything as yet."

"That's because I am her elder and her superior," said Beau. Janus hissed and took a swipe at him with extended claws.

"I will have my breakfast and then I must speak to your uncle for a brief moment before we start," René promised Simon. His pupils had now increased by three – a dragon and two kittens. He could only imagine the Duke's face when his Grace learned of this. And Chenevix would be even less pleased when he learned of what the conversation with Lyon would be about. But René would try his level best to keep that from the Duke as long as was possible.

After breakfast, which he ate with only Simon and the kittens for company, René went up to the Tower, where he found Lyon rather gloomily studying the fair copy of the binding spell.

"Ah, there you are," said Lyon, his tone implying 'at last'. "Finished Simon's lesson, have you?"

"Not at all," René answered, "but I must speak to you about the binding spell. If I could pass the *Magus Magistra*

380

sitting I would be qualified to be the locus for the spell," he said this in a rush, wanting to get it over with.

Lyon stared at him in consternation. "You're a virgin?" he said in disbelief. "At your age?"

René felt himself flushing and silently cursed the necessity of this admission. Why was it so shameful for a man but so desirable for a woman? And how could he explain to this always wealthy man how little one thought of the opposite sex when one was at times so hungry that nothing else mattered, particularly during adolescence, when one was hungry all of the time? And too, he had been told by more than one farmer, bluntly, not to tamper with his daughter, for the farmer did not wish to see his girl obliged to wed a poverty-stricken foreigner with a mad mother. And of course, there was no money to pay a *fille de joie*, even if he had not found the thought of such repulsive. The only female who qualified as a *fille de joie* in this small neighborhood was Bessie, the innkeeper's fat and slovenly daughter. Bessie, who was not particularly clean, would lay with anyone for a shilling or two. René found that he was far and away too fastidious to avail himself of her services.

Some of this must have showed in his face, for Lyon said quickly and uncharacteristically, "It's none of my affair, anyway. But do you know what you are letting yourself in for? It could be dangerous!"

"But there is no one else, *n'est-ce pas?*" René said. "Lord Oberon spoke to me of a task that only I would be fitted for and I think, *à bon droit*, that this is the task of which he spoke."

"England would owe you a huge debt," said Lyon slowly. "If you are absolutely certain that you wish to do this..."

"*De plein gré* – willingly," René said firmly, even though his heart beat so fast and so loud that he thought Lyon must be able to hear it.

"Well, then, we have a great deal to do," Lyon drew a piece of parchment towards him and picked up a pencil. "You'll have to take the *Magistra* exam in Dublin the day after tomorrow. It takes three days. I for one, think you're ready for it. There is so little time, for I am come to agree that it must be Lammastide." He sighed and pushed a hand through his hair. "Two more Wizards were killed last night," he said. "There was a 'griffe express rider awaiting me this morning from Warwickshire. Something must be done and this is the best chance we have. 'Tis a good thing that we can now scry over water, thanks to you Druids of Brittany – I'll speak to Conchobar this morning and he will get all in train for you. The other two Wizards that were prospects, you know, were not suitable. The invalid is too ill and the other one has set up a mistress just recently. And Mag Uidhir got married just a se'enight ago."

René was well aware of this last happening, for the two young men had become friends over the course of the last few weeks and he had had a letter from Diarmait not two days earlier, extolling the virtues of his bride, Aisling.

But there remained one more thing to discuss with Lyon. "If we may, *M'sieur*, keep this between ourselves until it is necessary to tell the others? My grandmother and mother would be much distressed..."

"Not to mention Chenevix. He might actually show some emotion," said Lyon dryly. "We shall have to inform the Vicar – he is driving himself to distraction trying to find a likely candidate. But he's a parson and knows how to be discreet."

"As I see it, though, even do you pass your Mastery – and you will – there is still one insurmountable problem," Lyon continued. "Where are we going to find a live unicorn so that you might pass the unicorn test? No one has seen a unicorn in Britain for several hundred years. It is supposed that they are extinct. That is a problem that may prove impossible to solve."

The Duke of Chenevix watched from the window in the library as his son and heir made a spectacle of himself with an audience of a young boy, a green dragon and two kittens. Several of the grooms were watching as well. If he must play at being a tutor why did he not send the servants about their business? They had hauled a table, some jars, chemicals and a bellows out to the dragon pen and were conducting chemical experiments – scarcely the behavior of a gentleman!

His Grace was more than a little angry with Keir. He had refused the services of Mariposa and had refused flat out to accompany his parents to London to begin their necessary transformation into members of the British *Ton*. Keir claimed that there was too much important work to do here and perhaps after the present crisis was resolved he might consider a trip to London. *Might consider it!* Chenevix's lips twisted in a sour grimace. Everything that was proposed to that young man was politely but firmly refused. He possessed no filial obedience whatever – he would not even listen to Lucie, who, the Duke admitted, did not try very hard to persuade him.

Keir needed to be broke to bridle, in vulgar parlance. He must learn that his Grace knew best.

From another window Ninon, too, watched the events in the dragon pen. Unlike Chenevix she smiled and laughed when the gasses ignited and Tuathail trumpeted and reared back on his tail, almost falling over backwards. She was so glad for René – he and Simon both looked as if they were enjoying themselves immensely. René was a natural teacher and Simon was full of intellectual curiosity. She could not see why Chenevix found it so disgraceful that René wished to teach Simon and continue working with Lyon. Did Chenevix want his son to turn into a lazy wastrel like that Goodbody creature, good for little save running up debts and assaulting females? In Ninon's view, Chenevix should stop fretting over what René was not and be grateful for what he was.

Ninon was a little worried about her grandson. He had seemed a trifle abstracted yester eve after the spell had been translated and its particulars discussed. She wondered what was wrong but thought that she knew. She was very much afraid that René was falling in love with Lady Diana Stillfield. Ninon had nothing against Lady Diana, not any more, but she saw no future in it. They were too different in background. At one time she would have added 'breeding' to that, but recent developments had changed her mind. She had always thought that René should marry a Frenchwoman – there were probably many ex-patriate Frenchwomen in London and its environs of suitable lineage of Huguenot leanings and of the Old Blood. Perhaps even a woman of Provence or Brittany where the Old Blood ran the strongest.

Now she was very much afraid that this Duke of Lucie's was going to interfere. But she knew that René would only stand for so much. He had been his own man since he was fifteen and she could not see him submitting to be ruled by someone like Chenevix.

Simon had a successful and satisfying first new lesson – they covered quite a bit of ground – as well as chemistry he learned, amongst other things, more about the use of his wand, and how to ask a favor of a tree. He was in alt – René had complimented him on what he had learned from Mama and Simon had had many of his questions answered on things he had read on his own. The two kittens had listened intently to Simon's lesson. "Rascal and Neige should be here, as well," commented Beau, "for this is important arcane knowledge that they should have." Both kittens decided that they would attend Simon's lessons and get him to read to them until they could read themselves.

The time was early afternoon and they were heading back towards the house. It was such a nice day that the lesson had taken place entirely out of doors. It was a cool day, for early July, and the high thin mares' tails in the sky spoke of rain to come.

Simon thought he heard the wings of a humming bird and looked about him eagerly. He exclaimed in delight when he saw the little blue Faerie, Medb.

"Hello, Wizard. Hello, little boy," said the Faerie, hanging in the air in front of their faces, making them stop precipitately. "I have a message for you from Father Oak," she continued, facing René. "He was going to send it through the trees but I happened to be heading this way to visit my sisters on the other sides of mans' village (by this she meant Silverbridge) and I thought that I would do him a favor. He wants to see you. Right now. It's very important."

"Many thanks, lady Faerie. I shall be sure and tell Father Oak what an excellent messenger he chose," René said very politely, with an elegant bow.

The little blue Faerie glowed. "When will you come?"

"Now," said René. "Simon, do you go and tell my grandmother where I have gone and that I shall return before she misses me." And he disappeared in a haze of violet.

"I want to learn to do that!" said Beau eagerly.

"So do I!" agreed Simon.

"All Faeries can do that!" Medb informed them in a complacent voice and disappeared in a wink of blue.

Simon had scarcely time to find Ninon and give her the message before René returned.

He returned to the Tower workroom, which by now he knew well enough to get a firm picture of it in his mind before teleporting. He found Lyon by himself, bent over the scry bowl that stood in a large tripod fashioned to look like three leaping dolphins supporting the scry bowl on their tails.

René's entrance startled Lyon, who whirled around clapping a hand to his heart. "I've GOT to be able to do that!" he declared, unconsciously echoing Simon and Beau.

"When all of this is over," René promised, "I shall teach you, *ne vous en faites pas.*"

"I shall hold you to that." said Lyon.

"I have this moment been to visit Father Oak. He promises that all of the trees shall seek out a unicorn for us. And the trees have promised to watch for the black magician as well," René announced. "He is certain that there are unicorns in some remote area. And the trees shall be able to find them."

"How did Father Oak come to know that we need a unicorn?" Lyon asked.

"The oak outside this window overheard our conversation, and told him," answered René.

"We're dashed lucky the trees are on our side," Lyon mused, thinking of how easy it was for a tree to listen to human plans.

"All of them will not help," René warned, "for many of the trees, especially firs, align themselves with the Unselighe Court."

"There is good and bad in everything, I dareswear," said Lyon. Abruptly changing the subject he said, "You'll leave for Ireland first thing in the morning. I would dearly love to go, but I can't be easy about leaving here with only two females to protect everyone. If only Chenevix had not lapsed —"

385

"Does anyone know why he has done this thing?" René could not imagine giving up magic for any reason whatsoever.

Lyon shook his head. "It was over twenty years ago – he made a public announcement of it, without stating a reason, and has not been a friend to magic – or magicians – ever since. He's behaved better that I thought he would during our present crisis, though."

Which wasn't saying much, René thought.

Lyon glanced at the case clock in the corner. "Nearly time for our nuncheon!" He rubbed his hands together briskly. "I'm famished! Let's go and see what that French chef has for us today. He makes bang-up meals, I'll give him that."

As they headed towards the stairs he said, "After we have our meal I'll try and give you an idea of what will be on the *Magistra* exam. As I've said, I don't anticipate you'll have any problems, but it doesn't hurt to be prepared."

32

The Quarrel

Lyon announced at dinner that evening that he was sending René to Ireland on important business. He said nothing of the *Magistra* examination, for he thought that someone might put two and two together and realize what René was planning to do. That someone would probably be Ninon. Lyon had come, in the past few weeks, to respect her intelligence – in many ways she reminded him of his late wife. Chenevix would more than likely tumble it too – the Duke was awake upon every suit – except that of how to handle his son. There had been an argument between them in the library that afternoon – no one knew what it was about, but the Duke wore a heavy frown this evening His Duchess looked as if she had been crying, and kept her head bent over her plate. René seemed unperturbed by the contretemps, for he kept up a conversation with Lady Diana and Simon, about the boy's lessons.

"What is needed to do in Ireland?" Ninon asked skeptically, giving Lyon a shrewd glance, as if she knew he was not telling the exact truth.

"Oh, dispatches and things," said Lyon vaguely. "We can't scry everything – some things need to be seen and studied."

"How long will René be gone?" Ninon wanted to know.

"It shouldn't be any longer than three or four days," Lyon said, motioning to Seppings that he would like some more roast beef. "And before you ask, *Madame*, that is probably because the weather prognostication for over the Irish sea is for two days of bad thunderstorms and Tuathail

387

won't be able to fly in that sort of weather. And Tuathail wants to visit his parents."

"A *dragon* wants to *visit his parents* and you accommodate this?" said the Duke incredulously. "Do you give your carriage horses leave to visit their relatives, Lyonshall?"

"If they asked me, I would!" Lyon grinned at Chenevix. "A dragon is a thinking, sentient creature, Chenevix, with as many ties to his family as you have, I daresay. More," he added thoughtfully, "when one considers what one has heard about your late father."

The Duke's looks became arctic. Only the realization that he was a guest in this house and no gentleman would violate the sacred ties of hospitality prevented him from uttering "How dare you!" Lyonshall had gone far beyond the bounds of what was pleasing. The Duke needed an outlet for his rage – it seemed that he had been angry all of the day today – and his glance lit on his heir.

René had been having a interesting conversation with Lady Diana and Simon about wands. Simon was eager to get a handle and a tip for his wand and wanted to know what sort of gemstone was the best to get.

As René explained, like so much else in magic, this was the Wizard's personal choice and no one stone was better than the other. Diana had just proposed that the three of them go into Knightswold, to *The Cauldron*, and help Simon choose, after Lammastide, for his birthday was in September.

It was so pleasant to be able to have a conversation with Lady Diana without hostility. René found her sense of humor delightful and her understanding quick and insightful. She did not flirt but was straight-forward and truthful. She was not afraid to show her intelligence as too many females were.

They were laughing together with Simon when the Duke's sharp voice cut into their enjoyment. "Keir!" he said in cutting tones. "You are eating improperly."

It seemed to René as if everyone turned to look at him. He had no idea what the Duke was talking about. Ninon had drummed good manners into his head at an early age and it had been quite a long time since she had rapped him on the knuckles for a *faux pas* at the dining table. "*Je ne vous comprends pas,*" he said blankly, taken by surprise.

"In society, one places a small piece of each food on the plate on one's fork and conveys it to the mouth. To ingest but a piece of beef or a potato as you are doing is vulgar. Only a servant would eat so," Chenevix stated peremptorily. And then added in high irritation, "Stop speaking so much French! You're an Englishman – it is time you started sounding like one!"

It was too much to be borne. René stood so swiftly that the dishes on the table rattled and the crystal chimed. "If the ladies will excuse me – *je vous demande pardon* – I will go and eat with the servants since that is all that I am fit for." And he left the room.

"Lucien!" Lucie cried, her eyes full of re-proach.

"*Tu peux l'assommer, il ne s'en rendra pas compte!*" said Ninon savagely, glaring at the Duke.

Lyon choked – she had told Lucie to hit her husband in the head – he'd never notice it.

Simon, who thought his hero perfect, glared at the Duke.

"That was not well done in you, your Grace!" said Diana, outraged. "Lord Keir is not a child to be corrected at table. And if I were to correct Simon's manners, it should be done in private, not with intent to humiliate!" She rose swiftly, throwing her linen serviette on the table and hurried after René.

At this point Chenevix finally lost control of his temper. "What might I expect, allying myself with the *bourgeoisie*?" he snarled. "Bad manners and –"

To everyone's surprise Lucie, the ever gentle, said in heat, "*Bourgeoisie*? We should be addressing my Maman as *la Duchesse* de Mont du Mer! My *Grandmère* on Papa's side was a Valois! Our family could sit on the throne of France!" She stood abruptly and threw her balled-up serviette in the Duke's face. "I thought that I was *lowering myself* to marry you!" She began sobbing wildly, looking from one to the other of them. With a cry she ran from the room. Ninon followed her, shooting the Duke a glance of fury as if to say "*Now* look what you have done!"

With a breathless "Pray excuse me," Simon left the room, presumably in search of his mother.

This left Chenevix and Lyonshall at the table. Seppings and Robert the footman were trying to remain expressionless.

Lyon took a slow slip of his wine. Chenevix was on his feet, the crumpled serviette adorning his shoulder.

"And you think that *I* cause theatrical scenes!" Lyon said, shaking his head. "That one was as good as any farce I've ever seen at the play! Dramatic quarrels! Startling revelations! Hysterical histrionics! All that's needed is to write it down and present it at Drury Lane."

Chenevix turned his frostiest glare on Lyon. He jerked the serviette from his shoulder and snapped, "*Pas devant les domestiques!*" with a significant glance at the servants.

"It's a little late for that, don't you think?" said Lyon mildly, pouring him self more wine. "And Chenevix – you're speaking French. As an Englishman, should you be doing that?"

The Duke threw a dagger-look at him and stalked from the room. He was shaking with anger.

As he was leaving the room another footman, Charles, entered, carrying a silver salver with a note upon it. "Excuse me, my lord," he said to Lyon, "but this note has come just this minute by express. It is marked 'urgent'.

With a sigh, Lyon took it. He expected it to be notification of the deaths of more Wizards.

But it was not. The sealing wax bore the seal of the Sheriff of the district, and as Lyon lifted it with the letter opener provided by Charles, he wondered what urgent matter the Sheriff could be writing to him about.

It did not take him long to find out. Sir Piers Mildmay had escaped from gaol.

René had not gone to the servants' hall. Diana found him on the terrace that looked out over the rose garden. He was leaning on the stone balustrade, looking out at the garden. His seemingly relaxed posture was spoiled by the tension in his shoulders and the way he gripped the railing as he stared out over the garden watching as the sun was beginning to slip down the horizon behind a bank of clouds, outlining the edges with rose-gold. There were few stars in sight, for it had begun to cloud over.

Diana did not quite know what to say to him. Was he still angry? Should she try to soothe him?

But he said, without turning to face her, "The weather should hold off, do you not think, until the morning? *Si le temps le permet, nous comptons partir à l'aube.*" He turned to face her. "I beg your pardon, Lady Diana. I am not supposed to speak French. Weather permitting, we will leave at dawn."

"I understood you the first time," she said with a sigh. "That man is impossible! Perhaps it is for the best that you go to Ireland and give him some chance to recover from his fit of the sulks. He certainly is in a bad skin!"

René, warmed buy her solicitude, felt as if he wanted to confide in her. The eyes looking into his were kind and sympathetic He had never noticed before how deeply violet in colour her eyes were, even in the dying light.

"This morning, we had the argument – he wants me to give up magic and become an 'ornament to society'," he quoted bitterly.

"But that is outrageous!" Diana said indig-nantly. "My uncle says that you are one of the most talented Wizards he has come across in years – it would be a crime for you to give up magic! And that is my opinion as well!"

"*Je vous remercie,*" he said, and coming closer, took her hand. In a gesture that was becoming old fashioned, he kissed her hand quickly and then allowed her hand to drop.

Diana's heart beat wildly and she opened her lips to speak, but was forestalled by the arrival of Simon.

Simon did not notice anything out of the ordinary. "Everyone is so angry!" he informed them. "Sir, your Mama threw a serviette at the Duke and she yelled at him! Is it true your grandmother is a Duchess too?"

"*Qu'est-ce que c'est que ça?* Where had you, that, Simon? It is my *Maman* who is the Duchess," said René.

"Twas your Mama who said it – she said that we had ought to be addressing your grandmother as the *Ducheez dee Mont do Mare.*" Simon repeated the French title as best he could.

"There must be a mistake," said René. His grand-mother was not a Duchess! Then came the memory of Ninon telling him that he looked like one of the peasants at Chateau Mont du Mer. Close on this came the recollection of a Faerie voice saying *"Your grandmother has many secrets,"* If this was true, why had she never told him?

"Is my grandmother still in the dining room?" he asked Simon.

"She ran out of the room after the Duchess," Simon answered.

That meant Ninon was probably comforting Lucie. René felt torn. This ongoing quarrel between himself and the Duke was hurting Lucie dreadfully. She simply could not understand why they could not get along. He could tell this evening that she had been crying. In fact, she had had tears in her eyes earlier when she had asked him to please try and bear with the Duke. He had promised her he would do so but that irritating man kept demanding the impossible or attacking silly inconsequential things such as this evening's complaint. Not eating correctly! Were such silly things so important in society that one was judged by them? It gave René a very poor opinion of society.

The Duke had been angry earlier today when, upon questioning, René told him that he could neither ride nor drive nor had ever fired a gun nor gone hunting. All of these were necessary for a gentleman to do, to be able to take his proper place in society, Chenevix had stated coldly. He had talked of lessons in all of these arts. The only lessons René was interested in were those pertaining to magic. And then the Duke had demanded that he give up magic and tutoring Simon as well, citing the humiliation he had felt at seeing his heir showing off for a pair of grooms, two kittens and a dragon.

That had torn it. René said simply "No," and left the library. As much as he could, he kept his promise to Lucie and did not openly quarrel with the Duke. But it was becoming harder and harder.

Lyon joined them then, before anything more could be said, looking agitated. "Sir Piers Mildmay has escaped from gaol!" he announced without warning.

"How?" Diana gasped. English gaols were not only stoutly built but bespelled as well.

"The Sheriff gives me little information, but from what he does say, Mildmay bribed a guard," answered Lyon. "If I judge Mildmay correctly, he'll be burning for revenge against us, but especially against you, Keir. He probably sees you as the author of all his misfortune. I hope they capture him before you return from Ireland."

"Surely he cannot hope to return here and evade recapture? *Est-ce possible!*" said René. "Surely the Sheriff will have all of his men out for the search, *non?*"

"He's called out the militia," Lyon waved the paper in his fist. "And how difficult will it be to find a one–armed man?"

"One-armed?" Diana repeated, puzzled. She remembered that the Cremave had shriveled and blackened the unfortunate baronet's arm, arm but had not removed it.

"The surgeon thought it best to amputate his arm. There was a danger of gangrene," Lyon explained.

René and Diana exchanged glances. Sir Piers would hate them much the more for causing the loss of a limb. Diana shivered and drew Simon closer to her.

Simon could sense her fear. "Will not the militia find him, Mama?" he said worriedly.

The adults leaped to reassure him. René put a hand on his shoulder, giving it a squeeze. "*Voyons comment ce tournera.* The good soldiers will do doubt take him with little trouble."

"You needn't worry, Simon," soothed Diana. "There are many guards here that will protect us."

"What if he follows you to Ireland, sir?" Simon looked up at René anxiously.

"No danger in that," said Lyon confidently. "The ports will be watched and Mildmay hasn't access to a dragon. The dragons will be watching for him too, you may be assured. I have no doubt that his likeness is being posted in every receiving office for miles around, even as we speak. Have no fear, Simon, they'll have him back in gaol in two twists of a lamb's tail."

When at last they separated to go to their respective bedchambers René went along to Ninon's room, for he wanted answers to his questions. Although he waited nearly two hours she failed to materialize. He could only assume that she was still with Lucio, soothing her. He neither knew nor cared where Chenevix was.

393

At length, René had to retire to bed. He needed to rest, as dawn came early and he hoped to be in the air as soon as Tuathail could safely fly. Perhaps she would be there to see him off.

But the next morning it was only Diana, Simon and Lyon who were there to bid him Godspeed. Diana had ransacked Lyon's closets and found a flying hat complete with protective spectacles, a wooly scarf, fleece-lined gloves, jacket and flying boots to wear over the flying suit. In order to avoid the lowering clouds with their promise of thunder, Tuathail was going to fly up above them, where it was quite cold. René had to be warmly dressed to avoid suffering from exposure. Lyon's things were a trifle large but they would serve to protect him.

As Tuathail spiraled up into the clouds René watched the figures below him disappear. He watched until he could no longer see them and the altitude made his head swim. They had all become dear to him in one way or another.

Sir Piers Mildmay felt as if he had been running forever. His breath came in great gasps and his heart thumped erratically. Cold sweat ran down his back. He was well into the forest so he sank down beneath a tree to catch his breath.

It had not been easy to find a guard that was amenable to bribery. Most of them took their oaths of office very seriously. But a new young guard, who stood watch during the small hours of the morning, had money troubles. Locked in the Sheriff's safe were Mildmay's personal effects, amongst these, some two hundred pounds in cash and a valuable watch, a diamond tie-pin, an onyx fob and a gold seal. Recklessly, Mildmay promised all of this to the young guard. For this, the guard was to leave the cell door unlocked, as well as the back door and lift the spell that alerted the Sheriff and his deputies if a prisoner attempted escape. The guard, as did all the guards, knew the simple but effective spell and had access to the safe as well, for any prisoner brought in was relived of the contents of his purse and pockets and this was put in a storage sack, labeled and placed in the safe.

To quit his prison in the hours before dawn suited Sir Piers down to the ground. The back door of the gaol led into an alley – this was where the Black Maria was brought up to bring prisoners in and take them to court or to the gallows. Stabling was directly behind the gaol for the horses who drew the prison wagon. Mildmay at first thought to steal a horse, but soon realized that with but one arm he probably could not tack up. So as soon as he was clear of the prison (the guard conveniently looking the other way) he began to run.

It was a lurching, desperate run. It was at times all that he could do to stay on his feet, for he was far from recovered from the anger of the Cremave. His lungs were like broken bellows and sweat ran into his eyes, blinding him. He had obtained a cloak from the guard and it disguised the fact that he had but one arm.

One arm! He wanted to weep and scream and curse about that. He had begged the surgeon finally, not to take it, when all of his blustering and swearing had not moved the sawbones. Mildmay had cherished the fancy that perhaps someone could restore his arm to what it had been. But if there was no arm, there was no possibility of that.

It was all, every bit of it, those Froggies' fault! If, as his attorney informed him, he would swing for his current crimes, he would wish to kill as many of them as he could before they took him again. He might as well be hung for a sheep as for a lamb. It would be worth it, when he climbed the gallows steps, to know that he had punished them for bringing him to this pass.

But it was twenty miles to Silverbridge. Fortunately, he knew this area thoroughly. He knew of a cave in the hills where he could hide and rest. There was water there, also. No food, but he could steal that if he had to do so. All that mattered was revenge. He was not certain how he would manage to kill Wizards but he would find a way – perhaps Cold Iron, although he knew little of the method. He had to do it – he could never rest in peace until he had his redress.

With the aid of the tree trunk he staggered to his feet again, and began moving ever west, towards Silverbridge, stumbling and gasping, but determined.

He did not know that he was watched by two bright and sly eyes set in an evil and ugly face.

Magus Magistra

It was a rough ride over the ocean. It was probably just as well that neither René nor Tuathail could see the waters below them through the thick cloud cover, for the sea was gray and angry with turbulent, white-topped waves. Tuathail flew straight out from Gloucestershire, over Saint David's Head in Wales to George's Channel, the narrowest part of the Irish Sea, to Cransore Point in Ireland. Once they were over land again the air was less agitated. Soon they left the clouds behind and René was able to see some of the beautiful emerald green land that passed beneath them as Tuathail flew north.

René was grateful for the flying clothes Diana had found for him, for it was very cold over the tops of the clouds, which fortunately were just forming and were not the full 35,000 feet that a mature thunder cloud could reach. Dragons, especially those carrying passengers, hardly ever flew more than a mile above the earth. Since they were almost impervious to both heat and cold, a dragon could fly higher in the cold air, which dropped 4 degrees for every 1,000 feet of altitude. But dragons understood that their human charges could not bear the cold, even in the very best of flying gear.

Tara lay to the north and west of Dublin, in County Meath on the Boyne River. The eons-old Druid enclave of *Temair na Ríg*, Tara of the Kings — sat atop a hill five hundred feet above sea level in the Boyne Valley. It was a sacred site, the most sacred in all of Ireland. In the millennia it had stood there Tara had grown from a simple complex of buildings with a formidable rampart around the rim of the hill, to a small and bustling city. The very top of the emerald hill was left bare, for here were the barrows of the *Túatha dé Danaan*, from whom the *Sidhe* descended, some of these barrows seven thousand years old. The *Lia Fàil*, the Stone of Destiny, stood there too, in the very center of the old walls. Perched as it was on the Plain of Meath, the rounded hill of Tara looked over some of the most fertile and green land in all of Europe. Dublin lay twenty miles to the south of Tara. Dublin, at Trinity University, was where the *Magus Magistra* examination would be held.

René was to stay at Tara, the guest of Diarmait and Aisling, They inhabited a snug little house, one of several in a row belonging to the Druidical Collegium, which were available to married staff. There was a large University-type Collegium of Druidical studies at Tara — the Wizards' university was at Dublin, at Trinity. There was a draconic Collegium as well, where dragons studied, at Tara.

Diarmait and Aisling met René at the Dragon Port just outside Dublin. It was a busy place, almost as busy as had been the London Port in Hounslow Heath.

Tuathail only waited for René's cases to be unloaded and to be to be unharnessed, and then flew off again, eager to see his parents, who lived at Dún Loaghaire on the coast south of Dublin. His harness could be stored at the port until it was needed again, for a modest fee. He was to return in four days time.

Aisling, Diarmiat's bride, proved to be every bit as charming as his letters had claimed and soon she was chattering away to René as if they had known one another for years. She was a small girl, and had the clear, creamy Irish complexion, bright blue eyes, long lashes put in with a sooty finger and a huge mass of naturally curling copper coloured hair that seemed to have a mind of its own. "Sure, and 'tis the bane of me existence!" she said with a wry smile as she pushed it out of her face for the fourth time. " 'Twill not stay up, no matter the pins I stick into it. I'd like fine to cut it all off, but me lad won't hear of it." Unfashionably, it hung down her back, tied round with a black velvet band.

They were walking towards a hackney that would convey them to the town and the wind was brisk. "To cut it off would be a crime, *Madame*, so beautiful as it is," said René gallantly, thinking of dusky curls and how they would look unbound.

"Tis certain ye are that you're not an Irishman?" Aisling teased him. "For ye've surly kissed the Blarney Stone! And I'm not *Madame*, I'm Aisling – we're not after standing on formality here."

Diarmait had many questions about the binding spell and what was being done to implement it. He had not been told that René was to be the locus as yet. Thus far, only Lyonshall knew — even the Vicar had not been told. Diarmait was to take his Mastery so that he could assist in the gathering of the Irish ley lines to send a cone of power to Avalon, where the binding ceremony was to be held. He assumed that was why René was to sit for the exam as well. There were so few Masters nowadays that were not well along in years. Such a gathering of power required as many Masters as was possible.

The Mag Uidhir's home was soon reached – a white-washed, thatched cottage of two stories, surrounded by trees and gardens. Aisling, Diarmait proudly informed René, was a Witch who specialized in agrimony and had already coaxed the flower and vegetable gardens into riotous bloom. Aisling's father, Brian Ó Comraidhe, was an *ócaire*, a small farmer, as well as a Wizard, and she came by her talent naturally.

They had decided to devote the day to sight-seeing rather than study, for as Diarmait said, "If we don't know our business by now, we never will." Thus René was able to see things he had only read about, among these the Book of Kells, in the Treasure Room of Tara, under a powerful preservation spell so that it was as fresh as when it was penned in the seventh century. There were relics of the early Celts and of the invading Vikings as well as those of the Saints such as Pádraig and Brighid, and a fabulous collection of Druidical jewelry, most of it well over one thousand years old. There was a gold torque that had supposedly been worn by Merlin.

Diarmait and Aisling made certain that René saw a good deal of the beautiful countryside as well. Pádraig offered his services, so they were able to cover a great deal of ground. Aisling packed a picnic basket and they ate a nuncheon at the edge of the passage graves near of the Boyne River at Newgrange. This 3,000 year old site was said to be a passage to the Otherworld and the dwelling place of the ancient Irish Gods. It had an atmosphere of great power – all three of them could feel the ley lines leading to the node and the node itself beneath the earth's surface throbbing with ancient energies.

At a Holy Well dedicated to Saint Brighid René drank an icy, pure cup of water from an archaic cup of beautiful crystal, thought to be of *Sidhe* crafting. The waters of the well were said to impart wisdom. After the meal they flew to Dublin and toured the ancient city and did some shopping. The Irish woolens and embroideries were among the best in the world and René could not resist buying shawls and scarves for his mother and grandmother.

They also toured the Papal palace, and saw the art treasures and rare books that the Irish Popes had collected over the centuries. Since King Arthur had removed the Catholic Church of Rome from England nearly one thousand years earlier, the Irish had followed suit but remained true to the Catholic faith and had their own Pope and College of Cardinals in Dublin. The Irish Pope, a venerable and holy man named Librán Mac Giolla Phádraiga, occupied the throne of Saint Pádraig, in the Saint's own Cathedral.

In no time at all the afternoon passed and it was time to return to Tara, for Aisling had invited Conchobar, his wife Roane and their daughter Sióbhan to dine with them. She felt it would be a good thing if neither her husband nor their guest had a minute to worry over the examination to come. Diarmiat's specialty was Geomancy – the powers of the earth and manipulating the elements and elemental creatures of it. Although a fully robed Druid he had yet to obtain his Wizard's mastery, for Druidical training was done differently in Ireland. In England, one obtained one's *Magistra* before applying to a Druidical college. In Ireland, a child was chosen by the Druids and sent to a Druid enclave at the age of ten, and after a long apprenticeship was made journeyman, then master. Usually during the journeyman phase the young Druid studied Wizardry as well at Trinity. It was not an easy discipline, and as Lyon had so often complained, it seemed every year that fewer people were willing to commit to the endeavor.

Diarmait 's family had a long tradition of one son or daughter in each generation devoted to Druidical training.

Normally, it would have taken him another year to study for his Wizardly *Magistra*, but these were not normal times and everything was accelerated.

Over tea, they talked a little of the examination to come. Diarmait was amazed when René told him that he was sitting for the General examination. "Did you know," Diarmait demanded as Aisling served hot Irish tea and her own tender soda bread with currants, "that the last person to sit for a General *Magistra* was Lord Lyonshall? Even people who have a General *Majori* don't sit for the General *Magistra*. 'Tis fearsome difficult, they do say. Most go for a specialty."

"Now, Diar," Aisling scolded, "ye should not fright our guest! He'll be wishing you at the Devil!"

"Lord Lyonshall has warned me," said René, wondering what was in the tea that gave it such a spirited flavor. Ailing could have told him it was a drop of the Irish.

"And you're still determined to do it?" Diarmait shook his head. "Man, we'll have to be sending you to a rest-cure in Bath!" His tone was teasing, but he was more than a little worried. The Geomancy exam, he had heard, was difficult enough – he could not imagine taking the General, which had the reputation of causing nervous breakdowns and once, even a suicide.

They would be tested for three days. On the first day, which they would be allowed to do with any other candidates, was the written portion. The next day they would be tested separately, in the Oral exams, in which a panel of at least two Masters were free to ask any questions they thought pertinent. Often one was expected to answer to several Masters at once. The third day was the worst, everyone said – the Practicals – in which one was to demonstrate all of the theory, spells and knowledge one had learned. This was done before the *Taoiseach* of all Ireland, a rank equivalent to the British Prime Minister and was by tradition a *Magus Magistra* and a Druid, and usually one of the most learned persons in all of Ireland. The *Taoiseach* was currently Aoife Ui Néill, descended in direct line from the ancient Irish Kings of Tara. She was a stern and brilliant lady, much feared in the Houses of Parliament in Dublin for her caustic wit. She was a trained *brehon* – a lawgiver and judge – as well. In Ireland, as in Wales and Brittany, there seemed to be no barrier to a woman obtaining an ultimate position of power. There were no female Druids in Britain, Scotland, Cornwall or Manx, and in those countries females were confined to becoming Witches, which did not enjoy the same rank or respect as did a Wizard. In countries such as Ireland it was up to the woman which path – Witchcraft or Wizardry and Druidry, she wished to pursue. Many females in Britain resented these limitations – about ten years earlier a Witch, Mary Wollestonecraft, had written a controversial volume – *A Vindication of the Rights of Female Wizards*, which was not well received by the male establishment.

They discussed these and other subjects over tea, no one admitting to any nervousness over the grueling three days to come. In no time at all it was time to dress for dinner, and Conchobar and his family had arrived.

Conchobar's wife, Roane, was a tall, dark woman who walked as if she was moving through water. When she gave her hand to René he saw that she had webbing between her fingers. He tried not to stare, but she said, "Aye, I'm a Roane in name and in nature. That will be Irish for 'seal', and I am using it for a name because a human tongue cannot get around the name I have when I am with the seal-folk."

René had read of the creatures who were human on land and a sleek seal, or Selchie, in the water, but he had never thought to meet one, especially at a dinner party.

Conchobar's daughter Sióbhan, was a lovely combination of her mother's brown seal eyes and her father's black Irish looks. She too had webbed fingers. She used her long lashed eyes to flirt with René, her dinner partner, over the meal.

The potato and leek soup, roast of pork with parsnips, carrots and green peas that Aisling served had been roasted over a peat fire which gave it a subtle, smoky flavor, and made it delicious. There was brown bread as well and a fine wine. Dessert was a concoction of blackberries, pastry and cream and a Saint Clement's cake – three layers of lemon curd, in a tender cake, its icing full of slices of oranges and lemons and crystallized candies.

Conversation was general over the meal, but light, avoiding by unspoken agreement the current troubles. They discussed the differences in Druidical training in Brittany and Ireland – they were amazed to learn that René had done most of his Druidical training through the medium of a scry bowl, with additional learning from his grand-mother and Father Oak.

Conchobar was eager to have someone come and teach the language of the trees to the Druidical Collegium, for it was a skill lost with the age of Merlin, save to the Druids of Brittany.

And after dessert had been cleared away, there was music. Aisling played the fifty-stringed Irish harp, while the guests had brought their instruments with them – Conchobar played the Uilleann pipes, while his daughter played the *tiompán*, a stringed instrument much like a hammered dulcimer and Diarmait proved a dab hand on the Irish drum, the *bohdran*. They played gigs and reels and Conchobar sang ballads of the Golden Age of Ireland. René wished that he had brought his violin or his flute. The impromptu concert was finished by Aisling's playing of the harp music of Turlough O'Carolan, the blind composer of County Meath, who had flourished in the early part of the previous century. It was a very pleasant evening and ended too soon with cups of Irish coffee and thick slices of Pratie Apple, an apple and mashed potato pie, sweetened with butter and brown sugar under a flaky crust.

Contrary to his expectations René slept soundly and awakened early in the morning to the smell of coffee and bacon.

Aisling had made then a hearty breakfast of fried back bacon, fried eggs and soda bread, with tomatoes and mushrooms fried in the bacon grease. This was accompanied by a steaming bowl of Irish porridge with sugar and cream. She gave each of them a bag of sandwiches and apples, for they would be allowed two short breaks during the course of the examination, as well as a nuncheon, provided by the University. "Fattening us for the slaughter?" Diarmait joked as they boarded Pádraig.

This would probably be the only day Pádraig could fly them to Dublin, for in the east the storm clouds hung heavy over the sea and the anvil shaped thunderheads had swollen to monster proportions. Thunder growled threateningly. The prognostications were still for two days of violent thunderstorms over most of the Irish sea and eastern Ireland. That meant two days of getting up early to take a horse and chaise to Dublin, for the sweep of a dragon's wings could have then in Dublin in under ten minutes, whereas a horse and chaise would take an hour or more.

By special permission Pádraig was allowed to land on the Campanile of Trinity as he was not a dragon employed by any member of the faculty.

A Proctor met them as they landed and took them at once to the small room where the examinations would be conducted. He also took charge of their food pouches and magically searched them for any evidence of cheating materials. They were then required to swear an oath that the examinations would be answered honestly and to the best of their abilities. They were also required to hand over their lapel pins, which would be augmented (or not) with their new ranks.

"How many people are sitting today?" asked Diarmait, a little nervously.

"But you two," the Proctor, a stout, balding man who looked as if he had never smiled, answered brusquely.

They were seated at opposite ends of the room, told what they were expected to do in what length of time and given a quill, an inkstand and an examination book and a pile of parchment. To give them as much time as was possible, the quill was magiced so that it would not need trimming and the inkwell would never run dry. The parchment was magiced so that it would not blot and would dry immediately.

The Proctor stood in the center of the room and withdrew a large hunter watch from his waistcoat pocket. "Time, gentlemen, please. Open your examination books to the first page. You will have three hours to complete Part One. When you have finished Part One, close your book and put down your quill. Do not go on or look further in the book. You may begin."

René opened his book. The first question was: *"Describe as best you can, Merlin's Master Spell for Adepts. All incantations should be in the original Welsh, with translations provided. Use diagrams when necessary Points will be taken for incorrect spellings, punctuation and grammar."*

He picked up his quill and began to write.

404

When Sir Piers tried to rise from his seat beneath the tree it was if he were tied to the trunk. He could move very little. He was terrified and strained against the invisible bonds. He could see nothing that would impede his getting up from the ground. Had his body completely failed him? He cursed and struggled, but at last had to admit defeat. To his horror and chagrin, tears were rolling down his cheeks. He would be caught and captured if he could not get up and move!

"Caught, ain't you, me buck?" came a voice from behind him. It was a particularly nasty voice, with a sibilant hiss like that of a snake.

"Damn you!" Mildmay blustered. "Who are you? Was it you who did this to me? Let me go at once! If it's money you want –". He had no idea how he could pay anything to his captor, if captor he was, but most people were amenable to a bribe.

"Money!" hissed the horrible voice. "What good's money to the likes o' me? Nay, money's for the humans. Ye've the stink o'magic on ye – powerful magic – an' me master's allus interested in such-like things."

"Who are you?" Mildmay demanded "And who is this Master of yours? Show yourself to me!"

There was a snort and a scrambling sound, and around the tree came a creature from Mildmay's nightmares.

It vaguely resembled a man – if a man could be made from a flash of lightning. It was brown in colour, covered with short, rank hair and was all angles and sharp points. Its sharp-cornered shoulders stood above its flat head and it had yellow, snake-like eyes over a long nose that jutted from its face. Lengthy tufts of hair decorated its skull, two large clumps that lay back over towards its neck, two locks like goat horns over its eyes and two mustache-like tussocks on its upper lip. It had a mouthful of razor-sharp teeth, and long arms that ended in large hands – four-fingered hands with sharp talons. Short-legged, with enormous feet, it also had a extended spindly tail which was twitching back and forth much as a hungry cat's on the trail of a mouse. And it was drooling – slimy spittle dripped from its lips and onto the fur of its chest, unnoticed.

"What are you?" Mildmay whispered, horror-struck. Being a non-magical he had never studied the Unselighe creatures. In this he was not alone. Many Wizards had never studied the Unselighe creatures, thinking them contained for all time.

"Don't ye know me, mortal man?" it taunted. "'Tis a bogle I am. Liars and murderers be my fare."

"What has that to do with me?" Mildmay said with false bravado.

It laughed – a stomach-turning sound, for it sounded what one might imagine a snake would sound like if it could feel mirth. It also licked its lips as it stared at Mildmay. "I'd have gobbled ye by now, elsewise my Master wants ye. Maybe I still will gobble ye…"

"And mayhap you will not," came a new voice, one that sounded so much like an educated gentleman that Mildmay nearly fainted in relief. That is, until he looked up and met the mad eyes of another inhuman being, this one as beautiful as the bogle was ugly.

It was an Elf – that pointed-eared beautiful being was right out of the Faerie-tale books Mildmay's nurse had read to him as a child. The Elf was golden-haired, green-eyed, with pupils slit like a cat's, and clad in old fashioned scarlet silks. He stared at Mildmay in amusement as the bogle abased himself on the ground. "You did well, Ainsel," said the Elf. "I am indeed interested in a human who reeks of the Cremave. And he did not fare well in the encounter."

"He's a liar an' a murderer, Lord Sluagh," put in the bogle eagerly, his face still plastered to the ground in the homage Sluagh required of his minions.

"And you would know, Ainsel. Do you go back Under-the-Hill – there will be a reward for you. Tell one of the Gwyllion I said you were to have a tasty treat."

"Not a rat, Lord Sluagh," begged the bogle.

"No, Ainsel, a lovely plump human child," Sluagh said. "We took some captive this morning."

Nauseated, Sir Piers watched the bogle's yellow eyes begin to glow as it licked the spittle from its lips in anticipation of the treat. It vanished as suddenly as it had come.

"And now, you and I, my dear mortal, will talk," said Sluagh.

34

Plots

When Ninon at last awoke the first thing she remembered was that she must go and wish René *bon voyage.* But the chiming of a clock somewhere in the house told her that it was far too late, for the clock rang out eight in silvery tones.

Ninon grumbled silently. She sat up and stretched, gasping as a sore neck and back made themselves known. She had fallen asleep in a chair by Lucie's bed. How many times had she done that over the years? This time was different, however. This time Lucie, though tearful, had been rational and they had been able to talk.

Well, nearly rational. Lucie could not understand why her husband and son were not getting along and nothing could convince her that their reaction to one another, given their per-sonalities, and the newness of their acquaintance, was only natural and inevitable. René was a grown man, well used to running his own life, and of course resented being corrected and being told what to do as if he were an idiot child. And the Duke was a inborn tyrant, a despot who thought he knew best for all concerned. He seemed, to Ninon, to view his wife and son as his property. She had never heard him call René by his Christian name or even refer to him as his son. It was always "Keir" or "my heir." His attitude towards Lucie was protective, but Ninon had no idea how they behaved towards one another in private. Lucie seemed happy, but Ninon had come to recognize that her daughter was more than content to have 'Lucien' tell her what to do.

Over and over yester eve she had demanded of Ninon why did René not just do as his father bade him and stop all these arguments? Ninon had thought the grounds of her argument fallible – why should René do what Lucie herself had not done? Lucie had run away from school and made a clandestine marriage because she did not wish to do as her parents desired – at the age of fourteen – not five and twenty! And Ninon agreed with René – *she* would not have put up with the Duke's ridiculous demands either! Not eating correctly! What a stupid thing to pick out a quarrel over! Really, when she thought of it, René had restrained himself admirably. She would have thrown her full plate at the Duke's head.

Lucie was still asleep, her cheeks stained by tears. Ninon decided against wakening her. Ninon had no idea where the Duke had slept last night and she did not care. She hoped it had been someplace uncomfortable – as uncomfortable as this chair.

Stiffly she rose from the chair and as silently as possible left the room for her own bedchamber.

Half an hour later, Ninon, feeling refreshed by a quick sponge bath and a change of clothes, went down to breakfast. She expected to find no one there, for it was now nearly nine in the morning, but Diana and Simon were still at the table, making a leisurely meal.

Already the French doors of the breakfast room stood open to the day, for it was going to be hot. Looking out the doors over the garden one could see a heat haze on the distant hills and the sun shone brightly in a brilliant brassy sky of blue. Not a breeze blew and the flowers drooped in the heat. Gardeners were moving slowly through the ranks of the flowers, with watering pots brimming with cool drinks for the flora.

Diana, like Ninon, wore a muslin frock, light in colour, short of sleeve, with an open neck. Simon was informal in shirtsleeves.

"Good morning, ma'am!" Simon greeted Ninon cheerfully. "Neige has been waiting for you!"

As he spoke the white kitten ran forward from in front of the open door where she had been sitting with her siblings. She impatiently waited for Ninon to sit and then

408

jumped into her lap, meowing for attention. She slept with Ninon at night and yesterday had been shut out of Lucie's room. She had ended in sleeping with Janus and Simon so that she would not be alone, and now she had to complain to Ninon about this distressing fact.

As Ninon petted her little familiar she asked if any one knew if René had begun his journey. She was gratified to learn that Diana, Simon and Lord Lyonshall had seen him off and that they had already had a scry from Ireland, telling then of his and Tuathail's safe arrival.

"I still do not see, me, why the Lord Lyonshall must send René all of the way to Ireland. *tout court*," she grumbled, as Simon very politely offered her as basket of fragrant muffins and Diana poured her a cup of steaming coffee.

This was a rhetorical question, for she knew that neither Diana nor Simon had any more idea than she did herself. "Where are the others?" she then asked.

"My uncle has gone to see Mr. Arabin," Diana explained. "And I gather that his Grace spent the night in the library and awoke this morning in a most disagreeable humor. He is now out riding, which will hopefully put him in a better skin."

Ninon murmured something rather savagely in French, which Diana translated to mean "I hope he chokes on it!"

"How is the Duchess this morning?" Diana asked carefully. She did not want to intrude, but she felt that Ninon should be aware of what Chenevix had demanded of his heir – to give up magic. She had told Lyon early this morning and his reaction had been such that she was surprised he had not awakened everyone in the surrounding counties. His solution was to wish to have Chenevix committed to Bedlam or killed outright.

Ninon shrugged. "She still sleeps, *non*? She thinks that René should just do as his father wishes and everyone will then be happy."

"His father wants him to give up magic," Diana said.

"*Foutasse!*" Ninon cried, her face thunderous. She struck the table with the flat of her hand. "*Cet homme* – he is insane! I will kill him myself!"

409

"And my uncle will be glad to help you," said Diana.
"He was incensed at even the thought of such a suggestion. It
would be a terrible waste. He has a very high opinion of Lord
Keir's abilities. As do I."

"*Vous êtes très gentil*," Ninon said.

"I'm not being kind – it is the truth," Diana insisted.
After being at Bryn Myrrdin and hearing from her uncle and
Tuathail what René had done, she was more than convinced
of his talents.

"Me, I shall have a thing to say to that Duke," Ninon
muttered, as Neige put a tender paw on her friend's face and
mewed a query of concern. She could tell that Ninon was
upset. How she wished that she could speak! She felt as if she
were on the edge of being able to talk but it was just not time
yet. So far, Beau, the oldest of the four kittens, was the only
one who could talk.

Ninon decided that she would go and find the Duke –
she had a few choice words for him. He was making both
Lucie and René unhappy and she, Ninon, was not about to
stand for that.

"Ma'am," asked Simon suddenly, "is it true that you
are a Duchess also, as the Duchess of Chenevix said yester
eve?"

"Simon!" protested Diana. "That is impolite –"

"No, let the boy speak," said Ninon. "And, *oui*, Simon,
it is true."

"But why did you never tell anyone?" Simon wanted to
know. "Surely it is a good thing to be a Duchess?"

"Not if one is poor and wished to pass unknown in a
small village. Not if one's husband is on the list of the
Inquisition, which does not scruple to send agents into those
countries that do not admit to her laws and snatch people
away from their families to be dragged back to France and
burned alive at the stake," Ninon answered sadly, using no
French so that Simon might understand. And there was
another reason as well, of which she did not speak. How does
one tell one's beloved grandson that while his grandparents
and mother were of the highest nobility he was probably
illegitimate, his father unknown? Of course. that was no
longer true.

Now she said, "Please, do not begin to call me *Madame la Duchesse*. It matters little. The title and all that it meant is without meaning now. *Cela m'est égal* – a *Duchesse* or *Madame* de Varien – who cares?"

The others, seeing her sincerity, agreed to this and by the time that the end of the meal was reached, the two ladies were Ninon and Diana to each other and Ninon was "Aunt' to Simon.

By the time they reached the foothills Mildmay was ready to collapse. Sluagh made little of the increasing elevation or the undergrowth of bracken, vines and shrubs. His silks never caught on the thorns and branches, nor had he to stop and draw in air in great panting gulps, wiping sweat from his eyes. He stood impatiently, while Mildmay did so.

There was something about the Elf that prevented Mildmay from making even the feeblest protest. The green eyes were strange – wild and mad, and Mildmay wondered more than once if he had done right to trust this inhuman being. But it had taken little encouragement from Sluagh for Sir Piers to pour out his tale of woe and the many injustices done him – not the least of which was the loss of his arm.

Sluagh found it most interesting that the Arch Druid of Britain had a French secretary – and furthermore, one who was loyal to England. He wanted to see Malcoeur's reaction to that piece of news. for Malcoeur, in spite of all the blows France had dealt him, still had a deep (and, in Sluagh's view, misplaced) love for his native land.

It was fortunate hat Ainsel had come across this poor wreck. He was a fountain of information, although Sluagh had had to listen to far too much self-pity. In his view, Mildmay deserved what he had got from the Cremave. But he would keep this pathetic excuse for a man alive, Sluagh decided. He might prove useful again.

Sluagh's madness was driving him to greater ill-judged folly. He was beginning to resent Malcoeur and his smooth assumption of authority. The Jongleur had not approved any of the things Sluagh had done, nor had he professed any admiration, only rejection of several brilliant plans proposed by the Elf. The Unselighe Court was more afraid of Malcoeur than they were of their own master, set over them by the Dark Lord himself.

Sluagh was determined to out do Malcoeur in one fashion or another. And perhaps this business with the Arch Druid might prove his key. For some odd reason, the Jongleur had declared the Arch Druid of Britain off limits to the Unselighe Court. He would deal with the Arch Druid his own self. A very odd look came into Malcoeur's eyes when they spoke of Lyonshall – a look Sluagh understood all too well – the Jongleur lusted for revenge. What Malcoeur held against the Arch Druid Sluagh had been unable to find out. The Jongleur hid his secrets well – Sluagh had learned little of him other than his plans for the eventual conquest of the British Isles by the French. To his anger and chagrin Sluagh was aware that Malcoeur had adroitly learned quite a bit about him – Sluagh, when in the grip of strong emotion, could not hold his tongue, and on some level, was aware of this. But his mania did not allow him discretion. His emotions were too raw and too powerful.

Sluagh had the glimmerings of a plot in his head, a plot that would permit him to show Malcoeur who was the real master of the Unselighe Court, who was the more clever at eliminating the threat from the Druids and Wizards. He needed this wretch, Mildmay, to implement it. So he would provide the baronet with comforts and keep him alive and safe from the militia who were even now searching for him. Sluagh would also set Ainsel to guard Sir Piers. Ainsel would keep the mortal cowed and terrified, for Ainsel would want to gobble his human charge and would let him see that only by Sluagh's grace did he remain alive.

On the day that René and Diarmait had their first sitting there arrived in Knightswold a cavalcade of carriages that stopped at the *Green Man* Inn. A traveling carriage, pulled by four high-bred Cleveland bays arrived first, driven by a livery-clad coachman with a groom up beside him, holding a yard of tin. This horn was used to blow up the occupants of the various toll-houses *en route* so that the Quality in the carriage need not be obliged to wait at the toll-gate. Perched up behind the body of the carriage, above the rear wheels, were a pair of supercilious, bewigged and powdered footmen.

A smart curricle, picked out in yellow, with a pair of showy chestnuts, followed this carriage, occupied by an exquisitely turned-out gentleman in a driving coat of no less that twelve capes, despite the heat of the day. Behind these, moving somewhat slower, were two heavily laden baggage coaches.

The landlord of the *Green Man*, being apprised of the arrival of this procession by an ostler loitering in the yard, wasted no time in bustling out into the yard and greeting what he hoped would be long- term guests.

He did not much look like the picture of a genial host, for he was a thin, dyspeptic man of middle years, by name Jonas Milburn. But he was hard-working and conscientious and ran a decent inn that gave good value. Mothers in the area were not afraid that their daughters would be corrupted if they became chambermaids at the *Green Man*. Mrs. Milburn kept an eagle eye on her girls. She was a devout Christian woman and allowed no havey-cavey activities – the grooms, pot-boys, maids and servers kept the line and attended church on Sundays. Mrs. Milburn, known to her intimates as Grace, was an excellent cook and an exacting housekeeper. In appearance she was tall and gaunt, with grey hair completely covered by a spotless mob cap and wore a perpetual frown. But underneath the severity of her exterior she had a good heart, as did her husband.

She followed her husband out into the yard at a more leisurely pace, for she had not his optimism that these Nobs would be staying for any length of time. More usually, they had a meal, and perhaps they baited their horses. The Green Man was not a large enough establishment to provide changes of horse, although Mr. Milburn dreamed of doing so. Grace Milburn, far more practical than her spouse, always pointed out that they were too far from any posting road to justify having hoards of horses and ostlers eating their heads off. Why, until the current Lord Lyonshall had come into the area, one seldom even saw dragons in the sky, so far were they from any major posting route. She had had to quash her eager husband's plans for a landing pen for dragon traffic. She did not want any dragons near the Green Man. Being entirely unacquainted with any dragons personally, she thought them to be dangerous, with all that flame and smoke.

Wanda Wycherley was tired, hot and beginning to be in an ill-humor. She certainly hoped that this trip was going to prove worth all her efforts. She had had several new gowns made for this venture, and had to endure three boring days of fittings and being poked with pins. The trip itself had proved tedious – not the least tedious of it was the behavior of Augustus Goodbody. She had banished him to the curricle after the first morning and he had sulked all the way here. He had seemed to think that they would spend the entire trip making love behind the drawn shades of the coach. That was a privilege she reserved for Culver Grindle. At least once a day she called him into the coach and they indulged themselves. It amused her that the coachman and the footmen could hear everything that was going on. Most times, she did not bother to draw the blinds.

In order to keep Goodbody somewhat satisfied, she had had to let him into her bed at night. They had taken separate rooms at each inn of course – she had her reputation to consider – they were passing as 'cousins'. But late at night when everyone was asleep, she admitted him to her chamber. Culver lay in wait – when Goodbody returned to his room, Culver joined her, for as she had feared, Goodbody was no one's idea of a talented lover. By the time she rid herself of him she was frustrated and only Culver's rough handling could satisfy her. Gentlemen! They were far and away too dainty for her taste.

This inn they were to stop at whilst she conducted her campaign of ensnaring the Marquis of Keir looked at least clean and even somewhat pretty, set about by gardens and near a river, at the end of the main street of the village. The latest edition of *Paterson's British Itinerary* had praised this inn, so she assumed it would be free of fleas and the food would at the very least be edible.

She was not best pleased that she had to finance this entire undertaking. Goodbody was all to pieces – in vulgar parlance he had swallowed a spider and she had even had to lay out funds to prevent his being taken up for debt. He had a broker's man installed in his flat – for a debt of £26, 9d. 4p. to a vintner, and there was a possibility of there being an execution in the house for debts owed to various tradesman, including an astronomical bill to his tailor. She had paid up the worst of what he owed, for he was of little use to her if he was in the Fleet for debt. She had taken his snuff box collection as surety that she would be repaid when he was in possession of Lady Diana's fortune. It was only money, though, of which she had a more than adequate supply. As the old saying went, one had to break eggs to make an omelet. And every expenditure, even enduring Goodbody's inexpert fumblings, would be worth those strawberry leaves and being addressed, one day, as "your Grace".

She now alighted from the carriage, handed down by one of the footmen, Henry. Like the other footman, John, he looked hot and bothered, but not from the weather.

Wanda laughed to herself, relishing his discomfort. Less than an hour ago she and Culver had disported themselves in the carriage. Goodbody and the coachman as well, were no doubt in a state of frustrated arousal. Goodbody had been shocked that she slept with her groom. He could accept another gentleman, but not a groom.

Jonas Milburn rushed forward to greet Wanda. "What may I do for you, ma'am?" he queried eagerly, bowing so low as to almost scrape his nose on the ground. There was no crest on the carriage panel, so she was not "my lady", but her clothes, servants and turnout proclaimed money as loudly as if she had announced it.

Removing her gloves, Wanda said, "I shall want your two best rooms, for myself and my cousin, who escorts me. I shall want a private parlour as well – your best, mind you."

Visions of largesse dancing in his brain, Milburn said, "It will be as you wish, ma'am! Our inn, though small, is very fine and you will find everything of the very best! We have even a bathing chamber!"

"That would be most refreshing," Wanda said. Getting out of these hot clothes would be refreshing, too. Her head was beginning to ache from the too tight rim of her plume-laden bonnet, which was bright blue to match the traveling costume. The heat was quite appalling. Laying naked in a tub of cool water, scented by the patchouli scent she favored – utter bliss.

But she supposed that she would have to meet with Augustus Goodbody this afternoon and discuss the how and whys of their little plot. Perhaps she would let him watch her bathe. There were things she could do with a bath sponge that would make him agree to anything she suggested. She had come to realize that most of his ideas were stupid. She needed him but for the magic help he could supply. It was perhaps fortunate for him that she had not as yet seem him perform any magics.

At the look that came over Wanda's face as she thought about her bath sponge, Mrs. Milburn gave an audible sniff. *No better than she should be, that one,* she thought, not impressed by Wanda. It was obvious that the baggage was *not* Quality. She'd better mind her manners here, or she'd find herself on the road on her well-padded rump. And the so-called gentlemen with her, Grace Milburn thought as she eyed Augustus Goodbody – he was a dandy, a type of creature she had no use for, and he was probably that *Madame's* procurer. They'd soon find out this was a good Christian inn if they started any of their wicked Town ways here!

Reverend Arabin sat in front of a small fire. The day had been hot, but the evening was chill, a chill swept in with the thunder that could be heard rumbling in the distance. It looked as if they were going to get some of the violent storms that plagued the Irish Sea.

The Vicar had spent the late afternoon and early evening with Merlin's little book, hoping to find out more about the spell of binding. Ever since that morning, when Lord Lyonshall had visited him and told him the true reason René had gone to Ireland and why, he had felt compelled to search further on in the little volume. He wanted to find if Merlin had written of the aftermath of the spell. It had taken a bit of work – until he found a single page, stuck to the others, written in Medieval Welsh, not in runes. With the aid of a dictionary to make absolutely certain that his translations were indeed accurate, he had rendered it into modern English. And when he finished with it, he wished he had not.

Now, in the firelight, with Plato on his knee and Minou on his shoulder, he held before him the translation. It was written by Merlin, there was no doubt of that. But it was not triumphant, outlining th success of binding the Unselighe Court to the Otherworld. It was a lament.

He had read it once, twice, three times. Now he held it to the firelight so that Plato could read it.

Spectacles gleaming in the dancing light of the flames, Plato read silently to the end. "This is not good," he said at last, "especially given the news Lord Lyonshall brought this morning."

"It is the worst possible news!" the Vicar said. He put the paper down upon his knee and withdrew a large handkerchief from his breast pocket. He removed his spectacles and wiped them, but the difficulties with his vision were moisture in his eyes, not dirty lenses. He wiped his eyes and for good measure, blew his nose noisily. "But if I try to dissuade him," he said miserably, "he will pay me no heed."

He did not have to tell Plato whom he meant – they both understood that he was talking about René.

Mr. Arabin replaced his spectacles on his nose and took up hi translation, to read it once again.

I am heavy hearted and near dry of tears, Merlin had written. *My dear Ninian, he who is like to a son, my natural successor and friend, is dead after three days of horrible suffering. Since the binding, he has sunk further, until there was no return from the depths of pain and madness. He first went blind from the intense white light of power of the ley lines, and weakened by the d-mands of the binding, was easy prey to a virulent fever. At the last he was mad, seeing horrid visions that his outer eyes could no longer see, on the paths of dreams. Naught I could do eased his sufferings. I prayed for his death, for I could do naught else. Oh, Ninian forgive me! It does not seem to matter that his was a willing sacrifice and he whispered to me at the last, when his mind seemed to return, that he had no sorrow in his heart for having given his life to the service of his King and country. We have bound the creatures that have plagued us but at what a price! What a price!*

"That last part was particularly difficult to read," said the Vicar. "The ink was blurred and had run dreadfully."

"Damage from the weather?" Plato inquired.

417

"No," answered the Vicar. "I realized that the damage was from Merlin's tears."

35

The Plots Thicken

In spite of the heat, the Duke of Chenevix rode fast and furiously. He set the horse – Lyon's riding horse, which he had not scrupled to borrow – at every obstacle in their path.

It was not until he noticed the animal's growing distress that he pulled up, cursing himself for a fool. He never mistreated an animal and despised and corrected those who did. He swung off the sweated horse, loosened the girth and began to walk the horse so that it might cool off. When it was completely cool he would find some water for it.

He had ridden a long way. The sun was growing high in the sky, but he had ridden into the woods and beneath the trees it was a trifle cooler.

The wild ride had suited his mood, however. His Grace had awoken in a foul mood – the anger of yester eve still burned fiercely in him and mingled with the anger was shock at Lucie's revelation. Why had she kept this from him? Once she knew that he was of the nobility why had she let him still believe that her background – and that of his heir – was of the *bourgeoisie* – or, as he had sometimes worried – of the peasantry? Marrying her, in spite of the love he felt for her, had been the one impulsive act of his life. He had fought against his feelings for her as well. Stuart had been appalled that his younger brother had married a little French girl. He thought that Carlisle should have taken her as a mistress – to get over his infatuation. But there was something about Lucie – something good and pure that he could not besmirch and remain honorable. No, he had to admit that he did not regret taking her to wife. And to find her again had been a miracle. He would not willingly let her go again.

But his heir – almost he wished that there had been no issue of their union. Why could the boy not see that everything he had been asked to do was for the best? Keir did not know his way about English society. He had no idea how savage the *Beau Monde* could be to one who did not meet their standards. All of this was for his own good.

It was incomprehensible to the Duke that Keir did not want to take his rightful place in Society. To want to keep working as a lowly secretary, to want to teach – it was inconceivable! Chenevix found his heir beyond understanding – stubborn, willful and unreasonable. Chenevix did not realize that his arrogant orders were not the calm reasoning that he imagined them to be. He was far too used to dealing with servants and underlings who had to obey him. He had no idea how to deal with am equal. He gave orders and expected them to be obeyed.

Now he felt that he was at *point non plus*. It was even more incomprehensible to him that everyone else – including Lucie – had taken Keir's side in this matter. No one could see that he, Chenevix, was correct in showing his heir the proper way to go on.

He had expected no better of Lyonshall, of course. There was a man who had flouted the conventions of society all of his life. Only look at that ridiculous beard and the pipe he affected! And never mind the rudeness that was in every utterance – the man had no breeding, no proper feeling, no restraint! And yet he and Keir talked easily together – even laughing with one another. When *he* tried to talk to Keir it was as if a wall of ice stood between them, and there was no laughter. Involuntarily the Duke's fist tightened on the reins, pulling at the horse's mouth.The horse gave a snort of annoyance, letting his rider know that he did not appreciate his mouth being abused.

Chenevix could not admit to himself that he was jealous of the easy relationship between Lyonshall and his heir. It was far less painful to blame Lyonshall or Keir for the failure of what should be a blood affinity.

Scowling, he felt behind the horse's front legs and on his neck. He was cool and no longer blowing. The Duke tightened the girth again and mounted lightly. It was time to go back – time to talk to Lucie and to Keir.

He frowned again as he belatedly remembered that Keir had probably by now departed for Ireland on some trumped-up errand for Lyonshall. He would however, make it clear to Lyonshall that Keir would no longer be working as a secretary to anyone. And his heir was not going to be a Wizard any longer. Lyonshall could handle this upcoming spell to bind the Unselighe Court. Chenevix, his wife and heir would be departing for Chenevix Duchis in Dorset, where tutors and tailors would be hired, to ready them for the Little Season. His Grace intended to resign as Chancellor of Magic – it had been a mistake to accept the post. Readying his dependents to face society so that he need not be put to shame by them was far more important.

The atmosphere at the Abbey during the next three days was as stormy as the weather out of doors. The thunderstorms and pouring rain kept everyone indoors and tempers frayed. Chenevix had argued with everyone – a huge quarrel with Lyonshall, who refused to accept the resignation the Duke penned for René – "I'll accept that when *he* gives it to me!" he snarled at the Duke, "And not before that!"

Ninon had wasted little time before telling the Duke exactly what she thought of his heavy-handed tactics and his unreasonable demands. That argument had not gone well, either, for she was a formidable opponent with a sharp tongue. To his mortification he had ended in slamming out of the room, when she laughed at his plan to take them to Chenevix Duchis. "René will never go, *je vous assure!*" she stated. "To be treated as a schoolboy and give up the magic which all of his life he has wished to practice! You are a fool if you think that he will do this!"

Lady Diana, who he thought might have supported him, was adamant in her refusal to see reason. He had told her that he had thought she had been properly brought up and the respect he had felt for her parents was considerably diminished by her attitude. He realized later that that was most ungentlemanly, but could not bring himself to apologize.

And Lucie – Lucie had merely said that she would ask her son if he would not obey his father. She was subdued and sad and did not wish to talk about anything. "It will be as you say, Lucien," she said listlessly.

And that was the worst of all. That light that shone in her – the laughter, the gaiety, seemed to have gone out. She was no longer so sweet and loving, and rather than do the needlework she delighted in, sat in front of the window for hours, watching the raindrops splash against the glass.

To add to this atmosphere was worry. Due to the very poor atmospheric conditions scrying was virtually impossible, particularly over water as it was so new to the Wizards of the Six Nations They heard nothing from Ireland after the first day. There was little news – even hippogriffes had trouble flying in this weather and the dragon post was disrupted by the heavy lightning and thunder. Such violent weather had not been seen in many a year and many older folk in the village called it unnatural – more than like caused by those Unselighe creatures that were roaming so free.

The *Wizards' Times*, which arrived like clockwork every morning, did not come for two days, and Lyon was driven to use his crystal ball to see what was going on elsewhere. He had never liked the crystal – he thought it wildly inaccurate and ambiguous, with a mind of its own. He longed to know how René had fared in Ireland and was kept from visiting the Vicar and indulging in fruitless speculation, by the violence of the storms. It was simply too dangerous to venture forth. Lightning had actually struck the Abbey and only the fact that Lyon had caused the American Wizard, Mr. Benjamin Franklin's lightning rods to be placed on the roof saved them from a fire.

But the crystal proved to be as disturbed as the scry bowl or any other method. There was nothing to do save wait until the storms passed.

Wanda Wycherley stared morosely out the mullioned window of the *Green Man*. Rain poured from the heavens, obliterating the view of the street. The rain was so heavy that no one was out on the street, not even daring to walk the covered kerb that ran in front of the shops. There were no carriages on the street, either. It was as if everyone and everything had vanished and the whole world was now confined to this wretched inn.

She was both bored and frustrated. Their plan had been decided upon and gone over again and again. She was eager to begin, but this unexpected weather had drawn rein on everything. Not only was the rain too difficult to go out in, but the incessant thunder and lightning was dangerous. Even the regulars in the tap room had failed to show up the last two evenings.

Wanda had never felt such mind-numbing boredom. There was little to do and for one of the first times in her life she was spending all of her hours in the bedroom entirely by herself. That cursed landlady! Mrs. Milburn made certain that no man set a foot inside Wanda's bedchamber – and she had been unable to slip out to the stables to seek Culver, nor even creep into Goodbody's room – even *he* would be a relief at this point! Mrs. Milburn had ears like a cat and the eyes of a hawk. She could not understand that a woman like Wanda needed male companionship – she was in danger of going insane without it.

Behind her at the table of their private parlor Goodbody played yet another game of Patience. He had no skill at it – nor had he any skill at the endless games of piquet to which they were reduced, to make an evening's entertainment. Little wonder he owed debts of honour to all and sundry.

Goodbody would have it that her enforced celibacy was a good thing – she'd have an excellent reputation at this inn without any nonsense – she'd do best not to be in bad loaf with the local moralists until she had a ring on her finger and her marriage lines in her pocket.

Privately, he was in alt that she was such a light-skirt. Proper little ladybird she was! He could only imagine the looks on their faces – all of them who had treated him so badly – when they realized what kind of woman the new Lord Keir had married. If his plan worked properly – and he saw no reason why it should not – Wanda would be a Duchess and he would have Lady Diana and her lovely, lovely money. And he would give Lyonshall and that Froggie their comeuppance.

In a cave in the hills Piers Mildmay too, watched the rain come down. He was as comfortable as was possible in the cave, with said comforts supplied by Sluagh. A fire burned for warmth, a thick pile of bedding lay on a bed of bracken, and he had plenty of good food. The bogle was stealing it from various farms. The bogle was the only creature who did not seem to mind this appalling weather.

Mildmay's only wish was for a news-sheet. He wanted to know what was being said and done about his escape. He had tried to explain to Ainsel what a news-sheet was and how important it could be, but the bogle did not comprehend and brought back a large sheet of coarse brown wrapping paper smelling like a fishmonger's shop. When Mildmay had indicated that this was not what he wanted, the bogle had eaten the paper with every evidence of enjoyment.

Mildmay had seen little of Sluagh – the Elf appeared once – to ask more questions of the man – about the habits of the Arch Druid, most of which Mildmay could not really answer. But the Elf had been surprisingly cooperative with the plan Mildmay had hatched.

He had to get those Frenchies out into the open where he could kill them, and he had woken two nights ago with the plot crystal clear in his brain. He would probably be killed, but if he could take then with him, it would be worth it. Sluagh had been able to get him a gun – Mildmay did not ask where it had been obtained. And Sluagh had promised that Ainsel would help him – that would make it far easier. Mildmay did not know nor care why the Elf was so eager to aid him – he accepted what was offered.

Another thing he missed and would have felt the better for was something fit to drink. The bogle drank some nasty stuff from a flask and, surprisingly, loved milk – he went to a farm at least once a day and stole a pannikin or a pail of milk and brought it back to the cave, smacking his thick lips in satisfaction after he gulped it down. For Piers he brought small beer or cider, when what the baronet wanted was port or better yet, gin.

Gin would help him sleep. Night after night he dreamed of the encounter with the Cremave and awoke shuddering and shaking. His vanished arm gave him an immense amount of pain for something that was no longer there. But the bogle could not understand what Mildmay wanted, and the baronet had to content himself with cider.

How he hated this rain! He blamed it for putting a crimp in his plans. He burned to set them in motion. He could think of nothing else than punishing those Frenchies for his loss and incarceration. He wished that there were some way to punish the Vicar and Lyonshall and his mouse of a sister, too. She had not come to see him the entire time he had been in gaol, nor even sent him a basket of comforts. No, it had been Reverend Arabin who had done that – Mildmay had refused to see him, of course. He did not want the Vicar's sanctimonious piety. Mildmay broke into a torrent of abuse when the guard had informed him that the Vicar was praying for him. He had actually thrown his dinner tray at the guard's head when he was told that Lyonshall had paid for the attorney that had consulted with him and was paying for the extra comforts he was enjoying – better food than the standard gaol fare and a softer bed and bedclothes.

No one else came to see him. His gambling cronies had all deserted him. He had thought they were his friends. Goodbody had returned to London, he presumed. This desertion rankled and he brooded on it whilst in gaol and in the cave, for there was little else to do. The bogle was ill company. He had no conversation other than staring at Piers and whispering "Gobble, gobble," with a lick of his lips. There were no cards or books – not that Mildmay had ever read anything other than pornography or sporting subjects. So he nursed his sense of injury and the wrongs he thought done to himself, fanning them to a flame, cursing the rain and plotting and planning.

The tests had been quite as bad as everyone had warned them, René and Diarmait found. Each day saw them worn out and drained of energy. The second day had been difficult. In separate rooms, each of them had faced a panel of three Masters who felt free to demand lengthy oral answers about every aspect of magic. They were allowed to draw in the air as a visual aid to the answers, but that only – no chalk board or paper was allowed. The questions came rapidly and it was hungry work. They ate all of Aisling's snacks at the rest periods and ate heartily of the delicious fare provided by the University at nuncheon. Each day after they were done, René went with Diarmait to a little pub where they had good Irish stout and thick corned beef sandwiches with pickles, and terrified one another with tales of the difficulty of their particular tests.

The last day was the Practical, where they would actually be doing magic before the *Taoiseach*. This was done in the same room where they had been separately tested on the Orals – since working magic was so fatiguing, they would alternate in demonstrating the problems put to them. Neither would be asked to do the same thing as the other.

The *Taoiseach*, a stern-faced woman, stricken in years, with iron – grey hair, did not make it easy for them. She asked to see everything from the Babylonian Incantation to the raising of the Druid's Mist, threw a demon at René for him to banish and commanded Diarmait to turn water into wine and actually drank it, telling him she would take points away from him if it was corked or not a good year.

At the end of the day both young men were ready to collapse. They had been on their feet all day, save for the brief breaks and nuncheon. The *Taoiseach* could see this and finally announced that she had seen enough. She would meet with the other Masters and a decision would be made as to their grades. Not by the merest flicker of an expression did she let them know whether or not she was pleased with their performances. And fortunately for their nerves they would know before the evening was over exactly how they had scored in each section of the tests, and whether or not they had both made *Magistra*.

She stood up from where she sat behind a long oaken table and gathered up the notes she had made. As she tapped these into order, preparatory to putting them into a leather folder, she said abruptly, "Lord Keir, Conchobar Ó Cléirigh tells me that you are able to dematerialize. Is this so?"

"Yes, your Worship," said René. Diarmait had informed him that this was the proper mode of address for the *Taoiseach*.

"I know you are fatigued, but I would dearly love to see a small demonstration," she said almost wistfully.

"From one side of the room to the other?" he suggested, "I really do not think, *je vous assure*, that I could manage much more than that at this moment."

"That will be more than ample, thank you," she said.

426

He then vanished and reappeared on the other side of the room.

"Fascinating!" she murmured. "Some day I should like to discus with you exactly how that is done. I imagine there are a great many Wizards who would like to discuss it with you. But now I suggest you go and eat something and rest. I can promise you both that we shall have your rankings before eight of the clock this evening. Your lapel pins will be returned at that time." She bowed to then and they bowed in return as she left the room.

"By Paddy's beard, I feel as if I've been doing the magics for a fortnight!" exclaimed Diarmait as they heard the door close behind her.

"I too," René confessed, stretching and rubbing his shoulder. Magic could be very physical. He had held his wand most of the day and now he stowed it in the breast pocket made into every Wizard's jacket that concealed and protected the wand.

Diarmait did the same and said, "D'ye think 'twas more difficult with all of this thunder in the air? I've never seen such lightning in me life!"

"It was certainly not easy to tap the ley lines, yes," René agreed. "There was much power in the air that fought with me."

"They'll be saying that this is unnatural weather – Unselighe weather brought about by the doings of the dark *Sidhe*," said Diarmait.

René was not certain. But he could not recall such violent weather – even as they spoke a huge crash of thunder made the entire ancient building shake and was followed by a flash of lurid green light as an immense bolt of lightning hurtled itself from the clouds.

"That was too close!" Diarmait exclaimed. "Every hair on me head is standing at attention! I tell you, René, we'd best spend the night here. The Augurs claim 'twill clear by tomorrow. This is the worst it's been yet and I'm thinking we'll not get a sensible horse to go out in this. I'll try to scry Aisling at the pub and tell her we're staying."

René agreed with this wholeheartedly. As tired as he was he had not looked forward to the drive back to Tara at a late hour in this terrible storm. Yesterday and this morning had been bad enough. Diarmait was right – it was indeed much worse out than it had been.

It was also nice to think that he had enough money in his pocket to not have to worry about whether or not he could pay for a room. He had plenty to book a good room, tip the servants and pay for a dinner and stand Diarmait a drink or two, and still enough to give Pádraig a thank you tip and still some left over. It was a good feeling, to be independent.

They headed for the cloakroom, for hats and rain capes. Umbrellas had proved useless in the strong winds, even for Wizards.

But before they had quite reached the cloakroom, they heard someone hurrying along the stone passageway and calling, "Lord Keir! Lord Keir! Pray, may I have a moment?"

René and Diarmait exchanged glances. Had the results from their examinations come so soon? Surely not! They turned to face the caller and saw Niáll Mac Cárthaigh, secretary to the Dean of Trinity College of Magical Studies, Declan Ó Floinn.

The secretary was a short, bald, chubby man, with a round face and a pair of always askew spectacles. He speeded up as he drew near them, his blue Wizard's robes flying out behind him. He skidded to a stop before then and panted a moment before he got out, "Most important message! The Dean has been after authorizing me to offer you, Lord Keir, a teaching position in our faculty, with especial attention being given to teaching the ancient language of trees and their magic, and the teaching of dematerialization. There would be after being a handsome numeration, a house available near the University, and an honorary baccalaureate should you be accepting the position!" he beamed at René. "We were wanting to get our bid in before those Englishers at Oxford and Cambridge did so!"

René was stunned. Here what he had always wanted was being handed to him! And he could not accept immediately as he wanted to.

"Please to be after saying yes," said Mac Cárthaigh beguilingly. "The staff was being impressed with ye and we know ye would like living in *Dubh Linn*," he added, giving the city its Irish name.

"I must give this some thought," René said slowly, "I had not expected – *je vous suis très reconnaissant.* I am most grateful for the offer."

"You can be taking all the time you need!" said the secretary agreeably. "'Tis an important decision, after all. I wish you good day, young sirs. Ye'll contact me as soon as you make your decision?"

"Without fail, *je vous promesse,*" promised René.

"Man, are ye crazed?" Diarmait burst out as Mac Cárthaigh bustled off down the hall. "Ye told me it was always your greatest wish to teach at University – now here's your chance and ye've got to think on it! And Aisling and I would like it fine if you were to settle this near us!"

"I want to say yes, *mon ami,*" said René, "but I can not in all honour accept a position that I may not be here to fill."

"Whatever are you meaning by that?" Diarmait's voice was sharp. He did not like the look on his friend's face.

"I have agreed to be the locus for the spell of binding," René said quickly.

"Holy Máire, Mother of God!" swore Diarmait. "Ye *are* insane!"

36

Scraping Up An Acquaintance

When Simon awoke it was, for the first time in three days, to a room flooded with sunlight. And something was jumping up and down on his chest.

"Hello! Hello!" said a squeaky little voice.

Simon rubbed his eyes to fully awaken and stared into Janus' bi-coloured face. "You're talking!" he exclaimed in delight, sitting up against the pillows. Janus bounded from his chest to the top of the bedclothes, stiff-legged. Her little tail was straight up, every hair standing out as if she had been struck by the recent lightning. She jumped up and down, repeating "Hello! Hello!" over and over again, delighted with herself.

It was only with difficulty that Simon was able to grab her and stop her. "When did you start talking?" he asked, catching her up in his arms and cuddling her against him.

"When I woke up!" she said excitedly. "I woke up a little while ago and yawned and then I said to myself, out loud 'I wonder what is for breakfast this morning?' and realized I was talking like a human! And now that brother of mine can't be so superior!" she added in satisfaction.

The Reverend Arabin had voiced the opinion that the kittens were speaking so early because of all the magicians in the Abbey, The process by which a familiar learned to talk was not really understood. It was thought they somehow tapped into the magic of their particular Witch or Wizard. They should have not been able to speak, for animals lacked the vocal equipment necessary for human speech. But all familiars could and did speak, and they began speaking in fully articulated sentences, unlike a human child. They learned to read as easily – a familiar that on Monday was using a primer could be reading Aristotle by Friday. Many Wizards at University level were studying the phenomenon, eager to apply it to human learning. But so far their endeavors had come to naught. How and why a familiar learned was still a mystery.

Simon was thrilled – it would be fun having a furry best friend to study, talk and play with. As much as he liked most of the adults in the household he often longed for someone near his own age. And a talking kitten would fill the bill nicely.

"Hurry, Simon!" urged Janus. "Hurry and get dressed so that I can show the others I can talk! It is too bad humans have to wear clothing! Fur is so much easier!"

Laughing, Simon reached for the bell-pull by the bed to summon Sanders. He felt his spirits rising. He had spent much of the past several days here in his room. The constant arguing that had gone on in the house had made him feel rather sick. He could not help but think that some of it was his fault, particularly when he heard the Duke and Uncle Lyon talking – no, talking was far and away too mild a word for what had passed between them – about Mr. Roussillon still teaching Simon his lessons. Simon could never remember to say or even think 'Lord Keir'. Hopefully, his tutor would return from his Irish errands today and their lessons could resume.

Simon missed Tuathail also – he spent a good amount of time with the dragon, listening to Irish legends and tales of the *Sidhe*. Tuathail would be full of new stories, for his father was a dragon-bard, and Simon found the stories about the dragon's family, a large and active one, fascinating as well.

It seemed as if everyone had slept late this morning, for the breakfast table was full when Simon went belowstairs. This was not surprising, for the sheer savagery of the storm had made sleep difficult. Last night had been the worst – fright-ening in its intensity, with constant thunder that shook even the stone walls and floors of the Abbey and a strange, unearthly lightning repeatedly flashing.

But this morning everything had changed. As was so often the case after a wild, ferocious storm the sky was astonishingly clear. The entire out-of-doors sparkled in the sunlight. There were many signs of the severity of weather just past. In the garden outside the French doors many flowers were flattened by the force of the rain and wind and would have to be staked up or cut today. Branches and leaves were scattered here and there over the lawns and Uncle Lyon was planning to ride out this morning to survey the damage, for his bailiff had already called with reports of flooding, damaged buildings and ruined crops.

But everything looked clean and fresh and brand-new. It even smelled new.

"I had an early scry from Ireland this morning," said Lyon, in a most amiable mood. "René should be back about noon-time, barring bad weather over the Irish sea. However, it seems as though the weather in Ireland is as beautiful as it is here and he anticipates no problems."

Chenevix looked at him sourly. When had Lyonshall become on Christian name terms with his heir?

Lyon ignored Chenevix's displeasure and said, "Simon, you look as if you are bursting with news! Pray what is it?"

"Janus has begun talking!" Simon said proudly.

He was roundly congratulated by Ninon and Diana, as well as Lyon. Lucie had been paying no attention to what anyone said, pushing a bit of egg back and forth on her plate with her fork as if she had no interest in aught else.

"I can talk, too!" came another voice rather indignantly, and Rascal came trotting across the room from the cats' breakfast bowls, and demanded that Diana pick him up. Even though he could jump he preferred that she help him into her lap, stretching out an imperative paw.

"*Moi aussi,*" came a second voice as Neige made herself heard. "And I," she added smugly "can speak French!"

"Are we to waste the morning listening to the babble of animals?" demanded the Duke. "Duchess, you'd best direct your abigail to pack your things. Once Keir has arrived the three of us will be departing for Chenevix Duchis."

Ninon and Diana exchanged looks that to the Duke appeared amused and disbelieving. He was further enraged when Lyon snorted and said, "You'll catch cold at that, Chenevix. I've already discussed this morning, with the man

432

himself, what René will be doing when he gets back today and believe me, it is not leaving for Dorsetshire! But there's no reason why you and the Duchess cannot leave!" he added hopefully.

Lucie had raised her head slowly when the Duke ordered her to get ready to leave. She disliked the way he always called her Duchess in public. He had scolded her for calling him Lucien in front of family and friends. Christian names, for people of their rank, were only to be used in the most intimate of settings. And she must learn to call their son Keir, not René. Her mother too, was to be *Madame la Duchesse*. To use intimate terms in front of servants and inferiors was simply insupportable.

"I do not wish," she said, "to go to Dorset at all. *Je vais rester ici.*"

"We are leaving for Dorset – all of us – by one this afternoon, Duchess, and you had best be ready," said the Duke in his iciest tones. "I shall not scruple to direct the footmen to carry you to the carriage if necessitated by this stupid obstinacy."

"Now look here, Chenevix!" roared Lyon. "Those are MY footmen you are talking about and you'll tell them to do no such thing! The Duchess is more than welcome to stay does she choose not to go with you! But as for you – you've worn out your welcome long ago – what is the saying – dead fish and guests stink after three days? We've had just about enough of what you want, and you riding roughshod over all and sundry."

"How dare you!" said the Duke his voice shaking in rage," How dare you interfere in my affairs!"

"You've been interfering in my affairs since you came here – unwanted – back in May!" returned Lyon heatedly. "I think I've been the soul of forbearance! So many times I wanted to pitch you out of the window! I bloody well wish I had!"

Seeing that this quarrel was about to descend to nursery level or fisticuffs, Diana judged it best to intervene. "That will be quite enough!" she said sharply. "There is no excuse for this sort of rudeness. Uncle, you will remember that his Grace is a guest in this house. And as for you, my Lord Duke, your wife and son are of age and capable of making their own decisions. This should be discussed in private."

Both Chenevix and Lyon glared at her but nonetheless subsided, resuming their seats, for in the violence of their passions they had come to their feet. Ninon looked at Diana approvingly while Simon's eyes seemed to fill his whole face. Lucie had gone back to chasing her egg about her plate.

"Why don't they just roll around on the floor and scratch and hiss?" came Beau's voice. He had been quiet since it had been revealed that his brother and sisters could speak. He was not in a good mood – he missed René dreadfully and was taken aback that his siblings were now at his level. He would have to come up with something to reassert his superiority as the eldest. "Human quarrels are so stupid," he added blightingly.

The Duke stood abruptly. "I will not be taught my manners by a kitten!" and he stalked from the room, with an abrupt bow to the ladies.

"*That* was a wonderful display of manners!" said Lyon.

"Oh, Uncle, do be quiet!" Diana begged, rubbing her forehead tiredly. There had been so many raised voices lately, so many arguments – it had become wearisome indeed. And for the last few days she had felt as if something was missing, something vital. When she arose in the morning it was to a feeling that the day stretching out before her was flat and dull. She supposed that it was this wretched weather. Witness how much better she felt this morning with the incredible improvement in the meteorological conditions – if there were only an end to these wretched altercations!

Wanda Wycherley rose at, what was for her, an unusually early hour – eight in the morning. She pushed her maid, an aptly named angular female named Grimstock, who had hitherto traveled in the baggage coach, to have her baggage packed in record time and had the footmen loading it on the coach by nine. She wanted to implement her plan immediately and she could not bear another hour in this inn under the gimlet eye of Mrs. Milburn. As soon as the coach was out of sight of the inn she intended to stop it and have Culver in. She had purposely donned a gown that was not at

434

all difficult to shed and had not worn any underpinnings – not that she ever wore much besides a body stocking, usually flesh-coloured. She also damped the few petticoats she wore, so that they would cling to her figure. But today she wore naught but a light frock, silk stockings, and garters. It made her feel delightfully sinful and eager for Culver's embraces. She had gone as long as she could without a man and intended to remedy this appalling situation as soon as possible. In fact, she planned to stop the coach in the forest of Knyghtwood she had heard about and sample the delights of the footmen and the coachman as well. Thus fortified, she could go onto the Abbey and arrive there just before nuncheon. With Culver's and the coachman's help her carriage was going to break down right at the gates. They would be obliged to offer her hospitality, particularly if she was so much shaken by the 'accident' that she could not go on. Augustus had put a spell on the carriage to make it even worse than Culver's meddling with it. In her reticule was his irresistible perfume – he had taught her the Words to activate its enchantment. She was quite confident of winning her objective – she might not have been so, had she realized how untalented a Wizard was Augustus Goodbody.

Grimstock packed a portmanteau for her mistress with a somewhat more demure gown in it to wear after her encounter in the forest. It mattered little to Grimstock how many men her mistress entertained. She turned not a hair at the sight of a regular orgy. She was exceedingly well-paid to dress and undress – primarily *undress* – Wanda and to keep her mouth shut as well. She was fully aware of the plan to ensnare the Marquis of Keir – since Goodbody had blotted his copybook with those at the Abbey Wanda needed a confederate and Hannah Grimstock was ideal – being completely without scruples. Grimstock liked the idea of being maid to a Duchess – it would increase her status amongst other servants and she was growing rich from all the vails gathered from Wanda's male 'friends'. And Wanda had promised her a considerable rise in salary once the Marquis was well and firmly caught.

Grimstock had already made a small fortune from allowing certain men to view Wanda's 'activities' when her mistress was entertaining the lower class men she favored, such as grooms and laborers. The maid made certain that they greased her palm thoroughly before she let them watch Wanda and her 'friends' from a hidden room. Wanda's bedroom was as heavily trafficked as was Hyde Park at the hour of the fashionable promenade, since Wanda's tastes were eclectic and her appetite insatiable. Wanda was fully aware that Grimstock allowed viewings of her amorous encounters – she thought it a great joke and an added fillip of excitement. Wanda neither knew nor cared if any of the men knew they were being viewed

To leave the inn, for her thin muslin was almost transparent, she had to wrap herself in a large Norwich silk shawl. That old besom, the landlady, sniffed disapprovingly as Augustus handed Wanda into the coach. Wanda could tell by the way Goodbody sweated and licked his lips that he knew just how little she was wearing. He was remaining behind – 'twas best if they were not seen together.

Culver was to be their messenger. The groom did not care whom she married, or even whom she welcomed to her bed, as long as she ended up with him. Since she found him and his rough ways the most satisfying of all her partners, there was little danger of him being ousted from what few real affections she possessed.

The carriage was scarcely well into the woods before she shed her gown and called to Culver and the three other menservants to join her. She had three, almost four days of deprivation to make up in only a few hours.

Simon was at the dragon pen, patiently waiting. The time was near noon and at any moment Tuathail would come down from the sky with his passenger. It was so clear that Simon would be able to see the green dragon coming a long ways off.

Behind him, near the house, Ninon and Simon's Mama were at work in the gardens. The house was going to be bursting with blooms, for many of them had been too beaten down by the blows of the rain and wind and could not be salvaged as ornaments to the garden. With judicious cutting, however, they might be able to adorn the house.

Simon could hear the two women talking softly and laughing as they worked. It was not at all hot today and being out of doors was so pleasant, especially after being shut up inside for the last few days.

With Simon waited all four kittens. They made a great deal more noise now that they could talk and seemed to squabble quite a bit. Beau held himself aloof from the others, sitting upright on the edge of the dragon pen, staring into the sky. After all, it was *his* Wizard that was arriving. Simon had been amazed to find out that the kittens considered the humans their property – the Wizards belonged to the kittens, not the other way around.

"I see the dragon!" Beau squeaked, sitting up on his hind legs and nearly tumbling over. They were still at he awkward stage and did bit have the bodily control they would have when they were fully grown.

But their eyesight was excellent. Simon had to shade his eyes and squint to make out a faint speck in the sky. But as it drew closer and closer he could see that yes, it was a dragon and most definitely Tuathail.

"Come on," he said to the kittens. They must needs clear the dragon pen area so that Tuathail had room to land.

They scampered after him as he ran towards the garden calling "Mama! Aunt Ninon! They're coming!"

They all stood in a group watching as the dragon came closer and closer and then began to spiral down, landing at last with an audible thump in front of the dragon pen.

As soon as Tuathail folded his great wings they ran forward. René scarcely had time to slid off Tuathail and remove his flying helmet and gloves before Ninon was hanging about his neck, Simon clung to his waist and Beau was trying to climb up his leg. Diana hung back a little, smiling brightly. It was indeed a wonderful day – the sun was suddenly brighter, the air sweeter and the summer chorus of birds more beguiling. She had never known herself to be so affected by weather before.

"*Doucement! Doucement!*" said René, laughing. "It as if I have been gone a year and it was feared I was dead!"

He returned their embraces and looked at Diana over the tops of their heads. He caught his breath almost painfully as he looked at her, for the look on her face was everything that he could have wished to see. She seemed every bit as glad to see him as did Ninon, Simon and Beau.

437

"Welcome back," she said, with a still deeper smile. "How did you find Ireland?"

"It is a beautiful country," he answered, "with friendly people. I liked it very much."

"Come inside, René!" said Ninon impatiently. "You must be hungry and you may tell us all about Ireland."

"First I must make Tuathail comfortable and see that he has his dinner –"

Daniel, Simons' groom, came up and touched the brim of his cap. "Me an' Sam 'll take care o' that, me lord. We'll get his harness off an' give him a nice oil bath while he eats his meal. Promised to tell us all about Ireland, he did."

René thanked him and Tuathail sighed in bliss. Dragons' skin could dry out and they needed to be oiled regularly to prevent itching.

René retrieved some packages from the breast harness and thanked Tuathail for a wonderful trip. It had indeed been enjoyable – even the flight over the ocean, for the air was clear, the deep blue sea covered in sun diamonds and the air temperature just right for long glides. At one point they had skimmed the surface of the sea and swung low over a fleet of fishing ships. There were many dragons and hippogriffes in the air and once, far off, they saw an entire herd of flying horses. Below them, mermaids and mermen, sea-horses and other Sea-Folk had leaped up to the dragon's shadow. Having grown up on the coast, Tuathail was acquainted with many of the Sea-Folk and they all seemed to want to greet him. Even a sea serpent had raised its great head to rumble a greeting as they flew over the blue waters, which today were calm and peaceful.

They paused briefly in the hall for René to shed his flying suit and give it into the care of as footman. Seppings bowed and said, "It is very gratifying to have your Lordship returned to us. I trust you found Ireland agreeable?"

"Most agreeable, thank you, Seppings," said René. "But I am glad to have returned."

Lucie came running down the stairs and flung herself at her son.

"René, René!" she almost sobbed. Then, in French too rapid for Diana to follow she said, "I do not wish to go to

438

Dorset! You do not wish to go to Dorset, do you? Tell your Papa that we will not go to Dorset! He will not listen to me!"

"Dorset?" René repeated blankly, distressed at her outburst, for although he did not know why she was so upset, he could hear the anguish in her voice.

He lifted his eyes to the Duke, who had followed Lucie down the stairs at a more sedate and proper pace. His Grace wore a deep frown as he watched Lucie's actions.

"We are going to Dorsetshire, to Chenevix Duchis, this afternoon – all of us," said Chenevix in answer to René's unspoken inquiry. "There we will begin preparing for your entry into Society."

"It is always what *you* want!" said Ninon scornfully. "As if no one has the right to think even their own thoughts! *Pipette venimeuse!*" She took Lucie from René's arms and took her daughter into her own embrace, patting Lucie soothingly on the shoulder, assuring her in French that she need not go anywhere.

Lyon entered at this moment and took in the situation at a glance. "Not again!" he groaned. "Chenevix, can you not ever be reasonable? Only look at all of the fuss and furor you are causing!"

"Be so good as to be quiet, Lyonshall!" snapped the Duke. "This is none of your affair!"

"It is my affair when you attempt to take my secretary from me – and no gentleman would stand aside and see a lady made so unhappy," Lyon returned in a far more moderate tone than he usually employed in taking to Chenevix.

"He is no longer your secretary, Lyonshall!" the Duke was rapidly losing what little control he still had over his temper. "I had thought that I made that perfectly clear – even to one of your limited intellect!"

"But of course I am still Lord Lyonshall's secretary!" protested René in some heat. "I have no wish to end the association at the present time and you, your Grace, have not the right to decide for me!"

His Grace drew a long breath. This was defiance and filial disobedience taken to its length! He went closer to René and gave him his most arctic stare. They were of a height – grey eyes met silver.

Look at him! Chenevix thought in disgust, surveying his heir. He had ought to have retreated to his chamber to repair the ravages of dragon flight – his hair was in need of combing, his cravat a crumpled wreck and his coat wrinkled. How dare he present himself to his parents in such a state? And now this recalcitrance!

"You, sirrah –" he began and then his disdainful glance fell on René's lapel, where a pin gleamed with enameled mistletoe leaves, a tapered Wizard's crystal and a new addition – a tiny golden dragon with fully outstretched wings and sapphire eyes perched on the crystal.

"Where had you that?" Chenevix demanded, almost hissing in his rage. "I told you that you were to give up magic – not obtain your Mastery! Is that what you were doing in Ireland?" He turned on his heel and looked daggers at Lyon. "This is, all of it, your fault!" he accused.

"I only helped him to what he wanted," said Lyon. He was growing very tired of Chenevix. "Which you would have done if you were any sort of decent father."

At the look of absolute rage that came over the Duke's face Simon shrank back against Diana's skirts, his hand rapidly inserted into hers. How could Mr. Roussillon be so calm when his father was so angry?

"You will cease your interference at once!" ordered Chenevix, leveling a finger at Lyonshall.

"No!" said René harshly. "*You* will cease your interference in my life! I am of age and I am not feeble-minded! I will make the decision of what I wish to do! *Laissez-moi tranquille!*"

Leave me in peace. It was out in the open at last. No more just walking away from the tyrannical commands. It was time to settle this for once and all.

As if this were not enough to put the Duke into the first stages of an apoplexy, Beau, who had climbed up to René's shoulder, stuck out his little pink tongue at the Duke and made a very rude noise.

His Grace lunged at the kitten, but René moved backwards very quickly, tucking the kitten into the curve of his arm and placing a protective had over him. It was very naughty of Beau, but one part of René agreed with the kitten's ill-manners.

At this rather inauspicious moment Seppings, a silent audience to the argument, cleared his throat loudly. "Pray excuse me, your Graces, my lords and lady, but Robert informs me there is a carriage come to grief at our gates and there is a lady and her servants, perhaps injured." No one, in the throes of violent disagreement, had heard the knock upon the door, nor heard Robert's quiet conversation with a liveried manservant.

"We must offer her our hospitality," said Diana quickly. "Is anyone in need of a physician?"

"That has not as yet been ascertained, my lady," said Seppings. "But Robert tells me a wheel is come off the vehicle and it lies upon its side."

"We'd best go and see what we may do at once!" announced Lyon, nodding at René. They were out the door before he had finished speaking.

"I shall see to having rooms readied and Simon, do you go to the still room and fetch the vinaigrette I keep there." Diana, not prone to fainting fits, seldom carried smelling salts on her person as did many ladies, to whom a swoon was as common as a yawn.

As Simon ran off and Diana began to confer with Seppings, Ninon took the opportunity to lead Lucy into the drawing room. She was certain that Lucie would be the better for a glass of sherry.

Chenevix was left standing in the hall, with no outlet for his continued rage.

Augustus Goodbody was an incompetent idiot! He was a humbug, a Friday-faced mooncalf! Wanda was disgusted with him. She struggled to right herself. The carriage lay upon its side and she could tell that the damage was extensive. It was supposed to have merely dropped upon the rear axle when the wheel came off, and bent the axle. That would take a wheelwright and a blacksmith to fix the damage – which probably would have meant spending at least one night at the Abbey. If she could not inveigle Lord Keir into compromising her virtue in a day and a night's worth of time it would seem that she had lost her touch. After all, that was how she had snared all of her five husbands into Parson's mousetrap. None of them had actually wished to marry her.

Now, due to Goodbody's bungling, she lay atop Grimstock, both of them covered in broken glass. Wanda had struck her elbow on the ornate dressing case Grimstock always carried in her lap. And her right ankle gave sharp stabs of pain. Her gown was torn, her bonnet ruined, and she was missing one sandal – not the one on the injured foot.

Beneath her Grimstock moaned piteously. Wanda had no pity for her, however. The stupid woman had refused to let go the holding strap – what sporting young gentlemen called the Jesus-strap because one prayed so hard when clutching it during a turn-over – and had wrenched her shoulder – in fact it was probably dislocated.

From outside Wanda could hear the horses, terror stricken, and one of the wheelers was trying to kick the carriage to flinders. She thought of how much she had paid for the coach and determined to add it to the sum of Goodbody's debts, unless she wrung his scrawny neck first.

Someone was screaming in pain and the coachman was shouting directions to cut the team loose. She heard someone climbing over the body of the coach and then Culver looked in at the window, looking down on them.

"You all right?" he demanded.

"Do I *look* all right?" she snapped. "Get me out of here!"

He moved slightly, sending more shards of glass raining down upon them. Wanda shrieked. "Get me out of here!"

"Need help t' do that," he pointed out. "Coachman 'as 'is 'ands full wi' th' 'orses. Footman's got a broke leg; t'other's out cold – fainted dead away after walkin' up to the 'ouse. 'elp's comin', though."

Wanda had never much patience at the best of times and the present circumstances wore what little she had left dangerously thin. She wanted out of this catastrophe now!

She managed to get herself off of Grimstock, who was grey-faced with pain.

A second face appeared by Culver's. Although she had never met him, she recognized Lord Lyonshall at once. Engravings of his distinctive bearded face had been in all of the news-sheets as of late.

"Good day, ma'am," he said politely. "We'll have you out of there in a trice. Your maid looks to be in bad case."

Grimstock opened her eyes and looked at him in a dazed fashion. "It's my shoulder," she moaned, as a single tear rolled down her gaunt cheek.

"I've sent for a physician," said Lyon. "Now, we'll fetch you ladies from this dilemma and make you comfortable in the Abbey." He turned his head and spoke to someone behind him. "We'll need a rope – no, don't go to the stables – we'll make one. 'Twill be more comfortable. Send me a good strong strand."

Almost immediately a double twisted violet rope began to snake its way down to Wanda. She grabbed at it.

"No, no, ma'am!" admonished Lyonshall. "Let the rope do the work – it knows what it is about."

Indeed it did, for it inserted itself about her and tied itself in a neat knot.

"Both hands on the rope now and we'll have you up!" encouraged Lyonshall.

And as the rope lifted her Wanda spoiled what was supposed to be a grand entrance by fainting dead away.

37

The Trap Is Sprung

As Wanda Wycherley, fainting, was borne into the Abbey, Augustus Goodbody was reconnoitering in the forest of Knyghtwood. His plan called for a specific place in which to lay a trap for his intended victim. It had to be a place where it was not easy to turn in or to escape – perhaps a place that was rather dark and intimidating to female sensibilities. Augustus Goodbody, like far too many men, had little opinion of female courage or resourcefulness. Women were easily frightened, easily manipulated, poor-spirited creatures.

He had hired a horse from the small livery in Knightswold and soon thought of it as the greatest slug he had crossed in his life. The horse thought him the worst rider she had ever endured. He ended in tying her to a tree and walking through the forest, casting about for a suitable place.

Knyghtwood was a friendly wood, full of ancient trees, pools of sunlight and a fast-running, sparkling river that emptied eventually into the Severn. The terrain was hilly and there were rocky outcroppings here and there. The road was narrow in places but it was not until Goodbody, limping slightly, for his fashionable be-tasseled Hessian boots were rather tight, went around a sharp turn and found the ideal place for his heinous plan.

There were rocks on each side of the road, making it almost like a tunnel. A carriage could not be turned here, even one driven by a Nonesuch, and to Goodbody's delight, the entire atmosphere of the forest changed in this little stretch. For not only did the large escarpments of rock block the sunlight but the trees here were dark and twisted – bent

444

firs who clung precariously to the rock, with little sustenance save for the small patch of soil to which they desperately held. Had Goodbody but known it, these sour, bitter trees had aligned themselves with the Unselighe Court and that was what gave the area its dark, oppressive feeling. Anyone driving this part of the road drove quickly, for horses were uneasy and liked to linger no more than did their drivers. The only ones like to linger were creatures such as Ainsel the bogle or highwaymen.

Goodbody was thrilled with the place he selected. It might have been made for just such an operation as he contemplated. There was even a stand of scrub pine in which to hide.

He was glad of this hiding place a few moments later, for he heard a sudden fall of rock as something came down the rock face, cursing and swearing. Goodbody dived into the protective cover of the scrub, inserting himself into the thickest part of it, and lying as flat as he could.

Looking out upon the road he could see naught but a pair of dusty boots, scratched and worn. They had once been very good boots – the type worn in the hunting field, with turned down white tops – and Goodbody recognized the master hand of Hoby of London.

He then heard a voice angrily ordering. "You – Ainsel! Bring your greasy hide down here! This looks as if it would be just the place we are looking for!"

Goodbody blinked in surprise. He knew that voice! He had thought never to hear it again – for was not Sir Piers Mildmay in gaol – awaiting the assizes?

There was another scrambling noise and something landed on the road, heavily. Goodbody could not make out what it was. He judged it better to remain where he was, rather than make himself known to the baronet.

Then Goodbody heard a quite horrible hissing voice say "Someone's a–spyin' on us, he is! I smells him! Right there in that bush!"

A loud click sounded And then Mildmay shouted, "Out of there at once! I've a pistol and 'tis cocked and loaded!"

A pistol! With an alacrity he seldom exhibited Goodbody was up and out of the brush, oblivious to the pine needles and other debris clinging to his as yet unpaid for bottle-green coat and exquisitely tinted fawn breeches. He had lost his bell-crowned hat in the brush.

"Goodbody!" swore Sir Piers. "What are you doing here?" He did not lower the gun.

"I might ask you the same question!" Goodbody was emboldened by the fact that Mildmay was more than likely a fugitive from justice and in no position to be making demands. Emboldened, that is, until his eyes focused on what stood behind Mildmay.

It was a creature from his worst nightmares. Unlike Mildmay, he knew what it was, for his Wizard's studies, minimal as they had been, had included a semester of academics on the Unselighe creatures of old. He had been young enough at that time for them to make a sizeable impression on his small brain. It could be naught else but a bogle. As he stared at it in trepidation it hissed at him and whispered, "Gobble, gobble," licking its lips in a particularly revolting fashion.

It was obviously in company with Mildmay, for the baronet barked at it, "Give over! He may be useful to us."

Mildmay then turned his attention back to Goodbody. "I want an explanation as to what you are doing here, Goodbody, and I want it now, or, by God, I'll shoot you where you stand! I'm already wanted for attempted murder and I care not if I kill you."

Goodbody ran his tongue over suddenly dry lips and felt his heart careening wildly. He did not doubt for one minute that Mildmay would shoot him without a qualm, for the baronet looked haggard and desperate.

"I am here for my revenge," he said and outlined to Mildmay what he and Wanda had planned.

Sir Piers cared naught for Wanda Wycherley and her chances of obtaining a coronet, but he thought that some elements of Goodbody's plan might serve to draw the Frenchies and perhaps Lyonshall as well into his clutches, where he might then dispose of them all. The more aid he had, the easier it would be.

He at last lowered the gun and said, "I think we can be of mutual benefit, Goodbody. I have the help of Ainsel here and I have the advantage of knowing every inch of these woods. We should talk. I've a snug little cave and some cider. We'll talk over a keg."

"My horse – " began Goodbody, gesturing to where the horse was tethered.

"Ainsel will take care of it," said Mildmay, and turned to glare at the bogle. "And I don't mean for you to eat it! Take it to where no one can see it!"

Ainsel looked disappointed but ran off to do Mildmay's bidding. Sluagh had told him to obey the baronet, but promised that Ainsel could gobble him when the baronet's usefulness was at an end.

"And now you, sirrah, come with me," Sir Piers pointed the pistol to a cliff above the road. "We must needs talk further."

Within two hours Wanda Wycherley had the Abbey at sixes and sevens, the servants run off their feet and everyone wishing her at Jericho.

No one had ever suffered such pain – she was certain that she was crippled for life. She paid no attention to her far more seriously injured servants – the Wizard Healer fetched from Cheltenham via the scry bowl *had* to attend her first.

But he was a sensible man and a cursory examination of Wanda reveled a bumped elbow and a slightly sprained ankle. He was far more concerned with the continued unconsciousness of one footman, the broken leg of the other, and Grimstock's dislocated shoulder. Dr. Paget was well aware of Ninon's skills with herbology and took her aside to request that she brew a cup of valerian tea for Mrs. Wycherley and quiet the incessant whining while he tended to others who needed his help far more urgently.

Ninon was glad to do so, for she had taken an instant dislike to Wanda. She knew the type all too well – she had seen just such opportunistic *chiens méchant* at Versailles on the few occasions she had Louis had attended the King and Queen. She did not like the speculative way that *prositutée* looked at René when they were introduced.

Diana accompanied her to the still-room, leaving Giselle and Susan, the maids, to attend to Wanda.

Diana lit the brazier with a quick flame from her fingertips while Ninon drew water from the small cistern that was kept full of purified water for the easy preparation of spells and *tisanes*. She poured this into a small copper kettle, which she handed to Diana.

"I have seen her type before," said Ninon darkly as she put some valerian, chamomile and mint into a mortar and began to grind it vigorously with the pestle. "She needs no magic to entice men into her nets!"

"She has no magic at all – in fact her aura is a sickly colour," Diana remarked. "Any of the gentlemen in this household would not disregard that, even should they be attracted to her. And I doubt any of them have taste in females that poor!" Like Ninon, she had not been enamored of Mrs. Wycherley. Diana hoped her stay was a very short one.

"All the same, me, I will keep the eye to her," stated Ninon.

"Perhaps the gentlemen will stay in the Tower – and keep Simon there with them," Diana suggested. She had not wanted Simon exposed to the dubious charms of Mrs. Wycherley, particularly when some less than lady-like expressions had escaped her lips.

"*C'est très ennuyeux!*" sighed Ninon. "Do you know of this woman, Diana? Is she of good *Ton*?"

Diana had begun to cut a small square of muslin which would serve as a steeping bag for the tea. "I shouldn't think she is of any breeding whatsoever. There is something rather vulgar about the cut of her gown and her toenails are gilded!"

"And she wears *les cosmétiques*," Ninon added. That high colour in her cheeks was rouge, of a certainty, and her darkened lashes had left smudges on her cheeks.

A meow sounded ay her feet and Neige jumped up on the worktable, followed by Rascal.

"You two are being *catty*," said Rascal severely. "Perhaps she is a nice woman when one comes to know her."

"No, she is not!" said Neige in protest. "Did you not hear her when Beau went up to her? 'Get that thing away from me!' she said to the doctor. 'I hate cats! They're nasty, sneaky and dirty!'"

"Dirty!" exclaimed Rascal in heat. "Why, we cats are the cleanest animals that there are! How dare she! She's an old cow!"

"Even our cats have the good taste, *non?*" laughed Ninon as the water began to boil. "This valerian will shut her mouth for the while, *n'est-ce pas?*"

Dr Paget declared Wanda's ankle to be slightly strained and her elbow in good condition – she would have bruises, but no real damage. He set the footman's leg, and put Grimstock's shoulder back into place. Once this was done the maid-servant was nearly as good as new. The other footman he removed by dragon transport to his surgery. The young man had a concussion and Dr Paget wanted to keep a close watch on him. Culver and the coachman sustained little injury other than cuts and bruises. The carriage, however, was nearly a total loss.

After a long sleep Wanda awoke in the morning ready to get on with her plan. She had slept so deeply that she was suspicious of what had been in that *tisane* that old Witch had offered her. She would have to watch that old woman – her *and* Chenevix, who had turned cold eyes upon her when she was carried into the house and awoke from her faint. He frankly scared her. She had never encountered such a frigid stare that seemed to say he saw straight down into her soul and that he despised what he saw.

She had not much opinion of her soon-to-be spouse. She disliked his physical type – tall and slender – and he did not pay her too much attention, which she found both insulting and unfathomable, particularly when she compared herself to Lady Diana. Now there was a female who had little or no bosom, compared to Wanda's overly ample charms, and she used no arts to attract. She had no idea how to use her body or her eyes, although Wanda did have to admit that those violet eyes were very fine. What she, Wanda, could do with a pair of eyes that size and colour! But they were wasted on Miss Prunes and Prisms. She'd probably be a hatchet-faced, skinny old tough before she was forty, Wanda thought in satisfaction. She could not understand what Augustus saw in her.

Wanda did not like the way Lyonshall looked at her either, as if he found her amusing. Nor did she like the fact that the house was over run with cats. And talking cats at that! It only wanted that to make them completely obnoxious.

Grimstock, up and about again, did a little discreet questioning of the servants and found out the routine of the household. Wanda's original plan had been to talk Keir into taking her for a walk, where it could be arranged for her to entrap him in a convenient barn, and Culver would lock them in with a bar of Cold Iron so Keir could not magic it away. There they would remain until they were missed and when the rescuers came she would be in a state of dishevelment. As a gentleman, Keir would have to offer for her.

But her injury would not allow her to walk that far. Dr. Paget had given her a stick to walk with – like a dowager! – and she found that she needed its support at times.

Grimstock looked the house over and found that the still-room suited their purposes the best. It was in the hall leading towards the kitchens – although not the hall used by the servants in their passage to and from the main rooms of the house. The windows were clerestory style – small and high – and but one door opened into the room. The walls were thick in that part of the house and it would be a long while before anyone heard cries for help. And best of all, Grimstock could drop an iron bar, which Wanda had concealed in her luggage, across the door. In the days when this building had been an actual Abbey, the still room was kept locked and barred. Grimstock had purloined the key from the key-holder in the kitchen. They were all conveniently labeled. It was a large key, of copper alloy, so the housekeeper did not wear it on the chatelaine at her waist.

All that remained was to lure Keir into her trap.

That day, most of the inhabitants of the Abbey met for luncheon, save Chenevix and Lucie. They had ordered a tray above stairs. Chenevix had decided to put off the trip to Dorset, for Lucie was nearly ill from constant crying and he had called Dr Paget into look at her. The doctor had recommended bed rest and freedom from stress for a few days and James' Powders for the headache. It would not do for the Duchess of Chenevix to travel in her current state – she was in a very low frame of mind and the doctor talked gravely of melancholia. This frightened Chenevix enough that he saw Lucie put to bed, tenderly administered to by Giselle, who had been promoted to lady's maid, much to her satisfaction. The Duke decided to stay near to his wife, and wrote letters in the dressing room while she slept the sleep of exhaustion and too many tears.

Grimstock's inquiries had revealed that most afternoons Lady Diana spent at the little gazebo, doing needlework. Diana insisted that Simon take a nap after nuncheon, after which they usually went riding. Ninon lay down, too, for the heat had returned and it exhausted her. Lyonshall took a stroll after nuncheon, whilst blowing a cloud. And Keir usually had a second cup of tea and fed the kittens tidbits, before joining Lyon in the Tower for the afternoon's work. With the Duke and Duchess above stairs it offered Wanda a marvelous opportunity to cast her net and pull it in.

René had not been pleased to be left alone with Wanda Wycherley at the nuncheon table. Everyone else had seemed all too willing to flee her company. Even Ninon, who he had hoped would stay, was forced to seek her bed. It looked as if she was getting one of her heat headaches, for which the only cure was to lay in a darkened room with a lavender soaked cloth upon her brow. She had sent the kittens a significant glance before leaving and Neige, rather than going with her, remained behind.

René gave this little thought, for he had fallen into the habit of treating the kittens with little bits of meat and a platter of cream, and he merely thought that Neige wanted to remain behind for the treat. Alphonse, as it turned out, was a great feline fancier and made up little surprises of meat and fish exquisitely cooked to tempt the kittens' palettes. René always gave them the last of the cream from the table, which today had been used not only for the tea and coffee but to cover a large bowl of raspberries.

Wanda, thankfully remained silent while he fed the kittens. They preferred to take the little fish or meat balls from his fingers rather than eat from a bowl, and there was much jumping up and down and squeaking as he made certain no one got more than the others. Of course, Beau felt that *he* ought to have the most as it was *his* Wizard who was feeding them. The others soon let him know what they thought of this idea.

Wanda gave René an uneasy feeling. He did not find her attractive in the least. She was overblown and coming – a *chien méchant* as Ninon would have said. Oberon's gift, still hanging on its chain around his neck, was warm against his skin and it tingled slightly. True to the Elf King's orders, he never removed it, not even when bathing. He felt as if it were warning him of something.

The kittens had finished eating and were neatly lined up at his feet, washing their faces and whiskers, each a mirror image of each other as they lapped a paw and used it to scrub a face.

Beau suddenly wrinkled his nose. "What is that stench?" he asked, sniffing the air. "It is awful!"

The other kittens agreed. René, not having their power of smell, was conscious only of a vague unpleasantness.

Wanda flushed. That addlepate Goodbody! Before nuncheon (for he had told her it took an hour to come into blossom) she had doused herself in his supposedly irresistible perfume and repeated the magic Words to activate it. Now instead of enticing Keir it would seem to be repelling him. But it was her own fault, she conceded, for after the fiasco Goodbody's spells had made of the carriage accident, she ought to have tossed the perfume into the trash, rather than using it.

But Keir was a gentleman and if she were pathetic enough...

Accordingly, she pushed back her chair and attempted to stand up and gave a small shriek. "Ow!" she screamed and almost fell.

As she had hoped, Keir was on his feet in a trice and caught her.

"Oh, thank you, my lord!" she said coyly, fluttering her eyelashes at him. The voice she affected, husky, low and full of promise, had usually an instant effect on most gentlemen – they would return her burning gaze with one of their own. And if she leaned on one of her *amours* as she was leaning on Keir they usually started sweating, panting or both. It seemed to have no effect whatsoever on Keir. The things she had to do to gain a coronet! It seemed she would have to marry a eunuch!

In truth, her perfume made René slightly ill. The amulet tingled stronger, warmer, almost hot. Its meaning was clear – she was a danger.

He said *"Madame*, would you care to be seated once more and I shall call your maid to you?"

"Oh, no," she said breathlessly, with a simper he found rather sickening. Thank *le bon Dieu* that Diana did not simper, but met one's gaze with openness and honesty. "Pray, my lord, will you allow me to lean upon your arm? I am still in a little pain and I wish to go to the still-room and brew myself a *tisane*. I have an old family recipe, a restorative, that I could make."

"If you asked Lady Diana, *Madame*, I am certain that she would be glad to brew it for you –" René began.

"Oh, I cannot do that! This is a family recipe, you must know, and I promised my mother that I would never reveal it to anyone!" The only thing that Wanda had ever promised her mother was to save herself for marriage and that promise had not been kept a fortnight before she succumbed to the manly charms of Culver Grindle.

René resigned himself to being the gentleman and escorting her to the still-room. It was an honor he could have done without. Once she was in the still-room he would go find her maid.

Wanda chattered all the way to the still-room, limping , and assuring him that the pain was not so very bad. She was being brave.

The kittens followed them, tails high. This was not part of Wanda's plan but she could not think of a good reason why they should be excluded. That little black and white one in particular had an annoying habit of asking "Why?" at every turn.

The still-room was reached and the kittens streamed in ahead of them. No one noticed Grimstock lurking just around the corner where the hall turned to the kitchens. Under her apron she held an iron bar.

Still leaning heavily on René's arm Wanda led him to the worktable in the middle of the room. Sighing theatrically, she slid onto a stool. "I wonder if you would be so good as to fetch me some herbs from the shelf?" she queried, with what she thought was a brave smile of pain nobly endured. "I shall need some mint, horehound and some vervain, and rosemary," she said, naming some herbs at random.

The kittens jumped up on th shelves, looking at the neatly labeled bottles. They had been learning to read and were eager to show off their skills. "Here is the vervain!" squeaked Beau, and pushed it with his paw so that René had to catch the bottle.

The others thought this great sport, and none of them gave any attention to Wanda.

She took this opportunity to leap up, showing that her ankle had mended very well indeed and closed the door swiftly and had the satisfaction of hearing the iron bar thump home in the brackets on the other side. She removed the key from the inside pocket of her skirt and turned it in the lock.

"What is she doing?" cried Beau.

René, who had just caught the bottle of rosemary tipped by Neige, turned around rapidly just in time to see Wanda, standing on both feet, insert a large copper key into her bodice. "What are you doing?" he demanded.

"I've a mind to have a title," she said impudently "and you will eventually be a Duke. We shall stay in here until we are missed and I am compromised. When they find us I will look as if you had your way with me and as a gentleman, you will have to offer for me." She was very smug. "And you needn't think that you can magic your way out of this, my lord Wizard! There is iron wire mesh over the windows and an iron bar across the door. And I have the key as well!" she patted her bosom. The wire mesh had been Culver's idea and he had covered the windows with it last night while everyone slept.

The kittens set up a yowl of protest and then hissed at her. "Let's scratch her eyes out!" said Beau.

"*Non, mon ami,*" said René. "It is the law that animals who attack people must be destroyed. It is a stupid law, especially for the life of this *chien méchant* – but it is the law."

"That means wicked dog!" Neige exclaimed in delight. "She is a *dog*! A wicked dog!"

Lucie had lamented that there was no likeness, other than their height between her son and her husband. Had she been there at this moment she would have seen a marked likeness between Chenevix and René, for René's eyes had gone hard and cold as his father's could and his jaw was as tight and set as the Duke's could be when he was angered "You are welcome to a title, *Madame*," he said in frigid tones, "but not mine, I think."

He said to the kittens. "I will send someone who can touch Cold Iron to free you. Please be patient and do not kill her. I will have that key," he said, turning to Wanda.

She patted her bosom. Whatever did he think he was going to do? "Not from where it is, my lord! Unless you are man enough to wrest it from me," she added, giving him a provocative look. She was certain that the Cold Iron would keep him here.

For an answer, René put out his hand and the key burst from her bosom and flew to him as if he had had it on a string. Then with a last admonition to the kittens, he disappeared, leaving Wanda open-mouthed and shocked.

For some reason, the clearest destination René had in his mind was the little gazebo on the side lawn. He had taken an early walk there only this morning. Only this morning! How long ago that seemed now!

He reappeared on the lawn just beside the gazebo – between it and a bed of marigolds.

Diana, who had been doing embroidery in the shelter of the gazebo, jumped to her feet, her needlework falling unheeded to the ground. "What is it?" she cried, for he looked both angry and harassed.

"*Cette femme!*" he exclaimed. "*Elle est dangereux!* She has tried to entrap me – nut she did not know that I can teleport –"

"Entrap –?" Diana repeated blankly. She knew at once what dangerous woman of which he spoke. "She hoped to compromise herself?"

"She will do anything, I think, to obtain a title, including a husband who would never cease hating her!" said René disgustedly. He suddenly staggered.

"Here, come and sit down!" Diana ran forward and helped him into the gazebo, where he sank down on one of the rustic benches that ran around each side of the structure.

455

"She had put the Cold Iron at the doors and windows," he explained. "But I am out before it hurt too badly. *Ne vous en faites pas.*"

Diana *was* worried. He looked rather grey and she was suddenly shaken by anger. How she hated scheming women! They gave the rest of their sex a terrible name.

"The kittens, they are in there with her," murmured René. "They wanted to scratch her, *non*? They must be let out by someone who can touch Cold Iron."

"I will ring for Robert," said Diana. "And I shall have him bring you a cordial as well. I wish the kittens *had* scratched her!" she added viciously.

But it was not necessary to ring for Robert magically, for across the lawn streamed the kittens. And close behind then was Wanda.

"She isn't even limping!" said Diana in outrage. She put out her hand and grasped René's arm. "Go along with whatever I say and do not be surprised at what I may say! Promise me!"

"I promise," said René, puzzled by what she might mean.

"Here," she reached into her work table and pulled out a slim volume of verse. "Read a poem out loud – start in the middle."

Although he did not understand why she wanted him to do this he opened the volume and selected a poem at random. As she had directed, he began to read in the middle of the piece, while she hurriedly restored her embroidery to her lap and picked up the needle again.

"And now good morrow to our waking souls,
Which watch not one another out of fear;
For love all love of other sights controls,
And makes one little room an everywhere
Let self-discoverers to new worlds have gone,
Let maps to other worlds on worlds have shown.
Let us possess one world, each hath one and is one...

"You!" shrieked Wanda, breathing heavily, for she was unused to running. Her unrestrained bosom bobbed up and down painfully.

456

"He attempted to compromise me!" she screamed, pointing at René.

She had thumped on the closed door until Grimstock, still lurking outside, had fetched the spare key from the housekeeper. During all of this time the kittens had hissed, spit and swiped at her.

"Liar! Liar!" clamored the kittens.

"Quiet, please," said Diana calmly. " I shall take care of this." She turned her haughtiest look on Wanda, the very one used by her mother to depress the pretensions of toad-eaters. "I am glad to see your ankle so recovered," she said dryly.

Wanda flushed angrily. Things were not going as she had planned.

"And what is this nonsense you are babbling, Mrs. Wycherley?" Diana continued. "As you can see, Lord Keir is here with me – indeed he has been here with me since shortly after nuncheon. He has been reading me poetry."

"He was just in the still-room with me where he tried to compromise my virtue!" Wanda retorted angrily. "He owes me an offer! If he calls himself a gentleman!"

"I doubt you have any virtue to compromise," Diana returned, still in that dry voice "But even a gentleman, Mrs. Wycherley, cannot be betrothed to two females at once.
And Lord Keir and I have been betrothed this past fortnight. So I really think that my claims outweigh any of yours."

The kittens cheered.

38

Eminently Suitable

"There has been no announcement!" Wanda riposted. "I read all of the society news – daily! And there has been naught!"

"There are reasons why it has not as yet been puffed in the journals –" Diana began.

"And what are those, pray?" Wanda sneered. "I'll tell you why! Because you just made it up out of whole cloth to save him behaving as he ought and coming up to scratch!"

"The reasons, Mrs. Wycherley, which by the bye, are none of your affair, but since you appear to be laboring under some sort of delusion," came an icy voice, "I shall tell you. The reasons are to do with the fact that the Chenevix betrothal ring is being resized for Lady Diana's slender hand. Furthermore, it is a ring of great antiquity and Rundell and Bridge discovered the main sapphire to be cracked."

They all turned to look at the Duke of Chenevix, who seemed to have magically appeared. He walked into the gazebo to join them. "I have just received a selection of sapphires from Rundell and Bridge and Lady Diana was to make her choice this very afternoon, had you not interrupted us with this wild and improbable story." With this he reached into his breast pocket and withdrew a small leather sack, which indeed bore the legend of the famous jewelers on its side. This he opened and shook out, onto the top of Diana's work table, a collection of sapphires of all sizes, including one of an immensity that caused Wanda to gasp in longing.

These jewels were in actuality, for a necklace for Lucie. Chenevix thought blue her best colour. The huge sapphire was to be the center stone of the necklace. The Duke wanted her to choose which stones she would like to compliment the large one and choose stones for earrings as well.

He had been walking in the garden, feeling in need of fresh air, when he had overheard Wanda and Diana. It had not taken him a minute to decide to lend verisimilitude to Diana's claims, and the sapphires presented a marvelous ring of truth. Even less than René did he desire such a trollop in his family. Indeed, had his heir been entrapped by such a strumpet he would not have hesitated in buying her off, or even, if necessary, making certain that she would never appear at the wedding ceremony.

Wanda was taken aback. She could not imagine why else Chenevix would be carrying sapphires about. She knew that the Nobs set great store by their traditions and that ancient and sometimes ugly betrothal rings were a large part of these traditions. She had read of elaborate ceremonies where the bride to be was gifted with the family ring, which stayed upon her finger until the wedding, and was then returned to the vault until the next heir to the title chose a bride.

Ignoring Wanda, the Duke turned to Diana and said, "These are all stones of the first water, my dear. If you will be so good to make your choice, I will have it expressed to Rundell and Bridge. They assure me that the ring will be ready in two days after they receive the stone."

Diana took a deep breath and played along with the Duke. "They are all so beautiful!" Turning to René, she said "Which one do you like, dearest?"

To her delight he was quick to fall into his role and not by a flicker of surprise did he hint to Wanda that this was all a charade for her benefit. He looked at the stone critically for a moment and then picked out a mid-sized stone. "That one, I think," he said, "but it is not nearly as beautiful as are your eyes."

Diana managed to look suitably struck by this compliment and agreed with his selection.

Chenevix withdrew a jeweler's loupe from his pocket and picking up the stone, looked at it closely through this instrument. It sparkled and gleamed in the sunlight as he held it up. "Flawless," he murmured. "I shall express this to London at once. We shall have the rest of the stones made into a parure for the betrothal ball."

Wanda was a sick as a cushion. That should have been her with those beautiful jewels! It should have been her having a betrothal ball! It was all that noddy Goodbody's fault! He should have known about the betrothal! Any one without wind-mills in his head would have sent someone to spy out the land before going to all of this trouble – all for naught! When she thought of how much he had cost her first and last – all the debts she had covered and how his ineptitude had ruined her new carriage – not even a six-month old and it was little better than kindling! And she had had to endure his inept fumblings as well.

"Walk with me, Mrs. Wycherley," came the Duke's voice, interrupting her fit of high dudgeon. "I think I am correct in assuming that my heir and his betrothed would rather be alone."

Wanda had little choice. The expression on his face gave pause. It was haughty and not at all friendly.

She executed a stiff curtsey in the direction of Lady Diana and Lord Keir. "I am sure I wish you very happy," she said stiffly and untruthfully. She was sure she wished them in Hell.

"My *fiancé* and I thank you," Diana graciously inclined her head, and stretched a hand out to René, who took it and kissed it. Wanda gritted her teeth.

As they walked away from the gazebo Chenevix said in a low, hard voice, "Allow me to place some plain facts before you, Mrs. Wycherley. No doubt you have thoroughly researched my title and fortune. Females of your stamp have all of the facts about their matrimonial prospects at their fingertips."

"Females of my stamp? What do you mean by that, pray?"

"Strumpets," he said coldly, ignoring her gasp of outrage. "You have no doubt entertained more men than Wellesley has in the Peninsula. But that is beside the point."

"The Dukedom of Chenevix is an old one," he continued. "It is the second creation after Edward III made the Black Prince Duke of Cornwall in 1337. The patent of Dux

Chenevix is an unusual one, Mrs. Wycherley, and you would have done well to read on it further. For you see, the holder of the title has absolute discretion in choosing his heir. It need not descend in direct line – the law of primogeniture has no effect upon it. In other words, should my heir marry to disoblige me, I may completely cut him off, not only from my personal fortune, but from the succession as well. Had he been so foolish as to succumb to the blandishments of a trollop such as yourself, he would have been a penniless commoner, with no hopes of ever stepping into my room, or inheriting one single penny-piece. I trust I have made myself sufficiently clear upon this point, Mrs. Wycherley?"

"Yes," muttered Wanda sullenly. How she hated this man!

"And to further dissuade you, *Madame,* I should inform you that after your patently false fainting fit in front of my house in Grosvernor Square, I had Bow Street investigate you. You seem to have more gentlemen callers than most Covent Gardens brothels. Should you at any time attempt to importune any member of my family, I shall have no hesitation in revealing your doings to the scandal sheets. You will then lose what little place you cling to on the fringes of society." He stared at her with those cold eyes. "You do understand me, do you not?"

"But that is blackmail!" she protested.

"I prefer to think of it as insurance," he said coolly. "I bid you good day, Mrs. Wycherley." Without even the barest of bows, he strode off, leaving her seething in the middle of the lawn.

Lucie was still sleeping when Chenevix entered their rooms. Beside the bed Giselle sat dozing in a chair. The windows stood wide to catch the afternoon breezes and the sheer curtains blew slightly as a light wind lifted them. Lucie lay beneath but a sheet. She seemed to be sleeping naturally however, and her brow was cool to the Duke's soft touch. He would not disturb her.

He went into the dressing room where he had spent most of the morning writing letters on a small desk set up by Mariposa. He opened a drawer and pulled out a fresh sheet of stationary.

461

He picked up a pen and dipped it into the inkwell.

A marriage has been arranged and will take place shortly, he wrote in his flowing copperplate script, *between Lady Diana Stillfield, widow of the late Captain Jonathan Stillfield and daughter of the Earl and Countess of Eastcote, and René Alain Delamar, Marquis of Keir, heir to the Duke of Chenevix and his Duchess. The marriage will take place at Chenevix Duchis, in Dorsetshire; the date to be announced in the very near future.*

Chenevix surveyed this in satisfaction. The match was eminently suitable. The only thing that he disliked about it was that Lady Diana was a widow. He would have preferred a bride fresh from the schoolroom – one who could be molded into a proper Duchess. But Lady Diana's family was an old and excellent one, free of scandal, vice or madness. She was beautiful as well, had a handsome fortune of her own and would look well in the family jewels.

And by inserting this in the papers, he could bend them to his will. Keir could not, in all honour, withdraw from the engagement. And she would be branded a jill-flirt and impossible to please should she jilt a matrimonial prize such as Keir.

He made two more copies of this announcement and then rang for Mariposa after he had sanded all three. Chenevix lit a candle with a flint device found in the drawer and prepared to melt a wafer of sealing wax. He took off his signet ring.

The valet appeared swiftly and silently as always. "Your Grace desires?" he said with a low bow,

"I have here several notices to insert in the newspapers, Mariposa. Specifically, in the *Journal*, the *Morning Post* and the *London Times* – *not* the *Wizards' Times*, though. I shall also need you to go to my bank and fetch the black lacquer box from my vault," Chenevix directed.

"Very good, your Grace." Mariposa took the proffered sheets, now shut with a blob of sealing wax and the Duke's seal pressed into it. "I assume your Grace wishes this accomplished with all dispatch?"

"I should like the notices to appear tomorrow, if at all possible."

Chenevix reached into the desk and withdrew a locked money box. This he opened with a small key that hung from his fob. A well-filled sack lay on the top of a large pile of banknotes. "Hire a hippogriffe if you must," He tossed the sack to Mariposa who adroitly caught it in mid-air.

"As your Grace wishes," said the valet as he bowed himself out.

Chenevix was quite pleased with himself. He did not consider that he had taken ruthless advantage of the situation. Now, at last things would start going his way.

"*C'est épatant!*" said René, in relief as soon as he was certain that Wanda was out of earshot. "This was clever of you! She believed that it is so!"

"I think she might not have believed it were it not for the Duke," said Diana reflectively. "How fortunate that he happened to have those gems on his person! They certainly lent truth to our claim."

"You shall have to keep pretending until she leaves," remarked Beau from where three of the kittens sat at their feet. "I sent Janus to go and tell the others so if that awful cow asks – they'll tell her it is true."

"I hope you won't mind – she will probably be with us only a few more days," Diana said apolo-getically to René.

Mind! It would be the dearest wish of his heart were it true! When she called him 'dearest' his heart had nearly turned over in his chest. How he wished he could speak of his feelings to her! But not only was Lammas night ahead but he was certain that she did not reciprocate his feelings. She was warm and friendly, but there was nothing deeper.

"Oh, no, I will not mind at all," he managed to say casually.

"I cannot abide females such as she that scheme and connive to catch a titled, wealthy husband!" Diana took up her embroidery again and stabbed her needle into it almost viciously. "I would do as much for anyone."

"Oh, anyone," he repeated hollowly. Beau looked up sharply at his voice and demanded to be picked up. "You still look tired," he accused, touching a velvet soft paw to René's face.

"How remiss of me!" Diana exclaimed. "I was going to have you brought a cordial! To dematerialize near so much Cold Iron must have been extremely difficult. I cannot imagine how you managed it!" She made a gesture in the air and far away they heard a bell ring.

In truth, René could not now imagine how he had managed. He had seldom been so angry – perhaps that had something to do with it. He would talk to Ninon. All of a sudden he was extremely tired. A cordial would be good. All he wanted now was to sit in the shade and look at Diana and imagine that the false betrothal was real.

A little later that afternoon, Mariposa hired a hippogriffe in Cheltenham and left for London, bearing the Duke's notices and a letter of authorization for the Duke's bank.

Since he had wasted no time in lifting the Duke's seal with a hot knife and reading the notice, he was well aware of what he carried. He also knew what a furor it would cause. Nothing happened in any house that Mariposa occupied that he did not know all about. He knew that Lord Keir had not made an offer to Lady Diana – it was one of his master's ploys. Mariposa was also up to snuff on what was in the black lacquer box.

39

A Treat for Simon

Diana was immensely relieved not to have to face Wanda Wycherley at the dinner table that evening. Her uncle had wasted no time in having his traveling chariot poled up and Wanda's baggage packed and put on it. He told Wanda that his coachman and horses would take her and the servants who were still able to travel anywhere she desired – even to John O'Groats! Riding roughshod over her sensibilities he packed her and Grimstock into the coach, saw her coachman up onto the box beside the Abbey coachman and promised her that the two footmen would be well taken care of, and then bade her farewell, and stepped back to wave at the carriage as it headed off in the direction of Knyghtwood. He then uttered an "Aha!" of satisfaction and rubbed his hands together. There was one problem resolved! If only the others that faced them were as easily put to rights.

Culver Grindle stayed behind, ostensibly to accompany the broken-limbed footman into Cheltenham, where he would recuperate at Dr. Paget's surgery. But Grindle's real reason – for he cared nothing for the footman – was to be Wanda's spy. She had still not given up on her plot, for if Goodbody succeeded, Lady Diana would be removed from the equation and Keir would be available once more. And she was certain that she could find a way around the Duke's edict. After some reflection she really doubted that he would disinherit his only son – that was to scare her off. Well his Grace would catch cold at that. She did not scare so easily.

Again, the Duke and Duchess absented themselves from the meal. Ninon was not there either, for she indeed had one of her heat headaches and Neige reported that her human was dozing. René was thus thwarted – he wanted to have a long conversation with his grandmother, wishing to know, among other things, why she had never informed him that she was a Duchess.

Lyon was loud in his praise of their rout of Wanda Wycherley. "Conniving females such as that one need to be put firmly in their place!" he declared allowing Seppings to help him to a bowl of Mulligatawny soup, fragrant with curry powder. "It would have been a scandal, my boy," he said to René, "if you had been found in a locked room with a disheveled female – and I'll go bail she would have been extremely disheveled!"

Simon, who had spent the earlier part of the afternoon napping, could not seem to eat much of the spicy soup which he had learned to love since coming to live in the Abbey. He had been awakened by Janus who had excitedly told him of the betrothal. Simon had been cast into alt. He could not imagine anything better! Mr. Roussillon would then be his Papa – and he would have a real family!

A little while before, on a rainy evening, he had dreamed of just such a future. While Mama sat in front of the fire with her needlework, and Mr. Roussillon read aloud from a book about unicorns, Simon lay on the floor between them, on his stomach. Although he looked as if he was reading Halkyut's *Voyages* and petting the kittens, in reality he was watching them – how she smiled or made a comment, the way he looked at her and how they both would look at him, Simon. It was all of his dearest wishes come true – to be part of a real family that he could love and loved him in return.

But then Janus had told him that it was not a real betrothal – they were not really going to married. There would be no family.

The sense of disappointment was crushing. Simon struggled not to cry as Janus recounted the good joke on that awful woman. Why could it not be real? He loved both of them so much and he thought they all should be together.

Now listening to Uncle Lyon laugh was almost too much to bear. *How could he laugh about it?* Simon thought resentfully, dragging his spoon aimlessly back and forth through the soup.

"Simon, are you not feeling well?" came Mama's soft voice. "That is your favorite soup!"

He raised his eyes to hers, which were full of love and concern. He wanted to cry out that she should marry Mr. Roussillon, that it should be real and they would be a family. But the words stuck in his throat. He knew what they would say – that it was grown-ups' business and he did not understand.

Diana felt Simon looked tired and sad. She thought she understood. He was sensitive and the air in the Abbey had been full of hostility as of late. He had even asked her if it was his fault that everyone quarreled so.

"I have to run an errand in Knightswold tomorrow," she said, smiling at him. "I have had a note from the *Cauldron*, advertising robes for Lammastide. Uncle's is worn out, mine is discoloured from storage and you haven't one, I daresay. Why do you not accompany me and we may have a treat at the tea shop? There is a lovely bookshop!"

"Could Lord Keir come as well?" Simon said eagerly, remembering to use the title.

Lyon overheard this and shook his head. "We are drowning in work at the Tower. I need him here. We are still scrying and pendulum dowsing for unicorns, you must know!"

René smiled at Simon. "Another time I shall be happy to go to Knightswold with you when there is not so much work to do. We are to chose the tip and handle for your wand very soon."

Simon was disappointed but tried not to let it show. He did not want Mama to think that he did not desire her company. Accordingly he smiled back at her and assured her that he would like it above all things if they went into Knightswold and visited the shops. At her suggestion, he applied himself to his soup and made a good dinner.

The next morning was again hot and the sky sullen. Diana's new pair, matched grays that she had christened Phoebus and Apollo, had been lunged by Daniel before being poled up, for they were very fresh after an extended stay in the stables during the thunderstorms.

"Looks as if we'll be getting' some more nasty weather, my lady," said Daniel as he handed her into the phaeton. "Don't like th' look of that sky. We're in for some foul weather by night-fall."

"I expect to be home again by noon-tide, Daniel," said Diana as the groom handed Simon up to the seat beside her. Hers was not one of the high-perch phaetons so popular with young bloods, but the so-called ladies' phaeton, sturdy and low to the ground. Diana had no desire to cut a dash in a dangerous, swaying carriage unsuited to country roads.

Simon settled into the seat by her. In spite of his continued sadness over the false betrothal, he was looking forward to the outing. Uncle Lyon had given him a golden guinea this morning, warning him that it was only to be spent on frivolity. Seppings had told him that the tea-shop also served a very good lemon ice – so refreshing on a hot day such as this one looked to be. Mr. Roussillon had given him some suggestions for books to read – all of them story books, not lesson books. The only discord was the behavior of Janus and Rascal – the kittens could not see why they could not go on this expedition as well. They kept trying to sneak into the carriage. In the end Ninon was forced to take them in her arms and threaten to lock them into the buttery. They were only reconciled to remaining behind when, shortly before Simon and Diana were to leave, Mr. Arabin arrived, with Plato, and they decided to visit with their father.

In spite of the look of the sky, which although blue, had a heavy quality about it, it was a beautiful, if rather hot and breathless day. The way to Knightswold lay through an area of farms where they could see the men haying, racing to get the hay cut and stacked before the threatening weather broke. The sweet smell of freshly-cut hay was heavy in the air.

It was a relief to get into the coolness of the wood, however. The pair trotted along, well up to their bits, and made little of the miles to the village. Simon and Diana talked in a desultory fashion, sometimes talking eagerly, at others just silent enjoying the day and one another's company.

Diana chose to go by the good broad road that led through he wood. As she explained to Simon, there was another road, a narrow one through the rocks. Although it was shorter route she did not like it – it had a nasty feel to it and made the horses uneasy. "If there were to be any Unselighe creatures about, that is where they would be," she explained.

Perhaps they were not being careful enough – to go out like this when the country was in such uproar, but they could not stop living and cower in their bedchambers. Diana was confident that she could overcome any Unselighe creature, at least in the daylight, for she could borrow magic from Simon if needs be. Simon still wore his dragon whistle and with the incredibly keen hearing of all dragons, Tuathail could hear it even at this distance and be with them in a trice. There were griffins in the woods as well who would spring to their defense. And Unselighe creatures usually attacked at night. That time at Bryn Mryddin seemed to have been an aberration.

Knightswold was soon reached, and as before, Diana put up her horses at the *Green Man*. She did not see either Wanda Wycherley or Augustus Goodbody, for they had gone out in a little trap rented from Mr. Milburn, into the woods. Nor did Mrs. Milburn mention her less than illustrious guests to her ladyship. Truth to tell, Mrs. Milburn was more than a little ashamed of having two such odious characters in her inn. She had been extremely chagrined when Wanda had returned. But they paid their shot ahead and in good coin of the realm. Mrs. Milburn doubted the validity of bank notes.

Diana ordered the Lammas robes first and Simon was entranced by the goods available in the *Cauldron*. Resolutely, he avoided looking at the large selection of tips, handles and gemstones. That was for another time, when Mr. Roussillon would come with them. Mama gave him another guinea, and feeling rich, he bought Janus a collar of jet and onyx. Diana bought him his own mortar and pestle, as he would soon begin studying herbology and a small armillary, or astrolabe, as well, that folded neatly into a conveniently carried package for he would be beginning his celestial studies, so important to magic.

They then spent several happy hours in the well-stocked bookshop, which was called *Bell, Book and Candle*. Simon found a stack of storybooks, including one he had been longing to read about the boyhood of Merlin. Diana bought more lesson books for Simon, and several novels for herself, including a newly published three-volume novel entitled "*Sense and Sensibility*" by a Lady. The clerk praised it as very true to life and quite amusing. Sampling several pages, Diana agreed with him and added it to the pile – a not inconsiderable one – that was growing on the counter. She let Simon have free rein and placed no objections to his gathering a formidable pile of volumes. Money spent on books was never wasted, she had been raised to believe. Simon should start amassing his very own library. He had found every book that his tutor had suggested and Diana thought well of René's choices. It was good of him to think that small boys needed more than just lesson books. The books chosen were those of adventure and humor. And Simon had chosen more books about dragons, a subject that seemed to interest him keenly.

After the books were paid for and tied up in brown paper – for ease in handling the clerk made three bulky packages – arrangements were made to send the books to the inn – Diana and Simon went to the *Ladies' Emporium*. Simon thought it would be a dead bore, but he was entranced by the colour of the beads and the ribbons and most of all by the musical instruments. He shook the tambourines, ran a stick over the bells of the glockenspiel and fell in love with the dulcimers, which a clerk obligingly demonstrated. Diana sat down at the pianoforte and tried some new songs. Simon loved to hear her sing and was pleased when she bought a number of new song sheets and promised some music of an evening at the Abbey. "Perhaps we can coax Lord Keir into playing his violin for us as well," she suggested to Simon,

Simon was thrilled. Pastimes such as these were what a family did. The new books could be read aloud as well – together. Perhaps if Mama and Mr. Roussillon did a great many of these activities they would come to see that they *ought* to be married!

After making the same arrangements for their purchases – Diana also bought a length of muslin to make handkerchiefs for all the gentlemen, which would be embroidered with white work crests – and a vast quantity of white silk floss, they adjourned to the tea shop.

The promise of heat to come had been more than fulfilled and the thoughts of an ice were compelling. The tea-shop was somewhat crowded but Diana found a table away from the glare of the window and she and Simon were soon enjoying an ice. Simon had a difficult time making up his mind, for there were no less than three flavors to choose from, which, the waitress told them proudly, was as good as Gunter's in London. Simon could not decide which would be better, lemon, orange or cherry. The waitress suggested one scoop of each and Simon was in bliss as he allowed the cold treat to melt on his tongue.

All too soon, the ices were eaten and it was time to leave. When they emerged from the shop it was to see a huge dark cloud on the horizon over the mountains. The air was oppressively hot and not a breeze stirred.

"Oh, dear!" said Diana. "We'd best head for home at once, Simon. I meant to give you a driving lesson this afternoon, for the pair is no longer fresh, but I think we had best concentrate on getting back to the Abbey before we are caught in this rain-storm. I think it is still a ways off – we may probably outrun it."

The ostler at the *Green Man* was quick and had the pair harnessed in no time flat. The horses had been baited and watered and brushed till they shone. Much pleased, Diana gave the ostler a good tip and thanked him for his services. He had also secured their purchases in the boot of the phaeton.

They left Knightswold at a brisk trot. Diana planned to let the pair out once they were clear of the forest. If she judged it right they could be home just before the huge cloud cleared the mountains. It was definitely a thunderhead and Diana hoped that it did not presage another storm of the ferocity of the ones just past.

But from the time the entered the greenwood, things began to go wrong. Halfway through the wood, near where Diana had found William and his Grandmama earlier in the year, there was a barrier, a tree trunk, across the road. A rustic fellow, sturdy in smock and gaiters, stood by it and waved them down.

"What is it?" Diana demanded, pulling her pair to a halt.

"Nay, then, missus," he replied, a rather dirty hand pulling at his forelock. "There's been mishap here – hay

471

wain's overturned an' carter taken up all over blood. No fit sight for little 'un or a lady. Have to take t'other road, you will."

"Is the carter all right?" she asked. "Perhaps I can help?"

"Nay then," he said again. "Doctor's on his way. Best you get home afore th' storm comes."

Diana's horses were restive, not standing still. Their ears were pinned back, and they were snorting and jibbing at their bits. It was the coming storm that disturbed then, she thought, agreeing with the rustic's advice. It was better to get home.

She turned the carriage easily in the broad road and found her horses were more than eager to leave the barricade area. It took all of her strength to hold them to a trot.

Had she or Simon looked behind them they would have seen a strange and frightening sight. For the rustic shimmered and changed, becoming taller and slimmer. The smock and gaiters became scarlet silks and the homely face became Elfin and mad.

Sluagh laughed to himself as he watched the carriage drive away. Those horses had nearly queered his game, for they sensed his disguise and his madness and reacted to it. Even Elvensteeds did not like to be near him. He had the same effect on most domestic animals, Elven or human.

Simon did not like the narrow trail through the forest. It was a dark and secretive place, darker still, now, for the sun had abruptly disappeared behind the massive cloud.

And a wind had suddenly sprung up – Diana remembered her grandfather Lyons, who lived in Sherwood Forest, teaching them that when the forest whispered there would be rain soon, for the noise of the trees came from gusting winds with downdrafts. And the wind was south to southeast, which usually meant a severe storm was coming.

What the trees were whispering on this shadowy trail was mocking and evil. The gloomy firs seemed to be leaning in towards them, almost as if the trees wanted to grab at them. The horses were sweating and whickering uneasily, but obeyed Diana's firm hands on the ribbons.

"I don't like this road, Mama," said Simon in a small, frightened voice. He moved closer to her on the seat.

472

"I don't either, Simon," she replied, her attention on her horses, for the road was rutted – she could not imagine why the road Wizards (who were paid a munificent sum to make certain that every road in England, even the smallest tracks and trails, were in superior condition) were about to let it come to this state. "But we shall be through it very soon and then it is a clear road for home. I shall spring them when we are done with the forest."

Simon agreed with this plan. He wanted to be at home as soon as was possible. The day which had been so wonderful had turned ugly. He did not like those trees at all! Surely they were not friends of Father Oak!

"One more turn ahead," Diana promised, "and then the road improves and very soon after that we shall be out of the forest." As she spoke, she directed the horses to make a sharp right. She avoided using the long thronged whip, for the team was quite nervous enough, even though she was quite capable of taking a fly off her leader's ear and neatly winding the thong around the stock, all in one deft motion.

Eagerly, the pair trotted around the corner, for Phoebus and Apollo knew their stable was not far off now.

Therefore they shied all the more violently when a caped and masked figure, pistol in hand, jumped out from the shrubs at the side of the road and shouted, "Stand and deliver!"

A highwayman! Diana could not give him a more than cursory glance for she was occupied with a plunging, rearing pair. "Hold on to the carriage rail, Simon!" she shouted, attempting to bring the terrified horses under control.

A second cloaked figure sprang from the shrubbery and leaped at the horses' heads, grabbing the reins near Apollo's tender mouth and wrenching the animal's head down, forcing him to be still. When Apollo quieted, so did Phoebus, but both horses remained shocked, their eyes rolling and uttering distressed noises.

"Drop the ribbons," ordered the first highwayman, leveling his barker at Diana and Simon.

Had it not been for Simon Diana would have used her whip and wrenched the control of the horses from the highwayman, but faster than she could react, a third figure ran to the side of the phaeton and grabbed Simon. "Mama,

Mama!" he shrieked, struggling futilely in the grasp of this new threat.

"Let him go!" Diana shouted frantically. "I'll give you all the money I have – only let my son go!"

"You must promise to use no magic against us, for we know you are a Witch," said the first highwayman. His voice was muffled and distorted by the scarf he wore wrapped around his face. "Elsewise, we shall use Cold Iron on the boy." He nodded at the second road rogue, who let go the horses long enough to pull a formidable length of iron bar from beneath his cloak.

Diana paled. Even a short exposure to that would probably kill Simon. An adult Wizard would be sickened almost to death. She was aware of it weakening her, even from this distance.

"I give you my word," she said, for she had no other choice. "I swear by all I hold sacred that I will not use magic against you."

With this oath, the third criminal let Simon go and, with a sob of relief, he ran to the carriage and flung himself into Diana's arms.

Pulling him tightly against her she looked at the three miscreants with hot, angry eyes. "If you harm one hair on my son's head," she vowed " I shall kill you myself!"

"No one shall be injured if you do as you're told," said number one. "Now, climb down from that carriage, you and the boy. And don't think to bamboozle me – I ain't a flat – you can't make a May game of me."

Diana, with Simon still clinging to her, obeyed. Number two had produced a horse weight from somewhere and had tethered Phoebus and Apollo, who still showed signs of wanting to flee. Number three took the whip from its socket and snapped it in thirds.

There was something odd about these highwaymen. Number one talked as if he were a gentleman – he sounded like one of Peter's friends, who laced their speech with cant. The second highwayman, she noticed, seemed to be crippled in some way and the third, she was beginning to feel, was not human.

With the aid of the pistol, number one waved her to the side of the road. Simon clung to her tightly; he was no longer crying but he was shivering in fear and that circumstance made her so angry that she wanted to hurl magic at them.

Looking at her stormy eyes, number one said, "My friend here is very fast. Before you could summon your magics, he'd have the boy up against that iron bar."

As if to demonstrate, the third cloaked figure moved so quickly that Diana was *certain* he was not human. No human could move like that. But what he was, she did not know.

She watched as number two drew an envelope from his pocket. It had a loop of ribbon affixed and this he dropped over the empty whip socket. Then he removed the horse weight and yelled "Gee up!" and took a bit of the broken whip to lash at the pair.

They bolted, taking off at a gallop, the phaeton lurching and swinging violently behind them.

"Them looked delicious, they did," said number three wistfully, as he watched the phaeton disappear in the direction of the Abbey.

"You'll get your share of things to gobble," said number two in disgust." That's all you think about – your stomach!"

"I'm fair gut-foundered," said the third member of the highwaymen. He spoke in sibilant syllables.

Diana had given a start when number two had spoken, for she recognized that voice. It was Sir Piers Mildmay! Little wonder that he had appeared to be crippled! She had been right – these were no ordinary highwaymen, intent on relieving her of her well-filled purse. They meant something far worse. Her grip on Simon tightened. She was suddenly very afraid.

40

The Dark Stair

It had not been a happy morning at the Tower. After wrestling with the rightness of his decision, Mr. Arabin had decided that Lord Lyonshall and René needed to see what he had found. And he had come across one other piece of information that might be very helpful indeed, since they had not as yet located any unicorns.

He joined the others in the Tower, leaving Plato and the kittens in the kitchen, where Alphonse was preparing *timbales de poulet* for them. Mr. Arabin was just as glad that the kittens would not be present for he could not trust their discretion.

The Duke of Chenevix, too, was absent. He had not been to the Tower in several days, Lyon informed the Vicar as he poured three cups of coffee and offered a basket of orange and date muffins as well.

The Vicar was nothing loath – breakfast had been quite a while ago.

"Not that we miss him much," Lyon went on. "I don't mean to insult your father, my boy," he said to René, unapologetically.

"*Je m'en fiche,*" said René. Indeed, he did not care tuppence if the Duke were to be insulted. His pity was all for his mother, who seemed to be suffering more than the two protagonists in all of this arguing. The Duke had been strangely silent since yesterday, though, with no new demands or criticisms. Perhaps worry for his wife's tender sensibilities had held his tongue. René certainly hoped so.

He had also noticed the effect of all the quarreling on Simon as well as Lucie. Some people were not made to bear quarrels – it hurt them almost physically. Lyon seemed to revel in arguing, as did Ninon. He himself did not care for loud, angry voices and incessant altercations and preferred not to indulge in such, but he was not made sick by them and could give as goods as he got, were he driven to it. Chenevix did not *like* to argue – he was surprised and angered that one did not leap to obey his dictums.

Reverend Arabin interrupted these thoughts. "I believe I have been able to gain us some time in our search for the unicorns!" he announced, pulling a sheaf of papers from his breast coat pocket. "I have become convinced that we must perform this ceremony on *Old* Lammas!"

Lyon looked at him in surprise over the rim of his coffee cup. "August sixth?" he asked. "As that Coven in Cornwall insists is right?"

"Yes," said the Vicar "for, as you must know, in Merlin's time the calendar used was the Julian, reformed by Julius Caesar from the one made by Numa Pompilius in the seventh century B.C. That was in 46 B.C. – and then in 1582 Pope Gregory XIII reformed the calendar yet again, making it 365 days a year, with a leap year every four years. And since we here in Britain did not accept Gregory's calendar until the 1750s, there was a further adjustment. If my calculations are correct, August 6th is the day we should perform our binding ceremony, to do as exactly as did Merlin, at the same time. I wish that you will check my calculations, my dear boy," he said to René, "for you are a far better mathematician than I ."

René took the papers and bent to his task. Reverend Arabin took a closely folded paper from his tail pocket and said gravely and quietly to Lyon, "You had best read this."

Lyon took it and unfolded it, wondering at the look on the Vicar's face. When he had done reading it, he no longer wondered.

At this moment René finished the calculations and said, "You are correct, we must do this on the 6th of August." He glanced at the large calendar that hung on the wall. Today was Friday, the 26th of July. This gave them almost another week and a half to find a unicorn. "And," he added, thinking aloud, "the moon will be but two days past the full." It was always better to perform magical ceremonies as near to the time of the full moon as was possible, with a few exceptions to this rule.

He turned to face the others. They were regarding him with identical expressions, both sad and speculative.

"What is it?" said René lightly. "Is it that I have grown two heads?"

Lyon thrust a much folded paper at him. "Read this," he ordered.

René obeyed. He had a feeling that he knew what sort of news it might contain.

When he had finished it, quickly, for he was a fast reader, he sighed and put it down upon the counter. *"Il faut casser le noyau pour en avior l'amande.* There is no helping this, *mon amis,* for I must do this thing," he said simply. "He who would eat the nut must first crack the shell – the Gods grant naught without labor – and sacrifice."

"You could die!" burst out Mr. Arabin "And such a death!"

"Do you not think that I have not thought of this – so many times. Almost I did not decide to offer myself," said René quietly. All of his fears had been faced and he had decided upon his course. He knew the risks and thought the outcome worth them. Again he repeated what Oberon had said. "There is no one else," he said now, "no one that can help to end this curse. And that is worth a sacrifice, I think."

"Do not worry, my boy!" Lyon declared. "We have learned a trick or two since Merlin's time and I shall safeguard you with every spell I know. I shall also scry a colleague of mine at Oxford, an expert on ley lines and their use, and ask his recommendations. Naught shall happen to you if I can prevent it! We want you around for a long time – and you must be here when Prinny will no doubt present you with the Order of the Garter or some such thing!" he added, trying to make light of it.

But the joke fell sadly flat.

Diana did not let Sir Piers know that she had recognized him. She decided to let them think her frightened and cowed. In truth, it would not be difficult to act so. She was deeply afraid for both herself and Simon. She did not know what the baronet had in mind – he would be ripe for revenge, that was certain. Were she and Simon to be merely tools for his vengeance? Or were they to be part of it?

Who were his confederates? One of them was not human – how had Sir Piers gained the cooperation of a non-human? He had no magic – a necromancer could bend demons or some Unselighe creatures to his will, but it took a powerful black magician to do so – something that Mildmay definitely was not.

They were taken through the woods under an increasingly darkening sky. The wind was picking up, and, for a southern wind, was chill in advance of the storm.

Ahead somewhere lay water, for Diana could hear it rushing over the stones in the bed of the river. The river was full and swollen still after all of the recent rainstorms.

The sound grew louder and louder until at last they came to an old mill on the bend of the river where it widened into a weed-choked mill pond.

The mill had been abandoned these twenty years and more. Diana remembered having a conversation with Lyon about it, for it was within the purlieu of the Abbey and her uncle felt strongly that it should be put into operation once more. His tenants now had a long way to go to grind their corn and grains. He was looking for an honest, hard-working miller who would be willing to oversee its reconstruction. But she had never seen the mill before, only its location on the estate map.

It was a stone building, some three stories in height and perched right upon the bank of the river. A large wheel, now leaning drunkenly, sat partly submerged in the water. Most of the windows were broken and the door was gaping wide. It had an atmosphere of melancholy about it, as if it were waiting for someone who never came. At one time it must have been a handsome building, bustling with life. Now the wheel creaked in the wind, also moving slightly because of the volume of water rushing through the race, which was in ill-repair.

It was an eerie sound and Simon shivered and drew closer to Diana. He had kept a tight grip on her hand since he had been restored to her side. He was trying his best to be brave but he was very frightened. He did not know how Mama could be so calm.

If Simon had but known it, Diana was far from calm. She had to find a way to escape from this perilous situation. She decided not to speak, but to let Sir Piers reveal his plans.

Diana and Simon were pushed into the mill ahead of number one, who waved the pistol about so carelessly that Diana had to bite her tongue to keep from screaming at him. It was a good quality Manton, no doubt with a hair-trigger, and in inexperienced hands it could go off without warning. It was too much to hope for that the wielder of the gun would be the one injured did the gun indeed go off. More than likely it would be her or Simon that was hurt.

It was as dark as a tomb inside the mill. Outside, the sky was growing steadily blacker and the windows let in little light. Simon made a small noise – he was still rather afraid of the dark and practiced conjuring up a mage light every night that hung comfortingly over his bed until the morning.

Diana put an arm around his shoulders. This was intolerable – scaring him like this!

Just as she was about to quit her resolve and demand that there be a light – for surely they had a lantern – a mage light blossomed from the fingertips of number one. It was a very poor excuse for a mage light – it was lopsided and burned fitfully with a sickly orange glow. It revealed the deserted, cobweb infested mill and it also revealed the identity of number one, for he had removed his concealing scarf.

"You!" Diana said in loathing as she recognized Augustus Goodbody. Little wonder his mage light was such a poor thing!

He grinned idiotically at her. "Not so cock-sure now, ain't you?" he said. "And you'll be even less so when we're standing over the anvil!"

"Standing over the anvil!" Diana repeated incredulously. " Do you think I will accompany you to Gretna Green and marry you there? You must be bosky if you even think for one minute that such a thing would come to pass! You're beneath my touch!" she added contemptuously.

"Oh, you'll have me, right enough," said Goodbody "elsewise the nipperkin here will be properly in the basket.

There's plenty of places that he could disappear and no questions asked. Small for his age, ain't he? Make a good climbing boy."

Diana had often read of someone's blood running cold, particularly in the more lurid gothick novels of the Minerva Press, which she had read endlessly to her sister Selena when that damsel had been sick in bed with influenza, the marble-backed horrid novels being Selena's favorite form of literature. But she thought the description was but a tool of the gothick authors, to terrify their readers. She now found out that the sensation was all too real as she thought of Simon handed over to a sweep, and made to crawl in and out of chimneys to clean them. She would do anything to save Simon from that fate –even marry Goodbody.

"Enough of this foolishness!" growled Sir Piers. "You're a tattle-box, Goodbody! We've a deal to do before they arrive and we'd best get to it." He raised his voice suddenly and bellowed, "Bevis! Where are you! Get in here!"

Down the stairs came the oddest creature Simon had ever seen. A lanky body bore a flat head that was all nose and little else, His eyes were small, set in mid-face and his ears were enormous, sweeping back from his face amidst a welter of straggly hairs. The ears came to points which curved towards his back. His nostrils were huge, and appeared to be located on his chin, and his thin neck seemed too fragile to hold up such a great head and nose. Oddest of all, he had no mouth that Simon could see. For clothing, he wore old grain sacks, cobbled into the semblance of a suit made with knee breeches and a long-skirted coat in the style of the previous century.

He appeared to have been crying, for he gave a loud sniff as he came up to Sir Piers and wiped a sleeve across that immensity of a nose. *Here I be,* he said.

Simon gave a start before he could help it, for the creature was not speaking – for how could he, without a mouth? But Simon could hear him nonetheless.

"You have your instructions," said the baronet. "You'll do as we want, or you know what will happen."

You'll kills my Molly, said that voice that seemed to be coming from inside Simon's head. The creature turned and looked at Simon and Diana.

You didn't tells me there was a child! I'll not hurt a child! You said a lady! he protested. To terrify a lady was bad enough.

Number three came forward and threw aside his cloak. "You does as we tells ye!" he hissed.

A bogle! Diana gasped. She would give a great deal to learn how Mildmay had fallen in with a bogle. And why had the bogle not eaten Mildmay – for liars and murderers were their fare of choice.

"Guard them!" snapped Mildmay. "Or it will be the worse for you *and* your Molly! Come!" he ordered the others. "They'll be getting that note soon and we have to be ready when they come. You watch them well, Bevis!" he directed as they left.

Diana was suddenly angry at herself. Why had she believed them when they told her that the bogle could have Simon against that Cold Iron before she could say Jack Robinson? A bogle could no more touch Cold Iron that she could. Of the entire party only Mildmay could touch Cold Iron and he was one-armed. If she had only known he was a bogle...

"Mama, what *is* that thing?" Simon whispered, interrupting her thoughts.

"He's a killmoulis, Simon," she explained. "Most mills have them – they're a type of Hob or brownie."

"Like the Hob that lives in the chimney at the Abbey?" Simon had chatted with the Hob quite often. Hobs were shy, but they liked children and would even take them for rides on the chimney smoke, but Simon had not yet taken advantage of the Hob's offer. Hobs were hearth brownies, beneficial spirits who helped keep order in the chimneys, pantry and buttery. Each night cook put out a pannikin of rich milk for him.

"Very like the Hob," Diana agreed. "The killmoulis helps the miller and his family. Sometimes they can be mischievous –"

I ain't never made no mischief! protested the killmoulis. *Me an' Molly, we was always helpin' – an' the miller treated us fair – plenty o' grain an' corn leavin's to snuff up an' even milk an' butter! We loves butter!* he added wistfully.

"Then why are you helping these bad people?" Diana asked. "I know killmoulises – they are never evil!"

He gave a loud wail. *Acos they got my Molly – my wife! They're goin' to kills her iffen I doesn't do what they wants – to guard you an' makes certain sure ye don't gets away! Ye can't climb over th' window cause there's Cold Iron on th' sills an' th' doors is barred with Cold Iron.*

That explained why she was beginning to feel weak and as if she needed to sit down. Simon was drooping visibly. Surely having a guard was gilding the lily. She was not surprised that the Cold Iron did not bother Goodbody – his Wizarding blood was weak. But should it not have bothered the bogle more?

"Is there another way out of here? Some little door that they wouldn't know about – that only you would know?" she asked.

Bevis shook his flat head. *They'll kill me Molly*, he repeated.

"I can help you find Molly and rescue her!" Diana pledged recklessly. "I am a Witch and my son is a Wizard! Only get us away from this Cold Iron! My uncle, the Marquis of Lyonshall, owns this mill and if you were to help us he would be so grateful that he would bring a new miller here to live and restore the mill!"

A miller – a real miller wi' a family an' children? Bevis looked at her with a sudden hopeful light in his eyes. Then a crafty look came over his face. *They thinks they're so clever an' poor old Bevis is addle-pated! There is a door, a little door, down by the wheel. We could go down there!* He went over to where the cobweb-festooned gears that drove the grindstones in the lowest level hung. *Right here!* he pulled open a little door that they had not noticed.

A smell of damp and mold drifted up the stairwell. *Won't be able to use mage light*, Bevis said, *for that bogle would be smelling' it. But I've got a few magics of me own an' he'll never figger out how we went!* He laughed, a sort of wheezing sound as if he had not laughed in a long time.

Simon shivered. Even it meant escaping he could not go down that stair in the dark. He simply could not do it.

483

41

The Kittens' Adventure

The kittens were bored. There had not been much going on in the Tower that morning. Lyon was busy scrying all parts of the kingdom, asking if there were any trace of unicorns. René and Mr. Arabin, who had stayed to help, were bent over a map, each with a pendulum in hand. A piece of unicorn horn was attached to each pendulum. They were trying by means of sympathetic magic to dowse the location of unicorns. They had not much hope of this, for pendulum dowsing worked best when the Wizard had a bit of hair or a belonging of the actual living person or animal to use as a locator. The unicorn who had borne this horn was long dead. They were hoping for an empathetic vibration. But nothing had happened, and Beau had been scolded away when he jumped up on the map and pawed at the shining pendulum.

The kittens had attempted to tease Leander, Lyon's familiar, but the great owl had stared them down with his large yellow eyes and lifted a huge talon. They had wisely retreated.

They at last decided to go out of doors to visit Tuathail. They always enjoyed talking to the dragon.

No one noticed them leave, for the three Wizards were deep in concentration and Leander had gone back to sleep. Their father, Plato, who was not needed in his duties, had curled up on the window seat and was enjoying the last of the sun, for it was clouding over rapidly. Out on his back, with his belly caressed by sunbeams, he did not notice the kittens slip through the cat door and tumble headlong down the stairs.

"We mustn't miss nuncheon," cautioned Rascal as they ran outside. Robert, the footman on duty at the Tower door, opened the heavy door for them. "Alphonse is making *Rissoles de Veau* and has promised to make enough for us!"

"All you think about is your stomach!" grumbled Beau. As usual, he was in the lead as they bounded across the lawn and through the gardens.

"We're growing kittens – we need our food!" Rascal returned.

Neige was looking about her as the two girls brought up the rear. "Oh, dear, it looks as if we are going to have some bad weather! Again!" She shivered and her fur stood on end. She could already feel the electricity in the air. She felt a sudden longing to be with Ninon, cuddled and safe. Like a great many white cats, she was rather timid and fearful. Fortunately, she was not deaf, as some of her colour were.

Janus did not like this either. "I hope Simon gets home before it breaks!" she said worriedly.

"You girls are scaredy cats!" jeered Beau and then laughed at his own pun.

The girls ignored him. He was such a brat at times!

They had now reached the dragon pen and found Tuathail just awakening from a nap. Like cats, dragons spent a good deal of time sleeping, and, like cats, dragons liked to bask in the sun.

But a huge dark cloud, looming up from the west, had reached out long tentacles of darkness and was beginning to block the noon day sun high overhead. It was the drop of temperature that had awoken Tuathail.

"I'm not after liking the looks of that cloud at all," remarked the dragon, after a yawn that cracked his jaws and showed huge white teeth, each one of which was larger than any of the kittens.

"Do you think it will be as bad as it was?" asked Janus anxiously, for dragons had great weather sense.

It was a question that was destined to remain unanswered, for with a pounding of hooves and the clatter of wheels on gravel, Diana's phaeton, pulled by fear-maddened Phoebus and Apollo, careened into the stable yard.

Tuathail reared back on his tail and gave a great bellow of warning. The kittens, paws to their ears, flattened against the ground as the grooms began to stream out of the stable. Daniel and Joseph, another of the grooms, leaped to the heads of the pair and managed to get them stopped. Young John, an apprentice groom, ran to the horse bell and began ringing it loudly. People rushed from the house, faces full of consternation and fear. Soon the stableyard was full of Wizards, ladies and servants.

As soon as Daniel and Joseph had the team under control Lyon and René examined the carriage for signs of an accident, since that was their first thought. Although they found some damage from the flight of the horses, there was no sign of an overturn, nor was the body much scraped, nor was there a broken wheel or an axle. "Perhaps they alighted for some reason and something spooked the pair," Lyon suggested.

"What is this?" said René sharply. He had found the note attached to the whip socket. He wasted no time in ripping it open. It was sealed with a virulent pink wafer.

In block letters it read:

WE HAVE THE WOMAN. HAVE THE FRENCHIES BRING £10,000 TO THE OLD MILL BY 5 PM IF YOU WANT TO SEE HER ALIVE AGAIN. DO NOT SEND FOR THE SHERIFF.

"They have been kidnapped!" said Ninon. She stood with her arms around Lucie, who had run out of doors in her night-rail and dressing gown.

"It says nothing about Simon," said René, frowning, and turning the note over and over as if there was something, some clue, that he might have overlooked.

"Give that to me," the Duke of Chenevix ordered. "Why are these criminals specifying you as the instrument of delivery, Keir? And in such insulting fashion?" No one seemed to notice that the kidnappers had employed the plural. Chenevix took the note from his son and studied it with his quizzing glass. "We must send for the sheriff immediately," he said at last, distaste in his voice. "The militia must be called out."

"Don't be more of an ass than you can help, Chenevix!" growled Lyon. "They more than likely have someone watching us, to see if we comply with their demands! I won't take a chance with Diana's – or Simon's – life. We'll do exactly as they say."

"Have you ten thousand pounds at hand?" asked the Vicar worriedly.

Lyon shook his mane of hair. "I shall have to go to my bank in Cheltenham. If it were quarter day and all of the rents were in, I might have part of that sum, but now, in mid quarter... there is no need to keep a sum like that at hand."

"Pray allow me to go to Cheltenham for you," said the Vicar eagerly. "If you would be so good as to give me a letter of authorization..."

"And I'll be taking the reverend gentleman to the town," said Tuathail eagerly.

"A good idea!" said Lyon. "Much faster than your dog cart, Reverend!"

Before they had finished speaking, René had gone into the stable and emerged with Tuathail's riding harness. With Joe's help he had the dragon ready for flight before Lyon had finished the letter of authorization. Then with some trepidation the Vicar mounted the dragon (it had been some years since he had ridden dragon-back) and took off for Cheltenham.

Chenevix stood by, angrily. He was incensed that all of these people, including his wife and son, were paying no attention to his orders. Plans were going ahead without his advice being asked. Already Keir was talking of going to the old mill as soon as the Vicar returned with the ransom. And the Duke was made angrier still when he offered Lyon's horse to Keir and was refused.

"I shall teleport," René said. "I cannot ride the horse and I know that area very well – it was an old playground of mine."

"That is the best idea," Ninon agreed. "We may follow with a wagon and comforts. They will be hungry and frightened."

"And probably wet as well," grunted Lyon, looking at the clouds. "Damn it!" he burst out, "who could have done this and why? It is unconscionable! To subject a gently-born female and a child to such terror!"

487

René could picture little else besides Diana and Simon in the hands of some fiends. Had they been hurt? Were they frightened? Had they been separated? His hands balled into fists as he thought of getting them on the people who had dared to hurt those he cared about.

"*Un instant, s'il vous plait!*" said Ninon. "Why do we not dowse with the pendulum and locate them? Then René can teleport to where they are and rescue them! Then we follow on the dragon, no? Several Wizards and a Witch may easily overcome these criminals!"

Lyon clapped a hand to his forehead. "Why didn't I think of that?" he cried and took off for the Tower. "Get something of Diana's!" he called to Ninon.

René was before all of them, for he disappeared in shards of violet light and by the time the rest of them reached the Tower he was already spreading out a map of the estate on the top of a work table.

The kittens had watched and listened to everything that was going on. Janus had a tendency to mew pitifully, worried about Simon. Rascal was all for going along with the rescuers, there to scratch eyes out and bite if necessary. Neige wanted Ninon to pick her up and cuddle her against her face.

Beau was already hatching a plan. He knew they would never be allowed to go. Everyone thought they were too young. But he would show them all! He wasn't actually certain what they could do, but they were not going to sit idly by while everyone faced danger in an exciting adventure. And besides, they *needed* him!

Ninon soon appeared with a scarf belonging to Diana. This René would around the long gold strand of the pendulum above the faceted elongated plumb. Everyone crowded around the table as René held the pendulum over the map of the Abbey lands and said the Words to invoke the spell. Outside in the hall the servants crowded against the door.

The pendulum began moving almost at once, swinging violently to the location of the old mill. And then it moved slower, moving away from the mill site till it came to a stop in what was marked 'Mill Woods'.

"Surely they cannot have been stupid enough to keep them where they intend to collect the ransom – the very first place any one would look!" said Lyon in disbelief.

"But they are moving now," René pointed out, as the pendulum began to move again, slowly this time, and cautiously.

"I have not known Diana long, *du vrai*," said Ninon, "but I do not think, me, that she would let these *couchons* do as they wish with her and *le petit* Simon!"

"My niece is a most redoubtable female," agreed Lyon with a smile.

"You must go at once, René," said Ninon decidedly.

"Without the ransom money?" said Chenevix.

"If they may be rescued there is no need of the ransom," said Lyon. "We know where they are – and that is to our advantage."

They had all been so intent on the scrying that they had not noticed the day outside changing for much the worse. It had become more ominous with every passing moment, the sky darkening in intensity. Now, suddenly, there was a great crack of thunder that startled everyone. All turned to look at the window to find the bright sky gone as dark as night and electricity flickering amongst the clouds.

"Damn!" swore Lyon. "Might you travel in this weather, my boy?"

"If I have to do so, I can," René said grimly. In truth, it was rather dangerous to teleport in a bad electrical storm. Only Ninon understood this and she looked anxious as the thunder pealed once again. "Perhaps you should wait, René," she said.

"I cannot, *Grandmère*," he said. He was as anxious as she, but not about the storm. He *had* to do something to help them and standing about, endlessly discussing what to do was not helping.

"Excuse me, your Graces, my lords, but I took the liberty of having Alphonse prepare a stone bottle of soup and another of tea," Seppings' soft voice interrupted them. He held a slim rucksack, which, if he had but known it, was not as slim as it had been.

"*C'est magnifique*, Seppings!" said Ninon. "You will remember, René, what Guénolé has said about expanding your field. If you hold this *sac* against you, it will teleport with you. For it begins to look as if we will not be with you directly."

489

Lyon had gone to the crystal and said, "You may need to find shelter out there. for the Augurs predict a violent storm of immense intensity, lasting into the early morning hours."

"I will beg shelter of Father Oak," said René, "for the Sacred Grove is not far from the Mill Woods."

Outside the wind began to shriek, rising suddenly. "Go quickly!" said Ninon as Seppings came forward with a rain cape.

"May *le bon Dieu* protect you, *mon fils*," whispered Lucie. She had come to stand behind Chenevix and he looked down at her in surprise as her hand crept into his.

René picked up the rucksack and held it tightly against him. He allowed Seppings to put the rain cloak over his shoulders and said briefly, "Say a prayer for us," and then vanished.

Barely seconds after he disappeared a huge flash of lightning split the sky and the wind seemed determined to rip the roof off the Tower.

"Pray the rain will hold off until he finds them and gets them to shelter," said Lyon peering out the window. "This is going to be a bad one. We won't be able to get out until morning, I dareswear. And Mr. Arabin will have to pass the night in Cheltenham. Tuathail can't fly in this."

Chenevix was in a foul temper. "Why did you not go. Lyonshall?" he burst out. "She is your niece! Why must it be Keir? He is risking his life!"

"I can't dematerialize," said Lyon simply. "He is the only one who can do this –"

"I can teleport also," said Ninon, "but not to the Old Mill, for that is a place I have never been."

"*You* can dematerialize?" cried Lyon. "My dear ma'am! Perhaps to pass the anxiety of waiting, you will explain to me some of the things I do not understand?"

Ninon agreed, for sitting and wringing her hands would accomplish naught and soon they were involved in a conversation that no one else in the room understood.

Seppings directed the servants to return to their duties. Dinner must still be served and the discipline of the house maintained, but he determined to hold a prayer service in the servant's hall that evening to ensure the safe return of all concerned.

Chenevix, who was still angered at what he thought Lyonshall's cavalier attitude to his heir's safety, felt a tug on his arm and looked down to see Lucie looking up at him. "Come, Lucien," she said, "there is a chapel here. We go to pray for our son's safety and that of the Lady Diana and the little one, *non*?"

The Duke was not a great believer in prayer – his regular attendance at Church was a matter of form rather than inclination, but there was nothing else he could do. And for the first time in days, Lucie was again touching him and acting as if she cared about him.

"Very well, my dear," he at last agreed, patting her hand which now lay on his arm. It felt good there.

Simon could not help it. His lip quivered and his eyes filled with tears. He could not go down that dark stair, not even with Mama holding his hand.

All of his life he had been afraid of the dark. He had always needed a candle at night and one of the reasons he had been so happy at the Abbey was because of the well-lit corridors and rooms. The bright mage lights lit up all of the nooks and crannies and he was allowed to have as large a mage light in his room as he could cast. Mr. Roussillon had taught him how to expand it and move it around the room, so if there were any odd shadows that seemed to be moving in a threatening manner, he could make his room as bright as day. This was a great comfort.

When he had lived in Norfolk, his cousins had made game of him, jeered and called him "baby" – his uncle admonishing him to be a man, and saying that his father, a brave soldier, would be ashamed to have such a namby-pamby for a son. But Mama had never said he was too old for a night light, nor had Mr. Roussillon. Simon had shyly confessed his fears to his tutor, when he wished to know how to enlarge his mage light. Simon had been grateful to them both

But now Bevis said they could not use mage light, that the bogle would smell it and they had to go down the stairs in the dark. And he just could not do it!

"Won't the bogle be able to sniff us out?" Diana was asking the killmoulis. In truth, Simon was more than a little afraid of him, too. Not only was he grotesque in appearance, but Simon was not certain that he liked the way the creature's voice buzzed in his head. It seemed a very strange way to talk.

Bevis gave a short laugh. *Not if I was to carry you down! He's just be a-smelling old killmoulis! No tracks for un t' sniff, ye sees*!

Simon shivered and looked piteously at Diana. He did not want that thing touching him! And then another thought struck him. Probably the killmoulis could only carry one of them at a time! That meant he would be left alone up here – and those wicked men and that thing with them might come back! Or he would have to wait at the bottom of the stairs – in the dark! There might be spiders and even ghosts! He began to shiver uncontrollably and wanted to be sick.

"Simon!" said Diana, noticing his distress. "What is it?" She came to kneel beside him, and put her arms around him.

"Oh, Mama!" he said, burying his face against her soft neck. "I'm so frightened! Uncle Frederick would call me a coward! Tom and my cousins would not be frightened."

"No, for they are too stupid to be frightened!" Diana said fiercely. "You are not a coward, Simon! Only a chuckle-head would not be afraid – we are in a great deal of danger and we must get ourselves out of it. I am certain that everyone at the Tower is already looking for us, but we need to help them."

Bevis was quite distressed by Simon's tears, and came to kneel beside them. *Don't be afeered, little 'un*! he said coaxingly. *Old Bevis is a-goin' to help ye an' yer ma, an' we'll find my Molly too!* He reached out his large, work-worn hand and placed it on Simon's thistledown hair.

Simons first impulse was to shrink away from the killmoulis. But as Bevis continued to rest his hand on Simon's head, the boy began to feel differently. A feeling of peace and quiet began to steal over his senses. The killmoulis was suddenly a friendly creature, his eyes full of love and compassion. He even smelled nice to Simon, redolent of good

492

ripe grain. And when Bevis took him in his arms and stood, Simon trustingly put his arms around the killmoulis's neck.

That's the dandy! said the voice in Simon's head, which no longer seemed so odd or frightening. *I'm a –goin' t' take ye down th' stairs an' out th' door an' then I'll bring yer ma down faster than you can say killmoulis! There's a nice old beech tree outside that'll be glad to watch over ye! We're great friends, him an' me.*

"I know Father Oak," Simon offered as they headed for the little door.

Well, then, my friend will be happy to meet ye, for he's a friend o' Father Oak's too, said Bevis, as they began going down the stairs, leaving Diana behind. She was so glad to see the look of fear disappear from Simon's face.

True to his word, Bevis had Simon down the stairs and out of doors before he had time to become fearful of the dark stair.

It was gloomy out of doors too, for the clouds had completely covered the sky and hung heavy and deep, inky in colour. The wind was quite strong.

Bevis deposited Simon amongst the lower branches of the enormous beech tree. *Now bide ye there,* he directed. *Iffen those bad 'uns come back, my friend here'll make certain sure they can't see ye!*

The beech rustled its long pointed leaves as if to agree and Simon sensed the protection the tree offered.

In no time at all Bevis was back with Diana. *We'll make for th' Grove,* Bevis said. *A penny to a florin th' trees know where they took my Molly!*

An' we'll need shelter soon, he added as thunder rumbled and rain began to spit, as he shepherded them in front of him, looking about for signs of the return of the kidnappers. But they were alone in an increasingly wild landscape. As the wind began to moan chillingly through he trees, they went deeper into the woods, not knowing what lay ahead, placing their trust in the killmoulis.

The kittens had not known what to expect when they climbed into the sack. It had been Beau's idea, of course. Seppings had had one of the footmen bring the sack to the Tower and put it on the floor near the door. What with all of the attention being given to the pendulum dowsing, no one noticed as three of the kittens crawled into the sack.

Neige refused to go, in spite of the jeers of Beau and Rascal. She was not afraid, she insisted – she thought it her duty to stay with Ninon. After all, Ninon was her Witch and might be worried if her familiar went missing.

Janus was not concerned with the adventure, as were the boys. She had to find Simon and make certain that he was safe. Had she but known it, her brothers were just as concerned about their humans, but they were even more thrilled about the chance for a daring exploit.

With their acute hearing they could discern everyone's speech as they found places amongst the stone bottles and silverware, serviettes, cups and bowls. There was also a package of fresh bread and a crock of butter, all carefully packed by Alphonse to be as flat as possible.

The kittens were still small enough to curl into little balls of fur and they did so at Beau's direction. "Run your claws into the side of the sack," he ordered.

"Why do you get to give the orders?" grumbled Rascal.

"Because I know about teleporting and you don't!" said Beau smugly. Actually, he knew little more than they did, but it would not do to let them know this. "We have to be very still and quiet so René will not tumble us."

Accordingly, they were motionless and silent as the sack was passed and then they felt René holding it against himself.

They heard the snap of the rain cape as Seppings threw it around René's shoulders, and heard René utter: "Say a prayer for us."

And then there was the sensation of being pulled apart. They seemed to go down a long tunnel, spinning faster and faster. The three kittens held on for grim life, uncurling and grabbing with their rear as well as their fore claws. "I'm going to be sick!" screamed Janus, but the others could not hear her, for a huge wind seemed to be roaring in their ears.

Then, as quickly as it was begun, it was done. They sensed that they were once again on solid ground and their sensitive noses told them that they were in a wood. All three of them felt dizzy and a little disoriented, but Beau was determined not to show it. As if he was used to being teleported every day he commanded in a whisper, "We'd best keep low and quiet still. I'll let you know when we can come out."

As the other two wanted nothing more than to keep their eyes closed and recover, they did not give him an argument.

The Friendly Trees

Earlier that day, on the Kentish Downs it was a lovely morning. The sun entered the breakfast parlor of the Eastcote estate and shone on the gleaming porcelain, glassware and silverware on the highly polished Sheraton table. From an open window came the sound of birdsong and the tinkle of sheep bells, high on the Downs. It was a perfect summer day.

Four people sat at the table, each immersed in a news-sheet. Lord and Lady Eastcote took the *Morning Post*, the *Wizards' Times* and the *London Journal*, so there were enough to go around.

Lord Eastcote's sister Lady Amabel, and her husband, George, Baron Renfrew, were at present visiting in Kent. Every July they came down from Northumberland and stayed with the Eastcotes for a seven-day, the two families then going onto Brighton for a fortnight. As usual, a house on the Marine Parade had been hired by the Renfrews – Lord Eastcote owned a house on the Steyne. There they tasted the delights of sea-bathing, military reviews on the Downs, balls at the Old Ship and evenings at the Regent's Chinoiserie Pavilion. This year they would be admitting to the ranks of the adults Lady Harriet Bryant and Miss Cecelia Renfrew. Lady Eastcote and Lady Amabel were presenting their seventeen–year-old daughters next spring, and both fond Mamas thought their daughters would take all the better should they have some experience of company before being thrust into the maws of the *Beau Ton*.

The family resemblance between Lady Amabel Renfrew and her brother was strong – tall, sandy-haired and

496

blue-eyed, spare of flesh and with a strong chin and the rather Roman Bryant nose. She dressed fashionably but suitably for one of her years in a gown of orange crepe, with a delicate *fraise* of fluting about her throat and a little Alexandrian cap perched on a coronet of braids. Her Lord was a bluff country gentleman who could not be called handsome, but was good natured to a fault, and, as much as he disliked being away from his estate, he liked to give this treat to his family, which consisted of Francis, the eldest, at two and twenty, Cecelia, and the younger two, Cyril, eleven, and Fanny, nine. These had, along with Harriet and Cecilia all had made up a large riding party with the younger Bryants this morning, leaving their parents in peace for a while.

Lady Eastcote was currently searching the *Wizards' Times* for news of the Augury Corps in the Peninsula. Peter was a poor correspondent and his last letter – misspelt and very difficult to decipher – had left his Mama with the impression that the Augury Corps was in the thick of the fighting. Lord Eastcote had doubted if this were indeed true – Lord Wellington was not such a fool as to expose his valuable Augurs to enemy fire. It was more than likely Peter putting on airs to be interesting. All the same, Lady Eastcote was worried. She wished that Peter had taken a position with the Bureau of Prognostication and been safely stationed at Dover or some such place, close to home, on the watch for storms and fog in his crystal.

The gentlemen were reading about the latest folly of Lord Liverpool's government – denying that there was any danger from the incursions of the Unselighe Court – and the news of yet another riot in Hyde Park, which had to be put down by the Life Guards. Several people had been trampled in the resulting *mêlée*.

"It is a great pity that the government seems to have its head in a hole," Lord Renfrew had just remarked when his wife, who had been reading the Society News, gave a great shriek.

Jorrocks, who had been pouring more tea for the company, gave a start and narrowly missed pouring tea upon his employer.

"Amabel!" protested her brother. "My ears, I beg you!"

She ignored him. "Gussie, you slyboots!" she said to her sister-in-law. "Not a word to any of us! But you have pulled off the *coup* of the Season! All the old cats in Brighton will be at hair-pulling with you, I daresay!"

"What are you talking about, Amabel?" demanded Lady Bryant rather crossly, for she had just located an article about the Wizard Augury Corps and wished to read it in peace.

Lady Amabel was practically bouncing up and down in her seat. "Why, this announcement of Diana's engagement to the biggest matrimonial prize in all of the Isles!" she said excitedly.

Lady Eastcote looked blankly at her. "Diana is not engaged," she said, "Why, we had a letter but yesterday and she said naught of any attachment–"

"Here it is in black and white!" said Lady Amabel, thrusting the news-sheet at her. "Do you doubt the evidence of your own eyes?"

Lord Renfrew, a man of few words, wasted no time in arguing. He turned to the Society News in the journal he was reading and read there, even as Lady Eastcote was reading, with her husband leaning over her shoulder:

A marriage has been arranged and will take place shortly between Lady Diana Stillfield, widow of the late Captain Jonathan Stillfield, daughter of the Earl and Countess of Eastcote and René Alain Delamar, Marquis of Keir, heir to the Duke of Chenevix and his Duchess. The marriage will take place at Chenevix Duchis, in Dorsetshire; the date to be announced in the very near future.

"Good God!" said Lord Eastcote in his wife's ear.

"Robert!" she clutched at his sleeve. "What can this mean? I cannot think Diana would do such a thing without telling us!"

Lady Amabel was suddenly round–eyed. "You did not know of this? I thought perhaps your brother Lyonshall had promoted the match!"

"We have had letters and scrys, from both of them –" began Lord Eastcote

"And letters from dear little Simon, as well!" his lady interrupted. "And not in any of those has there been even one hint that this young man had offered for her, or was even paying his addresses to her. Nor have we received a letter or a scry from him, requesting our consent. Not that Diana needs our consent, of course, for she is a widow and of age, but it would have been a gentlemanlike thing to do!" Angrily, she dabbed at her eyes with a bit of lacy handkerchief. "We must scry my brother at once!" she determined." I must speak to Diana!"

"Perhaps this is a mistake on the part of the news-sheets," suggested Lord Renfrew. "Why do I not scry the journals and inquire from whence they had this news?"

Both were tried – Lord and Lady Eastcote were unsuccessful in contacting Lyonshall, for it had become increasingly difficult to scry Lyonshall, with all of the others scrying him in his capacity as Arch Druid.

Lord Renfrew was more successful in obtaining information from the journals in London. The notice in each case had been delivered by a manservant in the livery of the Duke of Chenevix.

As they cautiously made their way through the wood near the mill, Diana noticed with dismay that the sky was growing steadily darker. It was beginning to spit rain as well. Neither she not Simon was clad for inclement weather – she wore a light gown of spotted muslin without a Spencer or pelisse, and a fabric capote on her head, while Simon was in a light nankeen suit. Somewhere, in his tussle with the bogle he had lost his flat tasseled cap.

She recalled being told by old Nurse that Simon's colds always went to his chest and the doctor's warning that he might be considered of a delicate constitution. How would he survive a night out in the open, in a thunderstorm, with an icy rain and perhaps hail? There was nothing she could do to protect him! Beneath the trees as the worst place one could possibly be in a lightning storm. They were far from any friendly farm or even from Knightswold. And they were in danger of being recaptured by Mildmay and his confederates. She wouldn't hesitate to use her magic on them this time. The dragon whistle could not be used here in the deep woods where Tuathail could not land, nor could the dragon fly in a thunderstorm. Diana was afraid of going out in the open where they might be more easily seen by their captors.

The killmoulis knew his way through the woods. He herded them in front of him, stepping over their small tracks with his big feet. He hoped to confuse the bogle of whom he was rather scornful. *Prides themselves on their noses, they do!* he said. *Huh! I coulds teach 'em a thing or two 'bout sniffin' out tracks!* He tapped his big nose with one gnarled finger. *Ain't nobody got the nose what a killmoulis got! And ain't nobody can hide tracks like a killmoulis!*

Beneath his big feet Simon and Diana's small footprints vanished as if they had never existed. *They'll be knowin' that ye escaped,* Bevis explained, *but happen it'll take 'em a mort o' time to figger out how an' where. Rain'll help too, aye, an' mebbe keeps 'em from comin' after us!*

Diana was more concerned at the moment to find shelter. The rain drops were coming more frequently and the lowering sky looked as if it would burst at any moment. Thunder rumbled not too far away and at that precise moment, a bolt of lightning shot across the sky.

And just ahead of them, violet light sparked and flared.

Simon let go Diana's hand abruptly and ran forward eagerly.

"Simon!" Diana attempted to grab at him and almost fell. The killmoulis steadied her. She pulled away from him and ran after her Simon in the gloom, terror stricken for her son.

To her immense relief, she found, in a little glade not too far ahead, Simon being held by René, who had dropped to one knee in order to embrace the boy. "I *knew* you would come!" Simon was saying happily.

René looked up as Diana and the killmoulis approached. "Both my *Grandmère* and your uncle said that you would rescue yourselves!" he said with a smile of relief at Diana.

"Our rescue was entirely due to Bevis," said Diana, pushing the killmoulis forward.

To her surprise, René said, "*Bonjour*, Bevis! I have not seen you in some time!"

Nigh on ten year, the killmoulis agreed. *You an' your friend Will ain't been around in a long, long while. Played hereabouts regular they did,* he added, turning to Diana.

"The old mill was a playground most *magnifique,*" René said. "But we may reminisce later, my old friend. We must now get to shelter as fast as we may."

"Where might we go?" Diana asked worriedly, for a sudden sweep of rain had come out of nowhere and more would come soon.

"I will ask Father Oak for shelter," René promised. He stood up, Simon still in his arms.

"You will have it, child of ours," a voice came through the trees, on the sigh of the wind. "The vines weave you a shelter and the moss makes you a bed. But you must hurry. The storm grows close and it is monstrous and hungry. Kilmoullis!" he then called out. "Your Molly is safe – she has been rescued! When the storm has passed you may go to her."

Bevis gave a great sigh, compounded of relief and happiness that echoed in everyone's head.

They ran through the last bit of the woods, René carrying Simon. As they neared the grove, the vines parted in front of them and they were on the painted floor.

There stood, or rather lay a little hut, almost in the center of the floor. It was made of tightly woven vines, with a mound of dried leaves covering it.

"But it is so exposed!" cried Diana. "Surely the lightning..."

"It is on the top of the node," René explained, " and the node will repel the lightning as well as provide warmth for us. In you go!" he put Simon down and gave him a little push towards a portion of the vines that were lifting. "Cast your mage light, Simon."

It was a small space, just enough room for the four of them to stretch out, and not really high enough for René or Bevis to stand upright. But it was snug and dry and the floor was covered in bright green springy moss, more comfortable than many a carpet Diana had trod upon. It smelled delightfully of the woods and proved rain proof, for with a horrendous crash, the heavens opened up and the sound of an avalanche of water cascaded upon the vine roof.

501

Inside the rucksack the kittens clung to one another, even Beau admitting, but only to himself, that he was frightened. They had been jostled when René ran through the woods and terrified by the roll of thunder. They now felt René put down the sack, and they waited in trepidation for him to open it and discover them. Now this adventure seemed a very bad idea.

But they were granted a respite, for it was judged that the most important thing was to create warmth.

"Might we have a fire in here, sir?" they heard Simon ask.

"No, for it would hurt this moss, which is so generously making us comfortable," René answered. "I shall borrow some of the natural warmth of the node to heat us. Watch, Simon."

Beau was frustrated that he could not see what was going on for he liked to see any act of magic performed. He heard Simon say "Oh!" in wonder and a very few moments warmth stole into the little shelter.

"I wish that I might do that," Diana said rather enviously. "Witches are not taught to use ley lines. We raise our cones of power the power of the Lady Moon and the crystals."

"I shall teach you," René promised, "for it seems foolish that you should not know."

"Mama," Simon's voice interrupted, "this is a very nice place, but I am so hungry!" It had been a long while, in more ways than one since the ices in Knightswold.

"I have brought tea and soup," said René.

The kittens felt him lift the bag and open the top. The moment was here – they were about to be discovered and the adventure was over – scoldings and recriminations would begin.

For the first thing that René's hand encountered was not a stone bottle of soup or tea, but a ball of fur.

"*Qu'est-ce que c'est que ça?*" René demanded and pulled Beau out into the light.

The kitten blinked, his eyes enormous, and looked from one of them to the other. When he saw the killmoulis's huge mouthless face, he swelled to twice his normal size and laid back his ears, spitting and hissing.

"He is a friend, Beau!" said Simon quickly.

René held the kitten up to his face. "What are you doing here, Beau?" he said severely. "This is no place for you – there is much danger!"

"We're your familiars!" Beau was indignant. "Where else should we –"

"We!" René interrupted. "You have all come?"

"Not Neige – she's afraid," the kitten explained, "but Rascal and Janus..."

Simon went to the rucksack and pulled it open. Out tumbled Janus and Rascal, trying to look as innocent as was possible. Once freed from the sack they ran to their humans, pausing only to hiss at Bevis.

The killmoulis seemed hurt by their attitude. *I likes little cats, I do, 'specially kittens!*

"They are not as yet accustomed to you," René soothed the killmoulis as he busied himself emptying the sack. "Are you able to ingest soup, Bevis?"

Nay then, lad, I've me grain sack I can snuff,. The killmoulis replied and pulled a sack out from under his coat. *Th' farmers here abouts been real good t' Molly an' me, an' brings grain by regular. Still, it ain't like havin' a miller, but this lady has promised that the Marquis 'll fetch in a miller – one wi' children, we hopes!* He pulled some grain form his sack and snuffed it up into his nose, rather in the manner of a gentleman taking snuff. He then began to explain to René about Molly and how he had come to rescue Diana and Simon. René assured him that he as well, would help him find Molly and thank whoever had rescued her. Father Oak had said no more than that. That Bevis was still worried about his wife, they all could see. *I was after hopin' Father Oak could tell me where Molly was bein' now, since th' trees know nearly everything,* he said. *But us has to waits out this storm, I reckon.*

Diana reached forward and took the stone bottle of tea and poured it into one of the cups. She wanted Simon to have something hot as soon as possible. He was slightly damp, but the warmth of the node was rapidly drying them all.

The tea was strong and sweetened, with no milk in it. Simon had not as yet graduated from Cambric tea – which was more than three parts milk – but under these

503

circumstances it was probably the best thing that he could drink. She pressed it on him, making the kittens, who had been clambering all over him, get down. "You are all very naughty kittens!" she said severely, at which they stared at her with big, sorrow-filled eyes and she found it impossible to remain angry with something so adorable, which was just as they intended. They knew full well how their humans could be swayed by sweet, cuddly kittens.

When Bevis and René had finished talking about where Molly might be, the soup was served. There was plenty of it, rich with large pieces of chicken and carrots, potatoes, onions and peas in a thick stock. There was fresh bread and butter as well, and Bevis did not refuse a lump of butter, which he snuffed up with a sigh of bliss. The kittens were fed chunks of chicken from the soup and the tea was drunk to the last drop. They all felt much better for the hot food and soon Simon, with all of the kittens snuggled up against him, fell asleep. It had been a long day for him.

Shortly after that, Bevis fell asleep as well, in spite of his anxiety over Molly. Diana was afraid that any creature possessed of such a nose would snore loudly, but to her surprise he slept quietly, neither snoring nor moving about much.

Outside the rain still hurled itself against the shelter of vines. There was still the boom of thunder and the flash of lightning, seen but dimly through the tightly woven vines.

Diana, whose nerves had been screaming all afternoon as she tried to cope with the kidnapping, found herself telling René exactly what had happened and how she had felt that day, and as she told it, she could feel the tension draining away. He told her of the ransom note they received and they speculated what the alliance between Mildmay, Goodbody and a bogle might mean, and what the villains had hoped to accomplish besides forcing Diana to wed Goodbody.

Such speculation proved fruitless, for they did not have enough information.

A particularly violent thunderclap sounded, followed immediately by a bolt of lightning. The storm was right on top of them.

Diana shrieked involuntarily and then wrapped her arms around herself, shuddering.

René wished that he dared take her in his arms to comfort her. He contented himself with passing her the rain cape, which she gratefully folded about herself. "This reminds me – oh, so much! – of that night in Spain – when Jonathan died," she said, almost to herself, and not looking at René at all, but rather, he thought, into the past.

"I have hated thunder and lightning ever since," she said. "I was used to enjoy watching it – the brilliance of it, and the noise. My old nurse told me that the thunder was the angels playing at bowls." She smiled faintly for a moment. "But now all I see is the men bearing his body back to camp, blackened and broken. And I blamed the French for that – even you, René –" she added, unconsciously using his Christian name for the first time, "– when in truth it was my fault, all my fault!" She wiped angrily at her eyes, for tears were beginning to stream down her cheeks.

"Diana –" René began, "Your husband was a soldier, *non*? And he had his duty to do..."

"You don't understand!" For the first time she really looked at him. "You see, I was the one who killed him!"

43

Confessions

From her bed Lucie watched as her husband strode back and forth in front of the long Gothic windows. The golden tassels on his Hessian boots swung wildly from the violence of his pacing. Lucie could hear the rain lashing the mullioned windows and every few minutes, or so it seemed, a terrible roar of thunder sounded out, shaking her to her bones, followed by a flash of lightning so intense that she inadvertently jumped in fear.

They had spent a good hour in the Chapel. Although praying had offered Lucie comfort, she had seen, with disappointment, that it had not done the same for her husband. She had placed her beloved son's life in God's hands. But Lucien was still angry – at Lyonshall, at *Maman*, at everyone, even God, or so it seemed. Lucie was not certain why he was so angry. Was it because René had once again disobeyed him? Or because Lord Lyonshall had not gone after his niece his own self? Of one thing she was certain – Lucien was not angry from anxiety over René's safety because he loved his son and did not wish anything to happen to him. No, she thought bleakly – Lord Lyonshall cared more for René's happiness and well-being than did his own father.

"It will be morning before we can hope to hear anything," muttered Chenevix. "This ill-weather shows no sign of letting up any time soon." As soon as he said this there was another awful boom of thunder followed right on its heels by a great flash of light.

"Oh, please, Lucien, come away from the windows!" Lucie begged. "I have heard the lightning will come into the window and kill people! Please – I am so frightened!" She turned eyes shadowed with anxiety on him and jumped visibly as a blazing dazzle split the sky.

He was beside her at once, pulling her against him and letting her bury her face in his cravat. He felt a deep surge of protectiveness as she shuddered against him.

"I did not mean to frighten you, Lucie – I cannot bear this infernal waiting without knowing what is going on!" he explained, beginning to stroke her hair. "Damn this storm!"

"Are you worried about René?" she asked rather timidly.

"Of course I am worried about Keir! He is my heir, after all. I confess to you, my dear, that I did not used to care that the title would go to my dissolute cousin Alfred, but now I find such an idea insupportable. That is why I am so upset that Keir insists on taking this risk and continues to practice magic – which in this day and age is scarcely safe. He is putting himself at needless risk."

"But are you not proud of him?" Lucie said in French, which language she always reverted to when emotionally distraught. "To have become so accomplished at an early age – *milord* Lyonshall has told *Maman* that most Wizards do not become *Magistra* before thirty and very few pass the General examination! But our son has done this at five and twenty, with the highest scores!"

He let go of her rather abruptly. "Lucie, I do not wish for any one in this family to practice magic! Magic is a snare and a delusion! Idiots like Lyonshall think that magic may accomplish anything. Well, it cannot. It cannot save the persons one loves from dying a horrible death," he added in a lowered voice, looking away from her.

She put a nervous hand to her throat. He looked at once sad and angry. "Do you speak of Stuart, your brother?" she inquired timidly. He had not told her why or how Stuart had died in his place in the *auto de fé* and somehow she had never dared to ask. Instinctively she felt that Stuart's death was perhaps the root of all his hatred of magic, perhaps even of his coldness towards everyone except herself.

She waited breathlessly as the storm continued. She really thought that he would not answer her, perhaps even tell her it was none of her affair.

507

At long last he spoke. "That evening, when the Inquisition came – that was Stuart who came home to you – not I. He had sent me upon some trumped-up errand and had come to see if you were good enough to be in our family. You must remember that I told you he did not approve of my marrying. We were identical twins, you know – not a hairsbreadth of difference between us. All of our lives no one could tell us apart, save our father."

"But he let me think he was you!" Lucie said indignantly.

"That was not well done in him," said Chenevix. He would not tell Lucie the shameful thing that he had found out afterwards – that Stuart had a bet with a friend – that he could deceive Lucie and actually take her to bed without her knowing the difference.

"I would have known – if he had time to kiss me," said Lucie thoughtfully. "But he was scarce inside the door before the Inquisition came – me, I think that they were watching for you."

"When I returned from my errand it was to be greeted with the news that Stuart had been taken up by the Inquisition," Chenevix continued. "His manservant had followed him to our flat and waited outside in the street. He saw the officers of the Inquisition drag Stuart away."

He looked at her sadly. "Forgive me, Lucie," he said softly. "When I heard about Stuart's arrest I could think of naught else. All of my energies went to wards getting Stuart released or rescuing him. Dealing with the officials of the Inquisition was as dealing with a solid wall of granite. They would listen to nothing I said. They would not allow me to see Stuart, nor would they let the British Ambassador see him. They cared naught that our father was a Duke and that Stuart was his heir. Foreigners, they told me, should know the Church's penalties for the practice of magic and be aware of the consequences should they make magic within the sway of Mother Church! They would not believe that it was I who was the guilty one. And all for a mage light! A mage light!" he repeated bitterly. "I was not even allowed to be present at his trial! I sent for my father and our man-at–law as well, but the attorney arrived too late; Stuart was gone. My father, of course, would not bestir himself to come."

508

He rose from the bed and began to pace once again. "I used every magical trick I knew, Lucie! But he was kept behind walls of Cold Iron, and was burnt in shackles. I could not cast a spell to relieve his suffering when they burned him! And I thought that I, a newly qualified *Magus Majori*, could at least save him that, with a mercy spell – but it did not work and he died in agony, screaming for me to help him! And I could do nothing! Nothing!"

"That is the reason you have given up the magics?" said Lucie softly.

"Yes," he said harshly. "For it is worthless. And because I used magic I lost both you and Stuart and earned my father's everlasting hatred and contempt."

From what Lucie had heard about the old Duke he had held her husband in hatred and contempt *before* Stuart's death. In fact he had treated both his sons in much the manner Lucien was treating René.

But she had no idea as to what to do to stop the cycle.

That Sluagh was up to something Malcoeur was certain. The Elf disappeared for hours at a time and had a tendency to look sideways at Malcoeur and dissolve in a cascade of giggles, his eyes bright and gaze darting back and forth. Malcoeur grew increasingly tired of him.

It had been a while since the Jongleur had attacked any of the Druid enclaves, or even a higher-ranking Wizard. There was a two-fold reason for this – it put them off their guard and the attack in Scotland had taken more from him than he had counted upon. To outsiders, the murders looked effortless. Only Malcoeur knew what it had cost him first and last in energies. It would take time and blood to build up his strength before another attack like that.

And he had failed in Ireland. He had not told Sluagh but he had attempted to attack Tara and the place itself had repelled him. He could not even draw near to that cursed hill without severe pain, pain such as he had never felt. He had not understood this until he did some more reading about Tara. It was not known for certain, but legend had it that the pagan Goddess Dana had the hill beneath her protection. For were not the *Tuatha de Danaan*, the *Sidhe*, her children and the now closed doors to the kingdom of the Shining Ones there on that hill?

Malcoeur knew nothing of the *Sidhe,* save what he had read. And that indicated that they were all powerful, could manipulate time and distance and were immortal. If what he had felt was any indication of their powers, he wanted naught to do with them.

So the Irish Arch Druid remained alive. He would have to be caught outside the protection of Tara. Malcoeur had set a phouka to spy upon the Arch Druid.

In the meantime he would rest and gather strength. He accompanied many of the Unselighe creatures up on their killing sprees and fed upon the blood and terror they inflicted. Even the non-magicals could feed his blood lust. He still had the Arch Druid of Man to deal with, and then the Arch Druid of Britain, a man whom Malcoeur hated more than any one he had ever hated in his entire life – more so than even Bishop de Cavillon – Eliot Lyons , Marquis of Lyonshall. He had a score of many years standing to settle with that gentleman and Lyonshall's death would be neither short nor pleasant.

Wanda moved voluptuously against silken sheets and arched her naked body in a languid stretch. Beneath half-closed eyes she regarded the man – if one could call him that – she had just entertained, which was Wanda's euphemism for having intercourse.

She had never been so sated in her life. For once she had found someone to match her desires and someone who seemed to know just what she most liked without having to be told or shown – a process she found boring when all she wanted was someone to get to it and satisfy her. Only Culver had ever come close. But this Elf, or whatever he was, – was rough and wild and more than a little mad. He was dangerous and bad, but he made her feel as no one ever had before – she wanted to both scream and convulse — and she wanted him again – even thought they had been in bed since the morning hours and she had lost track of how many times he had pleasured her. He was every bit as insatiable as she.

Sluagh lay beside her with his arms crossed behind his head. Like Wanda, he was more than satisfied. Elfin women had always, it seemed to him, given into his desires but infrequently and acted as if they were lowering themselves because he was not of pure Elfin blood. This of course, lay all in his mind. He did not usually couple with mortal women because they were afraid of him and unlike some, he found no satisfaction with a fear-stricken partner. But this woman –! She matched him equally and never grew tired of the most erotic and depraved games he could imagine. He turned his head on the silken pillows and saw her watching him, with a slight smile on her lips, and a look in her eyes that told him she was ready to fall into his arms again.

"I have a gift for you," he said abruptly "for you have pleasured me greatly."

"I only hope this will be the first of many, many times that I can pleasure you," she said in the husky voice he found enticing.

He rose from the bed and went across the room to a cabinet, ornately carved. From this he withdrew a small casket and took this to where Wanda still lay. He swiftly turned it upside down and poured the contents out upon her.

Wanda cried aloud in pleasure, for upon her body now lay the most beautiful jewels she had ever seen – jewels of every type and size. There were rings and bracelets, necklaces and even a tiara, all glittering and shining, set in gold and silver. Eagerly, she sat up and began putting them on – the diamond and ruby tiara on her mussed and tumbled hair, rings on each finger, a multitude of bracelets up each arm and a huge. old fashioned diamond waterfall at her throat. The diamonds cascaded over her breasts nearly down to her waist. There were many more that she could not even wear.

But Sluagh fastened jewels about her ankles and hips and put rings on her toes, making them fit magically. And when he was done he pulled her to her feet and waved his hand. A triple mirror appeared and she gasped at her reflection. She was beautiful – covered in glitter!

"Lovely!" said Sluagh, slipping his arms around her waist. " I have seldom seen jewels look so well on anyone." He nuzzled her neck above the diamond waterfall. "The time is coming, my lovely one, when I shall be all powerful here in England and even abroad, I want you beside me, just as you are now, to share my triumph and my bed. You shall be my Queen!"

"A Queen!" repeated Wanda, dazzled. She could not take her eyes off her reflection. Even her body seemed to shine golden beneath the fire of the jewels.

"Everyone will bow to you and worship your beauty – but only I shall possess you," Sluagh said, moving his hand over her back in a very promising fashion.

She was melting inside already. She had never imagined when she had accompanied Goodbody to that dank cave this morning and met that horrid Mildmay that she would end up in bed with this glorious being. The minute he had entered the cave she had felt something vibrate between them and knew that they would soon be in bed together. And now he wanted to make her a Queen!

"Come back to bed," Sluagh demanded.

Wanda, regretfully, began to take off the jewels.

"No," he ordered. "Leave them on. For you look like one of the Shining Ones."

This reference had little meaning for Wanda, but she did not wish to remove a single jewel, afraid that he night change his mind and take them back. She determined to be very, very good for him.

"*You* killed him?" René repeated blankly. "But how is this possible? You have always said that it was the French – was it then some sort of accident? Surely you could not do such a thing to someone you loved!"

"It was all my doing that he went out that night and was captured by the French and tortured," she said, her eyes filled with tears once more. "He had no need to go out again – his patrol had come in and we were bivouacked for the night. But I drove him out into the rain and into the hands of the enemy. I and my dreadful sharp tongue!" she paused and looked down at Simon, laying a hand on his forehead. He slept peacefully with no sign of fever.

"You had a quarrel?" René prompted. "But all couples quarrel – surely he did not set out to be captured because you had the argument?"

"I said very horrible things to him," she said in a small voice. "I have a temper, I know. They were always scolding me at school about my hasty temper. Only observe how I treated you without knowing all the facts," she added. "I still don't understand how you can forgive me for the terrible things I said."

"It matters little," he returned. He felt as if he were treading on boggy ground. Clearly she needed to unburden herself, but whether or not she would be willing to do so to him was a moot point.

As if to echo his thoughts she said almost crossly, "I cannot conceive why I am telling you all of this!" *You, of all people* her tone almost seemed to say.

He took a deep breath and forged on ahead. "Because you need to tell someone, *non*? And you have been through the terrible time today and it has reminded you of that other time?"

She nodded, a little reluctantly. She turned back to contemplation of Simon, who slept on, oblivious, as did the kittens and Bevis. Soft kitten snores filled the space, while the rain still crashed upon the roof and the thunder growled and roared. The mage lights had been dimmed for the sleepers and the only other source of light was the purple-white bolts of lightning. It was a curiously intimate setting and Diana found that she wanted – needed – to go on. She had never told anyone – not even her mother – what had happened that night and why. It was as if it had become a completely intolerable burden and she must tell or explode.

"Do you know what a *baile* is?" she inquired. "I daresay you do not, for it is a Spanish term – it means a place for gentlemen to drink and play cards and watch the Gypsy girls dance. Near to our encampment was a small village and it had its *baile* – the *Baile Flamenco* it was called. Jonathan was used to go there with some of the other officers. He would never take me for he said that it was not a respectable place for a lady of quality. I thought nothing of it, for there are many places that a respectable female may not go, such as Cribbs' Parlor and the Fives Court or the Cockpit Royal. Indeed, no female would wish to go to such places."

"There was a Gypsy girl who danced there called *La Golodrina* – that means 'swallow'. I saw her dance in a more respectable milieu and she was very talented – she darted

513

about just like a bird. She was the featured performer at the *Baile Flamenco* and the officers all went and cheered her on.

"I do not know if you are familiar with the dance they call the *faruca*, but it is a dance of the grossest indecency, particularly if one does not wear any clothing while dancing. *La Golodrina* did this for a select handful of officers who were willing to pay for the privilege. It is a most suggestive dance and what it seems to have suggested to my husband was that he form an intimate connection with this dancer."

She had been staring at Simon the entire time she spoke, gently stroking his forehead.

"The reason we quarreled," she continued, "was that I found out that he was unfaithful to me. I overheard his batman boasting about his master's 'tidy little bit' to our groom. And I felt completely betrayed and dirtied. He was everything to me and he had been with another woman – who was little better than a common prostitute! My dear friend in the regiment, Anne Richmond, told me to ignore it, for all men have these little adventures – little adventures! – to call a break of faith with one's martial vows a little adventure! My father has never — I know for a fact — treated my mother so! But I could not ignore it – I confronted him and he told me it was none of my business, that I had no right to chide him, for he had his needs and I was increasing, after all, and would soon be of little use to him!" Her voice broke on a sob.

René wisely said nothing, but gave her his hand-kerchief.

"Thank you." She blew her nose, and still unable to look at him, continued. "I told him he could go to her, and he had best do it, for he was never going to touch me again! And he said that that suited him very well, for virtuous prigs such as I was were dead bores and *La Golodrina* wasn't adverse to a slap and tickle without being so bloody high-minded about it. And then he left, and I never saw him alive again. He died, with that between and all I have thought about ever since is that if I had taken Anne's advice he might still be alive. So you see, I killed him."

"No, I do not see that at all," said René firmly. "I do not think that you would have been happy, to accept his adultery. It is a tragic circumstance that he decided to ride back out but this is his decision, no? He might just have as easily ridden out and taken a chill and died from that. He might have decided to spend the night with another officer, or at the headquarters. You did not make him do what he chose to do." He wanted to ask her what had happened to the child she had carried but it was obvious that she had miscarried. That had probably added to her burden of grief. "What did your parents say when you told them of this?"

Her violet eyes were swimming with tears. "I never told anyone about this," she said. "I couldn't. But it seemed as if I had to tell someone tonight or run mad."

Oddly enough, it did not occur to her to swear him to secrecy. Somehow she knew that he would never tell anyone, unless she allowed it.

Just then thunder and lightning seemed to converge in one and the wind attempted to sweep the vine hut away. It was terrifying, and Diana, her emotions still raw, gave a scream of pure fright and ended up in René's arms. It seemed comforting and natural to be there and her overwrought nerves found solace in tears and she sobbed herself to sleep on his shoulder. And he, ever the gentleman, merely soothed her with nonsense and stroked her hair, when he longed to kiss her and love her. But this was the wrong, the very worst time for that. He felt both pity and admiration for her, as well as love.

But it was going to be a long night.

44

Cluny

"*Will* you wake up?" said a cross little voice.

René woke abruptly from a very pleasant dream of holding Diana in his arms and found that he was actually doing so. She slept against his chest, with his arm about her and Simon snuggled against her, with the kittens on top of him. René's back was up against Bevis. It was very warm and cozy.

"It's about time!" said the same cross little voice. "I've been trying to wake you up for fifteen minutes! You sleep like the dead!"

Diana seemed to be very deeply asleep, as did the rest of the occupants of the little vine room.

"They'll none of them awake before I let them," said Medb, for it was the tiny blue bell Faerie that muttered in René's ear. "Now get up, Wizard, do! Father Oak needs to speak to you!"

Carefully, much to Medb's impatience, René disentangled himself from Diana and stood up, remembering to bend to accommodate the low roof. Moving as quietly as possible, he left them slumbering.

Outside, the rain had ceased. It was very early morning – dawn was just beginning to touch the horizon with pink and gold. The air was slightly chill and everything was very wet. A few sleepy birds were beginning to sing as René walked to where Father Oak stood on the eastern side of the Grove, where the rising sun would soon outline his venerable branches with living gold.

As was proper, René thanked Father Oak for his hospitality and wished him a good morning. The trees, like the *Sidhe*, much appreciated good manners.

"I have excellent news, child of ours," said the tree. Father Oak spoke much like Bevis, but his voice was borne on the wind and in the rustle of the leaves or the creak of the branches. "We have located a unicorn and persuaded her to come to you. She will be here within the next three days."

René felt a wave of relief wash over him. "*Je vous suis très reconnaissant,*" he said. He did not ask where the unicorn had been found – the unicorns had disappeared for their own reasons. It was enough that they had found one willing to leave her solitary wood and help in this endeavor.

"It is a dangerous thing you do," said Father Oak. "to be a locus for so much magic. Others have died. We are not happy that you must do this, child of ours, but we know that you must do it."

René was happy that Father Oak understood. Soon, he would have to tell Ninon and his parents what he intended to do. That would not be easy. He well remembered the appalled look on Diarmiat's face, and the angry protests of his friend. He wondered what Diana's and Simon's reaction would be.

"They are coming," said Father Oak abruptly, "those from the Old Abbey – they will be here by the time the sun is full up. I shall send Medb to guide them."

Again, René was relieved. He would not have to try and scry in a puddle or teleport back to the Abbey. Last night in the coming thunderstorm had been difficult and he would not care to try to teleport again so soon after that experience.

Since Father Oak had finished speaking, what René now wanted more than anything else was some time alone to think over what Diana had revealed yester eve.

He had been surprised, very much so. From what he had heard in the servants' hall, from Lyon and from Diana herself, he had thought her marriage a love match, with perfect contentment on both sides. But he also knew that in the course of an argument people could say hurtful, ugly things to one another, things that when not in the grip of passion they would never say.

He also felt differently about adultery than did most gentlemen, probably due to his upbringing and his early desire to take Holy Orders. No doubt Captain Stillfield would have called him a high-minded prig as well. It seemed to René that many gentlemen regarded the betrayal of marriage vows as little more than an annoyance if their spouse were to find out. These were the very same men who would toss a fellow they had known for years out of their club and shun him forever because he cheated at cards. A betrayal was a betrayal, as his grandfather had said.

Grandpère Louis had been an unusual man – although a genius with the sword, he was shy and diffident, not dashing and daring as might have been expected. Although his and Ninon's had been an arranged marriage, they had fallen in love, and as he told René, he had never wanted another woman – she was friend, lover, wife and mistress. One took vows when one married, before God and family and friends. Vows, of whatever kind, were meant to be kept, or one should not make them.

René had also the example of Mr. Arabin before him, whom, it was well-known in the parish, had lost his beloved young wife in childbed long before René and his family had come to Silverbridge, and had never had a relationship with another woman.

He could not understand a man like Jonathan Stillfield, who had a wife who loved him so passionately and wholeheartedly, and because she was carrying his child, and therefore not always readily available, could casually take a mistress. If Diana was carrying *his* child, René thought, he would be in awe and in alt, happy beyond belief. And not at all eager to run out and find a *fille de joie*. He had a feeling that he would have despised Captain Stillfield, both for his betrayal of Diana and his treatment of Simon.

He had wandered to the other side of the Grove, lost in these thoughts, when Father Oak had finished giving his news. The sun was higher now, rising above a thin wisp of smoke-blue cloud that only moments ago had been tinged with golden edges. The sky was washed clean, blue into infinity. Far away, a lark sang for pure joy.

The others were emerging from the shelter. Medb had left, and had obviously removed her sleep spell from them.

Bevis came out first, yawning and stretching, his great loose joints audibly cracking in the chill air, which was rapidly warming as the sun rose. All of the signs pointed to another hot day.

Diana and Simon came out together, Diana looking about anxiously. When she saw René her face lit up and she said something to Simon, bending quickly to whisper in his ear.

Simon took off at a run, followed by three balls of fur on legs. He launched himself at René, and was caught and whirled around, the kittens jumping up and down at their feet.

"Oh, sir!" Simon said breathlessly, when at last set on his feet. "We thought the bogle had gotten you!"

"Don't be a noddy!" said Beau severely. "He's a great Wizard! There's no bogle can defeat him!"

"And as long as we stay in this Grove, no harm may come to us, *n'est-ce pas?*" said René. "The bogle cannot set a foot in here, such is the good it provides."

"Perhaps we should all live here," suggested Janus as Diana joined them.

Beau jeered at her. "You're a noddy, too! Where would we sleep or eat, pray?"

"I'm hungry!" announced Rascal, pawing at Diana's skirt, which was sadly crumpled.

Diana and René exchanged looks of pure amusement over the kittens' heads. "Father Oak tells me that help is coming. And my *Grandmère* will not forget to bring food, *je vous assure!*" René informed them.

The kittens jumped up and down excitedly. "You could try and catch a mouse," Simon suggested.

The kittens looked at him as if he were the prize exhibit at a raree show. "A mouse?" Beau said at last. "A mouse? Those dirty little squeaking rodents? You expect us to eat a dirty *rodent*? They're not even cooked!"

"Most cats do eat mice," said Simon.

"Not us!" said Beau smugly. "We're gourmets!"

"Someone's coming!" Janus squeaked, her little body at attention, with tail held high.

The trees and vines were parting, so they knew that whoever was coming was a friend.

It was quite a procession that arrived. First came Lyon and Ninon in Lyon's carriage, followed closely by a farm wagon, and then Chenevix and Lucie in the barouche.

The farm wagon was driven by Jim Cerne, And riding in the back, to Bevis's delight, was his Molly.

When they saw one another they let out a simultaneous squeal of pure joy. Bevis ran towards the wagon, and Molly clambered down. When they met in the middle of the painted floor, they touched the tips of their enormous noses, rubbing them back and forth. Then they rubbed each side of each other's face, slowly and lovingly, cheek to cheek, finally to rest their face in the hollow of one another's throats, arms tight about each other, in perfect bliss and contentment.

"Someone locked her in my hay barn," Jim explained. "Found her there last night. Sarah took her in an' we gave her a good feed o' sweet grain –"

Molasses feed! Molly's high sweet voice interrupted. *An' Bevis, he's after givin' us a whole sack of it – I been sittin' on it!*

"An' I was bringin' her back t' th'old mill when I met up wi' his lordship an' he told me what had happened," Jim continued.

Thank you! Thank you! Bevis said, sounding tearful. "*I thought them wicked men would kill my Molly!*

Like Bevis, Molly's clothing consisted of old grain sacks, but hers made an old fashioned gown with a natural waistline, a fichu about her shoulders and an apron. Her ankles were bare, and like Bevis, she wore no shoes. She had little more hair on her head than did her husband but what there was was neatly braided under a grain sack cap.

The kilmoullises' happiness was infectious. There were greetings all around and expressions of relief. Even Chenevix unbent enough to congraulate his heir on a job well done.

But René disclaimed any part in the rescue – it was all Bevis's doing. The killmoulis was the hero of the hour and Molly beamed with pride as he was thanked and praised. It was agreed that it was too dangerous for them to go back to the mill for a while, for there might be reprisals. They accepted an invitation from Jim Cerne to stay with him for a while, quite eagerly, when Molly told Bevis of Jim's children and of all of the young animals at the farm.

Ninon then brought out baskets of foodstuffs, even food for the kittens, whose absence had been discovered when Neige, conscience – stricken, had confessed to Ninon. She stayed on Ninon's shoulder as the rescued party ate tender bits of chicken, thick ham sandwiches and fruit pasties, washed down with strong tea. Neige was afraid that here siblings would regard her as a tattle-tale, but even Beau was too busy eating to berate her. As it usually did, the food tasted good in the out of doors, for last night's soup and tea seemed a very long time ago.

They all listened to Diana and Simon's account of the kidnapping and all were shocked by the alliance of Goodbody and Mildmay with a bogle.

"What did they hope to gain by it?" Lyon mused, accepting a third cup of tea from Ninon. Everyone sat on the Painted Floor, on rugs from the carriages.

"It is well known in Town that Goodbody is all to pieces. He expected to gain Lady Diana's fortune, of course," said Chenevix dryly.

He was rather disconcerted to be sitting on the ground in company with a farmer and the killmoulises. He was not certain which made him more uncomfortable.

"What was Mildmay's motive? Even his half of the ransom could not spirit him from the country – not with every dragon in the island on the lookout for him. He might have been able to hire a smuggler, but he could not enter Holland without a passport. He'd have to go to France and with the smell of the Cremave on him he'd soon be brought to the notice of the Inquisition. Their Witch-Sniffers have long noses." Lyon took another fruit pastie.

"I know why," said Simon softly. "I heard him muttering. He wanted you to deliver the money, sir, so that he could kill you," he said, turning to René. "And he expected you to come, too, Aunt Ninon."

"*La vengeance*," said Ninon. "He blames us for all of his troubles, *non?*"

Lucie shivered. She felt rather overwhelmed by all that was going on and she was a little frightened by the killmoulises. They were so very strange – unlike anything she

521

had ever seen. But as she watched them her fears lessened. Her son and Lady Diana seemed to be perfectly at ease with them, and Simon adored them – and they adored him. They were very tender with the boy and Lucie realized that they were smiling, even though they had no lips to smile with. In some strange fashion she could *hear* them smiling.

"Is there any more tea?" Lyon asked, waving his cup at Ninon.

"It is fortunate, *n'est-ce pas*? – that I have brought much tea!" she grumbled, but smiled at him as she refilled his cup.

"What we have conjectured explains both Mildmay's and Goodbody's motives," said Lyon very thoughtfully. "But none of this explains the bogle. Bogles do not help human-kind. This makes me very uneasy. That bogle should have eaten Mildmay, not be his assistant in a kidnapping!"

The would-be kidnappers were angry, to put it mildly. Nothing had gone the way it was planned. They had been caught in the storm, and drenched to the skin. When they had reached the shelter of the old mill again it was to find their prizes had flown. Ainsel could not find a trace of them and when the storm had ended all scent had completely disap-peared. Nearly frothing at the mouth, Sir Piers had gone to the hay barn to kill Molly, for killing something at this point would greatly relieve his feelings, only to find that she, too, had escaped.

Ainsel thought it a huge joke, but Goodbody was afraid of the look on Mildmay's face. The baronet was red and choleric with rage and muttered angrily as he downed mug after mug of strong cider.

As far as Goodbody was concerned, the brilliant plan was done and over. From now on, Lady Diana would be watched and guarded. There would be no other opportunity for her to be snatched. They would guard the boy as well, for fear he could be used against Diana.

And where was Wanda? She had gone off with that Elf creature. Now there was another one who sent a chill down Goodbody's spine, for one look had told him the Elf was completely mad. Goodbody had once toured Bedlam with a party of young bloods, who found the mad men and women amusing. Goodbody had not found it so – it was frightening to him.

And he suspected that Wanda had not returned to the cave because she was sleeping with that Elf. Goodbody found this completely inexplicable – not only was the Elf mad but he was not even human! The thought of bedding a non-human creature gave Goodbody a rolling stomach. Wanda, he thought bitterly as he watched Mildmay down cider, would sleep with anything! He could not now imagine why he had found her so attractive. And she had gone off with the trap, too, so he was stuck here with a bogle and an angry drunk. If he wanted to go back to the Inn he would be forced to walk miles in tight boots. Could it get any worse than this?

Worse was to happen to Goodbody, for his man Thompson, tired of waiting for his back pay, absconded with all of Goodbody's clothing, boots, hats and fobs, seals and rings.

René told no one but Lyon Father Oak's good news about the unicorn. Mr. Arabin was also let in on the secret, for he would be needed to bless the unicorn test.

As Goodbody had thought, guards were put on Simon and Diana, and Lyon strictly forbade them to go to Knights-wold again without a griffin and armed grooms in attendance. Efforts had been stepped up to find Mildmay but had not been successful, and Goodbody seemed to have disappeared. He had not come back to the Inn – his man had vanished in the night with most of his master's traps. Wanda Wycherley had vanished as well. But no one was concerned with the whereabouts of Mrs. Wycherley.

Diana had been relieved to find her pair unharmed without even a strained hock between them. There was minor damage to her carriage, and their purchases were still in the boot, unharmed.

But she had nightmares for days about Simon being sold to a sweep, and what she should have done when the kidnapping took place, She reproached herself bitterly for not having had the wits to have Simon blow the dragon whistle, or having sent up a magical flare to call one of the griffins or simply annihilating all of them with a stunning spell. Her comfort during this time was René – she had thought that she might be self-conscious with him, after burdening him with the details of that horrible night on which Jonathan died, but she was not and she seemed to have a curious feeling of lightness, as if a large weight had been lifted from her spirits. They were now completely on Christian name terms.

Therefore she was disappointed, when on the third day after their return to the Abbey, she went in search of René and found he had gone off, quite early with Lyon. Even Beau did not know where they had gone. The kitten was quite indignant, for he thought he should have been informed or better yet. gone along. Even Leander had been left behind. A note, left by Lyon on the main work table said briefly: *"Back by mid-afternoon. Don't wait nuncheon."*

She had planned a picnic for herself, René, and Simon – not in the woods, but in the enclosed herb garden. She felt rather more cast-down that might have been thought possible when she found the Tower empty of Wizards.

But she was not allowed to brood for long, for she heard running steps on the stairs and a footman, Robert, burst into the room, panting from the speed with which he had mounted the spiral stair

"Oh, my lady!" he puffed. "You'd best come at once! Lord and Lady Eastcote have arrived! And her Ladyship is much distressed!"

Diana's first thought was that something had happened to Peter on the Peninsula. She paled and agreed to come at once.

She was at once everything they had expected and nothing like their dreams.

To begin with, she was very, very old, silver of hide, with mane and tail yellowed very slightly from age. As in the old tapestries, she had a goat-like beard, but there all resemblance to the goat ended. Her hooves were cloven, her legs thin and elegant as a deer's. Her head and neck were arched and refined like the finest Barbary steed's and her tail was like a lion's with a thick tassel at the end. She had green eyes – a deep, dark, emerald green that seemed to be filled with the woods and little creatures dancing. And her horn – it was at the very least four feet long, of a pure pale ivory, striated with bands of gold to its quite sharp tip. It seemed too big and heavy for her frail head and neck. For she was so old that in some light she seemed almost transparent. She was serene and good, wise beyond belief and heartbreakingly beautiful.

She stood in the middle of the Painted Floor regarding the three of them thoughtfully. When Medb had arrived to tell René that the unicorn had come, they had set out at once, sending Medb on to notify the Vicar, who met them at the Grove.

She had been there, waiting. Somehow, they could not approach her any closer, for she cast such a spell of awe on all three of them.

The unicorn at last spoke. Her voice was sweet and low, like the softest of breezes through the new leaves of spring trees. "I an Cluny," she said, "It is a long time since we unicorns were asked to discern a virgin. And it was never a young man. Perhaps you, Holy man," she said to the Vicar, "might tell us why we are now summoned."

The Vicar rather nervously explained what they wished to do. When he was done the Unicorn sighed. "The Unselighe Court – long our foes. For by killing us and drinking of our blood they can become immortal, nearly indestructible. It is difficult to decide who has done us more harm – the Unselighe Court or mankind."

"I have come here today," she said, "because I was assured by Father Oak that you were good men and did not intend to capture me and take my horn. My mother named me Cluny, after those appalling tapestries of the *Captive Unicorn*, so that I would never forget that men cannot see beauty without wanting to possess it and destroy it. That was what they did, you must know. When we in our bliss, had fallen to sleep in the virgin's lap, lulled by her scent of chastity and her caresses, men appeared and killed us for our blood and most of all for our horns. They imputed to the horn all sorts of talents that it did not have – not without one of us attached to it. A lonely horn can only purify– not cure the diseases that men think it can. Only we can do that," she added proudly. "And this was the grossest betrayal, for we trusted these young virgins and even loved them, and they led us to our deaths, or what might be worse, to live in captivity in a golden collar. Death is preferable, for a unicorn must be free!"

"We give our word to you that you will not be captured killed, or abused in any way," said Lyon softly.

"Father Oak, whom I have known for many years," said Cluny, "assures me that you may be trusted. You must know, young man, that if you are trying to deceive me I will know at once, and I will impale you upon my horn for the betrayal," she said, looking at René.

"I am not deceiving you, *je vous promesse*," he returned sincerely.

"Then come here," she pointed with her horn, "and sit upon the ground."

Where she indicated was still a distance from her and she watched him closely as he sat down. She regarded him for a moment and then took a deep breath. "Ahh!" she said, "The scent of chastity!" She came closer and circled about him, and at last came close. Like a horse, she went to her knees and lay down, carefully, so that her horn did not endanger René. Then she lay her head in his lap. "You may caress me if you like," she said, closing her eyes, as the Vicar began the blessing.

Almost timidly, he did so, stroking her silver neck. He had never in his life felt anything so soft or seen anything so beautiful. This close, she shone with a silvered light.

René ceased to be conscious of anything save her. He heard no other sound other than her quiet breathing and little sighs of contentment. All he felt was the velvet purity of her skin. He was being filled with peace and contentment, not untinged with awe.

How long they sat like that he never knew for certain, although Lyon insisted it was over an hour, while Mr. Arabin said it was less than fifteen minutes. But Cluny at last rose and lay her horn briefly on René's forehead. "That may serve to protect you in your ordeal," she said. "Thank you, my dear. We need the touch of a virgin every once in a while." She sighed and looked about her. "I am too old," she said "to return to my former home. I do think that this Knyghtwood will once again become a Unicorn wood."

45

The Black Lacquer Box

When Diana arrived at the bottom of the stairs and ran out the door she was more certain than ever that something must have happened. A Cornish Copper, wearing a harness that proclaimed him an employee of Dover Dragon Transports, Ltd had landed near the dragon pen. He had been hired because the Eastcotes did not keep a dragon. Lady Eastcote much disliked dragon flight – she became dragon-sick and she was terrified of heights. Therefore, Diana reasoned, something horrible must have happened to Peter, or some other member of the family if Lady Eastcote consented to get on a dragon.

Lady Eastcote did not look well – she had a greenish tinge to her face and leaned heavily on her husband's arm. Nonetheless, she managed to thank the dragon for a pleasant flight.

The dragon politely wished her well and apologized for any roughness in the flight.

"No need, my good fellow," said Lord Eastcote. "Her ladyship becomes ill looking out of a first storey window. Now I will see if I may arrange a meal for you before you return to Dover – ah, here is my daughter! She is the one we want. Diana!" her father demanded as she drew near, "Have you a meal for this stout fellow? He has flown quite a distance today!"

Diana was not the only one who had come out of doors when the dragon arrived. Seppings had been among the first to arrive, and now he stepped forward and said, "If you will allow me, my lord, I will take care of that. And perhaps a bath might be in order as well."

The dragon assented eagerly as Seppings nodded to a groom and told the man to show their visitor the dragon pen.

Ninon came out of the house next, followed by Simon and all of the kittens. "Oh, *le pauvre!*" Ninon exclaimed with one look at Lady Eastcote, just as Diana reached her mother and put an arm about her shoulders,

"What has happened?" Diana asked worriedly. "Is it Peter?"

"Peter!" Lady Eastcote, who had been pressing a handkerchief to her lips and moaning, looked up at this. "No, it is this! Why did you never tell us?" she asked piteously as she fumbled at the breast of her flying suit and withdrew a much-creased news-sheet and thrust it at her daughter.

The first thing Diana saw was an advertisement for '*Boot Blacking – As used by Mr. Brummel and other notables about Town.*'

"Boot blacking?" she said in utter confusion. "Mama, you climbed on a dragon to come and ask me about boot blacking?"

Lady Eastcote moaned again. "The other side!" she wailed, through her handkerchief.

Lord Eastcote took the news-sheet from his daughter and very obligingly turned it to the correct side, where the announcement of Diana's engagement had been circled in red ink.

"But this is impossible!" Diana said when she had read it. "We pretended to be engaged, it is true, but we never sent in a notice…"

"*Pretended to be engaged!*" Lady Eastcote shrieked. "I knew I should have never let you come here! It is my brother's influence – complete moral disintegration!"

"Now, my dear…" Lord Eastcote patted her hand.

"Let us go indoors, where we might have a cup of tea and talk this over like sensible persons," Diana pleaded, conscious of several servants, grooms and gardeners within earshot. And her Mama did not look well at all.

Ninon, who after hearing what little she had heard, rapidly discerned that Simon and the kittens would be quite *de trop,* sent them to the dragon pen over their protests.

She then went to Lady Eastcote and said soothingly, "I shall brew you a *tisane*, which will settle your stomach, *non*? And when you are feeling better, we shall talk."

Lady Eastcote, stomach rolling and head aching, looked at her suspiciously. "Who are you?"

"I am René's *Grandmère*," answered Ninon, "and I assure you that we knew nothing of this. It is most likely the work of that Duke."

"We found out that the notices were delivered by a manservant in the livery of the Duke of Chenevix," Lord Eastcote informed them as they began to move slowly towards the house.

Diana was so angered by this revelation that she could not speak. Her eyes glittered dangerously. Chenevix and Lucie had gone into Cheltenham for the day. It was as if he KNEW he would be called upon the carpet today! And where were René and her uncle when one needed them?

Lady Eastcote, removed from the discomfort of her flying suit, (which fit none too well as it too, was hired) and ensconced in the most comfortable chair in the drawing room, derived great comfort from a long vituperation on the character of the Duke of Chenevix; the shame of having such a falsehood printed in the paper; how the family honor would never survive when it became known that the engagement was a hoax and how this might affect Harriet's come-out. She then burst into tears, just as Ninon appeared with a fragrant *tisane*. Lady Eastcote was persuaded to drink this and then tenderly escorted above stairs by her daughter to a hastily prepared room, where she was laid down upon her bed and coaxed to go to sleep.

When Diana went below stairs again it was to find her father talking quietly with Ninon.

"How is she?" inquired Lord Eastcote at once.

"Sleeping," said Diana tiredly. She had never imagined her Mama to be capable of such histrionics. "Why was she put so out of frame by this, Papa? We can soon rectify such a mistake by a notice in the papers that we have mutually decided that we shall not suit —"

"She was deeply hurt, my dear, by the idea of you not telling us first, and being given no chance to meet and approve the young man. And given the fact that we were unable to scry you, for there have been severe electrical storms until today and we had to fly over the North Sea to avoid another one building up, rather than flying straight across –"

"Oh, poor Mama!"

"She had too much time to brood," finished Lord Eastcote. "And your fool of a brother has given us the impression that he is in the thick of the fighting…"

Diana stared at him. "The Augury Corps is kept well to the rear, back with the baggage train!"

Lord Eastcote nodded. "It is just as I thought. Peter thinks to make himself interesting by exaggeration. But your Mama will worry so. Perhaps she will believe you, my dear, for you have been in the Peninsula and have seen how things are done."

"Me, I wish to know why this Duke of Lucie's has done this thing and why we did not know about it before this?" Ninon scowled.

"I believe my brother-in-law Lyonshall takes only the *Wizards' Times*," said Lord Eastcote. "The notice was in every journal save that one."

"Very clever of his Grace of Chenevix," Diana said, her tone boding ill for the peer. She was wondering what it would feel like to strangle a Duke.

Once again, Simon felt ill-used. He – and the kittens – had been banished from an interesting conversation. Ninon had not allowed even Neige to stay and had warned them, looking fiercely at Beau, not to be caught eavesdropping under the open windows. Simon had not really understood what all of the fuss was about – something in the news-sheet – and it involved something Mama had done and the pretend engagement. He and the kittens talked about it all the way to the dragon pen, but could make no real sense of it, for they had not seen the news-sheet. Simon was sorry that Lady Eastcote was sick – he liked her very much, but he wished that people – adults – would stop hiding things from him. Not knowing was so much worse that knowing something, even if that something were bad. The kittens felt the same way. Of course, being cats and naturally curious, they felt that *everything* was their business, whether it actually was or not.

They found the dragon from the Transport service just finishing up a dragon-sized snack – half a cow, nicely cooked on a spit with herbs and gravy. Tuathail introduced the guest as Meleager, a Cornish Copper. The two dragons were comparing stories of 'where I have flown' and Simon and the kittens listened until the conversation, as shop talk usually does, took a technical turn The dragons began talking about air currents, wind velocity, thermals and how to prevent icing-up in the higher elevations. This held no interest to their auditors but just as they were going to look for something else to do, a clatter was heard and Lyon's carriage, closely followed by Mr. Arabin's dog cart, came into the stable yard. Simon, with his faithful furry followers, ran to met them.

"What's this, Simon? A dragon?" Lyon asked as he pulled up his horses. "Have we a visitor?"

"'Tis Lord and Lady Eastcote," Simon informed him.

Lyon stared at him in disbelief. "My sister came here dragon-back? Something terrible must have happened! My sister becomes extremely dragon-sick!"

"She did look rather green," put in Beau.

Lyon handed over the reins to René, who was sitting beside him, and jumped down from the carriage. Fortunately for René, who had never driven a pair and therefore no idea what to do with the ribbons given to him, Daniel came out of the stable and took the horses, as one of the other grooms took the dogcart. René was then able to follow Lyon and Mr. Arabin into the Abbey. The Vicar, of course, would be a help if there was indeed bad news.

The Duke of Chenevix and his lady had spent a moderately pleasant day in Cheltenham. It was a charming town, with wide, tree-lined streets, Georgian buildings, many open spaces and three pump rooms for the mineral springs that had been discovered in 1716. That was their primary reason for visiting the town – the Duke had determined that Lucie needed strengthening and decided that a course of the waters would do her good.

After her first sip of the decidedly nasty stuff, Lucie knew that they would do her no good at all, but might instead make her violently ill. To please her husband she sipped nearly half a glass before her stomach and taste buds rebelled, but talked him into immediately afterwards taking her to a tea-room, where good Bohea and cream rolls took the taste from her mouth. She could not understand why people thought mineral waters so beneficial – perhaps to bathe in, but surely drinking them would only hasten one's demise.

They visited the shops and Lucie bought gifts for everyone, as well as a number of useless and expensive trifles for herself, urged to do so by her husband.

When at last in the late afternoon they left to return to the Abbey Lucie was happy and content. If only Lucien could be always as he had been today – loving, teasing her, generous, laughing – !

She was not to be happy and contented for long. When they returned to the Abbey the storm burst over their heads.

"How could you do such a thing, Chenevix?" roared Lyon. "By God, it passes all bounds, even for you!"

Lady Eastcote was still abed, but the Duke faced a formidable array of angry persons. The Duke and Duchess had scarcely put a foot in the drawing room before Lyon and Lord Eastcote demanded to know what he thought he was about and Diana thrust the news-sheet under Chenevix's nose and demanded to know what he meant by doing such a thing.

He looked at her in his cold fashion. "I have arranged a very suitable and advantageous match for you and my heir, madam. Probably a finer match that you, the widow of an obscure Army Captain, could hope to expect."

At Diana's gasp of outrage, René said quickly and firmly, "You will not insult Lady Diana!" offering an icy stare back at Chenevix. He had come to stand beside her, rather protectively, as she faced the Duke. "You have done enough harm, I think," he added. Although to have a real betrothal was the dearest wish of his heart he was all too aware it was probably the last thing that Diana desired.

The Duke turned his arctic glare on his heir. "You continue to amaze me," he said sarcastically. "I have made it possible for you to have a socially acceptable, beautiful bride, one, moreover, who has a tidy fortune, and to whom, I think you are not indifferent, and you are telling me you do not want this union!" He shook his head.

Lucie, who all this time had remained silent while recriminations and accusations had been voiced – loudly – by nearly everyone else in the room, finally found her voice.

"But Lucien," she said, putting a hand on her husband's rigid arm, "They are adults, *non*? If they wish to marry, or not to marry, it is up to them."

"The days of arranged marriages are long past –" began Lord Eastcote.

"And only see what allowing your children to make their own choice has lead to in your family, Eastcote," said the Duke acidly. "Your daughter throwing herself away on a penniless serving soldier and your heir espousing an equally penniless nobody – the daughter of a country parson named Smith! Unions that brought little or no lustre to your family nor lucrative settlements or land to enrich your coffers."

Lord Eastcote's face darkened. "You have a powerful knowledge of my family's private business, my Lord Duke. And I cannot conceive why you have made it your business to know these things when it is none of your affair."

"Common knowledge," snapped his Grace. "The *on dits* of the season!"

"Scandal broth!" said Ninon scornfully.

The Duke turned on her. "Yes, *Madame*, scandal broth! Should this betrothal be broken there will be an immense scandal. I am certain that Lady Diana will not wish to be declared by all to be a jilt, nor might my heir in honor withdraw – no gentleman would do so." He strode to the embroidered bell pull and gave it two sharp pulls.

Seppings, who had been outside in the hall, as near to listening to the key hole as his dignity would allow, came in at once.

"Yes, your Grace?" He bowed.

"Have my manservant Mariposa fetched at once. And have him bring the black lacquer box with him. He will know what I mean," Chenevix directed.

"Very good, your Grace." The butler disappeared.

"And you think that the threat of a scandal will make us honor this betrothal?" said René in a deceptively quiet voice that made Ninon look at him uneasily.

533

Lord Eastcote had begun to look troubled. "Diana, this may reflect upon your sister's come—out. If your betrothal is announced and then quickly withdrawn, there is little doubt that the *Ton* will think the worst – that you are at the least a jill-flirt, and at the best a complete flat for whistling away such a match. And there are already any amount of rather ill-informed tales circulating about Lord Keir – what with you being French and all," he added apologetically to René. "Why, old Hurstmonceaux writ me a letter the other day, saying it was widely known that Keir had been one of Napoleon's marshals and was here to spy upon us."

This was so patently foolish that the others could only stare at him. The Duke's brow grew thunderous. "This is why I have wished to introduce you into Society!" he said between gritted teeth. "People will believe these absurdities, par-ticularly when they do not have proof of the falsehood in front of their eyes!"

Diana and René stared at one another, appalled.

"Perhaps," suggested Mr. Arabin, who like Lucie, had very little to say, "it might be best to maintain the *semblance* of a betrothal, until these vile calumnies may be put to rest. And too, the interest in the engagement will fade in time and a small notice as to the withdrawal of the suit might be inserted into the news-sheets. By then there will be some new scandal or interest to draw people's attention."

At this moment, the door opened, and Mariposa en-tered, bright in his gypsy garb and holding a black lacquer box, small in size and highly polished.

Lord Eastcote was startled to learn that this flamboyant person was Chenevix's valet. He was not at all what the Earl imagined a manservant of an austere fellow like Chenevix would be. Lord Eastcote had never seen anyone more likely to have a gold tooth – if not two.

Without a word, Mariposa bowed and presented the box to his master.

"We are agreed, then – the betrothal will stand for the nonce?" Chenevix said smoothly.

"You take too much for granted," said René harshly. "This is a sham!" he cried, reverting to French. "Why does anyone but us who are involved care about this? And do you think that I care that there are silly stories circulating about me amongst a group of equally silly people?" He felt as if he had dragged Diana into a quagmire, simply by having such a parent as the Duke of Chenevix.

A hand crept into his, out of view of the rest of the room. "*I* care what is said of you," Diana said in a small voice. "Please, René, perhaps it is best to do as Mr. Arabin suggests. I would not wish to ruin your reputation, or spoil my sister's come-out." She all too well remembered the furor of speculation that had erupted when it became known that the daughter of an Earl was to marry a soldier unequal to her in birth or fortune.

René did not look best pleased with his decision. Ninon and Lyon added their voices to Diana's. "Come Lammastide every one will forget about this!" said Lyon,

This was true. And the dilemma might be resolved in another way altogether.

"Very well," he at last agreed. "but I do not like it."

Gratefully, Diana squeezed his hand and smiled at him.

"Then you will need this," the Duke handed René the black lacquer box. René regretfully let go of Diana's hand.

"What is this?" he demanded.

"The Chenevix betrothal ring," answered the Duke. "I trust you are aware of what finger it goes upon and how to put it there?"

René opened the box to reveal a beautiful square-cut sapphire ring, set in a frame of diamonds.

You knew this is how it would end, René thought angrily, looking at the Duke. He had to have sent for the ring – one did not just carry one's family betrothal ring about. They had let themselves be manipulated. He had listened to Lord Eastcote when that gentleman told Chenevix how upset his wife was with the sudden news. Everyone was upset.

He had never ever wished to harm Diana, not even when she hated him so unjustly. And now it seemed he was doing nothing but hurting her, for this sham betrothal would no doubt, as the more worldly-wise amongst them said, have its ramifications.

As the others crowded around to see, Diana held out her left hand to him, lifting her ring finger.

As he slid the ring onto her hand, René vowed to himself that he would never again do anything to hurt her.

And Lucie, looking at her husband, felt a chill. He wore the smug satisfied look of a cat who has just successfully raided the dairy. How could he be stopped from this course he was so set upon, of bending everyone to his will? What could she do? Was there even anything she *could* do?

46

Encounter At Avalon

The date was now Wednesday, the thirty-first of July. If not for Mr. Arabin's calculations, tonight would have been the night that the binding would be attempted.

All the criteria had been met and all the components assembled. All of the Druid enclaves, the Witches' Covens and the Wizards were ready to cast the greatest Working undertaken in modern times. Tonight, however, would still be the Lammas celebration. And everyone needed a celebration to keep their minds from what was to come.

All anyone knew was that a suitable young man had been found – and passed the unicorn test – to be the locus. His identity had not been released. Even Lyon's household had no idea of who it might be. Speculation was rife, but no one succeeded in guessing correctly.

In one way René wished that it was over and done with – the waiting grated upon the nerves. But the later date gave him more time with Diana.

He also used the time to tie-up loose ends. He finally spoke to Ninon about the revelation of her noble rank, listened to her reasons, and if not quite understanding, accepted them. He spent time worked with Beau on his reading. And he spent time with Simon, teaching him as much as he could and with Lucie. He even tried to become reconciled with his father, a process which was less than successful, for Chenevix had had reports from London about the completely idiotish stories that were circulating about his heir and his temper was volatile, to say the least. René also got to know the Eastcotes, who had decided to remain at the

Abbey for a few days so that Lady Eastcote might recover from her ordeal.

During this time Lyon and Mr. Arabin were busy looking for and devising spells that would protect René during the great working. Lyon finally decided, on the afternoon of July 31ˢᵗ, to visit Avalon and study the books there, perhaps even go to Bryn Myrrdin. He would journey by himself, on Tuathail. Being unusually kind and considerate he left René behind to go on an outing with Diana, Simon and the Eastcotes to visit the Cernes, who still had their killmoulis guests. The Eastcotes wanted to meet and thank the creature who had saved their daughter and step-grandson. Mr. Arabin, who might have come along to Avalon, was busy with neglected parish duties.

Lyon was not really worried about a daytime attack on his person. He was confident in his ability to defend himself and at any rate, he was flying straight from the Abbey to Avalon – one of the most heavily guarded and powerful spots in the British Isles. Only Tara had more natural defenses. Like Tara, Avalon had protections not of this world, both Christian and pagan.

Avalon lay in Somersetshire, at Glastonbury. A monastery had once stood near the Isle of Apples and this was now home to the training school of the British Druids. The sacred Grove of Oak trees and the library, as well as the dwelling places of the Arch Druid and his assistants were on the Isle itself, as was the enormous node of magic that most ley lines in Britain converged upon.

Lyon had not spent as much time at the Isle as he had thought he would when first he had been appointed Arch Druid. He had not expected to inherit the Marquisate, nor had he known the affairs of the Abbey to be at such a sorry pass. He had hoped to put in a good steward and make a trip once a year to the estate while he remained at Avalon. Instead he was back and forth, unable to give full attention to either the Arch Driudship or the Marquisate. The situation was becoming intolerable. How he wished that he still had Amelia to guide him! He missed her wise counsel more than he could say.

These and other thoughts occupied him as he flew to Avalon. It was a quick flight, for Gloucestershire and Somersetshire were not far distant from one another and Tuathail caught what the dragon referred as a 'tail wind' and they were pushed along rapidly.

Lyon was greeted with cries of delight when he arrived. His second, a man in his forties named Hugh Bowden, had many questions about the coming Working and other problems to consult on with his superior. It was some two hours after his arrival before Lyon had the leisure to visit the library, for he had to deal with a myriad of problems from a possible disease in the sacred mistletoe to a dispute between two young Druids. He also spent time carefully questioning the Druids as to what had been seen in the area – anything unusual at all. But no one reported anything. The area had been relatively free of Unselighe creatures.

At nearly three o'clock in the afternoon Lyon was finally able to escape to the library. It was calm and quiet there. The long mullioned windows stood open to the afternoon air and sunlight poured in as well through the stained glass and lit up the rich wood paneling. The library had been outfitted in the Middle Ages and very little had been changed over the years, save for the addition of more and more volumes of arcane knowledge. Some of the books were more than five hundred years old, themselves copies of still older volumes. There were books in all tongues, ancient as well as modern, but a clever translation spell table enabled anyone to read a book in any language, whether the reader was fluent in that tongue or not. One merely inserted the book in the bespelled slot and the reader saw the contents in his native language. But it was a difficult spell to make and maintain. Two Master Druids, who were also *Magus Magistrii*, were kept busy in maintaining it.

Lyon found several useful spells that might be incorporated in the protective measures. He was determined that René would come out of this alive.

It was nearly five when at last he returned the last book to its proper place on the shelf. It was too bad, he thought as he hefted the heavy tome into a shelf over his head, that there was not a spell that would return the books to the shelves. He had had an interesting conversation with Ninon about the impracticality of most magic.

Most of the Druids were at their afternoon tea as he walked out to the ferry that would convey him to Glastonbury, to the dragon pen where Tuathail dozed in the sun. Lyon had declined an invitation to stay, for he wanted to get back and discuss what he had learned with the Vicar.

There was always a ferryman on duty, usually one of the novice Druids, who took this duty in turns. A rather morose young man rowed Lyon to the shore of the lake, where a stone pier jutted out into the water.

It was a beautiful lake, surrounding the Isle where ancient apple trees hung over the waters. Even on a clear, hot day though, a rather mysterious mist wisped over the lake's surface. Once the lake had been the dwelling place of the Lady of the Lake and her maidens, she who had given King Arthur the glorious sword Excalibur.

But the Lady and her court of maidens had long vanished, to where no one now living knew. The Isle of Apples had then been the Isle of Glass, visible only when it wanted to be so or needed to be. Somewhere on the Isle slept Arthur until Britain needed him once again, and with him his knights. But no one had ever been able to find his resting place. The Isle kept her secrets well.

It was a green and restful area that Lyon saw as he walked towards Glastonbury. The Druidry, which had once been a Benedictine Abbey before Arthur had expelled the Catholic Church from England, lay in the Mendips, on land that sloped up from the Brue Valley up to a tor of some 522 feet in height. Glastonbury Tor was itself a sacred spot. It was open, agricultural country and afterwards Lyon chided himself for not being more alert, as he would have been if the scenery had been heavily treed.

Out of nowhere came a bolt of pure energy that knocked him off his feet before he was able to step off the pier. He saw in his peripheral vision the young ferryman pushed back into the lake with a scream and a huge splash, the boat sinking beside him.

Lyon quickly gathered his magic and tapped into the ley lines, feeling the power of the lines converging in the node run through his veins. But he remained on his back on the pier, wanting whoever had attacked him to think that he was helpless or even injured.

540

A red bolt broke on either side of him, so close together that they seemed simultaneous, missing a strike by only a hairsbreadth. With that warning, Lyon knew better than to move. "Who are you?" he called. "Show yourself! What do you want?" It was a necromancer, that he was sure – probably the very necromancer they were looking for.

The air in front of him seemed to shimmer and a tall, thin figure in a red cloak and a bicorne hat was revealed. The figure swept the cloak dramatically away from his face and stood, staring at Lyon with a malicious gaze. "*Show-off!*" Lyon thought.

"Ah, I see that you remember me," the black magician said.

In truth, Lyon did not remember him. There was something vaguely familiar about the man, but it was just beyond his immediate memory. Right now he was more concerned with how to get out of this situation. The other Druids would be of no help – they were all at tea over on the island. And the ferryman and his boat were gone. Even Druids could not walk upon water. If the necromancer was worth his salt he would have already made it impossible for either his fellow Druids or Tuathail to help Lyon. Lyon could see his death in that long malicious face in front of him.

"Since the last time we met, Lyons, I have grown in power and cunning. You will no longer find it as easy to defeat me as when I was a youth. I was but eighteen when you met me and interfered in what was none of your affair, there in Constantinople," the necromancer said, his eyes black and full of hate.

Lyon blinked. Constantinople? He had toured Greece, the Levant and the Near East years before. It must have been nearly twenty – five years ago! Since the Continent was closed to English Wizards – for the Inquisition did not care if one was not a native of the region, or even Catholic. Under such conditions the Grand Tour was quite different for Wizards than for non-magicals. Both the Greek Orthodox faith and that of Islam did not frown upon magic. While the Greeks did not encourage the practice of magic, there were nonetheless many of those who practiced the Art on the Peloponnesus, the Isles, Delphi, Illyria and the northern areas. The lands of the Prophet abounded with sorcerers,

Djinns, flying carpets and other fascinating magics. Lyon had learned a good deal there, for he had a deep intellectual curiosity.

But he could not remember Constantinople. He had done something to this necromancer, something so meaningful that the man had cherished a deep hatred towards him for all these years! It seemed ironic to Lyon that he had no idea why he was about to die.

For he was not certain that he could win out in this encounter. He could put up a very good fight, but in the end, the blood magic might overtake him. This necromancer, to Lyon's Othersight, glowed with power, the power of many deaths and pain. His aura was blood red, his soul black. Lyon suddenly remembered Diana's description of the juggler she had seen at the Horse Fair. What was it he had called himself? The Jongleur! That was it! Lyon cursed himself for not taking her more seriously. She had seen real evil, not a boggart. Fleetingly, Lyon wondered if this was how Iain had felt, before he and his people were slaughtered. Had Myfanwy seen her slayer and known him for what he was?

"I have dreamed of this for years, *M'sieur*," said the Jongleur, coming closer so that he night look down upon his victim. "No one has ever bested me before or since and you will pay dearly for my humiliation! Your death will be neither short nor painless."

His French accent tipped something in Lyon's mind and he almost remembered – a French accent in a place where one would not expect it.

Lyon began to gather his magics quickly, for a bolt of pure energy at the necromancer, but he suddenly lost the power of the node. And then, behind him, the lake began to boil. He could hear it, as if it were a gigantic kettle.

Lyon turned on his side and stared at the rolling waters. Even the Jongleur looked at it with narrowed eyes.

Swiftly, a shining object, pointed and silver shot from the water. It was a sword of immense beauty and antiquity. Holding the sword was a female hand. Still it came, until an extraordinarily beautiful woman stood on the surface of the lake.

She was not wet, Lyon thought in amazement. Her fair hair, hanging over her shoulder to well below waist length was bound with pearls and her white gown, with gold cord binding it to her body from beneath her breasts to her waistline, was as dry as if she had been out walking upon the land. She shone white and pure from her head to her gold-slippered feet. She was flawlessly, exquisitely lovely.

"Who is it that violates the sanctity of my lake with blood magic?" she demanded, her brilliant green eyes flashing. She had lowered the sword to shoulder level, but still leveled it in a threatening manner.

Lyon felt a shiver of awe run over him. Surely this was the Lady of the Lake herself and that must be Excalibur in her hand! He was seeing sights that no one had seen since Merlin's time!

"I do not know who you are, *Madame,*" began Malcoeur, " but this is none of your –"

"Be silent!" she ordered, pointing the sword at him. Suddenly he could not move or barely even breath.

Lyon found himself in a similar condition.

"You will remove yourselves from this Holy place," she directed. "I will not allow you to profane it with your petty quarrels. I warn you, necromancer, if you do not take yourself away, I shall bestow Excalibur upon the Arch Druid and let him put an end to you. And be aware that Excalibur can and will kill you! Now go!"

With a wave of her other hand she pushed Malcoeur backwards until he was swept up in a whirlwind and taken out of sight.

The Lady then turned her attention to Lyon. "Arch Druid," she said formally, at last lowering the sword. A gem encrusted belt and scabbard appeared at her waist and she put Excalibur to rest in it. "if you must meet the necromancer, you must do so under the terms laid down for the Duel Arcane set out by Merlinus Ambrosius. And you are not to do so in a Holy Place such as this."

At the look in her eyes Lyon decided not to tell her that it had not been his idea. She had released him as well, and he got to his feet slowly.

Her gaze was still hostile.

"He must be stopped," she said. "But I fear you will not be the one to do it."

"I won't?" he said in some surprise. "But who –?"

She had already begun to disappear beneath the lake, faster than could be imagined. In no time at all she was gone, leaving not even a ripple behind and many questions unanswered.

47

Vignettes

It was not until later that evening that Lyon remembered what had happened in Constatinople.

The encounter at Avalon had been the topic of conversation ever since Lyon had returned to the Abbey late in the afternoon. The Vicar had been invited to dinner to hear about the necromancer.

Most of the company was in awe at the reappearance of the Lady of the Lake and of the fact that she interfered in mortal affairs.

"But that is her duty," said the Vicar. "She is the protectoress of the sanctity of the Isle where Arthur sleeps as well as the guardian of Excalibur. It would be sacrilege to allow black magic to be done near so Holy a place." He took another sip of his coffee and leaned back with a sigh of satisfaction. Alphonse made splendid dinners!

The Abbey household had fallen into the habit of a post-dinner cup of coffee and something very light, such as madeleines, in the drawing room. Simon was allowed to remain with the adults for this but his bed-time came shortly afterwards. Diana was worried that tonight after hearing Lyon's story he would have nightmares. The story had certainly horrified her. Lyon had apologized to her for doubting what she had seen. Now he, too, had seen the trapped souls in the aura of the Jongleur and realized that it was he who had stolen the souls of so many victims.

"But why did not the Lady kill this evil magician?" Lucie said, puzzled. She sat by Chenevix, who had had very little to say about the entire affair, for once.

"Because she *cannot* kill, my dear Duchess," answered the Vicar, "Her nature is noble and good, and killing, even though in this case it would have been a favor to us all had she done so, is foreign to her nature. She is of Faerie blood and creatures such as Faeries and naturals – Hobgoblins, or elementals such as salamanders – must remain true to their nature. Unlike humans, who have a wider range of emotions for good or evil, those creatures are *either* good or evil. They cannot change. Therefore you will never find a good and helpful Redcap, nor an evil unicorn."

"She should have given Uncle Lyon the sword, then," stated Simon, his eyes shining. To think, his uncle had actually seen the Lady of the Lake and Excalibur!

"That was quite clever of her, to threaten the necromancer with Excalibur, but it was an empty threat," the Vicar said with a chuckle. "Lord Lyonshall could not even pick up the sword, for only the crowned and anointed true King of Britain may yield it."

"Then why does not our King George have Excalibur?" Simon wanted to know. The adults exchanged uneasy glances. No one wanted to become involved in a lengthy discussion of whether or not the House of Hanover had a right to the throne and if indeed anyone since Arthur had a real right to the sword. The Lady of the Lake had never offered it to anyone else.

Perhaps fortunately, Lyon, who had taken little part in the recent conversation and indeed, seemed lost in a brown study, suddenly leaped to his feet and shouted "Constantinople!"

"Really, Lyonshall," Chenevix began. Startled by Lyon's actions, he had nearly spilled his coffee.

"I knew I'd remember it!" Lyon drove a fist into his open opposite hand. "I had an encounter with that gentleman before! It was in the Ottoman Empire. I had been exploring a magician's bazaar – fascinating place! – when I heard some screams. I went at once to investigate and found this necromancer – he was only about seventeen or eighteen, – mistreating a child." He had been about to say 'torturing' but one look at Simon's eager little face changed his mind. "I could tell at once that it was for purposes of blood magic. Put a stop to it of course. I took the young fellow back to his lodgings and destroyed his black grimoires and then turned him over to the Pasha. Black magic isn't illegal in the Empire the way it is here, but they rather frown on it, particularly of it is practiced by foreigners. I'd give my eyeteeth to find out how he got away from a Turkish prison! And he has held this against me these twenty years and more!"

"We now know who has been doing the killings, *non?*" said René quietly.

Lyon collapsed again in his chair, causing it to creak alarmingly. "But, now knowing that our killer is quite human, the binding ceremony will probably have no effect on him at all," he said gloomily. "But I have a glimmer of an understanding how the creatures got out in the first place. When Myfanwy was killed –"

"The blood magic tore a rent in the binding!" the Vicar finished eagerly. "Oh, why did we not see this before?"

"Ah, bah!" Ninon said. "Because nobody is certain that there is a human necromancer!

"One thing at a time," Lyon said. "First of all, we rid ourselves of the Unselighe Court. And then we shall bring down this Jongleur as he calls himself."

Malcoeur was swept all the way back to Snowdonia, not that far from Avalon, but an impressive distance. And he could so nothing to stop it. It was if he was held in a giant fist. He could neither move nor speak and it was not until he was dropped rather unceremoniously in the valley near Sluagh's underground kingdom that he regained the use of his tongue and his limbs.

He was completely enraged. He had had Lyons in his power! Unversed in Arthurian lore, Malcoeur had no idea who that interfering woman might be. That she was otherworldly he was well aware. He had not missed how she had emerged from the waters bone-dry and breathing normally. Where had her power come from? What was she?

Sluagh had better have the answers.

As the sun was lighting the valley with its rays there were no creatures about. At this time of day they would be hiding from the daylight within the depths of the caverns, sleeping, more than likely, until darkness came and they emerged to search for human prey. There was no telling where Sluagh might be – although for the last few days he had spent all of his time in bed with that *poule.*

Malcoeur was no admirer of Wanda's – he thought her a vulgar piece of goods. Last night she had come to the dinner table naked, of all things, save for a superfluity of jewels. To do Wanda justice, she thought she was wearing a gown of heavy cloth of gold. It was Sluagh's little joke to have it be transparent to everyone but her. Sluagh, so pleased with his new *inamorata*, wanted Malcoeur to be jealous, and what better way to accomplish that than by showing off her charms?

Malcoeur found Sluagh and his mistress at tea in the main chamber. She was still unclothed, with a different set of jewels, these mostly sapphires. Sluagh was feeding her tidbits of what looked like chicken. With no little satisfaction Malcoeur realized that she was probably eating rat.

Wanda, who saw on her person a beautiful blue brocade gown with a high gauze collar, could not understand why the other man did not look at her in admiration. In the mirror, the gown had seemed very becoming indeed. She did not realize what Sluagh had done.

"Where have you been?" Sluagh cried as Malcoeur entered. "The Gwyllion took several mortals just before dawn, among them a young Witch. I was certain that you would be here to suck her dry of her powers!"

"Who may be *la femme* that lives in the lake at Avalon?" Malcoeur demanded. Sluagh's playful tone grated on his nerves.

Sluagh, who had been tickling Wanda's breast, looked up sharply at this.

"You saw a woman in the lake at Avalon?" His manner changed at once, all the playfulness vanishing. "You actually saw the Lady of the Lake? Tell me everything!"

Avoiding even looking at Wanda (naked women had their place, but it was not at the tea table) Malcoeur flung aside his cape and bicorne. They were caught in mid air by a Gwyllion.

He helped himself to tea, preferring not to ask the naked slut to do so. And then he told Sluagh exactly what had happened in the terminated encounter.

548

"My friend, you are fortunate to be alive!" Sluagh said, shaking his head at Malcoeur's folly. "To try to harm the Arch Druid of Britain at Avalon is criminally stupid! She might have called on Lancelot or one of the other knights from their long sleep to dispatch you."

"A knight!" said Malcoeur scornfully. "Me, I am not worried about a knight!"

"Lancelot was unbeatable while he was alive, now that he is dead he is probably invulnerable," said Sluagh, frowning.

Malcoeur scowled. What was all this nonsense about dead knights? "Is that woman a sorceress?"

"Sorceress, enchantress, Faerie, the guardian of the Matter of Britain." Then, quickly and briefly, he outlined the history of Arthur, Merlin and the Lady of the Lake to Malcoeur.

"This country is insane," said Malcoeur flatly when Sluagh had finished. "These are fables for children, n'est-ce pas? Do all of these peoples believe this?"

"Yes, to the smallest child," Sluagh was paying little attention now to Malcoeur. Already in his diseased mind the wonder of the Lady of the Lake had faded and he was thinking more of Wanda. It was such a good joke, her being naked and not knowing it. She was so fetching in her jewels and naught else. He was thinking about taking her back to bed. Unlike some women he had bedded she never grew tired of the exercise.

Disgustedly, Malcoeur could see that he would get no more information from Sluagh, not if the look in his eyes was anything to go by. There was always the book shop in the village.

Early the next morning Beau galloped down the hall towards Simon's room. It was early indeed, the sun only up a little in another blue sky. In spite of the fact that all had attended the Lammas celebration the night before, and stayed up late, there was work to be done today. Guests – Wizards and other Druids who were to take part in the sending on Lammas old style would be arriving starting today. There had to be a ceremony of blessing and cleansing at the Sacred Grove – for it had been decided that it was there that the sending would take place, for to the astonishment of all, Father Oak had informed them that the Painted Floor was the very place Merlin had done the first binding. Father Oak had been but a sapling at the time. The stars had directed Merlin to the place and the node, for as well as Wizard, Merlin was a noted astrologer.

Beau slid in the slightly opened door of Simon's room and skidded to a halt. "It's time!" he announced.

Simon, who was being helped into his dressing gown by a yawning Sanders, looked up at the black and white kitten.

"Don't you ever knock?" Janus looked disapprovingly at her brother.

"Cats don't knock on doors!" he returned.

"Then you should at least meow politely until someone lets you in," she informed him.

Beau ignored her, saying instead to Simon," Come on, then, you don't want to miss anything!"

Shoving his slippers on his feet, Simon thanked Sanders and took off down the hall with Beau, Janus trailing behind, grumbling to herself.

Like many small boys Simon found the ritual of shaving fascinating and as of late had developed the habit of observing René at the shaving stand each morning. Simon enjoyed this immensely – they talked about 'man things' which one could of course not talk to Mama about, even as wonderful as she was. And it was a part of Simon's family fantasy – he could pretend that he was talking with his own Papa.

Beau had given himself the task of letting Simon know when the ceremony would start. The kitten found shaving fascinating as well – but why would one want to remove fur? The kittens liked Lyon's beard – it was fun to climb up his chest and knead it with their paws.

As usual, Simon climbed on René's bed and lay on his stomach, with his chin propped on his hands, a kitten on either side of him. Simon had some questions about the Lammas celebration and René taught him a simple spell to reheat water, for the water in the pitcher had not been very hot this morning. Not only had all in the household stayed up late, but the staff was all at sixes and sevens preparing for the guests.

René had finished shaving, and donned his shirt and waistcoat and was preparing to tie his cravat – another mystery Simon found fascinating – when Simon said, all in a rush, "If Mama is wearing the Chenevix betrothal ring, does that mean you are *really* going to get married?" His tone was hopeful and his eyes shone with longing.

Dismayed, René turned away from the mirror to face Simon. And something in his face told the little boy the truth, for he burst into tears at once, burying his face in the bedclothes.

"Simon!" René said, appalled. He strode to the bed and took Simon into his arms and sat on the edge of the bed holding the child close. Simon at once wound his arms about René's neck and sobbed into his shoulder.

With little mews of distress, the kittens climbed up on René's lap and from there to Simon's face, patting him with their paws and attempting to lick his cheeks.

"Simon, what is it?" René held him close, stroking his back.

"I wanted you to be my Papa!" Simon wailed though his tears, sniffing loudly.

Beau jumped down and ran to the dresser, jumping to the top of it by leaping to the seat of a chair and from there to the top of the dresser where a fresh handkerchief lay, ready to go into René's pocket. This he dragged to the bed and with a quick, *"Merci,"* René took it from him and wiped Simon's face and then told him to blow his nose.

Simon obeyed and then looked up into the face so near his with tragic eyes. "Why can you and Mama not be married? I don't understand! Why tell everyone you are going to be married if it is not real?" His tone was accusatory.

"Oh, Simon..." René sighed. How could he explain this whole complicated affair to a child – and an interested pair of kittens?

"We never understood it, either!" said Janus.

"Speak for yourself!" said Beau in some scorn "It was so René would not have to marry that awful Wycherley woman – the one who hated cats..." It was obvious to *him*.

551

"I think I understood that," said Simon, making use of the handkerchief again. His voice was still full of tears. "But I don't understand it now."

As simply as he could, René told Simon, what the Duke had done and the scandal it would cause if the betrothal was withdrawn too quickly. He could tell that Simon did not really comprehend what a scandal might mean, but the little boy accepted it. It was just another of those incomprehensible things adults did.

"I really wanted you to be my Papa," said Simon wistfully, a tear trickled down his cheek and he snuggled against René trustingly.

"I would like nothing better than to be your Papa, Simon," said René huskily. It was true. He could not imagine loving a son of his own body more than he loved this child. He had to explain to him why it could never be, though. "You see, when two people marry, they should love one another dearly, to make a family. It is not enough that one wants a family –"

"But I love you *and* Mama!" Simon protested.

"And I love you and your Mama. But she does not love me," said René with difficulty. "And no, Simon," he said as the boy was about to speak, "I cannot *make* her love me. That cannot be done, *n'est-ce pas?* We are friends now, that is all. There must be love on both sides for a proper, a good marriage."

"It isn't fair!" said Simon with a long sigh. He sniffed again.

"Life is not fair, no matter how much we wish it to be so," said René with a sigh as deep as Simon's. He took the handkerchief from Simon and tenderly wiped his face. "We must let Sanders make you presentable; you will not wish the others to know that you have been crying. Now, what would you like to do today? I am at your disposal – I have no duties in the Tower and we shall do whatever you like."

Simon's tear clouded face brightened visibly. "I would like to work with my wand."

"Then that is what we shall do," René promised. "Come, let Sanders wash your face and get you dressed."

With a last hug, Simon and Janus ran off to his room. He was thrilled that he was to have René all to himself for the

552

day. With the resiliency of youth he thought still that perhaps he could still have his wish.

René continued to sit on the edge of the bed, twisting the wet handkerchief between his fingers.

He had been a fool. He hadn't realized the depths of Simon's attachment. He had thought that only Ninon and Lucie would grieve if the ceremony had a fatal outcome. Now it seemed Simon would suffer another devastating loss.

But it was too late to turn back. He was committed. He had to do this, for the current state of affairs could not continue.

Beau looked at him sharply. The kitten could sense that something was wrong, but he did not question René. The kitten had already learned that his Wizard could be remarkably reticent. He contented himself with climbing into René's lap and purring.

Absentmindedly, René stroked the little cat. It was comforting – the feel of his soft fur and the gentle purring. But nothing comforted the ache in his heart.

Lord and lady Eastcote were leaving for Kent this morning. Lady Eastcote had somewhat recovered from her dragon-back ordeal and they needed to go home, for they had their own preparations to make for the upcoming ceremony. Lord Eastcote was a Wizard – a *Magus Majori* – he would be gathering with the other local Wizards to raise their own power to join with the rest of England. Lady Eastcote's Coven would do the same.

They had an early breakfast with their daughter. Lord Eastcote was well-used to early rising, for he liked to be out upon the land as early as his farmers, but his lady, used to more civilized hours, had to stifle yawns behind her lace-edged handkerchief.

After cutting a swathe through muffins, several rashers of bacon, kippers, ham, grilled tomatoes, buttered eggs and golden triangle of toast dripping with butter, Lord Eastcote cleared his throat portentously. Putting his finger-tips together he looked at his daughter. "Diana, if you will take my advice you will go ahead and marry that young man. I like him – fortunately he is nothing like his father –he seems to think just as he ought –"

"And handsome and charming as well!" put in Lady Eastcote. "That accent – so romantic!"

"I own, I cannot really like the Chenevix connection – that man can be insufferable," Lord Eastcote continued, " but Chenevix has hinted that he will come down handsome in the settlements –"

"And the Duchess is a sweet female – you will have no mama-in-law problems! And at any rate, Chenevix owns so many properties that he may very well make one over to you and your husband and you may live there and see little of your in-laws!" Diana's mother suggested.

Aghast, Diana looked from one parent to the other. "But there is no question of such a thing! The betrothal is a pretence, as you well know. We are not in the least attracted to one another in that way!"

Lord Eastcote snorted. "Ho! If he is not nutty upon you, you may take me for a flat! No man looks at a female that way unless he is seriously *épris*!"

"But I have never seen –" Diana began.

"But my dear, he looks at you when he thinks no one else is looking!" her Mama said in an arch voice Diana found particularly annoying.

"The match has our approval," her father continued. "The more I think on it the more I like the scheme. You could not do better for yourself."

Sourly, Diana thought her dear Papa sounded a great deal like the Duke of Chenevix.

"I intend never to remarry," she said, rather viciously slathering butter on an innocent muffin.

"Do you not wish a home of your own again and perhaps a little one – a brother or sister for dear little Simon?" queried Lady Eastcote. "Despite the fact that you have put on your caps you are as yet a young woman and not yet at your last prayers! Surely you do not to become an ape-leader!" Everyone knew that it was the fate of single females and childless wives to lead apes in Hell. Diana had come to consider the person who wrote that to be a certifiable idiot.

"And knowing that such a union would please your family and friends, not to mention the opportunities that you could throw in your sisters' ways, moving as you would in the first circles of fashion!" her mother continued.

"I am perfectly happy here, keeping house for my uncle – " Diana began, only to be interrupted by her father who said, "Aye, and what sort of society do you have here, pray tell? Lyonshall don't even attend the Assembly rooms! What if Lyonshall marries again? You'll probably get odd and keep cats, exactly like your Aunt Agatha. Had forty-two felines before she cocked up her toes!"

Rascal, who had been beneath the table begging bits of bacon, gave a loud hiss and demanded, "What's wrong with keeping cats? But Diana doesn't need any cats but me!"

Diana put her uneaten muffin down on the plate. "I do not intend to marry again," she said flatly and slowly, as if explaining something to the village idiot. "Whether or not I shall marry is my business and I shall not allow anyone to make up my mind for me." Then afraid of hurting their feelings, she added in a kinder voice, "I know that you both mean well, but I am the one who will have to live with any decision. And I could not marry without love, and in spite of the fact that René is everything you say he is, the plain fact is that I do not love him. We are friends, that is all."

Lord and Lady Eastcote exchanged glances and the subject was allowed to drop. Conversation turned to the preparations for the coming binding.

An hour later Diana saw her parents off. Lady Eastcote was looking as she suffered from *mal de dragonne* before even stepping onto Tuathail's back. The green dragon had volunteered to fly them home, for a carriage ride would get them to Kent with no time to spare before Lammas Old Style was upon them.

Diana had lost her anger by that time, but one thing still troubled her. Her father had said the René was 'nutty upon her'. Could that possibly be true? Was he in fact in love with her?

Oh, no, it couldn't be! Surely she would know. She had known instantly when Jonathan was attracted to her.

She thought how much it would hurt – unrequited love had always seemed to her one of the worst things that could happen to a person. She did not want to hurt him – she had come to value him as a friend. But actually marry him – no, it would never work. She would not marry again until she was head over heels in love, as she had been with Jonathan.

555

But she felt a strong need to talk with someone – someone older and wiser, but someone who would not tell her what to do. She at last hit on Ninon. Ninon would not hold it against Diana that she could not love her grandson. Diana and Ninon had come to quite a good understanding.

But she had to laugh at the notion of her uncle Lyon marrying again! Pray, whom would he find to marry? He was a rather difficult man to live with – no female in her right mind would take him on!

48

The Secret Revealed

Since they were singularly bereft of qualified Wizards in the immediate neighborhood Conchobar sent Diarmiat to help Lyon and the Vicar at the Sacred Grove. Diarmiat's specialty was geomancy, which meant a deep study of ley lines. Even with the addition of two Druids from the Île de Sein they needed another Master to complete a circle of power – one for each cardinal point and one who was free to move back and forth lighting candles, seeing to the incense and such. Few other Wizards could be spared from anywhere else. Lyon had been appalled when he added up how few Masters there were left and how many Wizards, Witches – and Druids – had been killed by the Jongleur. When this was all over, there would have to be some serious talks and plans about the future of Wizardry in the Six Nations.

The Covens were even more badly off, for thirteen Witches were needed to raise a cone of power and in many cases there were not enough Witches in each Coven to make their power circle. All over Britain there had been a furor of scrying and 'griffe' expresses to coordinate the Covens and combine them for the proper numbers to raise the cones. Diana was to join the Cheltenham Coven, with Ninon, which brought their number up to just the right amount. Diana had hoped to go to the Grove, but she was needed in Cheltenham, where the Coven was to meet at the local stone circle.

The identity of the Locus was still a secret, but was not to remain so for very long, which was to be Beau's fault.

The kittens were to accomplish their first real tasks as familiars on Lammas Old Style. They would fetch, carry and prompt the Wizards or Witches as necessary. They were more than a trifle nervous, but had been drilled by their father, and would have as well, the direction of both Leander and Diarmiat's familiar Ó Dálaigh, whom the kittens had met earlier. Although a rather stout, pleasant looking marmalade cat, he nevertheless had a quick and stern eye for mischief. Since the Druids of the Île de Sein did not follow English tradition, they did not employ familiars. The two kittens who would accompany their Witches to Cheltenham would have the guidance of the eleven other familiar animals in the Coven.

Diarmait and Ó Dàlaigh arrived on August fourth, on Pàdraig. Diarmait brought greetings from Aisling, who had desperately wanted to come along, but she was needed at her own Coven. Although Ireland had lost less of her magical personnel than had Britain, Wales, Scotland, Cornwall or even Man, everyone who could contribute power was needed. He also carried a packet of letters from Conchobar to Lyon – the final arrangements for the power to be raised from all over Ireland and routed through Tara and then to the Grove. This Conchobar had not wanted to scry, for scrying was not a secure method of communication and could be tapped by the wrong persons. The scrying between Covens had used the cover of a 'fertility ritual', in case anyone was listening who had no business doing so.

After a tasty nuncheon, Diarmait and René took a walk in the shrubbery. Ó Dálaigh went with them, but Beau was told to stay behind and study his prompts by the older cat.

Beau smarted under this treatment. He knew the whole ceremony backwards and forwards from memory! He did not see why he was treated so shabbily – he felt as if they were hiding things from him. His actual prompts, he noticed, were nothing compared to the others. They had pages and pages to learn, even Janus, for Simon had a small part to play in what was to come. It seemed as if René had very little to do in this ceremony and it seemed very odd to Beau. Mr. Arabin, Lyon, Diarmait, and François, one of the Druids from the Île de Sein, were to be the cardinal points while the other Druid, Marcel, was to light the candles and the other tasks that would be done outside the circle, according to what the kittens had been told. What was *his* Wizard going to be doing? Beau determined to find out.

Accordingly, he waited until the other kittens were deep in a post-nuncheon nap. Alphonse had outdone himself and even Leander, who usually confined himself to snacking nocturnally on the rodent family, had partaken of a rich *beouf bourguignon* and now slept with his head beneath his wing.

Beau felt sleepy, but his curiosity overcame any impulse he had to lay down and snooze the afternoon away. Everyone else in the household was busy or gone. Lyon was going over things with the two French Druids. Chenevix had taken his Duchess into Cheltenham for another course of the waters. Diana and Ninon were busy with household tasks. There would be a huge breakfast after the ceremony, for raising power made for hungry magicians. Simon was running errands for them.

No one stopped Beau as he slipped out of the Tower. He had been going to explain, if asked, that he had to use the earth box that was kept for the kittens in the Tower foyer.

But no one asked. Since it was a hot, sleepy day, Robert was dozing at his post and Beau did not wake him. The black and white kitten trotted out the recently installed cat door and with his acute hearing, followed the first of several conversations he could hear. The first proved to be several of the grooms idly talking as they cleaned tack. They were talking about Culver Grindle — how much they had disliked him and how glad they were to see the backside of him when he had finally left. He had, they were sure, cheated them at the dice, for he had the devil's own luck.

That was of no interest to Beau, so he went on to the herb garden where he found several maids sitting outside, sent there by Diana for a short break to cool down. They were sipping lemonade and eating fresh baked fruit tarts. Beau was tempted by the tarts, for he had a sweet tooth, but he passed them by.

At last he tracked down the Wizards. They were strolling around in the shrubbery, talking seriously in low voices. Ó Dálaigh sat on a stone bench, paws and tail tucked neatly under him. He looked half asleep, but Beau knew better. The older cat was alert and listening and could react in an instant to any threat.

Therefore Beau had to be doubly cautious. The kitten sank to his stomach and slid carefully along the ground under the cover of a large rhododendron. The gardeners had been busy; no leaf litter lay beneath the 'alpine rose' which had stood in this place since the late seventeenth century.

Beau slid to within a few feet of the two Wizards. He could probably hear what they were talking about further away, but he wanted to make certain that he heard everything. He could actually hear things in the higher ranges with more clarity and René had a baritone voice, while Diarmait was nearly a basso.

Beau settled into a comfortable position and pricked his ears forward. He was rewarded almost at once for his efforts.

"Do they know what you're planning on doing?" asked Diarmait, concern in his soft Irish voice.

"*Non*," René shook his head, not looking at his friend but at the neatly raked gravel they slowly walked upon. "Only Lord Lyonshall and the Vicar know."

"And it's not happy about it they are, I'm thinking," Diarmait observed. "As neither am I – nor Aisling."

"I *must* do it, Diarmait," René said, a little desperately. "There is no one else! Lord Lyonshall has found several spells that he is certain that will protect me – spells Merlin did not use, for all that we can find out."

"Oh, aye, and Conchobar has sent me with a few tricks as well. We are all determined you will come out of this alive and in full possession of all your senses," his friend informed him.

A chill ran over the listening kitten. Come out of this alive? What did they mean?

"Have ye heard enough then?" came a throaty voice from behind Beau.

Surprised, the kitten whirled and saw Ó Dálaigh regarding him through narrowed eyes. How had the tabby done that? Beau had seen or heard nothing.

As if he could read the kitten's mind, Ó Dálaigh said, "I'll be having a wee bit of the magic meself, young one. Were ye not told to study your prompts so ye can be helping your Wizard on the Great Day?"

"I've got it memorized," Beau said defensively. "I had very little to learn and I wanted to know why that is! René is a brilliant Wizard – everyone says so – and why he had so little part in the ceremony? Even Neige and Rascal have more prompts to learn than I do, and they are only Witches' familiars!"

Ó Dálaigh looked severely at the kitten. "There is no such thing as *only* a Witch, boyo. Every magician is important. Ye'll do well to remember that. And ye should be grateful, not cocky, that ye are privileged to work with a fine Wizard such as yours. He's a brave one, to be offering himself as the Locus for this working."

"The Locus!" said Beau, shocked. "But he could *die* – they all said how serious it was to be the Locus!"

"They'll not be letting him die," said the marmalade cat sharply. "There's a lot been learned since Merlin's time and it's certain I am that he'll be protected from harm."

"You *can't* be certain!" Beau protested angrily. "There has not been a human locus since that last binding! Nobody knows for certain what will happen! I know – I read about it and I have heard them talking!"

"Eavesdropping, no doubt," Ó Dálaigh sighed. "'Tis an excellent way to hear things ye don't or can't understand. I tell ye this now, kitten, we'll be after doin' our very best to protect your Wizard, ye can count on that." He went on to tell Beau that his Wizard had passed the Unicorn test and that Cluny was now living in Knyghtwood.

But then Ó Dálaigh made an error. He did not forbid Beau to speak of this to anyone else and Beau, once released from the older cat's company, promptly went to find his siblings and inform them.

"What did you say?" Diana said in horror, almost dropping the ceramic bowl she held on the floor.

In order to impart their news Neige and Rascal had scrambled up to the top of the work table in the still room where Diana and Ninon were decanting more honey mead. Ninon had paused in her task as well and drew in her breath sharply. "*Non*, this cannot be true! Surely you have heard wrong!"

Neige looked distressed and put out a paw to Ninon. "Beau overheard the Irish Wizard and René talking about it. And then Ó Dálaigh confirmed it – René is to be the Locus!" she said. She hated being the one to bring this news to Ninon, but felt her Witch should know.

Ninon went deathly pale and suddenly leaned heavily on the table. Diana went at once to her side and offered support.

"Why must it always be René?" Ninon moaned. "Why does he feel he has to save the world?"

"Beau says he is the only one who can do it," offered Rascal.

"But the unicorn test –" said Diana in confusion.

"He passed it and there is now a unicorn living in our wood!" said Rascal. "I want to go see it!"

"Oh, *mon Dieu!*" Ninon moaned again, dropping her face into her hands.

Diana had never seen the older woman so distressed. And she had no idea how to offer any comfort. She could think of nothing comforting about this situation. She herself was horrified – he couldn't do this! It was too chancy, too dangerous! What if something went wrong?

"This is much worse than the business with the Cremave!" Ninon said, in French. "At least then I was confident that he would win out, for I knew he was telling the truth and that the Cremave would know so. But this –" She lifted a face suddenly haggard to Diana. "Oh, Diana, what if he is killed? I do not think I can bear it!"

Diana could not bear it either. She had found a friend and she did not wish to lose him. And Simon! What effect would this have on him, so soon after losing his father? She had to admit, Simon was far closer to René than he had ever been to Jonathan.

"Let us find René and try to talk him out of this," she now suggested to Ninon. "Surely he will listen to reason."

Ninon nodded, hastily wiping away a tear that had trickled down her cheek. "I want so much for everything to be the way it was! We were poor, but we were happy. It was good that Lucie was restored to us, but nothing else that has happened has been good at all."

Diana understood what she meant. When bad things happened one was tempted to retreat into the past, to wish that things had remained the same.

"Come," she said to Ninon, putting a comforting arm around her shoulder. "We shall find him and talk some sense into his head!"

Ninon smiled very slightly and put her hand on Diana's gratefully. She felt every one of her years suddenly. And if she lost René, she would be bereft indeed, for Lucie, too was lost to her, now in the clutches of that Duke.

"I will not have this, sirrah! I refuse to allow you to commit such folly!" thundered the Duke of Chenevix. "Do you desire to put a period to your existence? You shall not do this!"

He was in the library with René, the doors locked against all intrusion. Sunlight poured in the windows and the windows themselves were open, filmy curtains stirring in a very light breeze. Idly, René thought how lovely a sight were the sheer curtains, stirring slightly, showing glimpses of the sun – the very epitome of summer.

How the Duke had learned of his role in the coming binding he had no idea. All he knew was that barely ten minutes after the Duke and Duchess had returned from Cheltenham he had been summoned to the library by a demand delivered by Mariposa.

It was Mariposa who had informed his master. The manservant had overheard the kittens talking and, telling no one else, had gone to his master's suite to wait for the Duke. He had privately informed Chenevix in the dressing room, away from Lucie's presence.

And Chenevix had become completely enraged. He had at once ordered Mariposa to find his heir and bring him to the library where they might be private. His Grace was not going to put up with this nonsense. The heir to the Dukedom of Chenevix was not going to be used as a sacrificial lamb. Let them get some commoner for their use!

René had scarcely entered the room before the harangue began. How dared he do such a thing? Was he mad? It would not be allowed, even should the Duke have to have his heir committed to a mad-house, where he obviously belonged!

René bore up well under the onslaught, for he knew there was actually little the Duke could do. If, as the Duke was threatening, he was locked into a room, he could teleport out. He was of age, and of sound mind

But he had never seem Chenevix so angry. A vein throbbed in the Duke's forehead and his face was high in colour. His brow was thunderous as he paced around the room, only pausing to deliver another order, in high dudgeon.

It was René's quiet and calm that at last caused Chenevix to wind down. Usually persons melted beneath one of his diatribes.

"*C'est ça*. I *am* going to do this," René stated, looking the Duke full in the face. "There is no one else and it must be done. *Je ne vous comprends pas* – to you I am naught but a commodity – the heir – you do not even seem to know that I have a Christian name –"

"A commodity?" Chenevix snarled, and then paused to rub at his chest. He had been feeling an uncomfortable pressure for some little time now and pain was spreading to his shoulders and arms, even into his neck and back. What had he eaten for breakfast that could effect him like this? "Commodity..." he repeated, rubbing harder. The pain was now running down his left arm.

On the periphery of his consciousness he heard René get up from his chair so quickly that it fell over backwards, and as he began to crumple he felt a strong arm around him and heard René demand in a frantic voice,
"*Qu'est-ce qu'il y a ?*"

"Speak... English..." Chenevix grated out, moments before he went down into darkness.

49

Lammas Old Style I

"Apoplexy," declared Dr. Paget, hastily summoned from Cheltenham. "Not surprising in one of his choleric temperament. Unbridled passions lead to ill health."

René's quick actions had saved the Duke's life. He had laid the Chenevix upon a sopha, loosened his cravat and waistcoat and magically flung open the locked door. He sent Mariposa, hanging about in the hall for no discernible reason, to fetch Ninon and a dose of willow bark tea. This was given at once to the stricken peer while René used what small healing magics he had to sustain the Duke's life, tapping into the ley lines to augment his energies.

At Lucie's insistence they sent to London for Sir William Knighton, the Regent's own physician. The famous Wizard Healer arrived dragon-back, on a Royal dragon, by early evening.

Sir William, a bluff, genial man whom everyone liked and trusted at once (save Dr Paget who was rather miffed that another doctor had been called in) concurred with his learned colleague and soothed the other's ruffled sensibilities by deferring to him. Sir William also brought messages of sympathy from the Regent and a mandate that he was to facilitate the recovery of the Chancellor of Magic with all dispatch.

Sir William was a great believer in the healing power of sleep and placed Chenevix under a powerful spell that would allow him to rest and avoid further agitation. He thought it best that his patient remain in this condition for at least forty-eight hours – perhaps even until the binding ceremony which upset him so was completed. Knighton was confident that the Duke would make a full recovery, but – and he was adamant on this point – his Grace must be kept quiet, not allowed to become agitated, and when he had recovered, he must learn to govern his temper, else there would be a repeat of this attack, the next one perhaps fatal.

Lucie, to the surprise of nearly everyone, suddenly dry-eyed and capable, promised the doctors that she herself would see that her husband abided by these new rules. The doctors had a long list of dietary changes and imparted these to Lucie, Mariposa and Alphonse, Wizard Healers had long known that a diet low in salt and equally low in rich fatty foods was far better for one in the Duke's situation.

At first René felt guilty – that it was his fault that Chenevix's temper had flared in such fashion as to cause an apoplexy. But both doctors assured him that this was not the case. It was always so with those of angry disposition. This worst of humors damaged the heart, the arteries and the brain. Chenevix was indeed fortunate that René had been with him at the time, and had been so quick to think of the willow bark tea and remove his restrictive clothing.

Lammas Eve, old style, dawned bright and hot. This night would see the beginning of the binding of the Unselighe Court and all over the British Isles preparations were being made.

After the Duke's collapse there was no hiding René's part in the coming ceremony from Simon. The boy had sobbed himself to sleep in his mother's arms. She had felt as if her heart was breaking for him. And for herself as well – she had come to depend on René's friendship and would miss it sorely if the worst happened, for somehow the friends of her youth had all drifted away – not that she had many particular friends, for Diana was not the sort to give her heart and friendship too lightly. It gave her a rather sick feeling to realize that after tonight she might never see him again. The talks both she and Ninon had had with him had not swayed him in the least. He was determined to do what he saw as his duty to his adopted country.

A pall seemed to hang over the entire house all day. The servants went about their tasks talking in whispers.

Upstairs, the Duke lay in a spell-induced sleep, attended by his wife, valet and Sir William Knighton. Simon and the kittens were quiet and morose, neither with much appetite.

René was to be sequestered most of the day. He was to eat but a light, proscribed diet, and remain in quiet and contemplation. Before the ceremony and the donning of the special silken robes he would take a ritual bath of purification and be blessed by Mr. Arabin and in a Druidical ceremony with the two Druids of his own order. Merlin had not mentioned whether the blessing had been Christian or pagan – Mr. Arabin saw no harm in having both – it could only help.

Though all expected that the day would go by slowly as it usually does when something is greatly anticipated, but it seemed no time at all before the sun was descending and it was time to begin the preparations.

Before they were to leave for the Grove René had a visitor – a small blue Faerie who sped into the open window of his room.

"Hallo, Wizard," Medb said. "I am sent to remind you of the King's gift. Read the parchment and obey what it says to the letter. Do it now. And no matter what ANY ONE tells you, do not remove your chain from about your neck! You'll be sorry if you do!" she added severely.

Obediently, René went to his dresser drawer and withdrew the little box. Inside was a tiny bejeweled jar atop a folded parchment. On the parchment in spidery Elfin writing were "Instructions for Use": *"One third to be applied liberally around eyes on each succeeding evening"* it read. René unscrewed the top of the jar and found a green ointment that smelled pleasantly of some sort of herbs that he could not identify.

There were directions as to what to do after the ceremony was complete.

"Your grandmother is an herb woman – she can help you with that part," said Medb – she was reading over his shoulder by this time.

"This is Faerie ointment, *non*?" he asked.

"It certainly is!" she said. "And whatever you do, don't use your Othersight when you first put it on or you'll walk into a wall or some such thing. Go ahead and put it on – they'll be coming for you soon." She reached out a little blue hand and took the parchment, which was almost as big as she was. "I'll see that your grandmother gets this."

René went to the mirror above his shaving stand and dipped a finger into the ointment. It was warm to the touch and had the weight and texture of honey. Gingerly, with one finger he stroked it around his eye socket and over the lid as the instructions directed. It caused a tingling feeling and remained warm. As he finished spreading it – being careful to use exactly one third of the stuff as the directions bade – his vision suddenly shifted and he saw things that he had never seen before.

Colours were more intense and in deeper, almost dizzying perspective and as he watched suddenly all about him were the elementals of which even Othersight gave but a dim vision. There were the creatures of all four elements – air, water, earth and fire – salamanders, naiads, nymphs and nereids of the air and water and dryads from the trees – all more clear and vivid than he had ever seen them before: a quiet salamander in the logs laid for the fire, miniature nereids in the water in the wash basin, sprites of the air in the breeze that came in the window where he could see a dryad in the sheltering tree outside and even a gnomish face in the earth of the pot plant that stood on the dresser. These creatures could be seen with Othersight, but they were but pale reflections of what René now saw. And there were other Faeries too – part of the invisible host that no mortal ever was privileged to see – all achingly beautiful and brilliant in colour.

Gradually the world righted itself and he once again stood on the floor of his bedchamber. The elementals faded and went away, but his sight was keener than normal and everything looked sharper and brighter.

"That's better," said Medb in satisfaction. "It's time – I hear them coming."

Everyone involved in the ceremonies had their own rites of purification to undergo. Candles were anointed and lit, herb-scented baths were taken and incense burned as the preparations went forward throughout the Six Nations.

Sluagh had noted the unusual activity but dismissed it as the fertility ritual that had been seen in the scrying bowls. He thought it quite amusing – they were attempting to repopulate their numbers! He thought of perhaps spying on them at one of their sacred sites – it might be diverting to watch a fertility ritual with Wanda at his side – it might prove stimulating as well. But Wanda had finally decided to collect her things from the Inn where Culver and her menservants were still staying in Cheltenham – why should she continue to pay their shot when she could send them back to London? She intended to stay with Sluagh – she was not about to give up on the most satisfying erotic experiences she had ever had. The fact that he gave her new jewels almost daily had a bit to do with her decision as well. She also enjoyed the subservient attitude of the Unselighe creatures – she could order them about as she had never been able to treat human servants. If they were insolent, Sluagh punished them. She had discovered she enjoyed watching that and Sluagh was even a better lover after he had tortured a Gwyllion or a bogle.

She did not, however, like Malcoeur and wished that Sluagh would rid himself of the necromancer. She did not like the look of contempt in his eyes, nor the fact that he did not seem to envy Sluagh for possessing her. She would have preferred them to be fighting over her as most men did – a situation she usually resolved by sleeping with both of them.

But Sluagh had suggested yesterday that she sleep with some of the creatures so that he could watch and she found herself eager to do so, especially when she took a good look at some of them. The fact that most of the creatures did not wear clothing helped a great deal in this regard.

Malcoeur was not at all perturbed by the goings on in the Wizards' world. He had always worked alone and had no tradition of working with others to raise power. He actually thought it rather pitiful that they had to work in such a fashion. Fertility ritual! Like Sluagh, he felt that they were trying to perhaps replenish their numbers – a foolish, futile effort, for babies were even easier to kill than were adults.

Wanda left for Cheltenham in the trap she had never returned to the *Green Man* in the late afternoon. She intended to spend the night at the inn, the *Happy Parrot,* where Culver Grindle was lodging. Her things had been taken to a more tonnish inn. But Culver had been very patient and deserved a reward – herself. But she was all impatient to return to Sluagh.

Malcoeur, with the aid of a glamourie he cast about himself spent the evening in the village inn, the *Gwragged Annwn*, for he had grown tired of Sluagh's company, particularly since the Elf showed a lamentable tendency to boast of what he and Wanda had been doing. Malcoeur found this more than a little disgusting. An evening spent amongst Welsh-speaking shepherds seemed enticing in comparison. And he needed quiet to think about this problem of how he was to kill the Irish and English Arch Druids who seemed so well protected. He did not notice that the Inn seemed deserted, so intent was he upon the problem before him. A 'don't look at me' spell guaranteed him privacy in a dark corner.

Lammas was celebrated as the beginning of harvest when the year began to go into he darkness. Days were shorter now, well past Midsummer's' Day and the greatest length of daylight. The wind was cooler, telling of the cold to come. It was a festival to celebrate the bounty of the Old Earth Goddess and the colours and scents used reflected the fruitfulness of the earth.

The incenses used were frankincense, heather and oak, denoting awareness, balance and protection. For both clarity and harmony the anointing oil was lilac, bringing a touch of late spring to the proceedings. The altar would be decked with sunflowers, ears of wheat and rye as well as late blooming flowers. Save for the white robes of the Druids, all wore yellow in honour of the season, but the Druid's sashes were yellow, of Celtic knot-work.

Near to the Sacred Grove lay a pool in the woods – or what appeared to be a pool. In Roman times it had been a bath house, but all semblance to that had disappeared over the centuries. Nature had filled in around it with trees, ferns and moss and it was only when one stepped into it that it became apparent that the bottom and sides were of marble, not of earth. It had been cleaned by the Druids for today's use and purified by Cluny's horn.

This was where René would take his ritual bath and don the white silk robes specified by Merlin. There would be two blessing ceremonies – one Christian conducted by Mr.

Arabin in his yellow robes and a second, by the Druids under Lyon's direction. At this time spells of protection would be cast.

A great calm had descended upon René. All the worries of the past weeks had drifted away – his feelings – still unexpressed to her – for Diana, how Simon would react, his worries over his parents and grandmother and the fear of his own death – all seemed to have vanished. He felt uplifted and somewhat unreal as he bathed, was anointed with oil and robed as the chanting began. He almost seemed to hear the chanting all over England as if his senses were preternaturally sharpened. As he was led to the altar, he scarcely heard Lyon's reassurances that if he, Lyon, had anything to do with this, René would come out of this well and hearty.

The top of the altar had been left clear, adorned only with a cloth of seasonal colour. The smells of incense and candles were all about, as well as the night scents and the smell of the flowers. René saw only the altar as he was laid upon it – flat on his back. He did not see the anxious faces of Simon and two of the kittens, who stood to one side. He would have to say a brief spell to open the full power of the ley lines, but after that his role was to be a conduit for the power raised all over Britain.

Although the time was now nearly midnight – when all of the power should converge upon the Grove – it was dark, save for the flickering of candles. The moon, at the full, would not rise until nearly two AM, by which time the ritual would have ended. The power was sustained for one hour exactly – if they had done everything correctly the ritual will have done its work properly.

Simon's part in the ritual was simple – he was to keep the candles lit while Marcel would be busy with other duties. The Druid would light them first with special purifying magic. Simon had been given a spell to keep the lights burning. Both he and Janus had spent hours committing this to memory. The ritual candles had to be lit manually to begin the spell, but must be kept lit as well as those needed for illumination. Mage lights would also be used.

Simon looked with trepidation at the figure of René, outstretched on the altar. His friend seemed transfigured, not entirely aware of his surroundings. Simon was reminded of the effigy of a Crusader knight he had once seen in a church. He suddenly wished that his mother had been able to be here. He needed her comfort. He heard a soft "Mew!' at his feet and looked down to see Beau and Janus looking up at him with sympathy on their furry faces. He reached down and petted them, each deriving comfort from the contact.

A few moments later Lyon called Beau over to sit near the altar. In case René faltered in his remembrance of the spell Beau would be there to prompt him.

As the time drew nearer to midnight they cast their Circle about the altar. It seemed to Mr. Arabin as each cardinal point was raised that he could see *something* there and could hear the rustle of great wings as the cardinal angels gathered to help in this endeavor. A weight lifted from his heart as he felt their presence. They would protect René.

Since the purpose of this circle was to guide the power to its locus, the ritual here at the grove was different from any other in the British Isles that night.

"Time!" announced Lyon and power flared out from his hands towards the altar. The other three in the circle added theirs to his at precisely the same moment.

On the altar René, who had been feeling a tingling in his bones from being directly over a node, let go his shields as he had been told to do. This was very difficult – one's mental shields and grounding were a part of a Wizard, as natural as breathing, and one of the first things a mage learned. He had been well surrounded with the protective spells that would expel the heat of the pulled ley lines but he must be completely open to receive the ley lines' power and the power that was to be shunted from all over the islands. Surendering his shields made him feel vulnerable.

He then spoke the words of the spell, needing no prompting from Beau. This ancient spell was designed to draw all of the ley lines to him, first making him aware of all of the nodes, and the maze of ley lines that tapped into each. To his inner eye, these nodes were brilliant points of light like diamonds on a necklace of smaller stones. As directed he kept his eyes firmly shut – indeed, Lyon had placed a thick silk scarf over his eyes.

René felt power begin to run through his veins. It felt like the one and only time he had had a glass of brandy –

fiery, intoxicating – only much more so. He opened himself further to the ley lines and began to pull them in to him. As he had rehearsed with Lyon, he braced himself for the shock of all that raw power, but no rehearsal could have prepared him for the dizziness of that overwhelming rapture, a feeling of all his senses at once being boosted to a height they had never known The power of it! For one moment he was a colossus, astride the world like a god and he was almost drunk with it.

But he had to control it into its proper channel. It must leave him and do its work. As he felt the power go through him he was also aware, briefly, of another power meeting with it and surging back out again. René held fiercely onto all of the lines of power, controlling them and guiding them, weaving them into one smooth unit, till it burst back out in a fountain of brilliant light.

To those watching it was as if all of the light in the world had shot up into the sky. They could no longer see René at all – just a pillar of light that began to spread out over their heads as if it were an immense umbrella.

"It's working!" Lyon whispered to himself. "It's working!"

And then a third band of light – this one green rather than the white of the ley lines and the purple-blue from the cones of power – joined the others – this broad, like a ribbon and undulating, joining itself seamlessly to the power from the raised cones and the ley lines. It seemed to come from the earth itself People said later that it was very like the aurora borealis.

No one expected this. What was it and where had it come from?

But Mr. Arabin, looking up at it, breathed, "The *Sidhe*! The *Sidhe* are helping us!"

50

Lammas Old Style II

All over the British Isles the huge ring of power spread out as if it were a dome, until it encompassed the entire area – out to the Isles of the Hebrides, the Orkneys and the Shetlands, over all of Ireland, even the tiny Arran Isles, from Land's End in Cornwall to John O'Groat's on Scotland, to the Isles of Man and Wight and the Channel Islands. And when the great dome descended, it took from every nook and cranny every Unselighe creature abroad on the hunt, and, as if in a whirlwind, took the shrieking creatures and drove them underground into their lairs, literally pushing many of them through the earth.

The first Malcoeur knew of any thing out of the ordinary happening was a stirring amongst the shepherds and drovers who frequented the inn. Despite all his best efforts Malcoeur had been unable to master more than a few words of Welsh, which had to be the most fiendishly difficult lan-guage he had ever come across Therefore when a young shepherd came into the tap, waving his arms excitedly and yelling, the Jongleur had no idea what was happening. But almost *en masse*, the men in the tap left their tankards and went out of doors. He followed, idly curious.

The power and the light struck him the moment he stepped outside. It was overwhelming in its intensity and almost blinding to the eye. It sang to him, but he could not touch it – for it was the antithesis of the magic he carried with him. This was magic of the earth, of all that was good and incorrupt. And something inside him yearned after it.

Ruthlessly, he quashed those feelings, angered at himself. Was this their fertility ritual? He somehow doubted it. This was not sex magic – that idiot Sluagh had been wrong again.

Then the shrieking began. He recognized the voices of the Gwyllion, of the bogles and the Fachan. What was happening? Malcoeur had remained in the shadows near the Inn. The men were cheering – how he wished he knew a spell to translate Welsh into an understandable language, such as there were for Arabic or even Hindu. But they had not found one and all of his efforts to concoct one had come to naught.

They were binding the creatures he realized with a shock and an ungovernable rage filled him. Those were HIS creatures – they were meant to help the Emperor of the French become invincible! Without caring that he might be seen, he flung aside his cloak and spread wide his hands, calling on his powers.

But nothing happened – no blood red energies flowed though his fingers. It was as if he had been again immobilized by the Lady of the Lake. He could do nothing – it was as if he had been stripped of his powers, negated.

He could do nothing to help the Unselighe Court. His anger grew and he wondered where Sluagh night be.

Sluagh had gone to meet Wanda, halfway between Cheltenham and Silverbridge. Just to the side of the road was a dark little copse of nasty fur trees, an excellent place for a lover's *rendezvous*, for Sluagh did not think that he could wait for her return to possess her again. It was odd, but the more he had her the more he wanted her. This had never happened to him before. She had been gone far too long. Even with the magical 'nudge' he had given her travels, it was still a long way from Wales to Cheltenham.

It was near midnight before she came at last, her trunks piled high on the trap. She had dallied with Culver Grindle, finding him rather unsatisfying after Sluagh. So she was nothing loath when the Elf suggested a tryst in the copse, shedding her clothing eagerly as Sluagh hid the horse and trap well off the road.

She was still far from being satiated when the light began to appear in the sky. They had been discussing, in

575

between bouts, of which of the creatures she would first take to her bed – she favored the Fachan for it was so hideous – when huge arcs of blue-white light began to streak through the sky, some of them originating quite close and meeting others that seem to come from all directions at once. They came down to earth again, not that far from where the Elf and Wanda lay on a bed of pine needles.

Sluagh let out a string of curses and jumped to his feet. "What is that?" he demanded angrily. "What are they up to?"

Wanda wore a *moue* of annoyance. The talk of her laying with a Fachan had excited Sluagh again and they had been just about to consummate another attack of lust. "I'm sure I don't know," she said tartly. "I'm not magical!"

"That is not a fertility ritual!" he snarled. "*We've* done more sex magic here tonight than that!"

And then they heard the screams of fright. Sluagh knew instantly what they meant.

"NO!" he screamed in rage. "NO! You can't do this to me!" He raised clenched fists to the heavens, shaking them at the lights and become even more maddened when he saw the green aurora-like bands joining the blue-white.

He should have looked ridiculous, naked, covered in pine needles and quivering and jumping in transports of anger, but he did not. For the first time Wanda actually felt fear as she looked at him. But as she watched, the strangest thing happened. He was still shouting and cursing but it was if he were acting in a pantomime, for although his mouth still moved she could no longer hear him. And then, very abruptly, as if someone had blown out a candle, he disappeared, leaving Wanda alone and suddenly cold.

To those watching at the Scared Grove, it was as if a huge fount of light had sprung up in the place of the altar. From beneath the earth through the altar – and René – thrust the light of the ley lines. From the heavens arced down from every direction the lines of power from the Covens and Wizards' gatherings. And joining that from the Hollow Hills came the green bands of the *Sidhe* power, all to surge up again and spread out over the countryside.

They could feel the power – it burned in their bones. At Mr. Arabin's suggestion all of them wore darkened spectacles such as astronomers used to watch the sun. Even with this protection their eyes stung and smarted. In dismay, Mr. Arabin wondered how René's eyes could survive such an assault, for he wore but a thin silk scarf. But the Vicar doubted that even darkened spectacles would have offered much protection.

Mr. Arabin was conscious that Simon and the two kittens were right behind him, crouched on the ground. He could dimly hear someone crying and little mews of distress, but he could not break the Circle nor let go of the power he was sending to the altar. His outstretched arms had begun to ache clear up to his shoulders but the Circle must be unbroken for an hour exactly. Once he heard Simon mutter the spell for keeping the candles lit and he was proud of the boy, that even in his distress he could remember his duty.

At long last he heard Marcel say *"Termenare,"* in Wizards' Latin and gratefully began the chant that would cease the spell and close down the Circle.

The lights suddenly reversed, the ley lines disappearing in to the earth, the light from the cones of power flowing backwards to their origins and the green bands snaking back into the Hollow Hills.

With the breaking of the Circle everyone rushed to the altar where René lay deathly still. He was obviously deeply unconscious.

Simon and the two kittens were the first to reach his side. Simon moaned as he looked upon his friend, for there seemed to be no sign of life.

Mr. Arabin was next to arrive and he withdrew a small mirror from the pocket of his robe and held to René's lips. A dim mist appeared on the mirror's surface and when the Vicar put his ear to his young friend's chest he could hear the faintest of heartbeats. "He lives!" he announced joyfully.

"He looks awful," said Lyon grimly, while Diarmait crossed himself and murmured a prayer.

René had a gray pallor and breathed so shallowly that it looked as if he were not breathing at all. One hand lay upon his chest, as if curled about something while the other hung limply at his side. He was as still and as stiff as an effigy as Lyon gently removed th silken scarf.

"Are ye seein' any damage?" Diarmait asked anxiously.

Lyon shook his head. "I had a little talk with Sir William about eye damage – he says sometimes you cannot see any apparent damage. He will perform an examination when René regains consciousness."Unspoken was the thought in all of their minds – *if he ever does.*

The two older familiars and come up to sit with the kittens and Plato was licking Beau and Janus in a soothing manner. Mr. Arabin had dropped an arm around Simon's shoulders, for which the boy was grateful. He had begun to shiver and could not seem to stop, in spite of the fact that the night was relatively warm.

Lyon had arranged that Tuathail, after bringing Diana and Ninon home from Cheltenham, would fly to the Grove and from there bear René back to the Abbey. This would be both faster and less jarring that a wagon ride through the forest.

"The dragon comes," announced Father Oak, who all through the proceedings had remained a silent spectator. The treetops bent aside to allow Tuathail access to the floor of the Grove.

As it was still some little while until moon-rise Lyon threw up a circle of mage lights so that the dragon might see where to land. A dragon's night sight was better than a man's but still could use help when landing in a dark forest.

But before the dragon could land, a brilliant flair of green light near the altar took everyone by surprise. There stood a glorious figure –whom he might be was known at once, for it could be no one else – Oberon.

Without preamble he said to the awed assembly, "You have done the thing. The Unselighe creatures have been bound to their underground hole."

"We could not have done it without your help, my lord King," said Mr. Arabin, with the deepest of bows. He was the first to recover from the shock of seeing the High King of Faerie appear so unexpectedly.

Oberon inclined his head graciously. "And I am glad to tell you, for the sake of my kinsman here –" this with a nod towards René – "that it will not be necessary to repeat this ceremony again. The Unselighe Court will trouble you no more. You have my word and surety on that."

He walked to the altar and lay a long-fingered hand on René's forehead. "We have done what we could to safeguard him. Now it is up to love to do the rest. Follow our instructions carefully and all will be well."

"Instructions?" repeated Lyon blankly.

But the Elf had disappeared in a swirl of green, just minutes before Tuathail landed on the Painted Floor with a thump.

To Lyon's surprise Ninon rode the dragon. "Have you touched him?" she asked sharply as Diarmait hurried forward and helped her from Tuathail's back.

"Oberon laid his hand upon his forehead," Mr. Arabin offered. He quickly explained to Ninon what had happened during the Elf King's visit.

Ninon looked as if she was sorely disappointed that she had not seen the Elf King, but just as quickly dismissed her regret and unfolded a piece of parchment that she had been carrying in the pocket of her robe. It was closely covered in fine script. "We must move him carefully, by magic, and keep his head flat and level, non? These are the Elves' instructions, given to me by the blue Faerie."

A spell was included to facilitate the removal to the dragon's harness. All the magicians in the Grove were needed to participate in this, for not one amongst them had the strength of a brand new apprentice, and all were exhausted and sweating by the time the maneuver was accomplished. But none of them begrudged the effort. Ninon and Lyon went with the dragon, who took off with far more care than was usual, leaving the others to put the Sacred Grove to rights before returning to the Abbey, where a large meal had been prepared.

Sluagh had no idea where he was . He lay in a meadow filled with flowers of all sorts.It was no longer night time. Judging by the angle of the sun it was perhaps mid-morning on a soft and lovely day. The area he lay in was ringed about by young, slender birches holding leafy arms to the blue sky. A crystal stream, bubbling over a pebbly bottom, reflected white puffy clouds drifting overhead.

Sluagh looked down at himself. He was no longer naked nor was there any sign of the pine needles in which he had lain with Wanda. He wore a simple tunic, leggings and boots of green, woven from spider web silk. His face twisted in a grimace. So that was where he was – in *his* domain! What did his damned brother want with him? Sluagh gave no thought of what might have happened to Wanda.

He would not stay here. He could not stay here. The familiar terror that the Faerie lands engendered was beginning to choke him. He had to get away and there seemed to be nothing stopping him. But as he walked in the direction that the little brook flowed he walked into an invisible wall. There was nothing that he could see but there was a wall there, up over his head and down into the ground.

And it was the same in each direction he tried. He was in a space of about ten by ten feet – walls seemingly of glass, although it did not feel like glass nor chime like it when repeatedly struck with his fists as his hysteria rose. He screamed until he was hoarse and then dropped to the ground amidst the flowers, rocking back and forth in a crunched-up ball as if he were a small child trying to comfort himself. He was all alone – locked in an invisible box.

And then he felt eyes upon him. He looked up sharply, scrubbing at his face with a sleeve.

There on the other side of the clear wall was a unicorn, regarding him with grave dark eyes.

51

Oberon's Justice

Mr. Arabin had returned to the Vicarage in the small hours of the new day, completely exhausted. For the first time since he had been Vicar of the parish of St. Swithin's he had not celebrated Matins, but had slept right through most of the morning. The grueling conditions of the major Working, his worries over René (who, when he had at last left the Abbey, had not as yet regained consciousness) and the feeling of exultation that also animated him – for accomplishing their task and actually seeing Oberon – all of these had combined to make sleep difficult to achieve and when it at last came, restless and light.

It was nearly eleven before he was at last able to drag himself from bed and dress and go belowstairs. Perhaps Lord Lyonshall was right – the peer had suggested that what Mr. Arabin needed was a young curate. He thought this over as he went down the stairs, uncertain as to whether to ask Mrs. Parker to prepare breakfast or a nuncheon.

The housekeeper met him at the foot of the stairs, looking distressed, hands wrapped in her snowy white apron.

"Oh, sir!" she exclaimed as he reached the bottom step. "Such a to – do!"

Mr. Arabin's first thought — and it made him reel — was that the news had come that René had succumbed to the hardship of the working and the face he turned to his housekeeper was pale with trepidation.

She at once discerned his fear. "Oh, no, 'tis not the young gentleman! Plato has been to the Abbey and back – there is no change but he seems to be holding his own and resting as comfortably as can be expected. I'm that sorry to give you such a fright! 'Tis Miss Mildmay – she's been sitting here awaiting you since just after breakfast. She seems dreadful upset about something – wouldn't eat anything but I did manage to get her to drink a cup of tea."

The Vicar at once felt a pang of guilt. He had had every intention of calling upon Miss Mildmay to see how she was going on, but, as had happened to so many things in the past weeks, he had not attended to it.

"Where have you put her?" Mr. Arabin asked.

Mrs. Parker bobbed a curtsey. "In the summer parlor. 'Tis a lovely day and the windows are open to the garden."

"Pray bring a tray of wine and biscuits for two," he directed and walked to the summer parlor and opened the door.

The summer parlor was a handsome room, with wide French doors open to the back garden. Like most rooms in the Vicarage the walls were lined with bookcases, well stuffed with a multitude of volumes.

Miss Mildmay, in an exceedingly ugly gown of brown fustian, sat on a shabby sopha, staring blindly out at the sunlit flowers. She twisted a handkerchief between her fingers and looked as if she had been crying. She had removed her bonnet and at her feet lay Minou's basket and a battered band-box. The little white cat had gone back to her mistress when Sir Piers had been taken to gaol. Minou could be heard crying distressfully. Plato sat by the basket, attempting to soothe his mate. He looked up sharply as the Vicar entered the room.

"My dear Miss Mildmay!" Reverend Arabin exclaimed. "How sorry I am to have kept you waiting for so long. But I am afraid I was from my bed very late last night."

Hester had whirled about when he spoke and now looked at him with wide, frightened eyes, her breast heaving.

"Why, my dear, what is it?" he asked gently, and coming up to her, took one mittened hand in his. It trembled in his grasp.

Her eyes filled with tears. "Forgive me," she said, "I did not know what else to do or where to go. You have always been so kind and patient with me..." Her voice, full of tears, trailed off.

582

"What has happened to distress you so? Has the Sheriff perhaps captured your brother?" he asked.

"There has been an execution in the house," said Plato harshly. "They are turned out of the house by Sir Piers' creditors."

"What!" The Vicar was aghast.

Miss Mildmay removed her hand from his and put both of them up to her face and began to sob disjointedly about gambling debts and unpaid bills to merchants and even smugglers demanding their due.

"They even took the hair brooch that was all I had left of Mama! I was only allowed to take the clothes I stood up in and some items of intimate apparel!" She blushed as she mentioned this, casting down her eyes. "They even wanted to take Minou but she bit and scratched so fiercely that the broker's men did not think it worth the effort to take her."

Mr. Arabin sank down on the sopha beside her. "My dear Miss Mildmay – I am truly appalled! I could have never guessed that things would have come to such a pass! And I must hold myself to blame that I did not do more for you!"

"Oh, no, oh, no!" she cried. "You have been such a kind, such a good friend! I did not know that his debts were so high – he was all to pieces! The gambling debts alone were in excess of £10,000! And he owed merchants half again as much. They told me that he had been living on post-obit bonds for years. He always expected to inherit from his Godpapa, Baron Heston, but the Baron changed his will when Piers was arrested. And my brother used up my portion as well! There is nothing left!"

Mr. Arabin gave her his large, soft linen handkerchief. She took it gratefully, for she had managed to shred her smaller lace-edged one in her distress.

As she wiped her face he said, "Have you anyone to go to, anyone to succor you and perhaps give you a home?"

She shook her head, setting the curls at the sides of her face bobbing. With a sense of shock he noticed that there were bits of straw in her hair. The poor lady must have spent the night in a barn!

"There is no one – what little family we had Piers managed to quarrel with them and most of them are dead now. I never had any friends," she said sadly, "for I am very dull, you must know. Bu that is why I have come here. I remember that once you told me of a Home for Decayed Gentlewomen near Bath. Perhaps I might be eligible for such a place. I haven't any money at all – they even took what little I had in my purse – but if you would be so kind as to lend me the fare of the public coach to Bath I will find some way to repay it –" the look on her face was so humble, so resigned that it tore at his heart.

"My dear, the Home of which you speak," he said, "requires a financial endowment from the female or her family." And as he said this he felt a great choking rage rising in him. Had not this poor lady stood enough in her life? Merely living with Sir Piers would have been enough for anyone to endure, never mind the physical abuse she had suffered at his hands. Mr. Arabin guessed that there had been countless humiliations as well, and her sensibilities had no doubt been assaulted aging and again, considering the type of companion that Sir Piers brought into the house.

"Then what am I to do?" she cried, tears spilling down her cheeks. She was not one of those fortunate women who looked attractive when she cried. Her nose was red and swollen, with a drip at the end and her eyes were red as well.

Mr. Arabin reached over and took both her hands in his. In a blinding rush he knew what the right thing to do was – not just the right thing, but the best thing – the perfect solution. "You, my dear Miss Mildmay — Hester – are going to marry me!"

Her mouth fell open. She had very pretty teeth, he thought inconsequently. "M – m – marry you?" she stammered. "But, but.."

"It is the ideal solution!" he said enthusiastically. "I think that we share a mutual regard and moral outlook. You have long been a tireless worker in this parish – you have already the knowledge and skills that a Vicar's wife ought – you would be the perfect helpmeet!"

"But you do not love me!" she protested, leaving unspoken '*nor I you.*'

"Perhaps not with the passion I should have felt as a young man, but I do hold you in a most sincere affection. Many successful unions have been based on less."

She pulled her hands away and turned to face the window. "There is someone I care for," she said in a low, choked voice, twisting her hands together again.

He had to be very careful here, Mr. Arabin thought. "I know, my dear," he said very compassionately "but rest assured, that no one else does, particularly the young gentleman you hold in regard. And he need never know."

The gaze she turned on him was stricken. "Am I as transparent as all that?" she cried.

"No, you are not. But it is my job, you must know, to notice these things. You are to be greatly commended for making such a worthy choice as the object of your affections. When one considers the example you had before you, once Sir Jason had taken to his bed –!"

"I could never love someone like Piers," she said in a low voice. "Indeed, I never regarded him with the affection a sister ought to have for her brother. Nor could I bear Geoffrey, my own nephew. That surely makes me a bad person, unfit to be a Vicar's wife."

"Nonsense!" he said. "I could not abide them either!"

Shocked, she looked at him speechlessly.

"Christian charity is one thing, but when every opportunity to walk the paths of righteousness are offered and spurned...you did well, my dear, to survive such baleful influences. It cannot have been easy."

She grew pink with pleasure and looked down at her hands.

"So please, my dear Hester, do me the honour of consenting to be my bride and I shall every day try to make you as happy as humanly possible," Mr. Arabin begged.

She thought fleetingly of her impossible love – just how impossible she had realized when first he was elevated in position and then when the notice of the betrothal appeared in the news-sheets.

She had always liked and respected Mr. Arabin – he was kind and thoughtful and cared deeply for the same things as did she. She would like to be a married lady. And the brutal truth was that this was the only option she had been given. She would be cared for and free from fear for the first time in a long time – since before dear Papa had his stroke.

"I will marry you," she said shyly.

"Huzza!" cried the Vicar, and picked up her hand and kissed it, causing Hester to blush. *"Why, she could be quite pretty if she were properly dressed in becoming colours,"* Mr. Arabin thought and at once resolved to give his bride over to Ninon to help her chose a trousseau.

A knock was heard upon the door and Mrs. Parker entered with a tray of wine and biscuits.

"Wish us happy, Mrs. Parker!" said the Vicar joyfully. "Behold the promised Mrs. Arabin!"

Mrs. Parker nearly dropped the tray.

The unicorn sank down into the flowers outside Sluagh's glass prison, never taking her eyes from him.

He hated unicorns. He had always fantasized about killing one and drinking its blood. He couldn't stand this one just lying there, only looking at him – as if she knew everything about him. He turned his back to her, leaning against the invisible wall, trying to steady his nerves.

But he could not seem to help turning again and again to look at her. In spite of his agitation and his longing to get from this cage a sense of peace gradually came over him and he grew calm. That was the effect of the unicorn, he knew.

"Did my brother send you to placate me?" he demanded of the beast. "Does he think that a unicorn can change me? To make me into what he approves?"

But the unicorn did not answer him – she merely regarded him with those unfathomable eyes – today, dark green in colour. He could not tell what she was thinking.

It seemed forever that they stared at one another – Sluagh and the unicorn. The sun grew higher in the sky and began to wester. Sluagh drank from the stream and discovered a little tree full of different fruits, obviously enchanted. He was hungry, so he ate them, all the while despising the magic that had created such a thing.

The sun was low in the sky, sending long beams across the flowers and grass, turning it to green-gold, when at last the one Sluagh had been expecting came.

He was suddenly there, standing behind the unicorn, in shining splendor of white court dress and his silver crown set with gleaming opals. "My greeting to you, Aubrey my brother," Oberon said softly.

Sluagh scrambled to his feet. "That is no longer my name!" he snapped. "I left all of that behind when you tossed me aside!"

"You would name yourself for the Host of the Unforgiven Dead," said Oberon, "rather than a name given you in love and honor?"

"Little did you love me!" Sluagh cried. "You were only too eager to rid yourself of me and usurp my powers!"

"You defied our laws, Aubrey. Murder cannot be forgiven – you had to be punished and I was as lenient as I dared. And as for usurping your powers – you had no natural powers save what you have now. The others were a gift granted to you as long as you used them wisely. And you did not do so – you used them for pain, torture and killing." Oberon's beautiful face looked sad.

"And what are you going to do with me now?" Sluagh demanded. "Am I to be kept here like a beast in a menagerie for this unicorn to gaze upon? I want to return to my kingdom!"

"Your kingdom is no more, Aubrey," said his brother gravely. "The Unselighe Court has been bound to the earth once more and the Dark Lord knows that he must ultimately answer to me. He will not step outside his bounds again as he did when he offered you rule of the Unselighe Court. It is over."

Sluagh gave a howl of rage and began to beat his fists on the wall. To his surprise there was nothing there and he fell forward to land on his hands and knees among the flowers, almost at his brother's feet.

The unicorn had stood up – she was still looking at him, but now he saw pity in her eyes.

Sluagh struggled to his feet. "You'll not defeat me," he said thickly, backing away from Oberon. "I have friends – people you don't know about – "

"The Frenchman?" said Oberon, arching one slim brow. "He'll have little use for you now that you cannot deliver the troops his Emperor wants."

"I had hoped it could be otherwise, Aubrey," he continued and then said briefly, "Cluny, if you please – forgive me, my brother."

She moved so quickly that Sluagh never saw her, not until the sharp ivory horn pierced his heart. They exchanged one glance before he died.

Cluny drew back from the crumpled form amongst the flowers.

"Thank you," said Oberon, closing his eyes against the sight and looking rather ill.

"You had no choice," she said. "He was a madman. To die upon my horn is a painless death. And far better to die than remain locked away for the balance of his existence."

"Nonetheless –" he said on a sigh, opening his eyes.

"You loved him," she said.

"Yes – for it is a rare thing for an Elf to have a sibling and I had such hopes for him. In childhood — how long ago!— we were close companions and I thought that he loved me as I loved him. I never saw his jealousy, his madness – not until he killed. And still I could not bring myself to do what needed to be done."

He waved his hand over Aubrey's corpse and it straightened out so that the dead Elf seemed to be sleeping quietly, a tender smile on his face, all traces of madness and evil gone. That was the effect of Cluny's horn. Wherever Aubrey had gone he was now at peace.

Oberon waved his hand again and the flowers began to cover the body rapidly taking it from view. When it was completely covered, the mound of flowers sank into the ground, leaving no trace behind.

Then the Elf King and the unicorn slowly walked away as the last rays of the setting sun lit the flowers from within over the enchanted spot.

The bogle had not come this morning and there was little left to eat in the cave. Mildmay had eaten the last of the cheese and drained the small keg of cider.

Where was that thrice-be-damned creature? He had always been almost as regular as clockwork!

Mildmay had been deserted by everyone. Goodbody had wasted no time in leaving, the Elf had not been seen since he took up with that lightskirt and now Ainsel had taken it into his head to go off somewhere.

Brooding upon this and the failure of his plans, Sir Piers stood it until the over-head sun told him it was noon-time. He was both hungry and thirsty. He no longer cared that the sheriff might be still hunting him. Something had happened last night – he had seem all of the strange lights in the sky. Having completely lost track of the time he had no idea that Lammas had come and gone, and he actually flattered himself that the lights had something to do with their desperation to capture him.

He would go to his home. He would bully his sister into giving him a horse and money. If he knew that sly slut she would have wasted no time in availing herself of his bank account and was probably living high on money to which she had no right. That would change!

The first thing that struck him about the Hall was its air of desolation. No one was about at all. There were none of the noises that should have greeted him, even though he had sneaked around the rear entrance. There were no horses in the paddock, no voices of the servants as they went about their tasks. No one challenged him as he came closer.

He entered the house through the kitchen and immediately knew that something was amiss.

For the kitchen, a great stone vault of a room, echoed with emptiness. There was no furniture to be seen, no settle, no massive table or chairs. No Welsh dresser laden with crockery, no copper pans hanging from the ceiling hooks. No great hams and ropes of vegetables hung from the smoke-darkened beams. Even the closed stove was gone.

It was the same throughout the rest of the house. It had been picked cleaner than a whistle. Sir Piers knew immediately what had happened.

Those damned vultures – men whom he had thought his friends! They had wasted no time in coming to claim what they thought was theirs. He spared no thought for his sister and what might have happened to her. He checked his secret hiding place – beneath a floor board in the book room – and it to, was empty of the roll of soft and bag of coins he hid there.

589

He went to the stables next – all that remained there was dirty straw. All of the horses were gone, his carriages and all of the tack. The feed and hay had gone as well. A mouse would have had extreme difficulty finding a morsel in that empty stable.

He was filled with a black rage and at the same time, a sinking terror. Where was he to go — how was he to survive without friends or funds? They would capture him and he would swing – to be shamed in front of everyone he knew. He writhed at the thought of that Frenchwoman looking at him contemptuously as the executioner put the rope about his neck.

No! He would not endure such a fate! He would be the one to make the decision as to what happened to him. They would have no satisfaction from him.

His gun was useless – he had no shot nor powder now – Goodbody had taken it.

He climbed the ladder to the loft and found what he sought – a coil of rope left behind, for it was rather old and had been used to haul hay into the loft. But it was stout enough as he found out when he tested it. It would do admirably. It was difficult to manipulate the rope with but one hand, Tying it to the edge of a stall helped, as did his teeth.

It was a full sevenight before anyone found the body swinging from the rafters. The hangman's noose had come to Sir Piers Mildmay after all.

52

Lord Lyonshall Writes a Letter

Diana awaited anxiously as Ninon flew off on Tuathail to the Sacred Grove. She was a little worried, she told herself, but had confidence in her uncle and Mr. Arabin's power to protect her friend from the consequences of the Working. And too, René had Oberon's gift. But still she found herself pacing back and forth in the front hall where the door, set on either side by glazed panels of glass, looked out towards the dragon pen. Seppings had insisted on bringing her a cup of tea but it sat untouched on the hall table.

When they had first arrived at the Hall after the Working Ninon had immediately gone above stairs to check on Lucie and the Duke. Sir William was still in attendance on his patient and reported him doing as well as could be expected. Indeed, Sir William thought in another day he would let Chenevix awaken and ascertain at that time any damages from the apoplexy. The doctor was hopeful of a good outcome.

He also promised Ninon that he would tend to René as soon as he was brought back to the Abbey. Sir William was very experienced with the fatigue and illness that sometime came after a major Working. Of course, René had gone through a great deal more than just participating in a major Working. Diana herself was exhausted – it had been a while since she had summoned so much magic or Worked with a Coven. She was glad to have her little familiar along – Rascal had had to prompt her more than once for her mind kept skittering off to what was happening at the Grove. Rascal had done a most excellent job and was presently, along with Neige, dozing off a tasty treat from Alphonse.

Ninon had showed Diana a parchment covered in Elfin writing – it was a set of directions in how to care for René once the ceremony had ended and Ninon insisted on going with Tuathail so that the directions might be carried out properly from the very beginning.

There was only one female flying suit at the Abbey – Diana's own – and it would be cold dragonback, for the temperature had fallen. As much as she wanted to go to the Grove, Diana offered the suit to Ninon – Ninon was worn out also and a great deal older than Diana – indeed Diana could not even conjecture where Ninon got her energy.

Diana was also worried about Simon. Had he been frightened? Had he been able to do his part in the ceremony? She paced back and forth in the hall, still clad in her sunflower embroidered yellow robes that she had worn at the meeting of the Coven. She was chilly, for protocol demanded that naught be worn under the robes – indeed the rituals of the Witches were conducted sky-clad – naked – in order for their bodies to fully absorb the powers of the moon. She actually felt her heart racing and found herself wringing her hands, like the silly heroine in a marble-backed novel from the Minerva Press.

It seemed to take forever for Tuathail to arrive. The moon was now rising and being so near the full, cast its silver light over the landscape, making it possible for Tuathail to see and make a nice soft landing. Sir William, too, had thought that to bring René back to the Abbey by dragon litter far less jarring than miles in a wagon.

As soon as she saw the dragon begin to descend Diana ran out onto the lawn. Rather than land near the dragon pen Tuathail landed as close to the door of the Abbey as was possible. One part of Diana's mind appreciated the skill of the dragon – he spiraled down easily, gently putting down on his hind legs so that he could hold the litter, strapped to his chest, straight and still.

Ninon, the Vicar, Diarmait and Simon, with their three familiars, all in flying gear, even Simon in a cut-down suit, also rode the dragon. Lyon and the two French Druids would return by wagon. They waited to dismount until

Seppings, with several footmen had come from the house. Cautioned by Ninon and aided by mage lights that Diana conjured, they lifted the litter and began to bear it to the house.

He was so still – so limp! Diana put a hand to her throat and gasped, her heart pounding. His head was held immobile between two solid-appearing cushions. She would have followed the litter into the house at once had it not been for a cry of "Mama!".

She turned back to see Simon, with the kittens clinging to him, being lifted down from Tuathail's back by Diarmait. As soon as he was on his feet, Simon put the kittens down (Beau ran after René) and sped towards her and hugged her around the waist. "He's going to be all right, Mama, is he not?" Simon choked out, begging for reassurance. Even in the moonlight Diana could see traces of tears on his cheeks.

She had no reassurance to offer him. She looked at the Vicar, who wore a rather grim look on his face.

"He's alive – barely," Mr. Arabin said. He looked gray with fatigue and suddenly a great deal older. "The good news is that this Working will not have to be repeated – we have Oberon's word on that. That will give René a far better chance to survive this. We're most worried about his vision at this point, since he *is* alive. The power and brightness of that light was far beyond anything we have ever seen! And when the *Sidhe* joined with us – " his voice trailed away and then he shook his head as if trying to wake up. "I am offering up a general prayer service tomorrow afternoon." He looked as if he had gone beyond the limits of his strength. He held a completely limp Plato.

"And there'll be a service at Saint Patrick's in Dublin," put in Diarmait. He too, was worn out and had Ó Dàlaigh slung over his shoulder. The big cat snored loudly. Indeed they all looked ready for their beds. "I was arranging that with His Holiness before I was leaving Ireland."

At this morning the wagon rattled up – Lyon had driven so furiously that they had made almost as good as time as had Tuathail.

"Is there anything to eat?" asked Lyon rather plaintively after inquiring about René's well-being. "I imagine

Sir William will be with René for a while – surely we can eat while we are waiting to hear what he has to say? There is little use in making ourselves ill."

Seppings had come back outside and announced that his lordship had been carefully put into bed and Sir William was with him now. There was a buffet laid out in the dining room for the party, and a dragon snack for Tuathail in the dragon pen.

This announcement caused a general exodus into the Abbey. Diana put her arm around Simon's shoulders as they walked in together. The boy was nearly asleep on his feet but it was important that he eat before retiring. He was not used to Working magic – even so little as he had done tonight. And the Working would have drawn from him, also, for he was part of the Circle.

All of the time that she played hostess and saw that everyone was taken care of – save Ninon, who had gone to show Sir William Oberon's instructions – Diana's mind was in the sickroom. She had caused a room on the ground floor to be made up as a bed chamber – easier on the servants and the patient.

Would he live? She kept thinking. And thought with her over active imagination – what if he did not survive – what if she had no chance to tell him...

It was at this moment, just as she was passing a dish of a haricot of mutton to her uncle that Diana had an epiphany. In later years she would laugh about it, for so life-changing a revelation to come under such prosaic circumstances.

She wanted to tell René that she loved him – had loved him for a long time but was too stupid to realize it!

What a ninny she had been! She thought as the wonder and the terror of it swept over her! When he had returned to Ireland it had not been the weather that had so improved her spirits – it was *his* return!

And now she might lose him. But she was going to help nurse him, she thought determinedly. If love could pull someone back from the valley of the shadow, she would do it. As she moved her hands, the great sapphire on her finger flashed. If she had any say in the matter – that was going to

594

soon mean a *real* betrothal – and a wedding. But first her bridegroom had to be well.

Sir William was sanguine about René's chances of recovery. "If this exercise had been repeated two more times as originally planned I would have told you to order up a shroud for him. But *Madame* tells me that it is not necessary. About his eyesight I am less certain. Following the Elves' directions as we did, did not allow me to examine his eyes closely. But the mere fact that the ointment he used was Elfin in origin is highly significant. Their knowledge of eye care is far beyond ours and I shall trust to their knowledge and we shall follow their instructions to the letter."

"For now I am letting him sleep," the doctor continued, looking at the ring of anxious faces about the table. "There is no doubt about it – when he awakens he will be in pain – how could it be otherwise when one's body is used as a channel for that much power? I have seen crystals shatter under that pressure. I have remedies for pain, of course, but I cannot stress enough that he must be kept quiet and still. But with careful nursing..."

"I shall nurse him myself!" said Ninon fiercely.

"And I shall help you," Diana declared.

Ninon looked at her sharply and then almost exclaimed aloud at the look on Diana's face. So she had finally realized it! That was an excellent reason for René to get well and Ninon was suddenly certain that when Diana confessed her feelings to him they would see a remarkable improvement in his health.

Sir William accepted a laden plate of food from Lyon. "Of course," he said thoughtfully, "he will have to remain an invalid for some time. One does not recover from such an undertaking over night Working much magic at all is out of the question for the near future and other activities had ought to be curtailed as well."

"When will he be able to marry, *M'sieur le docteur?*" Ninon boldly.

Diana gasped and her cheeks turned crimson. Ninon was smiling at her and the rest of them looked at her in surprise. Simon, in spite of a huge yawn that cracked his jaws, beamed at her in utter joy.

595

Sir William laughed. "Samhain, if all goes well," he said. "Three months."

Samhain was considered an excellent time to marry, for it was a time when the Faerie world and that of the mortal touched and one was apt to receive Faerie gifts and blessings at that time of year.

"Come," said Ninon to Diana, "you may sit with him for a while. Me, I think that you will not sleep until you do so."

"Oh, thank you!" said Diana, her eyes blazing with joy. This was generosity indeed, for Diana knew that the older woman wanted nothing else than to be near her grandson.

Diarmait offered to carry Simon up to bed and this had the effect of breaking up the party, the Druids retiring to their respective rooms, and Diana going to the sickroom. Mr. Arabin and Plato left – Tuathail was to make one last flight to the Vicarage. At last only Lyon and Seppings were left.

The butler looked so tired that Lyon ordered him and the rest of the staff to bed. He would put a preservation spell on the leftover food so that it could be dealt with in the morning.

Lyon was bone-weary. He thought he might have trouble sleeping, though – as he had gotten older it sometimes seemed that he would become too tired to fall asleep. But a nice glass of port would tip the scales towards sleep and relax his tired muscles as well.

Accordingly he went to his bookroom where a small mage light always burned. The fire had died but Lyon magiced a small log onto tit and lit this. Even this small magic and the earlier preservation spell made him feel as if he were five hundred years old.

He had gone to the wine tray and poured a crystal goblet of porter when he heard a small sound. "A house full of cats," he thought ruefully "and yet we still have mice."

But the sound came again and this time Lyon was certain that it was not a mouse. It sounded suspiciously like a sob and was coming from a wing chair that was out of place, its back turned from the fire.

Quietly, for he could move very silently when he needed to do so, Lyon went to the chair and peered over the top of it.

There, huddled in a ball, tears streaming down her face, was Ninon. She had no handkerchief, for she was wiping her face on the sleeve of her robe.

"What is it?" he inquired very gently.

"I am a silly old woman, me," she said, looking up at him. "I am glad that your Diana and René will have each other, *non*? But I suddenly have wondered, so selfishly, what will happen to me, *n'est-ce pas?* For that Duke, he does not want me to live with him and Lucie. And, *je vous assure*, I do not think young people need the in-law to live with them when first they are married."

"That's not selfish, it's practical," Lyon remarked. "Here, have some port." He gave her the as yet untasted glass he carried and went back to the wine tray and poured himself another. Then he turned another chair to face the fire and sat down opposite her. He took a long draught of the port, feeling it warm him inside.

Ninon sipped at the ruby liquid. It was just what she needed. And she was suddenly glad not to be alone.

"I have decided to resign as Arch Druid," Lyon announced abruptly.

Ninon looked at him in astonishment. *"Porquoi?"*

"Why?" he gave her a lopsided grin. "Because I have no talent for it, my dear! As I have been told repeatedly, I have no tact, no gift for handling people and I hate paperwork and dealing with idiot politicians – the only requirement I meet is that I am one of the finest magicians in the Isles." This was said in no false modesty.

Ninon snorted.

"And besides that, I have a little project in mind, something that you inspired," he continued.

"Moi? I have inspired you?" she asked curiously.

"Indeed you have. Do you remember a conversation – several – we had about how impractical magic really is? Why there are no spells to really make life easier – say spells to wring laundry and draw water?"

Ninon nodded and sipped some more port.

"Well," he went on, "I have decided I'm going to bend my not inconsiderable talents" – Ninon stuck out her tongue at him – "to devising such spells. And you could stay here at the Abbey and help me? I enjoy your company –"

"But we quarrel *toujours le temps!*" Ninon said in surprise.

"Yes," he said happily, "that's the best part."

"But to stay here with you – it is improper – that Duke, he would never let me see Lucie again!"

"Damn it, woman, I'm not suggesting setting you up as my mistress! I'm asking you to marry me!"

"Marry you?" Ninon nearly choked on the last of her port. "But I am too old for you!"

"I doubt it," he said dryly. "One never asks a lady her age, but –"

"Me, I am very near to being sixty!" she announced.

"And I can give you ten years. I shall be seventy on my next birthday. And yes, I know I don't look it, but that 's partly my family heritage and partly practicing so much magic. Magic extends youth and life. And I've had a relatively easy life," he informed her. "Now, what do you say? I know you think I'm an idiot in a lot of ways, but I think we could be happy."

Ninon could not help it – she laughed at him and said "Ah, bah! What can I say but *mais oui*, thank you, *M'sieur*, in the face of this oh so romantic proposal?"

He beamed at her. "I think we shall go on very well. We've interesting work to do and hopefully many quarrels and making up ahead of us."

Thinking about it, Ninon thought it would do very well – she was not in what she thought of as love, but she found him stimulating – she enjoyed their arguments as much a he did. As of late she woke up wondering what they would quarrel about that day with keen anticipation... And the thought of interesting, useful work – she had dreaded dwindling into a great grandmother to the children René and Diana would no doubt have, and to hang on her grandson's sleeve as his pensioner. She would be independent – and she had missed being married and all it entailed. She had married for duty once and it had turned to love – perhaps marrying for Work to do might turn out just as well.

They had another glass of port to seal their bargain, Ninon informing him that she expected an excellent settlement, pin-money and a handsome widow's jointure since he was so old. He laughed at her, but promised that it would be done, and told her he would accept her modest dowry of a cat and several dozen bottles of herbs.

They then went their separate ways to bed, very pleased with themselves.

Lyon was among the first to rise next morning and after checking in on Chenevix and René (both doing well, although not as yet conscious) he went to his bookroom, where he took parchment and pens from a drawer, and pulled an inkwell close to hand.

He had a letter to write. It was one he had meant to write long since, but he had not known precisely what to say. He had sent Seppings to nose about in Knightswold and see what he could learn about Wanda Wycherley. What Seppings had learned from the other servants was very interesting. One of her footmen had very loose lips and had told all sorts of *crim. com* stories to the other servants at the Inn.

Accordingly, Lyon sharpened his quill and began to write:

>*My dear Viscount Ffoillot ,*
>*I feel that you should be made aware of the goings-on between your son, the Honorable Augustus Goodbody and a respectable wealthy widow....*

Wanda waited quite a long time for Sluagh to return. She soon grew cold laying naked on a bed of pine needles and at last somewhere near three in the morning she rose and brushed off the pine needles and dressed. She was sexually frustrated as well and exceedingly angry at being abandoned just when she was most eager and ready for his embraces. She would have a thing or two to say to him when she next saw him.

There was nothing to do but to return to Cheltenham tonight. It was too far to go onto Wales and at any rate, she wasn't sure exactly where Under-the-Hill lay. She had really hoped to bed that Fachan tonight – she had peeked beneath his deerskins – most impressive!

It took longer than she thought to return to Cheltenham and a sleepy porter let her in to the Inn she had but recently left. They were only open because of the celebrations, he explained, yawning in her face, elsewise the Inn, the *Prince's Three Feathers,* would be shut up tighter than a drum. And the room she had previously rented had gone to another traveler. She would have to make do with what was left.

Wanda did not even ask what celebrations. Probably some stupid magical festival. Those people were always having them. It wasn't as if it were a real holiday, such as the King's birthday.

The porter refused her request for a bath and put her in a decidedly inferior room. He did however, bring up one bag and her dressing case. Wanda wished she had not sent both Culver Grindle and Grimstock back to London. She was not used to waiting on herself and did not like it.

The dressing case was an absolute necessity. It was home to an amazing jewel case that Sluagh had given her. It was small in size, but bottomless. No matter how many jewels were placed in it, it never became full.

To comfort herself she decided to bedeck her body in jewels and wear them and nothing else but a smile of satisfaction and greed to bed. She had become accustomed to this – for it was Sluagh's favorite dress – and it made her feel both wicked and decadent.

After dismissing the porter without a tip she opened the dressing case and took out the little box. She would wear the diamond waterfall – the one that came down over her breasts, almost to her navel – and tickled her erotically.

When she opened the little enameled box – decorated with flowers – her scream of rage could be heard all over the inn. For there was not in the box but ashes and when she put down the little box, it, too, crumbled into nothingness. Too late she remembered nursery warnings about Faerie gifts fading away.

Worse was to come when she returned to London – miserable and unhappy, for she missed the erotic delights of pleasure with Sluagh as much as she missed his jewels.

For waiting for her in London, was Viscount Ffoillot, Augustus Goodbody, a Vicar and a special license. In no uncertain terms the Viscount (who looked as like his son as he could stare) informed her that she and Augustus were to be married – he had already cut off Augustus' allowance and he personally would ruin what little reputation Wanda had left if she refused. The Viscount had received an anonymous letter detailing Wanda's relationship with Augustus. The Viscount had not liked the shady reputation Wanda had, but his greedy heart had thrilled to the figures in her bank balance. That would guarantee Augustus would never need to pick his father's pocket again. Indeed, the Viscount might borrow from his son.

Over both their protests the Viscount saw them married. It was a poor start for a union and it never prospered. She never forgot Sluagh's lovemaking and spent the rest of her life looking for its equal. Several young wits named her "the Whore of London" for she became increasingly desperate and obvious as time went on.

And as for Augustus, he soon found that her elderly merchant husbands had tied up her money so that she had the most use of it. They had not wanted the ready wasted by some young sprig of the nobility. He, who should have had control of her money by law, was forced to exist on a miserly allowance paid out by his wife, and must needs have every trip to his club rendered horrible listening to the ribald remarks and sneers from his contemporaries about the prominent pair of horns on his brow. The couple had naught in common, quarreled bitterly and incessantly and soon learned to loathe one another.

It was perhaps one of the most miserable marriages in the history of humankind. Fortunately, there was no issue of the union.

53

Awakenings

When Chenevix first awoke he could not imagine what had happened to him. He had no memory of anything beyond becoming incensed with Keir yet again.

It was a struggle to open his eyes and his limbs seemed heavy and leaden. He involuntarily moaned as he attempted to fully awaken. Why was he so weak and tired?

"Lucien!" It was Lucie's voice and her anxious face was the first thing he saw when he at last won the struggle to open his eyes.

"What –" he began, but found that his voice was hoarse and his tongue felt curiously thick. Even turning his head upon the pillow took a great deal of effort.

"Shh! Shh!" Lucie laid a finger on his lips. "Do not try to speak, *mon cher*." Her face was full of concern.

"Awake, is he, your Grace?" came a voice that Chenevix did not recognize and another person came into view. It seemed to the Duke as if he ought to know the identity of the gentleman, but his brain seemed equally clouded. But suddenly he remembered – he was Sir William Knighton – the famous Wizard Healer.

Sir William bent over him as the Duke tried to speak again. "No, no, your Grace – best be quiet. I can see by your face that you recognize both your lady and myself. You may relax while I examine you and then I shall give you a draught to wake you up a little more. Then will be the time for talking."

An examination by a talented Wizard Healer was a pleasant experience by and large. The green light of healing that flowed from the physician's hands was warm and

602

soothing. It went deep into all parts of the body, searching out abnormalities, and allowing the doctor to read what was wrong as well as if he could see inside the body.

Chenevix felt markedly better by the time Sir William had completed the examination.

The physician appeared pleased by the results and allowed Chenevix, with Lucie's help, to sit up against the pillows. He then turned away to prepare a draught.

Mariposa had been in the background, doing something beyond the edges of Chenevix's vision. Now he came forward with a steaming kettle. "I am very glad to see your Grace recovered!" he said fervently, a smile showing his gold tooth. "The water is precisely at a full rolling boil as you requested, Sir William."

"Very good. Thank you, Mariposa," said the doctor. He then tipped a blend of herbs into a chalice – he had first ground them together with a silver pestle in mortar of the same metal — and then poured the water over the herbs. A aromatic aroma rose from the chalice. A silent incantation, a tap of his wand to make it a drinkable temperature and it was ready.

Mariposa helped his master take this potion. "Drink every drop!" ordered Sir William – and the Duke obeyed. He was willing to do anything that would make him feel better. The taste was not unpleasant and it really was no hardship to finish it.

Almost immediately Chenevix began to feel better – clearer in mind and he felt his tongue untangle.

"What happened to me?" he asked. He still did not sound his old self but it was good to be able to speak and feel rational.

"Oh, Lucien! You had *la apoplexie!*" said Lucie, her eyes filling with tears. She sat on the edge of the bed, so that she could be close to him.

"Nonsense!" he said, frowning. "I am in perfect health!"

"That might have been true at one time, your Grace, but you can claim that distinction no longer," said Sir William dryly. "You have had what we are starting to call a heart attack – a minor one, to be sure, but a cardiac event no less.

603

You were very fortunate that your son was with you when it happened – he no doubt saved your life."

"Keir saved my life?" he repeated and then he fully remembered. Keir – the ceremony! "What day is today?" he asked hurriedly. "Keir – did he take part in that – is he alright?" He looked rather wildly from one to the other.

"That was two days ago, your Grace," answered Sir William. "Today is the eighth of August. And Lord Keir is as right as one may be after undergoing such an ordeal. I hope to wake him up today or tomorrow."

"He was so brave, Lucien," said Lucie putting her hand over his on top of the counterpane. "Everyone says so – we have had the letters from *M'sieur* the Prince and the Prime Minister and a – what was that thing from London, Mariposa?"

"A special commendation from the Houses of Parliament, your Grace," said Mariposa proudly.

"I want to see him," said Chenevix, restlessly moving his head on the pillow.

"As neither of you can be moved at the moment that is inadvisable," Sir William informed him. "Within a few days, if your recovery goes well, I shall allow an invalid chair, which you shall use until I give you leave to cease. Then you may visit your son. It will be a while longer before he can be moved."

Chenevix frowned at this. "But he *will* recover?" he asked sharply.

"Undoubtedly." Sir William felt no need to tell the sick Duke that they were worried about Lord Keir's eyesight and precisely how long it would take for him to become well again. Let the Duke make his own recovery first.

Chenevix turned his gaze on Lucie, who pressed his hand. "I thank *le bon Dieu* that you were both spared to me," she said, and lifted his hand to her cheek as tears spilled down.

Diana and Ninon had taken turns, round the clock, sitting by René's bed. Against her better judgment Diana allowed Simon in to the sickroom – he pleaded so earnestly that she could not refuse. She was very much afraid that the sight of René, so pale and still, would frighten the boy, but

Simon took it very well and said he was going to pray extra hard that all would be well.

Their constant companion was Beau. He refused to leave his Wizard at all and an earth box had to be set up in t the room for his use. He also had to be coaxed to eat. He insinuated himself beneath René's right hand and tried to purr without much success. He was as worried as the rest of them.

To keep her nerves from shattering Diana sat by the bedside and did needlework – handkerchiefs for the gentlemen – one never had enough handkerchiefs — and the same for the ladies – she found herself embroidering handkerchiefs for herself with the initials DED – Diana Elaine Delamar.

When Ninon saw these her mobile brow shot up but she did not say anything.

Sir William, after leaving Chenevix, came to exam René and gave him a small draught of herbs – much the same as he had administered to the Duke, but in a much smaller quantity. This, he explained to Ninon Diana and Lyon, was to help René wake up slowly. Sir William thought that the next day would be soon enough. Even unconscious, René was in pain – they could all see it.

According to Oberon's instructions René lay flat on his back, his head held immobile by pillows and his eyes covered by an herbal poultice that was changed twice a day. The Elfin eye ointment had been applied each of the two days following the working as well.

They were all disappointed that it would be another day before they would be able to actually talk to René. Lyon was eager to find out what the experience of channeling that much power had been like. Ninon wanted to tell him her news and assure herself of his full recovery.

And Diana wanted to tell him that she loved him — indeed was more certain of it every day. To tell him would be to defy all of the proper lady-like tenets she had ever learned. The lady was to wait for the gentleman to express interest. Only a bold hussy would profess her love first. Even did she receive an offer the properly brought-up young lady would refuse the first time, only modestly accepting the second time that the gentleman laid his heart at her feet. Diana had always thought this rather hard on the suitor, for how was he to know if the young lady would grant him his desire the second time he girded up his loins to approach her?

She had not made Jonathan wait for his answer. And she had let him know that she returned his interest. That love had been so overwhelming and had been born almost the instant they had laid eyes on each other.

This was different – it had been born gradually, deepening from friendship. When she spoke of this to Ninon, wondering if it could be true love, since she was not in the heights and depths of tempestuous passion, but felt a quiet, growing, steady certainty that this man was the one she wanted to spend her life with.

Ninon had laughed at her. "Ah, child!" she said "There are many kinds of love, *n'est-ce pas*? And me, I think the love that grows from friendship is the best, the most lasting. But you two will find passion when at last you come together – you will see! You have worked magic together – remember how that was?"

Diana remembered well – and it woke her up at night.

After three days of healing sleep René at last awoke. Diana was sitting with him at the time, embroidering a Samhain robe for Simon. It was amazing how many robes both Wizards and Witches needed in the course of a year. Sometimes she envied the Druids – all of their robes were white with only a different coloured waist cord for each festival or ceremony.

She knew he was awake when she heard a whispered. *"Mon Dieu!"* and saw his hands clutch on the bedclothes. Beau sat up at once with an inquiring "Mrrp?"

Sir William had warned them that René would no doubt be in a great deal of pain when he woke up. The doctor had left a draught that could be easily heated by magic so that René could be offered ready relief.

Diana cast aside her embroidery and went at once to the bedside table. She tapped the draught with her wand and readied it. The draught was in an invalid cup with a long spout on it so that the patient could sip without having to sit up.

"Here," she said quietly, "this will help. Do not move your head. Let me help you."

With some little difficulty he managed to get a good amount of it down, Beau watching anxiously. Diana could see when it took effect, for he relaxed visibly.

"Diana?" he asked anxiously, trying to move his head." Did we succeed?"

"Oh, yes – we succeeded beautifully!" she assured him. "There have been no reports of any Unselighe creatures whatsoever and Lord Oberon assures us that we have done the thing."

"I cannot see you." He made a movement as if to lift his hand to his eyes but was too weak to complete it.

"No, dearest, you must not disturb the bandages!" she said firmly "And try not to move your head – Lord Oberon says that if we follow his instructions and use the poultices for a fortnight your vision will be unimpaired."

"What did you call me?" he said incredulously.

"Dearest," Diana whispered, feeling suddenly shy. She could feel a blush rising all the way from her toes.

"But why – do we pretend again?" he said bitterly.

"Oh, for Bastet's sake, TELL him!" said Beau impatiently. Humans! If they were cats they'd be happily licking each other's heads by now.

"I love you," she said in a rush. "I want to have a real betrothal. "

"And hopefully get married and have kittens before we all expire of old age," Beau remarked in his know it all voice.

René laughed at the little cat. It was a laugh of sheer happiness. "How I wish I could see your face and take you in my arms!" he said. "*Ma migonne* – you are certain of this?"

"She's been mooning around here for days!" said the kitten.

Diana gave the kitten a tap on the nose." I may speak for myself. Mr. Impudence!"

He gave a little growl. "Humans! We cats do these things much better!"

"And this is from your vast experience, *non?*" René asked his familiar.

"Well, I haven't had a female friend as yet but when I do I am certain I won't take as long as you two have!" the kitten retorted.

607

"Hold my hand," René ordered Diana."I want to make certain that you will not fly away like a dream." As she obeyed, he asked that she tell him all about what had happened.

Sometime during her recital he fell asleep, but Diana's heart was singing with happiness. She felt hat everything was going to be fine and there was much to look forward to.

The next few weeks were a time of quiet happiness for René, Diana and Simon. They were becoming a family. René continued to improve daily and at the end of a fortnight when the poultices were removed, he was able to see all of the people who had crowded into the room while the doctor removed the bandages. In fact, his declared his eyesight to be sharper than ever it had been.

One of the first things he had wanted to know when he awoke for the second time was how the Duke went on. It had been a week before Chenevix was allowed to visit his son and he had been shocked at the sight of him, having to keep still and his eyes bandaged tightly. He could not believe it when they assured him that René looked a great deal better than he had.

The first time they met after René had regained consciousness had been awkward. Their last words to one another had been in anger. But both were anxious to be conciliatory and the Duke, in the past week had become aware that his heir had indeed done a very brave thing, indeed, was a hero, and he began to feel stirrings of pride. And René had realized when he saw that aggravating man collapse that he had come to care for him – at least a bit and would not like to see him laid out in his coffin. Chenevix, under stern orders from Sir William and Dr Paget to mend his ways, and with the earnest entreaties of Lucie, was trying his best. To both Lucie's and Diana's joy, they both seemed to be making an effort. Perhaps there would never be real love or understanding between them, but perchance there could be amity. When Mr. Arabin chanced to mention that René had always had a keen interest in incunabula, but had never the money to indulge in this passion for old manuscripts, a common bond was struck, for the Duke was an avid collector.

As September began René was well enough to visit *The Cauldron* and help Simon chose his birthday handles and tips — although Diana insisted that he go to bed the minute they returned from the excursion. He still tired easily and Sir William, who made periodic visits to check on the progress of his patients, forbade using magic — he would not be able to participate in the Grand design at Samhain — and recommended spending the winter in a warm climate.

It was decide that they would marry at the end of October, spend a week in a private honeymoon at a property of Chenevix's in Cornwall, and then, with Simon, take the Duke's yacht, the *Sea Spray*, for an extended honeymoon to Greece and the Levant. A winter in the Greek Isles should see René restored to full health.

In September Ninon and Lyon went up to London one day and married with a special license, the ceremony conducted by the Bishop of London, who was an old friend of Mr. Arabin's from school days. Neither Lyon or Ninon wanted any fuss since it was the second marriage for both of them.

The Vicar and Miss Mildmay were married in grand style, which her romantic heart craved, with all of the village in attendance. Everyone was amazed by the difference being happy made in Hester. With a gown chosen by Ninon, a smile and sparkling eyes she was actually pretty.

All of this time there was no sign of the Jongleur. No more Wizards or Druids were killed and life seemed to be returning to what it had been before the attacks had begun.

But Malcoeur was biding his time. He had gone into hiding — and when he wished to hide not even a *Sidhe* could find him. Even the trees were unaware where he might be, for he cast a mighty glamourie about himself.

He had been angered beyond belief by the binding. All his plans were in chaos. He had had word from Paris that the assault on Russia would soon begin and he had had to notify Napoleon that no creatures would march with the *Grand Armée*. Sluagh had disappeared and the creatures were locked beneath the earth once again.

But Malcoeur waited. He still much desired the death of Eliot Lyons. It seemed to him that this festival they called Samhain was the perfect time to kill Lyons, who after all, was responsible for the ruination of Malcoeur's dreams of conquest. Too, the Jongleur had read of the young man, half French, who had contributed so much to the Working. Malcoeur wanted him dead as well. He was a filthy traitor – to be working for the English!

So the Jongleur watched and waited and plotted patiently until just the right time.

54

The Duel Arcane

It was one of the most beautiful autumns in recent memory. Each day shone brilliant blue and the trees flamed into a living glory of red, gold and yellow – they had seldom been so brilliant. The days were warm and the nights – which seemed to be the only time it rained – were cool. René, Diana and Simon took walks in the woods and orchards during the day and sat by a cozy fire at night. As René's health returned he and Diana made music together with her voice and his violin – a circumstance that made both of them long for the honey-moon. But Lucie and Ninon were assiduous chaperones.

René had been more than a little surprised that Ninon chose to marry Lyonshall – he had thought – as most of them had – that the two did not like one another very well. But the more he saw them together the more pleased he was. Ninon, he knew, would have refused to make her home with him and Diana, as much as she would have been welcomed. She had had to live with her in-laws when first wed to Louis and it had been an unhappy situation. She had vowed never to inflict herself upon her children in such a fashion. Lyon and Ninon were busy and happy devising new spells for practical magic and enjoyed their not infrequent disagreements and enjoyed even more making up after the quarrel was done.

And Simon was in alt. He already addressed René as 'Papa', even though the vows were yet to be said. And he was thrilled about another circumstance as well.

René had refused the offer from Trinity University to teach there, being reasonably certain that he would not survive to fulfill his obligation. But the University renewed its offer, telling René that they would hold the position open until the Michaelmas (autumn) term of 1812, by which time he should have completely recovered his health. Urged by his bride-to-be and Diarmait, he accepted. By that time Simon would be ten and that was a good age to start as a day pupil at the Tara Druidry. They would live in Dublin and he could take a dragon to Tara each day. Diana and Simon both liked this idea very much. Diana found the idea of a busy life as the wife of a fellow at University much more to her taste than to be an ornament of society. She and Aisling began a correspondence and Diana learned of the active Coven in Dublin and the many charities and work with orphans Aisling did. By the time they finally met they were firm friends.

Chenevix was not as keen – but he had come to finally realize – largely through Lucie's efforts – that he must let his son go his own way, and teaching, while not being quite what he would like for his son and heir, was a noble profession.

At the beginning of October, at the recommendation of Sir William Knighton, both Chenevix and René went to Bath for a course of the waters, leaving Diana behind to make the final preparations for the wedding. It was to be a small, private ceremony at Diana's childhood home where she could have her sisters as bridesmaids, and the new Mrs. Arabin (to her delight) as Matron of Honor. Mr. Arabin would officiate in tandem with Mr. Onslow, the Rector of St Barnabas. Chenevix had wanted St George's, Hanover Square in London, but Diana had been married there the first time and it had been a far from intimate ceremony with most of the *Ton* attending. Both she and René wanted only the people they cared for at this wedding. Simon was to be ring-bearer and there were to be two rings. This was considered quite unusual but it was what they wanted.

Naturally there were daily scrys and letters from Bath and Diana found an unexpected turn for comedy in her love as he described the society of Bath and its hypo-chondriacs and valetudinarians, and the Duke's reaction to the many hangers-on and toad-eaters that frequented the watering place.

René was to return alone to the Abbey by himself while his parents went back to Chenevix Duchis – at long last, said Lyon. Then they would all go to Kent for the wedding. They would be married on Samhain Eve.

On the golden afternoon in which René was to return Diana found herself nearly alone at the house. Her trunks were packed except for last minute items such as a toothbrush – as were Simon's. They would go by dragon transport to Kent – they would leave for the wedding tomorrow and be married the next day. Lady Eastcote had scryed that morning that guests were already arriving – among them Diarmait and Aisling – Diarmait was to be René's groomsman..

Simon, with Neige and Janus, (Beau, of course, had gone to Bath) had gone to the Vicarage and Lyon and his new Marchioness were gone into Cheltenham in search of arcane supplies for a spell that they were working on to make laundry easier. For days now the entire Abbey had smelled like wet laundry.

Diana was out in the garden picking asters and chrysanthemums. The latter had been introduced to England recently, but had already become immensely popular. Diana loved their spicy scent and autumn colours. They looked handsome in an urn of copper or bronze with the purple asters for contrast.

It was another beautiful day – the kind of day to be stored up ion memory for the winter ahead. The weather Augurs predicted this weather to last another week, so Diana could be confident that her wedding day would be equally lovely

Rascal was out with his Witch. He had been exceedingly playful all morning, making Diana laugh at his antics, such as chasing his tail until he was dizzy. The kittens would go to Greece as well – they had threatened to stow away, but would stay in Kent with Simon while Diana and René were in Cornwall.

Diana expected René to arrive on dragon-back – Bath had a large dragon transport firm – and when she became conscious of a shadow she at first thought it was a dragon spiraling down and she came to her feet, shading her eyes with one hand to look up into the bright blue sky. But there was nothing there.

She knew she was not alone when she heard Rascal hiss – a long rising hiss that ended in a defiant spit. She looked down at him and he was twice his normal size, back arched and ears laid back, every bit of fur on his body standing straight out. He glared at a tall man who had magically appeared as if he, too, could teleport like Ninon and René.

She felt suddenly terror stricken. On the surface he appeared innocuous, although somewhat strangely clad in a black cloak and some sort of spangled suit, with a bicorne *à la* Napoleon –parallel to the shoulder. Why anyone would actively seek to copy the Emperor of the French Diana could not comprehend.

Now he swept this hat from his head and bowed to her. "I seek the Marquis of Lyonshall and the Marquis of Keir. Are they at home?" He had a long, rather sad face, but the coldest eyes she had ever seen. He also had a French accent.

Diana wanted desperately to use her Othersight on this caller, but she could not seem to do aught but stare at him like a gaby. Something about him frightened her and made her think of darkness and evil. She knew she had seen him before but her mind was working slowly. "They are neither of them here at the moment," she finally got out. At her feet Rascal continued to spit and hiss, backed up against her skirts. "Perhaps you should come back another day." She desperately hoped that he would go and *never* come back.

At this moment a dragon began to circle down from the sky. Diana, after longing all day for René's return, now wished that he had come home much later.

"Ah!" said her visitor, "This, *sans doubte*, will be one of them."

Malcoeur had, after the encounter with the Lady of the Lake, read of the Duel Arcane, the requirements of which he had read in a book about Merlin and Arthur and the Lady. It had amused him and he decided to challenge these poor pathetic Wizards on their own playing field with their own rules. It would be like a cat playing with a mouse, for they could not hope to best him. When he tired of the game he would end it with blood magic.

Therefore he waited for René to dismount from the transport dragon, who instantly went skywards again. Tuathail was not in evidence – he was in Cheltenham, having flown Ninon and Lyon there.

It seemed strangely quiet at the Abbey – no grooms came out from the stable and René, as he shed his flying suit, could see Diana and Rascal standing near the garden, booth looking odd and a tall, thin man whom René did not know. René put Beau, who had traveled inside his jacket, down on the ground and the kitten scampered towards his brother.

Suddenly, with the Sight given him by the Elfin eye ointment, René saw the true aura of the man threatening Diana and ran forward, placing himself between the man and his *fiancée*.

"Very commendable," said the stranger dryly, in French. "One must always protect the women and children. I have always wondered why this must be so."

"But my quarrel is with you," he continued, "If you are the traitor to France who calls himself the Marquis of Keir."

"He is no traitor!" Diana managed to get out. "He is as English as I, for his father is an Englishman."

"Be quiet, woman!" Malcoeur ground out. "This is none of your affair!"

Beau had joined his brother at Diana's feet and now he too, spat and hissed and said "I'll scratch your eyes out, you bad man!"

Malcoeur had never liked cats. To him they always looked at him as if they despised him and thought themselves better than him. He had never been able to manipulate a cat.

Now he looked at the kittens with hatred. "Remove them, *Madame*, or I shall kill them. I have no use for vermin."

Diana snatched up both her kittens over their protests and pressed them to her bosom, begging Beau to be quiet, for the kitten was throwing insults at Malcoeur.

"I challenge you, *M'sieur*, to the Duel rcane."Malcoeur made a handsome leg and a flourish of his hat towards René.

"I accept your challenge," returned René, owing in return.

"René! No!" cried Diana in protest. "You can't –"

"I have told you to be quiet!" snapped Malcoeur, "Hold your tongue or I shall –"

"You will do nothing to her – or the kittens! She will leave us – do you hear me, Diana, I want you to go!" cried René, his eyes flashing. "Your quarrel is with me, *M'sieur*! Do we duel or not?"

"*Très bien*," Malcoeur acquiesced, losing interest in Diana and the kittens. "Let the duel begin."

According to the rules, they stood back to back, paced off twenty steps and fired the opening volley.

From the very beginning René knew that he hadn't a chance. His only hope was to hold Malcoeur off until Diana could get away or perhaps Lyon returned. But Diana refused to run.

It was all René could do to dodge the bolts of raw energy that the Jongleur threw at him. He was still weak and when he reached for the ley lines he could barely tap them. There was a little malicious smile on the thin lips of the necromancer as he toyed with his opponent.

Diana, hugging the kittens to her breast, watched with her heart in her throat. Trying to remain secretive, she willed as much of her magic to René as was possible. Witches were well used to sharing power and doing it unobtrusively. But she could tell that it was doing little good. It was still too soon after Lammas night.

Malcoeur easily destroyed the attacks on him from his opponent. Deliberately he had not unleashed his full powers, nor had he used the full spectrum of his blood magic. This was an amusing, taunting game with him.

Then abruptly, he tired of the game and unleashed a last bolt of pure red energy that easily pierced the violet shield René had thrown up.

The bolt took René and whirled him about, lifting him from his feet and tossing him against a nearby elm tree. He fell and lay still on the grass, as limp as a rag doll.

Both the kittens and Diana screamed, the kittens scrambling from her hold and racing towards René's body.

"*Pathetique!*" said Malcoeur. "Victory is not victory when it is too easy. But now I will end this farce." And raising his hands, he began to draw his blood magic.

"NO!" Diana screamed again and without conscious thought she pulled the silver oak leaf from beneath her gown, and gripping it so tight that it bit into her hand, pulled her wand from her skirt pocket and pointed it at the Jongleur.

Pure white light poured from her wand and surrounded him. It held him for a moment in its grip and Diana saw his shocked face. The blood magic was scattered into a million pieces and swept away on the breeze. As the white magic held him his body began to empty of the souls he had stolen – Diana could see them, faint and ephemeral, heading skywards and his own soul, solid black and corrupt, lightened to ash-grey.

The white light then seem to fold in on itself and with a sudden crack, was gone, taking every trace of Malcoeur with it.

Diana fell to her knees, gasping. She felt as if she had been trampled. But she could not surrender to her weakness. She staggered to her feet and went to René.

"He's alive! Only barely –" Beau said in answer to her unspoken query. He and Rascal had been licking as much of René face as they could reach, from where he lay crumpled on his side.

Diana fell down rather than knelt beside him. With some difficulty he turned him onto his back, helped by the kittens, who inserted their little teeth into his clothes and tugged.

She knew what to do, although she was not conscious of how she was aware of this. She ripped his cravat off and reached inside his shirt to find the golden acorn. This she held to her silver oak leaf and the two sprang together, to form one piece. These she lay on his heart.

A green light of healing at once began to ripple and shimmer over him.

"What are you doing?" Beau squeaked anxiously. "Is this helping?"

"I know what I'm doing," she said confidently, although everything she had done had come from a power outside herself. "Look!"

Even as she spoke René's eyes were opening and he looked up at her. She grabbed his hand and pressed it to her cheek. With glad cries and purrs the kittens climbed onto his chest.

"Don't try to sit up," said Diana as he tried to rise. "Rest a moment. I think I brought you back from the brink of death."

"You —" he managed and then was glad to do as she suggested. "What happened?"

Briefly she told him of the white light and the disappearance of the necromancer.

"It was Lord Oberon," René whispered "We are fortunate in his friendship."

Diana shivered. If they had not received those Faerie gifts, if the King and Queen had not chosen to honour them with their friendship — the outcome could have been very different.

"Did you kill him?" Rascal wanted to know.

"I don't know," Diana admitted, wondering. "All of the poor souls he enslaved for his blood magic were released — I saw that. There were so many of them!"

"I hope he is dead," said Beau viciously. No one reprimanded him, for they all felt the same.

Fifteen minutes later, when Lyon, Ninon and Simon returned, they found the little group on the lawn, still rejoicing.

But it was to be some years before they found out the true fate of the Jongleur.

55

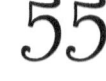

Aftermath

"Well, you two have managed to create quite a tempest in the teapot!"

Lyon poked his head in the door of the sunny bedchamber where Diana and René sat in the window seat. Simon sat at their feet and their three kittens were curled up in a tangled mass of furry bodies in the sun.

It was a fortnight since the defeat of the Jongleur and the first day that the doctor had let René rise from bed. Over his protests everyone had persisted in treating him as an invalid. The wedding had been postponed and everything put on hold.

Lyon pushed open the door and entered, closely followed by Ninon. Their familiars following them.

"I have never in my entire life spent so much time in front of a scry bowl!" Lyon announced. He found a chair and let himself drop into it. Leander perched on the back of it. "But I think I have prevented my niece from being tried for murder."

"What!" Diana and René said as one. The kittens awoke and began to protest

"Oh, *oui*, by the so-stupid British law, Diana can be accused of murdering that *socerier!*" said Ninon indignantly as Neige snuggled into her lap. "To kill in the Duel Arcane is legal, but she was not a participant to the challenge –"

"The law is a jackass," grunted Lyon, raking his hands through his mane of hair. "I knew I should not have reported the entire thing to the authorities! But once I showed them the futility of a murder trial without a body – .

At any rate, the official version now will be that René killed him, all legal and proper in the Duel Arcane. Of course, they cut up stiff that there were no seconds and no doctor in attendance and no notice to the proper authorities. But they're willing to look the other way since it rid us of a necromancer. I am very much afraid, my boy that you may be knighted."

"Afraid that he will be honoured?" Ninon said in surprise.

"It's a burden, not an honour," said Lyon. "Every time there's a national crisis they'll expect René to do something about it or at least be consulted. He'll have to trot out his medals on the appropriate holidays and they'll always be after him to take government posts – most of which will pay naught and involve an inordinate amount of work."

Diana exchanged a smile with her *fiancé*. Only her irascible uncle could see the ills in receiving an honour from one's government.

"But the important thing, now is that everyone has now arrived and we are all set for the ceremony!" said Ninon, clapping here hands.

"Ceremony?" said René.

"You are going to be married this evening!" Lyon announced with a grin. "All the guests have arrived and you'd best get dressed, my boy, unless you want to be wed in your dressing gown. It might set a new trend – ready for the honeymoon the instant that the vows are made."

"And Susan has your gown all laid out," Ninon told Diana.

"But there is no question of such a thing!" Diana protested, "We had thought to wait until after Christmas –"

Lyon pooh-poohed this. "If I ever saw a pair smelling of April and May and eager for the honeymoon, it is you two!"

"You should be wed, *n'est-ce pas*, before anything else happens!" Ninon stated firmly.

"Why are they so eager for the honeymoon?" Simon whispered to Janus.

"Ask Ninon," Janus said, feeling unable to explain it.

"Simon, you must wash and dress too," said Ninon firmly and bore him away to do just that. Neige and Janus, more interested in what was going on here, stayed behind.

620

"Come along, you two," ordered Lyon. "We've a wedding to attend and we certainly can't do it without you!"

"*Un moment, s'il vous plait,*" said René, with a significant look.

"Oh!" said Lyon. "Well, I've got to get into my own wedding togs – I'll leave you two alone, shall I? But don't be too long about it!" He left followed by Leander, who winked at the kittens as he flew from the room.

Once they were alone – save for four interested kittens, René took Diana in his arms and said seriously, "Do you wish to do this now, *cherie?*"

"More than anything!" she returned. "I did not see how I could wait until Christmas!"

This answer deserved a kiss and she leaned into him, looking forward to the night.

"I will help you out tonight –" Beau an-nounced.

"That you will not do!" said René tightening his hold on Diana, who burst into laughter. "There are some things for which I need no prompts from my familiar!"

"Find your own girl!" said Rascal and Janus in chorus.

"And they all lived happily ever after!" sighed the romantic Neige.

621

Epilogue
July 24ᵗʰ, 1815

The ships were coming into Tor Bay.

No one who was there that day ever forgot the sight. The declining sun shone around clouds of smoke-blue and gilded every mast, rope and sail of the ships in gold and rose and blue. The great ships, sails taut in the wind, seemed to glide over the water in a magical fashion.

In the center was H.M.S. *Bellerophon*. She was flanked on either side by frigates guarding the grey-coated captive who stood on the deck looking towards England – Napoleon Bonaparte.

The hillside town of Torquay was filled with spectators, all trying to catch a glimpse of the fallen Emperor of the French. Some of then had been there for days, hoping to see him. They crowded the streets and quays and filled the harbor with over crowded little boats.

Among the spectators were several who would not have been there at all unless their very special guests had not requested that they go and look upon the former Emperor. They had driven down from Dorsetshire that morning.

"So that is the little man who tried to conquer the world," said Oberon, snapping shut a spy-glass that he had used to observe the man on the deck. Since it was of Elfin origin, he had seen every detail clearly, even though the landau in which he sat with his wife and his hosts, the Marquis and Marchioness of Keir, was high upon a hill overlooking the Channel inlet.

"He almost succeeded," said René, thinking that the battle of Waterloo had been a close-run thing. At one point advance news had declared the battle lost, causing a panic in the City and a frenzy of selling on the Exchange.

Diana exchanged smiles with Tatania. The Elf Queen and King looked wonderfully well in the guise of ordinary English gentlefolk. They had expressed a wish to see the man they had helped defeat – for the transfer of power to the Russian magicals had no doubt helped bring about the catastrophe that was Napoleon's Russian campaign. Oberon and René had been playing 'what if' since that left Chenevix Duchis, where Lord and Lady Keir and their family were spending the summer with the Duke and Duchess. The Duke, much mellowed, was the proud grandfather of nearly three year old Stuart Robert Louis Eliot Delamar. And the Duchess was happily knitting baby items, for another child was due come Christmas.

Alongside the carriage rode Simon, now tall for his age of almost thirteen. He was a star pupil at the Tara Druidry and had decided to make the study of dragons his life's work.

He had been formally adopted by Diana and René and thoroughly enjoyed being a big brother to Stuart. Stuart adored him as well. Simon and his parents were very happy in Dublin – it was 'home' to all of them.

"It is a very good thing that Napoleon did not achieve his ambition of enslaving all of Europe," said Tatania in her musical voice. "For that would have affected us as well as you mortals."

"His defeat was at a terrible cost," said Diana, thinking of the thousands dead on the battlefield and the many civilians whose lives had been ruined.

"A necessary cost, I am afraid," the Elf King said. "There is always a cost to defeat evil." He looked thoughtful for a moment and then said "The time has come to let you know what became of the necromancer."

René and Diana exchanged glances. They had always known that the *Sidhe* had played a part in that encounter, for it had been the Faerie gifts that had put an end to him and restored René to life. But what had happened to Malcoeur they had never known. They had assumed him dead.

"He is in my care," said the Elf King. "I have placed him where he can do no harm. And his blood magic is gone from him. He shall trouble you no more."

It was a tidy little French *chateau,* spotlessly neat and well supplied. There was a well-stocked library, beautiful formal gardens, a little lake with a boat house and horses in the stable.

Food appeared on the dining room table at exactly the right time and bath water was drawn when needed. The bed – luxuriously soft – smelled of lavender and was made up each day.

But Malcoeur saw no one. He had looked for them, calling for someone, anyone. But there was no one that he could see, in spite of the fact that the house was kept and food prepared for him.

One day, angered beyond belief, he had mounted a horse and ridden as fast and as far as he could. In all of that time he had seen no other signs of life. There were no other *chateaux,* no farms, no villages. Just endless forest, which was teeming with birds and animals but no people. He did not understand how he had gotten here or where he was. It was a beautiful spot, no doubt of that and the food was delicious. Each day was a perfect summer's day. There were interesting books in the library, weapons to hunt with and equipment to fish the stream that ran through the woods and the lake. There was even a small Wizard's laboratory.

But he ached to know where he was and more important WHY he was there and how he had gotten there. The last thing he remembered was that duel – he had just been about to finish off that poor excuse for a sorcerer. The next thing he knew he had woken up in the fragrant big bed.

But there was no one to answer his questions.

On the fourth day of his captivity he had just finished breakfast – the finest omelet and croissants he had ever eaten, served with fresh fruits and perfect coffee – when he was suddenly aware that he was not alone. He leaped from his chair and whirled around to find himself being regarded by a being – the like of whom he had never seen before.

"Who are you or what are you?" he demanded in French.

"Oberon. I am your host," the being answered in the same language. He was tall and slender, clad in shining white with a huge moon-stone about his neck. His hair was dark and he had emerald eyes slitted like a cat's and pointed ears.

"And as to what I am, I am the Lord of the *Sidhe* – an Elf, your people would call me."

"Where am I?" Malcoeur demanded.

"You are in one of my domains. I have created it for you. Here you will remain for the rest of your life, for I cannot allow you to wreak havoc in the World Above. It was my magic that brought you here – Lady Diana was but a conduit. I have removed all of your blood magic and restored the stolen souls to their afterlives. It is a pleasant prison – you have only to ask if you desire something – even company or a woman," the Elf King told him.

"Why have you made me wait four days to tell me this?" Malcoeur said sourly.

Oberon smiled slightly. "My dear mortal, you have been here for four *years*. Time is not the same in my domain as it is in the world above."

He waved his hand and a pile of news-sheets appeared before the bemused Malcoeur. "You will wish to know what has happened in your world."

He turned away for a moment, obviously thinking and then looked back at the Jongleur intently. "Understand this and understand it well. I have allowed you to retain your powers – you will find arcane books in your library and you may study to your heart's content. But there will be no blood magic of any sort. And there will be no escape. You may ride for days in any direction but you shall never come to the end of this domain. You are here unless I chose to release you – and that will never happen. And do not forget – your powers are but the candlelight to the sun in comparison with mine." And then he was gone in a shimmer of rainbow light.

Here forever? Malcoeur's lips twisted bitterly. He would find a way out. He was clever and intelligent and would study those books in the library.

He would become totally familiar with this place – its strengths and its weaknesses. Somehow he would find a way out. He had been in difficult situations before, but he had always won out. This time would be no exception.

www.ingramcontent.com/pod-product-compliance
Lightning Source LLC
Chambersburg PA
CBHW020453020726
47493CB00001B/16